D1098056

NOBLE HOUSE

Volume 1

NOBLE HOUSE
is the fourth novel in the Asian Saga
that so far consists of:

James Clavell

NOBLE HOUSE

A Novel of Contemporary Hong Kong

Volume 1

DELACORTE PRESS/NEW YORK

I would like to offer this
work as a tribute to
Her Britannic Majesty,
Elizabeth II, to the people
of Her Crown Colony of
Hong Kong—*and perdition
to their enemies.*

Of course this is a novel. It is peopled with imaginary persons and companies and no reference to any person or company that was, or is, part of Hong Kong or Asia is intended.

I would also like to apologize at once to all Hong Kong *yan*—all Hong Kong *persons*—for rearranging their beautiful city, for taking incidents out of context, for inventing people and places and streets and companies and incidents that, hopefully, may appear to have existed but have never existed, for this, truly, is a story. . . .

June 8, 1960

PROLOGUE

His name was Ian Dunross and in the torrential rain he drove his old MG sports car cautiously around the corner into Dirk's Street that skirted the Struan Building on the waterfront of Hong Kong. The night was dark and foul. Throughout the Colony—here on Hong Kong Island, across the harbor in Kowloon and the New Territories that were part of the China Mainland—streets were almost totally deserted, everyone and everything battened down, waiting for Typhoon Mary. The number nine storm warning had been hoisted at dusk and already eighty- to a hundred-knot gusts came out of the tempest that stretched a thousand miles southward to send the rain horizontal against the roofs and hillsides where tens of thousands of squatters huddled defenseless in their shantytowns of make-shift hovels.

Dunross slowed, blinded, the wipers unable to cope with the quantity of rain, the wind tearing at the canvas roof and side screens. Then the windshield cleared momentarily. At the end of Dirk's Street, directly ahead, was Connaught Road and the praya, then sea walls and the squat bulk of the Golden Ferry Terminal. Beyond in the vast, well-protected harbor, half a thousand ships were snug with all anchors out.

Ahead on the praya, he saw an abandoned street stall ripped bodily off the ground by a gust and hurled at a parked car, wrecking it. Then the car and the stall were sent skittering out of sight. His wrists were very strong and he held the wheel against the eddies that trembled his car violently. The car was old but well kept, the souped-up engine and brakes perfect. He waited, his heart beating nicely, loving storm, then eased up onto the sidewalk to park in the lee, well against the building, and got out.

He was fair-haired with blue eyes, in his early forties, lean and trim and he wore an old raincoat and cap. Rain drenched him as he hurried along the side street then ducked around the corner to hurry for the main entrance of the twenty-two-story building. Over the huge doorway was the Struan crest—the Red Lion of Scotland entwined with the Green Dragon of China. Gathering himself he strode up the broad steps and went in.

"Evening, Mr. Dunross," the Chinese concierge said.

"The tai-pan sent for me."

"Yes sir." The man pressed the elevator button for him.

When the elevator stopped, Dunross walked across the small hall, knocked and went into the penthouse living room. "Evening, tai-pan," he said with cold formality.

Alastair Struan was leaning against the fine fireplace. He was a big, ruddy, well-kept Scotsman with a slight paunch and white hair, in his sixties, and he had ruled Struan's for eleven years. "Drink?" He waved a hand at the Dom Pérignon in the silver bucket.

"Thank you." Dunross had never been in the tai-pan's private quarters before. The room was spacious and well furnished, with Chinese lacquer and good carpets, old oils of their early clipper ships and steamers on the walls. The big picture windows that would normally overlook all Hong Kong, the harbor and Kowloon across the harbor were now black and rain streaked.

He poured. "Health," he said formally.

Alastair Struan nodded and, equally coldly, raised his glass in return. "You're early."

"Five minutes early is on time, tai-pan. Isn't that what Father hammered into me? Is it important that we meet at midnight?"

"Yes. It's part of our custom. Dirk's custom."

Dunross sipped his wine, waiting in silence. The antique ship's clock ticked loudly. His excitement increased, not knowing what to expect. Over the fireplace was a marriage portrait of a young girl. This was Tess Struan who had married Culum, second tai-pan and son of their founder Dirk Struan, when she was sixteen.

Dunross studied it. A squall dashed the windows. "Filthy night," he said.

The older man just looked at him, hating him. The silence grew. Then the old clock chimed eight bells, midnight.

There was a knock on the door.

"Come in," Alastair Struan said with relief, glad that now they could begin.

The door was opened by Lim Chu, the tai-pan's personal servant. He stepped aside to admit Phillip Chen, compradore of Struan's, then closed the door after him.

"Ah, Phillip, you're on time as usual," Alastair Struan said, trying to sound jovial. "Champagne?"

"Thank you, tai-pan. Yes, thank you. Good evening, Ian Struan Dunross," Phillip Chen said to the younger man with unusual formality, his English very upper-class British. He was Eurasian, in his late sixties, spare, rather more Chinese than European, a very handsome man with gray hair and high cheekbones, fair skin, and dark, very dark Chinese eyes. "Dreadful night, what?"

"Yes, it is indeed, Uncle Chen," Dunross replied, using the polite Chinese form of address for Phillip, liking him and respecting him as much as he despised his cousin Alastair.

"They say this typhoon's going to be a bastard." Alastair Struan was pouring the champagne into fine glasses. He handed Phillip Chen a glass first, then Dunross. "Health!"

They drank. A rain squall rattled the windows. "Glad I'm not afloat tonight," Alastair Struan said thoughtfully. "So, Phillip, here you are again."

"Yes, tai-pan. I'm honored. Yes, very honored." He sensed the violence between the two men but dismissed it. Violence is a pattern, he thought, when a tai-pan of the Noble House hands over power.

Alastair Struan sipped again, enjoying the wine. At length he said, "Ian, it's our custom that there be a witness to a handing over from tai-pan to tai-pan. It's always—and only—our current compradore. Phillip, how many times does this make?"

"I've been witness four times, tai-pan."

"Phillip has known almost all of us. He knows too many of our secrets. Eh, old friend?" Phillip Chen just smiled. "Trust him, Ian. His counsel's wise. You can trust him."

As much as any tai-pan should trust anyone, Dunross thought grimly. "Yes sir."

Alastair Struan set down his glass. "First: Ian Struan Dunross, I ask you formally, do you want to be tai-pan of Struan's?"

"Yes sir."

"You swear by God that all of these proceedings will be kept secret by you and not divulged to anyone but your successor?"

"Yes sir."

"Swear it formally."

"I swear by God these proceedings will be secret and never divulged to anyone but my successor."

"Here." The tai-pan handed him a parchment, yellow with age. "Read it aloud."

Dunross took it. The writing was spidery, but perfectly legible. He glanced at the date—August 30, 1841—his excitement soaring. "Is this Dirk Struan's writing?"

"Aye. Most of it—part was added by his son, Culum Struan. Of course we've photocopies in case of damage. Read it!"

" 'My Legacy shall bind every tai-pan that succeedeth me and he shall read it aloud and shall swear before God in front of witnesses in the manner set forth by me, Dirk Struan, founder of Struan and Company, to accept them, and to ever keep them secret, prior to taking to himself my mantle. I require this to ensure a pleasing continuity and in anticipation of difficulties which will, in the following years, beset my successors because of the blood I have spilled, because of my debts of honor, and because of the vagaries of the ways of China to which we are wedded, which are without doubt unique on this earth. This is my Legacy:

" 'First: There shall be only one tai-pan at one time and he hath total, absolute authority over the Company, power to employ or remove from employment all others, authority over all our captains and our ships and companies wherever they may be. The tai-pan is always alone, that being the joy and the hurt of it. His privacy must be guarded by all and his back protected by all. Whatsoever he orders, it shall be obeyed, and no committees or courts or inner circles shall ever be formed or allowed in the Company to curb this absolute power.

" 'Second: When the tai-pan stands on the quarterdeck of any of our ships he takes precedence over the captain thereof, and his battle orders or sailing orders are law. All captains will be so sworn before God, before appointment to any of our ships.

" 'Third: The tai-pan alone chooses his successor who shall be selected only from an Inner Court of six men. Of these, one shall be our compradore who shall, in perpetuity, be from the House of Chen. The other five shall be worthy to be tai-pan, shall be good men and true with at least five whole years of service in the Company as China Traders, and shall be wholesome in spirit. They must be Christian and must be kinsmen to the clan Struan by birth or marriage—my line and my brother Robb's line not taking precedence, unless by fortitude or qualities over and above all others. This Inner Court may be advisors to the tai-pan if he so desires, but let it be said again, the vote of the tai-pan shall weight seven against one for each of them.

" 'Fourth: If the tai-pan be lost at sea, or killed in battle, or vanished for six lunar months, before he hath his successor chosen, then the Inner Court shall elect one of their members to succeed, each having one vote, except the vote of the compradore shall count four. The tai-pan shall then be sworn in the same manner set forth before his fellows—those who voted against his election in open ballot being expelled at once, without remuneration, from the Company forever.

" 'Fifth: Election to the Inner Court, or removal therefrom, shall be solely at the tai-pan's pleasure and, on his retirement which shall be at a time when it pleasures him, he shall take no more than ten parts of every hundred of all value for himself, except that all our ships shall always be excluded from any valuation . . . our ships, their captains and their crews being our lifeblood and our lifeline into future times.

" 'Sixth: Each tai-pan shall approve the election of the compradore. The compradore shall acknowledge in writing prior to his election that he may be removed at any time, without need for explanations, that he will step aside should the tai-pan wish it.

" 'Last: The tai-pan shall swear his successor, whom he alone chooses, in the presence of the compradore using the words set down under my hand in our family Bible, here in Hong Kong, this thirtieth day of August in the year of our Lord 1841.' "

Dunross exhaled. "It's signed by Dirk Struan and witnessed by— I can't read the chop characters, sir, they're archaic."

Alastair glanced at Phillip Chen who said, "The first witness is my grandfather's foster father, Chen Sheng Arn, our first compradore. The second, my great-aunt, T'Chung Jin May-may."

"Then the legend's true!" Dunross said.

"Some of it. Yes, some of it." Phillip Chen added, "Talk to my auntie Sarah. Now that you're to be tai-pan she'll tell you lots of secrets. She's eighty-four this year. She remembers my grandfather, Sir Gordon Chen, very well, and Duncan and Kate T'Chung, May-may's children by Dirk Struan. Yes. She remembers many things. . . ."

Alastair Struan went over to the lacquered bureau and very carefully picked out the heavy threadbare Bible. He put on his spectacles and Dunross felt the hackles on his neck rise. "Repeat after me: I, Ian Struan Dunross, kinsman to the Struans, Christian, sweareth before God in the presence of Alastair McKenzie Duncan Struan, eleventh tai-pan, and Phillip T'Chung Sheng Chen, fourth compradore, that I shall obey all the Legacy read out by me in their presence here in Hong Kong, that I shall further bind the Company to Hong Kong and to the China trade, that I shall maintain my main place of business here in Hong Kong while tai-pan, that, before God, I assume the promises, responsibility and the gentleman's word of honor of Dirk Struan to his eternal friend Chen-tse Jin Arn, also known as Jin-qua, or to his successors; further, that I w—"

"What promises?"

"You swear before God, blind, like all the tai-pans did before you! You'll learn soon enough what you inherit."

"And if I won't?"

"You know the answer to that!"

The rain was battering the windows and its violence seemed to Dunross to equal the thumping in his chest as he weighed the insanity of such an open-ended commitment. But he knew he could not be tai-pan unless he did, and so he said the words and made the commitment before God, and continued to say the words read out to him.

". . . further that I will use all powers, and any means, to keep the Company steadfast as the First House, the Noble House of Asia, that I swear before God to commit any deed necessary to vanquish, destroy and cast out from Asia the company called Brock and Sons and particularly my enemy, the founder, Tyler Brock, his son Morgan, their heirs or any of their line excepting only Tess Brock and her issue, the wife of my son Culum, from the face of Asia. . . ." Dunross stopped again.

"When you've finished you can ask any questions you want," Alastair Struan said. "Finish it!"

"Very well. Lastly: I swear before God that my successor as tai-pan will also be sworn, before God, to all of this Legacy, so help me God!"

Now the silence was broken only by the rain slashing the windows. Dunross could feel the sweat on his back.

Alastair Struan put down the Bible and took off his spectacles. "There, it's done." Tautly he put out his hand. "I'd like to be the first to wish you well, tai-pan. Anything I can do to help, you have."

"And I'm honored to be second, tai-pan," Phillip Chen said with a slight bow, equally formally.

"Thank you." Dunross's tension was great.

"I think we all need a drink," Alastair Struan said. "With your permission, I'll pour," he added to Dunross with untoward formality. "Phillip?"

"Yes, tai-pan. I—"

"No. Ian's tai-pan now." Alastair Struan poured the champagne and gave the first glass to Dunross.

"Thank you," Dunross said, savoring the compliment, knowing nothing had changed. "Here's to the Noble House," he said, raising his glass.

The three men drank, then Alastair Struan took out an envelope. "This is my resignation from the sixty-odd chairmanships, managing directorships and directorships that automatically go with the tai-pan position. Your appointment in my stead is equally automatic. By custom I become chairman of our London subsidiary—but you can terminate that anytime you wish."

"It's terminated," Dunross said at once.

"Whatever you say," the old man muttered, but his neck was purple.

"I think you'd be more useful to Struan's as deputy chairman of the First Central Bank of Edinburgh."

Struan looked up sharply. "What?"

"That's one of our appointments, isn't it?"

"Yes," Alastair Struan said. "Why that?"

"I'm going to need help. Struan's goes public next year."

Both men stared at him, astounded. "What!"

"We're going publ—"

"We've been a private company for 132 years!" the old man roared. "Jesus bloody Christ I've told you a hundred times that's our strength, with no god-cursed stockholders or outsiders prying into our private affairs!" His face was flushed and he fought to control his anger. "Don't you ever listen?"

"All the time. Very carefully," Dunross said in an unemotional voice. "The only way we can survive is to go public . . . that's the only way we can get the capital we need."

"Talk to him, Phillip—get some sense into him."

Nervously the compradore said, "How will this affect the House of Chen?"

"Our formal compradore system is ended from tonight." He saw Phillip

Chen's face go white but he continued, "I have a plan for you—in writing. It changes nothing, and everything. Officially you'll still be compradore, unofficially we'll operate differently. The major change is that instead of making about a million a year, in ten years your share will bring you 20, in fifteen years about 30."

"Impossible!" Alastair Struan burst out.

"Our net worth today's about 20 million U.S. In ten years it'll be 200 million and in fifteen, with joss, it'll be 400 million—and our yearly turnover approaching a billion."

"You've gone mad," Struan said.

"No. The Noble House is going international—the days of being solely a Hong Kong trading company are gone forever."

"Remember your oath, by God! We're Hong Kong based!"

"I won't forget. Next: What responsibility do I inherit from Dirk Struan?"

"It's all in the safe. Written down in a sealed envelope marked 'The Legacy.' Also the Hag's 'Instructions to future tai-pans.'"

"Where's the safe?"

"Behind the painting in the Great House. In the study." Sourly Alastair Struan pointed to an envelope beside the clock on the mantelpiece. "That contains the special key—and the present combination. You will of course change it. Put the figures into one of the tai-pan's private safety deposit boxes at the bank, in case of accidents. Give Phillip one of the two keys."

Phillip Chen said, "By our rules, while you're alive, the bank is obliged to refuse me permission to open it."

"Next: Tyler Brock and his sons—those bastards were obliterated almost a hundred years ago."

"Aye, the legitimate male line was. But Dirk Struan was vindictive and his vengeance reaches out from his grave. There's an up-to-date list of Tyler Brock's descendents, also in the safe. It makes interesting reading, eh Phillip?"

"Yes, yes it does."

"The Rothwells and the Tomms, Yadegar and his brood, you know about. But Tusker's on the list though he doesn't know it, Jason Plumm, Lord Depford-Smyth and, most of all, Quillan Gornt."

"Impossible!"

"Not only is Gornt tai-pan of Rothwell-Gornt, our main enemy, but he's also a secret, direct male descendent of Morgan Brock—direct though illegitimate. He's the last of the Brocks."

"But he's always claimed his great-grandfather was Edward Gornt, the American China Trader."

"He comes from Edward Gornt all right. But Sir Morgan Brock was really Edward's father and Kristian Gornt his mother. She was an American from Virginia. Of course it was kept secret—society wasn't any more forgiving then than now. When Sir Morgan became tai-pan of Brock's in

1859, he fetched this illegitimate son of his out of Virginia, bought him a
partnership in the old American trading firm of Rothwell and Company
in Shanghai, and then he and Edward bided their time to destroy us.
They almost did—certainly they caused the death of Culum Struan. But
then Lochlin and Hag Struan broke Sir Morgan and smashed Brock and
Sons. Edward Gornt never forgave us, his descendents never will either—
I'd wager they too have a pact with their founder."

"Does he know we know?"

"I don't know. But he's enemy. His genealogy's in the safe, with all the
others. My grandfather was the one who discovered it, quite by chance,
during the Boxer Rebellion in '99. The list is interesting, Ian, very. One
particular person for you. The head of—"

A sudden violent gust shook the building. One of the ivory bric-a-brac
on the marble table toppled over. Nervously Phillip Chen stood it up.
They all stared at the windows, watching their reflections twist nauseatingly as the gusts stretched the huge panes of glass.

"*Tai-fun!*" Phillip muttered, sweat beading him.

"Yes." They waited breathlessly for the "Devil Wind" to cease. These
sudden squalls came haphazardly from all points of the compass, sometimes gusting to a hundred and fifty knots. In their wake was always dev-
astation.

The violence passed. Dunross went over to the barometer, checked it
and tapped it. 980.3.

"Still falling," he said.

"Christ!"

Dunross squinted at the windows. Now the rain streaks were almost
horizontal. "*Lasting Cloud* is due to dock tomorrow night."

"Yes, but now she'll be hove to somewhere off the Philippines. Captain
Moffatt's too canny to get caught," Struan said.

"I don't agree. Moffatt likes hitting schedules. This typhoon's unsched-
uled. You . . . he should have been ordered." Dunross sipped his wine
thoughtfully. "*Lasting Cloud* better not get caught."

Phillip Chen heard the undercurrent of fury. "Why?"

"We've our new computer aboard and two million pounds' worth of jet
engines. Uninsured—at least the engines are." Dunross glanced at Alastair
Struan.

Defensively the old man said, "It was that or lose the contract. The engines are consigned to Canton. You know we can't insure them, Phillip,
since they're going to Red China." Then he added irritably, "They're, er,
they're South American owned and there're no export restrictions from
South America to China. Even so, no one's willing to insure them."

After a pause Phillip Chen said, "I thought the new computer was coming in March."

"It was but I managed to jump it forward," Alastair said.

"Who's carrying the paper on the engines?" Phillip Chen asked.

"We are."

"That's a lot of risk." Phillip Chen was very uneasy. "Don't you agree, Ian?"

Dunross said nothing.

"It was that or lose the contract," Alastair Struan said, even more irritably. "We stand to double our money, Phillip. We need the money. But more than that the Chinese need the engines, they made that more than clear when I was in Canton last month. And we need China—they made that clear too."

"Yes, but 12 million, that's . . . a lot of risk in one ship," Phillip Chen insisted.

Dunross said, "Anything we can do to take business away from the Soviets is to our advantage. Besides, it's done. You were saying, Alastair, there's someone on the list I should know about? The head of?"

"Marlborough Motors."

"Ah," Dunross said with sudden grim delight. "I've detested those sods for years. Father and son."

"I know."

"So the Nikklins're descendents of Tyler Brock? Well it won't be long before we can wipe them off the list. Good, very good. Do they know they're on Dirk Struan's oblit list?"

"I don't think so."

"That's even better."

"I don't agree! You hate young Nikklin because he beat you." Angrily Alastair Struan stabbed a finger at Dunross. "It's time you gave up car racing. Leave all the hill climbs and Macao Grand Prix to the semiprofessionals. The Nikklins have more time to spend on their cars, it's their life, and now you've other races to run, more important ones."

"Macao's amateur and those bastards cheated last year."

"That was never proved—your engine blew up. A lot of engines blow up, Ian. That was just joss!"

"My car was tampered with."

"And that was never proved either! For Christ's sake, you talk about bad blood? You're as stupid about some things as Devil Struan himself!"

"Oh?"

"Yes, and—"

Phillip Chen interrupted quickly, wanting an end to the violence in the room. "If it's so important, please let me see if I can find out the truth. I've sources not available to either of you. My Chinese friends will know, should know, if either Tom or young Donald Nikklin were involved. Of course," he added delicately, "if the tai-pan wishes to race, then that's up to the tai-pan. Isn't it, Alastair?"

The older man controlled his rage though his neck was still choleric. "Yes, yes you're right. Still, Ian, my advice is you cease. They'll be after you even more because they detest you equally."

"Are there others I should know about—on the list?"

After a pause, Struan said, "No, not now." He opened the second bottle and poured as he talked. "Well, now it's all yours—all the fun and all the sweat. I'm glad to pass everything over to you. After you've been through the safe you'll know the best, and the worst." He gave them each a glass and sipped his. "By the Lord Jesus, that's as fine a wine as ever came out of France."

"Yes," Phillip Chen said.

Dunross thought Dom Pérignon overpriced and overrated and knew the year, '54, was not a particularly good one. But he held his peace.

Struan went over to the barometer. It read 979.2. "We're in for a bad one. Well, never mind that. Ian, Claudia Chen has a file for you on important matters, and a complete list of our stockholdings—with names of the nominees. Any questions, have them for me before the day after tomorrow—I'm booked for London then. You'll keep Claudia on, of course."

"Of course." Claudia Chen was the second link from tai-pan to tai-pan after Phillip Chen. She was executive secretary to the tai-pan, a distant cousin to Phillip Chen.

"What about our bank—the Victoria Bank of Hong Kong and China?" Dunross asked, savoring the question. "I don't know our exact holdings."

"That's always been tai-pan knowledge only."

Dunross turned to Phillip Chen. "What's your holding, openly or through nominees?"

The compradore hesitated, shocked.

"In future I'm going to vote your holdings as a block with ours." Dunross kept his eyes on the compradore's. "I want to know now and I'll expect a formal transfer of perpetual voting power, in writing, to me and following tai-pans, tomorrow by noon, and first refusal on the shares should you ever decide to sell."

The silence grew.

"Ian," Phillip Chen began, "those shares . . ." But his resolve wavered under the power of Dunross's will. "6 percent . . . a little over 6 percent. I . . . you'll have it as you wish."

"You won't regret it." Dunross put his attention on Alastair Struan and the older man's heart missed a beat. "How much stock have we? How much's held by nominees?"

Alastair hesitated. "That's tai-pan knowledge only."

"Of course. But our compradore is to be trusted, absolutely," Dunross said, giving the old man face, knowing how much it had hurt to be dominated in front of Alastair Struan. "How much?"

Struan said, "15 percent."

Dunross gasped and so did Phillip Chen and he wanted to shout, Jesus bloody Christ, we have 15 percent and Phillip another 6 percent and you haven't had the sodding intelligence to use what's got to be a major interest to get us major funding when we're almost bankrupt?

But instead he reached forward and poured the remains of the bottle into the three glasses and this gave him time to stop the pounding of his heart.

"Good," he said with his flat unemotional voice. "I was hoping together we'd make it better than ever." He sipped his wine. "I'm bringing forward the Special Meeting. To next week."

Both men looked up sharply. Since 1880, the tai-pans of Struan's, Rothwell-Gornt and the Victoria Bank had, despite their rivalry, met annually in secret to discuss matters that affected the future of Hong Kong and Asia.

"They may not agree to bring the meeting forward," Alastair said.

"I phoned everyone this morning. It's set for Monday next at 9 A.M. here."

"Who's coming from the bank?"

"Deputy Chief Manager Havergill—the old man's in Japan then England on leave." Dunross's face hardened. "I'll have to make do."

"Paul's all right," Alastair said. "He'll be the next chief."

"Not if I can help it," Dunross said.

"You've never liked Paul Havergill, have you, Ian?" Phillip Chen said.

"No. He's too insular, too Hong Kong, too out of date, and too pompous."

"And he supported your father against you."

"Yes. But that's not the reason he should go, Phillip. He should go because he's in the way of the Noble House. He's too conservative, far too generous to Asian Properties and I think he's a secret ally of Rothwell-Gornt."

"I don't agree," Alastair said.

"I know. But we need money to expand and I intend to get the money. So I intend to use *my* 21 percent very seriously."

The storm outside had intensified but they did not seem to notice.

"I don't advise you to set your cap against the Victoria," Phillip Chen said gravely.

"I agree," Alastair Struan said.

"I won't. Provided *my* bank cooperates." Dunross watched the rain streaks for a moment. "By the way, I've also invited Jason Plumm to the meeting."

"What the hell for?" Struan asked, his neck reddening again.

"Between us and his Asian Properties we—"

"Plumm's on Dirk Struan's oblit list, as you call it, and absolutely opposed to us."

"Between the four of us we have a majority say in Hong Kong—" Dunross broke off as the phone rang loudly. They all looked at it.

Alastair Struan said sourly, "It's your phone now, not mine."

Dunross picked it up. "Dunross!" He listened for a moment then said, "No, Mr. Alastair Struan has retired, I'm tai-pan of Struan's now. Yes. Ian Dunross. What's the telex say?" Again he listened. "Yes, thank you."

He put down the phone. At length he broke the silence. "It was from our office in Taipei. *Lasting Cloud* has foundered off the north coast of Formosa. They think she's gone down with all hands. . . ."

SUNDAY,
August 18, 1963

1

The police officer was leaning against one corner of the information counter watching the tall Eurasian without watching him. He wore a light tropical suit and a police tie and white shirt, and it was hot within the brightly lit terminal building, the air humid and smell laden, milling noisy Chinese as always. Men, women, children, babes. An abundance of Cantonese, some Asians, a few Europeans.

"Superintendent?"

One of the information girls was offering him a phone. "It's for you, sir," she said and smiled prettily, white teeth, dark hair, dark sloe eyes, lovely golden skin.

"Thanks," he said, noticing that she was Cantonese and new, and did not mind that the reality of her smile was empty, with nothing behind it but a Cantonese obscenity. "Yes?" he said into the phone.

"Superintendent Armstrong? This is the tower—*Yankee* 2's just landed. On time."

"Still Gate 16?"

"Yes. She'll be there in six minutes."

"Thanks." Robert Armstrong was a big man and he leaned across the counter and replaced the phone. He noticed her long legs and the curve of her rump in the sleek, just too tight, uniformed *chong-sam* and he wondered briefly what she would be like in bed. "What's your name?" he asked, knowing that any Chinese hated to be named to any policeman, let alone a European.

"Mona Leung, sir."

"Thank you, Mona Leung." He nodded to her, kept his pale blue eyes on her and saw a slight shiver of apprehension go through her. This pleased him. Up yours too, he thought, then turned his attention back to his prey.

The Eurasian, John Chen, was standing beside one of the exits, alone, and this surprised him. Also that he was nervous. Usually John Chen was unperturbable, but now every few moments he would glance at his watch, then up at the arrivals board, then back to his watch again.

Another minute and then we'll begin, Armstrong thought.

He began to reach into his pocket for a cigarette, then remembered that he had given up smoking two weeks ago as a birthday present to his wife, so he cursed briefly and stuck his hands deeper into his pockets.

Around the information counter harassed passengers and meeters-of-passengers rushed up and pushed and went away and came back again, loudly asking the where and when and how and why and where once more in myriad dialects. Cantonese he understood well. Shanghainese and Mandarin a little. A few Chu Chow expressions and most of their swear words. A little Taiwanese.

He left the counter now, a head taller than most of the crowd, a big, broad-shouldered man with an easy, athletic stride, seventeen years in the Hong Kong Police Force, now head of CID—Criminal Investigation Department—of Kowloon.

"Evening, John," he said. "How're things?"

"Oh hi, Robert," John Chen said, instantly on guard, his English American-accented. "Everything's great, thanks. You?"

"Fine. Your airport contact mentioned to Immigration that you were meeting a special plane. A charter—*Yankee 2.*"

"Yes—but it's not a charter. It's privately owned. By Lincoln Bartlett—the American millionaire."

"He's aboard?" Armstrong asked, knowing he was.

"Yes."

"With an entourage?"

"Just his Executive VP—and hatchet man."

"Mr. Bartlett's a friend?" he asked, knowing he was not.

"A guest. We hope to do business with him."

"Oh? Well, his plane's just landed. Why don't you come with me? We'll bypass all the red tape for you. It's the least we can do for the Noble House, isn't it?"

"Thanks for your trouble."

"No trouble." Armstrong led the way through a side door in the Customs barrier. Uniformed police looked up, saluting him instantly and watched John Chen thoughtfully, recognizing him at once.

"This Lincoln Bartlett," Armstrong continued with pretended geniality, "doesn't mean anything to me. Should it?"

"Not unless you were in business," John Chen said, then rushed on nervously, "He's nicknamed 'Raider'—because of his successful raids and takeovers of other companies, most times much bigger than himself. Interesting man, I met him in New York last year. His conglomerate grosses almost half a billion dollars a year. He says he started in '45 with two thousand borrowed dollars. Now he's into petrochemicals, heavy engineering, electronics, missiles—lots of U.S. Government work—foam, polyurethane foam products, fertilizers—he even has one company that makes and sells skis, sports goods. His group's Par-Con Industries. You name it, he has it."

"I thought your company owned everything already."

John Chen smiled politely. "Not in America," he said, "and it is not my company. I'm just a minor stockholder of Struan's, an employee."

"But you're a director and you're the eldest son of Noble House Chen so you'll be next compradore." By historic custom the compradore was a Chinese or Eurasian businessman who acted as the exclusive intermediary between the European trading house and the Chinese. All business went through his hands and a little of everything stuck there.

So much wealth and so much power, Armstrong thought, yet with a little luck, we can bring you down like Humpty-Dumpty and Struan's with you. Jesus Christ, he told himself, the anticipation sickly sweet, if that happens the scandal's going to blow Hong Kong apart. "You'll be compradore, like your father and grandfather and great-grandfather before you. Your great-grandfather was the first, wasn't he? Sir Gordon Chen, compradore to the great Dirk Struan who founded the Noble House and damn nearly founded Hong Kong."

"No. Dirk's compradore was a man called Chen Sheng. Sir Gordon Chen was compradore to Dirk's son, Culum Struan."

"They were half-brothers weren't they?"

"So the legend goes."

"Ah yes, legends—the stuff we feed on. Culum Struan, another legend of Hong Kong. But Sir Gordon, he's a legend too—you're lucky."

Lucky? John Chen asked himself bitterly. To be descended from an illegitimate son of a Scots pirate—an opium runner, a whoring evil genius and murderer if some of the stories are true—and a Cantonese singsong girl bought out of a filthy little cathouse that still exists in a filthy little Macao alley? To have almost everyone in Hong Kong know your lineage and to be despised for it by both races? "Not lucky," he said, trying to be outwardly calm. His hair was gray-flecked and dark, his face Anglo-Saxon and handsome, though a little slack at the jowls, and his dark eyes only slightly Asian. He was forty-two and wore tropicals, impeccably cut as always, with Hermès shoes and Rolex watch.

"I don't agree," Armstrong said, meaning it. "To be compradore to Struan's, the Noble House of Asia . . . that's something. Something special."

"Yes, that's special." John Chen said it flat. Ever since he could think, he had been bedeviled by his heritage. He could feel eyes watching him—him, the eldest son, the next in line—he could feel the everlasting greed and the envy. It had terrified him continuously, however much he tried to conquer the terror. He had never wanted any of the power or any of the responsibility. Only yesterday he had had another grinding row with his father, worse than ever before. "I don't want any part of Struan's!" he had shouted. "For the hundredth time I want to get the hell out of Hong Kong, I want to go back to the States, I want to lead my own life, as I want, where I want, and how I want!"

"For the thousandth time, you'll listen to me. I sent you to Am—"

"Let me run our American interests, Father. Please. There's more than enough to do! You could let me have a couple of mill—"

"*Ayeeyah* you will listen to me! It's here, here in Hong Kong and Asia we make our money! I sent you to school in America to prepare the family for the modern world. You are prepared, it's your duty to the fam—"

"There's Richard, Father, and young Kevin—Richard's ten times the businessman I am and chomping at the bit. What about Uncle Jam—"

"You'll do as I say! Good God, you know this American Bartlett is vital to us. We need your knowl—"

"—Uncle James or Uncle Thomas. Uncle James'd be the best for you; best for the family and the bes—"

"You're my eldest son. You're the next head of the family and the next compradore!"

"I won't be by God!"

"Then you won't get another copper cash!"

"And that won't be much of a change! We're all kept on a pittance, whatever outsiders think! What are you worth? How many millions? Fifty? Seventy? A hun—"

"Unless you apologize at once and finish with all this nonsense, finish with it once and for all, I'll cut you off right now! Right now!"

"I apologize for making you angry but I'll never change! Never!"

"I'll give you until my birthday. Eight days. Eight days to become a dutiful son. That's my last word. Unless you become obedient by my birthday I'll chop you and your line off our tree forever! Now get out!"

John Chen's stomach twisted uneasily. He hated the interminable quarreling, his father apoplectic with rage, his wife in tears, his children petrified, his stepmother and brothers and cousins all gloating, wanting him gone, all of his sisters, most of his uncles, all their wives. Envy, greed. The hell with it and them, he thought. But Father's right about Bartlett, though not the way he thinks. No. This one is for me. This deal. Just this one then I'll be free forever.

They were almost through the long, brightly lit Customs Hall now.

"You going racing Saturday?" John Chen asked.

"Who isn't!" The week before, to the ecstasy of all, the immensely powerful Turf Club with its exclusive monopoly on horse racing—the only legal form of gambling allowed in the Colony—had put out a special bulletin: "Though our formal season does not start this year until October 5, with the kind permission of our illustrious Governor, Sir Geoffrey Allison, the Stewards have decided to declare Saturday, August 24 a Very Special Race Day for the enjoyment of all and as a salute to our hardworking population who are bearing the heavy weight of the second worst drought in our history with fortitude. . . ."

"I hear you've got Golden Lady running in the fifth," Armstrong said.

"The trainer says she's got a chance. Please come by Father's box and have a drink with us. I could use some of your tips. You're a great punter."

"Just lucky. But my ten dollars each way hardly compares with your ten thousand."

"But that's only when we've one of our horses running. Last season was a disaster. . . . I could use a winner."

"So could I." Oh Christ how I need a winner, Armstrong thought. But you, Johnny Chen, it doesn't matter a twopenny tick in hell if you win or lose ten thousand or a hundred thousand. He tried to curb his soaring jealousy. Calm down, he told himself. Crooks're a fact and it's your job to catch them if you can—however rich, however powerful—and to be content with your rotten pay when every street corner's groaning with free silver. Why envy this bastard—he's for the chopper one way or another. "Oh by the way, I sent a constable to your car to take it through the gate. It'll be waiting at the gangway for you and your guests."

"Oh, that's great, thanks. Sorry for the trouble."

"No trouble. It's a matter of face. Isn't it. I thought it must be pretty special for you to come yourself." Armstrong could not resist another barb. "As I said, nothing's too much trouble for the Noble House."

John Chen kept his polite smile but screw you, he thought. We tolerate you because of what you are, a very important cop, filled with envy, heavily in debt, surely corrupt and you know nothing about horses. Screw you in spades. *Dew neh loh moh* on all your generations, John Chen thought, but he kept the obscenity hidden carefully, for though Armstrong was roundly hated by all Hong Kong *yan,* John Chen knew from long experience that Armstrong's ruthless, vengeful cunning was worthy of a filthy Manchu. He reached up to the half-coin he wore on a thin leather thong around his neck. His fingers trembled as they touched the metal through his shirt. He shivered involuntarily.

"What's the matter?" Armstrong asked.

"Nothing. Nothing at all." Get hold of yourself, John Chen thought.

Now they were through the Customs Hall and into the Immigration area, the night dark outside. Lines of anxious, unsettled, tired people waited in front of the neat, small desks of the cold-faced, uniformed Immigration officers. These men saluted Armstrong. John Chen felt their searching eyes.

As always, his stomach turned queasy under their scrutiny even though he was safe from their probing questions. He held a proper British passport, not just a second-class Hong Kong passport, also an American Green Card—the Alien Card—that most priceless of possessions that gave him free access to work and play and live in the U.S.A., all the privileges of a born American except the right to vote. Who needs to vote, he thought, and stared back at one of the men, trying to feel brave, but still feeling naked under the man's gaze.

"Superintendent?" One of the officers was holding up a phone. "It's for you, sir."

He watched Armstrong walk back to take the call and he wondered what it would be like to be a policeman with so much opportunity for so much graft, and, for the millionth time, what it would be like to be all British or all Chinese, and not a Eurasian despised by both.

He watched Armstrong listening intently, then heard him say above the hubbub, "No, just stall. I'll deal with it personally. Thanks, Tom."

Armstrong came back. "Sorry," he said, then headed past the Immigration cordon, up a small corridor and into the VIP Lounge. It was neat and expansive, with bar facilities and a good view of the airport and the city and the bay. The lounge was empty except for two Immigration and Customs officers and one of Armstrong's men waiting beside Gate 16—a glass door that let out onto the floodlit tarmac. They could see the 707 coming onto her parking marks.

"Evening, Sergeant Lee," Armstrong said. "All set?"

"Yes sir. *Yankee* 2's just shutting down her engines." Sergeant Lee saluted again and opened the gate for them.

Armstrong glanced at John Chen, knowing the neck of the trap was almost closed. "After you."

"Thanks." John Chen walked out onto the tarmac.

Yankee 2 towered over them, its dying jets now a muted growl. A ground crew was easing the tall, motor-driven gangway into place. Through the small cockpit windows they could see the dimly lit pilots. To one side, in the shadows, was John Chen's dark blue Silver Cloud Rolls, the uniformed Chinese chauffeur standing beside the door, a policeman nearby.

The main cabin door of the aircraft swung open and a uniformed steward came out to greet the two airport officials who were waiting on the platform. He handed one of the officials a pouch with the airplane's documents and arrival manifests, and they began to chat affably. Then they all stopped. Deferentially. And saluted politely.

The girl was tall, smart, exquisite and American.

Armstrong whistled quietly. "*Ayeeyah!*"

"Bartlett's got taste," John Chen muttered, his heart quickening.

They watched her come down the stairs, both men lost in masculine musings.

"You think she's a model?"

"She moves like one. A movie star, maybe?"

John Chen walked forward. "Good evening. I'm John Chen of Struan's. I'm meeting Mr. Bartlett and Mr. Tchuluck."

"Oh yes of course, Mr. Chen. This's very kind of you, sir, particularly on a Sunday. I'm pleased to meet you. I'm K.C. Tcholok. Linc says if you . . ."

"Casey Tchuluck?" John Chen gaped at her. "Eh?"

"Yes," she said, her smile nice, patiently passing over the mispronunciation. "You see my initials are K.C., Mr. Chen, so *Casey* became my nickname." She turned her eyes on Armstrong. "Evening. You're also from Struan's?" Her voice was melodious.

"Oh, er, excuse me, this, this is Superintendent Armstrong," John Chen stuttered, still trying to recover.

"Evening," Armstrong said, noticing that she was even more attractive close up. "Welcome to Hong Kong."

"Thank you. Superintendent? That's police?" Then the name clicked into place. "Ah, Armstrong. Robert Armstrong? Chief of CID Kowloon?"

He covered his surprise. "You're very well informed, Miss Tcholok."

She laughed. "Just part of my routine. When I go to a new place, particularly one like Hong Kong, it's my job to be prepared . . . so I just sent for your current listings."

"We don't have published listings."

"I know. But the Hong Kong Government puts out a government phone book which anyone can buy for a few pennies. I just sent for one of those. All police departments are listed—heads of departments, most with their home numbers—along with every other government office. I got one through your Hong Kong PR office in New York."

"Who's head of Special Branch?" he asked, testing her.

"I don't know. I don't think that department was listed. Is it?"

"Sometimes."

A slight frown stood in her eyes. "You greet all private airplanes, Superintendent?"

"Only those I wish to." He smiled at her. "Only those with pretty, well-informed ladies aboard."

"Something's wrong? There's trouble?"

"Oh no, just routine. Kai Tak's part of my responsibility," Armstrong said easily. "May I see your passport please?"

"Of course." Her frown deepened as she opened her handbag and handed her U.S. passport over.

Years of experience made his inspection very detailed indeed. "Born Providence, Rhode Island, November 25, 1936, height 5 feet 8 inches, hair blond, eyes hazel." Passport's valid with two years left to run. Twenty-six, eh? I'd've guessed younger, though there's a strangeness to her eyes if you look closely.

With apparent haphazardness he flipped carelessly through the pages. Her three-month Hong Kong visa was current and in order. A dozen immigration visa stamps, all England, France, Italy or South American. Except one. USSR, dated July this year. A seven-day visit. He recognized the Moscow frank. "Sergeant Lee!"

"Yes sir?"

"Get it stamped for her," he said casually, and smiled down at her. "You're all cleared. You may stay more or less as long as you like. Towards the end of three months just go to the nearest police station and we'll extend your visa for you."

"Thanks very much."

"You'll be with us for a while?"

"That depends on our business deal," Casey said after a pause. She smiled at John Chen. "We hope to be in business for a long time."

John Chen said, "Yes. Er, we hope so too." He was still nonplussed, his mind churning. It's surely not possible for Casey Tcholok to be a woman, he thought.

Behind them the steward, Sven Svensen, came bouncing down the stairs, carrying two air suitcases. "Here you are, Casey. You're sure this's enough for tonight?"

"Yes. Sure. Thanks, Sven."

"Linc said for you to go on. You need a hand through Customs?"

"No thanks. Mr. John Chen kindly met us. Also, Superintendent Armstrong, head of Kowloon CID."

"Okay." Sven studied the policeman thoughtfully for a moment. "I'd better get back."

"Everything all right?" she asked.

"I think so." Sven Svensen grinned. "Customs're just checking our stocks of booze and cigarettes." Only four things were subject to any import license or customs duty in the Colony—gold, liquor, tobacco and gasoline—and only one contraband—apart from narcotics—and totally forbidden: all forms of firearms and ammunition.

Casey smiled up at Armstrong. "We've no rice aboard, Superintendent. Linc doesn't eat it."

"Then he's in for a bad time here."

She laughed then turned back to Svensen. "See you tomorrow. Thanks."

"9 A.M. on the dot!" Svensen went back to the airplane and Casey turned to John Chen.

"Linc said for us not to wait for him. Hope that's all right," she said.

"Eh?"

"Shall we go? We're booked into the Victoria and Albert Hotel, Kowloon." She began to pick up her bags but a porter materialized out of the darkness and took them from her. "Linc'll come later . . . or tomorrow."

John Chen gawked at her. "Mr. Bartlett's not coming?"

"No. He's going to stay in the airplane overnight if he can get permission. If not, he'll follow us by cab. In any event he'll join us tomorrow for lunch as arranged. Lunch is still on, isn't it?"

"Oh yes, but . . ." John Chen was trying to get his mind working. "Then you'll want to cancel the 10 A.M. meeting?"

"Oh no. I'll attend that as arranged. Linc wasn't expected at that meeting. That's just financing—not policy. I'm sure you understand. Linc's very tired, Mr. Chen," she said. "He just got back yesterday from Europe." She looked back at Armstrong. "The captain asked the tower if Linc could sleep in, Superintendent. They checked with Immigration who said they'd get back to us but I presume our request'll come through channels to you. We'd certainly appreciate it if you'd approve. He's really been on the jet lag trail for too long."

Armstrong found himself saying, "I'll chat with him about it."

"Oh thanks. Thanks very much," she said, and then to John Chen, "Sorry for all this trouble, Mr. Chen. Shall we go?" She began to head for Gate 16, the porter following, but John Chen pointed to his Rolls. "No, this way, Miss Tchu—er, Casey."

Her eyes widened. "No Customs?"

"Not tonight," Armstrong said, liking her. "A present from Her Majesty's Government."

"I feel like visiting royalty."

"All part of the service."

She got into the car. Lovely smell of leather. And luxury. Then she saw the porter hurrying through the gate into the terminal building. "But what about my bags?"

"No need to worry about those," John Chen said irritably. "They'll be in your suite before you are."

Armstrong held on to the door for a moment. "John came with two cars. One for you and Mr. Bartlett—the other for luggage."

"Two cars?"

"Of course. Don't forget you're in Hong Kong now."

He watched the car drive off. Linc Bartlett's a lucky man, he thought, and wondered absently why Special Intelligence was interested in her.

"Just meet the airplane and go through her passport personally," the director of SI had told him this morning. "And Mr. Lincoln Bartlett's."

"May I ask why, sir?"

"No, Robert, you may not ask why. You're no longer in this branch—you're in a nice cushy job at Kowloon. A positive sinecure, what?"

"Yes sir."

"And Robert, kindly don't balls up this operation tonight—there may be a lot of very big names involved. We go to a great deal of trouble to keep you fellows abreast of what the nasties are doing."

"Yes sir."

Armstrong sighed as he walked up the gangway followed by Sergeant Lee. *Dew neh loh moh* on all senior officers, particularly the director of SI.

One of the Customs officials was waiting at the top of the gangway with Svensen. "Evening, sir," he said. "Everything's shipshape aboard. There's a .38 with a box of a hundred shells unopened as part of ship's stores. A Verey Light pistol. Also three hunting rifles and a twelve-bore with ammo belonging to Mr. Bartlett. They're all listed on the manifest and I inspected them. There's a locked gun cabinet in the main cabin. Captain has the key."

"Good."

"You need me anymore, sir?"

"No, thanks." Armstrong took the airplane's manifest and began to check it. Lots of wine, cigarettes, tobacco, beer and spirits. Ten cases of Dom Pérignon '59, fifteen Puligny Montrachet '53, nine Château Haut Brion '53. "No Lafite Rothschild 1916, Mr. Svensen?" he said with a small smile.

"No sir." Svensen grinned. "'16 was a very bad year. But there's half a case of the 1923. It's on the next page."

Armstrong flipped the page. More wines and the cigars were listed. "Good," he said. "Of course all this is in bond while you're on the ground."

"Yes sir. I'd already locked it—your man's tagged it. He said it was okay to leave a twelve-pack of beer in the cooler."

"If the owner wants to import any of the wines, just let me know. There's no fuss and just a modest contribution to Her Majesty's bottom drawer."

"Sir?" Svensen was perplexed.

"Eh? Oh, just an English pun. Refers to a lady's bottom drawer in a chest of drawers—where she puts away the things she needs in the future. Sorry. Your passport please." Svensen's passport was Canadian. "Thanks."

"May I introduce you to Mr. Bartlett? He's waiting for you."

Svensen led the way into the airplane. The interior was elegant and simple. Right off the small hallway was a sitting area with half a dozen deep leather chairs and a sofa. A central door closed off the rest of the airplane, aft. In one of the chairs a stewardess was half asleep, her travel bags beside her. Left was the cockpit door. It was open.

The captain and first officer/copilot were in their seats, still going through their paper work.

"Excuse me, Captain. This is Superintendent Armstrong," Svensen said, and stepped aside.

"Evening, Superintendent," the captain said. "I'm Captain Jannelli and this's my copilot, Bill O'Rourke."

"Evening. May I see your passports please?"

Both pilots had massed international visas and immigration stamps. No Iron Curtain countries. Armstrong handed them to Sergeant Lee for stamping. "Thank you, Captain. Is this your first visit to Hong Kong?"

"No sir. I was here a couple of times R and R during Korea. And I had a six-month tour with Far Eastern as first officer on their round-the-world route in '56, during the riots."

"What riots?" O'Rourke asked.

"The whole of Kowloon blew apart. Couple hundred thousand Chinese went on a sudden rampage, rioting, burning. The cops—sorry, the police tried to settle it with patience, then the mobs started killing so the cops, police, they got out a couple of Sten guns and killed half a dozen jokers and everything calmed down very fast. Only police have guns here which is a great idea." To Armstrong he said, "I think your guys did a hell of a job."

"Thank you, Captain Jannelli. Where did this flight emanate?"

"L.A.—Los Angeles. Linc's—Mr. Bartlett's head office's there."

"Your route was Honolulu, Tokyo, Hong Kong?"

"Yes sir."

"How long did you stop in Tokyo?"

Bill O'Rourke turned up the flight log at once. "Two hours and seventeen minutes. Just a refueling stop, sir."

"Just enough time to stretch your legs?"

Jannelli said, "I was the only one who got out. I always check my gear, the landing gear, and do an exterior inspection whenever we land."

"That's a good habit," the policeman said politely. "How long are you staying?"

"Don't know, that's up to Linc. Certainly overnight. We couldn't leave before 1400. Our orders're just to be ready to go anywhere at any time."

"You've a fine aircraft, Captain. You're approved to stay here till 1400. If you want an extension, call Ground Control before that time. When you're ready, just clear Customs through that gate. And would you clear all your crew together, please."

"Sure. Soon as we're refueled."

"You and all your crew know the importing of any firearms into the Colony is absolutely forbidden? We're very nervous about firearms in Hong Kong."

"So am I, Superintendent—anywhere. That's why I've the only key to the gun cabinet."

"Good. Any problems, please check with my office." Armstrong left and went into the anteroom, Svensen just ahead.

Jannelli watched him inspect the air hostess's passport. She was pretty, Jenny Pollard. "Son of a bitch," he muttered, then added quietly, "Something stinks around here."

"Huh?"

"Since when does CID brass check goddamn passports for chrissake? You sure we're not carrying anything curious?"

"Hell no. I always check everything. Including Sven's stores. Of course I don't go through Linc's stuff—or Casey's—but they wouldn't do anything stupid."

"I've flown him for four years and never once . . . Even so, something sure as hell stinks." Jannelli wearily twisted and settled himself in his pilot's seat more comfortably. "Jesus, I could use a massage and a week off."

In the anteroom Armstrong was handing the passport to Sergeant Lee who stamped it. "Thank you, Miss Pollard."

"Thank you."

"That's all the crew, sir," Svensen said. "Now Mr. Bartlett."

"Yes, please."

Svensen knocked on the central door and opened it without waiting. "Linc, this's Superintendent Armstrong," he said with easy informality.

"Hi," Linc Bartlett said, getting up from his desk. He put out his hand. "May I offer you a drink? Beer?"

"No thanks. Perhaps a cup of coffee."

Svensen turned for the galley at once. "Coming up," he said.

"Make yourself at home. Here's my passport," Bartlett said. "Won't be a moment." He went back to the typewriter and continued tapping the keys with two fingers.

Armstrong studied him leisurely. Bartlett was sandy haired with gray-flecked blue eyes, a strong good-looking face. Trim. Sports shirt and jeans. He checked the passport. Born Los Angeles, October 1, 1922. He looks young for forty, he thought. Moscow franking, same as Casey Tcholok, no other Iron Curtain visits.

His eyes wandered the room. It was spacious, the whole width of the airplane. There was a short central corridor aft with two cabins off it and two toilets. And at the end a final door which he presumed was the master suite.

The cabin was fitted as if it were a communications center. Teletype, international telephone capability, built-in typewriters. An illuminated world time clock on a bulkhead. Filing cabinets, duplicator and a built-in leather-topped desk strewn with papers. Shelves of books. Tax books. A few paperbacks. The rest were war books and books on generals or by generals. Dozens of them. Wellington and Napoleon and Patton, Eisenhower's *Crusade in Europe,* Sun Tzu's *The Art of War* . . .

"Here you are, sir," broke into Armstrong's inspection.

"Oh, thank you, Svensen." He took the coffee cup and added a little cream.

Svensen put a fresh, opened can of chilled beer beside Bartlett, picked up the empty, then went back to the galley, closing the door after him. Bartlett sipped the beer from the can, rereading what he had written, then pressed a buzzer. Svensen came at once. "Tell Jannelli to ask the tower to send this off." Svensen nodded and left. Bartlett eased his shoulders and swung around in the swivel chair. "Sorry—I had to get that right off."

"That's all right, Mr. Bartlett. Your request to stay overnight is approved."

"Thanks—thanks very much. Could Svensen stay as well?" Bartlett grinned. "I'm not much of a housekeeper."

"Very well. How long will your aircraft be here?"

"Depends on our meeting tomorrow, Superintendent. We hope to go into business with Struan's. A week, ten days."

"Then you'll need an alternate parking place tomorrow. We've another VIP flight coming in at 1600 hours. I told Captain Jannelli to phone Ground Control before 1400 hours."

"Thanks. Does the head of CID Kowloon usually deal with parking around here?"

Armstrong smiled. "I like to know what's going on in my division. It's a tedious habit but ingrained. We don't often have private aircraft visiting us—or Mr. Chen meeting someone personally. We like to be accommodating if we can. Struan's owns most of the airport and John's a personal friend. He's an old friend of yours?"

"I spent time with him in New York and L.A. and liked him a lot. Say, Superintendent, this airplane's my comm—" One of the phones rang. Bartlett picked it up. "Oh hello Charlie, what's happening in New York? . . . Jesus, that's great. How much? . . . Okay Charlie, buy the whole block. . . . Yes, the whole 200,000 shares. . . . Sure, first thing Monday morning, soon as the market opens. Send me a confirm by telex. . . ." Bartlett put the phone down and turned to Armstrong. "Sorry. Say, Superintendent, this's my communications center and I'll be lost without it. If we park for a week is it okay to come back and forth?"

"I'm afraid that might be dicey, Mr. Bartlett."

"Is that yes or no or maybe?"

"Oh that's slang for difficult. Sorry, but our security at Kai Tak's very particular."

"If you have to put on extra men, I'd be glad to pay."

"It's a matter of security, Mr. Bartlett, not money. You'll find Hong Kong's phone system first class." Also it will be far easier for Special Intelligence to monitor your calls, he thought.

"Well, if you can I'd appreciate it."

Armstrong sipped the coffee. "This's your first visit to Hong Kong?"

"Yes sir. My first time in Asia. Farthest I've gotten was Guadalcanal, in '43."

"Army?"

"Sergeant, Engineers. Construction—we used to build anything: hangars, bridges, camps, anything. A great experience." Bartlett sipped from the can. "Sure I can't give you a drink?"

"No thanks." Armstrong finished his cup, began to get up. "Thanks for the coffee."

"Now may I ask you a question?"

"Of course."

"What's Dunross like? Ian Dunross. The head of Struan's?"

"*The* tai-pan?" Armstrong laughed outright. "That depends whom you ask, Mr. Bartlett. You've never met him?"

"No, not yet. I do tomorrow. At lunch. Why do you call him *the tai-pan?*"

"*Tai-pan* means 'supreme leader' in Cantonese—the person with the ultimate power. The European heads of all the old trading companies are all tai-pans to the Chinese. But even among tai-pans there's always the greatest. *The* tai-pan. Struan's is nicknamed the 'Noble House' or 'Noble Hong,' *hong* meaning 'company.' It goes back to the beginning of the China trade and the early days of Hong Kong. Hong Kong was founded in 1841, January 26, actually. The founder of Struan and Company was a legend, still is in some ways—Dirk Struan. Some say he was a pirate, some a prince. In any event he made a fortune smuggling Indian opium into China, then converting that silver into China teas which he shipped to England in a fleet of China clippers. He became a merchant prince, earned the title of *the* tai-pan, and ever since, Struan's has always tried to be first in everything."

"Are they?"

"Oh a couple of companies dog their heels, Rothwell-Gornt particularly, but yes, I'd say they were first. Certainly not a thing comes into Hong Kong or goes out, is eaten or buried or made without Struan's, Rothwell-Gornt, Asian Properties, Blacs—the Bank of London and China—or the Victoria Bank having a finger in the stew somewhere."

"And Dunross himself? What's he like?"

Armstrong thought a moment, then said lightly, "Again it depends very much whom you ask, Mr. Bartlett. I know him just a little, socially—we meet from time to time at the races. I've had two official meetings with him. He's charming, very good at his job. . . . I suppose *brilliant* might sum him up."

"He and his family own a lot of Struan's?"

"I don't know that for certain. I doubt if anyone does, outside of the family. But his stockholdings aren't the key to the tai-pan's desk. Oh no. Not of Struan's. Of that I'm very certain." Armstrong locked his eyes on Bartlett's. "Some say Dunross is ruthless and ready to kill. I know I wouldn't like him as an enemy."

Bartlett sipped his beer and the little lines beside his eyes crinkled with a curious smile. "Sometimes an enemy's more valuable than a friend."

"Sometimes. I hope you have a profitable stay."

At once Bartlett got up. "Thanks. I'll see you out." He opened the door and ushered Armstrong and Sergeant Lee through it, then followed them out of the main cabin door onto the landing steps. He took a deep breath of air. Once again he caught a strangeness on the wind, neither pleasant nor unpleasant, neither odor nor perfume—just strange, and curiously exciting. "Superintendent, what's that smell? Casey noticed it too, the moment Sven opened the door."

Armstrong hesitated. Then he smiled. "That's Hong Kong's very own, Mr. Bartlett. It's money."

2

"All gods bear witness to the foul luck I'm having tonight," Four Finger Wu said and spat on the deck. He was aft, on the high poop of his ocean-going junk that was moored to one of the great clusters of boats that sprawled over Aberdeen harbor on the south coast of Hong Kong Island. The night was hot and humid and he was playing mah-jong with three of his friends. They were old and weatherbeaten like himself, all captains of junks that they owned. Even so, they sailed in his fleet and took orders from him. His formal name was Wu Sang Fang. He was a short, illiterate fisherman, with few teeth and no thumb on his left hand. His junk was old, battered and filthy. He was head of the seaborne Wu, captain of the fleets, and his flag, the Silver Lotus, flew on all the four seas.

When it was his turn again, he picked up another of the ivory tiles. He glanced at it and as it did not improve his hand, discarded it noisily and spat again. The spittle glistened on the deck. He wore a ragged old undershirt and black coolie pants, like his friends, and he had ten thousand dollars riding on this single game.

"*Ayeeyah*," Pockmark Tang said, pretending disgust though the tile he had just picked up made him only one short of a winning combination—the game somewhat like gin rummy. "Fornicate all mothers except ours if I don't win!" He discarded a tile with a flourish.

"Fornicate yours if you win and I don't!" another said and they all laughed.

"And fornicate those foreign devils from the Golden Mountain if they don't arrive tonight," Goodweather Poon said.

"They'll arrive," Four Finger Wu told him confidently. "Foreign devils are glued to schedules. Even so, I sent Seventh Son to the airport to make sure." He began to pick up a tile but stopped and looked over his shoulder and watched critically as a fishing junk eased past, chugging quietly, heading up the twisting, narrow access channel between the banks of boats toward the neck of the harbor. She had only riding lights, port and star-board. Ostensibly she was just going fishing but this junk was one of his and she was out to intercept a Thai trawler with a cargo of opium. When she was safely passed, he concentrated on the game once more. It was low tide now, but there was deep water around most of the boat islands. From the shore and flats came the stench of rotting seaweed, shellfish and human waste.

Most of the sampans and junks were dark now, their multitudes sleep-ing. There were a few oil lamps here and there. Boats of all sizes were moored precariously to each other, seemingly without order, with tiny sea alleys between the floating villages. These were the homes of the Tanka and Haklo people—the boat dwellers—who lived their lives afloat, were born afloat and died afloat. Many of these boats never moved from these moorings but stayed locked together until they sank or fell apart, or went down in a typhoon or were burnt in one of the spectacular conflagrations that frequently swept the clusters when a careless foot or hand knocked over a lamp or dropped something inflammable into the inevitable open fires.

"Grandfather!" the youthful lookout called.

"What is it?" Wu asked.

"On the jetty, look! Seventh Son!" The boy, barely twelve, was pointing to the shore.

Wu and the others got up and peered shorewards. The young Chinese was paying off a taxi. He wore jeans and a neat T-shirt and sneakers. The taxi had stopped near the gangway of one of the huge floating restaurants that were moored to the modern jetties, a hundred yards away. There were four of these gaudy floating palaces—three, four or five stories tall—ablaze with lights, splendiferous in scarlet and green and gold with fluted Chinese roofs and gods, gargoyles and dragons.

"You've good eyes, Number Three Grandson. Good. Go and meet Sev-enth Son." Instantly the child scurried off, sure-footed across the rickety planks that joined this junk to others. Four Fingers watched his seventh son head for one of the jetties where ferry sampans that serviced the harbor were clustered. When he saw that the boatman he had sent had inter-cepted him, he turned his back on the shore and sat down again. "Come on, let's finish the game," he said grimly. "This's my last fornicating hand. I've got to go ashore tonight."

They played for a moment, picking up tiles and discarding them.

"*Ayeeyah!*" Pockmark Tang said with a shout as he saw the face of the tile that he had just picked up. He slammed it onto the table face upwards with a flourish and laid down his other thirteen hidden tiles that made up his winning hand. "Look, by all the gods!"

Wu and the others gawked at the hand. "Pisss!" he said and hawked loudly. "Piss on all your generations, Pockmark Tang! What luck!"

"One more game? Twenty thousand, Four Finger Wu?" Tang said

gleefully, convinced that tonight old devil, Chi Kung, the god of gamblers, was sitting on his shoulder.

Wu began to shake his head, but at that moment a seabird flew overhead and called plaintively. "Forty," he said immediately, changing his mind, interpreting the call as a sign from heaven that his luck had changed. "Forty thousand or nothing! But it'll have to be dice because I've no time now."

"I haven't got forty cash by all gods, but with the twenty you owe me, I'll borrow against my junk tomorrow when the bank opens and give you all my fornicating profit on our next gold or opium shipment until you're paid, *heya?*"

Goodweather Poon said sourly, "That's too much on one game. You two fornicators've lost your minds!"

"Highest score, one throw?" Wu asked.

"*Ayeeyah,* you've gone mad, both of you," Poon said. Nonetheless, he was as excited as the others. "Where are the dice?"

Wu produced them. There were three. "Throw for your fornicating future, Pockmark Tang!"

Pockmark Tang spat on his hands, said a silent prayer, then threw them with a shout.

"Oh oh oh," he cried out in anguish. A four, a three and another four. "Eleven!" The other men were hardly breathing.

Wu spat on the dice, cursed them, blessed them and threw. A six, a two and a three. "Eleven! Oh all gods great and small! Again—throw again!"

Excitement gathered on the deck. Pockmark Tang threw. "Fourteen!"

Wu concentrated, the tension intoxicating, then threw the dice. "*Ayeeyah!*" he exploded, and they all exploded. A six, a four and a two.

"Eeeee," was all Pockmark Tang could say, holding his belly, laughing with glee as the others congratulated him and commiserated with the loser.

Wu shrugged, his heart still pounding in his chest. "Curse all seabirds that fly over my head at a time like that!"

"Ah, is that why you changed your mind, Four Finger Wu?"

"Yes—it was like a sign. How many seabirds call as they fly overhead at night?"

"That's right. I would have done the same."

"Joss!" Then Wu beamed. "Eeeee, but the gambling feeling's better than the Clouds and the Rain, *heya?*"

"Not at my age!"

"How old are you, Pockmark Tang?"

"Sixty—perhaps seventy. Almost as old as you are." Haklos did not have permanent records of births like all village land dwellers. "I don't feel more than thirty."

"Have you heard the Lucky Medicine Shop at Aberdeen Market's got a new shipment of Korean ginseng, some of it a hundred years old! That'll stick fire in your stalk!"

"His stalk's all right, Goodweather Poon! His third wife's with child again!" Wu grinned toothlessly and pulled out a big roll of 500-dollar notes. He began counting, his fingers nimble even though his left thumb was missing. Years ago it had been hacked off during a fight with river pirates during a smuggling expedition. He stopped momentarily as his number seven son came on deck. The young man was tall for a Chinese, twenty-six. He walked across the deck awkwardly. An incoming jet began to whine past overhead.

"Did they arrive, Seventh Son?"

"Yes, Father, yes they did."

Four Fingers pounded the upturned keg with glee. "Very good. Now we can begin!"

"Hey, Four Fingers," Pockmark Tang said thoughtfully, motioning at the dice. "A six, a four and a two—that's twelve, which's also three, the magic three."

"Yes, yes I saw."

Pockmark Tang beamed and pointed northwards and a little east to where Kai Tak airport would be—behind the Aberdeen mountains, across the harbor in Kowloon, six miles away. "Perhaps your luck has changed, *heya?*"

MONDAY

3

At half-dawn a jeep with two overalled mechanics aboard came around Gate 16 at the eastern end of the terminal and stopped close beside the main landing gear of *Yankee* 2. The gangway was still in place and the main door slightly ajar. The mechanics, both Chinese, got out and one began to inspect the eight-wheeled main gear while the other, equally carefully, scrutinized the nose gear. Methodically, they checked the tires and wheels and then the hydraulic couplings of the brakes, then peered into the landing bays. Both used flashlights. The mechanic at the main landing gear took out a spanner and stood on one of the wheels for a closer inspection, his head and shoulder now well into the belly of the airplane. After a moment he called out softly in Cantonese, *"Ayeeyah!* Hey, Lim, take a look at this."

The other man strolled back and peered up, sweat staining his white overalls. "Are they there or not, I can't see from down here."

"Brother, put your male stalk into your mouth and flush yourself down a sewer. Of course they're here. We're rich. We'll eat rice forever! But be quiet or you'll wake the dung-stained foreign devils above! Here . . ." The man handed down a long, canvas-wrapped package which Lim took and stowed quietly and quickly in the jeep. Then another and another small one, both men sweating and very nervous, working fast but quietly.

Another package. And another . . .

And then Lim saw the police jeep whirl around the corner and simultaneously other uniformed men come pouring out of Gate 16, among them Europeans. "We're betrayed," he gasped as he fled in a hopeless dash for freedom. The jeep intercepted him easily and he stopped, shivering with pent-up terror. Then he spat and cursed the gods and withdrew into himself.

The other man had jumped down at once and leaped into the driving seat. Before he could turn on the ignition he was swamped and handcuffed.

"So, little oily mouth," Sergeant Lee hissed, "where do you think you're going?"

"Nowhere, Officer, it was him, him there, that bastard son of a whore, Officer, he swore he'd cut my throat if I didn't help him. I don't know anything on my mother's grave!"

"You lying bastard, you never had a mother. You're going to go to jail for fifty years if you don't talk!"

"I swear, Officer, by all the gods th—"

"Piss on your lies, dungface. Who's paying you to do this job?"

Armstrong was walking slowly across the tarmac, the sick sweet taste of the kill in his mouth. "So," he said in English, "what have we here, Sergeant?" It had been a long night's vigil and he was tired and unshaven and in no mood for the mechanic's whining protestations of innocence, so he said softly in perfect gutter Cantonese, "One more tiny, insignificant word out of you, purveyor of leper dung, and I'll have my men jump on your Secret Sack."

The man froze.

"Good. What's your name?"

"Tan Shu Ta, lord."

"Liar! What's your friend's name?"

"Lim Ta-cheung, but he's not my friend, lord, I never met him before this morning."

"Liar! Who paid you to do this?"

"I don't know who paid him, lord. You see he swore he'd cut—"

"Liar! Your mouth's so full of dung you must be the god of dung himself. What's in those packages?"

"I don't know. I swear on my ancestor's gr—"

"Liar!" Armstrong said it automatically, knowing that the lies were inevitable.

"John *China*man's not the same as us," his first police teacher, an old China hand, had told him. "Oh I don't mean cut on the cross or anything like that—he's just different. He lies through his teeth all the time to a copper and when you nab a villain fair and square he'll still lie and be as slippery as a greased pole in a pile of shit. He's different. Take their names. All Chinese have four different names, one when he's born, one at puberty, one when he's an adult and one he chooses for himself, and they forget one or add another at the drop of a titfer. And their names—God stone the crows! Chinese call themselves *lao-tsi-sing*—the Ancient One Hundred Names. They've only got a basic hundred surnames in all China and of those there're twenty Yus, eight Yens, ten Wus and God knows how many Pings, Lis, Lees, Chens, Chins, Chings, Wongs and Fus and each one of them you pronounce five different ways so God knows who's who!"

"Then it's going to be difficult to identify a suspect, sir?"

"Full marks, young Armstrong! Full marks, lad. You can have fifty Lis, fifty Changs and four hundred Wongs and not one related to the other. God stone the crows! That's the problem here in Hong Kong."

Armstrong sighed. After eighteen years Chinese names were still as confusing as ever. And on top of that everyone seemed to have a nickname by which they were generally known.

"What's your name?" he asked again and didn't bother to listen to the answer. "Liar! Sergeant! Unwrap one of those! Let's see what we've got."

Sergeant Lee eased aside the last covering. Inside was an M14, an automatic rifle, U.S. Army. New and well greased.

"For this, you evil son of a whore's left tit," Armstrong grated, "you'll howl for fifty years!"

The man was staring at the gun stupidly, aghast. Then a low moan came from him. "Fornicate all gods I never knew they were guns."

"Ah, but you did know!" Armstrong said. "Sergeant, put this piece of dung in the wagon and book him for smuggling guns."

The man was dragged away roughly. One of the young Chinese policemen was unwrapping another package. It was small and square. "Hold it!" Armstrong ordered in English. The policeman and everyone in hearing distance froze. "One of them may be booby-trapped. Everyone get away from the jeep!" Sweating, the man did as he was ordered. "Sergeant, get our bomb disposal wallahs. There's no hurry now."

"Yes sir." Sergeant Lee hurried to the intercom in the police wagon.

Armstrong went under the airplane and peered into the main gear bay. He could see nothing untoward. Then he stood on one of the wheels. "Christ!" he gasped. Five snug racks were neatly bolted to each side of the inner bulkhead. One was almost empty, the others still full. From the size and shape of the packages he judged them to be more M14's and boxes of ammo—or grenades.

"Anything up there, sir?" Inspector Thomas asked. He was a young Englishman, three years in the force.

"Take a look! But don't touch anything."

"Christ! There's enough for a couple of riot squads!"

"Yes. But who?"

"Commies?"

"Or Nationalists—or villains. These'd—"

"What the hell's going on down there?"

Armstrong recognized Linc Bartlett's voice. His face closed and he jumped down, Thomas following him. He went to the foot of the gangway. "I'd like to know that too, Mr. Bartlett," he called up curtly.

Bartlett was standing at the main door of the airplane, Svensen beside him. Both men wore pajamas and robes and were sleep tousled.

"I'd like you to take a look at this." Armstrong pointed to the rifle that was now half hidden in the jeep.

At once Bartlett came down the gangway, Svensen following. "What?"

"Perhaps you'd be kind enough to wait in the airplane, Mr. Svensen."

Svensen started to reply, stopped. Then he glanced at Bartlett who nodded. "Fix some coffee, Sven, huh?"

"Sure, Linc."

"Now what's this all about, Superintendent?"

"That!" Armstrong pointed.

"That's an M14." Bartlett's eyes narrowed. "So?"

"So it seems your aircraft is bringing in guns."

"That's not possible."

"We've just caught two men unloading. There's one of the buggers"—Armstrong stabbed a finger at the handcuffed mechanic waiting sullenly beside the jeep—"and the other's in the wagon. Perhaps you'd be kind enough to look up in the main gear bay, sir."

"Sure. Where?"

"You'll have to stand on a wheel."

Bartlett did as he was told. Armstrong and Inspector Thomas watched exactly where he put his hands for fingerprint identification. Bartlett stared blankly at the racks. "I'll be goddamned! If these're more of the same, it's a goddamn arsenal!"

"Yes. Please don't touch them."

Bartlett studied the racks, then climbed down, wide awake now. "This isn't a simple smuggling job. Those racks are custom made."

"Yes. You've no objection if the aircraft's searched?"

"No. Of course not."

"Go ahead, Inspector," Armstrong said at once. "And do it very carefully indeed. Now, Mr. Bartlett, perhaps you'd be kind enough to explain."

"I don't run guns, Superintendent. I don't believe my captain would—or Bill O'Rourke. Or Svensen."

"What about Miss Tcholok?"

"Oh for chrissake!"

Armstrong said icily, "This is a very serious matter, Mr. Bartlett. Your aircraft is impounded and without police approval until further notice neither you nor any of your crew may leave the Colony pending our inquiries. Now, what about Miss Tcholok?"

"It's impossible, it's totally impossible that Casey is involved in any way with guns, gun smuggling or any kind of smuggling. Impossible." Bartlett was apologetic but quite unafraid. "Nor would any of the rest of us." His voice sharpened. "You were tipped off, weren't you?"

"How long did you stop at Honolulu?"

"An hour or two, just to refuel, I don't remember exactly." Bartlett thought for a moment. "Jannelli got off but he always does. Those racks couldn't've been loaded in an hour or so."

"Are you sure?"

"No, but I'd still bet it was done before we left the States. Though when and where and why and who I've no idea. Have you?"

"Not yet." Armstrong was watching him keenly. "Perhaps you'd like to go back to your office, Mr. Bartlett. We could take your statement there."

"Sure." Bartlett glanced at his watch. It was 5:43 A.M. "Let's do that now, then I can make a few calls. We're not wired into your system yet. There's a local phone there?" He pointed to the terminal.

"Yes. Of course we'd prefer to question Captain Jannelli and Mr. O'Rourke before you do—if you don't mind. Where are they staying?"

"At the Victoria and Albert."

"Sergeant Lee!"

"Yes sir."

"Get on to HQ."

"Yes sir."

"We'd also like to talk to Miss Tcholok first. Again if you don't mind."

Bartlett walked up the steps, Armstrong beside him. At length he said, "All right. Provided you do that personally, and not before 7:45. She's been working overtime and she's got a heavy day today and I don't want her disturbed unnecessarily."

They went into the airplane. Sven was waiting by the galley, dressed now and very perturbed. Uniformed and plainclothes police were everywhere, searching diligently.

"Sven, how about that coffee?" Bartlett led the way through the anteroom into his office-study. The central door, aft, at the end of the corridor, was open. Armstrong could see part of the master suite with its kingsize bed. Inspector Thomas was going through some drawers.

"Shit!" Bartlett muttered.

"Sorry," Armstrong said, "but this is necessary."

"That doesn't mean I have to like it, Superintendent. Never did like strangers peeking into my private life."

"Yes. I agree." The superintendent beckoned one of the plainclothes officers. "Sung!"

"Yes sir."

"Take this down will you please."

"Just a minute, let's save some time," Bartlett said. He turned to a bank of electronic gear and pressed two switches. A twin cassette tape deck clicked into operation. He plugged in a microphone and set it on the desk. "There'll be two tapes, one for you, one for me. After your man's typed it up—if you want a signature I'm here."

"Thank you."

"Okay, let's begin."

Armstrong was suddenly uneasy. "Would you please tell me what you know about the illegal cargo found in the main gear bay of your aircraft, Mr. Bartlett."

Bartlett repeated his denial of any knowledge. "I don't believe any of my crew or any of my people are involved in any way. None of them has ever been involved with the law as far as I know. And I would know."

"How long has Captain Jannelli been with you?"

"Four years. O'Rourke two. Svensen since I got the airplane in '58."

"And Miss Tcholok?"

After a pause Bartlett said, "Six—almost seven years."

"She's a senior executive in your company?"

"Yes. Very senior."

"That's unusual, isn't it, Mr. Bartlett?"

"Yes. But that has nothing to do with this problem."

"You're the owner of this aircraft?"

"My company is. Par-Con Industries Incorporated."

"Do you have any enemies—anyone who'd want to embarrass you seriously?"

Bartlett laughed. "Does a dog have fleas? You don't get to head a half-billion-dollar company by making friendships."

"No enemy in particular?"

"You tell me. Running guns is a special operation—this has to have been done by a professional."

"Who knew about your flight plan to Hong Kong?"

"The visit's been scheduled for a couple of months. My board knew. And my planning staff." Bartlett frowned. "It was no real secret. No reason to be." Then he added, "Of course Struan's knew—exactly. For at least two weeks. In fact we confirmed the date on the 12th by telex, exact ETD and ETA. I wanted it sooner but Dunross said Monday the 19th'd suit him better, which is today. Maybe you should ask him."

"I will, Mr. Bartlett. Thank you, sir. That will do for the moment."

"I've got some questions, Superintendent, if you don't mind. What's the penalty for smuggling guns?"

"Ten years without parole."

"What's the value of this cargo?"

"Priceless, to the right buyer, because no guns—absolutely none—are available to anyone."

"Who's the right buyer?"

"Anyone who wants to start a riot, insurrection, or commit mass murder, bank robbery, or some crime of whatever magnitude."

"Communists?"

Armstrong smiled and shook his head. "They don't have to shoot at us to take over the Colony, or smuggle M14's—they've got guns a-plenty of their own."

"Nationalists? Chiang Kai-shek's men?"

"They're more than well supplied with all sorts of armaments by the U.S. Government, Mr. Bartlett. Aren't they? So they don't need to smuggle this way either."

"A gang war maybe?"

"Good God, Mr. Bartlett, our gangs don't shoot each other. Our gangs—triads as we call them—our triads settle their differences in sensible, civilized Chinese fashion, with knives and axes and fighting irons and anonymous calls to the police."

"I'll bet it was someone in Struan's. That's where you'll find the answer to the riddle."

"Perhaps." Armstrong laughed strangely, then said again, "Perhaps. Now if you'll excuse me . . ."

"Of course." Bartlett turned off the recorder, took out the two cassettes and handed one over.

"Thank you, Mr. Bartlett."

"How long will this search go on?"

"That depends. Perhaps an hour. We may wish to bring in some experts. We'll try to make it as easy as possible. You'll be off the plane before lunch?"

"Yes."

"If you want access please check with my office. The number's 88-77-33. There'll be a permanent police guard here for the time being. You'll be staying at the Vic?"

"Yes. Am I free to go into town now, do what I like?"

"Yes sir, provided you don't leave the Colony, pending our inquiries."

Bartlett grinned. "I've got that message already, loud and clear."

Armstrong left. Bartlett showered and dressed and waited until all the police went away except the one who was guarding the gangway. Then he went back into his office suite and closed the door. Quite alone now he checked his watch. It was 7:37. He went over to his communications center and clicked on two micro switches and pressed the sending button.

In a moment there was a crackle of static and Casey's sleepy voice. "Yes, Linc?"

"Geronimo," he said clearly, into the mike.

There was a long pause. "Got it," she said. The loudspeaker went dead.

4

The Rolls came off the car ferry that linked Kowloon to Hong Kong Island and turned east along Connaught Road, joining the heavy traffic. The morning was very warm, humid and cloudless under a nice sun. Casey settled deeper into the back cushions. She glanced at her watch, her excitement growing.

"Plenty time, Missee," the sharp-eyed chauffeur said. "Noble House down street, tall building, ten, fifteen minutes never mind."

"Good."

This is the life, she told herself. One day I'll have a Rolls of my very own and a neat, polite, quiet Chinese chauffeur and I'll not have to worry about the price of gas. Not ever. Maybe—at long last—this is where I'm going to get my *drop dead* money. She smiled to herself. Linc was the first one who had explained about drop dead money. He had called it *screw you* money. Enough to say screw you to anybody or anything. "Screw you money's the most valuable in the world . . . but the most expensive," he had said. "If you work for me—with me but for me—I'll help you get your screw you money. But Casey, I don't know if you'll want to pay the cost."

"What's the cost?"

"I don't know. I only know it varies, person to person—and always costs you more than you're prepared to pay."

"Has yours?"

"Oh yes."

Well, she thought, the price hasn't been too high yet. I make $52,000 a year, my expense account is good and my job stretches my brain. But the government takes too much and there's not enough left to be drop dead money. "Drop dead money comes from a killing," Linc had said. "Not from cash flow."

How much do I need?

She had never asked herself the question before.

$500,000? At 7 percent that'll bring $35,000 a year forever but that's taxable. What about the Mexican Government guarantee of 11 percent, less 1 for them for their trouble? Still taxable. In tax free bonds at 4 percent it's $20,000 but bonds are dangerous and you don't gamble your drop dead money.

"That's the first rule, Casey," Linc had said. "You never risk it. Never." Then he had laughed that lovely laugh of his which disarmed her as always. "You never risk your screw you money except the once or twice you decide to."

A million? Two? Three?

Get your mind on the meeting and don't dream, she told herself. I won't but my price is 2 million cash in the bank. Tax free. That's what I want. 2 million at 5¼ percent tax free will bring $105,000 a year. And that will give me and the family everything I want with enough to spare forever. And I could better 5¼ percent on my money.

But how to get 2 million tax free?

I don't know. But somehow I know this's the place.

The Rolls stopped suddenly as a mass of pedestrians dodged through the tightly packed lines of cars and double-decker buses and taxis and trucks and carts and lorries and bicycles and handcarts and some rickshaws. Thousands of people scurried this way and that, pouring out of or into the alleys and side roads, spilling off the pavements onto the roadway in the morning rush hour. Rivers of human ants.

Casey had researched Hong Kong well, but she was still not prepared for the impact that the incredible overcrowding had made upon her.

"I never saw anything like it, Linc," she had said this morning when he had arrived at the hotel just before she left for the meeting. "It was after ten when we drove here from the airport, but there were thousands of people out—including kids—and everything—restaurants, markets, shops—were still open."

"People mean profit—why else're we here?"

"We're here to usurp the Noble House of Asia with the secret help and collusion of a Judas Iscariot, John Chen."

Linc had laughed with her. "Correction. We're here to make a deal with Struan's, and to look around."

"Then the plan's changed?"

"Tactically yes. The strategy's the same."

"Why the change, Linc?"

"Charlie called last night. We bought another 200,000 shares of Rothwell-Gornt."

"Then the bid for Struan's is just a blind and our real target's Rothwell-Gornt?"

"We still have three targets: Struan's, Rothwell-Gornt and Asian Properties. We look around and we wait. If things look good we attack. If

not, we can make 5, maybe 8 million this year on our straight deal with
Struan's. That's cream."

"You're not here for 5 or 8 million. What's the real reason?"

"Pleasure."

The Rolls gained a few yards then stopped again, the traffic heavier
now as they approached Central District. Ah Linc, she thought, your
pleasure covers a multitude of piracies.

"This first visit to Hong Kong, Missee?" broke into her thoughts.

"Yes, yes it is. I arrived last night," she said.

"Ah very good. Weather very bad never mind. Very smelly, very
humid. Always humid in summer. First day very pretty, *heya?*"

First day had started with the sharp buzz of her citizens band transceiver jerking her out of sleep. And *"Geronimo."*

It was their code word for danger—beware. She had showered and
dressed quickly, not knowing where the danger was coming from. She had
just put in her contact lenses when the phone rang. "This is Superintendent Armstrong. Sorry to bother you so early, Miss Tcholok, but could
I see you for a moment?"

"Certainly, Superintendent." She had hesitated. "Give me five minutes
—I'll meet you in the restaurant?"

They had met and he had questioned her, telling her only that contraband had been found aboard the airplane.

"How long have you worked for Mr. Bartlett?"

"Directly, six years."

"Have there ever been any police problems before? Of any sort?"

"You mean with him—or with me?"

"With him. Or with you."

"None. What's been found aboard, Superintendent?"

"You don't seem unduly worried, Miss Tcholok."

"Why should I be? I've done nothing illegal, neither has Linc. As to
the crew, they're carefully picked professionals, so I'd doubt they have
anything to do with smuggling. It's drugs, isn't it? What sort of drugs?"

"Why should it be drugs?"

"Isn't that what people smuggle in here?"

"It was a very large shipment of guns."

"What?"

There had been more questions, most of which she had answered, and
then Armstrong was gone. She had finished her coffee and refused, for the
fourth time, the home-baked, warm hard French rolls offered by a starched
and smiling boy-waiter. They reminded her of those she had had in the
south of France three years ago.

Ah, Nice and Cap D'Ail and the vin de Provence. And dear Linc, she
had thought, going back to the suite to wait for him to phone.

"Casey? Listen, th—"

"Ah Linc, I'm glad you called," she had said at once, deliberately interrupting him. "Superintendent Armstrong was here a few minutes ago—and I forgot to remind you last night to call Martin about the shares." *Martin* was also a code word, meaning, "I think this conversation's being overheard."

"I'd thought about him too. That's not important now. Tell me exactly what happened."

So she told him. He related briefly what had occurred. "I'll fill in the rest when I get there. I'm heading for the hotel right now. How's the suite?"

"Fantastic! Yours's called Fragrant Spring, my room's adjoining, guess it's normally part of it. Seems like there are ten houseboys per suite. I called room service for coffee and it arrived on a silver tray before I'd put the phone down. The bathrooms're big enough for a cocktail party for twenty with a three-piece combo."

"Good. Wait for me."

She sat in one of the deep leather sofas in the luxurious sitting room and began to wait, enjoying the quality that surrounded her. Beautiful Chinese lacquered chests, a well-stocked bar in a mirrored alcove, discreet flower arrangements and a bottle of monogrammed Scotch—Lincoln Bartlett—with the compliments of the chief manager. Her bedroom suite through an interlocking door was one side, his, the master suite, the other. Both were the biggest she had ever seen, with king-size beds.

Why were guns put on our airplane and by whom?

Lost in thought she glanced out of the wall-to-wall window and faced Hong Kong Island and the dominating Peak, the tallest mountain on the island. The city, called Victoria after Queen Victoria, began at the shoreline, then rose, tier on tier, on the skirts of the sharply rising mountain, lessening as the slopes soared, but there were apartment buildings near the crest. She could see one just above the terminal of the Peak's funicular. The view from there must be fantastic, she thought absently.

The blue water was sparkling nicely, the harbor as traffic-bound as the streets of Kowloon below. Liners and freighters were anchored or tied up alongside the wharves of Kowloon or steaming out or in, their sirens sounding merrily. Over at the dockyard Hong Kong side was a Royal Navy destroyer and, nearby at anchor, a dark-gray U.S. Navy frigate. There were hundreds of junks of every size and age—fishing vessels mostly—some powered, some ponderously sailing this way and that. Crammed double-decker ferries darted in and out of the traffic like so many dragonflies, and everywhere tiny sampans, oared or powered, scurried unafraid across the ordered sea-lanes.

Where do all these people live? she asked herself, appalled. *And how do they support themselves?*

A room boy opened the door with his passkey, without knocking, and Linc Bartlett strode in. "You look great, Casey," he said, shutting the door behind him.

"So do you. This gun thing's bad, isn't it?"

"Anyone here? Any maids in the rooms?"

"We're alone, but the houseboys seem to come in and out as they please."

"This one had his key out before I reached the door." Linc told her what had happened at the airport. Then he dropped his voice. "What about John Chen?"

"Nothing. He just made nervous, light conversation. He didn't want to talk shop. I don't think he'd recovered from the fact that I'd turned out to be a woman. He dropped me at the hotel and said they'd send a car at 9:15."

"So the plan worked fine?"

"Very fine."

"Good. Did you get it?"

"No. I said I was authorized by you to take delivery and offered the initial sight draft. But he pretended to be surprised and said he'd talk to you privately when he drives you back after the lunch. He seemed very nervous."

"Doesn't matter. Your car'll be here in a few minutes. I'll see you at lunch."

"Should I mention the guns to Struan's? To Dunross?"

"No. Let's wait and see who brings it up."

"You think it might be them?"

"Easily. They knew our flight plan, and they've a motive."

"What?"

"To discredit us."

"But why?"

"Maybe they think they know our battle plan."

"But then wouldn't it have been much wiser for them not to do any-thing—to sucker us in."

"Maybe. But this way they've made the opening move. Day One: Knight to King Bishop 3. The attack's launched on us."

"Yes. But by whom—and are we playing White or Black?"

His eyes hardened and lost their friendliness. "I don't care, Casey, as long as we win." He left.

Something's up, she told herself. Something dangerous he's not telling me about.

"Secrecy's vital, Casey," he had said back in the early days. "Napoleon, Caesar, Patton—any of the great generals—often hid their *real* plan from their staff. Just to keep them—and therefore enemy spies—off balance. If I withhold from you it's not mistrust, Casey. But you must never withhold from me."

"That's not fair."

"Life's not fair. Death's not fair. War's not fair. Big business is war. I'm playing it like it was war and that's why I'm going to win."

"Win what?"

"I want Par-Con Industries bigger than General Motors and Exxon combined."

"Why?"

"For my goddamn pleasure."

"Now tell me the real reason."

"Ah, Casey, that's why I love you. You listen and you know."

"Ah, Raider, I love you too."

Then they had both laughed together for they knew they did not love the other, not in the ordinary sense of that word. They had agreed, way back in the beginning, to put aside the ordinary for the extraordinary. For seven years.

Casey looked out of the window at the harbor and the ships in the harbor.

Crush, destroy, and win. Big Business, the most exciting Monopoly game in the world. And my leader's Raider Bartlett, Mastercraftsman. But time's running out on us, Linc. This year, the seventh year, the last year ends on my birthday, November 25, my twenty-seventh birthday. . . .

Her ears heard the half knock and the passkey in the lock and she turned to say come in but the starched houseboy was already in.

"Morning Missee I'm Number One Houseboy Daytime Chang." Chang was gray haired and solicitous. He beamed. "Tidy room plees?"

"Don't any of you ever wait for someone to say come in?" she asked sharply.

Chang stared at her blankly. "Missee?"

"Oh never mind," she said wearily.

"Pretty day, *heya?* Which first, Master's room or Missee's?"

"Mine. Mr. Bartlett hasn't used his yet."

Chang grinned toothily. *Ayeeyah,* did you and Master tumble together in yours, Missee, before he went out? But there were only fourteen minutes between Master's arrival and leaving and certainly he did not look flushed when he went away.

Ayeeyah, first it's supposed to be two men foreign devils sharing my suite and then one's a she—confirmed by Nighttime Ng, who of course went through her luggage and found serious proof that she was a true she —proof reconfirmed this morning with great gusto by Third Toiletmaid Fung.

Golden pubics! How vile!

And Golden Pubics is not only *not* the Master's chief wife—she is not even a second wife, and oh ko, worst of all she did not have the good manners to pretend she was so the hotel rules could be honored and everyone save face.

Chang chortled, for this hotel had always had astounding rules about ladies in men's rooms—oh gods what else is a bed for?—and now a female was living openly in barbarian sin! Oh how tempers had soared last night.

Barbarians! *Dew neh loh moh* on all barbarians! But this one is surely a dragon because she stared down the Eurasian assistant manager, and the Eurasian night manager, and even old mealy-mouth, Chief Manager Big Wind himself.

"No no no," he had wailed, so Chang had been told.

"Yes yes yes," she had replied, insisting that she have the adjoining half of the Fragrant Spring suite.

It was then that Honorable Mong, chief porter and chief triad and therefore leader of the hotel, solved the unsolvable. "The Fragrant Spring suite has three doors, *heya?*" he had said. "One for each bedroom, one for the main room. Let her be shown into Fragrant Spring B which is the inferior room anyway, through its own door. But the inner door to the main sitting room and thence to the Master's quarters shall be tight locked. But let a key be left nearby. If the mealy-mouthed whore unlocks the door herself . . . what can one do? And then, if there happens to be a mix-up in bookings tomorrow or the next day and our honorable chief manager has to ask the billionaire and his strumpet from the Land of the Golden Mountain to leave, well so sorry never mind, we have bookings enough and to spare and our face to protect."

And so it was done.

The outer door to B was unlocked and Golden Pubics invited in. That she took up the key and at once unlocked the inner door—who is to say? That the door is open now, well, certainly I would never tell any outsider, my lips are sealed. As always.

Ayeeyah, but though outer doors may be locked and be prudish, the inner ones may be flung wide and be luscious. Like her Jade Gate, he thought pensively. *Dew neh loh moh* I wonder what it would be like to storm a Jade Gate the size of hers? "Make bed, Missee?" he asked sweetly in English.

"Go right ahead."

Oh how truly awful the sound of their barbarian tongue is. Ugh!

Daytime Chang would have hawked and cleared the spit god from his mouth, but that was against hotel rules.

"*Heya,* Daytime Chang," Third Toiletmaid Fung said brightly as she came into the bedroom after knocking half-heartedly on the suite door long after she had opened it. "Yes, Missee, so sorry, Missee," in English, then again to Chang in Cantonese, "Haven't you finished yet? Is her dung so sweet you want to dawdle in her drawers?"

"*Dew neh loh moh* in yours, Sister. Watch your tongue or your old father may give you a good drubbing."

"The only drubbing your old mother wants, you can't help me with! Come on, let me help you make her bed quickly. There's a mah-jong game beginning in half an hour. Honorable Mong sent me for you."

"Oh, thank you, Sister. *Heya,* did you really see her pubics?"

"Haven't I told you already? Am I a liar? They're pure golden, lighter than her head hair. She was in the bath and I was as close as we are now. And, oh yes, her nipples're pinkish, not brown."

"Eeee! Imagine!"

"Just like a sow's."

"How awful!"

"Yes. Did you read today's *Commercial Daily?*"

"No, Sister, not yet. Why?"

"Well their astrologer says this is a very good week for me and today the financial editor says it looks as though there's a new boom beginning."

"Dew neh loh moh you don't say!"

"So I told my broker this morning to buy a thousand more Noble House, the same Golden Ferry, 40 of Second Great House and 50 Good Luck Properties. My bankers are generous but now I haven't a single brass cash left in Hong Kong I can beg or borrow!"

"Eeeee, you're plunging, Sister. I'm stretched out myself. Last week I borrowed from the bank on my shares and bought another 600 Noble House. That was Tuesday. I bought in at 25.23!"

"Ayeeyah, Honorable Chang, they were 29.14 at close last night." Third Toiletmaid Fung made an automatic calculation. "You're already 2,348 Hong Kong ahead! And they say Noble House's going to bid for Good Luck Properties. If they try, it will send their enemies' rage to boiling point. Ha! The tai-pan of Second Great House will fart dust!"

"Oh oh oh but meanwhile the shares will skyrocket! Of all three companies! Ha! *Dew neh loh moh,* where can I get more cash?"

"The races, Daytime Chang! Borrow 500 against your present winnings and put it on the daily double on Saturday or the double quinella. 4 and 5 are my lucky numbers. . . ."

They both looked up as Casey came into the bedroom. Chang switched to English. "Yes Missee?"

"There's some laundry in the bathroom. Can you have it picked up, please?"

"Oh yes I fix. Today six o'clock come by okay never mind." These foreign devils are so stupid, Chang thought contemptuously. What am I, an empty-headed dung heap? Of course I'll take care of the laundry if there's laundry.

"Thank you."

They both watched fascinated as she checked her makeup in the bedroom mirror, preparing to leave.

"Her tits don't droop at all, do they, Sister?" Chang said. "Pink nipples *heya?* Extraordinary!"

"Just like a sow's, I told you. Are your ears merely pots to piss in?"

"In your ear, Third Toiletmaid Fung."

"Has she tipped you yet?"

"No. The Master gave too much and she nothing. Disgusting *heya?*"

"Yes. What can you do? People from the Golden Mountain are really very uncivilized, aren't they, Daytime Chang?"

5

The tai-pan came over the rise and barreled down the Peak Road in his E-Type Jaguar, going east toward Magazine Gap. On the winding road there was but a single lane each side with few places to pass and precipitous on most corners. Today the surface was dry and, knowing the way so well, Ian Dunross rode the bends fast and sweetly, hugging the mountainside, his scarlet convertible tight to the inside curve. He did a racing shift down and braked hard as he swooped a bend and came up to an ancient, slow-moving truck. He waited patiently, then, at the perfect moment, swung out onto the wrong side and was past safely before the oncoming car had rounded the blind corner ahead.

Now Dunross was clear for a short stretch and could see that the snaking road ahead was empty. He jammed his foot down and slid some corners, usurping the whole of the road, taking the straightest line, using hand and eye and foot and brake and gearshift in unison, feeling the vast power of the engine and the wheels in all of him. Ahead, suddenly, was an oncoming truck from the far corner and his freedom vanished. He geared down and braked in split-second time, hugging his side, regretting the loss of freedom, then accelerated and was away again into more treacherous bends. Now another truck, this time ladened with passengers, and he waited a few yards behind, knowing there was no place to pass for a while. Then one of the passengers noticed his number plate, 1-1010, and she pointed and they all looked, chattering excitedly one to another, and one of them banged on the cabin of the truck. The driver obligingly squeezed off the road onto the tiny shoulder and flagged him on. Dunross made sure he was safe then passed, waving to them with a grin.

More corners, the speed and the waiting-to-pass and the passing and the danger pleasing him. Then he cut left into Magazine Gap Road, down the hill, the bends trickier, the traffic building up now and slower. He overtook a taxi and jumped three cars very fast and was back in line though still over the speed limit when he saw the traffic motorcycle police-men waiting ahead. He changed down and passed them going the regula-tion 30 mph. He waved good-naturedly. They waved back.

"You really must slow down, Ian," his friend, Henry Foxwell, Senior Superintendent of Traffic, had said recently. "You really should."

"I've never had an accident—yet. Or a ticket."

"Good God, Ian, there's not a traffic copper on the island who'd dare give you one! You, *the* tai-pan? Perish the thought. I meant for your own good. Keep that speed devil of yours bottled for Monaco, or your Macao Road Race."

"Monaco's professional. I don't take chances, and I don't drive that fast anyway."

"67 mph over Wongniechong isn't exactly slow, old chap. Admittedly it was 4:23 A.M. on an almost empty road. But it is a 30 mph zone."

"There're lots of E-Types in Hong Kong."

"Yes, I agree. Seven. Scarlet convertibles with a special number plate? With a black canvas roof, racing wheels and tires, that goes like the clappers of hell? It was last Thursday, old chap. Radar and all that. You'd been to . . . to visit friends. In Sinclair Road I believe."

Dunross had contained his sudden rage. "Oh?" he said, the surface of his face smiling. "Thursday? I seem to remember I had dinner with John Chen then. At his apartment in Sinclair Towers. But I thought I was home long before 4:23."

"Oh I'm sure you were. I'm sure the constable got the number plate and color and everything all wrong." Foxwell clapped him on the back in friendly style. "Even so, slow down a little will you? It'd be so boring if you killed yourself during my term. Wait till I'm transferred back to Spe-cial Branch—or the police college, eh? Yes, I'm sure he made a mistake."

But there was no mistake, Dunross had said to himself. You know it, I know it, and John Chen would know it and so would Wei-wei.

So you fellows know about Wei-wei! That's interesting.

"Are you fellows watching me?" he had asked bluntly.

"Good God no!" Foxwell had been shocked. "Special Intelligence was watching a villain who's got a flat at Sinclair Towers. You happened to be seen. You're very important here, you know that. I happened to pick it up through channels. You know how it is."

"No, I don't."

"They say one word to the wise is sufficient, old chap."

"Yes they do. So perhaps you'd better tell your Intelligence fellows to be more intelligent in future."

"Fortunately they're very discreet."

"Even so I wouldn't like my movements a matter of record."

"I'm sure they're not. Not a matter of record."

"Good. What villain in Sinclair Towers?"

"One of our important capitalist dogs but suspected secret Commie fellows. Very boring but SI have to earn their daily bread, don't they?"

"Do I know him?"

"I imagine you know everyone."

"Shanghainese or Cantonese?"

"What makes you think he's either?"

"Ah, then he's European?"

"He's just a villain, Ian. Sorry, it's all very hush-hush at the moment."

"Come on, we own that block. Who? I won't tell anyone."

"I know. Sorry old boy, but I can't. However, I've another hypothetical idea for you. Say a hypothetical married VIP had a lady friend whose uncle happened to be the undercover deputy chief of the illegal Kuomintang Secret Police for Hong Kong. Say, hypothetically, the Kuomintang wanted this VIP on their side. Certainly he could be pressured by such a lady. Couldn't he?"

"Yes," Dunross had said easily. "If he was stupid." He already knew about Wei-wei Jen's uncle and had met him at a number of private parties several times in Taipei. And liked him. No problem there, he had thought, because she's not my mistress or even a lady friend, however beautiful and desirable. And tempting.

He smiled to himself as he drove in the stream of traffic down Magazine Gap Road then waited in line to circle the roundabout and head down Garden Road toward Central, half a mile below, and to the sea.

Now he could see the soaring modern office block that was Struan's. It was twenty-two stories high and fronted Connaught Road and the sea, almost opposite the Terminal of the Golden Ferries that plied between Hong Kong and Kowloon. As always, the sight pleased him.

He weaved in and out of heavy traffic where he could, crawled past the Hilton Hotel and the Cricket Ground on his left, then turned into Connaught Road, the sidewalks jammed with pedestrians. He stopped outside his front entrance.

This's the big day, he thought. The Americans have arrived.

And, with joss, Bartlett's the noose that'll strangle Quillan Gornt once and for all time. Christ, if we can pull this off!

"Morning, sir." The uniformed doorman saluted crisply.

"Morning, Tom." Dunross eased himself out of the low-slung car and ran up the marble steps, two at a time, toward the huge glass entrance. Another doorman drove the car off to its underground parking and still another opened the glass door for him. He caught the reflection of the Rolls drawing up. Recognizing it, he glanced back. Casey got out and he whistled involuntarily. She carried a briefcase. Her sea-green silk suit was tailored and very conservative, but even so, it hid none of the trim of her figure or the dance to her stride and the sea green enhanced the tawny gold of her hair.

She looked around, feeling his eyes. Her recognition was immediate and she measured him as he measured her and though the instant was short it seemed long to both of them. Long and leisurely.

She moved first and walked toward him. He met her halfway.

"Hello, Mr. Dunross."

"Hello. We've never met, have we?"

"No. But you're easy to recognize from your photos. I didn't expect to have the pleasure of meeting you till later. I'm Cas—"

"Yes," he said and grinned. "I had a deranged call from John Chen last night. Welcome to Hong Kong, Miss Tcholok. It is Miss, isn't it?"

"Yes. I hope my being a woman won't upset things too much."

"Oh yes it will, very much. But we'll try to accommodate the problem. Would you and Mr. Bartlett care to be my guests at the races on Saturday? Lunch and all that?"

"I think that would be lovely. But I have to check with Linc—may I confirm this afternoon?"

"Of course." He looked down at her. She looked back. The doorman still held the door open.

"Well, come along, Miss Tcholok, and let battle commence."

She glanced at him quickly. "Why should we battle? We're here to do business."

"Oh yes, of course. Sorry, it's just a Sam Ackroyd saying. I'll explain another time." He ushered her in and headed for the bank of elevators. The many people already lined up and waiting immediately moved aside for them to get into the first elevator, to Casey's embarrassment.

"Thanks," Dunross said, not noticing anything out of the ordinary. He guided her in, pressed 20, the top button, noticing absently that she wore no perfume or jewelry, just a thin gold chain around her neck.

"Why's the front door at an angle?" she asked.

"Sorry?"

"The front entrance seems to be on a slight tilt—it's not quite straight—I was wondering why."

"You're very observant. The answer is *fung sui*. When the building was put up four years ago, somehow or other we forgot to consult our house *fung sui* man. He's like an astrologer, a man who specializes in heaven, earth, water currents, and devils, that sort of thing, and makes sure you're building on the Earth Dragon's back and not on his head."

"What?"

"Oh yes. You see every building in the whole of China's on some part of the Earth Dragon. To be on his back's perfect, but if you're on his head it's very bad, and terrible if you're on his eyeball. Anyway, when we did get around to asking, our *fung sui* man said we were on the Dragon's back —thank God, otherwise we'd've had to move—but that devils were getting in the door and this was what was causing all the trouble. He advised me to reposition the door, and so, under his direction we changed the angle and now the devils are all deflected."

She laughed. "Now tell me the real reason."

"*Fung sui.* We had very bad joss here—bad luck—rotten in fact until the door was changed." His face hardened momentarily then the shadow passed. "The moment we changed the angle, everything became good again."

"You're telling me you really believe that? Devils and dragons?"

"I believe none of it. But you learn the hard way when you're in China that it's best to act a little Chinese. Never forget that though Hong Kong's British it's still China."

"Did you learn th—"

The elevator stopped and opened on a paneled hallway and a desk and a neat, efficient Chinese receptionist. Her eyes priced Casey's clothes and jewelry instantly.

Cow, Casey thought, reading her loud and clear, and smiled back as sweetly.

"Morning, tai-pan," the receptionist said smoothly.

"Mary, this is Miss K. C. Tcholok. Please show her into Mr. Struan's office."

"Oh but—" Mary Li tried to cover her shock. "They're, they're waiting for a . . ." She picked up the phone but he stopped her. "Just show her in. Now. No need to announce her." He turned back to Casey and smiled. "You're launched. I'll see you shortly."

"Yes, thanks. See you."

"Please follow me, Miss Tchuluck," Mary Li said and started down the hall, her *chong-sam* tight and slit high on her thighs, long silk-stockinged legs and saucy walk. Casey watched her for a moment. It must be the cut that makes their walk so blatantly sexual, she thought, amused by such obviousness. She glanced at Dunross and raised an eyebrow.

He grinned. "See you later, Miss Tcholok."

"Please call me Casey."

"Perhaps I'd prefer Kamalian Ciranoush."

She gaped at him. "How do you know my names? I doubt if even Linc remembers."

"Ah, it pays to have friends in high places, doesn't it?" he said with a smile. "*À bientôt.*"

"*Oui, merci,*" she replied automatically.

He strode for the elevator opposite and pressed the button. The doors opened instantly and closed after him.

Thoughtfully Casey walked after Mary Li who was waiting, ears still tuned for every nuance.

Inside the elevator Dunross took out a key and inserted it into the lock and twisted it. Now the elevator was activated. It serviced the top two floors only. He pressed the lower button. Only three other persons had similar keys: Claudia Chen, his executive secretary; his personal secretary, Sandra Yi; and his Number One Houseboy, Lim Chu.

The twenty-first floor contained his private offices, and the Inner Court boardroom. The twenty-second, the penthouse, was the tai-pan's personal suite. And he alone had the key to the last private elevator that connected the basement garage directly with the penthouse.

"Ian," his predecessor tai-pan, Alastair Struan, had said when he handed over the keys after Phillip Chen had left them, "your privacy's the most valuable thing you have. That too Dirk Struan laid down in his legacy and how wise he was! Never forget, the private lifts aren't for luxury or ostentation, any more than the tai-pan's suite is. They're there just to give you the measure of secrecy you'll need, perhaps even a place to hide yourself. You'll understand better after you've read the legacy and been through the tai-pan's safe. Guard that safe with all you've got. You can't be too careful, there's lots of secrets there—too many I think sometimes— and some are not so pretty."

"I hope I won't fail," he had said politely, detesting his cousin, his excitement huge that at long last he had the prize he had worked so hard to achieve and gambled so much for.

"You won't. Not you," the old man had said tautly. "You've been tested, and you've wanted the job ever since you could think. Eh?"

"Yes," Dunross had said. "I've tried to train for it. Yes. I'm only surprised you've given it to me."

"You're being given the ultimate in Struan's not because of your birthright—that only made you eligible for the Inner Court—but because I think you're the best we've got to follow me, and you've been conniving and pushing and shoving for years. That's the truth, isn't it?"

"Struan's needs changing. Let's have more truth: The Noble House is in a mess. It's not all your fault, there was the war, then Korea, then Suez —you've had bad joss for several years. It'll take years to make us safe. If Quillan Gornt—or any one of twenty enemies—knew half the truth, knew how far we're overextended, we'd be drowned in our own useless paper within the week."

"Our paper's good—it's not useless! You're exaggerating—as usual!"

"It's worth twenty cents on the dollar because we've insufficient capital, not enough cash flow and we're absolutely in mortal danger."

"Rubbish!"

"Is it?" Dunross's voice had sharpened for the first time. "Rothwell-Gornt could swallow us in a month if they knew the value of our present accounts receivable, against our pressing liabilities."

The old man had just stared at him without answering. Then he said, "It's a temporary condition. Seasonable and temporary."

"Rubbish! You know very well you're giving me the job because I'm the only man who can clean up the mess you leave, you, my father, and your brother."

"Aye, I'm gambling you can. That's true enough," Alastair had flared at him. "Aye. You've surely got the right amount of Devil Struan in your blood to serve that master if you've a mind."

"Thank you. I admit I'll let nothing stand in my way. And since this is a night for truth, I can tell you why you've always hated me, why my own father has also hated me."

"Can you now?"

"Yes. It's because I survived the war and your son didn't and your nephew, Linbar, the last of your branch of the Struan's, is a nice lad but useless. Yes, I survived but my poor brothers didn't, and that's still sending my father around the bend. It's the truth, isn't it?"

"Yes," Alastair Struan had said. "Aye, I'm afraid it is."

"I'm not afraid it is. I'm not afraid of anything. Granny Dunross saw to that."

"*Heya*, tai-pan," Claudia Chen said brightly as the elevator door opened. She was a jolly, gray-haired Eurasian woman in her mid-sixties, and she sat behind a huge desk that dominated the twenty-first-floor foyer. She had served the Noble House for forty-two years and succeeding tai-pans, exclusively, for twenty-five of them. "*Neh hoh mah?*" How're you?

"*Ho ho,*" he replied absently. Good. Then in English, "Did Bartlett call?"

"No." She frowned. "He's not expected until lunch. Do you want me to try to reach him?"

"No, never mind. What about my call to Foster in Sydney?"

"That's not through either. Or your call to Mr. MacStruan in Edinburgh. Something's troubling you?" she asked, having instantly sensed his mood.

"What? Oh, no, nothing." He threw off his tension and walked past her desk into his office that overlooked the harbor and sat in an easy chair beside the phone. She closed the door and sat down nearby, her notepad ready.

"I was just remembering my D Day," he said. "The day I took over."

"Oh. Joss, tai-pan."

"Yes."

"Joss," she repeated, "and a long time ago."

He laughed. "Long time? It's forty lifetimes. It's barely three years but the whole world's changed and it's going so fast. What's the next couple of years going to be like?"

"More of the same, tai-pan. I hear you met Miss Casey Tcholok at our front door."

"Eh, who told you that?" he asked sharply.

"Great good God, tai-pan, I can't reveal my sources. But I heard you stared at her and she stared at you. *Heya?*"

"Nonsense! Who told you about her?"

"Last night I called the hotel to see that everything was all right. The manager told me. Do you know that silly man was going to be 'overbooked'? Huh, if they share a suite or a bed or don't, never mind I told him. This is 1963 and the modern age with lots of liberations, and anyway it's a fine suite with two entrances and separate rooms and most important they're our guests." She chortled. "I pulled a little rank. . . . *Ayeeyah*, power is a pretty toy."

"Did you tell young Linbar or the others, about K. C. being female?"

"No. No one. I knew you knew. Barbara Chen told me Master John had already phoned you about Casey Tcholok. What's she like?"

"*Beddable* would be one word," he said and grinned.

"Yes—but what else?"

Dunross thought a moment. "She's very attractive, very well dressed—though subdued today, for our benefit I imagine. Very confident and very observant—she noticed the front door was out of whack and asked about it." He picked up an ivory paper knife and toyed with it. "John didn't like her at all. He said he'd bet she was one of those pathetic American women who're like California fruit: great to look at, with plenty of body, but no taste whatsoever!"

"Poor Master John, much as he likes America, he does prefer certain, er, aspects of Asia!"

Dunross laughed. "How clever a negotiator she is we'll soon find out." He smiled. "I sent her in unannounced."

"I'll wager 50 HK at least one of them knew in advance she was a she."

"Phillip Chen of course—but that old fox wouldn't tell the others. A hundred says neither Linbar, Jacques or Andrew Gavallan knew."

"Done," Claudia said happily. "You can pay me now, tai-pan. I checked very discreetly, this morning."

"Take it out of petty cash," he told her sourly.

"So sorry." She held out her hand. "A bet is a bet, tai-pan."

Reluctantly he gave her the red one-hundred-dollar note.

"Thank you. Now, a hundred says Casey Tcholok will walk all over Master Linbar, Master Jacques and Andrew Gavallan."

"What do you know?" he asked her suspiciously. "Eh?"

"A hundred?"

"All right."

"Excellent!" she said briskly, changing the subject. "What about the dinners for Mr. Bartlett? The golf match and the trip to Taipei? Of course, you can't take a woman along on those. Shall I cancel them?"

"No. I'll talk to Bartlett—he'll understand. I did invite her to Saturday's races though, with him."

"Oh, that's two too many. I'll cancel the Pangs, they won't mind. Do you want to sit them together at your table?"

Dunross frowned. "She should be at my table, guest of honor, and sit him next to Penelope, guest of honor."

"Very well. I'll call Mrs. Dunross and tell her. Oh and Barbara—Master John's wife—wants to talk with you." Claudia sighed and smoothed a crease in her neat dark blue *chong-sam.* "Master John didn't come back last night—not that that's anything out of the ordinary. But it's 10:10 now and I can't find him either. It seems he wasn't at Morning Prayers."

"Yes, I know. Since he dealt with Bartlett last night I told him to skip them." Morning Prayers was the jocular way that insiders in Struan's referred to the daily obligatory 8:00 A.M. meeting with the tai-pan of all managing directors of all Struan's subsidiaries. "No need for him to come today, there's nothing for him to do until lunch." Dunross pointed out of the window at the harbor. "He's probably on his boat. It's a great day for a sail."

"Her temperature's very high, tai-pan, even for her."

"Her temperature's always high, poor bugger! John's on his boat—or at Ming-li's flat. Did you try her flat?"

She sniffed. "Your father used to say a closed mouth catches no wee beasties. Even so, I suppose I can tell you now, Ming-li's been Number Two Girl Friend for almost two months. The new favorite calls herself Fragrant Flower, and she occupies one of his 'private flats' off Aberdeen Main Road."

"Ah, conveniently near his mooring!"

"Oh very yes. She's a flower all right, a Fallen Flower from the Good Luck Dragon Dance Hall in Wanchai. But she doesn't know where Master John is either. He didn't visit either of them though he had a date with Miss Fallen Flower, so she says, at midnight."

"How did you find out all this?" he asked, filled with admiration.

"Power, tai-pan—and a network of relations built up over five generations. How else do we survive, *heya?*" She chuckled. "Of course if you want a little real scandal, John Chen doesn't know she wasn't the virgin she and the broker claimed she was when he first pillowed her."

"Eh?"

"No. He paid the broker . . ." One of the phones rang and she picked it up and said "Please hold one moment," clicked on the hold button and continued happily in the same breath, ". . . 500 cash, U.S. dollars, but all her tears and all the, er, evidence, was a pretend. Poor fellow, but it serves him right, eh, tai-pan? What should a man like him at his age want virginity to nourish the yang for—he's only forty-two, *heya?*" She pressed the *on* connection. "Tai-pan's office, good morning," she said attentively.

He watched her. He was amused and bemused, astounded as always at her sources of information, pithy and otherwise, and her delight in knowing secrets. And passing them on. But only to clan members and special insiders.

"Just one moment please." She clicked the hold button. "Superintendent Armstrong would like to see you. He's downstairs with Superintendent Kwok. He's sorry to come without an appointment but could you spare them a moment?"

"Ah, the guns. Our police're getting more efficient every day," he said with a grim smile. "I didn't expect them till after lunch."

At seven this morning he had had a detailed report from Phillip Chen who had been called by one of the police sergeants who made the raid and was a relation of the Chens.

"You'd better put all our private sources on finding out the who and the why, Phillip," he had said, very concerned.

"I already have. It's too much of a coincidence that guns should be on Bartlett's plane."

"It could be highly embarrassing if we're found to be connected with it in any way."

"Yes."

He saw Claudia waiting patiently. "Ask Armstrong to give me ten minutes. Bring them up then."

She dealt with that, then said, "If Superintendent Kwok's been brought in so soon, it must be more serious than we thought, *heya*, tai-pan?"

"Special Branch or Special Intelligence has to be involved at once. I'll bet the FBI and CIA have already been contacted. Brian Kwok's logical because he's an old mate of Armstrong's—and one of the best they've got."

"Yes," Claudia agreed proudly. "Eeeee what a lovely husband he'd make for someone."

"Provided she's a Chen—all that extra power, *heya*?" It was common knowledge that Brian Kwok was being groomed to be the first Chinese assistant commissioner.

"Of course such power has to be kept in the family." The phone rang. She answered it. "Yes, I'll tell him, thank you." She replaced the phone huffily. "The governor's equerry—he called to remind you about cocktails at 6:00 P.M.—huh, as if I'd forget!"

Dunross picked up one of the phones and dialed.

"*Weyyyy?*" came the coarse voice of the *amah*, the Chinese servant. Hello?

"Chen *tai-tai*," he said into the phone, his Cantonese perfect. "Mrs. Chen please, this is Mr. Dunross."

He waited. "Ah, Barbara, good morning."

"Oh hello, Ian. Have you heard from John yet? Sorry to bother you," she said.

"No bother. No, not yet. But the moment I do I'll get him to call you. He might have gone down to the track early to watch Golden Lady work out. Have you tried the Turf Club?"

"Yes, but they don't remember him breakfasting there, and the workout's between 5:00 and 6:00. Damn him! He's so inconsiderate. *Ayeeyah*, men!"

"He's probably out on his boat. He's got nothing here until lunch and it's a great day for a sail. You know how he is—have you checked the mooring?"

"I can't, Ian, not without going there, there's no phone. I have a hairdressing appointment which I simply can't break—all Hong Kong will be at your party tonight—I simply can't go rushing off to Aberdeen."

"Send one of your chauffeurs," Dunross said dryly.

"Tang's off today and I need Wu-chat to drive me around, Ian. I simply can't send him over to Aberdeen—that could take an hour and I've a mah-jong game from two till four."

"I'll get John to call you. It'll be around lunch."

"I won't be back till five at the earliest. When I catch up with him he's going to get what for never mind. Oh well, thanks, sorry to bother you. 'Bye."

"'Bye." Dunross put the phone down and sighed. "I feel like a bloody nursemaid."

"Talk to John's father, tai-pan," Claudia Chen said.

"I have. Once. And that's enough. It's not all John's fault. That lady's enough to drive anyone bonkers." He grinned. "But I agree her temperature's gone to the moon—this time it's going to cost John an emerald ring or at least a mink coat."

The phone rang again. Claudia picked it up. "Hello, the tai-pan's office! Yes? Oh!" Her happiness vanished and she hardened. "Just a moment, please." She punched the hold button. "It's a person to person from Hiro Toda in Yokohama."

Dunross knew how she felt about him, knew she hated the Japanese and loathed the Noble House's connection with them. He could never forgive the Japanese either for what they had done to Asia during the war. To those they had conquered. To the defenseless. Men, women and children. The prison camps and unnecessary deaths. Soldier to soldier he had no quarrel with them. None. War was war.

His own war had been against the Germans. But Claudia's war had been here in Hong Kong. During the Japanese Occupation, because she was Eurasian, she had not been put into Stanley Prison with all European civilians. She and her sister and brother had tried to help the POWs with food and drugs and money, smuggling it into the camp. The Kampeitai, the Japanese military police, had caught her. Now she could have no children.

"Shall I say you're out?" she asked.

"No." Two years before Dunross had committed an enormous amount of capital to Toda Shipping Industries of Yokohama for two giant bulk ships to build up the Struan fleet that had been decimated in the war. He had chosen this Japanese shipyard because their product was the finest, their terms the best, they guaranteed delivery and all the things the British shipyards would not, and because he knew it was time to forget.

"Hello, Hiro," he said, liking the man personally. "Nice to hear from you. How's Japan?"

"Please excuse me for interrupting you, tai-pan. Japan's fine though hot and humid. No change."

"How're my ships coming along?"

"Perfectly, tai-pan. Everything is as we arranged. I just wanted to advise you that I will be coming to Hong Kong on Saturday morning for a business trip. I will be staying for the weekend, then on to Singapore and Sydney, back in time for our closing in Hong Kong. You'll still be coming to Yokohama for both launchings?"

"Oh yes. Yes, absolutely. What time do you arrive Saturday?"

"At 11:10, Japan Air Lines."

"I'll send a car to meet you. What about coming directly to Happy Valley to the races? You could join us for lunch, then my car will take you to the hotel. You're staying at the Victoria and Albert?"

"This time at the Hilton, Hong Kong side. Tai-pan, please excuse me, I do not wish to put you to any trouble, so sorry."

"It's nothing. I'll have one of my people meet you. Probably Andrew Gavallan."

"Ah, very good. Then thank you, tai-pan. I look forward to seeing you, so sorry to inconvenience you."

Dunross put the phone down. I wonder why he called, the real reason? he asked himself. Hiro Toda, managing director of the most go-ahead shipbuilding complex in Japan, never does anything suddenly or unpremeditated.

Dunross thought about the closing of their ship deal and the three payments of 2 million each that were due imminently on September 1, 11 and 15, the balance in ninety days. $12 million U.S. in all that he didn't have at the moment. Or the charterer's signed contract that was necessary to support the bank loan that he did not have, yet. "Never mind," he said easily, "everything's going to be fine."

"For them, yes," Claudia said. "You know I don't trust them, tai-pan. Any of them."

"You can't fault them, Claudia. They're only trying to do economically what they failed to do militarily."

"By pricing everyone out of the world markets."

"They're working hard, they're making profits and they'll bury us, if we let them." His eyes hardened too. "But after all, Claudia, scratch an Englishman—or a Scot—and find a pirate. If we're such bloody fools to allow it we deserve to go under—isn't that what Hong Kong's all about?"

"Why help the enemy?"

"They were the enemy," he said kindly. "But that was only for twenty-odd years and our connections there go back a hundred. Weren't we the first traders into Japan? Didn't Hag Struan buy us the first plot offered for sale in Yokohama in 1860? Didn't she order that it be a cornerstone of Struan's policy to have the China-Japan-Hong Kong triangle?"

"Yes, tai-pan, but don't you thi—"

"No, Claudia, we've dealt with the Todas, the Kasigis, the Toranagas for a hundred years, and right now Toda Shipping's very important to us."

The phone rang again. She answered it. "Yes, I'll phone him back." Then to Dunross. "It's the caterers—about your party tonight."

"What's the problem?"

"None, tai-pan—they're moaning. After all, it's *the* tai-pan's twentieth wedding anniversary. All Hong Kong will be there and all Hong Kong better be impressed." Again the phone rang. She picked it up. "Ahh good! Put him through. . . . It's Bill Foster from Sydney."

Dunross took the phone. "Bill . . . no, you were top of the list. Have you closed on the Woolara Properties deal yet? . . . What's the hold-up? . . . I don't care about that." He glanced at his watch. "It's just past noon your time. Call them right now and offer then fifty cents Australian more a share, the offer good till the close of business today. Get on to the bank in Sydney at once and tell them to demand full repayment of all their loans at the close of business today. . . . I couldn't care less, they're thirty days overdue already. I want control of that company now. Without it our new bulk-carrier charter deal will fall apart and we'll have to begin all over again. And catch the Qantas Flight 543 on Thursday. I'd like you here for a conference." He put the phone down. "Get Linbar up here as soon as the Tcholok meeting's over. Book him on Qantas 716 for Sydney on Friday morning."

"Yes, tai-pan." She made a note and handed him a list. "Here're your appointments for today."

He glanced at it. Four board meetings of some subsidiary companies this morning: Golden Ferry at 10:30, Struan's Motor Imports of Hong Kong at 11:00, Chong-Li Foods at 11:15 and Kowloon Investments at 11:30. Lunch with Lincoln Bartlett and Miss Casey Tcholok 12:40 to 2:00 P.M. More board meetings this afternoon, Peter Marlowe at 4:00 P.M., Phillip Chen at 4:20, cocktails at 6:00 with the governor, his anniversary party beginning at 8:00, a reminder to call Alastair Struan in Scotland at 11:00, and at least fifteen other people to phone throughout Asia during the day.

"Marlowe?" he asked.

"He's a writer, staying at the Vic—remember, he wrote for an appointment a week ago. He's researching a book on Hong Kong."

"Oh yes—the ex-RAF type."

"Yes. Would you like him put off?"

"No. Keep everything as arranged, Claudia." He took out a thin black leather memo-card case from his back pocket and gave her a dozen cards covered with his shorthand. "Here're some cables and telexes to send off at once and notes for the various board meetings. Get me Jen in Taipei, then Havergill at the bank, then run down the list."

"Yes, tai-pan. I hear Havergill's going to retire."

"Marvelous. Who's taking over?"

"No one knows yet."

"Let's hope it's Johnjohn. Put your spies to work. A hundred says I find out before you do!"

"Done!"

"Good." Dunross held out his hand and said sweetly, "You can pay me now. It's Johnjohn."

"Eh?" She stared at him.

"We decided it last night—all the directors. I asked them to tell no one until eleven today."

Reluctantly she took out the hundred-dollar note and offered it. "*Ayeeyah*, I was particularly attached to this note."

"Thank you," Dunross said and pocketed it. "I'm particularly attached to that one myself."

There was a knock on the door. "Yes?" he said.

The door was opened by Sandra Yi, his private secretary. "Excuse me, tai-pan, but the market's up two points and Holdbrook's on line two." Alan Holdbrook was head of their in-house stockbroking company.

Dunross punched the line two button. "Claudia, soon as I'm through bring in Armstrong." She left with Sandra Yi.

"Yes, Alan?"

"Morning, tai-pan. First: There's a heavy rumor that we're going to make a bid for control of Asian Properties."

"That's probably put out by Jason Plumm to boost his shares before their annual meeting. You know what a canny bastard he is."

"Our stock's gone up ten cents, perhaps on the strength of it."

"Good. Buy me 20,000 at once."

"On margin?"

"Of course on margin."

"All right. Second rumor: We've closed a multimillion-dollar deal with Par-Con Industries—huge expansion."

"Pipe dreams," Dunross said easily, wondering furiously where the leaks were. Only Phillip Chen—and in Edinburgh, Alastair Struan and old Sean MacStruan—was supposed to know about the ploy to smash Asian Properties. And the Par-Con deal was top secret to the Inner Court only.

"Third: Someone's buying large parcels of our stock."

"Who?"

"I don't know. But there's something smelly going on, tai-pan. The way our stock's been creeping up the last month . . . There's no reason that I know of, except a buyer, or buyers. Same with Rothwell-Gornt. I heard a block of 200,000 was bought offshore."

"Find out who."

"Christ, I wish I knew how. The market's jittery, and very nervous. A lot of Chinese money's floating around. Lots of little deals going on . . . a few shares here, a few there, but multiplied by a hundred thousand or so . . . the market might start to fall apart . . . or to soar."

"Good. Then we'll all make a killing. Give me a call before the market closes. Thanks, Alan." He put the phone down, feeling the sweat on his back. "Shit," he said aloud. "What the hell's going on?"

In the outer office Claudia Chen was going over some papers with Sandra Yi who was her niece on her mother's side—and smart, very good to look at, twenty-seven with a mind like an abacus. Then she glanced at her watch and said in Cantonese, "Superintendent Brian Kwok's downstairs, Little Sister, why don't you fetch him up—in six minutes."

"*Ayeeyah*, yes, Elder Sister!" Sandra Yi hastily checked her makeup and swished away. Claudia smiled after her and thought Sandra Yi would be perfect—a perfect choice for Brian Kwok. Happily she sat behind her desk and began to type the telexes. Everything's done that should be done, she told herself. No, something the tai-pan said . . . what was it? Ah yes! She dialed her home number.

"*Weyyyyy?*" said her *amah*, Ah Sam.

"Listen, Ah Sam," she said in Cantonese, "isn't Third Toiletmaid Fung at the Vic your cousin three times removed?"

"Oh yes, Mother," Ah Sam replied, using the Chinese politeness of servant to mistress. "But she's four times removed, and from the Fung-tats, not the Fung-sams which is my branch."

"Never mind that, Ah Sam. You call her and find out all you can about two foreign devils from the Golden Mountain. They're in Fragrant Spring suite." Patiently she spelled their names, then added delicately, "I hear they have peculiar pillow habits."

"*Ayeeyah*, if anyone can find out, Third Toiletmaid Fung can. Ha! What peculiars?"

"Strange peculiars, Ah Sam. You get on with it, little oily mouth." She beamed and hung up.

The elevator doors opened and Sandra Yi ushered the two police officers in, then left reluctantly. Brian Kwok watched her go. He was thirty-nine, tall for a Chinese, just over six foot, very handsome, with blue-black hair. Both men wore civilian clothes. Claudia chatted with them politely, but the moment she saw the light on line two go out she ushered them in and closed the door.

"Sorry to come without an appointment," Armstrong said.

"No sweat, Robert. You look tired."

"A heavy night. It's all the villainy that goes on in Hong Kong," Armstrong said easily. "Nasties abound and saints get crucified."

Dunross smiled, then glanced across at Kwok. "How's life treating you, Brian?"

Brian Kwok smiled back. "Very good, thanks, Ian. Stock market's up—
I've a few dollars in the bank, my Porsche hasn't fallen apart yet, and ladies will be ladies."

"Thank God for that! Are you doing the hill climb on Sunday?"

"If I can get Lulu in shape. She's missing an offside hydraulic cou-
pling."

"Have you tried our shop?"

"Yes. No joy, tai-pan. Are you going?"

"Depends. I've got to go to Taipei Sunday afternoon—I will if I've got
time. I entered anyway. How's SI?"

Brian Kwok grinned. "It beats working for a living." Special Intelligence was a completely independent department within the elite, semi-
secret Special Branch responsible for preventing and detecting subversive
activities in the Colony. It had its own secret ways, secret funding and
overriding powers. And it was responsible to the governor alone.

Dunross leaned back in the chair. "What's up?"

Armstrong said, "I'm sure you already know. It's about the guns on
Bartlett's plane."

"Oh yes, I heard this morning," he said. "How can I help? Have you
any idea why and where they were destined? And by whom? You caught
two men?"

Armstrong sighed. "Yes. They were genuine mechanics all right—both
ex-Nationalist Air Force trained. No previous record, though they're suspected of being members of secret triads. Both have been here since the
exodus of '49. By the way, can we keep this all confidential, between the
three of us?"

"What about your superiors?"

"I'd like to include them in—but keep it just for your ears only."

"Why?"

"We have reason to believe the guns were destined for someone in
Struan's."

"Who?" Dunross asked sharply.

"Confidential?"

"Yes. Who?"

"How much do you know about Lincoln Bartlett and Casey Tcholok?"

"We've a detailed dossier on him—not on her. Would you like it? I can
give you a copy, providing it too is kept confidential."

"Of course. That would be very helpful."

Dunross pressed the intercom.

"Yes sir?" Claudia asked.

"Make a copy of the Bartlett dossier and give it to Superintendent
Armstrong on his way out." Dunross clicked the intercom off.

"We won't take much more of your time," Armstrong said. "Do you always dossier potential clients?"

"No. But we like to know who we're dealing with. If the Bartlett deal goes through it could mean millions to us, to him, a thousand new jobs to Hong Kong—factories here, warehouses, a very big expansion—along with equally big risks to us. Everyone in business does a confidential financial statement—perhaps we're a bit more thorough. I'll bet you fifty dollars to a broken hatpin he's done one on me."

"No criminal connections mentioned?"

Dunross was startled. "Mafia? That sort of thing? Good God no, nothing. Besides, if the Mafia were trying to come in here they wouldn't send a mere ten M14 rifles and two thousand rounds and a box of grenades."

"Your information's damn good," Brian Kwok interrupted. "Too damn good. We only unpacked the stuff an hour ago. Who's your informant?"

"You know there're no secrets in Hong Kong."

"Can't even trust your own coppers these days."

"The Mafia would surely send in a shipment twenty times that and they'd be handguns, American style. But the Mafia would be bound to fail here, whatever they did. They could never displace our triads. No, it can't be Mafia—only someone local. Who tipped you about the shipment, Brian?"

"Tokyo Airport Police," Kwok said. "One of their mechanics was doing a routine inspection—you know how thorough they are. He reported it to his superior, their police phoned us and we said to let it through."

"In that case get hold of the FBI and the CIA—get them to check back to Honolulu—or Los Angeles."

"You went through the flight plan too?"

"Of course. That's obvious. Why someone in Struan's?"

"Both of the villains said . . ." Armstrong took out his pad and referred to it. "Our question was, 'Where were you to take the packages?' Both answered using different words: 'To 15 go-down, we were to put the packages in Bay 7 at the back.'" He looked up at Dunross.

"That proves nothing. We've the biggest warehouse operation at Kai Tak—just because they take it to one of our go-downs proves nothing—other than they're smart. We've got so much merchandise going through, it'd be easy to send in an alien truck." Dunross thought a moment. "15's right at the exit—perfect placing." He reached for the phone. "I'll put my security folk on it right n—"

"Would you not, please, just for the moment."

"Why?"

"Our next question," Armstrong continued, "was, 'Who employed you?' Of course they gave fictitious names and descriptions and denied everything but they'll be more helpful soon." He smiled grimly. "One of them did say, however, when one of my sergeants was twisting his ear a little, figuratively speaking of course"—he read from the pad—"'You leave me alone, I've got very important friends!' 'You've no friends in the world,' the sergeant said. 'Maybe, but the Honorable Tsu-yan has and Noble House Chen has.'"

The silence became long and heavy. They waited.

Those God-cursed guns, Dunross thought furiously. But he held his face calm and his wits sharpened. "We've a hundred and more Chens working for us, related, unrelated—Chen's as common a name as Smith."

"And Tsu-yan?" Brian Kwok asked.

Dunross shrugged. "He's a director of Struan's—but he's also a director of Blacs, the Victoria Bank and forty other companies, one of the richest men in Hong Kong and a name anyone in Asia could pull out of a hat. Like Noble House Chen."

"Do you know he's suspected of being very high up in the triad hierarchy—specifically in the Green Pang?" Brian Kwok asked.

"Every important Shanghainese's equally suspect. Jesus Christ, Brian, you know Chiang Kai-shek was supposed to have given Shanghai to the Green Pang years ago as their exclusive bailiwick if they'd support his northern campaign against the warlords. Isn't the Green Pang still, more or less, an official Nationalist secret society?"

Brian Kwok said, "Where'd Tsu-yan make his money, Ian? His first fortune?"

"I don't know. You tell me, Brian."

"He made it during the Korean War smuggling penicillin, drugs and petrol—mostly penicillin—across the border to the Communists. Before Korea all he owned was a loincloth and a broken-down rickshaw."

"That's all hearsay, Brian."

"Struan's made a fortune too."

"Yes. But it would really be very unwise to imply we did it smuggling—publicly or privately," Dunross said mildly. "Very unwise indeed."

"Didn't you?"

"Struan's began with a little smuggling 120-odd years ago, so rumor has it, but it was an honorable profession and never against British law. We're law-abiding capitalists and China Traders and have been for years."

Brian Kwok did not smile. "More hearsay's that a lot of his penicillin was bad. Very bad."

"If it was, if that's the truth, then please go get him, Brian," Dunross said coldly. "Personally I think that's another rumor spread by jealous competitors. If it was true he'd be floating in the bay with the others who tried, or he'd be punished like Bad Powder Wong." He was referring to a Hong Kong smuggler who had sold a vast quantity of adulterated penicillin over the border during the Korean War and invested his fortune in stocks and land in Hong Kong. Within seven years he was very very rich. Then certain triads of Hong Kong were ordered to balance the books. Every week one member of his family vanished, or died. By drowning, car accident, strangulation, poison or knife. No assailant was ever caught. The killing went on for seventeen months and three weeks and then stopped. Only he and one semi-imbecile infant grandson remained alive. They lived today, still holed up in the same vast, once luxurious penthouse apartment with one servant and one cook, in terror, guarded night and day, never going out—knowing that no guards or any amount of money could ever prevent the inexorability of his sentence published in a tiny box in a local Chinese newspaper: Bad Powder Wong will be punished, he and all his generations.

Brian Kwok said, "We interviewed that sod once, Robert and I."

"Oh?"

"Yes. Scary. Every door's double locked and chained, every window nailed up and boarded over with planks—just spy holes here and there. He hasn't been out since the killing started. The place stank, my God did it stink! All he does is play Chinese checkers with his grandson and watch television."

"And wait," Armstrong said. "One day they'll come for both of them. His grandson must be six or seven now."

Dunross said, "I think you prove my point. Tsu-yan's not like him and never was. And what possible use could Tsu-yan have for a few M14's? If he wanted to, I imagine he could muster half the Nationalist army along with a battalion of tanks."

"In Taiwan but not in Hong Kong."

"Has Tsu-yan ever been involved with Bartlett?" Armstrong asked. "In your negotiations?"

"Yes. He was in New York once and in Los Angeles on our behalf. Both times with John Chen. They initialed the agreement between Struan's and Par-Con Industries which is to be finalized—or abandoned— here this month, and they formally invited Bartlett to Hong Kong on my behalf."

Armstrong glanced at his Chinese partner. Then he said, "When was this?"

"Four months ago. It's taken that time for both sides to prepare all the details."

"John Chen, eh?" Armstrong said. "He certainly could be Noble House Chen."

"You know John's not the type," Dunross said. "There's no reason why he should be mixed up in such a ploy. It must be just coincidence."

"There's another curious coincidence," Brian Kwok said. "Tsu-yan and John Chen both know an American called Banastasio, at least both have been seen in his company. Does that name mean anything?"

"No. Who's he?"

"A big-time gambler and suspected racketeer. He's also supposed to be closely connected with one of the Cosa Nostra families. Vincenzo Banastasio."

Dunross's eyes narrowed. "You said, 'seen in his company.' Who did the seeing?"

"The FBI."

The silence thickened a little.

Armstrong reached into his pocket for a cigarette.

Dunross pushed across the silver cigarette box. "Here."

"Oh, thanks. No, I won't—I wasn't thinking. I've stopped for the last couple of weeks. It's a killer." Then he added, trying to curb the desire, "The FBI passed the info on to us because Tsu-yan and Mr. John Chen are so prominent here. They asked us to keep an eye on them."

Then Dunross suddenly remembered Foxwell's remark about a prominent capitalist who was a secret Communist that they were watching in Sinclair Towers. Christ, he thought, Tsu-yan's got a flat there, and so has John Chen. Surely it's impossible either'd be mixed up with Communists.

"Of course heroin's big business," Armstrong was saying, his voice very hard.

"What does that mean, Robert?"

"The drug racket requires huge amounts of money to finance it. That kind of money can only come from banks or bankers, covertly of course. Tsu-yan's on the board of a number of banks—so's Mr. Chen."

"Robert, you'd better go very slow on that sort of remark," Dunross grated. "You are drawing very dangerous conclusions without any proof whatsoever. That's actionable I'd imagine and I won't have it."

"You're right, sorry. I withdraw the coincidence. Even so, the drug trade's big business, and it's here in Hong Kong in abundance, mostly for ultimate U.S. consumption. Somehow I'm going to find out who our nasties are."

"That's commendable. And you'll have all the help you want from Struan's and me. I hate the traffic too."

"Oh I don't hate it, tai-pan, or the traffickers. It's a fact of life. It's just another business—illegal certainly but still a business. I've been given the job of finding out who the tai-pans are. It's a matter of personal satisfaction, that's all."

"If you want help, just ask."

"Thank you." Armstrong got up wearily. "Before we go there're a couple more coincidences for you. When Tsu-yan and Noble House Chen were named this morning we thought we'd like to chat with them right away, but shortly after we ambushed the guns Tsu-yan caught the early flight to Taipei. Curious, eh?"

"He's back and forth all the time," Dunross said, his disquiet soaring. Tsu-yan was expected at his party this evening. It would be extraordinary if he did not appear.

Armstrong nodded. "It seems it was a last-minute decision—no reservation, no ticket, no luggage, just a few extra dollars under the counter and someone was bounced off and him on. He was carrying only a briefcase. Strange, eh?"

Brian Kwok said, "We haven't a hope in hell of extraditing him from Taiwan."

Dunross studied him then looked back at Armstrong, his eyes steady and the color of sea ice. "You said there were a couple of coincidences. What's the other?"

"We can't find John Chen."

"What're you talking about?"

"He's not at home, or at his lady friend's, or at any of his usual haunts. We've been watching him and Tsu-yan off and on for months, ever since the FBI tipped us."

The silence gathered. "You've checked his boat?" Dunross asked, sure that they had.

"She's at her moorings, hasn't been out since yesterday. His boat-boy hasn't seen him either."

"Golf course?"

"No, he's not there," Armstrong said. "Nor at the racetrack. He wasn't at the workout, though he was expected, his trainer said. He's gone, vanished, scarpered."

6

There was a stunned silence in the boardroom.

"What's wrong?" Casey asked. "The figures speak for themselves."

The four men around the table looked at her. Andrew Gavallan, Linbar Struan, Jacques deVille and Phillip Chen, all members of the Inner Court.

Andrew Gavallan was tall and thin and forty-seven. He glanced at the sheaf of papers in front of him. *Dew neh loh moh* on all women in business, he thought irritably. "Perhaps we should check with Mr. Bartlett," he said uneasily, still very unsettled that they were expected to deal with a woman.

"I've already told you I have authority in all these areas," she said, trying to be patient. "I'm treasurer and executive vice-president of Par-Con Industries and empowered to negotiate with you. We confirmed that in writing last month." Casey held her temper. The meeting had been very heavy going. From their initial shock that she was a woman to their inevitable, overpolite awkwardness, waiting for her to sit, waiting for her to talk, then not sitting until she had asked them to, making small talk, not wanting to get down to business, not wishing to negotiate with her as a person, a business person, at all, saying instead that their wives would be delighted to take her shopping, then gaping because she knew all the intimate details of their projected deal. It was all part of a pattern that, normally, she could deal with. But not today. Jesus, she thought, I've got to succeed. I've got to get through to them.

"It's really quite easy," she had said initially, trying to clear their awkwardness away, using her standard opening. "Forget that I'm a woman—judge me on my ability. Now, there are three subjects on our agenda: the polyurethane factories, our computer-leasing representation and last, general representation of our petrochemical products, fertilizers, pharmaceutical and sports goods throughout Asia. First let's sort out the polyurethane factories, the chemical mix supplies and a projected time schedule for the financing." At once she gave them graphics and prepared documentation, verbally synopsized all the facts, figures and percentages, bank charges and interest charges, simply and very quickly, so that even the slowest brain could grasp the project. And now they were staring at her.

Andrew Gavallan broke the silence. "That's . . . that's very impressive, my dear."

"Actually I'm not your 'dear,'" she said with a laugh. "I'm very hard-nosed for my corporation."

"But mademoiselle," Jacques deVille said with a suave Gallic charm, "your nose is perfect and not hard at all."

"*Merci, monsieur,*" she replied at once, and added lightly in passable French, "but please may we leave the shape of my nose for the moment and discuss the shape of this deal. It's better not to mix the two, don't you think?"

Another silence.

Linbar Struan said, "Would you like some coffee?"

"No thanks, Mr. Struan," Casey said, being careful to conform to their customs and not to call them by their Christian names too early. "May we zero in on this proposal? It's the one we sent you last month. . . . I've tried to cover your problems as well as ours."

There was another silence. Linbar Struan, thirty-four, very good-looking with sandy hair and blue eyes with a devil-may-care glint to them, persisted, "Are you sure you wouldn't like coffee? Tea perhaps?"

"No thanks. Then you accept our proposal as it stands?"

Phillip Chen coughed and said, "In principle we agree to want to be in business with Par-Con in several areas. The Heads of Agreement indicate that. As to the polyurethane factories . . ."

She listened to his generalizations, then once more tried to get to the specifics—the whole reason for this meeting. But the going was very hard and she could feel them squirming. This's the worst it's ever been. Perhaps it's because they're English, and I've never dealt with the English before.

"Is there anything specific that needs clarifying?" she asked. "If there's anything you don't understand . . ."

Gavallan said, "We understand very well. You present us with figures which are lopsided. We're financing the building of the factories. You provide the machines but their cost is amortized over three years which'll mess up any cash flow and mean no profits for five years at least."

"I'm told it is your custom in Hong Kong to amortize the full cost of a building over a three-year period," she replied equally sharply, glad to be challenged. "We're just proposing to follow your custom. If you want five —or ten years—you may have them, provided the same applies to the building."

"You're not paying for the machines—they're on a lease basis and the monthly charge to the joint venture is high."

"What's your bank prime rate today, Mr. Gavallan?"

They consulted, then told her. She used her pocket slide rule for a few seconds. "At today's rate you'd save 17,000 HK a week per machine if you take our deal which, over the period we're talking . . ." Another quick calculation. ". . . would jump your end of the profits 32 percent over the best you could do—and we're talking in millions of dollars."

They stared at her in silence.

Andrew Gavallan cross-questioned her about the figures but she never faltered. Their dislike for her increased.

Silence.

She was sure they were fogged by her figures. What else can I say to convince them? she thought, her anxiety growing. Struan's will make a bundle if they get off their asses, we'll make a fortune and I'll get my drop dead money at long last. The foam part of the deal alone will make Struan's rich and Par-Con nearly $80,000 net a month over the next ten years and Linc said I could have a piece.

"How much do you want?" he had asked her, just before they had left the States.

"51 percent," she had replied with a laugh, "since you're asking."

"3 percent."

"Come on, Linc, I need my drop dead money."

"Pull off the whole package and you've got a stock option of 100,000 Par-Con at four dollars below market."

"You're on. But I want the foam company too," she had said, holding her breath. "I started it and I want that. 51 percent. For me."

"In return for what?"

"Struan's."

"Done."

Casey waited outwardly calm. When she judged the moment correct she said innocently, "Are we agreed then, that our proposal stands as is? We're fifty-fifty with you, what could be better than that?"

"I still say you're not providing 50 percent of the financing of the joint venture," Andrew Gavallan replied sharply. "You're providing the machines and materials on a lease carry-back so your risk's not equivalent to ours."

"But that's for our tax purposes and to lessen the amount of cash outlay, gentlemen. We're financing from cash flow. The figures add up the same. The fact that we get a depreciation allowance and various rebates is neither here nor there." Even more innocently, baiting the trap, she added, "We finance in the States, where we've the expertise. You finance in Hong Kong where you're the experts."

* * *

Quillan Gornt turned back from his office window. "I repeat, we can better any arrangement you can make with Struan's, Mr. Bartlett. Any arrangement."

"You'd go dollar for dollar?"

"Dollar for dollar." The Englishman strolled back and sat behind his paperless desk and faced Bartlett again. They were on the top floor of the Rothwell-Gornt Building also fronting Connaught Road and the waterfront. Gornt was a thickset, hard-faced, bearded man, just under six feet, with graying black hair and graying bushy eyebrows and brown eyes. "It's no secret our companies are very serious rivals, but I assure you we can outbid them and outmatch them, and I'd arrange our side of the financing within the week. We could have a profitable partnership, you and I. I'd suggest we set up a joint company under Hong Kong law—the taxes here're really quite reasonable—15 percent of everything earned in Hong Kong, with the rest of the world free of all taxes." Gornt smiled. "Better than the U.S.A."

"Much better," Bartlett said. He was sitting in a high-backed leather chair. "Very much better."

"Is that why you're interested in Hong Kong?"

"One reason."

"What're the others?"

"There's no American outfit as big as mine here in strength yet, and there should be. This is the age of the Pacific. But you could benefit from our coming. We've a lot of expertise you don't have and a major say in areas of the U.S. market. On the other hand, Rothwell-Gornt—and Struan's—have the expertise we lack and a major say in the Asian markets."

"How can we cement a relationship?"

"First I have to find out what Struan's are after. I started negotiating with them, and I don't like changing airplanes in mid-ocean."

"I can tell you at once what they're after: profit for them and the hell with anyone else." Gornt's smile was hard.

"The deal we've discussed seems very fair."

"They're past masters at appearing to be very fair and putting up a half share, then selling out at their own choosing to skim the profit and yet retain control."

"That wouldn't be possible with us."

"They've been at it for almost a century and a half. They've learned a few tricks by now."

"So've you."

"Of course. But Struan's is very different from us. We own things and companies—they're percentagers. They've little more than a 5 percent holding in most of their subsidiaries yet they still exercise absolute control by special voting shares, or by making it mandatory in the Articles of Association that their tai-pan's also tai-pan of the subsidiary with overriding say."

"That sounds smart."

"It is. And they are. But we're better and straighter—and our contacts and influence in China and throughout the Pacific Rim, except for the U.S. and Canada, are stronger than theirs and growing stronger every day."

"Why?"

"Because our company operations originated in Shanghai—the greatest city in Asia—where we were dominant. Struan's has always concentrated on Hong Kong which, until recently, was almost a provincial backwater."

"But Shanghai's a dead issue and has been since the Commies closed off the Mainland in '49. There's no foreign trade going through Shanghai today—it's all through Canton."

"Yes. But it's the Shanghainese who left China and came south with money, brains and guts, who made Hong Kong what it is today and what it'll be tomorrow: the now and future metropolis of the whole Pacific."

"Better than Singapore?"

"Absolutely."

"Manila?"

"Absolutely."

"Tokyo?"

"That will ever only be for Japanese." Gornt's eyes sparkled, the lines on his face crinkled. "Hong Kong is the greatest city in Asia, Mr. Bartlett. Whoever masters it will eventually master Asia. . . . Of course I'm talking about trade, financing, shipping and big business."

"What about Red China?"

"We think Hong Kong benefits the PRC—as we call the People's Republic of China. We're the controlled 'open door' for them. Hong Kong and Rothwell-Gornt represent the future."

"Why?"

"Because since Shanghai was the business and industrial center of China, the pacesetter, Shanghainese are the go-getters of China, always have been and always will be. And now the best are with us here. You'll soon see the difference between Cantonese and Shanghainese. Shanghainese're the entrepreneurs, the industrialists, promoters and internationalists. There's not a great textile or shipping magnate or industrialist who isn't Shanghainese. Cantonese-run family businesses, Mr. Bartlett, they're loners, but Shanghainese understand partnerships, corporate situations and above all, banking and financing." Gornt lit another cigarette. "That's where our strength is, why we're better than Struan's—why we'll be number one eventually."

Linc Bartlett studied the man opposite him. From the dossier that Casey had prepared he knew that Gornt had been born in Shanghai of British parents, was forty-eight, a widower with two grown children, and that he had served as a captain in the Australian infantry '42–'45 in the Pacific. He knew too that he ruled Rothwell-Gornt very successfully as a private fief and had done so for eight years since he took over from his father.

Bartlett shifted in the deep leather chair. "If you've got this rivalry with Struan's and you're so sure you'll be number one eventually, why wait? Why not take them now?"

Gornt was watching him, his craggy face set. "There's nothing in the world that I'd like to do more. But I can't, not yet. I nearly did three years ago—they'd overreached themselves, the previous tai-pan's joss had run out."

"Joss?"

"It's a Chinese word meaning luck, fate, but a bit more." Gornt watched him thoughtfully. "We're very superstitious out here. Joss is very important, like timing. Alastair Struan's joss ran out, or changed. He had a disastrous last year, and then, in desperation, handed over to Ian Dunross. They almost went under that time. A run had started on their stock. I went after them, but Dunross squeezed out of the run and stabilized the market."

"How?"

"Let's say he exercised an undue amount of influence in certain banking circles." Gornt remembered with cold fury how Havergill at the bank had suddenly, against all their private, secret agreements, not opposed Struan's request for a temporary, enormous line of credit that had given Dunross the time to recover.

Gornt remembered his blinding rage when he had called Havergill. "What the hell did you do that for?" he had asked him. "A hundred million as an Extraordinary Credit? You've saved their necks for chrissake! We had them. Why?" Havergill had told him that Dunross had mustered enough votes on the board and put an extreme amount of personal pressure on him. "There was nothing I could do. . . ."

Yes, Gornt thought, looking at the American. I lost that time but I think you're the twenty-four-carat explosive key that will trigger the bomb to blow Struan's to hell out of Asia forever. "Dunross went to the edge that time, Mr. Bartlett. He made some implacable enemies. But now we're equally strong. It's what you'd call a standoff. They can't take us and we can't take them."

"Unless they make a mistake."

"Or we make a mistake." The older man blew a smoke ring and studied it. At length he glanced back at Bartlett. "We'll win eventually. Time in Asia's a little different from time in the U.S.A."

"That's what people tell me."

"You don't believe it?"

"I know the same rules of survival apply here, there or where the hell ever. Only the degree changes."

Gornt watched the smoke from his cigarette curling to the ceiling. His office was large with well-used old leather chairs and excellent oils on the walls and it was filled with the smell of polished leather and good cigars. Gornt's high-backed chair, old oak and carved, with red plush fitted seat and back looked hard, functional and solid, Bartlett thought, like the man.

"We can outbid Struan's and we've time on our side, here, there, where the hell ever," Gornt said.

Bartlett laughed.

Gornt smiled too but Bartlett noticed his eyes weren't smiling. "Look around Hong Kong, Mr. Bartlett. Ask about us, and about them. Then make up your mind."

"Yes, I'll do that."

"I hear your aircraft's impounded."

"Yes. Yes it is. The airport cops found some guns aboard."

"I heard. Curious. Well, if you need any help to unimpound it, perhaps I can be of service."

"You could help right now by telling me why and who."

"I've no idea—but I'll wager someone in Struan's knows."

"Why?"

"They knew your exact movements."

"So did you."

"Yes. But it was nothing to do with us."

"Who knew we were to have this meeting, Mr. Gornt?"

"You and I. As we agreed. There was no leak from here, Mr. Bartlett. After our private meeting in New York last year, everything's been by telephone—not even a confirming telex. I subscribe to your wisdom of caution, secrecy and dealing face to face. In private. But who on your side knows of our . . . our continuing interest?"

"No one but me."

"Not even your lady treasurer executive vice-president?" Gornt asked with open surprise.

"No sir. When did you learn Casey was a she?"

"In New York. Come now, Mr. Bartlett, it's hardly likely we'd contemplate an association without ascertaining your credentials and those of your chief executives."

"Good. That will save time."

"Curious to have a woman in such a key position."

"She's my right and left arm and the best executive I've got."

"Then why wasn't she told of our meeting today?"

"One of the first rules of survival is to keep your options open."

"Meaning?"

"Meaning I don't run my business by committee. Besides, I like to play off the cuff, to keep certain operations secret." Bartlett thought a moment then added, "It's not lack of trust. Actually, I'm making it easier for her. If anyone at Struan's finds out and asks her why I'm meeting with you now, her surprise will be genuine."

After a pause Gornt said, "It's rare to find anyone really trustworthy. Very rare."

"Why would someone want M14's and grenades in Hong Kong and why would they use my plane?"

"I don't know but I'll make it my business to find out." Gornt stubbed out his cigarette. The ashtray was porcelain—Sung dynasty. "Do you know Tsu-yan?"

"I've met him a couple of times. Why?"

"He's a very good fellow, even though he's a director of Struan's."

"He's Shanghainese?"

"Yes. One of the best." Gornt looked up, his eyes very hard. "It's possible there could be peripheral benefit to dealing with us, Mr. Bartlett. I hear Struan's is quite extended just now—Dunross's gambling heavily on his fleet, particularly on the two super bulk cargo carriers he has on order from Japan. The first's due to be paid for substantially in a week or so. Then, too, there's a strong rumor he's going to make a bid for Asian Properties. You've heard of them?"

"A big land operation, real estate, all over Hong Kong."

"Yes. They're the biggest—even bigger than his own K.I."

"Kowloon Investments is part of Struan's? I thought they were a separate company."

"They are, outwardly. But Dunross is tai-pan of K.I.—they always have the same tai-pan."

"Always?"

"Always. It's in their Heads of Agreement. But Ian's overriding himself. The Noble House may soon become ignoble. He's very cash light at the moment."

Bartlett thought a moment, then he asked, "Why don't you join with another company, maybe Asian Properties, and take Struan's? That's what I'd do in the States if I wanted a company I couldn't take alone."

"Is that what you want to do here, Mr. Bartlett?" Gornt asked at once, pretending shock. "To 'take' Struan's?"

"Is it possible?"

Gornt looked at the ceiling carefully before answering. "Yes—but you'd have to have a partner. Perhaps you could do it with Asian Properties but I doubt it. Jason Plumm, the tai-pan, hasn't the balls. You'd need us. Only we have the perspicacity, the drive, the knowledge and the desire. Nevertheless, you'd have to risk a very great deal of money. Cash."

"How much?"

Gornt laughed outright. "I'll consider that. First you'll have to tell me how serious you are."

"And if I am, would you want in?"

Gornt stared back, his eyes equally level. "First I would have to be sure, very sure, how serious you are. It's no secret I detest Struan's generally and Ian Dunross personally, would want them obliterated. So you already know my long-term posture. I don't know yours. Yet."

"If we could take over Struan's—would it be worth it?"

"Oh yes, Mr. Bartlett. Oh yes—yes it'd be worth it," Gornt said jovially, then once more his voice iced. "But I still need to know how serious you are."

"I'll tell you when I've seen Dunross."

"Are you going to suggest the same thought to him—that together you can swallow Rothwell-Gornt?"

"My purpose here is to make Par-Con international, Mr. Gornt. Maybe up to a $30 million investment to cover a whole range of merchandising, factories and warehousing. Up to a short time ago I'd never heard of Struan's—or Rothwell-Gornt. Or your rivalry."

"Very well, Mr. Bartlett, we'll leave it at that. Whatever you do will be interesting. Yes. It will be interesting to see if you can hold a knife."

Bartlett stared at him, not understanding.

"That's an old Chinese cooking term, Mr. Bartlett. Do you cook?"

"No."

"It's a hobby of mine. The Chinese say it's important to know how to hold a knife, that you can't use one until you can hold it correctly. Otherwise you'll cut yourself and be off to a very bad start indeed. Won't you?"

Bartlett grinned. "Hold a knife, is it? I'll remember that. No, I can't cook. Never got around to learning—Casey can't cook worth a damn either."

"The Chinese say there're three arts in which no other civilization can compare to theirs—literature, brush painting and cooking. I'm inclined to agree. Do you like good food?"

"The best meal I ever had was in a restaurant just outside Rome on the Via Flaminia, the Casale."

"Then we've at least that in common, Mr. Bartlett. The Casale's one of my favorites too."

"Casey took me there once—*spaghetti alla matriciana al dente* and *buscetti* with an ice-cold bottle of beer followed by the *piccata* and more beer. I'll never forget it."

Gornt smiled. "Perhaps you'll have dinner with me while you're here. I can offer you *alla matriciana* too—actually it'll compare favorably, it's the very same recipe."

"I'd like that."

"And a bottle of Valpolicella, or a great Tuscany wine."

"Personally, I like beer with pasta. Iced American beer out of the can."

After a pause Gornt asked, "How long are you staying in Hong Kong?"

"As long as it takes," Bartlett said without hesitation.

"Good. Then dinner one day next week? Tuesday or Wednesday?"

"Tuesday'd be fine, thanks. May I bring Casey?"

"Of course." Then Gornt added, his voice flatter, "By that time perhaps you'll be more sure of what you want to do."

Bartlett laughed. "And by that time you'll find out if I can hold a knife."

"Perhaps. But just remember one thing, Mr. Bartlett. If we ever join forces to attack Struan's, once the battle is joined, there will be almost no way to withdraw without getting severely mauled. Very severely mauled indeed. I'd have to be very sure. After all, you can always retire hurt to the U.S.A. to fight another day. We stay—so the risks are unequal."

"But the spoils are unequal too. You'd gain something priceless which doesn't mean ten cents to me. You'd become the Noble House."

"Yes," Gornt said, his eyes lidding. He leaned forward to select another cigarette and his left foot moved behind the desk to press a hidden floor switch. "Let's leave everything until Tues—"

The intercom clicked on. "Excuse me, Mr. Gornt, would you like me to postpone the board meeting?" his secretary asked.

"No," Gornt said. "They can wait."

"Yes sir. Miss Ramos is here. Could you spare her a few minutes?"

Gornt pretended to be surprised. "Just a moment." He looked up at Bartlett. "Have we concluded?"

"Yes." Bartlett got up at once. "Tuesday's firm. Let's keep everything cooking till then." He turned to go but Gornt stopped him. "Just a moment, Mr. Bartlett," he said, then into the intercom, "ask her to come in." He clicked off the switch and stood up. "I'm glad to have had the meeting."

The door opened and the girl came in. She was twenty-five and stunning with short black hair and sloe eyes, clearly Eurasian, casually dressed in tight, American washed jeans and a shirt. "Hello, Quillan," she said with a smile that warmed the room, her English slightly American accented. "Sorry to interrupt but I've just got back from Bangkok and wanted to say hello."

"Glad you did, Orlanda." Gornt smiled at Bartlett who was staring at her. "This is Linc Bartlett, from America. Orlanda Ramos."

"Hello," Bartlett said.

"Hi . . . oh, Linc Bartlett? The American millionaire gun-runner?" she said and laughed.

"What?"

"Oh don't look so shocked, Mr. Bartlett. Everyone in Hong Kong knows—Hong Kong's just a village."

"Seriously—how did you know?"

"I read it in my morning paper."

"Impossible! It only happened at 5:30 this morning."

"It was in the *Fai Pao*—the *Express*—in the Stop Press column at nine o'clock. It's a Chinese paper and the Chinese know everything that's going on here. Don't worry, the English papers won't pick it up till the afternoon editions, but you can expect the press on your doorstep around the happy hour."

"Thanks." The last thing I want's the goddamn press after me, Bartlett thought sourly.

"Don't worry, Mr. Bartlett, I won't ask you for an interview, even though I am a free-lance reporter for the Chinese press. I'm really very discreet," she said. "Am I not, Quillan?"

"Absolutely. I'll vouch for that," Gornt said. "Orlanda's absolutely trustworthy."

"Of course if you want to *offer* an interview—I'll accept. Tomorrow."

"I'll consider it."

"I'll guarantee to make you look marvelous!"

"The Chinese really know everything here?"

"Of course," she said at once. "But *quai loh*—foreigners—don't read the Chinese papers, except for a handful of old China hands—like Quillan."

"And the whole of Special Intelligence, Special Branch and the police in general," Gornt said.

"And Ian Dunross," she added, the tip of her tongue touching her teeth.

"He's that sharp?" Bartlett asked.

"Oh yes. He's got Devil Struan's blood in him."

"I don't understand."

"You will, if you stay here long enough."

Bartlett thought about that, then frowned. "You knew about the guns too, Mr. Gornt?"

"Only that the police had intercepted contraband arms aboard 'the millionaire American's private jet which arrived last night.' It was in my Chinese paper this morning too. The *Sing Pao*." Gornt's smile was sardonic. "That's *The Times* in Cantonese. It was in their Stop Press column too. But, unlike Orlanda, I am surprised you haven't been intercepted by members of our English press already. They're very diligent here in Hong Kong. More diligent than Orlanda gives them credit for being."

Bartlett caught her perfume but persisted. "I'm surprised you didn't mention it, Mr. Gornt."

"Why should I? What do guns have to do with our possible future association?" Gornt chuckled. "If worst comes to worst we'll visit you in jail, Orlanda and I."

She laughed. "Yes indeed."

"Thanks a lot!" Again her perfume. Bartlett put aside the guns and concentrated on her. "Ramos—that's Spanish?"

"Portuguese. From Macao. My father worked for Rothwell-Gornt in Shanghai—my mother's Shanghainese. I was brought up in Shanghai until '49, then went to the States for a few years, to high school in San Francisco."

"Did you? L.A.'s my hometown—I went to high school in the Valley."

"I love California," she said. "How d'you like Hong Kong?"

"I've just arrived." Bartlett grinned. "Seems I made an explosive entrance."

She laughed. Lovely white teeth. "Hong Kong's all right—provided you can leave every month or so. You should visit Macao for a weekend—it's old worldly, very pretty, only forty miles away with good ferries. It's very different from Hong Kong." She turned back to Gornt. "Again, I'm sorry to interrupt, Quillan, just wanted to say hello. . . ." She started to leave.

"No, we're through—I was just going," Bartlett said, interrupting her. "Thanks again, Mr. Gornt. See you Tuesday if not before. . . . Hope to see you again, Miss Ramos."

"Yes, that would be nice. Here's my card—if you'll grant the interview I guarantee a good press." She held out her hand and he touched it and felt her warmth.

Gornt saw him to the door and then closed it and came back to his desk and took a cigarette. She lit the match for him and blew out the flame, then sat in the chair Bartlett had used.

"Nice-looking man," she said.

"Yes. But he's American, naive, and a very cocky bastard who may need taking down a peg."

"That's what you want me to do?"

"Perhaps. Did you read his dossier?"

"Oh yes. Very interesting." Orlanda smiled.

"You're not to ask him for money," Gornt said sharply.

"*Ayeeyah,* Quillan, am I that dumb?" she said as abrasively, her eyes flashing.

"Good."

"Why would he smuggle guns into Hong Kong?"

"Why indeed, my dear? Perhaps someone was just using him."

"That must be the answer. If I had all his money I wouldn't try something as stupid as that."

"No," Gornt said.

"Oh, did you like that bit about my being a free-lance reporter? I thought I did that very well."

"Yes, but don't underestimate him. He's no fool. He's very sharp. Very." He told her about the Casale. "That's too much of a coincidence. He must have a dossier on me too, a detailed one. Not many know of my liking for that place."

"Maybe I'm in it too."

"Perhaps. Don't let him catch you out. About the free lancing."

"Oh, come on, Quillan, who of the tai-pans except you and Dunross read the Chinese papers—and even then you can't read all of them. I've already done a column or two . . . 'by a Special Correspondent.' If he

grants me an interview I can write it. Don't worry." She moved the ashtray closer for him. "It went all right, didn't it? With Bartlett?"

"Perfectly. You're wasted. You should be in the movies."

"Then talk to your friend about me, please, please, Quillan dear. Charlie Wang's the biggest producer in Hong Kong and owes you lots of
favors. Charlie Wang has so many movies going that . . . just one chance
is all I need. . . . I could become a star! Please?"

"Why not?" he asked dryly. "But I don't think you're his type."

"I can adapt. Didn't I act exactly as you wanted with Bartlett? Am I not
dressed perfectly, American style?"

"Yes, yes you are." Gornt looked at her, then said delicately, "You could
be perfect for him. I was thinking you could perhaps have something
more permanent than an affair. . . ."

All her attention concentrated. "What?"

"You and he could fit together like a perfect Chinese puzzle. You're
good-humored, the right age, beautiful, clever, educated, marvelous at the
pillow, very smart in the head, with enough of an American patina to put
him at ease." Gornt exhaled smoke and added, "And of all the ladies I
know, you could really spend his money. Yes, you two could fit perfectly
. . . he'd be very good for you and you'd brighten his life considerably.
Wouldn't you?"

"Oh yes," she said at once. "Oh yes I would." She smiled then frowned.
"But what about the woman he has with him? They're sharing a suite at
the Vic. I heard she's gorgeous. What about her, Quillan?"

Gornt smiled thinly. "My spies say they don't sleep together though
they're better than friends."

Her face fell. "He's not queer, is he?"

Gornt laughed. It was a good rich laugh. "I wouldn't do that to you,
Orlanda! No, I'm sure he's not. He's just got a strange arrangement with
Casey."

"What is it?"

Gornt shrugged.

After a moment she said, "What do I do about her?"

"If Casey Tcholok's in your way, remove her. You've got claws."

"You're . . . Sometimes I don't like you at all."

"We're both realists, you and I. Aren't we." He said it very flat.

She recognized the undercurrent of violence. At once she got up and
leaned across the desk and kissed him lightly. "You're a devil," she said,
placating him. "That's for old times."

His hand strayed to her breast and he sighed, remembering, enjoying
the warmth that came through the thin material. *"Ayeeyah,* Orlanda, we
had some good times, didn't we?"

She had been his mistress when she was seventeen. He was her first
and he had kept her for almost five years and would have continued but
she went with a youth to Macao when he was away and he had been told

about it. And so he had stopped. At once. Even though they had a daughter then, he and she, one year old.

"Orlanda," he had told her as she had begged for forgiveness, "there's nothing to forgive. I've told you a dozen times that youth needs youth, and there'd come a day. . . . Dry your tears, marry the lad—I'll give you a dowry and my blessing. . . ." And throughout all her weepings he had remained firm. "We'll be friends," he had assured her, "and I'll take care of you when you need it. . . ."

The next day he had turned the heat of his covert fury on the youth, an Englishman, a minor executive in Asian Properties and, within the month, he had broken him.

"It's a matter of face," he had told her calmly.

"Oh I know, I understand but . . . what shall I do now?" she had wailed. "He's leaving tomorrow for England and he wants me to go with him and marry him but I can't marry now, he's got no money or future or job or money. . . ."

"Dry your tears, then go shopping."

"What?"

"Yes. Here's a present." He had given her a first-class, return ticket to London on the same airplane that the youth was traveling tourist. And a thousand pounds in crisp, new ten-pound notes. "Buy lots of pretty clothes, and go to the theater. You're booked into the Connaught for eleven days—just sign the bill—and your return's confirmed, so have a happy time and come back fresh and without problems!"

"Oh thank you, Quillan darling, oh thank you. . . . I'm so sorry. You forgive me?"

"There's nothing to forgive. But if you ever talk to him again, or see him privately . . . I won't be friendly to you or your family ever again."

She had thanked him profusely through her tears, cursing herself for her stupidity, begging for the wrath of heaven to descend upon whoever had betrayed her. The next day the youth had tried to speak to her at the airport and on the plane and in London but she just cursed him away. She knew where her rice bowl rested. The day she left London he committed suicide.

When Gornt heard about it, he lit a fine cigar and took her out to a dinner atop the Victoria and Albert with candelabra and fine linen and fine silver, and then, after he had had his Napoleon brandy and she her crème de menthe, he had sent her home, alone, to the apartment he still paid for. He had ordered another brandy and stayed, watching the lights of the harbor, and the Peak, feeling the glory of vengeance, the majesty of life, his face regained.

"Ayeeyah, we had some good times," Gornt said again now, still desiring her, though he had not pillowed with her from the time he had heard about Macao.

"Quillan . . ." she began, his hand warming her too.

"No."

Her eyes strayed to the inner door. "Please. It's three years, there's never been anyone . . ."

"Thank you but no." He held her away from him, his hands now firm on her arms but gentle. "We've already had the best," he said as a connoisseur would. "I don't like second best."

She sat back on the edge of the desk, watching him sullenly. "You always win, don't you."

"The day you become lovers with Bartlett I'll give you a present," he said calmly. "If he takes you to Macao and you stay openly with him for three days I'll give you a new Jag. If he asks you to marry him you get the apartment and everything in it, and a house in California as a wedding present."

She gasped, then smiled gloriously. "An XK-E, a black one, Quillan, oh that would be perfect!" Then her happiness evaporated. "What's so important about him? Why is he so important to you?"

He just stared at her.

"Sorry," she said, "sorry, I shouldn't have asked." Thoughtfully she reached for a cigarette and lit it and leaned over and gave it to him.

"Thanks," he said, seeing the curve of her breast, enjoying it, yet a little saddened that such beauty was so transient. "Oh, by the way, I wouldn't like Bartlett to know of our arrangement."

"Nor would I." She sighed and forced a smile. Then she got up and shrugged. "*Ayeeyah*, it would never have lasted with us anyway. Macao or not Macao. You would have changed—you'd have become bored, men always do."

She checked her makeup and her shirt and blew him a kiss and left him. He stared at the closed door then smiled and stubbed out the cigarette she had given him, never having puffed on it, not wanting the taint of her lips. He lit a fresh one and hummed a little tune.

Excellent, he thought happily. Now we'll see, Mr. Bloody Cocky Confident Yankee Bartlett, now we'll see how you handle that knife. Pasta with beer indeed!

Then Gornt caught a lingering whiff of her perfume and he was swept back momentarily into memories of their pillowing. When she was young, he reminded himself. Thank God there's no premium on youth or beauty out here, and a substitution's as close as a phone call or a hundred-dollar note.

He reached for the phone and dialed a special private number, glad that Orlanda was more Chinese than European. Chinese are such practical people.

The dial tone stopped and he heard Paul Havergill's crisp voice. "Yes?"

"Paul, Quillan. How're things?"

"Hello, Quillan—of course you know Johnjohn's taking over the bank in November?"

"Yes. Sorry about that."

"Damnable. I thought I was going to be confirmed but instead the board chose Johnjohn. It was official last night. It's Dunross again, his clique, and the damned stock they have. How did your meeting go?"

"Our American's chomping at the bit, just as I told you he would be." Gornt took a deep drag of his cigarette and tried to keep the excitement out of his voice. "How would you like a little special action before you retire?"

"What had you in mind?"

"You're leaving end of November?"

"Yes. After twenty-three years. In some ways I won't be sorry."

Nor will I, Gornt thought contentedly. You're out of date and too bloody conservative. The only thing in your favor is that you hate Dunross. "That's almost four months. That'd give us plenty of time. You, me and our American friend."

"What do you have in mind?"

"You remember one of my hypothetical game plans, the one I called 'Competition'?"

Havergill thought a moment. "That was how to take over or eliminate an opposition bank, wasn't it? Why?"

"Say someone dusted off the plan and made a few changes and pushed the go button . . . two days ago. Say someone knew Dunross and the others would vote you out and wanted some revenge. Competition would work perfectly."

"I don't see why. What's the point of attacking Blacs?" The Bank of London, Canton and Shanghai was the Victoria's main opposition. "Doesn't make sense."

"Ah, but say someone changed the target, Paul."

"To whom?"

"I'll come by at three and explain."

"To whom?"

"Richard." Richard Kwang controlled the Ho-Pak Bank—one of the largest of all the many Chinese banks in Hong Kong.

"Good God! But that's . . ." There was a long pause. "Quillan, you've really begun Competition . . . to put it into effect?"

"Yes, and no one knows about it except you and me."

"But how is that going to work against Dunross?"

"I'll explain later. Can Ian meet his commitments on his ships?"

There was a pause which Gornt noted. "Yes," he heard Havergill say. "Yes, but what?"

"But I'm sure he'll be all right."

"What other problems has Dunross got?"

"Sorry, but that wouldn't be ethical."

"Of course." Gornt added thinly, "Let me put it another way: Say their boat was a little rocked. Eh?"

There was a longer pause. "At the right moment, a smallish wave could scuttle them, or any company. Even you."

"But not the Victoria Bank."

"Oh no."

"Good. See you at three." Gornt hung up and mopped his brow again, his excitement vast. He stubbed out his cigarette, made a quick calculation, lit another cigarette, then dialed. "Charles, Quillan. Are you busy?"

"No. What can I do for you?"

"I want a balance sheet." A balance sheet was a private signal for the attorney to telephone eight nominees who would buy or sell on the stock market on Gornt's behalf, secretly, to avoid the trading being traced back to him. All shares and all monies would pass solely through the attorney's hands so that neither the nominees nor the brokers would know for whom the transactions were being made.

"A balance sheet it will be. What sort, Quillan?"

"I want to sell short." To sell short meant he sold shares he did not own on the presumption their value would go down. Then, before he had to buy them back—he had a maximum margin of two weeks in Hong Kong—if the stock had indeed gone down, he would pocket the difference. Of course if he gambled wrong and the stock had gone up, he would have to pay the difference.

"What shares and what numbers?"

"A hundred thousand shares of Ho-Pak . . ."

"Holy Christ . . ."

". . . the same, as soon as the market opens tomorrow, and another 200 during the day. I'll give you further instructions then."

There was a stunned silence. "You did say Ho-Pak?"

"Yes."

"It'll take time to borrow all those shares. Good God, Quillan, four hundred thousand?"

"While you're about it, get another hundred. A round half a million."

"But . . . but Ho-Pak's as blue a blue chip as we've got. It hasn't gone down in years."

"Yes."

"What've you heard?"

"Rumors," Gornt said gravely and chuckled to himself. "Would you like an early lunch, eat at the club?"

"I'll be there."

Gornt hung up, then dialed another private number.

"Yes?"

"It's me," Gornt said cautiously. "Are you alone?"

"Yes. And?"

"At our meeting, the Yankee suggested a raid."

"*Ayeeyah!* And?"

"And Paul's in," he said, the exaggeration coming easily. "Absolutely secretly, of course. I've just talked to him."

"Then I'm in. Provided I get control of Struan's ships, their Hong Kong property operation and 40 percent of their landholdings in Thailand and Singapore."

"You must be joking!"

"Nothing's too much to smash them. Is it, old boy?"

Gornt heard the well-bred, mocking laugh and hated Jason Plumm for it. "You despise him just as much as I do," Gornt said.

"Ah, but you'll need me and my special friends. Even with Paul on or off the fence, you and the Yankee can't pull it off, not without me and mine."

"Why else am I talking to you?"

"Listen, don't forget I'm not asking for any piece of the American's pie."

Gornt kept his voice calm. "What's that got to do with anything?"

"I know you. Oh yes. I know you, old boy."

"Do you now?"

"Yes. You won't be satisfied just with destructing our 'friend,' you'll want the whole pie."

"Will I now?"

"Yes. You've wanted a stake in the U.S. market too long."

"And you."

"No. We know where our toast's toasted. We're content to trail along behind. We're content with Asia. We don't want to be a noble anything."

"Oh?"

"No. Then it's a deal?"

"No," Gornt said.

"I'll drop the shipping totally. Instead I'll take Ian's Kowloon Investments, the Kai Tak operation, and 40 percent of the landholdings in Thailand and Singapore, and I'll accept 25 percent of Par-Con and three places on the board."

"Get stuffed!"

"The offer's good till Monday."

"Which Monday?"

"Next Monday."

"*Dew neh loh moh* on all your Mondays!"

"And yours! I'll make you a last offer. Kowloon Investments and their Kai Tak operation totally, 35 percent of all their landholdings in Thailand and Singapore, and 10 percent of the Yankee pie with three seats on the board."

"Is that all?"

"Yes. Again, the offer's good till next Monday. And don't think you can gobble us in the process."

"Have you gone mad?"

"I told you—I know you. Is it a deal?"

"No."

Again the soft, malevolent laugh. "Till Monday—next Monday. That's time enough for you to make up your mind."

"Will I see you at Ian's party tonight?" Gornt asked thinly.

"Have you gone bonkers! I wouldn't go if . . . Good God, Quillan, are you really going to accept? *In person?*"

"I wasn't going to—but now I think I will. I wouldn't want to miss perhaps the last great party of the Struans' last tai-pan. . . ."

7

12:01 P.M.:

In the boardroom it was still rough going for Casey. They would take none of the baits she offered. Her anxiety had increased and now as she waited she felt a wave of untoward fear go through her.

Phillip Chen was doodling, Linbar fiddling with his papers, Jacques deVille watching her thoughtfully. Then Andrew Gavallan stopped writing the latest percentages she had quoted. He sighed and looked up at her. "Clearly this should be a co-financing operation," he said, his voice sharp. Electricity in the room soared and Casey had difficulty suppressing a cheer as he added, "How much would Par-Con be prepared to put up, joint financing, for the whole deal?"

"18 million U.S. this year should cover it," she answered immediately, noting happily that they all covered a gasp.

The published net worth of Struan's last year was almost 28 million, and she and Bartlett had gauged their offer on this figure.

"Make the first offer 20 million," Linc had told her. "You should hook 'em at 25 which'd be great. It's essential we co-finance, but the suggestion's got to come from them."

"But look at their balance sheet, Linc. You can't tell for sure what their real net worth is. It could be 10 million either way, maybe more. We don't know how strong they really are . . . or how weak. Look at this item: '14.7 million retained in subsidiaries.' What subsidiaries, where and what for? Here's another one: '7.4 million transferred to—' "

"So what, Casey? So it's 30 million instead of 25. Our projection's still valid."

"Yes—but their accounting procedures . . . My God, Linc, if we did one percent of this in the States the SEC'd have our asses in a sling and we'd end up in jail for fifty years."

"Yes. But it's not against *their* law, which is a major reason for going to Hong Kong."

"20 is too much for openers."

"I'll leave it to you, Casey. Just remember in Hong Kong we play Hong Kong rules—whatever's legal. I want in their game."

"Why? And don't say 'for my goddamn pleasure.' "

Linc had laughed. "Okay—then for *your* goddamn pleasure. Just make the Struan deal!"

The humidity in the boardroom had increased. She would have liked to reach for a tissue but she kept still, willing them onward, pretending calm.

Gavallan broke the silence. "When would Mr. Bartlett confirm the offer of 18 million . . . if we accepted?"

"It's confirmed," she said sweetly, passing over the insult. "I have clearance to commit up to 20 million on this deal without consulting Linc or his board," she said, deliberately giving them room to maneuver. Then she added innocently, "Then it's all settled? Good." She began to sort out her papers. "Next: I'd—"

"Just a moment," Gavallan said, off balance. "I, er, 18 is . . . In any event we have to present the package to the tai-pan."

"Oh," she said, pretending surprise. "I thought we were negotiating as equals, that you four gentlemen had powers equal to mine. Perhaps I'd better talk to Mr. Dunross directly in the future."

Andrew Gavallan flushed. "The tai-pan has final say. In everything."

"I'm very glad to know it, Mr. Gavallan. I only have final say up to 20 million." She beamed at them. "Very well, put it to your tai-pan. Meanwhile, shall we set a time limit on the consideration period?"

Another silence.

"What do you suggest?" Gavallan said, feeling trapped.

"Whatever the minimum is. I don't know how fast you like to work," Casey said.

Phillip Chen said, "Why not table that answer until after lunch, Andrew?"

"Yes—good idea."

"That's fine with me," Casey said. I've done my job, she thought. I'll settle for 20 million when it could've been 30 and they're men and expert, and over twenty-one and they think I'm a sucker. But now I get my drop dead money. Dear God in heaven let this deal go through because then I'm free forever.

Free to do what?

Never mind, she told herself. I'll think about that later.

She heard herself continue the pattern: "Shall we go through the details of how you'd like the 18 million and . . ."

"18 is hardly adequate," Phillip Chen interrupted, the lie coming very easily. "There are all sorts of added costs. . . ."

In perfect negotiating style Casey argued and allowed them to push her to 20 million and then, with apparent reluctance, she said, "You gentlemen are exceptional businessmen. Very well, 20 million." She saw their hidden smiles and laughed to herself.

"Good," Gavallan said, very satisfied.

"Now," she said, wanting to keep the pressure on, "how do you want our joint venture corporate structure to be? Of course subject to your tai-pan—sorry, subject to *the* tai-pan's approval," she said, correcting herself with just the right amount of humility.

Gavallan was watching her, irritably wishing she were a man. Then I could say, up yours, or go shit in your hat, and we'd laugh together because you know and I know you always have to check with the tai-pan in some way or another—whether it's Dunross or Bartlett or a board or your wife. Yes, and if you were a man we wouldn't have this bloody sexuality in the boardroom which doesn't belong here in the first place. Christ, if you were an old bag maybe that'd make a difference but, shit, a bird like you?

What the hell gets into American women? Why in the name of Christ don't they stay where they belong and be content with what they're great at? Stupid!

And stupid to concede financing so quickly, and even more stupid to give us an extra two million when ten would probably have been acceptable in the first place. For God's sake, you should have been more patient and you would have made a much better deal! That's the trouble with you Americans, you've—no finesse and no patience and no style and you don't understand the art of negotiation, and you, dear lady, you're much too impatient to prove yourself. So now I know how to play you.

He glanced at Linbar Struan who was watching Casey covertly, waiting for him or Phillip or Jacques to continue. When I'm tai-pan, Gavallan thought grimly, I'm going to break you, young Linbar, break you or make you. You need shoving out into the world on your own, to make you think for yourself, to rely on yourself, not on your name and your heritage. Yes, with a lot more hard work to take some of the heat out of your yang—the sooner you remarry the better.

His eyes switched to Jacques deVille who smiled back at him. Ah Jacques, he thought without rancor, you're my main opposition. You're doing what you usually do: saying little, watching everything, thinking a lot—rough, tough and mean if necessary. But what's in your mind about this deal? Have I missed something? What does your canny legal Parisian mind forecast? Ah but she stopped you in your tracks with her joke about your joke about her nose, eh?

I'd like to bed her too, he thought absently, knowing Linbar and Jacques had already decided the same. Of course—who wouldn't?

What about you, Phillip Chen?

Oh no. Not you. You like them very much younger and have it done to you, strangely, if there's any truth to the rumors, *heya?*

He looked back at Casey. He could read her impatience. You don't look lesbian, he thought and groaned inwardly. Is that your other weakness? Christ, that'd be a terrible waste!

"The joint venture should be set up under Hong Kong law," he said.

"Yes of course. There's—"

"Sims, Dawson and Dick can advise us how. I'll arrange an appointment for tomorrow or the day after."

"No need for that, Mr. Gavallan. I already got their tentative proposals, hypothetical and confidential, of course, just in case we decided to conclude."

"What?" They gaped at her as she took out five copies of a short form, legal contract and handed one to each of them.

"I found out they were your attorneys," she said brightly. "I had our people check them out and I was advised they're the best so they were fine with us. I asked them to consider our joint hypothetical needs—yours as well as ours. Is anything the matter?"

"No," Gavallan said, suddenly furious that their own firm had not told them of Par-Con's inquiries. He began to scan the letter.

Dew neh loh moh on Casey bloody whatever her names are, Phillip Chen was thinking, enraged at the loss of face. May your golden gully wither and be ever dry and dust-filled for your foul manners and your fresh, filthy, unfeminine habits!

God protect us from American women!

Ayeeyah, it is going to cost Lincoln Bartlett a pretty penny for daring to stick this . . . this creature upon us, he promised himself. How dare he!

Nevertheless, his mind was estimating the staggering value of the deal they were being offered. It has to be at least 100 million U.S., potentially, over the next few years, he told himself, his head reeling. This will give the Noble House the stability it needs.

Oh happy day, he gloated. And co-financing dollar for dollar! Unbelievable! Stupid to give us that so quickly without even a tiny concession in return. Stupid, but what can you expect from a stupid woman? *Ayeeyah*, the Pacific Rim will gorge on all the polyurethane foam products we can make—for packaging, building, bedding and insulating. One factory here, one in Taiwan, one in Singapore, one in Kuala Lumpur and a last, initially, in Jakarta. We'll make millions, tens of millions. And as to the computer-leasing agency, why at the rental these fools are offering us, 10 percent less than IBM's list price, less our 7½ percent commission—with just a little haggling we would have been delighted to agree to 5 percent—by next weekend I can sell three in Singapore, one here, one in Kuala Lumpur and one to that shipping pirate in Indonesia for a clear profit of $67,500 each, or $405,000 for six phone calls. And as to China . . .

And as to China . . .

Oh all gods great and small and very small, help this deal to go through and I will endow a new temple, a cathedral, in Tai-ping Shan, he promised, consumed with fervor. If China will drop some controls, or even ease them just a fraction, we can fertilize the paddy fields of Kwantung

Province and then of all China and over the next twelve years this deal will mean tens of hundreds of millions of dollars, U.S. dollars not Hong Kong dollars!

The thought of all this profit mollified his rage considerably. "I think this proposal can form the basis for further discussion," he said, finishing reading. "Don't you, Andrew?"

"Yes." Gavallan put the letter down. "I'll call them after lunch. When would it be convenient for Mr. Bartlett . . . and you of course . . . to meet?"

"This afternoon—the sooner the better—or anytime tomorrow but Linc won't come. I handle all the details, that's my job," Casey said crisply. "He sets policy—and will formally sign the final documents—after I've approved them. That's the function of the commander-in-chief, isn't it?" She beamed at them.

"I'll make an appointment and leave a message at your hotel," Gavallan was saying.

"Perhaps we could set it up now—then that's out of the way?"

Sourly Gavallan glanced at his watch. Almost lunch, thank God. "Jacques—how're you fixed tomorrow?"

"Morning's better than the afternoon."

"And for John too," Phillip Chen said.

Gavallan picked up the phone and dialed. "Mary? Call Dawson and make an appointment for eleven tomorrow to include Mr. deVille and Mr. John Chen and Miss Casey. At their offices." He put the phone down. "Jacques and John Chen handle all our corporate matters. John's sophisticated on American problems and Dawson's the expert. I'll send the car for you at 10:30."

"Thanks, but there's no need for you to trouble."

"Just as you wish," he said politely. "Perhaps this is a good time to break for lunch."

Casey said, "We've a quarter of an hour yet. Shall we start on how you'd like our financing? Or if you wish we can send out for a sandwich and work on through."

They stared at her, appalled. "Work through lunch?"

"Why not? It's an old American custom."

"Thank God it's not a custom here," Gavallan said.

"Yes," Phillip Chen snapped.

She felt their disapproval descend like a pall but she did not care. Shit on all of you, she thought irritably, then forced herself to put that attitude away. Listen, idiot, don't let these sons of bitches get you! She smiled sweetly. "If you want to stop now for lunch, that's fine with me."

"Good," Gavallan said at once and the others breathed a sigh of relief. "We begin lunch at 12:40. You'll probably want to powder your nose first."

"Yes, thank you," she said, knowing they wanted her gone so they could discuss her—and then the deal. It should be the other way around, she thought, but it won't be. No. It'll be the same as always: they'll lay bets as to who'll be the first to score. But it'll be none of them, because *I* don't want any of *them* at the moment, however attractive they are in their way. These men are like all the others I've met: they don't want love, they just want sex.

Except Linc.

Don't think about Linc and how much you love him and how rotten these years have been. Rotten and wonderful.

Remember your promise.

I won't think about Linc and love.

Not until my birthday which is ninety-eight days from now. The ninety-eighth day ends the seventh year and because of my darling by then I'll have my drop dead money and really be equal, and, God willing, we'll have the Noble House. Will that be my wedding present to him? Or his to me?

Or a good-bye present.

"Where's the ladies' room?" she asked, getting up, and they all stood and towered over her, except Phillip Chen whom she topped by an inch, and Gavallan directed her.

Linbar Struan opened the door for her and closed it behind her. Then he grinned. "A thousand says you'll never make it, Jacques."

"Another thousand," Gavallan said. "And ten that you won't, Linbar."

"You're on," Linbar replied, "provided she's here a month."

"You're slowing up, aren't you, old chap?" Gavallan said, then to Jacques, "Well?"

The Frenchman smiled. "Twenty that you, Andrew, will never charm such a lady into bed—and as to you, poor young Linbar. Fifty against your racehorse says the same."

"I like my filly for God's sake. Noble Star's got a great chance of being a winner. She's the best in our stable."

"Fifty."

"A hundred and I'll consider it."

"I don't want any horse that much." Jacques smiled at Phillip Chen. "What do you think, Phillip?"

Phillip Chen got up. "I think I'll go home to lunch and leave you stallions to your dreams. It's curious though that you're all betting the others won't—not that any of you could." Again they laughed.

"Stupid to give us the extra, eh?" Gavallan said.

"The deal's fantastic," Linbar Struan said. "Christ, Uncle Phillip, fantastic!"

"Like her *derrière*," deVille said as a connoisseur would. "Eh, Phillip?"

Good-naturedly Phillip Chen nodded and walked out, but as he saw Casey disappearing into the ladies' room, he thought, *Ayeeyah*, who'd want the big lump anyway?

Inside the ladies' room, Casey looked around, appalled. It was clean but smelled of old drains and there were pails piled one on top of another and some were filled with water. The floor was tiled but water-spotted and messy. I've heard the English are not very hygienic, she thought disgustedly, but here in the Noble House? Ugh! Astonishing!

She went into one of the cubicles, its floor wet and slippery, and after she had finished she pulled the handle and nothing happened. She tried it again, and again, and still nothing happened so she cursed and lifted off the top of the cistern. The cistern was dry and rusty. Irritably she unbolted the door and went to the basin and turned on the water but none came out.

What's the matter with this place? I'll bet those bastards sent me here deliberately!

There were clean hand towels so she poured a pail of water into the basin awkwardly, spilling some, washed her hands, then dried them, furious that her shoes had got splashed. At a sudden thought, she took another pail and flushed the toilet, then used still another bucket to clean her hands again. When she left, she felt very soiled.

I suppose the goddamn pipe's broken somewhere and the plumber won't come until tomorrow. Goddamn all water systems!

Calm down, she told herself. You'll start making mistakes.

The corridor was covered with fine Chinese silk carpet, and the walls were lined with oil paintings of clipper ships and Chinese landscapes. As she approached she could hear the muted voices from the boardroom and a laugh—the kind of laugh that comes from a ribald joke or a smutty remark. She knew the moment she opened the door, the good humor and comradeship would vanish and the awkward silence would return.

She opened the door and they all got up.

"Are you having trouble with your water mains?" she asked, holding her anger down.

"No, I don't think so," Gavallan said, startled.

"Well, there's no water. Didn't you know?"

"Of course there's no— Oh!" He stopped. "You're staying at the V and A so . . . Didn't anyone tell you about the water shortage?"

They all began talking at once but Gavallan dominated them. "The V and A has its own water supply—so do a couple of other hotels—but the rest of us're on four hours of water every fourth day, so you've got to use a pail. Never occurred to me you didn't know. Sorry."

"How do you manage? *Every fourth day?*"

"Yes. For four hours, 6:00 A.M. till 8:00 A.M., then 5:00 till 7:00 in the evening. It's a frightful bore because of course it means we've got to store four days' supply. Pails, or the bath, whatever you can. We're short of pails—it's our water day tomorrow. Oh my God, there was water for you, wasn't there?"

"Yes, but . . . You mean the water mains are turned off? Everywhere?" she asked incredulously.

"Yes," Gavallan said patiently. "Except for those four hours every fourth day. But you're all right at the V and A. As they're right on the waterfront they can refill their tanks daily from lighters—of course, they have to buy it."

"You can't shower or bathe?"

Linbar Struan laughed. "Everyone gets pretty grotty after three days in this heat but at least we're all in the same sewer. Still it's survival training to make sure there's a full pail before you go."

"I had no idea," she said, aghast that she had used *three* pails.

"Our reservoirs are empty," Gavallan explained. "We've had almost no rain this year and last year was dry too. Bloody nuisance but there you are. Just one of those things. Joss."

"Then where does your water come from?"

They stared at her blankly. "From China of course. By pipes over the border into the New Territories, or by tanker from the Pearl River. The government's just chartered a fleet of ten tankers that go up the Pearl River, by agreement with Peking. They bring us about 10 million gallons a day. It'll cost the government upwards of 25 million for this year's charter. Saturday's paper said our consumption's down to 30 million gallons a day for our 3½ million population—that includes industry. In your country, one person uses 150 gallons a day, so they say."

"It's the same for everyone? Four hours every fourth day?"

"Even at the Great House you use a pail." Gavallan shrugged again. "But the tai-pan's got a place at Shek-O that has its own well. We all pile over there when we're invited, to get the slime off."

She thought again of the three pails of water she had used. Jesus, she thought, did I use it all? I don't recall if there's any left.

"I guess I've a lot to learn," she said.

Yes, they all thought. Yes, you bloody have.

"Tai-pan?"

"Yes, Claudia?" Dunross said into the intercom.

"The meeting with Casey's just broken for lunch. Master Andrew is on line four. Master Linbar's on his way up."

"Cancel him till after lunch. Any luck on Tsu-yan?"

"No sir. The plane landed on time at 8:40. He's not at his office in Taipei. Or his flat. I'll keep trying, of course. Another thing, I've just had an interesting call, tai-pan. It seems that Mr. Bartlett went to Rothwell-Gornt this morning and had a private meeting with Mr. Gornt."

"Are you sure?" he asked, ice in his stomach suddenly.

"Yes, oh very yes."

Bastard, Dunross thought. Does Bartlett mean me to find out? "Thanks," he said, putting the question aside for the moment, but very glad to know. "You've got a thousand dollars on any horse on Saturday."

"Oh thank you, tai-pan."

"Back to work, Claudia!" He punched the number four button. "Yes, Andrew? What's the deal?"

Gavallan told him the important part.

"20 million in cash?" he asked with disbelief.

"In marvelous, beautiful U.S. cash!" Dunross could feel his beam down the phone. "And when I asked when Bartlett would confirm the deal the little scrubber had the bloody cheek to say, 'Oh it's confirmed now—I can commit up to 20 million on this deal without consulting him or anyone.' Do you think that's possible?"

"I don't know." Dunross felt a little weak in the knees. "Bartlett's due any moment. I'll ask."

"Hey, tai-pan, if this goes through . . ."

But Dunross was hardly listening as Gavallan ran on ecstatically. It's an unbelievable offer, he was telling himself.

It's too good. Where's the flaw?

Where's the flaw?

Ever since he had become tai-pan he had had to maneuver, lie, cajole and even threaten—Havergill of the bank for one—far more than ever he had expected, to stay ahead of the disasters he had inherited, and the natural and political ones that seemed to be besetting the world. Even going public had not given him the capital and time he had expected because a worldwide slump had ripped the markets to pieces. And last year in August, Typhoon Wanda had struck, leaving havoc in her wake, hundreds dead, a hundred thousand homeless, half a thousand fishing boats sunk, twenty ships sunk, one of their three thousand tonners flung ashore, their giant half-completed wharf wrecked and their entire building program smashed for six months. In the fall the Cuban crisis and more slump. This spring de Gaulle had vetoed Britain's entry into the Common Market and more slump. China and Russia quarreling and more slump. . . .

And now I've almost got 20 million U.S. but I think we're somehow involved in gun-running, Tsu-yan's apparently on the run and John Chen's God knows where!

"Christ all sodding mighty!" he said angrily.

"What?" Gavallan stopped, aghast, in midflow. "What's up?"

"Oh nothing—nothing, Andrew," he said. "Nothing to do with you. Tell me about her. What's she like?"

"Good at figures, fast and confident, but impatient. And she's the best-looking bird I've seen in years, with potentially the best pair of knockers in town." Gavallan told him about the bets. "I think Linbar's got the inside track."

"I'm going to fire Foster and send Linbar down to Sydney for six months, get him to sort everything out there."

"Good idea." Gavallan laughed. "That'll stop his farting in church—though they say the ladies Down Under are very accommodating."

"You think this deal will go through?"

"Yes. Phillip was ecstatic about it. But it's shitty dealing through a woman and that's the truth. Do you think we could bypass her and deal with Bartlett direct?"

"No. He was quite clear in his correspondence that K. C. Tcholok was his chief negotiator."

"Oh well . . . into the breach and all that! What we do for the Noble House!"

"Have you found her weak spot?"

"Impatience. She wants to 'belong'—to be one of the boys. I'd say her Achilles' heel is that she desperately wants acceptance in a man's world."

"No harm in wanting that—like the Holy Grail. The meeting with Dawson's set for eleven tomorrow?"

"Yes."

"Get Dawson to cancel it, but not until nine tomorrow morning. Tell him to make an excuse and reset it for Wednesday at noon."

"Good idea, keep her off balance, what?"

"Tell Jacques I'll take that meeting myself."

"Yes, tai-pan. What about John Chen? You'll want him there?"

After a pause Dunross said, "Yes. Have you seen him yet?"

"No. He's expected for lunch—you want me to chase him?"

"No. Where's Phillip?"

"He went home. He's coming back at 2:30."

Good, Dunross thought, and tabled John Chen until that time. "Listen . . ." The intercom buzzed. "Just a minute, Andrew." He punched the hold. "Yes, Claudia?"

"Sorry to interrupt, tai-pan, but I've got your call to Mr. Jen in Taipei on line two and Mr. Bartlett's just arrived downstairs."

"Bring him in as soon as I'm through with Jen." He stabbed line four again. "Andrew, I may be a couple of minutes late. Host drinks and that sort of thing for me. I'll bring Bartlett up myself."

"Okay."

Dunross stabbed line two. "*Tsaw an,*" he said in Mandarin dialect—How are you?—glad to talk to Wei-wei's uncle, General Jen Tang-wa, deputy chief of the illegal Kuomintang secret police for Hong Kong.

"*Shey-shey,*" then in English, "What's up, tai-pan?"

"I thought you should know . . ." Dunross told him briefly about the guns and Bartlett, that the police were involved, but not about Tsu-yan or John Chen.

"*Ayeeyah!* That's very curious indeed."

"Yes. I thought so too. Very curious."

"You're convinced it's not Bartlett?"

"Yes. There appears to be no reason. None at all. It'd be stupid to use your own plane. Bartlett's not stupid," Dunross said. "Who'd need that sort of armament here?"

There was a pause. "Criminal elements."

"Triads?"

"Not all triads are criminals."

"No," Dunross said.

"I'll see what I can find out. I'm sure it's nothing to do with us, Ian. Are you still coming Sunday?"

"Yes."

"Good. I'll see what I can find out. Drinks at 6:00 P.M.?"

"How about eight o'clock? Have you seen Tsu-yan yet?"

"I thought he wasn't due until the weekend. Isn't he making up our foursome on Monday with the American?"

"Yes. I heard he caught an early flight today." Dunross kept his voice matter-of-fact.

"He's sure to call—do you want him to phone?"

"Yes. Anytime. It's nothing important. See you Sunday at eight."

"Yes, and thanks for the information. If I get anything I'll phone at once. 'Bye."

Dunross put the phone down. He had been listening very carefully to the tone of Jen's voice but he had heard nothing untoward. Where the hell's Tsu-yan?

A knock.

"Come in." He got up and went to meet Bartlett. "Hello." He smiled and held out his hand. "I'm Ian Dunross."

"Linc Bartlett." They shook hands firmly. "Am I too early?"

"You're dead on time. You must know I like punctuality." Dunross laughed. "I heard the meeting went well."

"Good," Bartlett replied, wondering if Dunross meant the Gornt meeting. "Casey knows her facts and figures."

"My fellows were most impressed—she said she could finalize things herself. Can she, Mr. Bartlett?"

"She can negotiate and settle up to 20 million. Why?"

"Nothing. Just wanted to find out your form. Please sit down—we've a few minutes yet. Lunch won't begin till 12:40. It sounds as though we may have a profitable enterprise in front of us."

"I hope so. As soon as I've checked with Casey, perhaps you and I can get together?"

Dunross looked at his calendar. "Tomorrow at ten. Here?"

"You're on."

"Smoke?"

"No thanks. I quit a few years back."

"So did I—still want a cigarette though." Dunross leaned back in his chair. "Before we go to lunch, Mr. Bartlett, there're a couple of minor points. I'm going to Taipei on Sunday afternoon, will be back Tuesday in time for dinner, and I'd like you to come along. There're a couple of people I'd like you to meet, a golf match you might enjoy. We could chat leisurely, you could see the potential plant sites. It could be important. I've made all the arrangements, but it's not possible to take Miss Tcholok."

Bartlett frowned, wondering if Tuesday was just a coincidence. "According to Superintendent Armstrong I can't leave Hong Kong."

"I'm sure that could be changed."

"Then you know about the guns too?" Bartlett said and cursed himself for the slip. He managed to keep his eyes steady.

"Oh yes. Someone else's been bothering you about them?" Dunross asked, watching him.

"The police even chased Casey! Jesus! My airplane's seized, we're all suspect, and I don't know a goddamn thing about any guns."

"Well, there's no need to worry, Mr. Bartlett. Our police are very good."

"I'm not worried, just teed off."

"That's understandable," Dunross said, glad the Armstrong meeting was confidential. Very glad.

Christ, he thought queasily, if John Chen and Tsu-yan are involved somehow, Bartlett's going to be very teed off indeed, and we'll lose the deal and he'll throw in with Gornt and then . . .

"How did you hear about the guns?"

"We were informed by our office at Kai Tak this morning."

"Nothing like this ever happened before?"

"Yes." Dunross added lightly, "But there's no harm in smuggling or even a little gun-running—actually they're both very honorable professions —of course we do them elsewhere."

"Where?"

"Wherever Her Majesty's Government desires." Dunross laughed. "We're all pirates here, Mr. Bartlett, at least we are to outsiders." He paused. "Presuming I can make arrangements with the police, you're on for Taipei?"

Bartlett said, "Casey's very close-mouthed."

"I'm not suggesting she's not to be trusted."

"She's just not invited?"

"Certain of our customs here are a little different from yours, Mr. Bartlett. Most times she'll be welcome—but sometimes, well, it would save a lot of embarrassment if she were excluded."

"Casey doesn't embarrass easily."

"I wasn't thinking of her embarrassment. Sorry to be blunt but perhaps it's wiser in the long run."

"And if I can't 'conform'?"

"It will probably mean you cannot take advantage of a unique opportunity, which would be a very great pity—particularly if you intend a long-term association with Asia."

"I'll think about that."

"Sorry, but I have to have a yes or no now."

"You do?"

"Yes."

"Then go screw!"

Dunross grinned. "I won't. Meanwhile, finally: yes or no."

Bartlett broke out laughing. "Since you put it that way, I'm on for Taipei."

"Good. Of course I'll have my wife look after Miss Tcholok while we're away. There'll be no loss of face for her."

"Thank you. But you needn't worry about Casey. How are you going to fix Armstrong?"

"I'm not going to *fix* him, just ask the assistant commissioner to let me be responsible for you, there and back."

"Parole me in your custody?"

"Yes."

"How do you know I won't just leave town? Maybe I was gun-running."

Dunross watched him. "Maybe you are. Maybe you'll try—but I can deliver you back dead or alive, as they say in the movies. Hong Kong and Taipei are within my fief."

"Dead or alive, eh?"

"Hypothetically, of course."

"How many men have you killed in your lifetime?"

The mood in the room changed and both men felt the change deeply. It's not dangerous yet between him and me, Dunross thought, not yet.

"Twelve," he replied, his senses poised, though the question had surprised him. "Twelve that I'm sure of. I was a fighter pilot during the war. Spitfires. I got two single-seat fighters, a Stuka, and two bombers—they were Dornier 17s and they'd have a crew of four each. All the planes burned as they went down. Twelve that I'm sure of, Mr. Bartlett. Of course we shot up a lot of trains, convoys, troop concentrations. Why?"

"I'd heard you were a flier. I don't think I've killed anyone. I was building camps, bases in the Pacific, that sort of thing. Never shot a gun in anger."

"But you like hunting?"

"Yes. I went on a safari in '59 in Kenya. Got an elephant and a great kudu bull and lots of game for the pot."

Dunross said after a pause, "I think I prefer to kill planes and trains and boats. Men, in war, are incidental. Aren't they?"

"Once the general's been put into the field by the ruler, sure. That's a fact of war."

"Have you read Sun Tzu's *The Art of War*?"

"The best book on war I've ever read," Bartlett said enthusiastically.

"Better'n Clausewitz or Liddell Hart, even though it was written in 500 B.C."

"Oh?" Dunross leaned back, glad to get away from the killings. I haven't remembered the killing for years, he thought. That's not fair to those men, is it?

"Did you know Sun Tzu's book was published in French in 1782? I've a theory Napoleon had a copy."

"It's certainly in Russian—and Mao always carried a copy that was dog-eared with use," Dunross said.

"You've read it?"

"My father beat it into me. I had to read the original in characters—in Chinese. And then he'd question me on it, very seriously."

A fly began to batter itself irritatingly against the windowpane. "Your dad wanted you to be a soldier?"

"No. Sun Tzu, like Machiavelli, wrote about life more than death—and about survival more than war. . . ." Dunross glanced at the window then got up and went over to it and obliterated the fly with a controlled savagery that sent warning signals through Bartlett.

Dunross returned to his desk. "My father thought I should know about survival and how to handle large bodies of men. He wanted me to be worthy to become tai-pan one day, though he never thought I'd amount to much." He smiled.

"He was tai-pan too?"

"Yes. He was very good. At first."

"What happened?"

Dunross laughed sardonically. "Ah, skeletons so early, Mr. Bartlett? Well, briefly, we had a rather tedious, long-drawn-out difference of opinion. Eventually he handed over to Alastair Struan, my predecessor."

"He's still alive?"

"Yes."

"Does your British understatement mean you went to war with him?"

"Sun Tzu's very specific about going to war, Mr. Bartlett. Very bad to go to war he says, unless you need to. Quote: 'Supreme excellence of generalship consists in breaking the enemy's resistance without fighting.' "

"You broke him?"

"He removed himself from the field, Mr. Bartlett, like the wise man he was."

Dunross's face had hardened. Bartlett studied him. Both men knew they were drawing battle lines in spite of themselves.

"I'm glad I came to Hong Kong," the American said. "I'm glad to meet you."

"Thank you. Perhaps one day you won't be."

Bartlett shrugged. "Maybe. Meanwhile we've got a deal cooking—good for you, good for us." He grinned abruptly, thinking about Gornt and the cooking knife. "Yes. I'm glad I came to Hong Kong."

"Would you and Casey care to be my guests this evening? I'm having a modest bash, a party, at 8:30 odd."

"Formal?"

"Just dinner jacket—is that all right?"

"Fine. Casey said you like the tux and black tie bit." Then Bartlett noticed the painting on the wall: an old oil of a pretty Chinese boat girl carrying a little English boy, his fair hair tied in a queue. "That a Quance? An Aristotle Quance?"

"Yes, yes it is," Dunross said, barely covering his surprise.

Bartlett walked over and looked at it. "This the original?"

"Yes. You know much about art?"

"No, but Casey told me about Quance as we were coming out here. She said he's almost like a photographer, really a historian of the early times."

"Yes, yes he is."

"If I remember this one's supposed to be a portrait of a girl called May-may, May-may T'Chung, and the child is one of Dirk Struan's by her?"

Dunross said nothing, just watched Bartlett's back.

Bartlett peered a little closer. "Difficult to see the eyes. So the boy is Gordon Chen, Sir Gordon Chen to be?" He turned and looked at Dunross.

"I don't know for certain, Mr. Bartlett. That's one story."

Bartlett watched him for a moment. The two men were well matched, Dunross slightly taller but Bartlett wider in the shoulders. Both had blue eyes, Dunross's slightly more greenish, both wideset in lived-in faces.

"You enjoy being tai-pan of the Noble House?" Bartlett asked.

"Yes."

"I don't know for a fact what a tai-pan's powers are, but in Par-Con I can hire and fire anyone, and can close it down if I want."

"Then you're a tai-pan."

"Then I enjoy being a tai-pan too. I want in in Asia—you need an in in the States. Together we could sew up the whole Pacific Rim into a tote bag for both of us."

Or a shroud for one of us, Dunross thought, liking Bartlett despite the fact that he knew it was dangerous to like him.

"I've got what you lack, you've got what I lack."

"Yes," Dunross said. "And now what we both lack is lunch."

They turned for the door. Bartlett was there first. But he did not open it at once. "I know it's not your custom but since I'm going with you to Taipei, could you call me Linc and I call you Ian and we begin to figure out how much we're gonna bet on the golf match? I'm sure you know my handicap's thirteen, officially, and I know yours's ten, officially, which probably means at least one stroke off both of us for safety."

"Why not?" Dunross said at once. "But here we don't normally bet money, just balls."

"I'm goddamned if I'm betting mine on a golf match."

Dunross laughed. "Maybe you will, one day. We usually bet half a dozen golf balls here—something like that."

"It's a bad British custom to bet money, Ian?"

"No. How about five hundred a side, winning team take all?"

"U.S. or Hong Kong?"

"Hong Kong. Among friends it should be Hong Kong. Initially."

Lunch was served in the directors' private dining room on the nineteenth floor. It was an L-shaped corner room, with a high ceiling and blue drapes, mottled blue Chinese carpets and large windows from which they could see Kowloon and the airplanes taking off and landing at Kai Tak and as far west as Stonecutters Island and Tsing Yi Island, and, beyond, part of the New Territories. The great, antique oak dining table which could seat twenty easily was laid with placemats and fine silver, and Waterford's best crystal. For the six of them, there were four silent, very well-trained waiters in black trousers and white tunics embroidered with the Struan emblem.

Cocktails had been started before Bartlett and Dunross arrived. Casey was having a dry vodka martini with the others—except for Gavallan who had a double pink gin. Bartlett, without being asked, was served an ice-cold can of Anweiser, on a Georgian silver tray.

"Who told you?" Bartlett said, delighted.

"Compliments of Struan and Company," Dunross said. "We heard that's the way you like it." He introduced him to Gavallan, deVille and Linbar Struan, and accepted a glass of iced Chablis, then smiled at Casey. "How are you?"

"Fine, thanks."

"Excuse me," Bartlett said to the others, "but I have to give Casey a message before I forget. Casey, will you call Johnston in Washington tomorrow—find out who our best contact'd be at the consulate here."

"Certainly. If I can't get him I'll ask Tim Diller."

Anything to do with Johnston was code for: how's the deal progressing? In answer: Diller meant good, Tim Diller very good, Jones bad, George Jones very bad.

"Good idea," Bartlett said and smiled back, then to Dunross, "This is a beautiful room."

"It's adequate," Dunross said.

Casey laughed, getting the underplay. "The meeting went very well, Mr. Dunross," she said. "We came up with a proposal for your consideration."

How American to come out with it like that—no finesse! Doesn't she know business is for after lunch, not before. "Yes. Andrew gave me the outline," Dunross replied. "Would you care for another drink?"

"No thanks. I think the proposal covers everything, sir. Are there any points you'd like me to clarify?"

"I'm sure there will be, in due course," Dunross said, privately amused, as always, by the *sir* that many American women used conversationally, and often, incongruously, to waiters. "As soon as I've studied it I'll get back to you. A beer for Mr. Bartlett," he added, once more trying to divert business until later. Then to Jacques, "*Ça va?*"

"*Oui merci. A rien.*" Nothing yet.

"Not to worry," Dunross said. Yesterday Jacques's adored daughter and her husband had had a bad car accident while on holiday in France—how bad he was still waiting to hear. "Not to worry."

"No." Again the Gallic shrug, hiding the vastness of his concern.

Jacques was Dunross's first cousin and he had joined Struan's in '45. His war had been rotten. In 1940 he had sent his wife and two infants to England and had stayed in France. For the duration. Maquis and prison and condemned and escaped and Maquis again. Now he was fifty-four, a strong, quiet man but vicious when provoked, with a heavy chest and brown eyes and rough hands and many scars.

"In principle does the deal sound okay?" Casey asked.

Dunross sighed inwardly and put his full concentration on her. "I may have a counterproposal on a couple of minor points. Meanwhile," he added decisively, "you can proceed on the assumption that, in general terms, it's acceptable."

"Oh fine," Casey said happily.

"Great," Bartlett said, equally pleased, and raised his can of beer. "Here's to a successful conclusion and big profits—for you and for us."

They drank the toast, the others reading the danger signs in Dunross, wondering what the tai-pan's counterproposal would be.

"Will it take you long to finalize, Ian?" Bartlett asked, and all of them heard the *Ian.* Linbar Struan winced openly.

To their astonishment, Dunross just said, "No," as though the familiarity was quite ordinary, adding, "I doubt if the solicitors will come up with anything insurmountable."

"We're seeing them tomorrow at eleven o'clock," Casey said. "Mr. de-Ville, John Chen and I. We've already gotten their advance go-through . . . no problems there."

"Dawson's very good—particularly on U.S. tax law."

"Casey, maybe we should bring out our tax guy from New York," Bartlett said.

"Sure, Linc, soon as we're set. And Forrester." To Dunross she said, "He's head of our foam division."

"Good. And that's enough shoptalk before lunch," Dunross said. "House rules, Miss Casey: no shop with food, it's very bad for the digestion." He beckoned Lim. "We won't wait for Master John."

Instantly waiters materialized and chairs were held out and there were typed place names in silver holders and the soup was ladled.

The menu said sherry with the soup, Chablis with the fish—or claret with the roast beef and Yorkshire pudding if you preferred it—boiled string beans and boiled potatoes and boiled carrots. Sherry trifle as dessert. Port with the cheese tray.

"How long will you be staying, Mr. Bartlett?" Gavallan asked.

"As long as it takes. But Mr. Gavallan, since it looks as though we're going to be in business together a long time, how about you dropping the 'Mr.' Bartlett and the 'Miss' Casey and calling us Linc and Casey."

Gavallan kept his eyes on Bartlett. He would have liked to have said, Well Mr. Bartlett, we prefer to work up to these things around here—it's one of the few ways you tell your friends from your acquaintances. For us first names are a private thing. But as the tai-pan hasn't objected to the astonishing "Ian" there's not a thing I can do. "Why not, Mr. Bartlett?" he said blandly. "No need to stand on ceremony. Is there?"

Jacques deVille and Struan and Dunross chuckled inside at the "Mr. Bartlett," and the way Gavallan had neatly turned the unwanted acceptance into a put-down and a loss of face that neither of the Americans would ever understand.

"Thanks, Andrew," Bartlett said. Then he added, "Ian, may I bend the rules and ask one more question before lunch: Can you finalize by next Tuesday, one way or another?"

Instantly the currents in the room reversed. Lim and the other servants hesitated, shocked. All eyes went to Dunross. Bartlett thought he had gone too far and Casey was sure of it. She had been watching Dunross. His expression had not changed but his eyes had. Everyone in the room knew that the tai-pan had been called as a man will call another in a poker game. Put up or shut up. By next Tuesday.

They waited. The silence seemed to hang. And hang.

Then Dunross broke it. "I'll let you know tomorrow," he said, his voice calm, and the moment passed and everyone sighed inwardly and the waiters continued and everyone relaxed. Except Linbar. He could still feel the sweat on his hands because he alone of them knew the thread that went through all of the descendents of Dirk Struan—a strange, almost primeval, sudden urge to violence—and he had seen it almost surface then, almost but not quite. This time it had gone away. But the knowledge of it and its closeness terrified him.

His own line was descended from Robb Struan, Dirk Struan's halfbrother and partner, so he had none of Dirk Struan's blood in his veins. He bitterly regretted it and loathed Dunross even more for making him sick with envy.

Hag Struan on you, Ian bloody Dunross, and all your generations, he thought, and shuddered involuntarily at the thought of her.

"What's up, Linbar?" Dunross asked.

"Oh nothing, tai-pan," he said, almost jumping out of his skin. "Nothing—just a sudden thought. Sorry."

"What thought?"

"I was just thinking about Hag Struan."

Dunross's spoon hesitated in midair and the others stared at him. "That's not exactly good for your digestion."

"No sir."

Bartlett glanced at Linbar, then at Dunross. "Who's Hag Struan?"

"A skeleton," Dunross said with a dry laugh. "We've lots of skeletons in our family."

"Who hasn't?" Casey said.

"Hag Struan was our eternal bogeyman—still is."

"Not now, tai-pan, surely," Gavallan said. "She's been dead for almost fifty years."

"Maybe she'll die out with us, with Linbar, Kathy and me, with our generation, but I doubt it." Dunross looked at Linbar strangely. "Will Hag Struan get out of her coffin tonight and gobble us up?"

"I swear to God I don't like even joking about her like that, tai-pan."

"The pox on Hag Struan," Dunross said. "If she was alive I'd say it to her face."

"I think you would. Yes," Gavallan laughed suddenly. "That I'd like to have seen."

"So would I." Dunross laughed with him, then he saw Casey's expression. "Ah, just bravado, Casey. Hag Struan was a fiend from hell if you believe half the legends. She was Culum Struan's wife—he was Dirk Struan's son—our founder's son. Her maiden name was Tess, Tess Brock and she was the daughter of Dirk's hated enemy, Tyler Brock. Culum and Tess eloped in 1841, so the story goes. She was sweet sixteen and a beauty, and he heir to the Noble House. It was rather like Romeo and Juliet—except they lived and it made no difference whatsoever to the blood feud of Dirk against Tyler or the Struans versus the Brocks, it just heightened and complicated it. She was born Tess Brock in 1825 and died Hag Struan in 1917, aged ninety-two, toothless, hairless, besotten, vicious and dreadful to her very last day. Life's strange, *heya?*"

"Yes. Unbelievable sometimes," Casey said thoughtfully. "Why is it people change so much growing old—get so sour and bitter? Particularly women?"

Fashion, Dunross could have answered at once, and because men and women age differently. It's unfair—but an immortal fact. A woman sees the lines beginning and the sagging beginning and the skin no longer so fresh and firm but her man's still fine and sought after and then she sees the young dolly birds and she's petrified she'll lose him to them and eventually she will because he'll become bored with her carping and the self-fed agony of the self-mutilation—and too, because of his built-in uncontrollable urge toward youth. . . .

"*Ayeeyah*, there's no aphrodisiac in the world like youth," old Chen-Chen—Phillip Chen's father—Ian's mentor would always say. "None, young Ian, there's none. None none none. Listen to me. The yang needs the yin juices, but young juices, oh yes they should be young, the juices young to extend your life and nourish the yang—oh oh oh! Remember, the older your Male Stalk becomes the more it needs youth and change and young enthusiasm to perform exuberantly, and the more the merrier! But also remember that the Beauteous Box that nests between all their thighs, peerless though it is, delectable, delicious, unearthly, oh so sweet and oh so satisfying as it also is, beware! Ha! It's also a trap, ambush, torture chamber and your coffin!" Then the old, old man would chuckle and his belly would jump up and down and the tears would run down his face. "Oh the gods are marvelous, are they not? They grant us heaven on earth but it's living hell when you can't get your one-eyed monk to raise his head to enter paradise. Joss, my child! That's our joss—to crave the Greedy Gully until she eats you up, but oh oh oh . . ."

It must be very difficult for women, particularly Americans, Dunross thought, this trauma of growing old, the inevitability of it happening so early, too early—worse in America than anywhere else on earth.

Why should I tell you a truth you must already know in your bones, Dunross asked himself. Or say further that American fashion demands you try to grasp an eternal youth neither God nor devil nor surgeon can give you. You can't be twenty-five when you're thirty-five nor have a thirty-five-year-old youthfulness when you're forty-five, or forty-five when you're fifty-five. Sorry, I know it's unfair but it's a fact.

Ayeeyah, he thought fervently, thank God—if there is a God—thank all gods great and small I'm a man and not a woman. I pity you, American lady with the beautiful names.

But Dunross answered simply, "I suppose that's because life's no bed of roses and we're fed stupid pap and bad values growing up—not like the Chinese who're so sensible—Christ, how unbelievably sensible they are! In Hag Struan's case perhaps it was her rotten Brock blood. I think it was her joss—her fate or luck or unluck. She and Culum had seven children, four sons and three daughters. All her sons died violently, two of the 'flux' —probably plague—here in Hong Kong, one was murdered, knifed in Shanghai, and the last was drowned off Ayr in Scotland, where our family lands are. That'd be enough to send any mother around the bend, that and the hatred and envy that surrounded Culum and her all their lives. But when you add this to all the problems of living in Asia, the passing over of the Noble House to other people's sons . . . well, you can understand." Dunross thought a moment, then added, "Legend has it she ruled Culum Struan all his life and tyrannized the Noble House till the day she died—and all tai-pans, all daughters-in-law, all sons-in-law and all the children as well. Even after she died. I can remember one English nanny I had, may she burn in hell forever, saying to me, 'You better behave,

Master Ian, or I'll conjure up Hag Struan and she'll gobble you up. . . .'
I can't have been more than five or six."

"How terrible," Casey said.

Dunross shrugged. "Nannies do that to children."

"Not all of them, thank God," Gavallan said.

"I never had one who was any good at all. Or a *gan sun* who was ever
bad."

"What's a *gan sun?*" Casey asked.

"It means 'near body,' it's the correct name for an *amah*. In China pre-
'49, children of well-to-do families and most of the old European and Eurasian families out here always had their own 'near body' to look after them
—in many cases they kept them all their lives. Most *gan sun* take a vow of
celibacy. You can always recognize them by the long queue they wear
down their back. My *gan sun*'s called Ah Tat. She's a great old bird. She's
still with us," Dunross said.

Gavallan said, "Mine was more like a mother to me than my real
mother."

"So Hag Struan's your great-grandmother?" Casey said to Linbar.

"Christ no! No, I'm—I'm not from Dirk Struan's line," he replied and
she saw sweat on his forehead that she did not understand. "My line
comes from his half-brother, Robb Struan. Robb Struan was Dirk's partner. The tai-pan's descended directly from Dirk, but even so . . . none of
us're descended from the Hag."

"You're all related?" Casey asked, feeling curious tensions in the room.
She saw Linbar hesitate and glance at Dunross as she looked at him.

"Yes," he said. "Andrew's married to my sister, Kathy. Jacques is a
cousin, and Linbar . . . Linbar carries our name." Dunross laughed.
"There're still lots of people in Hong Kong who remember the Hag,
Casey. She always wore a long black dress with a big bustle and a funny
hat with a huge moth-eaten feather, everything totally out of fashion, and
she'd have a black stick with a silver handle on it with her. Most times she
was carried in a sort of palanquin by four bearers up and down the streets.
She wasn't much more than five foot but round and tough as a coolie's
foot. The Chinese were equally petrified of her. Her nickname was 'Honorable Old Foreign Devil Mother with the Evil Eye and Dragon's
Teeth.'"

"That's right," Gavallan said with a short laugh. "My father and grandmother knew her. They had their own trading company here and in
Shanghai, Casey, but got more or less wiped out in the Great War and
joined up with Struan's in '19. My old man told me that when he was a
boy he and his friends used to follow the Hag around the streets and
when she got particularly angry she'd take out her false teeth and chomp
them at them." They all laughed with him as he parodied her. "My old
man swore the teeth were two feet tall and on some form of spring and
they'd go, crunch crunch crunch!"

"Hey Andrew, I'd forgotten that," Linbar broke in with a grin. "My *gan sun*, old Ah Fu, knew Hag Struan well and every time you'd mention her, Ah Fu's eyes'd turn up and she'd petition the gods to protect her from the evil eye and magic teeth. My brother Kyle and I . . ." He stopped, then began again in a different voice. "We used to tease Ah Fu about her."

Dunross said to Casey, "There's a portrait of her up at the Great House —two in fact. If you're interested, I'll show them to you one day."

"Oh thanks—I'd like that. Is there one of Dirk Struan?"

"Several. And one of Robb, his half-brother."

"I'd love to see them."

"Me too," Bartlett said. "Hell, I've never even seen a photo of my grandparents, let alone a portrait of my great-great-grandfather. I've always wanted to know about my forebears, what they were like, where they came from. I know nothing about them except my grandpa was supposed to have run a freight company in the Old West in a place called Jerrico. Must be great to know where you're from. You're lucky." He had been sitting back listening to the undercurrents, fascinated by them, seeking clues against the time he'd have to decide: Dunross or Gornt. If it's Dunross, Andrew Gavallan's an enemy and will have to go, he told himself. Young Struan hates Dunross, the Frenchman's an enigma and Dunross himself is nitroglycerine and just as dangerous. "Your Hag Struan sounds fantastic," he said. "And Dirk Struan too must have been quite a character."

"Now that's a masterpiece of understatement!" Jacques deVille said, his dark eyes sparkling. "He was the greatest pirate in Asia! You wait—you look at Dirk's portrait and you'll see the family resemblance! Our tai-pan's the spitting image, and *ma foi*, he's inherited all the worst parts."

"Drop dead, Jacques," Dunross said good-naturedly. Then to Casey, "It's not true. Jacques is always ribbing me. I'm nothing like him at all."

"But you're descended from him."

"Yes. My great-grandmother was Winifred, Dirk's only legitimate daughter. She married Lechie Struan Dunross, a clansman. They had one son who was my grandfather—he was tai-pan after Culum. My family— the Dunrosses are Dirk Struan's only direct descendents, as far as we know."

"You, you said legitimate?"

Dunross smiled. "Dirk had other sons and daughters. One son, Gordon Chen, was from a lady called Shen actually, that you know of. That's the Chen line today. There's also the T'Chung line—from Duncan T'Chung and Kate T'Chung, his son and daughter by the famous May-may T'Chung. Anyway that's the legend, they're accepted legends here though no one can prove or disprove them." Dunross hesitated and his eyes crinkled with the depth of his smile. "In Hong Kong and Shanghai our predecessors were, well, friendly, and the Chinese ladies beautiful, then as now. But they married their ladies rarely and the pill's only a very recent invention—so you don't always know who you might be related to. We, ah, we don't discuss this sort of thing publicly—in true British fashion we pretend it doesn't exist though we all know it does, then no one loses face. Eurasian families of Hong Kong usually took the name of their mothers, in Shanghai their fathers. We all seem to have accommodated the problem."

"It's all very friendly," Gavallan said.

"Sometimes," Dunross said.

"Then John Chen's related to you?" Casey asked.

"If you go back to the garden of Eden everyone's related to everyone I suppose." Dunross was looking at the empty place. Not like John to run off, he thought uneasily, and he's not the sort to get involved in gun smuggling, for any reason. Or be so stupid as to get caught. Tsu-yan? Well he's Shanghainese and he could easily be panicked—if he's mixed up in this. John's too easily recognized not to have been seen getting on a plane this morning so it's not that way. It has to be by boat—if he has run off. A boat where? Macao—no, that's a dead end. Ship? Too easy, he thought, if it was planned or even not planned and arranged at an hour's notice. Any day of the year there'd be thirty or forty scheduled sailings to all parts of the world, big ships and little ships, let alone a thousand junks nonscheduled, and even if on the run, a few dollars here and there and too easy to smuggle out—out or in. Men, women, children. Drugs. Anything. But no reason to smuggle inward except humans and drugs and guns and liquor and cigarettes and petrol—everything else is duty free and unrestricted.

Except gold.

Dunross smiled to himself. You import gold legally under license at thirty-five dollars an ounce for transit to Macao and what happens then is nobody's business but immensely profitable. Yes, he thought, and our Nelson Trading board meeting's this afternoon. Good. That's one business venture that never fails.

As he took some of the fish from the proffered silver tray he noticed Casey staring at him. "Yes, Casey?"

"Oh I was just wondering how you knew my names." She turned to Bartlett. "The tai-pan surprised me, Linc. Before we were even introduced he called me Kamalian Ciranoush as though it were Mary Jane."

"That's Persian?" Gavallan asked at once.

"Armenian originally."

"Kamahly-arn Cirrrannoooossssh," Jacques said, liking the sibilance of the names. "*Très jolie, mademoiselle. Ils ne sont pas difficile sauf pour les cretins.*"

"*Ou les* English," Dunross said and they all laughed.

"How did you know, tai-pan?" Casey asked him, feeling more at home with *tai-pan* than with Ian. *Ian* doesn't belong, yet, she thought, swept by his past and Hag Struan and the shadows that seemed to be surrounding him.

"I asked your attorney."

"What do you mean?"

"John Chen called me last night around midnight. You hadn't told him what K.C. stood for and I wanted to know. It was too early to talk to your office in Los Angeles—just 8 A.M., L.A. time—so I called your attorney in New York. My father used to say, when in doubt ask."

"You got Seymour Steigler III on a Saturday?" Bartlett asked, amazed.

"Yes. At his home in White Plains."

"But his home number's not in the book."

"I know. I called a Chinese friend of mine in the UN. He tracked him down for me. I told Mr. Steigler I wanted to know because of invitations—which is, of course, the truth. One should be accurate, shouldn't one?"

"Yes," Casey said, admiring him greatly. "Yes one should."

"You knew Casey was . . . Casey was a woman, last night?" Gavallan asked.

"Yes. Actually I knew several months ago, though not what K.C. stood for. Why?"

"Nothing, tai-pan. Casey, you were saying about Armenia. Your family immigrated to the States after the war?"

"After the First World War in 1918," Casey said, beginning the oft-told story. "Originally our surname was Tcholokian. When my grandparents arrived in New York they dropped the *ian* for simplicity, to help Americans. I still got Kamalian Ciranoush though. As you know, Armenia is the southern part of Caucasus—just north of Iran and Turkey and south of Russian Georgia. It used to be a free sovereign nation but now it's all absorbed by Soviet Russia or Turkey. My grandmother was Georgian—there was lots of intermarriage in the old days. My people were spread all over the Ottoman Empire, about two million, but the massacres, particularly in 1915 and '16 . . ." Casey shivered. "It was genocide really. There're barely 500,000 of us left and now we're scattered throughout the world. Armenians were traders, artists, painters and jewelry makers, writers, warriors too. There were nearly 50,000 Armenians in the Turkish Army before they were disarmed, outcast and shot by the Turks during World War One—generals, officers and soldiers. They were an elite minority and had been for centuries."

"Is that why the Turks hated them?" deVille asked.

"They were hardworking and clannish and very good traders and businessmen for sure—they controlled lots of business and trade. My granddad said trading's in our blood. But perhaps the main reason is that Armenians are Christian—they were the first Christian state in history under the Romans—and of course the Turks are Mohammedan. The Turks conquered Armenia in the sixteenth century and there was always a border war going on between Christian Tsarist Russia and the 'Infidel' Turks.

Up to 1917 Tsarist Russia was our real protector. . . . The Ottoman Turks were always a strange people, very cruel, very strange."

"Your family got out before the trouble?"

"No. My grandparents were quite rich, and like a lot of people thought nothing could happen to them. They escaped just ahead of the soldiers, took two sons and a daughter out the back door with just what they could grab in their dash for freedom. The rest of the family never made it. My grandfather bribed his way out of Istanbul onto a fishing boat that smuggled him and my grandmother to Cyprus where, somehow, they got visas to the States. They had a little money and some jewelry—and lots of talent. Granny's still alive . . . she can still haggle with the best of them."

"Your grandfather was a trader?" Dunross asked. "Is that how you first got interested in business?"

"We certainly had it drummed into us as soon as we could think about being self-sufficient," Casey said. "My granddad started an optical company in Providence, making lenses and microscopes and an import-export company dealing mostly in carpets and perfumes, with a little gold and precious stones trading on the side. My dad designed and made jewelry. He's dead now but he had a small store of his own in Providence, and his brother, my uncle Bghos, worked with Granddad. Now, since Granddad died, my uncle runs the import-export company. It's small but stable. We grew up, my sister and I, around haggling, negotiating and the problem of profit. It was a great game and we were all equals."

"Where . . . oh, more trifle, Casey?"

"No thanks, I'm fine."

"Where did you take your business degree?"

"I suppose all over," she said. "After I got out of high school, I put myself through a two-year business course at Katharine Gibbs in Providence: shorthand, typing, simple accounting, filing, plus a few business fundamentals. But ever since I could count I worked nights and holidays and weekends with Granddad in his businesses. I was taught to think and plan and put the plan into effect, so most of my training's been in the field. Of course since I've gotten out of school I've kept up with specialized courses that I wanted to take—at night school mostly." Casey laughed. "Last year I even took one at the Harvard Business School which went down like an H-bomb with some members of the faculty, though it's getting a little easier now for a woman."

"How did you manage to become hatchetman—hatchetlady to Par-Con Industries?" Dunross said.

"Perspicacity," she said and they laughed with her.

Bartlett said, "Casey's a devil for work, Ian. Her speed reading's fantastic so she can cover more ground than two normal execs. She's got a great nose for danger, she's not afraid of a decision, she's more of a deal maker than a deal breaker, and she doesn't blush easily."

"That's my best point," Casey said. "Thanks, Linc."

"But isn't it very hard on you, Casey?" Gavallan asked. "Don't you have to concede a hell of a lot as a woman to keep up? It can't be easy for you to do a man's job."

"I don't consider my job a man's job, Andrew," she replied at once. "Women have just as good brains and work capacity as men."

There was an immediate hoot of friendly derision from Linbar and Gavallan and Dunross overrode them and said, "I think we'll table that one for later. But again, Casey, how did you get where you are at Par-Con?"

Shall I tell you the real story, Ian lookalike to Dirk Struan, the greatest pirate in Asia, or shall I tell you the one that's become legend, she asked herself.

Then she heard Bartlett begin and she knew she could safely drift for she had heard his version a hundred times before and it was part true, part false and part what he wanted to believe had happened. How many of *your* legends are true—Hag Struan and Dirk Struan and what's your real story and how did you become tai-pan? She sipped her port, enjoying the smooth sweetness, letting her mind wander.

There's something wrong here, she was thinking now. I can feel it strongly. Something's wrong with Dunross.

What?

"I first met Casey in Los Angeles, California—about seven years ago," Bartlett had begun. "I'd gotten a letter from a Casey Tcholok, president of Hed-Opticals of Providence, who wanted to discuss a merger. At that time I was in construction all over the L.A. area—residential, supermarkets, a couple of good-sized office buildings, industrial, shopping centers—you name it, I'd build it. We had a turnover of 3.2 million and I'd just gone public—but I was still a million miles away from the Big Board. I'd—"

"You mean the New York Stock Exchange?"

"Yes. Anyway, Casey comes in bright as a new penny and says she wants me to merge with Hed-Opticals which she says grossed $277,600 last year, and then together, we'd go after Randolf Opticals, the grand-daddy of them all—53 million in sales, quoted on the Big Board, a huge slice of the lens market and lots of cash in the bank—and I said you're crazy but why Randolf? She said because first she was a stockholder in Bartlett Constructions—she'd bought ten one-dollar shares—I'd capitalized at a million shares and sold 500,000 at par—and she figured it'd be dandy for Bartlett Construction to own Randolf, and second, 'because this son of a bitch George Toffer who runs Randolf Opticals is a liar, a cheat, a thief, and he's trying to put me out of business.' "

Bartlett grinned and paused for breath and Dunross broke in with a laugh. "This's true, Casey?"

Casey came back quickly. "Oh yes, I said that George Toffer was a liar, a cheat, thief and son of a bitch. He still is." Casey smiled without humor. "And he was certainly trying to put me out of business."

"Why?"

"Because I had told him to go—to drop dead."

"Why'd you do that?"

"I'd just taken over Hed-Opticals. My granddad had died the previous year and we'd flipped a coin, my uncle Bghos and I, who'd get which business. . . . I'd won Hed-Opticals. We'd had an offer from Randolf to buy us out a year or so back but we'd turned it down—we had a nice, small operation, a good work force, good technicians—a number of them Armenians—a little slice of the market. But no capital and no room to maneuver but we got by and the quality of Hed-Opticals was optimum. Just after I took over, George Toffer 'happened to drop by.' He fancied himself, my God how he fancied himself. He claimed he was a U.S. Army war hero but I found out he wasn't—he was that sort of guy. Anyway, he made me another ridiculous offer to take Hed-Opticals off my hands . . . the poor little girl who should be in the kitchen bit, along with the 'let's have dinner tonight in my suite and why don't we have a little fun because I'm here alone for a few days. . . .' I said no thanks and he was very put out. Very. But he said okay and went back to business and suggested that instead of a buy-out we subcontract some of his contracts. He made me a good offer and after haggling a bit we agreed on terms. If I performed on this one he said he'd double the deal. Over the next month we did the work better and cheaper than he could ever have done it—I delivered according to contract and he made a fantastic profit. But then he reneged on a verbal clause and deducted—stole—$20,378, and the next day five of my best customers left us for Randolf, and the next week another seven—they'd all been offered deals at less than cost. He let me sweat for a week or two then he phoned. 'Hi, baby,' he said, happy as a toad in a pail of mud, 'I'm spending the weekend alone at Martha's Vineyard.' That's a little island off the East Coast. Then he added, 'Why don't you come over and we'll have some fun and discuss the future and doubling our orders.' I asked for my money, and he laughed at me and told me to grow up and suggested I better reconsider his offer because at the rate I was going soon there'd be no Hed-Opticals.

"I cursed him," Casey said. "I can curse pretty good when I get mad and I told him what to do with himself in three languages. Within four more weeks I'd no customers left. Another month and the work force had to get other jobs. About that time I thought I'd try California. I didn't want to stay in the East." She smiled wryly. "It was a matter of face—if I'd known about face then. I thought I'd take a couple of weeks off to figure out what to do. Then one day I was wandering aimlessly around a state fair in Sacramento and Linc was there. He was selling shares in Bartlett Construction in a booth and I bought—"

"He what?" Dunross asked.

"Sure," Bartlett said. "I sold upwards of 20,000 shares that way. I covered state fairs, mail orders, supermarkets, stockbrokers, shopping centers—along with investment banks. Sure. Go on, Casey!"

"So I read his prospectus and watched him awhile and thought he had a lot of get up and go. His figures and balance sheet and expansion rate were exceptional and I thought anyone who'd pitch his own stock has got to have a future. So I bought ten shares, wrote him and went to see him. End of story."

"The hell it is, Casey," Gavallan said.

"You tell it, Linc," she said.

"Okay. Well, then—"

"Some port, Mr.—sorry, Linc?"

"Thanks Andrew, but, er, may I have another beer?" It arrived instantly. "So Casey'd come to see me. After she'd told it, almost like she's told it now, I said, 'One thing, Casey, Hed-Opticals grossed less than 300,000-odd last year. What's it going to do this year?'

"'Zero,' she said with that smile of hers. 'I'm Hed-Opticals' total asset. In fact, I'm all there is.'

"'Then what's the use of my merging with zero—I've got enough problems of my own.'

"'I know how to take Randolf Opticals to the cleaners.'

"'How?'

"'22 percent of Randolf's is owned by three men—all of whom despise Toffer. With 22 percent you could get control. I know how you could get their proxies, and most of all, I know the weakness of Toffer.'

"'What's that?'

"'Vanity, and he's a megalomaniac, but most of all he's stupid.'

"'He can't be stupid and run that company.'

"'Perhaps he wasn't once, but now he is. He's ready to be taken.'

"'And what do you want out of this, Casey?'

"'Toffer's head—I want to do the firing.'

"'What else?'

"'If I succeed in showing you how . . . if we succeed in taking over Randolf Opticals, say within six months, I'd like . . . I'd like a one-year deal with you, to be extended to seven, at a salary you think is commensurate with my ability, as your executive vice-president in charge of acquisitions. But I'd want it as a person, not as a woman, just as an equal person to you. You're the boss of course, but I'm to be equal as a man would be equal, as an individual . . . if I deliver.'"

Bartlett grinned and sipped his beer. "I said, okay you've got a deal. I thought, what've I got to lose—me with my lousy three-quarter million and her with her nothing zero balance for Randolf Opticals in six months, now that's one helluva steal. So we shook, man to woman." Bartlett laughed. "First time I'd ever made a deal with a woman, just like that—and I've never regretted it."

"Thanks, Linc," Casey said softly, and every one of them was envious.

And what happened after you fired Toffer, Dunross was thinking with all the others. Is that when you two began?

"The takeover," he said to Bartlett. "It was smooth?"

"Messy, but we got blooded and the lessons I learned, we learned, paid off a thousand percent. In five months we'd control. Casey and I had conquered a company 53½ times our size. At D-hour minus one I was down to minus 4 million dollars in the bank and goddamn near in jail, but the next hour I'd control. Man, that was a battle and a half. In a month and a half we'd reorganized it and now Par-Con's Randolf Division grosses $150 millions yearly and the stock's way up. It was a classic blitz-krieg and set the pattern for Par-Con Industries."

"And this George Toffer, Casey? How did you fire him?"

Casey took her tawny eyes off Linc and turned them on Dunross and he thought, Christ I'd like to possess you.

Casey said, "The hour we got control I—" She stopped as the single phone rang and there was a sudden tension in the room. Everyone, even the waiters, immediately switched their total attention to the phone—except Bartlett. The color had drained out of Gavallan's face and deVille's. "What's the matter?" Casey asked.

Dunross broke the silence. "It's one of our house rules. No phone calls are put through during lunch unless it's an emergency—a personal emergency—for one of us."

They watched Lim put down the coffee tray. It seemed to take him forever to walk across the room and pick up the phone. They all had wives and children and families and they all wondered what death or what disaster and please God, let the call be for someone else, remembering the last time the phone had rung, two days ago. For Jacques. Then another time last month, for Gavallan, his mother was dying. They had all had calls, over the years. All bad.

Andrew Gavallan was sure the call was for him. His wife, Kathren, Dunross's sister, was at the hospital for the results of exhaustive tests—she had been sick for weeks for no apparent reason. Jesus Christ, he thought, get hold of yourself, conscious of others watching him.

"*Weyyyy?*" Lim listened a moment. He turned and offered the phone. "It's for you, tai-pan."

The others breathed again and watched Dunross. His walk was tall. "Hello? . . . Oh hel— What? . . . . No . . . no, I'll be right there. . . . No, don't do anything, I'll be right there." They saw his shock as he replaced the phone in the dead silence. After a pause he said, "Andrew, tell Claudia to postpone my afternoon board meetings. You and Jacques continue with Casey. That was Phillip. I'm afraid poor John Chen's been kidnapped." He left.

8

Dunross got out of his car and hurried through the open door of the vast, Chinese-style mansion that was set high on the mountain crest called Struan's Lookout. He passed a glazed servant who closed the door after him, and went into the living room. The living room was Victorian and gaudy and overstuffed with bric-a-brac and ill-matched furniture.

"Hello, Phillip," he said. "I'm so sorry. Poor John! Where's the letter?"

"Here." Phillip picked it up from the sofa as he got up. "But first look at that." He pointed at a crumpled cardboard shoebox on a marble table beside the fireplace.

As Dunross crossed the room he noticed Dianne, Phillip Chen's wife, sitting in a high-backed chair in a far corner. "Oh, hello, Dianne, sorry about this," he said again.

She shrugged impassively. "Joss, tai-pan." She was fifty-two, Eurasian, Phillip Chen's second wife, an attractive, bejeweled matron who wore a dark brown *chong-sam,* a priceless jade bead necklace and a four-carat diamond ring—amid many other rings. "Yes, joss," she repeated.

Dunross nodded, disliking her a little more than usual. He peered down at the contents of the box without touching them. Among loose, crumpled newspaper he saw a fountain pen that he recognized as John Chen's, a driving license, some keys on a key ring, a letter addressed to John Chen, 14A Sinclair Towers, and a small plastic bag with a piece of cloth half-stuffed into it. With a pen that he took out of his pocket he flipped open the cover of the driving license. John Chen.

"Open the plastic bag," Phillip said.

"No. I might mess up any fingerprints that're on it," Dunross said, feeling stupid but saying it anyway.

"Oh—I'd forgotten about that. Damn. Of course, fingerprints! Mine are . . . I opened it of course. Mine must be all over it—all over everything."

"What's in it?"

"It's—" Phillip Chen came over and before Dunross could stop him pulled the cloth out of the plastic, without touching the plastic again. "You can't have fingerprints on cloth, can you? Look!" The cloth contained most of a severed human ear, the cut clean and sharp and not jagged.

Dunross cursed softly. "How did the box arrive?" he asked.

"It was hand delivered." Phillip Chen shakily rewrapped the ear and put it back in the box. "I just . . . I just opened the parcel as anyone would. It was hand delivered half an hour or so ago."

"By whom?"

"We don't know. He was just a youth, the servant said. A youth on a motor scooter. She didn't recognize him or take any number. We get lots of parcels delivered. It was nothing out of the ordinary—except the 'Mr. Phillip Chen, a matter of great importance, to open personally,' on the outside of the package, which she didn't notice at once. By the time I'd opened it and read the letter . . . it was just a youth who said, 'Parcel for Mr. Phillip Chen,' and went away."

"Have you called the police?"

"No, tai-pan, you said to do nothing."

Dunross went to the phone. "Have you got hold of John's wife yet?"

Dianne said at once, "Why should Phillip bear bad tidings to her? She'll throw a temperament that will raise the roof tiles never mind. Call Barbara? Oh dear no, tai-pan, not . . . not until we've informed the police. They should tell her. They know how to do these things."

Dunross's disgust increased. "You'd better get her here quickly." He dialed police headquarters and asked for Armstrong. He was not available. Dunross left his name then asked for Brian Kwok.

"Yes tai-pan?"

"Brian, can you come over here right away? I'm at Phillip Chen's house up on Struan's Lookout. John Chen's been kidnapped." He told him about the contents of the box.

There was a shocked silence, then Brian Kwok said, "I'll be there right away. Don't touch anything and don't let him talk to anyone."

"All right."

Dunross put the phone down. "Now give me the letter, Phillip." He handled it carefully, holding it by the edges. The Chinese characters were clearly written but not by a well-educated person. He read it slowly, knowing most of the characters:

> Mr. Phillip Chen, I beg to inform you that I am badly in need of 500,000 Hong Kong currency and I hereby consult you about it. You are so wealthy that this is like plucking one hair from nine oxen. Being afraid that you might refuse I therefore have no alternative but to hold your son hostage. By doing so there is not a fear of your refusal. I hope you will think it over carefully thrice and take it into se-

rious consideration. It is up to you whether you report to the police or not. I send herewith some articles which your son uses every day as proof of the situation your son is in. Also sent is a little bit of your son's ear. You should realize the mercilessness and cruelty of my actions. If you smoothly pay the money the safety of your son will be ensured. Written by the Werewolf.

Dunross motioned at the box. "Sorry, but do you recognize the, er . . . that?"

Phillip Chen laughed nervously and so did his wife. "Do you, Ian? You've known John all your life. That's . . . how does one recognize something like that, *heya?*"

"Does anyone else know about this?"

"No, except the servants of course, and Shitee T'Chung and some friends who were lunching with me here. They . . . they were here when the parcel arrived. They, yes, they were here. They left just before you arrived."

Dianne Chen shifted in her chair and said what Dunross was thinking. "So of course it will be all over Hong Kong by evening!"

"Yes. And banner headlines by dawn." Dunross tried to collate the multitude of questions and answers flooding his mind. "The press'll pick up about the, er, ear and the 'Werewolf' and make it a field day."

"Yes. Yes they will." Phillip Chen remembered what Shitee T'Chung had said the moment they had all read the letter. "Don't pay the ransom for at least a week, Phillip old friend, and you'll be world famous! *Ayeeyah,* fancy, a piece of his ear and Werewolf! Eeeee, you'll be world famous!"

"Perhaps it's not his ear at all and a trick," Phillip Chen said hopefully.

"Yes." If it is John's ear, Dunross thought, greatly perturbed, and if they've sent it on the first day before any negotiation or anything, I'll bet the poor sod's already dead. "No point in hurting him like that," he said. "Of course you'll pay."

"Of course. It's lucky we're not in Singapore, isn't it?"

"Yes." By law in Singapore now, the moment anyone was kidnapped all bank accounts of the family were frozen to prevent payment to the kidnappers. Kidnapping had become endemic there with almost no arrests, Chinese preferring to pay quickly and quietly and say nothing to the police. "What a bastard! Poor old John."

Phillip said, "Would you like some tea—or a drink? Are you hungry?"

"No thanks. I'll wait until Brian Kwok gets here then I'll be off." Dunross looked at the box and at the keys. He had seen the key ring many times. "The safety deposit key's missing," he said.

"What key?" Dianne Chen asked.

"John always had a deposit box key on his ring."

She did not move from her chair. "And it's not there now?"

"No."

"Perhaps you're mistaken. That he always had it on the ring."

Dunross looked at her and then at Phillip Chen. They both stared back at him. Well, he thought, if the crooks didn't take it, now Phillip or Dianne have, and if I were them I'd do the same. God knows what might be in such a box. "Perhaps I'm mistaken," he said levelly.

"Tea, tai-pan?" Dianne asked, and he saw the shadow of a smile in the back of her eyes.

"Yes, I think I will," he said, knowing they had taken the key.

She got up and ordered tea loudly and sat down again. "Eeee, I wish they'd hurry up . . . the police."

Phillip was looking out of the window at the parched garden. "I wish it would rain."

"I wonder how much it'll cost to get John back," she muttered.

After a pause, Dunross said, "Does it matter?"

"Of course it matters," Dianne said at once. "Really, tai-pan!"

"Oh yes," Phillip Chen echoed. "$500,000! *Ayeeyah*, $500,000—that's a fortune. Damn triads! Well, if they ask five I can settle for $150,000. Thank God they didn't ask a million!" His eyebrows soared and his face became more ashen. "*Dew neh loh moh* on all kidnappers. They should get the chop—all of them."

"Yes," Dianne said. "Filthy triads. The police should be more clever! More sharp and more clever and protect us better."

"Now that's not fair," Dunross said sharply. "There hasn't been a major kidnapping in Hong Kong for years and it happens every month in Singapore! Crime's fantastically low here—our police do a grand job—grand."

"Huh," Dianne sniffed. "They're all corrupt. Why else be a policeman if it's not to get rich? I don't trust any of them. . . . We know, oh yes we know. As to kidnapping, huh, the last one was six years ago. It was my third cousin, Fu San Sung—the family had to pay $600,000 to get him back safely. . . . It nearly bankrupted them."

"Ha!" Phillip Chen scoffed. "Bankrupt Hummingbird Sung? Impossible!" Hummingbird Sung was a very wealthy Shanghainese shipowner in his fifties with a sharp nose—long for a Chinese. He was nicknamed Hummingbird Sung because he was always darting from dance hall to dance hall, from flower to flower, in Singapore, Bangkok and Taipei, Hong Kong, dipping his manhood into a myriad of ladies' honey pots, the rumor being it wasn't his manhood because he enjoyed mutual cunnilingus.

"The police got most of the money back if I remember rightly, and sent the criminals to jail for twenty years."

"Yes, tai-pan, they did. But it took them months and months. And I wouldn't mind betting one or two of the police knew more than they said."

"Absolute nonsense!" Dunross said. "You've no cause to believe anything like that! None."

"Quite right!" Phillip Chen said irritably. "They caught them, Dianne." She looked at him. At once he changed his tone. "Of course, dear, some police may be corrupt but we're very lucky here, very lucky. I suppose I wouldn't mind so much about, about John—it's only a matter of ransom and as a family we've been very lucky so far—I wouldn't mind except for . . . for that." He motioned at the box disgustedly. "Terrible! And totally uncivilized."

"Yes," Dunross said, and wondered if it wasn't John Chen's ear, whose was it—where do you get an ear from? He almost laughed at the ridiculousness of his questions. Then he put his mind back to pondering if the kidnapping was somehow tied in with Tsu-yan and the guns and Bartlett. It's not like a Chinese to mutilate a victim. No, and certainly not so soon. Kidnapping's an ancient Chinese art and the rules have always been clear: pay and keep silent and no problem, delay and talk and many problems.

He stared out of the window at the gardens and at the vast northern panorama of city and seascape below. Ships and junks and sampans dotted the azure sea. There was a fine sky above and no promise of rain weather, the summer monsoon steady from the southwest and he wondered absently what the clippers had looked like as they sailed before the wind or beat up against the winds in his ancestors' time. Dirk Struan had always had a secret lookout atop the mountain above. There the man could see south and east and west and the great Sheung Sz Mun Channel which approached Hong Kong from the south—the only path inward bound for ships from home, from England. From Struan's Lookout, the man could secretly spot the incoming mail ship and secretly signal below. Then the tai-pan would dispatch a fast cutter to get the mails first, to have a few hours leeway over his rivals, the few hours perhaps meaning the trading difference between fortune and bankruptcy—so vast the time from home. Not like today with instant communication, Dunross thought. We're lucky—we don't have to wait almost two years for a reply like Dirk did. Christ, what a man he must have been.

I must not fail with Bartlett. I must have those 20 million.

"The deal looks very good, tai-pan," Phillip Chen said as though reading his mind.

"Yes. Yes it is."

"If they really put up cash we'll all make a fortune and it'll be *h'eung yau* for the Noble House," he added with a beam.

Dunross's smile was again sardonic. *H'eung yau* meant "fragrant grease" and normally referred to the money, the payoff, the squeeze, that was paid by all Chinese restaurants, most businesses, all gambling games, all dance halls, all ladies of easy virtue, to triads, some form of triad, throughout the world.

"I still find it staggering that *h'eung yau's* paid wherever a Chinese is in business."

"Really, tai-pan," Dianne said as though he were a child. "How can any business exist without protection? You expect to pay, naturally, so you pay never mind. Everyone gives *h'eung yau*—some form of *h'eung yau*." Her jade beads clicked as she shifted in her chair, her eyes dark in the whiteness of her face—so highly prized among Chinese. "But the Bartlett deal, tai-pan, do you think the Bartlett deal will go through?"

Dunross watched her. Ah Dianne, he told himself, you know every important detail that Phillip knows about his business and my business, and a lot Phillip would weep with fury if he knew you knew. So you know Struan's could be in very great trouble if there's no Bartlett deal, but if the deal is consummated then our stock will skyrocket and we'll be rich again —and so will you be, if you can get in early enough, to buy early enough.

Yes.

And I know you Hong Kong Chinese ladies like poor Phillip doesn't, because I'm not even a little part Chinese. I know you Hong Kong Chinese ladies are the roughest women on earth when it comes to money—or perhaps the most practical. And you, Dianne, I also know you are ecstatic now, however much you'll pretend otherwise. Because John Chen's not your son. With him eliminated, your own two sons will be direct in line and your eldest, Kevin, heir apparent. So you'll pray like you've never prayed before that John's gone forever. You're delighted. John's kidnapped and probably murdered but what about the Bartlett deal?

"Ladies are so practical," he said.

"How so, tai-pan?" she asked, her eyes narrowing.

"They keep things in perspective."

"Sometimes I don't understand you at all, tai-pan," she replied, an edge to her voice. "What more can we do now about John Chen? Nothing. We've done everything we can. When the ransom note arrives we negotiate and we pay and everything's as it was. But the Bartlett deal is important, very important, very very important whatever happens, *heya? Moh ching, moh meng.*" No money, no life.

"Quite. It is very important, tai-pan." Phillip caught sight of the box and shuddered. "I think under the circumstances, tai-pan, if you'll excuse us this evening . . . I don't th—"

"No, Phillip," his wife said firmly. "No. We must go. It's a matter of face for the whole House. We'll go as planned. As difficult as it will be for us—we will go as planned."

"Well, if you say so."

"Yes." Oh very yes she was thinking, replanning her whole ensemble to enhance the dramatic effect of their entrance. We'll go tonight and we'll be the talk of Hong Kong. We'll take Kevin of course. Perhaps he's heir now. *Ayeeyah!* Who should my son marry? I've got to think of the future now. Twenty-two's a perfect age and I have to think of his new future. Yes, a wife. Who? I'd better choose the right girl at once and quickly if he's heir, before some young filly with a fire between her legs and a rapacious mother does it for me. *Ayeeyah*, she thought, her temperature rising, gods forbid such a thing! "Yes," she said, and touched her eyes with her handkerchief as though a tear were there, "there's nothing more to be done for poor John but wait—and continue to work and plan and maneuver for the good of the Noble House." She looked up at Dunross, her eyes glittering. "The Bartlett deal would solve everything, wouldn't it?"

"Yes." And you're both right, Dunross thought. There's nothing more to be done at the moment. Chinese are very wise and very practical.

So put your mind on important things—he told himself. Important things—like do you gamble? Think. What better place or time than here and now could you find to begin the plan you've been toying with ever since you met Bartlett?

None.

"Listen," he said, deciding irrevocably, then looked around at the door that led to the servants' quarters, making sure that they were alone. He lowered his voice to a conspiratorial whisper and Phillip and his wife leaned forward to hear better. "I had a private meeting with Bartlett before lunch. We've made the deal. I'll need some minor changes, but we close the contract formally on Tuesday of next week. The 20 million's guaranteed and a further 20 million next year."

Phillip Chen's beam was huge. "Congratulations."

"Not so loud, Phillip," his wife hissed, equally pleased. "Those turtle mouth slaves in the kitchen have ears that can reach to Java. Oh but that's tremendous news, tai-pan."

"We'll keep this in the family," Dunross said softly. "This afternoon I'm instructing our brokers to start buying Struan's stock secretly—every spare penny we've got. You do the same, in small lots and spread the orders over different brokers and nominees—the usual."

"Yes. Oh yes."

"I bought 40 thousand this morning personally."

"How much will the stock go up?" Dianne Chen asked.

"Double!"

"How soon?"

"Thirty days."

"Eeeee," she chortled. "Think of that."

"Yes," Dunross said agreeably. "Think of that! Yes. And you two will only tell your very close relations, of which there are many, and they will only tell their very close relations, of which there are a multitude, and you'll all buy and buy because this is an inside-inside, gilt-edged tip and hardly any gamble at all which will further fuel the stock rise. The fact that it's only family will surely leak and more will jump in, then more, and then the formal announcement of the Par-Con deal will add fire and then, next week, I'll announce the takeover bid for Asian Properties and then all Hong Kong will buy. Our stock will skyrocket. Then, at the right moment, I dump Asian Properties and go after the real target."

"How many shares, tai-pan?" Phillip Chen asked—his mind swamped by his own calculations of the possible profits.

"Maximum. But it has to be family only. Our stocks'll lead the boom."

Dianne gasped. "There's going to be a boom?"

"Yes. We'll lead it. The time's ripe, everyone in Hong Kong's ready. We'll supply the means, we'll be the leader, and with a judicious shove here and there, there'll be a stampede."

There was a great silence. Dunross watched the avarice on her face.

Her fingers clicked the jade beads. He saw Phillip staring into the distance and he knew that part of his compradore's mind was on the various notes that he, Phillip, had countersigned for Struan's that were due in thirteen to thirty days: $12 million U.S. to Toda Shipping Industries of Yokohama for the two super bulk cargo freighters, $6,800,000 to the Orlin International Merchant Bank, and $750,000 to Tsu-yan, who had covered another problem for him. But most of Phillip's mind would be on Bartlett's 20 million and the stock rise—the doubling that he had arbitrarily forecast.

Double?

No way—no not at all, not a chance in hell . . .

Unless there's a boom. Unless there's a boom!

Dunross felt his heart quicken. "If there's a boom . . . Christ, Phillip, we can do it!"

"Yes—yes, I agree, Hong Kong's ripe. Ah yes." Phillip Chen's eyes sparkled and his fingers drummed. "How many shares, tai-pan?"

"Every bl—"

Excitedly Dianne overrode Dunross, "Phillip, last week my astrologer said this was going to be an important month for us! A boom! That's what he must have meant."

"That's right, I remember you telling me, Dianne. Oh oh oh! How many shares, tai-pan?" he asked again.

"Every bloody penny! We'll make this the big one. But family only until Friday. Absolutely until Friday. Then, after the market closes I'll leak the Bartlett deal. . . ."

"Eeeeee," Dianne hissed.

"Yes. Over the weekend I'll say 'no comment'—you make sure you're not available, Phillip—and come Monday morning, everyone'll be chomping at the bit. I'll still say 'no comment,' but Monday we buy openly. Then, just after close of business Monday, I'll announce the whole deal's confirmed. Then, come Tuesday . . ."

"The boom's on!"

"Yes."

"Oh happy day," Dianne croaked delightedly. "And every *amah*, houseboy, coolie, businessman, will decide their joss is perfect and out will come their savings and everything gets fed, all stocks will rocket. What a pity there won't be an editorial tomorrow . . . even better, an astrologer in one of the papers . . . say Hundred Year Fong . . . or . . ." Her eyes almost crossed with excitement. "What about *the* astrologer, Phillip?"

He stared at her, shocked. "Old Blind Tung?"

"Why not? Some *h'eung yau* in his palm . . . or the promise of a few shares of whatever stock you name. *Heya?*"

"Well, I—"

"Leave that one to me. Old Blind Tung owes me a favor or two, I've sent him enough clients! Yes. And he won't be far wrong announcing heavenly portents that herald the greatest boom in Hong Kong's history, will he?"

9

The police pathologist, Dr. Meng, adjusted the focus of the microscope and studied the sliver of flesh that he had cut from the ear. Brian Kwok watched him impatiently. The doctor was a small pedantic little Cantonese with thick-lensed glasses perched on his forehead. At length he looked up and his glasses fell conveniently onto his nose. "Well, Brian, it could have been sliced from a living person and not a corpse . . . possibly. Possibly within the last eight or ten hours. The bruising . . . here, look at the back"—Dr. Meng motioned delicately at the discoloration at the back and at the top—". . . that certainly indicates to me that the person was alive at the time."

"Why bruising, Dr. Meng? What caused it? The slash?"

"It could have been caused by someone holding the specimen tightly," Dr. Meng said cautiously, "while it was being removed."

"By what—knife, razor, zip knife, or Chinese chopper—cooking chopper?"

"By a sharp instrument."

Brian Kwok sighed. "Would that kill someone? The shock? Someone like John Chen?"

Dr. Meng steepled his fingers. "It could, possibly. Possibly not. Does he have a history of a weak heart?"

"His father said he hadn't—I haven't checked with his own doctor yet—the bugger's on holiday but John's never given any indication of being anything but healthy."

"This mutilation probably shouldn't kill a healthy man but he'd be very uncomfortable for a week or two." The doctor beamed. "Very uncomfortable indeed."

"Jesus!" Brian said. "Isn't there anything you can give me that'll help?"

"I'm a forensic pathologist, Brian, not a seer."

"Can you tell if the ear's Eurasian—or pure Chinese?"

"No. No, with this specimen that'd be almost impossible. But it's certainly not Anglo-Saxon, or Indian or Negroid." Dr. Meng took off his glasses and stared myopically up at the tall superintendent. "This could possibly cause quite a ripple in the House of Chen, *heya*?"

"Yes. And the Noble House." Brian Kwok thought a moment. "In your opinion, this Werewolf, this maniac, would you say he's Chinese?"

"The writing could have been a civilized person's, yes—equally it could have been done by a *quai loh* pretending to be a civilized person. But if he or she was a civilized person that doesn't necessarily mean that the same person who did the act wrote the letter."

"I know that. What are the odds that John Chen's dead?"

"From the mutilation?"

"From the fact that the Werewolf, or more probably Werewolves, sent the ear even before starting negotiations."

The little man smiled and said dryly, "You mean old Sun Tzu's 'kill one to terrorize ten thousand'? I don't know. I don't speculate on such imponderables. I only estimate odds on horses, Brian, or the stock market. What about John Chen's Golden Lady on Saturday?"

"She's got a great chance. Definitely. And Struan's Noble Star—Gornt's Pilot Fish and even more, Richard Kwang's Butterscotch Lass. She'll be the favorite I'll bet. But Golden Lady's a real goer. She'll start about three to one. She's a flier and the going'll be good for her. Dry. She's useless in the wet."

"Ah, any sign of rain?"

"Possible. They say there's a storm coming. Even a sprinkle could make all the difference."

"Then it better not rain till Sunday, *heya*?"

"It won't rain this month—not unless we're enormously lucky."

"Well if it rains it rains and if it doesn't it doesn't never mind! Winter's coming—then this cursed humidity will go away." Dr. Meng glanced at the wall clock. It was 5:35 P.M. "How about a quick one before we go home?"

"No thanks. I've still got a few things to do. Bloody nuisance this."

"Tomorrow I'll see what clues I can come up with from the cloth, or the wrapping paper or the other things. Perhaps fingerprinting will help you," the doctor added.

"I wouldn't bet on that. This whole operation is very smelly. Very smelly indeed."

Dr. Meng nodded and his voice lost its gentleness. "Anything to do with the Noble House and their puppet House of Chen's smelly. Isn't it?"

Brian Kwok switched to *sei yap*, one of the main dialects of the Kwantung Province, spoken by many Hong Kong Cantonese. "Eh, Brother, don't you mean any and all capitalist running dogs are smelly, of which the Noble House and the House of Chen are chief and dung heavy?" he said banteringly.

"Ah, Brother, don't you know yet, deep in your head, that the winds of change are whirling throughout the world? And China under the immortal guidance of Chairman Mao, and Mao Thought, is the lead—"

"Keep your proselytizing to yourself," Brian Kwok said coldly, switching back to English. "Most of the thoughts of Mao are out of the writings of Sun Tzu, Confucius, Marx, Lao Tsu and others. I know he's a poet—a great one—but he's usurped China and there's no freedom there now. None."

"Freedom?" the little man said defiantly. "What's freedom for a few years when, under the guidance of Chairman Mao, China's once more China and has taken back her rightful place in the world. Now China is feared by all filthy capitalists! Even by revisionist Russia."

"Yes. I agree. For that I thank him. Meanwhile if you don't like it here go home to Canton and sweat your balls off in your Communist paradise and *dew neh loh moh* on all Communists—and their fellow travelers!"

"You should go there, see for yourself. It's propaganda that communism's bad for China. Don't you read the newspapers? No one's starving now."

"What about the twenty-odd million who were murdered after the takeover? What about all the brainwashing?"

"More propaganda! Just because you've been to English and Canadian public schools and talk like a capitalist swine doesn't mean you're one of them. Remember your heritage."

"I do. I remember it very well."

"Your father was mistaken to send you away!" It was common knowledge that Brian Kwok had been born in Canton and, at the age of six, sent to school in Hong Kong. He was such a good student that in '37, when he was twelve, he had won a scholarship to a fine public school in England and had gone there, and then in '39, with the beginning of World War II, the whole school was evacuated to Canada. In '42, at eighteen, he had graduated top of his class, senior prefect, and had joined the Royal Canadian Mounted Police in their plainclothes branch in Vancouver's huge Chinatown. He spoke Cantonese, Mandarin, *sei yap,* and had served with distinction. In '45 he had requested a transfer to the Royal Hong Kong Police. With the reluctant approval of the RCMP, who had wanted him to stay on, he had returned. "You're wasted working for them, Brian," Dr. Meng continued. "You should serve the masses and work for the Party!"

"The Party murdered my father and my mother and most of my family in '43!"

"There was never proof of that! Never. It was hearsay. Perhaps the Kuomintang devils did it—there was chaos then in Canton. I was there, I know! Perhaps the Japanese swine were responsible—or triads—who knows? How can you be certain?"

"I'm certain, by God."

"Was there a witness? No! You told me that yourself!" Meng's voice rasped and he peered up at him myopically. *"Ayeeyah,* you're Chinese, use your education for China, for the masses, not for the capitalist overlord."

"Up yours!"

Dr. Meng laughed and his glasses fell on to the top of his nose. "You wait, Superintendent Kar-shun Kwok. One day your eyes will open. One day you will see the beauty of it all."

"Meanwhile get me some bloody answers!" Brian Kwok strode out of the laboratory and went up the corridor to the elevator, his shirt sticking to his back. I wish it would rain, he thought.

He got into the elevator. Other policemen greeted him and he them. At the third floor he got out and walked along the corridor to his office. Armstrong was waiting for him, idly reading a Chinese newspaper. "Hi, Robert," he said, pleased to see him. "What's new?"

"Nothing. How about you?"

Brian Kwok told him what Dr. Meng had said.

"That little bugger and his 'could possiblys'! The only thing he's ever emphatic about's a corpse—and even then he'll have to check a couple of times."

"Yes—or about Chairman Mao."

"Oh, he was on that broken record again?"

"Yes." Brian Kwok grinned. "I told him to go back to China."

"He'll never leave."

"I know." Brian stared at the pile of papers in his in tray and sighed. Then he said, "It's not like a local to cut off an ear so soon."

"No, not if it's a proper kidnapping."

"What?"

"It could be a grudge and the kidnapping a cover," Armstrong said, his well-used face hardening. "I agree with you and Dunross. I think they did him in."

"But why?"

"Perhaps John was trying to escape, started a fight, and they or he panicked and before they or he knew what was happening, they or he'd knifed him, or bonked him with a blunt instrument." Armstrong sighed and stretched to ease the knot in his shoulders. "In any event, old chap, our Great White Father wants this solved quickly. He honored me with a call to say the governor had phoned personally to express his concern."

Brian Kwok cursed softly. "Foul news travels quickly! Nothing in the press yet?"

"No, but it's all over Hong Kong and we'll have a red hot wind fanning our tails by morning. Mr. Bloody Werewolf Esquire—assisted by the pox-ridden, black-hearted, uncooperative Hong Kong press—will, I fear, cause us nothing but grief until we catch the bastard, or bastards."

"But catch him we will, oh yes, catch him we will!"

"Yes. How about a beer—or better, a very large gin and tonic? I could use one."

"Good idea. Your stomach off again?"

"Yes. Mary says it's all the good thoughts I keep bottled up." They laughed together and headed for the door and were in the corridor when the phone rang.

"Leave the bloody thing, don't answer it, it's only trouble," Armstrong said, knowing neither he nor Brian would ever leave it.

Brian Kwok picked up the phone and froze.

It was Roger Crosse, senior superintendent, director of Special Intelligence. "Yes sir?"

"Brian, would you please come up right away."

"Yes sir."

"Is Armstrong with you?"

"Yes sir."

"Bring him too." The phone clicked off.

"Yes sir." He replaced the receiver and felt the sweat on his back. "God wants us, on the double."

Armstrong's heart jumped a beat. "Eh? Me?" He caught up with Brian who was heading for the elevator. "What the hell does he want me for? I'm not in SI now."

"Ours not to reason why, ours just to shit when he murmurs." Brian Kwok pressed the *up* button. "What's up?"

"Got to be important. The Mainland perhaps?"

"Chou En-lai's ousted Mao and the moderates're in power?"

"Dreamer! Mao'll die in office—the Godhead of China."

"The only good thing you can say about Mao is that he's Chinese first and Commie second. God-cursed Commies!"

"Hey, Brian, maybe the Soviets are hotting up the border again. Another incident?"

"Could be. Yes. War's coming—yes, war's coming between Russia and China. Mao's right in that too."

"The Soviets aren't that stupid."

"Don't bet on it, old chum. I've said it before and I've said it again, the Soviets are the world enemy. There'll be war—you'll soon owe me a thousand dollars, Robert."

"I don't think I want to pay that bet. The killing'll be hideous."

"Yes. But it'll still happen. Again Mao's right in that. It'll be hideous all right—but not catastrophic." Irritably Brian Kwok punched the elevator button again. He looked up suddenly. "You don't think the invasion from Taiwan's launched at long last?"

"That old chestnut? That old pipe dream? Come off it, Brian! Chiang Kai-shek'll never get off Taiwan."

"If he doesn't the whole world's in the manure pile. If Mao gets thirty years to consolidate . . . Christ, you've no idea. A billion automatons?

Chiang was so right to go after the Commie bastards—they're the real enemy of China. They're the plague of China. Christ, if they get time to Pavlov all the kids."

Armstrong said mildly, "Anyone'd think you're a running dog Nationalist. Simmer down, lad, everything's lousy in the world which is now and ever shall be normal—but you, capitalist dog, you can go racing Saturday, hill climbing Sunday and there're lots of birds ready to be plucked. Eh?"

"Sorry." They got into the elevator. "That little bastard Meng caught me off balance," Brian said, stabbing the top-floor button.

Armstrong switched to Cantonese. "*Thy mother on your sorry, Brother.*"

"*And thine was stuffed by a vagrant monkey with one testicle in a pail of pig's nightsoil.*"

Armstrong beamed. "That's not bad, Brian," he said in English. "Not bad at all."

The elevator stopped. They walked along the drab corridor. At the door they prepared themselves. Brian knocked gently.

"Come in."

Roger Crosse was in his fifties, a thin tall man with pale blue eyes and fair thinning hair and small, long-fingered hands. His desk was meticulous, like his civilian clothes—his office spartan. He motioned to chairs. They sat. He continued to read a file. At length he closed it carefully and set it in front of him. The cover was drab, interoffice and ordinary. "An American millionaire arrives with smuggled guns, an ex-drug peddling, very suspect Shanghainese millionaire flees to Taiwan, and now a VIP kidnapping with, God help us, Werewolves and a mutilated ear. All in nineteen-odd hours. Where's the connection?"

Armstrong broke the silence. "Should there be one, sir?"

"Shouldn't there?"

"Sorry sir, I don't know. Yet."

"That's very boring, Robert, very boring indeed."

"Yes sir."

"Tedious in fact, particularly as the powers that be have already begun to breathe heavily down my neck. And when that happens . . ." He smiled at them and both suppressed a shudder. "Of course Robert, I did warn you yesterday that important names might be involved."

"Yes sir."

"Now Brian, we're grooming you for high office. Don't you think you could take your mind off horse racing, car racing and almost anything in skirts and apply some of your undoubted talents to solving this modest conundrum."

"Yes sir."

"Please do. Very quickly. You're assigned to the case with Robert because it might require your expertise—for the next few days. I want this out of the way very very quickly indeed because we've a slight problem.

One of our American friends in the consulate called me last night. Privately." He motioned at the file. "This is the result. With his tip we intercepted the original in the bleak hours—of course this's a copy, the original was naturally returned and the . . ." He hesitated, choosing the correct word, ". . . the courier, an amateur by the way, left undisturbed. It's a report, a sort of newsletter with different headings. They're all rather interesting. Yes. One's headed, 'The KGB in Asia.' It claims that they've a deep-cover spy ring I've never even heard of before, code name 'Sevrin,' with high-level hostiles in key positions in government, police, business—at the tai-pan level—throughout Southeast Asia, *particularly here in Hong Kong*."

The air hissed out of Brian Kwok's mouth.

"Quite," Crosse said agreeably. "If it's true."

"You think it is, sir?" Armstrong said.

"Really, Robert, perhaps you're in need of early retirement on medical grounds: softening of the brain. If I wasn't perturbed do you think I'd endure the unhappy pleasure of having to petition the assistance of the CID Kowloon?"

"No sir, sorry sir."

Crosse turned the file to face them and opened it to the title page. Both men gasped. It read, "*Confidential to Ian Dunross only. By hand, report 3/1963. One copy only.*"

"Yes," he continued. "Yes. This's the first time we've actual proof Struan's have their own intelligence system." He smiled at them and their flesh crawled. "I'd certainly like to know how tradesmen manage to be privy to all sorts of very intimate information we're supposed to know ages before them."

"Yes sir."

"The report's obviously one of a series. Oh yes, and this one's signed on behalf of Struan's Research Committee 16, by a certain A. M. Grant—dated in London three days ago."

Brian Kwok gasped again. "Grant? Would that be the Alan Medford Grant, the associate of the Institute for Strategic Planning in London?"

"Full marks, Brian, ten out of ten. Yes. Mr. AMG himself. Mr. VIP, Mr. Advisor to Her Majesty's Government for undercover affairs who really knows onions from leeks. You know him, Brian?"

Brian Kwok said, "I met him a couple of times in England last year, sir, when I was on the Senior Officers Course at the General Staff College. He gave a paper on advanced strategic considerations for the Far East. Brilliant. Quite brilliant."

"Fortunately he's English and on our side. Even so . . ." Crosse sighed again. "I certainly hope he's mistaken this time or we're in the mire deeper than even I imagined. It seems few of our secrets are secrets anymore. Tiring. Very. And as to this," he touched the file again, "I'm really quite shocked."

"Has the original been delivered, sir?" Armstrong asked.

"Yes. To Dunross personally at 4:18 this afternoon." His voice became even more silky. "Fortunately, thank God, my relations with our cousins across the water are first class. Like yours, Robert—unlike yours, Brian. You never did like America, did you, Brian?"

"No sir."

"Why, may I ask?"

"They talk too much, sir, you can't trust them with any secrets—they're loud, and I find them stupid."

Crosse smiled with his mouth. "That's no reason not to have good relations with them, Brian. Perhaps you're the stupid one."

"Yes sir."

"They're not all stupid, oh dear no." The director closed the file but left it facing them. Both men stared at it, mesmerized.

"Did the Americans say how they found out about the file, sir?" Armstrong asked without thinking.

"Robert, I really do believe your sinecure in Kowloon has addled your brain. Shall I recommend you for a medical retirement?"

The big man winced. "No sir, thank you sir."

"Would we reveal our sources to them?"

"No sir."

"Would they have told me if I'd been so crass as to ask them?"

"No sir."

"This whole business is very tedious and filled with loss of face. Mine. Don't you agree, Robert?"

"Yes sir."

"Good, that's something." Crosse leaned back in his chair, rocking it. His eyes ground into them. Both men were wondering who the tipster was, and why.

Can't be the CIA, Brian Kwok was thinking. They'd have done the intercept themselves, they don't need SI to do their dirty work for them. Those crazy bastards'll do anything, tread on any toes, he thought disgustedly. If not them, who?

Who?

Must be someone who's in Intelligence but who can't, or couldn't do the intercept, who's on good terms, safe terms with Crosse. A consular official? Possible. Johnny Mishauer, Naval Intelligence? Out of his channel. Who? There's not many . . . Ah, the FBI man, Crosse's protégé! Ed Langan. Now, how would Langan know about this file? Information from London? Possible, but the FBI doesn't have an office there. If the tip came from London, probably MI-5 or 6 would know it first and they'd've arranged to get the material at the source and would have telexed it to us, and given us hell for being inept in our own backyard. Did the courier's aircraft land at Lebanon? There's an FBI man there I seem to recall. If not from London or Lebanon, the information must have come from the aircraft itself. Ah, an accompanying friendly informer who saw the file, or the cover? Crew? *Ayeeyah!* Was the aircraft TWA or Pan Am? The FBI has all sorts of links, close links—with all sorts of ordinary businesses, rightly so. Oh yes. Is there a Sunday flight? Yes. Pan Am, ETA 2030. Too late for a night delivery by the time you've got to the hotel. Perfect.

"Strange that the courier came Pan Am and not BOAC—it's a much better flight," he said, pleased with the oblique way his mind worked.

"Yes. I thought the same," Crosse said as evenly. "Terribly un-British of him. Of course, Pan Am does land on time whereas you never know with poor old BOAC these days—" He nodded at Brian agreeably. "Full marks again. Go to the head of the class."

"Thank you sir."

"What else do you deduce?"

After a pause Brian Kwok said, "In return for the tip, you agreed to provide Langan with an exact copy of the file."

"And?"

"And you regret having honored that."

Crosse sighed. "Why?"

"I'll know only after I've read the file."

"Brian, you really are surpassing yourself this afternoon. Good." Absently the director fingered the file and both men knew he was titillating them, deliberately, but neither knew why. "There are one or two very curious coincidences in other sections of this. Names like Vincenzo Banastasio . . . meeting places like Sinclair Towers . . . Does Nelson Trading mean anything to either of you?"

They both shook their heads.

"All very curious. Commies to the right of us, commies to the left . . ." His eyes became even stonier. "It seems we even have a nasty in our own ranks, possibly at superintendent level."

"Impossible!" Armstrong said involuntarily.

"How long were you with us in SI, dear boy?"

Armstrong almost flinched. "Two tours, almost five years sir."

"The spy Sorge was impossible—Kim Philby was impossible—dear God Philby!" The sudden defection to Soviet Russia in January this year by this Englishman, this onetime top agent of MI-6—British military intelligence for overseas espionage and counterespionage—had sent shock waves throughout the Western world, particularly as, until recently, Philby had been first secretary at the British Embassy in Washington, responsible for liaison with U.S. Defense, State, and the CIA on all security matters at the highest level. "How in the name of all that's holy he could have been a Soviet agent for all those years and remain undetected is impossible, isn't it, Robert?"

"Yes sir."

"And yet he was, and privy to our innermost secrets for years. Certainly from '42 to '58. And where did he start spying? God save us, at Cambridge in 1931. Recruited into the Party by the other arch-traitor, Burgess, also of Cambridge, and his friend Maclean, may they both toast in hell for all eternity." Some years ago these two highly placed Foreign Office diplomats —both of whom had also been in Intelligence during the war—had abruptly fled to Russia only seconds ahead of British counterespionage agents and the ensuing scandal had rocked Britain and the whole of NATO. "Who else did they recruit?"

"I don't know, sir," Armstrong said carefully. "But you can bet that now they're all VIP's in government, the Foreign Office, education, the press, particularly the press—and, like Philby, all burrowed very bloody deep."

"With people nothing's impossible. Nothing. People are really very dreadful." Crosse sighed and straightened the file slightly. "Yes. But it's a privilege to be in SI, isn't it, Robert?"

"Yes sir."

"You have to be invited in, don't you? You can't volunteer, can you?"

"No sir."

"I never did ask why you didn't stay with us, did I?"

"No sir."

"Well?"

Armstrong groaned inwardly and took a deep breath. "It's because I like being a policeman, sir, not a cloak-and-dagger man. I like being in CID. I like pitting your wits against the villain, the chase and the capture and then the proving it in court, according to rules—to the law, sir."

"Ah but in SI we don't, eh? We're not concerned with courts or laws or anything, only results?"

"SI and SB have different rules, sir," Armstrong said carefully. "Without them the Colony'd be up the creek without a paddle."

"Yes. Yes it would. People are dreadful and fanatics multiply like maggots in a corpse. You were a good undercover man. Now it seems to me it's time to repay all the hours and months of careful training you've had at Her Majesty's expense."

Armstrong's heart missed twice but he said nothing, just held his breath and thanked God that even Crosse couldn't transfer him out of CID against his will. He had hated his tours in SI—in the beginning it had been exciting and to be chosen was a great vote of confidence, but quickly it had palled—the sudden swoop on the villain in the dark hours, hearings *in camera*, no worry about exact proof, just results and a quick, secret deportation order signed by the governor, then off to the border at once, or onto a junk to Taiwan, with no appeal and no return. Ever.

"It's not the British way, Brian," he had always said to his friend. "I'm for a fair, open trial."

"What's it matter? Be practical, Robert. You know the bastards're all guilty—that they're the enemy, Commie enemy agents who twist our rules to stay here, to destroy us and our society—aided and abetted by a few bastard lawyers who'd do anything for thirty pieces of silver, or less. The same in Canada. Christ, we had the hell of a time in the RCMP, our own lawyers and politicians were the enemy—and recent Canadians—curiously always British—all socialist trades unionists who were always in the forefront of any agitation. What does it matter so long as you get rid of the parasites?"

"It matters, that's what I think. And they're not all Commie villains here. There's a lot of Nationalist villains who want to—"

"The Nationalists want Commies out of Hong Kong, that's all."

"Balls! Chiang Kai-shek wanted to grab the Colony after the war. It was only the British navy that stopped him after the Americans gave us away. He still wants sovereignty over us. In that he's no different from Mao Tse-tung!"

"If SI doesn't have the same freedom as the enemy how are we going to keep us out of the creek?"

"Brian, lad, I just said *I* don't like being in SI. You're going to enjoy it. I just want to be a copper, not a bloody Bond!"

Yes, Armstrong thought grimly, just a copper, in CID until I retire to good old England. Christ, I've enough trouble now with the god-cursed Werewolves. He looked back at Crosse and kept his face carefully noncommittal and waited.

Crosse watched him then tapped the file. "According to this we're very much deeper in the mire than even I imagined. Very distressing. Yes." He looked up. "This report refers to previous ones sent to Dunross. I'd certainly like to see them as soon as possible. Quickly and quietly."

Armstrong glanced at Brian Kwok. "How about Claudia Chen?"

"No. No chance. None."

"Then what do you suggest, Brian?" Crosse asked. "I imagine my American friend will have the same idea . . . and if he's been misguided enough to pass on the file, a copy of the file, to the director of the CIA here . . . I really would be very depressed if they were there first again."

Brian Kwok thought a moment. "We could send a specialized team into the tai-pan's executive offices and his penthouse, but it'd take time—we just don't know where to look—and it would have to be at night. That one could be hairy, sir. The other reports—if they exist—might be in a safe up at the Great House, or at his place at Shek-O—even at his, er, at his private flat at Sinclair Towers or another one we don't even know about."

"Distressing," Crosse agreed. "Our intelligence is getting appallingly lax even in our own bailiwick. Pity. If we were Chinese we'd know everything, wouldn't we, Brian?"

"No sir, sorry sir."

"Well, if you don't know where to look you'll have to ask."

"Sir?"

"Ask. Dunross's always seemed to be cooperative in the past. After all he is a friend of yours. Ask to see them."

"And if he says no, or that they were destroyed?"

"You use your talented head. You cajole him a little, you use a little art, you warm to him, Brian. And you barter."

"Do we have something current to barter with, sir?"

"Nelson Trading."

"Sir?"

"Part's in the report. Plus a modest little piece of information I'll be delighted to give you later."

"Yes sir, thank you sir."

"Robert, what have you done to find John Chen and the Werewolf or Werewolves?"

"The whole of CID's been alerted, sir. We got the number of his car at once and that's on a 1098. We've interviewed his wife Mrs. Barbara Chen, among others—she was in hysterics most of the time, but lucid, very lucid under the flood."

"Oh?"

"Yes sir. She's . . . Well, you understand."

"Yes."

"She said it wasn't unusual for her husband to stay out late—she said he had many late business conferences and sometimes he'd go early to the track or to his boat. I'm fairly certain she knew he was a man about town. Retracing his movements last night's been fairly easy up to 2:00 A.M. He dropped Casey Tcholok at the Old Vic at about 10:30—"

"Did he see Bartlett last night?"

"No sir, Bartlett was in his aircraft at Kai Tak all the time."

"Did John Chen talk to him?"

"Not unless there's some way for the airplane to link up with our phone system. We had it under surveillance until the pickup this morning."

"Go on."

"After dropping Miss Tcholok—I discovered it was his father's Rolls by the way—he took the car ferry to the Hong Kong side where he went to a private Chinese club off Queen's Road and dismissed the car and chauffeur. . . ." Armstrong took out his pad and referred to it. ". . . It was the Tong Lau Club. There he met a friend and business colleague, Wo Sang Chi, and they began to play mah-jong. About midnight the game broke up. Then, with Wo Sang Chi and the two other players, both friends, Ta Pan Fat, a journalist, and Po Cha Sik, a stockbroker, they caught a taxi."

Robert Armstrong heard himself reporting the facts, falling into the familiar police pattern and this pleased him and took his mind off the file and all the secret knowledge he possessed, and the problem of the money that he needed so quickly. I wish to God I could just be a policeman, he thought, detesting Special Intelligence and the need for it. "Ta Pan Fat left the taxi first at his home on Queen's Road, then Wo Sang Chi left on the same road shortly afterwards. John Chen and Po Cha Sik—we think he's got triad connections, he's being checked out now very carefully—went to the Ting Ma Garage on Sunning Road, Causeway Bay, to collect John Chen's car, a 1960 Jaguar." Again he referred to his notebook, wanting to be accurate, finding the Chinese names confusing as always, even after so many years. "A garage apprentice, Tong Ta Wey, confirms this. Then John Chen drove his friend Po Cha Sik to his home at 17 Village Street in Happy Valley where the latter left the car. Meanwhile Wo Sang Chi, John Chen's business colleague, who, curiously, heads Struan's haulage company which has the monopoly of cartage to and from Kai Tak, had gone to the Sap Wah Restaurant on Fleming Road. He states that after being there for thirty minutes, John Chen joined him and they left the restaurant in Chen's car, intending to pick up some dancing girls in the street and take them to supper—"

"He wouldn't even go to the dance hall and buy the girls out?" Crosse asked thoughtfully. "What's the going rate, Brian?"

"Sixty dollars Hong Kong, sir, at that time of night."

"I know Phillip Chen's got the reputation of being a miser, but is John Chen the same?"

"At that time of night, sir," Brian Kwok said helpfully, "lots of girls start leaving the clubs if they haven't arranged a partner yet—most of the clubs close around 1:00 A.M.—Sunday's not a good pay night, sir. It's quite usual to cruise, there's certainly no point in wasting sixty, perhaps two or three times sixty dollars, because the decent girls are in twos or threes and you usually take two or three to dinner first. No point wasting all that money is there, sir?"

"Do you cruise, Brian?"

"No sir. No need—no sir."

Crosse sighed and turned back to Armstrong. "Go on, Robert."

"Well sir, they failed to pick up any girls and went to the Copacabana Night Club in the Sap Chuk Hotel in Gloucester Road for supper, getting there about one o'clock. About 1:45 A.M. they left and Wo Sang Chi said he saw John Chen get into his car, but he did not see him drive off—then he walked home, as he lived nearby. He said John Chen was not drunk or bad-tempered, anything like that, but seemed in good spirits, though earlier at the club, the Tong Lau Club, he'd appeared irritable and cut the mah-jong game short. There it ends. John Chen's not known to have been seen again by any of his friends—or family."

"Did he tell Wo Sang Chi where he was going?"

"No. Wo Sang Chi told us he presumed he was going home—but then he said, 'He might have gone to visit his girl friend.' We asked him who, but he said he didn't know. After pressing him he said he seemed to remember a name, Fragrant Flower, but no address or phone number—that's all."

"Fragrant Flower? That could cover a multitude of ladies of the night."

"Yes sir."

Crosse was lost in thought for a moment. "Why would Dunross want John Chen eliminated?"

The two police officers gaped at their superior.

"Put that in your abacus brain, Brian."

"Yes sir, but there's no reason. John Chen's no threat to Dunross, wouldn't possibly be—even if he became compradore. In the Noble House the tai-pan holds all the power."

"Does he?"

"Yes. By definition." Brian Kwok hesitated, thrown off balance again. "Well yes sir—I . . . in the Noble House, yes."

Crosse turned his attention to Armstrong. "Well?"

"No reason I can think of, sir. Yet."

"Well think about it."

Crosse lit a cigarette and Armstrong felt the smoke hunger pangs heavily. I'll never keep my vow, he thought. Bloody bastard Crosse-that-we-all-have-to-carry! What the hell's in his mind? He saw Crosse offer him a packet of Senior Service, the brand he always used to smoke—don't fool yourself, he thought, the brand you still smoke. "No thank you sir," he heard himself say, shafts of pain in his stomach and through all of him.

"You're not smoking, Robert?"

"No sir, I've stopped . . . I'm just trying to stop."

"Admirable! Why should Bartlett want John Chen eliminated?"

Again both police officers gawked at him. Then Armstrong said throatily, "Do you know why, sir?"

"If I knew, why should I ask you? That's for you to find out. There's a connection somewhere. Too many coincidences, too neat, too pat—and too smelly. Yes it smells of KGB involvement to me, and when that happens in my domain I must confess I get irritable."

"Yes sir."

"Well, so far so good. Put surveillance on Mrs. Phillip Chen—she could easily be implicated somewhere. The stakes for her are certainly high enough. Tail Phillip Chen for a day or two as well."

"That's already done, sir. Both of them. On Phillip Chen, not that I suspect him but just because I think they'll both do the usual—be uncooperative, keep mum, negotiate secretly, pay off secretly and breathe a sigh of relief once it's over."

"Quite. Why is it these fellows—however well educated—think they're so much smarter than we are and won't help us do the work we're paid to do?"

Brian Kwok felt the steely eyes grinding into him and the sweat trickled down his back. Control yourself, he thought. This bastard's only a foreign devil, an uncivilized, manure-eating, dung-ladened, motherless, *dew neh loh moh* saturated, monkey-descended foreign devil. "It's an old Chinese custom which I'm sure you know, sir," he said politely, "to distrust all police, all government officials—they've four thousand years of experience, sir."

"I agree with the hypothesis, but with one exception. The British. We have proved beyond all doubt we're to be trusted, we can govern, and, by and large, our bureaucracy's incorruptible."

"Yes sir."

Crosse watched him for a moment, puffing his cigarette. Then he said, "Robert, do you know what John Chen and Miss Tcholok said or talked about?"

"No sir. We haven't been able to interview her yet—she's been at Struan's all day. Could it be important?"

"Are you going to Dunross's party tonight?"

"No sir."

"Brian?"

"Yes sir."

"Good. Robert, I'm sure Dunross won't mind if I bring you with me, call for me at 8:00 P.M. All Hong Kong that counts will be there—you can keep your ears to the grindstone and your nose everywhere." He smiled at his own joke and did not mind that neither smiled with him. "Read the report now. I'll be back shortly. And Brian, please don't fail tonight. It really would be very boring."

"Yes sir."

Crosse left.

When they were alone Brian Kwok mopped his brow. "That bugger petrifies me."

"Yes. Same for me, old chum, always has."

"Would he really order a team into Struan's?" Brian Kwok asked incredulously. "Into the inner kernel of the Noble House?"

"Of course. He'd even lead it himself. This's your first tour with SI, old lad, so you don't know him like I do. That bugger'd lead a team of assassins into hell if he thought it important enough. Bet you he got the file himself. Christ, he's been over the border twice that I know of to chat to a friendly agent. He went alone, imagine that!"

Brian gasped. "Does the governor know?"

"I wouldn't think so. He'd have a hemorrhage, and if MI-6 ever heard, he'd be roasted and Crosse'd get sent to the Tower of London. He knows too many secrets to take that chance—but he's Crosse and not a thing you can do about it."

"Who was the agent?"

"Our guy in Canton."

"Wu Fong Fong?"

"No, a new one—at least he was new in my time. In the army."

"Captain Ta Quo Sa?"

Armstrong shrugged. "I forget."

Kwok smiled. "Quite right."

"Crosse still went over the border. He's a law unto himself."

"Christ, you can't even go to Macao because you were in SI a couple of years ago and he goes over the border. He's bonkers to take that risk."

"Yes." Armstrong began to mimic Crosse. "And how is it tradesmen know things before we do, dear boy? Bloody simple," he said, answering himself, and his voice lost its banter. "They spend money. They spend lots of bloody money, whereas we've sweet f.a. to spend. He knows it and I know it and the whole world knows it. Christ, how does the FBI, CIA, KGB or Korean CIA work? They spend money! Christ, it's too easy to get Alan Medford Grant on your team—Dunross hired him. Ten thousand pounds retainer, that'd buy lots of reports, that's more than enough, perhaps it was less. How much are we paid? Two thousand quid a year for three hundred and sixty-six, twenty-five hour days and a copper on the beat gets four hundred quid. Look at the red tape we'd have to go through to get a secret ten thousand quid to pay to one man to buy info. Where'd the FBI, CIA and god-cursed KGB be without unlimited funds? Christ," he added sourly, "it'd take us six months to get the money, if we could get it, whereas Dunross and fifty others can take it out of petty cash." The big man sat in his chair slouched and loose-limbed, dark shadows under his eyes that were red rimmed, his cheekbones etched by the overhead light. He glanced at the file on the desk in front of him but did not touch it yet, just wondered at the evil news it must contain. "It's easy for the Dunrosses of the world," he said.

Brian Kwok nodded and wiped his hands and put his kerchief away. "They say Dunross's got a secret fund—the tai-pan's fund—started by Dirk Struan in the beginning with the loot he got when he burned and sacked Foochow, a fund that only the current tai-pan can use for just this sort of thing, for *h'eung yau* and payoffs, anything—maybe even a little murder. They say it runs into millions."

"I'd heard that rumor too. Yes. I wish to Christ . . . oh well." Armstrong reached for the file, hesitated, then got up and went for the phone. "First things first," he told his Chinese friend with a sardonic smile. "First we'd better breathe on a few VIPs." He dialed Police HQ in Kowloon. "Armstrong—give me Divisional Staff Sergeant Tang-po please."

"Good evening, sir. Yes sir?" Divisional Staff Sergeant Tang-po's voice was warm and friendly.

"Evening, 'Major," he said sweetly using the contraction of Sergeant Major as was customary. "I need information. I need information on who the guns were destined for. I need information on who the kidnappers of John Chen are. I want John Chen—or his body—back in three days. And I want this Werewolf—or Werewolves, in the dock very quickly."

There was a slight pause. "Yes sir."

"Please spread the word. The Great White Father is very angry indeed. And when he gets even just a little angry superintendents get posted to other commands, and so do inspectors—even sergeants, even divisional staff sergeants class one. Some even get demoted to police constable and sent to the border. Some might even get discharged or deported or go to prison. Eh?"

There was an even longer pause. "Yes sir."

"And when he's very angry indeed wise men flee, if they can, before anticorruption falls on the guilty—and even on innocents."

Another pause. "Yes sir. I'll spread the word, sir, at once. Yes, at once."

"Thank you, 'Major. The Great White Father is really very angry indeed. And oh, yes." His voice became even thinner. "Perhaps you'd ask your brother sergeants to help. They'll surely understand, too, my modest problem is theirs as well." He switched to Cantonese. *"When the Dragons belch, all Hong Kong defecates. Heya?"*

A longer pause. "I'll take care of it, sir."

"Thank you." Armstrong replaced the receiver.

Brian Kwok grinned. "That's going to cause a few sphincter muscles to oscillate."

The Englishman nodded and sat down again but his face did not lose its hardness. "I don't like to pull that too often—actually that's only the second time I've ever done it—but I've no option. He made that clear, so did the Old Man. You better do the same with your sources."

"Of course. 'When the Dragons belch . . .' You were punning on the legendary Five Dragons?"

"Yes."

Now Brian Kwok's handsome face settled into a mold—cold black eyes in his golden skin, his square chin almost beardless. "Tang-po's one of them?"

"I don't know, not for certain. I've always thought he was, though I've nothing to go on. No, I'm not certain, Brian. Is he?"

"I don't know."

"Well, it doesn't matter if he is or isn't. The word'll get to one of them, which is all I'm concerned about. Personally I'm pretty certain the Five Dragons exist, that they're five Chinese divisional sergeants, perhaps even station sergeants, who run all the illegal street gambling of Hong Kong—and probably, possibly, some protection rackets, a few dance halls and girls—five out of eleven. Five senior sergeants out of eleven possibilities. Eh?"

"I'd say the Five Dragons're real, Robert—perhaps there are more, perhaps less, but all street gambling's run by police."

"Probably run by Chinese members of our Royal Police Force, lad," Armstrong said, correcting him. "We've still no proof, none—and we've been chasing that will o' the wisp for years. I doubt if we'll ever be able to prove it." He grinned. "Maybe you will when you're made assistant commissioner."

"Come off it, for God's sake, Robert."

"Christ, you're only thirty-nine, you've done the special bigwig Staff

College course and you're a super already. A hundred to ten says you'll end up with that rank."

"Done."

"I should have made it a hundred thousand," Armstrong said, pretending sourness. "Then you wouldn't have taken it."

"Try me."

"I won't. I can't afford to lose that amount of tootie—you might get killed or something, this year or next, or resign—but if you don't you're in for the big slot before you retire, presuming you want to go the distance."

"Both of us."

"Not me—I'm too mad dog English." Armstrong clapped him on the back happily. "That'll be a great day. But you won't close down the Dragons either—even if you'll be able to prove it, which I doubt."

"No?"

"No. I don't care about the gambling. All Chinese want to gamble and if some Chinese police sergeants run illegal street gambling it'll be mostly clean and mostly fair though bloody illegal. If they don't run it, triads will, and then the splinter groups of rotten little bastards we so carefully keep apart will join together again into one big *tong* and then we'll really have a real problem. You know me, lad, I'm not one to rock any boats, that's why I won't make assistant commissioner. I like the status quo. The Dragons run the gambling so we keep the triads splintered—and just so long as the police always stick together and are absolutely the strongest triad in Hong Kong, we'll always have peace in the streets, a well-ordered population and almost no crime, violent crime."

Brian Kwok studied him. "You really believe that, don't you?"

"Yes. In a funny sort of a way, right now the Dragons are one of our strongest supports. Let's face it, Brian, only Chinese can govern Chinese. The status quo's good for them too—violent crime's bad for them. So we get help when we need it—sometimes, probably—help that we foreign devils couldn't get any other way. I'm not in favor of their corruption or of breaking the law, not at all—or bribery or all the other shitty things we have to do, or informers, but what police force in the world could operate without dirty hands sometimes and snotty little bastard informers? So the evil the Dragons represent fills a need here, I think. Hong Kong's China and China's a special case. Just so long as it's just illegal gambling I don't care never mind. Me, if it was left up to me I'd make gambling legal tonight but I'd break anyone for any protection racket, any dance hall protection or girls or whatever. I can't stand pimps as you know. Gambling's different. How can you stop a Chinese gambling? You can't. So make it legal and everyone's happy. How many years have the Hong Kong police been advising that and every year we're turned down. Twenty that I know of. But oh no and why? Macao! Simple as that. Dear old Portuguese Macao feeds off illegal gambling and gold smuggling and that's what keeps them alive and we can't afford, we, the UK, we can't afford to have our old ally go down the spout."

"Robert Armstrong for prime minister!"

"Up yours! But it's true. The take on illegal gambling's our only slush fund—a lot of it goes to pay our ring of informers. Where else can we get quick money? From our grateful government? Don't make me laugh! From a few extra tax dollars from the grateful population we protect? Ha!"

"Perhaps. Perhaps not, Robert. But it's certainly going to backfire one day. The payoffs—the loose and uncounted money that 'happens' to be in a station drawer? Isn't it?"

"Yes, but not on me 'cause I'm not in on it, or a taker, and the vast majority aren't either. British *or Chinese*. Meanwhile how do we three hundred and twenty-seven poor foreign devil police officers control eight odd thousand civilized junior officers and coppers, and another three and a half million civilized little bastards who hate our guts never mind."

Brian Kwok laughed. It was an infectious laugh and Armstrong laughed with him and added, "Up yours again for getting me going."

"Likewise. Meanwhile are you going to read that first or am I?"

Armstrong looked down at the file he held in his hand. It was thin and contained twelve closely typewritten pages and seemed to be more of a newsletter with topics under different headings. The contents page read: Part One: The Political and Business Forecast of the United Kingdom. Part Two: The KGB in Asia. Part Three: Gold. Part Four: Recent CIA Developments.

Wearily Armstrong put his feet on the desk and eased himself more comfortably in his chair. Then he changed his mind and passed the file over. "Here, you can read it. You read faster than I do anyway. I'm tired of reading about disaster."

Brian Kwok took it, his impatience barely contained, his heart thumping heavily. He opened it and began to read.

Armstrong watched him. He saw his friend's face change immediately and lose color. That troubled him greatly. Brian Kwok was not easily shocked. He saw him read through to the end without comment, then flick back to check a paragraph here and there. He closed the file slowly.

"It's that bad," Armstrong said.

"It's worse. Some of it—well, if it wasn't signed by A. Medford Grant, I'd say he was off his rocker. He claims the CIA have a serious connection with the Mafia, that they're plotting and have plotted to knock off Castro, they're into Vietnam in strength, into drugs and Christ knows what else—here—read it for yourself."

"What about the mole?"

"We've a mole all right." Brian reopened the file and found the paragraph. "Listen: 'There's no doubt that presently there is a high-level Communist agent in the Hong Kong police. Top-secret documents brought to our side by General Hans Richter—second-in-command of the East German Department of Internal Security—when he defected to us in March of this year clearly state the agent's code name is "Our Friend," that he has been in situ for at least ten, probably fifteen years. His contact is probably a KGB officer in Hong Kong posing as a visiting friendly businessman from the Iron Curtain countries, possibly as a banker or journalist, or posing as a seaman off one of the Soviet freighters visiting or being repaired in Hong Kong. Among other documented information we now know "Our Friend" has provided the enemy with are: All restricted radio channels, all restricted private phone numbers of the governor, chief of police and top echelon of the Hong Kong Government, along with very private dossiers on most of them . . .'"

"Dossiers?" Armstrong interrupted. "Are they included?"

"No."

"Shit! Go on, Brian."

"'. . . most of them; the classified police battle plans against a Communist-provoked insurrection, or a recurrence of the Kowloon riots; copies of all private dossiers of all police officers above the rank of inspector; the names of the chief six Nationalist undercover agents of the Kuomintang operating in Hong Kong under the present authority of General Jen Tang-wa (Appendix A); a detailed list of Hong Kong's Special Intelligence agents in Kwantung under the general authority of Senior Agent Wu Fong Fong (Appendix B).'"

"Jesus!" Armstrong gasped. "We'd better get old Fong Fong and his lads out right smartly."

"Yes."

"Is Wu Tat-sing on the list?"

Kwok checked the appendix. "Yes. Listen, this section ends: '. . . It is the conclusion of your committee that until this traitor is eliminated, the internal security of Hong Kong is hazardous. Why this information has not yet been passed on to the police themselves we do not yet know. We presume this ties in with the current political Soviet infiltration of UK administration on all levels which enables the Philbys to exist, and permits such information as this to be buried, or toned down, or misrepresented (which was the material for Study 4/1962). We would suggest this report —or portions of it, should be leaked at once to the governor or the commissioner of police, Hong Kong, *if you consider them trustworthy.*'" Brian Kwok looked up, his mind rocking. "There's a couple of other pieces here, Christ, the political situation in the UK and then there's Sevrin. . . . Read it." He shook his head helplessly. "Christ, if this's true . . . we're in it up to our necks. God in Heaven!"

Armstrong swore softly. "Who? Who could the spy be? Got to be high up. Who?"

After a great silence, Brian said, "The only one . . . the only one who could know all of this's Crosse himself."

"Oh come on for chrissake!"

"Think about it, Robert. He knew Philby. Didn't he go to Cambridge also? Both have similar backgrounds, they're the same age group, both were in Intelligence during the war—like Burgess and Maclean. If Philby could get away with it for all those years, why not Crosse?"

"Impossible!"

"Who else but him? Hasn't he been in MI-6 all his life? Didn't he do a tour here in the early fifties and wasn't he brought back here to set up our SI as a separate branch of SB five years ago? Hasn't he been director ever since?"

"That proves nothing."

"Oh?"

There was a long silence. Armstrong was watching his friend closely. He knew him too well not to know when he was serious. "What've you got?" he asked uneasily.

"Say Crosse is homosexual."

"You're plain bonkers," Armstrong exploded. "He's married and . . . and he may be an evil son of a bitch but there's never been a smell of anything like that, never."

"Yes, but he's got no children, his wife's almost permanently in England and when she's here they have separate rooms."

"How do you know?"

"The *amah* would know so if I wanted to know it'd be easy to find out."

"That proves nothing. Lots of people have separate rooms. You're wrong about Crosse."

"Say I could give you proof?"

"What proof?"

"Where does he always go for part of his leave? The Cameron Highlands in Malaya. Say he had a friend there, a young Malayan, a known deviate."

"I'd need photos and we both know photos can be easily doctored," Armstrong said harshly. "I'd need tape recordings and we both know those can be doctored too. The youth himself? That proves nothing—it's the oldest trick in the book to produce false testimony and false witnesses. There's never been a hint . . . and even if he's AC-DC, that proves nothing—not all deviates are traitors."

"No. But all deviates lay themselves open to blackmail. And if he is, he'd be highly suspect. Highly suspect. Right?"

Armstrong looked around uneasily. "I don't even like talking about it here, he could have this place tapped."

"And if he has?"

"If he has and if it's true he can fry us so quickly your head would spin. He can fry us anyway."

"Perhaps—but if he is the one then he'll know we're on to him and if he's not he'll laugh at us and I'm out of SI. In any event, Robert, he can't fry every Chinese in the force."

Armstrong stared at him. "What's that supposed to mean?"

"Perhaps there's a file on him. Perhaps every Chinese above the rank of corporal's read it."

"What?"

"Come on, Robert, you know Chinese are great joiners. Perhaps there's a file, per—"

"You mean you're all organized into a brotherhood? A *tong*, a secret society? A triad within the force?"

"I said perhaps. This is all surmise, Robert. I said perhaps and maybe."

"Who's the High Dragon? You?"

"I never said there was such a grouping. I said perhaps."

"Are there other files? On me, for instance?"

"Perhaps."

"And?"

"And if there was, Robert," Brian Kwok said gently, "it'd say you were a fine policeman, uncorrupted, that you had gambled heavily on the stock market and gambled wrong and needed twenty-odd thousand to clean up some pressing debts—and a few other things."

"What other things?"

"This is China, old chum. We know almost everything that goes on with *quai loh* here. We have to, to survive, don't we?"

Armstrong looked at him strangely. "Why didn't you tell me before?"

"I haven't told you anything now. Nothing. I said perhaps and I repeat perhaps. But if this's all true . . ." He passed over the file and wiped the sweat off his upper lip. "Read it yourself. If it's true we're up the creek without a paddle and we'll need to work very quickly. What I said was all surmise. But not about Crosse. Listen Robert, I'll bet you a thousand . . . a thousand to one, he's the mole."

10

Dunross finished reading the blue-covered file for the third time. He had
read it as soon as it had arrived—as always—then again on the way to the
Governor's Palace. He closed the blue cover and set it onto his lap for a
moment, his mind possessed. Now he was in his study on the second floor
of the Great House that sat on a knoll on the upper levels of the Peak, the
leaded bay windows overlooking floodlit gardens, and then far below, the
city and the immensity of the harbor.

The ancient grandfather clock chimed a quarter to eight.

Fifteen minutes to go, he thought. Then our guests arrive and the party
begins and we all take part in a new charade. Or perhaps we just continue
the same one.

The room had high ceilings and old oak paneling, dark green velvet
curtains and Chinese silk rugs. It was a man's room, comfortable, old, a little worn and very cherished. He heard the muted voices of the servants
below. A car came up the hill and passed by.

The phone rang. "Yes? Oh hello, Claudia."

"I haven't reached Tsu-yan yet, tai-pan. He wasn't in his office. Has he
called?"

"No. No not yet. You keep trying."

"Yes. See you in a little while. 'Bye."

He was sitting in a deep, high-winged chair and wore a dinner jacket,
his tie not yet tied. Absently he stared out of the windows, the view ever
pleasing. But tonight he was filled with foreboding, thinking about Sevrin
and the traitor and all the other evil things the report had foretold.

What to do?

"Laugh," he said out loud. "And fight."

He got up and went with his easy stride to the oil painting of Dirk
Struan that was on the wall over the mantelpiece. Its frame was heavy
and carved gilt and old, the gilt chipped off here and there, and it was

secretly hinged on one side. He moved it away from the wall and opened the safe the painting covered. In the safe were many papers, some neatly tied with scarlet ribbons, some ancient, some new, a few small boxes, a neat, well-oiled, loaded Mauser in a clip attached to one of the sides, a box of ammunition, a vast old Bible with the Struan arms etched into the fine old leather and seven blue-covered files similar to the one he had in his hand.

Thoughtfully he slid the file alongside the others in sequence. He stared at them a moment, began to close the safe but changed his mind as his eyes fell on the ancient Bible. His fingers caressed it, then he lifted it out and opened it. Affixed to the thick flyleaf with old sealing wax were halves of two old Chinese bronze coins, crudely broken. Clearly, once upon a time, there had been four such half-coins for there was still the imprint of the missing two and the remains of the same red sealing wax attached to the ancient paper. The handwriting heading the page was beautiful copperplate: "I swear by the Lord God that whomsoever produces the other half of any of these coins, I will grant him whatsoever he asks." It was signed Dirk Struan, June 10, 1841, and below his signature was Culum Struan's and all the other tai-pans and the last name was Ian Dunross.

Alongside the first space where once a coin had been was written: "Wu Fang Choi, paid in part, August 16, Year of our Lord 1841," and signed again by Dirk Struan and cosigned below by Culum Struan and dated 18 June 1845 "paid in full." Alongside the second: "Sun Chen-yat, paid in full, October 10, 1911," and signed boldly, Hag Struan.

Ah, Dunross told himself, bemused, what lovely arrogance—to be so secure to be able to sign the book thus and not Tess Struan, for future generations to see.

How many more generations? he asked himself. How many more tai-pans will have to sign blindly and swear the Holy Oath to do the bidding of a man dead almost a century and a half?

Thoughtfully he ran his finger over the jagged edges of the two remaining half-coins. After a moment he closed the Bible firmly, put it into its place again, touched it once for luck and locked the safe. He swung the painting back into its place and stared up at the portrait, standing now with his hands deep in his pockets in front of the mantelpiece, the heavy old oak carved with the Struan arms, chipped and broken here and there, an old Chinese fire screen in front of the huge fireplace.

This oil of Dirk Struan was his favorite and he had taken it out of the long gallery when he became tai-pan and had hung it here in the place of honor—instead of the portrait of Hag Struan that had been over the mantelpiece in the tai-pan's study ever since there was a Great House. Both had been painted by Aristotle Quance. In this one, Dirk Struan was standing in front of a crimson curtain, broad-shouldered and arrogant, his high-cut coat black and his waistcoat and cravat and ruffled shirt white and high-cut. Heavy eyebrows and strong nose and clean-shaven, with reddish hair and muttonchop sideburns, lips curled and sensual and you could feel the eyes boring into you, their green enhanced by the black and white and crimson.

Dunross half-smiled, not afraid, not envious, more calmed than anything by his ancestor's gaze—knowing he was possessed, partially possessed by him. He raised his glass of champagne to the painting in half-mocking jest as he had done many times before: "Health!"

The eyes stared back at him.

What would you do, Dirk—Dirk o' the will o' the wisp, he thought.

"You'd probably say just find the traitors and kill them," he mused aloud, "and you'd probably be right."

The problem of the traitor in the police did not shatter him as much as the information about the Sevrin spy ring, its U.S. connections and the astonishing, secret gains made by the Communists in Britain. Where the hell does Grant get all his info? he asked himself for the hundredth time.

He remembered their first meeting. Alan Medford Grant was a short, elflike, balding man with large eyes and large teeth, in his neat pin-striped suit and bowler hat and he liked him immediately.

"Don't you worry, Mr. Dunross," Grant had said when Dunross had hired him in 1960, the moment he became tai-pan. "I assure you there'll be no conflict of interest with Her Majesty's Government if I chair your research committee on the nonexclusive basis we've discussed. I've already cleared it with them in fact. I'll only give you—confidentially of course, for you personally of course, and absolutely not for publication—I'll only give you classified material that does not, in my opinion, jeopardize the national interest. After all, our interests are the same there, aren't they?"

"I think so."

"May I ask how you heard of me?"

"We have friends in high places, Mr. Grant. In certain circles your name is quite famous. Perhaps even a foreign secretary would recommend you," he had added delicately.

"Ah yes."

"Our arrangement is satisfactory?"

"Yes—one year initially, extended to five if everything goes well. After five?"

"Another five," Dunross said. "If we achieve the results I want, your retainer will be doubled."

"Ah. That's very generous. But may I ask why you're being so generous —perhaps *extravagant* would be the word—with me and this projected committee?"

"Sun Tzu said: 'What enables a wise sovereign or good general to strike and to conquer and to achieve things beyond the reach of normal men is foreknowledge. Foreknowledge comes only through spies. Nothing is of more importance to the state than the quality of its spies. *It is ten thou-*

sand times cheaper to pay the best spies lavishly than even a tiny army poorly.' "

Alan Medford Grant beamed. "Quite right! My 8,500 pounds a year is lavish indeed, Mr. Dunross. Oh yes. Yes indeed."

"Can you think of a better investment for me?"

"Not if I perform correctly, if I and the ones I choose are the best to be had. Even so, 30-odd thousand pounds a year in salaries—a fund of up to 100,000 pounds to draw on for . . . for informants and information, all secret monies . . . well, I hope you will be satisfied with your investment."

"If you're the best I'll recoup a thousandfold. I expect to recoup a thousandfold," he had said, meaning it.

"I'll do everything in my power of course. Now, specifically what sort of information do you want?"

"Anything and everything, commercial, political, that'd help Struan's plan ahead, with accent on the Pacific Rim, on Russian, American and Japanese thinking. We'd probably know more about Chinese attitudes ourselves. Please give me more rather than less. Actually anything could be valuable because I want to take Struan's out of the China trade—more specifically I want the company international and want to diversify out of our present dependence on China trade."

"Very well. First: I would not like to trust our reports to the mails."

"I'll arrange a personal courier."

"Thank you. Second: I must have free range to select, appoint and remove the other members of the committee—and spend the money as I see fit?"

"Agreed."

"Five members will be sufficient."

"How much do you want to pay them?"

"5,000 pounds a year for a nonexclusive retainer each would be excellent. I can get top men for that. Yes. I'll appoint associate members for special studies as I need them. As, er, as most of our contacts will be abroad, many in Switzerland, could funds be available there?"

"Say I deposit the full amount we've agreed quarterly in a numbered Swiss account. You can draw funds as you need them—your signature or mine only. You account to me solely, quarterly in arrears. If you want to erect a code that's fine with me."

"Excellent. I won't be able to name anyone—I can't account to whom I give money."

After a pause Dunross had said, "All right."

"Thank you. We understand one another, I think. Can you give me an example of what you want?"

"For example, I don't want to get caught like my predecessor was over Suez."

"Oh! You mean the 1956 fiasco when Eisenhower betrayed us again and caused the failure of the British-French-Israeli attack on Egypt—because Nasser had nationalized the canal?"

"Yes. That cost us a fortune—it wrecked our Middle East interests, almost ruined us. If the previous tai-pan'd known about a possible closure of Suez we could have made a fortune booking cargo space—increasing our fleet . . . or if we'd had an advanced insight into American thinking, particularly that Eisenhower would side again with Soviet Russia against us, we could certainly have cut our losses."

The little man had said sadly, "You know he threatened to freeze all British, French and Israeli assets in the States instantly if we did not at once withdraw from Egypt when we were a few hours from victory? I think all our present problems in the Middle East stem from that U.S. decision. Yes. Inadvertently the U.S. approved international piracy for the first time and set a pattern for future piracies. Nationalization. What a joke! *Theft* is a better word—or piracy. Yes. Eisenhower was ill-advised. And very ill-advised to go along with the fatuous political Yalta agreement of an ailing Roosevelt, the incompetent Attlee to allow Stalin to gorge most of Europe, when it was militarily clear to even the most stupid politician or hidebound general that *it was contrary to our absolute national interest, ours and the United States to hold back.* I think Roosevelt hated us really, and our British Empire."

The little man steepled his fingers and beamed. "I'm afraid there's one big disadvantage in employing me, Mr. Dunross. I'm entirely pro-British, anti-Communist, and particularly anti-KGB which is the main instrument of Soviet foreign policy, which is openly and forever committed to our destruction, so some of my more peppery forecasts you can discount, if you wish. I'm entirely against a left-wing dominated Labour Party and I will constantly remind anyone who will listen that the anthem of the Labour Party's 'The Red Flag.' " Alan Medford Grant smiled in his pixy way. "It's best you know where you stand in the beginning. I'm royalist, loyalist and believe in the British parliamentary way. I'll never knowingly give you false information though my evaluations will be slanted. May I ask what your politics are?"

"We have none in Hong Kong, Mr. Grant. We don't vote, there are no elections—we're a colony, particularly a free-port colony, not a democracy. The Crown rules—actually the governor rules despotically for the Crown. He has a legislative council but it's a rubber-stamp council and the historic policy is *laissez-faire.* Wisely he leaves things alone. He listens to the business community, makes social changes very cautiously and leaves everyone to make money or not make money, to build, expand, go broke, to go or to come, to dream or to stay awake, to live or to die as best you can. And the maximum tax is 15 percent but only on money earned in Hong Kong. We don't have politics here, don't want politics here—neither does China want us to have any here. They're for the status quo too. My personal politics? I'm royalist, I'm for freedom, for freebooting and free trade. I'm a Scotsman, I'm for Struan's, I'm for *laissez-faire* in Hong Kong and freedom throughout the world."

"I think we understand one another. Good. I've never worked for an individual before—only the government. This will be a new experience for me. I hope I will satisfy you." Grant paused and thought a moment. "Like Suez in '56?" The lines beside the little man's eyes crinkled. "Very well, plan that the Panama Canal will be lost to America."

"That's ridiculous!"

"Oh don't look so shocked, Mr. Dunross! It's too easy. Give it ten or fifteen years of enemy spadework and lots of liberal talk in America, ably assisted by do-gooders who believe in the benevolence of human nature, add to all this a modest amount of calculated Panamanian agitation, students and so on—preferably, ah, always students—artfully and secretly assisted by a few highly trained, patient, professional agitators and oh so secret KGB expertise, finance and a long-range plan—ergo, in due course the canal could be out of U.S. hands into the enemy's."

"They'd never stand for it."

"You're right, Mr. Dunross, but they will sit for it. What could be a better garrotte in time of hostilities, or even crisis, against your main, openly stated capitalistic enemy than to be able to inhibit the Panama Canal or rock it a little? One ship sunk in any one of a hundred spots, or a lock wrecked, could dam up the canal for years."

Dunross remembered how he had poured two more drinks before answering, and then he had said, "You're seriously suggesting we should make contingency plans against that."

"Yes," the little man said with his extraordinary innocence. "I'm very serious about my job, Mr. Dunross. My job, the one I've chosen for me, is to seek out, to uncover and evaluate enemy moves. I'm not anti-Russian or anti-Chinese or anti-East German or anti any of that bloc—on the absolute contrary I want desperately to help them. I'm convinced that we're in a state of war, that the enemy of all the people is the Communist Party member, whether British, Soviet, Chinese, Hungarian, American, Irish . . . even Martian . . . and all are linked in one way or another; that the KGB, like it or not, is in the center of their web." He sipped the drink Dunross had just refilled for him. "This is marvelous whiskey, Mr. Dunross."

"It's Loch Vey—it comes from a small distillery near our homelands in Ayr. It's a Struan company."

"Marvelous!" Another appreciative sip of the whiskey and Dunross reminded himself to send Alan Medford Grant a case for Christmas—if the initial reports proved interesting.

"I'm not a fanatic, Mr. Dunross, nor a rabble-rouser. Just a sort of reporter and forecaster. Some people collect stamps, I collect secrets. . . ."

The lights of a car rounding the half-hidden curve of the road below distracted Dunross momentarily. He wandered over to the window and watched the car until it had gone, enjoying the sound of the highly tuned engine. Then he sat in a high-winged chair and let his mind drift again. Yes, Mr. Grant, you certainly collect secrets, he thought, staggered as usual by the scope of the little man's knowledge.

Sevrin—Christ almighty! If that's true . . .

How accurate are you this time? How far do I trust you this time—how far do I gamble?

In previous reports Grant had given two projections that, so far, could be proved. A year in advance, Grant had predicted that de Gaulle would veto Britain's effort to join the EEC, that the French general's posture would be increasingly anti-British, anti-American and pro-Soviet, and that de Gaulle would, prompted by outside influences and encouraged by one of his closest advisors—an immensely secret, covert KGB mole—mount a long-term attack on the U.S. economy by speculation in gold. Dunross had dismissed this as farfetched and so had lost a potential fortune.

Recently, six months in advance, Grant had forecast the missile crisis in Cuba, that Kennedy would slam down the gauntlet, blockade Cuba and exert the necessary pressure and not buckle under the strain of brinkmanship, that Khrushchev would back off under pressure. Gambling that Grant was correct this time—though a Cuban missile crisis had seemed highly unlikely at the time forecast—Dunross had made Struan's half a million pounds by buying Hawaiian sugar futures, another 600,000 on the stock market, plus 600,000 for the tai-pan's secret fund—and cemented a long-range plan to invest in Hawaiian sugar plantations as soon as he could find the financial tool. And you've got it now, he told himself gleefully. Par-Con.

"You've almost got it," he muttered, correcting himself.

How far do I trust this report? Thus far AMG's committee's been a gigantic investment for all his meanderings, he thought. Yes. But it's almost like having your own astrologer. A few accurate forecasts don't mean they'll all be. Hitler had his own forecaster. So did Julius Caesar. Be wise, be cautious, he reminded himself.

What to do? It's now or never.

Sevrin. Alan Medford Grant had written: "Documents brought to us and substantiated by the French spy Marie d'Orleans caught by the Sûreté June 16 indicate that the KGB Department V (Disinformation—FAR EAST) have in situ a hitherto unknown, deep-cover espionage network throughout the Far East, code name *Sevrin*. The purpose of Sevrin is clearly stated in the stolen Head Document:

"Aim: To cripple revisionist China—formally acknowledged by the Central Committee of the USSR as the main enemy, second only to capitalist U.S.A.

"Procedure: The permanent obliteration of Hong Kong as the bastion of capitalism in the Far East and China's preeminent source of all foreign currency, foreign assistance and all technical and manufactured assistance of every kind.

"Method: Long-term infiltration of the press and media, the government, police, business and education with friendly aliens controlled by Center—but only in accordance with most special procedures throughout Asia.

"Initiation date: Immediate.

"Duration of operation: Provisionally thirty years.

"Target date: 1980–83.

"Classification: *Red One*.

"Funding: Maximum.

"Approval: L.B. March 14, 1950.

"It's interesting to note," Grant had continued, "that the document is signed in 1950 by L.B.—presumed to be Lavrenti Beria—when Soviet Russia was openly allied with Communist China, and that, even in those days, China was secretly considered their Number Two enemy. (Our previous report 3/1962, Russia versus China refers.)

"China, historically, is the great prize that always was—and ever will be —sought by imperialistic and hegemonic Russia. Possession of China, or its mutilation into balkanized subject states, is the perpetual keystone of Russian foreign policy. First is, of course, the obliteration of Western Europe, for then, Russia believes, China can be swallowed at will.

"The documents reveal that the Hong Kong cell of Sevrin consists of a resident controller, code name Arthur, and six agents. We know nothing about Arthur, other than that he has been a KGB agent since recruitment in England in the thirties (it's not known if he was born in England, or if his parents are English, but he would be in his late forties or early fifties). His mission is, of course, a long-term, deep-cover operation.

"Supporting top-secret intelligence documents stolen from the Czechoslovak STB (State Secret Security) dated April 6, 1959, translate in part, '. . . between 1946 and 1959 six key, deep-cover agents have been recruited through information supplied by the controller, Arthur: one each in the Hong Kong Colonial Office (code name Charles), Treasury (code name Mason), Naval Base (John), the Bank of London and China (Vincent), the Hong Kong Telephone Company (William), and Struan and Company (Frederick). According to normal procedures only the controller knows the true identity of the others. Seven safe houses have been established. Among them are Sinclair Towers on Hong Kong Island and the Nine Dragons Hotel in Kowloon. Sevrin's New York contact, has the code name Guillio. He is very important to us because of his Mafia and CIA connections.'"

Grant had continued, "Guillio is believed to be Vincenzo Banastasio, a substantial racketeer and the present don of the Sallapione family. This is being checked through our U.S. sources. We don't know if the deep-cover enemy agent in the police (covered in detail in another section) is part of Sevrin or not but presume he is.

"In our opinion, China will be forced to seek ever-increasing amounts of trade with the West to counterbalance imperialist Soviet hegemony and to fill the void and chaos created by the sudden withdrawal in 1960 of all Soviet funding and technicians. China's armed forces badly need modernizing. Harvests have been bad. Therefore all forms of strategic materials and military hardware will find a ready market for many years to come, and food, basic foodstuffs. The long-range purchase of American rice futures is recommended.

"I have the honor to be, sir, your obedient servant, AMG, London, August 15, 1963."

Jets and tanks and nuts and bolts and rockets and engines and trucks and petrol and tires and electronics and food, Dunross thought, his mind soaring. A limitless spectrum of trade goods, easy to obtain, easy to ship, and nothing on earth like a war for profit if you can trade. But China's not buying now, whatever they need, whatever Grant says.

Who could Arthur be?

Who in Struan's? Jesus Christ! John Chen and Tsu-yan and smuggled guns and now a KGB agent within. Who? What about . . .

There was a gentle knock on the door.

"Come in," he said, recognizing his wife's knock.

"Ian, it's almost eight," Penelope, his wife, said, "I thought I'd better tell you. You know how you are."

"Yes."

"How did it go today? Awful about John Chen, isn't it? I suppose you read the papers? Are you coming down?"

"Yes. Champagne?"

"Thanks."

He poured for her and replenished his glass. "Oh by the way, Penn, I invited a fellow I met this afternoon, an ex-RAF type. He seemed a decent fellow—Peter Marlowe."

"Fighters?"

"Yes. But Hurricanes—not Spits. Is that a new dress?"

"Yes."

"You look pretty," he said.

"Thank you but I'm not. I feel so old, but thank you." She sat in the other winged chair, her perfume as delicate as her features. "Peter Marlowe, you said?"

"Yes. Poor bugger got caught in Java in '42. He was a POW for three and a half years."

"Oh, poor man. He was shot down?"

"No, the Japanese plastered the 'drome before he could scramble. Perhaps he was lucky. The Zeros got two on the ground and the last two just after they were airborne—the pilots flamed in. Seems those four Hurri-

canes were the last of the Few—the last of the whole air defense of the Far
East. What a balls-up that was!"

"Terrible."

"Yes. Thank God our war was in Europe." Dunross watched her. "He
said he was a year in Java, then the Japanese sent him to Singapore on a
work party."

"To Changi?" she asked, her voice different.

"Yes."

"Oh!"

"He was there for two and a half years." Changi in Malay meant
"clinging vine," and Changi was the name of the jail in Singapore that
was used by the Japanese in World War II for one of their infamous
prisoner-of-war camps.

She thought a moment, then smiled a little nervously. "Did he know
Robin there?" Robin Grey was her brother, her only living relative: her
parents had been killed in an air raid in London in 1943, just before she
and Dunross were married.

"Marlowe said yes, he seemed to remember him, but clearly he didn't
want to talk about those days so I let it drop."

"I can imagine. Did you tell him Robin was my brother?"

"No."

"When's Robin due back here?"

"I don't know exactly. In a few days. This afternoon the governor told
me the delegation's in Peking now." A British Parliamentary Trade Delegation drawn from MPs of the three parties—Conservative, Liberal and
Labour—had been invited out from London by Peking to discuss all manner of trade. The delegation had arrived in Hong Kong two weeks ago
and had gone directly on to Canton where all trade negotiations were conducted. It was very rare for anyone to get an invitation, let alone a parliamentary delegation—and even rarer to be invited on to Peking. Robin
Grey was one of the members—representative of the Labour Party. "Penn
darling, don't you think we should acknowledge Robin, give a reception
for him? After all, we haven't seen him for years, this's the first time he's
been to Asia—isn't it time you buried the hatchet and made peace?"

"He's not invited to my house. Any of my houses."

"Isn't it time you relaxed a little, let bygones be bygones?"

"No, I know him, you don't. Robin has his life and we have ours, that's
what he and I agreed years ago. No, I've no wish to see him ever again.
He's awful, dangerous, foul-mouthed and a bloody bore."

Dunross laughed. "I agree he's obnoxious and I detest his politics—but
he's only one of a half dozen MPs. This delegation's important. I should
do something to entertain them, Penn."

"Please do, Ian. But preferably not here—or else tell me in good time so
I can have the vapors and see that the children do the same. It's a matter
of face and that's the end of it." Penelope tossed her head and shook off

her mood. "God! Let's not let him spoil this evening! What's this Marlowe doing in Hong Kong?"

"He's a writer. Wants to do a book on Hong Kong, he said. He lives in America now. His wife's coming too. Oh, by the way, I also invited the Americans, Linc Bartlett and Casey Tcholok."

"Oh!" Penelope Dunross laughed. "Oh well, four or forty extra won't make any difference at all—I won't know most of them anyway, and Claudia's organized everything with her usual efficiency." She arched an eyebrow. "So! A gun-runner amongst the pirates! That won't even cause a ripple."

"Is he?"

"Everyone says so. Did you see the piece in this afternoon's *Mirror*, Ian? Ah Tat's convinced the American is bad joss—she informed the whole staff, the children and me—so that makes it official. Ah Tat told Adryon that her astrologer insisted she tell you to watch out for bad influence from the East. Ah Tat's sure that means the Yanks. Hasn't she bent your ear yet?"

"Not yet."

"God, I wish I could chatter Cantonese like you and the children. I'd tell that old harpy to keep her superstitions and opinions to herself—she's a bad influence."

"She'd give her life for the children."

"I know she's your *gan sun* and almost brought you up and thinks she's God's gift to the Dunross clan. But as far as I'm concerned she's a cantankerous, loathsome old bitch and I hate her." Penelope smiled sweetly. "I hear the American girl's pretty."

"Attractive—not pretty. She's giving Andrew a bad time."

"I can imagine. A lady talking business! What are we coming to in this great world of ours? Is she any good?"

"Too soon to tell. But she's very smart. She's—she'll make things awkward certainly."

"Have you seen Adryon tonight?"

"No—what's up?" he asked, instantly recognizing the tone of voice.

"She's been into my wardrobe again—half my best nylons are gone, the rest are scattered, my scarves are all jumbled up, my new blouse's missing and my new belt's disappeared. She's even whipped my best Hermès . . . that child's the end!"

"Nineteen's hardly a child," he said wearily.

"She's the end! The number of times I've told her!"

"I'll talk to her again."

"That won't do a bit of good."

"I know."

She laughed with him. "She's such a pill."

"Here." He handed her a slim box. "Happy twentieth!"

"Oh thank you, Ian. Yours is downstairs. You'll . . ." She stopped and opened the box. It contained a carved jade bracelet, the jade inset into silver filigree, very fine, very old—a collector's piece. "Oh how lovely, thank you, Ian." She put it on her wrist over the thin gold chain she was wearing and he heard neither real pleasure nor real disappointment under her voice, his ears tuned to her. "It's beautiful," she said and leaned forward and brushed her lips against his cheek. "Thank you, darling. Where did you get it? Taiwan?"

"No, here on Cat Street. At Wong Chun Kit's, he ga—"

The door flew open and a girl barreled in. She was tall and slim and oh so fair and she said in a breathless rush, "I hope it's all right I invited a date tonight and I just had the call that he's coming and he'll be late but I thought it'd be okay. He's cool. And very trick."

"For the love of God, Adryon," Dunross said mildly, "how many times do I have to ask you to knock before you charge in here and would you kindly talk English? What the hell's *trick?*"

"Good, great, cool, trick. Sorry, Father, but you really are rather square because cool and trick are very in, even in Hong Kong. See you soon, have to dash, after the party I'm going out—I'll be late so don't—"

"Wait a min—"

"That's my blouse, my new blouse," Penelope burst out. "Adryon, you take it off this minute! I've told you fifty times to stay the hell out of my wardrobe."

"Oh, Mother," Adryon said as sharply, "you don't need it, can't I borrow it for this evening?" Her tone changed. "Please? Pretty please? Father, talk to her." She switched to perfect *amah* Cantonese, "Honorable Father . . . please help your Number One Daughter to achieve the unachievable or I shall weep weep weep *oh ko* . . ." Then back into English in the same breath, "Mother . . . you don't need it and I'll look after it, truly. Please?"

"No."

"Come on, pretty please, I'll look after it, I promise."

"No."

"Mother!"

"Well if you pr—"

"Oh thanks." The girl beamed and turned and rushed out and the door slammed behind her.

"Jesus bloody Christ," Dunross said sourly, "why the hell does a door always happen to slam behind her!"

"Well at least it's not deliberate now." Penelope sighed. "I don't think I could go through that siege again."

"Nor me. Thank God Glenna's reasonable."

"It's purely temporary, Ian. She takes after her father, that one, like Adryon."

"Huh! I don't have a filthy temper," he said sharply. "And since we're on the subject I hope to God Adryon has found someone decent to date instead of the usual shower! Who is this she's bringing?"

"I don't know, Ian. This is the first I've heard of it too."

"They're always bloody awful! Her taste in men's appalling. . . . Remember that melon-headed berk with the neolithic arms that she was 'madly in love with'? Christ Jesus, she was barely fifteen an—"

"She was almost sixteen."

"What was his name? Ah yes, Byron. Byron for chrissake!"

"You really shouldn't have threatened to blow his head off, Ian. It was just puppy love."

"It was gorilla bloody love, by God," Dunross said even more sourly. "He was a bloody gorilla. . . . You remember that other one, the one before bloody Byron—the psychiatric bastard . . . what was his name?"

"Victor. Yes, Victor Hopper. He was the one . . . oh yes, I remember, he was the one who asked if it was all right if he slept with Adryon."

"He what?"

"Oh yes." She smiled up at him so innocently. "I didn't tell you at the time . . . thought I'd better not."

"He *what?*"

"Don't get yourself all worked up, Ian. That's at least four years ago. I told him no, not at the moment, Adryon's only fourteen, but yes, certainly, when she was twenty-one. That was another that died on the vine."

"Jesus Christ! *He asked* you if he co—"

"At least he asked, Ian! That was something. It's all so very ordinary." She got up and poured more champagne into his glass, and some for herself. "You've only got another ten years or so of purgatory, then there'll be the grandchildren. Happy anniversary and the best of British to you!" She laughed and touched his glass and drank and smiled at him.

"You're right again," he said and smiled back, liking her very much. So many years, good years. I've been lucky, he thought. Yes. I was blessed that first day. It was at his RAF station at Biggin Hill, a warm, sunny August morning in 1940 during the Battle of Britain and she was a WAAF and newly posted there. It was his eighth day at war, his third mission that day and first kill. His Spitfire was latticed with bullet holes, parts of his wing gone, his tail section tattooed. By all the rules of joss, he should be dead but he wasn't and the Messerschmitt was and her pilot was and he was home and safe and blood raging, drunk with fear and shame and relief that he had come back and the youth he had seen in the other cockpit, the enemy, had burned screaming as he spiraled.

"Hello, sir," Penelope Grey had said. "Welcome home sir. Here." She had given him a cup of hot sweet tea and she had said nothing else though she should have begun debriefing him at once—she was in Signals. She said nothing but smiled and gave him time to come out of the skies of death into life again. He had not thanked her, just drank the tea and it was the best he had ever had.

"I got a Messerschmitt," he had said when he could talk, his voice trembling like his knees. He could not remember unsnapping his harness or getting out of his cockpit or climbing into the truck with the other survivors. "It was a 109."

"Yes sir, Squadron Leader Miller has already confirmed the kill and he says to please get ready, you're to scramble any minute again. You're to take Poppa Mike Kilo this time. Thank you for the kill, sir, that's one less of those devils . . . oh how I wish I could go up with you to help you all kill those monsters. . . ."

But they weren't monsters, he thought, at least the first pilot and first plane that he had killed had not been—just a youth like himself, perhaps the same age, who had burned screaming, died screaming, a flaming falling leaf, and this afternoon or tomorrow or soon it would be his turn—too many of them, the enemy, too few of us.

"Did Tommy get back, Tom Lane?"

"No sir, sorry sir. He . . . the squadron leader said Flight Lieutenant Lane was jumped over Dover."

"I'm petrified of burning, going down," he had said.

"Oh you won't, sir, not you. They won't shoot you down. *I know*. You won't, sir, no, not you. They'll never get you, never never never," she had said, pale blue eyes, fair hair and fair of face, not quite eighteen but strong, very strong and very confident.

He had believed her and her faith had carried him through four more months of missions—sometimes five missions each day—and more kills and though she was wrong and later he was blown out of the sky, he lived and burned only a little. And then, when he came out of the hospital, grounded forever, they had married.

"Doesn't seem like twenty years," he said, holding in his happiness.

"Plus two before," she said, holding in her happiness.

"Plus two be—"

The door opened. Penelope sighed as Ah Tat stalked into the room, talking Cantonese fifty to the dozen, "*Ayeeyah*, my Son, but aren't you ready yet, our honored guests will be here any moment and your tie's not tied and that motherless foreigner from North Kwantung brought unnecessarily into our house to cook tonight . . . that smelly offspring of a one-dollar strumpet from North Kwantung where all the best thieves and worst whores come from who fancies himself a cook . . . ha! . . . This man and his equally despicable foreign staff is befouling our kitchen and stealing our peace. *Oh ko*," the tiny wizened old woman continued without a breath as her clawlike fingers reached up automatically and deftly tied his tie, "and that's not all! Number Two Daughter . . . Number Two Daughter just won't put on the dress that Honorable First Wife has chosen for her and her rage is flying to Java! Eeeee, this family! Here, my Son," she took the telex envelope out of her pocket and handed it to Dunross, "here's another barbarian message bringing more congratulations for this happy day that your poor old Mother had to carry up the stairs herself on her poor old legs because the other good-for-nothing servants are good for nothing and bone idle. . . ." She paused momentarily for breath.

"Thank you, Mother," he said politely.

"In your Honorable Father's day, the servants worked and knew what to do and your old Mother didn't have to endure dirty strangers in our Great House!" She walked out muttering more curses on the caterers. "Now don't you be late, my Son, otherwise . . ." She was still talking after she'd closed the door.

"What's up with *her?*" Penelope asked wearily.

"She's rattling on about the caterers, doesn't like strangers—you know what she's like." He opened the envelope. In it was the folded telex.

"What was she saying about Glenna?" his wife asked, having recognized *yee-chat*, Second Daughter, though her Cantonese was minimal.

"Just that she was having a fit about the dress you picked for her."

"What's wrong with it?"

"Ah Tat didn't say. Look, Penn, perhaps Glenna should just go to bed —it's almost past her bedtime now and sh—"

"Dreamer! No chance till hell freezes over. Even Hag Struan wouldn't keep Glenna from her first grown-up as she calls it! You did agree Ian, *you* agreed, I didn't, you did!"

"Yes, but don't you th—"

"No. She's quite old enough. After all she's thirteen going on thirty." Penelope calmly finished her champagne. "Even so I shall now deal with that young lady never mind." She got up. Then she saw his face. He was staring at the telex.

"What's the matter?"

"One of our people's been killed. In London. Grant. Alan Medford Grant."

"Oh. I don't know him, do I?"

"I think you met him once in Ayrshire. He was a small, pixyish man. He was at one of our parties at Castle Avisyard—it was on our last leave."

She frowned. "Don't remember." She took the offered telex. It read: "Regret to inform you A. M. Grant was killed in motorcycle accident this morning. Details will follow when I have them. Sorry. Regards, Kiernan." "Who's Kiernan?"

"His assistant."

"Grant's . . . he was a friend?"

"In a way."

"He's important to you?"

"Yes."

"Oh, sorry."

Dunross forced himself to shrug and keep his voice level. But in his mind he was cursing obscenely. "Just one of those things. Joss."

She wanted to commiserate with him, recognizing at once the depth of his shock. She knew he was greatly perturbed, trying to hide it—and she wanted to know immediately the who and the why of this unknown man. But she held her peace.

That's my job, she reminded herself. Not to ask questions, to be calm and to be there—to pick up the pieces, but only when I'm allowed to. "Are you coming down?"

"In a moment."

"Don't be long, Ian."

"Yes."

"Thanks again for my bracelet," she said, liking it very much and he said, "It's nothing," but she knew he had not really heard her. He was already at the phone asking for long distance. She walked out and closed the door quietly and stood miserably in the long corridor that led to the east and west wings, her heart thumping. Curse all telexes and all telephones and curse Struan's and curse Hong Kong and curse all parties and all hangers-on and oh how I wish we could leave forever and forget Hong Kong and forget work and the Noble House and Big Business and the Pacific Rim and the stock market and all curs—

"Motherrrrr!"

She heard Glenna's voice screeching from the depths of her room around the far corner in the east wing and at once all her senses concentrated. There was frustrated rage in Glenna's voice, but no danger, so she did not hurry, just called back, "I'm coming . . . what is it, Glenna?"

"Where are *youuuuu?*"

"I'm coming, darling," she called out, her mind now on important things. Glenna will look pretty in that dress, she thought. Oh I know, she told herself happily, I'll lend her my little rope of pearls. That'll make it perfect.

Her pace quickened.

Across the harbor in Kowloon, Divisional Staff Sergeant Tang-po, CID, the High Dragon, climbed the rickety stairs and went into the room. The inner core of his secret triad was already there. "Get this through that bone some of you carry between your ears: the Dragons want Noble House Chen found and these pox-dripping, dung-eating Werewolves caught so fast even gods will blink!"

"Yes, Lord," his underlings chorused, shocked at the quality of his voice.

They were in Tang-po's safe house, a small, drab, three-room apartment behind a drab front door on the fifth floor of an equally drab apartment building over very modest shops in a dirty alley just three blocks from their police headquarters of Tsim Sha Tsui District that faced the harbor and the Peak on the tip of Kowloon Peninsula. There were nine of them:

one sergeant, two corporals, the rest constables—all plainclothes detectives of the CID, all Cantonese, all handpicked and sworn with blood oaths to loyalty and secrecy. They were Tang-po's secret *tong* or Brotherhood, which protected all street gambling in Tsim Sha Tsui District.

"Look everywhere, talk to everyone. We have three days," Tang-po said. He was a strongly built man of fifty-five with slightly graying hair and heavy eyebrows and his rank was the highest he could have and not be an officer. "This is the order of me—all my Brother Dragons—and the High One himself. Apart from that," he added sourly, "Big Mountain of Dung has promised to demote and post us to the border or other places, all of us, if we fail, and that's the first time he's ever threatened that. All gods piss from a great height on all foreign devils, particularly those motherless fornicators who won't accept their rightful squeeze and behave like civilized persons!"

"Amen!" Sergeant Lee said with great fervor. He was a sometimes Catholic because in his youth he had gone to a Catholic school.

"Big Mountain of Dung made it quite clear this afternoon: results, or off to the border where there's not a pot to piss in and no squeeze within twenty miles. *Ayeeyah,* all gods protect us from failure!"

"Yes," Corporal Ho said for all of them, making a note in his book. He was a sharp-featured man who was studying at night school to become an accountant, and it was he who kept the Brotherhood's books and minutes of their meetings.

"Elder Brother," Sergeant Lee began politely, "is there a fixed reward we can offer our informers? Is there a minimum or a maximum?"

"Yes," Tang-po told them, then added carefully, "The High Dragon has said 100,000 HK if within three days . . ." The room was suddenly silent at the vastness of the reward. ". . . half for finding Noble House Chen, half for finding the kidnappers. And a bonus of 10,000 to the Brother whose informer produces either—and promotion."

"One 10,000 for Chen and one ten for the kidnappers?" the corporal asked. O gods grant me the prize, he prayed, as they all were praying. "Is that right, Elder Brother?"

"*Dew neh loh moh* that's what I said," Tang-po replied sharply, puffing his cigarette. "Are your ears filled with pus?"

"Oh no, sorry Honorable Sir. Please excuse me."

All their minds were on the prize. Sergeant Lee was thinking, Eeee, 10,000 and—and promotion if in three days! Ah, if within three days then it will be in time for Race Day and then . . . O all gods great and small bless me this once and a second time on Saturday's double quinella.

Tang-po was referring to his notes. "Now to other business. Through the cooperation of Daytime Chang and the Honorable Song, the Brotherhood can use their showers daily at the V and A between 8:00 A.M. and 9:00 A.M., not 7:00 A.M. to 8:00 A.M. as before. Wives and concubines on a roster basis. Corporal Ho, you rearrange the roster."

"Hey, Honored Lord," one of the young detectives called out, "did you hear about Golden Pubics?"

"Eh?"

The youth related what Daytime Chang had told him this morning when he went to the hotel kitchens for breakfast. They all guffawed.

"*Ayeeyah*, imagine that! Like gold, *heya*?"

"Have you ever pillowed a foreign devil, Honorable Lord?"

"No never. No. *Ayeeyah*, the very thought . . . ugh!"

"I'd like one," Lee said with a laugh, "just to see what was what!"

They laughed with him and one called out, "A Jade Gate's a Jade Gate but they say some foreign devils are lopsided!"

"I heard they were cleft sideways!"

"Honored Sir, there was another thing," the young detective said when the laughter had died down. "Daytime Chang told me to tell you Golden Pubics has a miniature transmitter-receiver—best he'd ever seen, better than anything we've got, even in Special Branch. She carries it around with her."

Tang-po stared at him. "That's curious. Now why should a foreign devil woman want a thing like that?"

Lee said, "Something to do with the guns?"

"I don't know, Younger Brother. Women with transceivers? Interesting. It wasn't in her luggage when our people went through it last night, so it must've been in her handbag. Good, very good. Corporal Ho, after our meeting leave a gift for Daytime Chang—a couple of reds." A red note was 100 HK. "I'd certainly like to know who those guns were for," he added thoughtfully. "Make sure all our informers know I'm very interested in that too."

"Is Noble House Chen tied into the guns and these two foreign devils?" Lee asked.

"I think so, Younger Brother. I think so. Yes. Another curiosity—to send an ear is not civilized—not so soon. Not civilized at all."

"Ah, then you think the Werewolves're foreign devils? Or fornicating half-persons? Or Portuguese?"

"I don't know," Tang-po said sourly. "But it happened in our district, so it's a matter of face for all of us. Big Mountain of Dung is very enraged. His face is in the mangle too."

"Eeee," Lee said, "that fornicator has such a very filthy temper."

"Yes. Perhaps the information about the transceiver will appease him. I think I'll ask all my Brothers to put surveillance on Golden Pubics and her gun-running friend just in case. Now, there was something else. . . ." Again Tang-po referred to his notes. "Ah yes, why is our contribution from the Happy Hostess Night Club down 30 percent?"

"A new ownership's just taken over, Honored Sir," Sergeant Lee, in whose area the dance hall was, said. "One Eye Pok sold out to a Shanghainese fornicator called Wang—Happy Wang. Happy Wang says the Fragrant Grease's too high, business is bad, very bad."

"*Dew neh loh moh* on all Shanghainese. Is it?"

"It's down, but not much."

"That's right, Honored Sir," Corporal Ho said. "I was there at midnight to collect the fornicating week's advance—the stink fornicating place was about half full."

"Any foreign devils there?"

"Two or three, Honored Lord. No one of importance."

"Give Honorable Happy Wang a message from me: He has three weeks to improve his business. Then we'll reconsider. Corporal Ho, tell some of the girls at the Great New Oriental to recommend the Happy Hostess for a month or so—they've plenty of foreign devil customers . . . and tell Wang that there's a nuclear aircraft carrier—the *Corregidor*—coming in the day after tomorrow for R and R . . ." He used the English letters, everyone understanding rest and recreation from the Korean War days. "I'll ask my Brother Dragon in Wanchai and the dock area if Happy Wang can send some visiting cards over there. A thousand or so Golden Country barbarians will certainly be a help! They're here for eight days."

"Honored Sir, I'll do that tonight," Corporal Ho promised.

"My friend in marine police told me that there are going to be lots of visiting warships soon—the American Seventh Fleet is being increased." Tang-po frowned. "Doubled, so he says. The talk from the Mainland is that American soldiers are going to go into Vietnam in strength—they already run an airline there—at least," he added, "their triad CIA does."

"Eeee, that's good for business! We'll have to repair their ships. And entertain their men. Good! Very good for us."

"Yes. Very good. But very stupid for them. Honorable Chou En-lai's sent them warnings, politely, for months that China doesn't want them there! Why won't they listen? Vietnam's our outer barbarian sphere! Stupid to pick that foul jungle and those detestable barbarians to fight against. If China couldn't subdue those outer barbarians for centuries, how can they?" Tang-po laughed and lit another cigarette. "Where's old One Eye Pok gone?"

"That old fox's permanent visa came through and he was off on the next airplane to San Francisco—him, his wife and eight kids."

Tang-po turned to his accountant. "Did he owe us any money?"

"Oh no Honored Sir. He was fully paid up-to-date, Sergeant Lee saw to that."

"How much did it cost that old fornicator? To get the visa?"

"His exit was smoothed by a gift of 3,000 HK to Corporal Sek Pun So in Immigration on our recommendation—our percentage was paid—we also assisted him to find the right diamond merchant to convert his wealth into the best blue whites available." Ho referred to his books. "Our 2 percent commission came to 8,960 HK."

"Good old One Eye!" Tang-po said, pleased for him. "He's done very well for himself. What was his 'unique services' job for his visa?"

Sergeant Lee said, "A cook in a restaurant in Chinatown—the Good Eating Place it's called. *Oh ko,* I've tasted his home cooking and old One Eye is very bad indeed."

"He'll hire another to take his place while he goes into real estate, or gambling and a nightclub," someone said. "Eeee, what joss!"

"But what did his U.S. visa cost him?"

"Ah, the golden gift to Paradise!" Ho sighed. "I heard he paid 5,000 U.S. to jump to the head of the list."

"*Ayeeyah*, that's more than usual! Why?"

"It seems there's also a promise of a U.S. passport as soon as the five years are up and not too much harassment about his English—old One Eye doesn't talk English as you know. . . ."

"Those fornicators from the Golden Country—they squeeze but they aren't organized. They've no style, none at all," Tang-po said scornfully. "One or two visas here and there—when everyone here knows you can buy one if you're at the right time with the right squeeze. So why don't they do it properly in a civilized way? Twenty visas a week—even forty— they're all mad these foreign devils!"

"*Dew neh loh moh* but you're right," Sergeant Lee said, his mind boggled at the potential amount of squeeze he could make if he were a vice-consul in the U.S. Consulate of Hong Kong in the Visa Department. "Eeeeee!"

"We should have a civilized person in that position, then we'd soon be set up like Mandarins and policing San Francisco!" Tang-po said, and they all guffawed with him. Then he added disgustedly, "At least they should have a man there, not one who likes a Steaming Stalk in his Ghastly Gulley, or his in another's!"

They laughed even more. "Hey," one of them called out, "I heard his partner's young Foreign Devil Stinknose Pork Belly in the Public Works— you know, the one who's selling building permits that shouldn't be!"

"That's old news, Chan, very old. They've both moved on to unwiser pastures. The latest rumor is our vice-consul devil's connected with a youth. . . ." Tang-po added delicately, "Son of a prominent accountant who's also a prominent Communist."

"Eeeee, that's not good," Sergeant Lee said, knowing at once who the man was.

"No," Tang-po agreed. "Particularly as I heard yesterday the youth has a secret flat around the corner. In my district! And my district has the least crime of any."

"That's right," they all said proudly.

"Should he be spoken to, Elder Brother?" Lee asked.

"No, just put under special surveillance. I want to know all about these two. Everything. Even if they belch." Tang-po sighed. He gave Sergeant

Lee the address and made the work assignments. "Since you're all here,
I've decided to bring payday forward from tomorrow." He opened the
large bag that contained bank notes. Each man received the equivalent of
his police pay plus authorized expenses.

300 HK a month salary with no expenses was not enough for a constable to feed even a small family and have a small flat, not even a two-room
apartment with one tap and no sanitation, and to send one child to school;
or enough to be able to send a little back to the home village in the
Kwantung to needy fathers and grandmothers and mothers and uncles
and grandfathers, many of whom, years upon years ago, had given their
life's saving to help launch him on the broken road to Hong Kong.

Tang-po had been one of these. He was very proud that he had survived the journey as a six-year-old, alone, and had found his relations and
then, when he was eighteen, had joined the police—thirty-six years ago.
He had served the Queen well, the police force impeccably, the Japanese
enemy during their occupation not at all and now was in charge of a key
division in the Colony of Hong Kong. Respected, rich, with one son in
college in San Francisco, another owning half a restaurant in Vancouver,
Canada, his family in Kwantung supported—and, most important, his Division of Tsim Sha Tsui with less unsolved robberies, less unsolved
woundings and maimings and triad wars than any other district—and only
three murders in four years and all solved and the culprits caught and sen-
tenced, and one of those a foreign devil seaman who'd killed another over
a dance-hall girl. And almost no petty theft and never a tourist foreign
devil harassed by beggars or sneak thieves and this the largest tourist area
with upward of also 300,000 civilized persons to police and protect from
evildoers and from themselves.

Ayeeyah, yes, Tang-po told himself. If it wasn't for us those bone-
headed fornicating peasants'd be at each other's throats, raging, looting,
killing, and then the inevitable mob cry would go up: Kill the foreign
devils! And they would try and then we would be back in the riots again.
Fornicate disgustingly all wrongdoers and unpeaceful persons!

"Now," he said affably, "we'll meet in three days. I've ordered a ten-
course feast from Great Food Chang's. Until then, let everyone put an eye
to the orifice of the gods and get me the answers. I want the Werewolves
—and I want John Chen back. Sergeant Lee, you stay a moment. Corporal
Ho, write up the minutes and let me have the accounts tomorrow at five."

"Yes, Honored Lord."

They all trooped out. Tang-po lit another cigarette. So did Sergeant
Lee. Tang-po coughed.

"You should quit smoking, Elder Brother."

"So should you!" Tang-po shrugged. "Joss! If I'm to go, I'm to go. Joss.
Even so, for peace I've told my Chief Wife I've stopped. She nags and
nags and nags."

"Show me one that doesn't and she'll turn out to be a he with a ghastly gulley."

They laughed together.

"That's the truth. *Heya,* last week she insisted I see a doctor and you know what that motherless fornicator said? He said, you'd better give up smoking, old friend, or you'll be nothing but a few cinders in a burial jar before you're twenty moons older and then I guarantee your Chief Wife'll be spending all your money on loose boys and your concubine'll be tasting another's fruits!"

"The swine! Oh the swine!"

"Yes. He really frightened me—I felt his words right down in my secret sack! But maybe he was speaking the truth."

He took out a handkerchief, blew his nose, his breath wheezing, cleared his throat noisily and spat into the spittoon. "Listen, Younger Brother, our High Dragon says the time has come to organize Smuggler Yuen, White Powder Lee, and his cousin Four Finger Wu."

Sergeant Lee stared at him in shock. These three men were believed to be the High Tigers of the opium trade in Hong Kong. Importers and exporters. For local use and also, rumor had it, for export to the Golden Country where the great money was. Opium brought in secretly and converted into morphine and then into heroin. "Bad, very bad. We've never touched that trade before."

"Yes," Tang-po said delicately.

"That'd be very dangerous. Narcotics Branch are very serious against it. Big Mountain of Dung himself is very seriously interested in catching those three—very fornicating serious."

Tang-po stared at the ceiling. Then he said, "The High Dragon explained it this way: A ton of opium in the Golden Triangle costs 67,000 U.S. Changed into fornicating morphine and then into fornicating heroin and the pure heroin diluted to 5 percent, the usual strength on the streets of the Golden Country, delivered there you have almost 680 million worth in American dollars. From one ton of opium." Tang-po coughed and lit another cigarette.

The sweat began on Lee's back. "How many tons could go through those three fornicators?"

"We don't know. But he's been told about 380 tons a year are grown in the whole Golden Triangle—Yunnan, Burma, Laos and Thailand. Much of it comes here. They'd handle 50 tons, he said. He's certain of 50 tons."

"*Oh ko!*"

"Yes." Tang-po was sweating too. "Our High Dragon says we should invest in the trade now. It's going to grow and grow. He has a plan to get Marine with us. . . ."

"*Dew neh loh moh,* you can't trust those seagoing bastards."

"That's what I said, but he said we need the seagoing bastards and we can trust a selected few, who else can snatch and intercept a token 20 percent—even 50 percent to appease Mountain of Dung himself at prearranged moments?" Tang-po spat deftly again. "If we could get Marine, Narcotics Branch, and the Gang of Three, our present *h'eung yau* would be like an infant's piddle in the harbor."

There was a serious silence in the room.

"We would have to recruit new members and that's always dangerous."

"Yes."

Lee helped himself to the teapot and poured some jasmine tea, sweat running down his back now, the smoke-ladened air sultry and overbearing. He waited.

"What do you think, Younger Brother?"

These two men were not related but used the Chinese politeness between themselves because they had trusted each other for more than fifteen years. Lee had saved his superior's life in the riots of 1956. He was thirty-five now and his heroism in the riots had earned him a police medal. He was married and had three children. He had served sixteen years in the force and his whole pay was 843 HK a month. He took the tram to work. Without supplementing his income through the Brotherhood, like all of them, he would have had to walk or bicycle, most days. The tram took two hours.

"I think the idea is very bad," he said. "Drugs, any drugs, that's fornicating bad—yes, very bad. Opium, that's bad though it's good for old people—the white powder, cocaine, that's bad, but not as bad as the death squirts. It'd be bad joss to deal in the death squirts."

"I told him the same."

"Are you going to obey him?"

"What's good for one Brother should be good for all," Tang-po said thoughtfully, avoiding an answer.

Again Lee waited. He did not know how a Dragon was elected, or exactly how many there were, or who the High Dragon was. He only knew that his Dragon was Tang-po who was a wise and cautious man who had their interests at heart.

"He also said one or two of our foreign devil superiors are getting itchy piles about their fornicating slice of the gambling money."

Lee spat disgustedly. "What do those fornicators do for their share? Nothing. Just close their fornicating eyes. Except the Snake." This was the nickname of Chief Inspector Donald C. C. Smyth who openly organized his district of East Aberdeen and sold favors and protection on all levels, in front of his Chinese underlings.

"Ah him! He should be stuffed down the sewer, that fornicator. Soon those who he pays off above him won't be able to hide his stink anymore. And his stench'll spread over all of us."

"He's due to retire in a couple of years," Lee said darkly. "Perhaps he'll finger his rear to all those high-ups until he leaves and there won't be a thing they can do. His friends are very high, so they say."

"Meanwhile?" Tang-po asked.

Lee sighed. "My advice, Elder Brother, is to be cautious, not to do it if you can avoid it. If you can't . . ." he shrugged. "Joss. Is it decided?"

"No, not yet. It was mentioned at our weekly meeting. For consideration."

"Has an approach been made to the Gang of Three?"

"I understand White Powder Lee made the approach, Younger Brother. It seems the three are going to join together."

Lee gasped. "With blood oaths?"

"It seems so."

"They're going to work together? Those devils?"

"So they said. I'll bet old Four Finger Wu will be the Highest Tiger."

"*Ayeeyah,* that one? They say he's murdered fifty men himself," Lee said darkly. He shivered at the danger. "They must have three hundred fighters in their pay. It'd be better for all of us if those three were dead—or behind bars."

"Yes. But meanwhile White Powder Lee says they're ready to expand, and for a little cooperation from us they can *guarantee* a giant return." Tang-po mopped his brow and coughed and lit another cigarette. "Listen, Little Brother," he said softly. "He swears they've been offered a very large source of American money, cash money and bank money, and a very large retail outlet for their goods there, based in this place called Manhattan."

Lee felt the sweat on his forehead. "A retail outlet there . . . *ayeeyah,* that means millions. They will guarantee?"

"Yes. With very little for us to do. Except close our eyes and make sure Marine and Narcotics Branch seize only the correct shipments and close their eyes when they're supposed to. Isn't it written in the Ancient Books: If you don't squeeze, lightning will strike you?"

Again a silence. "When does the decision . . . when's it going to be decided?"

"Next week. If it's decided yes, well, the flow of trade will take months to organize, perhaps a year." Tang-po glanced at the clock and got up. "Time for our shower. Nighttime Song has arranged dinner for us afterwards."

"Eeeee, very good." Uneasily Lee turned out the single overhead light. "And if the decision is no?"

Tang-po stubbed out his cigarette and coughed. "If no . . ." He shrugged. "We only have one life, gods notwithstanding, so it is our duty to think of our families. One of my relations is a captain with Four Finger Wu. . . ."

11

"Hello, Brian," Dunross said. "Welcome."

"Evening, tai-pan—congratulations—great night for a party," Brian Kwok said. A liveried waiter appeared out of nowhere and he accepted a glass of champagne in fine crystal. "Thanks for inviting me."

"You're very welcome." Dunross was standing beside the door of the ballroom in the Great House, tall and debonair, Penelope a few paces away greeting other guests. The half-full ballroom was open to crowded floodlit terraces and gardens where the majority of brightly dressed ladies and dinner-jacketed men stood in groups or sat at round tables. A cool breeze had come with nightfall.

"Penelope darling," Dunross called out, "you remember Superintendent Brian Kwok."

"Oh of course," she said, threading her way over to them with her happy smile, not remembering at all. "How're you?"

"Fine thanks—congratulations!"

"Thank you—make yourself at home. Dinner's at nine fifteen, Claudia has the seating lists if you've lost your card. Oh excuse me a moment. . . ." She turned away to intercept some other guests, her eyes trying to watch everywhere to see that everything was going well and that no one stood alone—knowing in her secret heart that if there was a disaster there was nothing for her to do, that others would make everything well again.

"You're very lucky, Ian," Brian Kwok said. "She gets younger every year."

"Yes."

"So. Here's to twenty more years! Health!" They touched glasses. They had been friends since the early fifties when they had met at the first racing hill climb and had been friendly rivals ever since—and founding members of the Hong Kong Sports Car and Rally Club.

"But you, Brian, no special girl friend? You arrive alone?"

"I'm playing the field." Brian Kwok dropped his voice. "Actually I'm staying single permanently."

"Dreamer! This's your year—you're the catch of Hong Kong. Even Claudia's got her eyes on you. You're a dead duck, old chap."

"Oh Christ!" Brian dropped the banter for a moment. "Say, tai-pan, could I have a couple of private minutes this evening?"

"John Chen?" Dunross asked at once.

"No. We've got every man looking, but nothing yet. It's something else."

"Business?"

"Yes."

"How private?"

"Private."

"All right," Dunross said, "I'll find you after dinner. What ab—"

A burst of laughter caused them to look around. Casey was standing in the center of an admiring group of men—Linbar Struan and Andrew Gavallan and Jacques deVille among them—just outside one of the tall French doors that led to the terrace.

"Eeeee," Brian Kwok muttered.

"Quite," Dunross said and grinned.

She was dressed in a floor-length sheath of emerald silk, molded just enough and sheer just enough.

"Christ, is she or isn't she?"

"What?"

"Wearing anything underneath?"

"Seek and ye shall find."

"I'd like to. She's stunning."

"I thought so too," Dunross said agreeably, "though I'd say 100 percent of the other ladies don't."

"Her breasts are perfect, you can see that."

"Actually you can't. Just. It's all in your mind."

"I'll bet there isn't a pair in Hong Kong to touch them."

"Fifty dollars to a copper cash says you're wrong—provided we include Eurasians."

"How can we prove who wins?"

"We can't. Actually I'm an ankle man myself."

"What?"

"Old Uncle Chen-Chen used to say, 'First look at the ankles, my son, then you tell her breeding, how she'll behave, how she'll ride, how she'll . . . like any filly. But remember, all crows under heaven are black!' "

Brian Kwok grinned with him then waved at someone in friendly style. Across the room a tall man with a lived-in face was waving back. Beside him was an extraordinarily beautiful woman, tall, fair, with gray eyes. She waved happily too.

"Now there's an English beauty at her best!"

"Who? Oh, Fleur Marlowe? Yes, yes she is. I didn't know you knew the Marlowes, tai-pan."

"Likewise! I met him this afternoon, Brian. You've known him long?"

"Oh a couple of months-odd. He's persona grata with us."

"Oh?"

"Yes. We're showing him the ropes."

"Oh? Why?"

"Some months ago he wrote to the commissioner, said he was coming to Hong Kong to research a novel and asked for our cooperation. Seems the Old Man happened to have read his first novel and had seen some of his films. Of course we checked him out and he appears all right." Brian Kwok's eyes went back to Casey. "The Old Man thought we could do with an improved image so he sent word down that, within limits, Peter was approved and to show him around." He glanced back at Dunross and smiled thinly. "Ours not to reason why!"

"What was his book?"

"Called *Changi*, about his POW days. The Old Man's brother died there, so I suppose it hit home."

"Have you read it?"

"Not me—I've too many mountains to climb! I did skim a few pages. Peter says it's fiction but I don't believe him." Brian Kwok laughed. "He can drink beer though. Robert had him on a couple of his Hundred Pinters and he held his end up." A Hundred Pinter was a police stag party to which the officers contributed a barrel of a hundred pints of beer. When the beer was gone, the party ended.

Brian Kwok's eyes were feasting on Casey, and Dunross wondered for the millionth time why Asians favored Anglo-Saxons and Anglo-Saxons favored Asians.

"Why the smile, tai-pan?"

"No reason. But Casey's not bad at all, is she?"

"Fifty dollars says she's *bat jam gai, heya?*"

Dunross thought a moment, weighing the bet carefully. *Bat jam gai* meant, literally, white chicken meat. This was the way Cantonese referred to ladies who shaved off their pubic hair. "Taken! You're wrong, Brian, she's *see yau gai*," which meant soya chicken, "or in her case red, tender and nicely spicy. I have it on the highest authority!"

Brian laughed. "Introduce me."

"Introduce yourself. You're over twenty-one."

"I'll let you win the hill climb on Sunday!"

"Dreamer! Off you go and a thousand says you won't."

"What odds'll you give me?"

"You must be joking!"

"No harm in asking. Christ, I'd like to carry the book on that one. Where's the lucky Mr. Bartlett?"

"I think he's in the garden—I told Adryon to chaperone him. Excuse me a moment. . . ." Dunross turned away to greet someone Brian Kwok did not recognize.

Upward of 150 guests had already arrived and been greeted personally. Dinner was for 217, each carefully seated according to face and custom at round tables that were already set and candlelit on the lawns. Candles and candelabra in the halls, liveried waiters offering champagne in cut glass crystal, or smoked salmon and caviar from silver trays and tureens.

A small band was playing on the dais and Brian Kwok saw a few uniforms among the dinner jackets, American and British, army, navy and air force. It was no surprise that Europeans were dominant. This party was strictly for the British inner circle that ruled Central District and were the power block of the Colony, their Caucasian friends, and a few very special Eurasians, Chinese and Indians. Brian Kwok recognized most of the guests: Paul Havergill of the Victoria Bank of Hong Kong, old Sir Samuel Samuels, multimillionaire, tai-pan of twenty real estate, banking, ferry and stockbroking companies; Christian Toxe, editor of the *China Guardian*, talking to Richard Kwang, chairman of the Ho-Pak Bank; multimillionaire shipowner V. K. Lam talking to Phillip and Dianne Chen, their son Kevin with them; the American Zeb Cooper, inheritor of the oldest American trading company, Cooper-Tillman, having his ear bent by Sir Dunstan Barre, tai-pan of Hong Kong and Lan Tao Farms. He noticed Ed Langan, the FBI man, among the guests and this surprised him. He had not known that Langan or the man he was talking to, Stanley Rosemont, a deputy director of the China-watching CIA contingent, were friends of Dunross. He let his eyes drift over the chattering group of men, and the mostly separate groups of their wives.

They're all here, he thought, all the tai-pans except Gornt and Plumm, all the pirates, all here in incestuous hatred to pay homage to *the* tai-pan.

Which one is the spy, the traitor, controller of Sevrin, *Arthur*?

He's got to be European.

I'll bet he's here. And I'll catch him. Yes. I'll catch him, soon, now that I know about him. We'll catch him and catch them all, he thought grimly. And we'll catch these crooks with their hands in their tills, we'll stamp out their piracies for the common good.

"Champagne, Honored Sir," the waiter asked in Cantonese with a toothy smile.

Brian accepted a full glass. "Thank you."

The waiter bowed to hide his lips. "The tai-pan had a blue-covered file among his papers when he came in tonight," he whispered quickly.

"Is there a safe, a secret hiding place here?" Brian asked equally cautiously in the same dialect.

"The servants say in his office on the next floor," the man said. His name was Wine Waiter Feng, and he was one of SI's undercover network of intelligence agents. His cover as a waiter for the company that catered all Hong Kong's best and most exclusive parties gave him great value.

"Perhaps it's behind the painting, I heard. . . ." He stopped suddenly and switched to pidgin English. "Champ-igy-nee Missee?" he asked tooth-ily, offering the tray to the tiny old Eurasian lady who was coming up to them. "Wery wery first class."

"Don't you Missee me, you impertinent young puppy," she rapped haughtily in Cantonese.

"Yes, Honored Great-Aunt, sorry, Honored Great-Aunt." He beamed and fled.

"So, young Brian Kwok," the old lady said, peering up at him. She was eighty-eight, Sarah Chen, Phillip Chen's aunt, a tiny birdlike person with pale white skin and Asian eyes that darted this way and that. And though she appeared frail her back was upright and her spirit very strong. "I'm glad to see you. Where's John Chen? Where's my poor grand-nephew?"

"I don't know, Great Lady," he said politely.

"When are you going to get my Number One Grand-nephew back?"

"Soon. We're doing everything we can."

"Good. And don't you interfere with young Phillip if he wants to pay John's ransom privately. You see to it."

"Yes. I'll do what I can. Is John's wife here?"

"Eh? Who? Speak up, boy!"

"Is Barbara Chen here?"

"No. She came earlier but as soon as *that* woman arrived she 'got a headache' and left. Huh, I don't blame her at all!" Her old rheumy eyes were watching Dianne Chen across the room. "Huh, that woman! Did you see her entrance?"

"No, Great Lady."

"Huh, like Dame Nellie Melba herself. She swept in, handkerchief to her eyes, her eldest son Kevin in tow—I don't like that boy—and my poor nephew Phillip like a second-class cook boy in the rear. Huh! The only time Dianne Chen ever wept was in the crash of '56 when her stocks went down and she lost a fortune and wet her drawers. Ha! Look at her now, preening herself! Pretending to be upset when everyone knows she's act-ing as though she's already Dowager Empress! I could pinch her cheeks! Disgusting!" She looked back at Brian Kwok. "You find my grand-nephew John—I don't want that woman or her brat *loh-pan* of our house."

"But he can be *tai-pan?*"

They laughed together. Very few Europeans knew that though *tai-pan* meant great leader, in the old days in China a *tai-pan* was the colloquial title of a man in charge of a whorehouse or public toilet. So no Chinese would ever call himself *tai-pan*, only *loh-pan*—which also meant great leader or head leader. Chinese and Eurasians were greatly amused that Europeans enjoyed calling themselves *tai-pan*, stupidly passing over the correct title.

"Yes. If he's the right *pan*," the old woman said and they chuckled. "You find my John Chen, young Brian Kwok!"

"Yes. Yes we'll find him."

"Good. Now, what do you think of Golden Lady's chances on Saturday?"

"Good, if the going's dry. At three to one she's worth a bundle. Watch Noble Star—she's got a chance too."

"Good. After dinner come and find me. I want to talk to you."

"Yes, Great Lady." He smiled and watched her go off and knew that all she wanted was to try to act the marriage broker for some great-niece. *Ayeeyah*, I'll have to do something about that soon, he thought.

His eyes strayed back to Casey. He was delighted by the disapproving looks from all the women—and the cautious covert admiration from all their escorts. Then Casey glanced up and saw him watching her across the room and she stared back at him briefly with equal frank appraisal.

Dew neh loh moh, he thought uneasily, feeling somehow undressed. I'd like to possess that one. Then he noticed Roger Crosse with Armstrong beside him. He put his mind together and headed for them.

"Evening, sir."

"Evening, Brian. You're looking very distinguished."

"Thank you, sir." He knew better than to volunteer anything pleasant in return. "I'm seeing the tai-pan after dinner."

"Good. As soon as you've seen him, find me."

"Yes sir."

"So you think the American girl stunning?"

"Yes sir." Brian sighed inwardly. He had forgotten that Crosse could lip-read English, French and some Arabic—he spoke no Chinese dailects—and that his eyesight was exceptional.

"Actually she's rather obvious," Crosse said.

"Yes sir." He saw Crosse concentrating on her lips and knew that he was overhearing her conversation from across the room and he was furious with himself that he had not developed the talent.

"She seems to have a passion for computers." Crosse turned his eyes back on them. "Curious, what?"

"Yes sir."

"What did Wine Waiter Feng say?"

Brian told him.

"Good. I'll see Feng gets a bonus. I didn't expect to see Langan and Rosemont here."

"It could be a coincidence, sir," Brian Kwok volunteered. "They're both keen punters. They've both been to the tai-pan's box."

"I don't trust coincidences," Crosse said. "As far as Langan's concerned, of course you know nothing, either of you."

"Yes sir."

"Good. Perhaps you'd both better be about our business."

"Yes sir." Thankfully the two men turned to leave but stopped as there was a sudden hush. All eyes went to the doorway. Quillan Gornt stood there, black-browed, black-bearded, conscious that he had been noticed. The other guests hastily picked up their conversations and kept their eyes averted but their ears concentrated.

Crosse whistled softly. "Now why is he here?"

"Fifty to one says he's up to no good," Brian Kwok said, equally astounded.

They watched Gornt come into the ballroom and put out his hand to Dunross and Penelope beside him. Claudia Chen who was nearby was in shock, wondering how she could reorganize Dunross's table at such short notice because of course Gornt would have to be seated there.

"I hope you don't mind my changing my mind at the last moment," Gornt was saying, his mouth smiling.

"Not at all," Dunross replied, his mouth smiling.

"Good evening, Penelope. I felt I had to give you my congratulations personally."

"Oh, thank you," she said. Her smile was intact but her heart was beating very fast now. "I, I was sorry to hear about your wife."

"Thank you." Emelda Gornt had been arthritic and confined to a wheelchair for some years. Early in the year she had caught pneumonia and had died. "She was very unlucky," Gornt said. He looked at Dunross. "Bad joss about John Chen too."

"Very."

"I suppose you read the afternoon *Gazette?*"

Dunross nodded and Penelope said, "Enough to frighten everyone out of their wits." All the afternoon papers had had huge headlines and dwelt at length on the mutilated ear and the Werewolves. There was a slight pause. She rushed to fill it. "Your children are well?"

"Yes. Annagrey's going to the University of California in September— Michael is here on his summer holiday. They're all in very good shape I'm glad to say. And yours?"

"They're fine. I do wish Adryon would go to university though. Dear me, children are very difficult these days, aren't they?"

"I think they always were." Gornt smiled thinly. "My father was always pointing out how difficult I was." He looked at Dunross again.

"Yes. How is your father?"

"Hale and hearty I'm glad to say. The English climate suits him, he says. He's coming out for Christmas." Gornt accepted a proffered glass of champagne. The waiter quailed under his look, and fled. He raised his glass. "A happy life and many congratulations."

Dunross toasted him in return, still astonished that Gornt had arrived. It was only for politeness and for face that Gornt and other enemies had been sent formal invitations. A polite refusal was all that was expected— and Gornt had already refused.

Why's he here?

He's come to gloat, Dunross thought. Like his bloody father. That must be the reason. But why? What devilment has he done to us? Bartlett? Is it through Bartlett?

"This's a lovely room, beautiful proportions," Gornt was saying. "And a lovely house. I've always envied you this house."

Yes, you bastard, I know, Dunross thought furiously, remembering the last time any of the Gornts had been in the Great House. Ten years ago, in 1953, when Ian's father, Colin Dunross, was still *the* tai-pan. It was during Struan's Christmas party, traditionally the biggest of the season, and Quillan Gornt had arrived with his father, William, then tai-pan of Rothwell-Gornt, again unexpectedly. After dinner there had been a bitter, public clash between the two tai-pans in the billiard room where a dozen or so of the men had gathered for a game. That was when Struan's had just been blocked by the Gornts and their Shanghainese friends in their attempt to take over South Orient Airways, which, because of the Communist conquest of the Mainland, had just become available. This feeder airline monopolized all air traffic in and out of Shanghai from Hong Kong, Singapore, Taipei, Tokyo and Bangkok, and if merged with Air Struan, their fledgling airline, Struan's would have virtual feeder monopoly in the Far East based out of Hong Kong. Both men had accused the other of underhand practices—both accusations were true.

Yes, Ian Dunross told himself, both men went to the brink that time. William Gornt had tried every way to become established in Hong Kong after Rothwell-Gornt's huge losses in Shanghai. And when Colin Dunross knew Struan's could not prevail, he had snatched South Orient out of William Gornt's grasp by throwing his weight to a safe Cantonese group.

"And so you did, Colin Dunross, so you did. You fell into the trap and you'll never stop us now," William Gornt had gloated. "We're here to stay. We'll hound you out of Asia, you and your god-cursed Noble House. South Orient's just the beginning. We've won!"

"The hell you have! The Yan-Wong-Sun group's associated with us. We have a contract."

"It's hereby canceled." William Gornt had motioned to Quillan, his eldest son and heir apparent, who took out the copy of an agreement. "This contract's between the Yan-Wong-Sun group who're nominees of the Tso-Wa-Feng group," he said happily, "who're nominees of Ta-Weng-Sap who sells control of South Orient to Rothwell-Gornt for one dollar more than the original cost!" Quillan Gornt had laid it on the billiard table with a flourish. "South Orient's ours!"

"I don't believe it!"

"You can. Happy Christmas!" William Gornt had given a great, scorn-filled laugh, and walked out. Quillan had replaced his billiard cue, laughing too. Ian Dunross had been near the door.

"One day I'll own this house," Quillan Gornt had hissed at him, then turned and called out to the others, "If any of you want jobs, come to us. Soon you'll all be out of work. Your Noble House won't be noble much longer." Andrew Gavallan had been there, Jacques deVille, Alastair Struan, Lechie and David MacStruan, Phillip Chen, even John Chen.

Dunross remembered how his father had raged that night, and blamed treachery and nominees and bad joss, knowing all the time that he himself had warned him, many times, and that his warnings had been shoved aside. Christ, how we lost face! All Hong Kong laughed at us that time— the Noble House peed on from a great height by the Gornts and their Shanghainese interlopers.

Yes. But that night finalized Colin Dunross's downfall. That was the night I decided that he had to go before the Noble House was lost forever. I used Alastair Struan. I helped him to shove my father aside. Alastair Struan had to become tai-pan. Until I was wise enough and strong enough to shove him aside.

Am I wise enough now?

I don't know, Dunross thought, concentrating on Quillan Gornt now, listening to his pleasantries, hearing himself react with equal charm, while his mind said, I haven't forgotten South Orient, or that we had to merge our airline with yours at a fire-sale price and lose control of the new line renamed All Asia Airways. Nothing's forgotten. We lost that time but this time we'll win. We'll win everything, by God.

Casey was watching both men with fascination. She had noticed Quillan Gornt from the first moment, recognizing him from the photographs of the dossier. She had sensed his strength and masculinity even from across the room and had been uneasily excited by him. As she watched, she could almost touch the tension between the two men squaring off—two bulls in challenge.

Andrew Gavallan had told her at once who Gornt was. She had volunteered nothing, just asked Gavallan and Linbar Struan why they were so shocked at Gornt's arrival. And then, as they were alone now, the four of them—Casey, Gavallan, deVille and Linbar Struan—they told her about the "Happy Christmas" and "One day I'll own this house."

"What did the tai-pan . . . what did Ian do?" she asked.

Gavallan said, "He just looked at Gornt. You knew if he had a gun or a knife or a cudgel he'd've used it, you just knew it, and as he hadn't a weapon you knew any moment he was going to use his hands or teeth. . . . He just stood rock still and looked at Gornt and Gornt went back a pace, out of range—literally. But that bugger Gornt's got *cojones*. He sort of gathered himself together and stared back at Ian for a moment. Then, without saying a word he went around him slowly, very cautiously, his eyes never leaving Ian, and he left."

"What's that bastard doing here tonight?" Linbar muttered.

Gavallan said, "It's got to be important."

"Which one?" Linbar asked. "Which important?"

Casey looked at him and at the edge of her peripheral vision she saw Jacques deVille shake his head warningly and at once the shades came down on Linbar and on Gavallan. Even so she asked, "What *is* Gornt doing here?"

"I don't know," Gavallan told her, and she believed him.

"Have they met since that Christmas?"

"Oh yes, many times, all the time," Gavallan told her. "Socially of course. Then, too, they're on the boards of companies, committees, councils together." Uneasily he added, "But . . . well I'm sure they're both just waiting."

She saw their eyes wander back to the two enemies and her eyes followed. Her heart was beating strongly. They saw Penelope move away to talk to Claudia Chen. In a moment, Dunross glanced across at them. She knew he was signaling Gavallan in some way. Then his eyes were on her. Gornt followed his glance. Now both men were looking at her. She felt their magnetism. It intoxicated her. A devil in her pushed her feet toward them. She was glad now that she had dressed as she had, more provocatively than she had planned, but Linc had told her this was a night to be less businesslike.

As she walked she felt the brush of the silk, and her nipples hardened. She felt their eyes flow over her, undressing her, and this time, strangely, she did not mind. Her walk became imperceptibly more feline.

"Hello, tai-pan," she said with pretended innocence. "You wanted me to join you?"

"Yes," he replied at once. "I believe you two know each other."

She shook her head and smiled at both of them, not noticing the trap. "No. We've never met. But of course I know who Mr. Gornt is. Andrew told me."

"Ah, then let me introduce you formally. Mr. Quillan Gornt, tai-pan of Rothwell-Gornt. Miss Tcholok—Ciranoush Tcholok—from America."

She held out her hand, knowing the danger of getting between the two men, half her mind warmed by the danger the other half shouting, Jesus, what're you doing here.

"I've heard a lot about you, Mr. Gornt," she said, pleased that her voice was controlled, pleased by the touch of his hand—different from Dunross's, rougher and not as strong. "I believe the rivalry of your firms goes back generations?"

"Only three. It was my grandfather who first felt the not so tender mercies of the Struans," Gornt said easily. "One day I'd enjoy telling you our side of the legends."

"Perhaps you two should smoke a pipe of peace," she said. "Surely Asia's wide enough for both of you."

"The whole world isn't," Dunross said affably.

"No," Gornt agreed, and if she had not heard the real story she would have presumed from their tone and manner they were just friendly rivals.

"In the States we've many huge companies—and they live together peacefully. In competition."

"This isn't America," Gornt said calmly. "How long will you be here, Miss Tcholok?"

"That depends on Linc—Linc Bartlett—I'm with Par-Con Industries."

"Yes, yes I know. Didn't he tell you we're having dinner on Tuesday?"

The danger signals poured through her. "Tuesday?"

"Yes. We arranged it this morning. At our meeting. Didn't he mention it?"

"No," she said, momentarily in shock. Both men were watching her intently and she wished she could back off and come back in five minutes when she had thought this through. Jesus, she thought and fought to retain her poise as all the implications swamped her. "No," she said again, "Linc didn't mention any meeting. What did you arrange?"

Gornt glanced at Dunross who still listened expressionlessly. "Just to have dinner next Tuesday. Mr. Bartlett and yourself—if you're free."

"That would be nice—thank you."

"Where's your Mr. Bartlett now?" he asked.

"In—in the garden, I think."

Dunross said, "Last time I saw him he was on the terrace. Adryon was with him. Why?"

Gornt took out a gold cigarette case and offered it to her.

"No thank you," she said. "I don't smoke."

"Does it bother you if I do?"

She shook her head.

Gornt lit a cigarette and looked at Dunross. "I'd just like to say hello to him, before I leave," he said pleasantly. "I hope you don't mind me coming for just a few minutes—if you'll excuse me I won't stay for dinner. I have some pressing business to attend to . . . you understand."

"Of course." Dunross added, "Sorry you can't stay."

Neither man showed anything in his face. Except the eyes. It was in their eyes. Hatred. Fury. The depth shocked her. "Ask Ian Dunross to show you the Long Gallery," Gornt was saying to her. "I hear there're some fine portraits there. I've never been in the Long Gallery—only the billiard room." A chill went down her spine as he looked again at Dunross who watched him back.

"This meeting this morning," Casey said, thinking clearly now, judging it wise to bring everything out in front of Dunross at once. "When was it arranged?"

"About three weeks ago," Gornt said. "I thought you were his chief executive, I'm surprised he didn't mention it to you."

"Linc's our tai-pan, Mr. Gornt. I work for him. He doesn't have to tell me everything," she said, calmer now. "Should he have told me, Mr. Gornt? I mean, was it important?"

"It could be. Yes. I confirmed, formally, that we can better any offer

Struan's can make. Any offer." Gornt glanced back at the tai-pan. His voice hardened a fraction. "Ian, I wanted to tell you, personally, that we're in the same marketplace."

"Is that why you came?"

"One reason."

"The other?"

"Pleasure."

"How long have you known Mr. Bartlett?"

"Six months or so. Why?"

Dunross shrugged, then looked at Casey and she could read nothing from his voice or face or manner other than friendliness. "You didn't know of any Rothwell-Gornt negotiations?"

Truthfully she shook her head, awed by Bartlett's skillful long-range planning. "No. Are negotiations in progress, Mr. Gornt?"

"I would say yes." Gornt smiled.

"Then we shall see, won't we," Dunross said. "We shall see who makes the best deal. Thank you for telling me personally, though there was no need. I knew, of course, that you'd be interested too. There's no need to belabor that."

"Actually there's a very good reason," Gornt said sharply. "Neither Mr. Bartlett nor this lady may realize how vital Par-Con is to you. I felt obliged to make the point personally to them. And to you. And of course to offer my congratulations."

"Why vital, Mr. Gornt?" Casey asked, committed now.

"Without your Par-Con deal and the cash flow it will generate, Struan's will go under, could easily go under in a few months."

Dunross laughed and those few who listened covertly shuddered and moved their own conversations up a decibel, aghast at the thought of Struan's failing, at the same time thinking, What deal? Par-Con? Should we sell or buy? Struan's or Rothwell-Gornt?

"No chance of that," Dunross said. "Not a chance in hell!"

"I think there's a very good chance." Gornt's tone changed. "In any event, as you say, we shall see."

"Yes, we will—meanwhile . . ." Dunross stopped as he saw Claudia approaching uneasily.

"Excuse me, tai-pan," she said, "your personal call to London's on the line."

"Oh thank you." Dunross turned and beckoned Penelope. She came over at once. "Penelope, would you entertain Quillan and Miss Tcholok for a moment. I've got a phone call—Quillan's not staying for dinner—he has pressing business." He waved cheerily and left them. Casey noticed the animal grace to his walk.

"You're not staying for dinner?" Penelope was saying, her relief evident though she tried to cover it.

"No. I'm sorry to inconvenience you—arriving so abruptly, after declining your kind invitation. Unfortunately I can't stay."

"Oh. Then . . . would you excuse me a moment, I'll be back in a second."

"There's no need to worry about us," Gornt said gently. "We can look after ourselves. Again, sorry to be a nuisance—you're looking marvelous, Penelope. You never change." She thanked him and he willed her away. Gratefully she went over to Claudia Chen who was waiting nearby.

"You're a curious man," Casey said. "One moment war, the next great charm."

"We have rules, we English, in peace and war. Just because you loathe someone, that's no reason to curse him, spit in his eye or abuse his lady." Gornt smiled down at her. "Shall we find your Mr. Bartlett? Then I really should go."

"Why did you do that? To the tai-pan? The battle challenge—the 'vital' bit. That was the formal gauntlet, wasn't it? In public."

"Life's a game," he said. "All life's a game and we English play it with different rules from you Americans. Yes. And life's to be enjoyed. Ciranoush—what a lovely name you have. May I use it?"

"Yes," she said after a pause. "But why the challenge now?"

"Now was the time. I didn't exaggerate about your importance to Struan's. Shall we go and find your Mr. Bartlett?"

That's the third time he's said *your* Mr. Bartlett, she thought. Is that to probe, or to needle? "Sure, why not?" She turned for the garden, conscious of the looks, overt and covert, of the other guests, feeling the danger pleasantly. "Do you always make dramatic entrances like this?"

Gornt laughed. "No. Sorry if I was abrupt, Ciranoush—if I distressed you."

"You mean about your private meeting with Linc? You didn't. It was very shrewd of Linc to approach the opposition without my knowledge. That gave me a freedom of action that otherwise I'd not have had this morning."

"Ah, then you're not irritated that he didn't trust you in this?"

"It has nothing to do with trust. I often withhold information from Linc, until the time's ripe, to protect him. He was obviously doing the same for me. Linc and I understand one another. At least I think I understand him."

"Then tell me how to finalize a deal."

"First I have to know what you want. Apart from Dunross's head."

"I don't want his head, or death or anything like that—just an early demise of their Noble House. Once Struan's is obliterated we become the Noble House." His face hardened. "Then all sorts of ghosts can sleep."

"Tell me about them."

"Now's not the time, Ciranoush, oh no. Too many hostile ears. That'd be for your ears only." They were out in the garden now, the gentle breeze grand, a fine night sky overhead, star filled. Linc Bartlett was not on this terrace so they went down the wide stone steps through other guests to the lower one, toward the paths that threaded the lawns. Then they were intercepted.

"Hello, Quillan, this's a pleasant surprise."

"Hello, Paul. Miss Tcholok, may I introduce you to Paul Havergill? Paul's presently in charge of the Victoria Bank."

"I'm afraid that's very temporary, Miss Tcholok, and only because our chief manager's on sick leave. I'm retiring in a few months."

"To our regret," Gornt said, then introduced Casey to the rest of this group: Lady Joanna Temple-Smith, a tall, stretched-faced woman in her fifties, and Richard Kwang and his wife Mai-ling. "Richard Kwang's chairman of the Ho-Pak, one of our finest Chinese banks."

"In banking we're all friendly competitors, Miss, er, Miss, except of course for Blacs," Havergill said.

"Sir?" Casey said.

"Blacs? Oh that's a nickname for the Bank of London, Canton and Shanghai. They may be bigger than we are, a month or so older, but we're the best bank here, Miss, er . . ."

"Blacs're my bankers," Gornt said to Casey. "They do me very well. They're first-class bankers."

"Second-class, Quillan."

Gornt turned back to Casey. "We've a saying here that Blacs consists of gentlemen trying to be bankers, and those at the Victoria are bankers trying to be gentlemen."

Casey laughed. The others smiled politely.

"You're all just friendly competition, Mr. Kwang?" she asked.

"Oh yes. We wouldn't dare oppose Blacs or the Victoria," Richard Kwang said amiably. He was short and stocky and middle-aged with gray-flecked black hair and an easy smile, his English perfect. "I hear Par-Con's going to invest in Hong Kong, Miss Tchelek."

"We're here to look around, Mr. Kwang. Nothing's firm yet." She passed over his mispronunciation.

Gornt lowered his voice. "Just between ourselves, I've formally told both Bartlett and Miss Tcholok that I will better any offer Struan's might make. Blacs are supporting me one hundred percent. And I've friendly bankers elsewhere. I'm hoping Par-Con will consider all possibilities before making any commitment."

"I imagine that would be very wise," Havergill said. "Of course Struan's does have the inside track."

"Blacs and most of Hong Kong would hardly agree with you," Gornt said.

"I hope it won't come to a clash, Quillan," Havergill said. "Struan's is our major customer."

Richard Kwang said, "Either way, Miss Tchelek, it would be good to have such a great American company as Par-Con here. Good for you, good for us. Let's hope that a deal can be found that suits Par-Con. If Mr. Bartlett would like any assistance . . ." The banker produced his business card. She took it, opened her silk handbag and offered hers with equal dexterity, having come prepared for the immediate card exchanging that is good manners and obligatory in Asia. The Chinese banker glanced at it then his eyes narrowed.

"Sorry I haven't had it translated into characters yet," she said. "Our bankers in the States are First Central New York and the California Merchant Bank and Trust Company." Casey mentioned them proudly, sure the combined assets of these banking giants were in excess of 6 billions. "I'd be gl—" She stopped, startled at the sudden chill surrounding her. "Is something wrong?"

"Yes and no," Gornt said after a moment. "It's just that the First Central New York Bank's not at all popular here."

"Why?"

Havergill said disdainfully, "They turned out to be a shower—that's, er, English for a bad lot, Miss, er, Miss. The First Central New York did some business here before the war, then expanded in the mid-forties while we at the Victoria and other British institutions were picking ourselves off the floor. In '49 when Chairman Mao threw Chiang Kai-shek off the Mainland to Taiwan, Mao's troops were massed on our border just a few miles north in the New Territories. It was touch and go whether or not the hordes would spill over and overrun the Colony. A lot of people cut and ran, none of us of course, but all the Chinese who could got out. Without any warning, the First Central New York called in all their loans, paid off their depositors, closed their doors and fled—all in the space of one week."

"I didn't know," Casey said, aghast.

"They were a bunch of yellow bastards, my dear, if you'll excuse the expression," Lady Joanna said with open contempt. "Of course, they were the *only* bank that scarpered—ran away. But then they were . . . well, what can you expect, my dear?"

"Probably better, Lady Joanna," Casey said, furious with the VP in charge of their account for not warning them. "Perhaps there were mitigating circumstances. Mr. Havergill, were the loans substantial?"

"At that time, very, I'm afraid. Yes. That bank ruined quite a lot of important businesses and people, caused an enormous amount of grief and loss of face. Still," he said with a smile, "we all benefited by their leaving. A couple of years ago they had the effrontery to apply to the financial secretary for a new charter!"

Richard Kwang added jovially, "That's one charter that'll never be renewed! You see, Miss Tchelek, all foreign banks operate on a renewable yearly charter. Certainly we can do very well without that one, or for that matter any other American bank. They're such . . . well, you'll find the

Victoria, Blacs or the Ho-Pak, perhaps all three Miss K.C., can fulfill all Par-Con's needs perfectly. If you and Mr. Bartlett would like to chat . . ."

"I'd be glad to visit with you, Mr. Kwang. Say tomorrow? Initially I handle most of our banking needs. Maybe sometime in the morning?"

"Yes, yes of course. You'll find us competitive," Richard Kwang said without a flicker. "At ten?"

"Great. We're at the V and A, Kowloon. If ten's not good for you just let me know," she said. "I'm pleased to meet you personally too, Mr. Havergill. I presume our appointment for tomorrow is still in order?"

"Of course. At four, isn't it? I look forward to chatting at length with Mr. Bartlett . . . and you, of course, my dear." He was a tall, lean man and she noticed his eyes rise from her cleavage. She dismissed her immediate dislike. I may need him, she thought, and his bank.

"Thank you," she said with the right amount of deference and turned her charm on Lady Joanna. "What a pretty dress, Lady Joanna," she said, loathing it and the row of small pearls that circled the woman's scrawny neck.

"Oh, thank you, my dear. Is yours from Paris too?"

"Indirectly. It's a Balmain but I got it in New York." She smiled down at Richard Kwang's wife, a solid, well-preserved Cantonese lady with an elaborate coiffure, very pale skin and narrow eyes. She was wearing an immense imperial jade pendant and a seven-carat diamond ring. "Pleased to meet you, Mrs. Kwang," she said, awed by the wealth that the jewelry represented. "We were looking for Linc Bartlett. Have you seen him?"

"Not for a while," Havergill volunteered. "I think he went into the east wing. Believe there's a bar there. He was with Adryon—Dunross's daughter."

"Adryon's turned out to be such a pretty girl," Lady Joanna said. "They make such a nice couple together. Charming man, Mr. Bartlett. He's not married, is he, dear?"

"No," Casey said, equally pleasantly, adding Lady Joanna Temple-Smith to her private list of loathsome people. "Linc's not married."

"He'll be gobbled up soon, mark my words. I really believe Adryon's quite smitten. Perhaps you'd like to come to tea on Thursday, my dear? I'd love you to meet some of the girls. That's the day of our Over Thirty Club."

"Thank you," Casey said. "I don't qualify—but I'd love to come anyway."

"Oh I'm sorry, dear! I'd presumed . . . I'll send a car for you. Quillan, are you staying for dinner?"

"No, can't. Got pressing business."

"Pity." Lady Joanna smiled and showed her bad teeth.

"If you'll excuse us—just want to find Bartlett and then I have to leave. See you Saturday." Gornt took Casey's arm and guided her away.

They watched them leave. "She's quite attractive in a common sort of way, isn't she?" Lady Joanna said. "Chuluk. That's Middle European, isn't it?"

"Possibly. It could be Mideastern, Joanna, you know, Turkish, something like that, possibly the Balkans. . . ." Havergill stopped. "Oh, I see what you mean. No, I don't think so. She certainly doesn't look Jewish."

"One really can't tell these days, can one? She might have had her nose fixed—they do marvelous things these days, don't they?"

"Never occurred to me to look. Hum! Do you think so?"

Richard Kwang passed Casey's card over to his wife who read it instantly and got the same message instantly. "Paul, her card says treasurer and executive VP of the holding company . . . that's quite impressive, isn't it? Par-Con's a big company."

"Oh my dear fellow, but they're American. They do extraordinary things in America. Surely it's just a title—that's all."

"Giving his mistress face?" Joanna asked.

12

The billiard cue struck the white ball and it shot across the green table and slashed the red into a far pocket and stopped perfectly behind another red.

Adryon clapped gleefully. "Oh Linc, that was super! I was sure you were just boasting. Oh do it again!"

Linc Bartlett grinned. "For one dollar that red around the table and into that pocket and the white here." He marked the spot with a flick of chalk.

"Done!"

He leaned over the table and sighted and the white stopped within a millimeter of his mark, the red sunk with marvelous inevitability.

"*Ayeeyah!* I haven't got a dollar with me. Damn! Can I owe it to you?"

"A lady—however beautiful—has to pay her gambling debts at once."

"I know. Father says the same. Can I pay you tomorrow?"

He watched her, enjoying her, pleased that his skill pleased her. She was wearing a knee-length black skirt and the lovely silk blouse. Her legs were long, very long, and perfect. "Nope!" He pretended ill humor and then they laughed together in the huge room, the vast lights low over the full-size billiard table, the rest of the room dark and intimate but for the shaft of light from the open door.

"You play incredibly well," she said.

"Don't tell anyone but I made my living in the Army playing pool."

"In Europe?"

"No. Pacific."

"My father was a fighter pilot. He got six planes before he was shot down and grounded."

"I guess that made him an ace, didn't it?"

"Were you part of those awful landings against the Japs?"

"No. I was in construction. We came in when everything was secured."

"Oh."

"We built bases, airfields in Guadalcanal, and islands all over the Pacific. My war was easy—nothing like your dad's." As he went over to the cue rack, he was sorry for the first time that he had not been in the Marines. Her expression when he had said construction made him feel unmanned. "We should go look for your boyfriend. Maybe he's here by now."

"Oh he's not important! He's not a real boyfriend, I just met him a week or so ago at a friend's party. Martin's a journalist on the *China Guardian*. He's not a lover."

"Are all young English ladies so open about their lovers?"

"It's the pill. It's released us from masculine servitude forever. Now we're equal."

"Are you?"

"I am."

"Then you're lucky."

"Yes I know I'm very lucky." She watched him. "How old are you, Linc?"

"Old." He snapped the cue into its rack. It was the first time in his life that he had not wanted to tell his age. Goddamn, he thought, curiously unsettled. What's your problem?

None. There's no problem. Is there?

"I'm nineteen," she was saying.

"When's your birthday?"

"October 27—I'm a Scorpio. When's yours?"

"October 1."

"Oh it's not! Tell me honestly!"

"Cross my heart and hope to die."

She clapped her hands with delight. "Oh that's marvelous! Father's the tenth. That's marvelous—a good omen."

"Why?"

"You'll see." Happily she opened her handbag and found a crumpled cigarette package and a battered gold lighter. He took the lighter and flicked it for her but it did not light. A second and a third time but nothing.

"Bloody thing," she said. "Bloody thing's never worked properly but Father gave it to me. I love it. Of course I dropped it a couple of times."

He peered at it, blew the wick and fiddled a moment. "You shouldn't smoke anyway."

"That's what Father always says."

"He's right."

"Yes. But I like smoking for the time being. How old are you, Linc?"

"Forty."

"Oh!" He saw the surprise. "Then you're the same age as Father! Well, almost. He's forty-one."

"Both were great years," Linc said dryly, and he thought, Whichever way you figure it, Adryon, I really am old enough to be your father.

Another frown creased her brow. "It's funny, you don't seem the same age at all." Then she added in a rush, "In two years I'll be twenty-one and that's practically over the hill, I just can't imagine being twenty-five let alone thirty and as to forty . . . God, I think I'd rather be pushing up daisies."

"Twenty-one's old—yes ma'am, mighty old," he said. And he thought, It's a long time since you spent time with such a young one. Watch yourself. This one's dynamite. He flicked the lighter and it lit. "What d'you know!"

"Thanks," she said and puffed her cigarette alight. "You don't smoke?" she asked.

"No, not now. Used to but Casey sent me illustrated pamphlets on cancer and smoking every hour on the hour until I got the message. Didn't phase me a bit to stop—once I'd decided. It sure as hell improved my golf and tennis and . . ." He smiled. "And all forms of sports."

"Casey is gorgeous. Is she really your executive vice-president?"

"Yes."

"She's going to . . . it'll be very difficult for her here. The men won't like dealing with her at all."

"Same in the States. But they're getting used to it. We built Par-Con in six years. Casey can work with the best of them. She's a winner."

"Is she your mistress?"

He sipped his beer. "Are all young English ladies so blunt?"

"No." She laughed. "I was just curious. Everyone says . . . everyone presumes she is."

"That a fact?"

"Yes. You're the talk of Hong Kong society, and tonight will cap everything. You both made rather a grand entrance, what with your private jet, the smuggled guns and Casey being the last European to see John Chen, so the papers said. I liked your interview."

"Eh, those bas—those press guys were waiting on the doorstep this afternoon. I tried to keep it short and sharp."

"Par-Con's really worth half a billion dollars?"

"No. About 300 million—but it'll be a billion-dollar company soon. Yes, it'll be soon now."

He saw her looking at him with those frank, gray-green eyes of hers, so adult yet so young. "You're a very interesting man, Mr. Linc Bartlett. I like talking to you. I like you too. Didn't at first. I screamed bloody murder when Father told me I had to chaperone you, introduce you around for a while. I haven't done a very good job, have I?"

"It's been *super*."

"Oh come on." She grinned too. "I've totally monopolized you."

"Not true. I met Christian Toxe the editor, Richard Kwang and those two Americans from the consulate. Lannan wasn't it?"

"Langan, Edward Langan. He's nice. I didn't catch the other one's name—I don't know them really, they've just been racing with us. Christian's nice and his wife's super. She's Chinese so she's not here tonight."

Bartlett frowned. "Because she's Chinese?"

"Oh, she was invited but she wouldn't come. It's face. To save her husband's face. The nobs don't approve of mixed marriages."

"Marrying the natives?"

"Something like that." She shrugged. "You'll see. I'd better introduce you to some more guests or I'll get hell!"

"How about to Havergill the banker? What about him?"

"Father thinks Havergill's a berk."

"Then by God he's a twenty-two-carat berk from here on in!"

"Good," she said and they laughed together.

"Linc?"

They looked around at the two figures silhouetted in the shaft of light from the doorway. He recognized Casey's voice and shape at once but not the man. It was not possible from where they were to see against the light.

"Hi, Casey! How's it going?"

He took Adryon's arm casually and propelled her toward the silhouette. "I've been teaching Adryon the finer points of pool."

Adryon laughed. "That's the understatement of the year, Casey. He's super at it, isn't he?"

"Yes. Oh Linc, Quillan Gornt wanted to say hi before he left."

Abruptly Adryon jerked to a stop and the color left her face. Linc stopped, startled. "What's wrong?" he asked her.

"Evening, Mr. Bartlett," Gornt said, moving toward them into the light. "Hello, Adryon."

"What're you doing here?" she said in a tiny voice.

"I just came for a few minutes," Gornt said.

"Have you seen Father?"

"Yes."

"Then get out. Get out and leave this house alone." Adryon said it in the same small voice.

Bartlett stared at her. "What the hell's up?"

Gornt said calmly, "It's a long story. It can wait until tomorrow—or next week. I just wanted to confirm our dinner on Tuesday—and if you're free over the weekend, perhaps you two would like to come out on my boat for the day. Sunday if the weather's good."

"Thanks, I think so, but may we confirm tomorrow?" Bartlett asked, still nonplussed by Adryon.

"Adryon," Gornt said gently, "Annagrey's leaving next week, she asked me to ask you to give her a call." Adryon did not answer, just stared at him, and Gornt added to the other two, "Annagrey's my daughter.

They're good friends—they've both gone to the same schools most of their lives. She's off to university in California."

"Oh—then if there's anything we could do for her . . ." Casey said.

"That's very kind of you," he said. "You'll meet her Tuesday. Perhaps we can talk about it then. I'll say g—"

The door at the far end of the billiard room swung open and Dunross stood there.

Gornt smiled and turned his attention back to them. "Good night, Mr. Bartlett—Ciranoush. See you both on Tuesday. Good night, Adryon." He bowed slightly to them and walked the length of the room and stopped. "Good night, Ian," he said politely. "Thank you for your hospitality."

"'Night," Dunross said, as politely, and stood aside, a slight smile twisting his lips.

He watched Gornt walk out of the front door and then turned his attention back to the billiard room. "Almost time for dinner," he said, his voice calm. And warm. "You must all be starving. I am."

"What . . . what did he want?" Adryon said shakily.

Dunross came up to her with a smile, gentling her. "Nothing. Nothing important, my pet. Quillan's mellowing in his old age."

"You're sure?"

"Sure." He put his arm around her and gave her a little hug. "No need to worry your pretty head."

"Has he gone?"

"Yes."

Bartlett started to say something but stopped instantly as he caught Dunross's eye over Adryon's head.

"Yes. Everything's grand, my darling," Dunross was saying as he gave her another little hug, and Bartlett saw Adryon gather herself within the warmth. "Nothing to worry about."

"Linc was showing me how he played pool and then . . . It was just so sudden. He was like an apparition."

"You could have knocked me down with a feather too when he appeared like the Bad Fairy." Dunross laughed, then added to Bartlett and Casey, "Quillan goes in for dramatics." Then to Bartlett alone, "We'll chat about that after dinner, you and I."

"Sure," Bartlett said, noticing the eyes weren't smiling.

The dinner gong sounded. "Ah, thank God!" Dunross said. "Come along, everyone, food at long last. Casey, you're at my table." He kept his arm around Adryon, loving her, and guided her out into the light.

Casey and Bartlett followed.

Gornt got into the driver's seat of the black Silver Cloud Rolls that he had parked just outside the Great House. The night was good, though the humidity had increased again. He was very pleased with himself. And now for dinner and Jason Plumm, he thought. Once that bugger's committed, Ian Dunross's as good as finished and I own this house and Struan's and the whole kit and caboodle!

It couldn't have been better: first Casey and Ian almost at once, and everything laid out in front of him and in front of her. Then Havergill and Richard Kwang together. Then Bartlett in the billiard room and then Ian himself again.

Perfect!

Now Ian's called, Bartlett's called, Casey, Havergill, Richard Kwang and so's Plumm. Ha! If they only knew.

Everything's perfect. Except for Adryon. Pity about her, pity that children have to inherit the feuds of the fathers. But that's life. Joss. Pity she won't go out into the world and leave Hong Kong, like Annagrey—at least until Ian Dunross and I have settled our differences, finally. Better she's not here to see him smashed—nor Penelope too. Joss if they're here, joss if they're not. I'd like him here when I take possession of his box at the races, the permanent seat on all boards, all the sinecures, the legislature—oh yes. Soon they'll all be mine. Along with the envy of all Asia.

He laughed. Yes. And about time. Then all the ghosts will sleep. God curse all ghosts!

He switched on the ignition and started the engine, enjoying the luxury of real leather and fine wood, the smell rich and exclusive. Then he put the car into gear and swung down the driveway, past the carpark where all the other cars were, down to the huge wrought-iron main gates with the Struan arms entwined. He stopped for passing traffic and caught sight of the Great House in his rear mirror. Tall, vast, the windows ablaze, welcoming.

Soon I really will own you, he thought. I'll throw parties there that Asia's never seen before and never will again. I suppose I should have a hostess.

What about the American girl?

He chuckled. "Ah, Ciranoush, what a lovely name," he said out loud with the same, perfect amount of husky charm that he had used previously. That one's a pushover, he told himself confidently. You just use old world charm and great wine, light but excellent food and patience—along with the very best of upper-class English, masculine sophistication and no swear words and she'll fall where and when you want her to. And then, if you choose the correct moment, you can use gutter English and a little judicious roughness, and you'll unlock all her pent-up passion like no man ever has done.

If I read her correctly she needs an expert pillowing rather badly. So either Bartlett's inadequate or they're really not lovers as the confidential report suggested. Interesting.

But do you want her? As a toy—perhaps. As a tool—of course. As a hostess no, much too pushy.

Now the road was clear so he pulled out and went down to the junction and turned left and soon he was on Peak Road going downhill toward Magazine Gap where Plumm's penthouse apartment was. After dinner with him he was going to a meeting, then to Wanchai, to one of his private apartments and the welcoming embrace of Mona Leung. His pulse quickened at the thought of her violent lovemaking, her barely hidden hatred for him and all *quai loh* that was ever in perpetual conflict with her love of luxury, the apartment that was on loan to her and the modest amount of money he gave her monthly.

"Never give 'em enough money," his father William had told him early on. "Clothes, jewelry, holidays—that's fine. But not too much money. Control them with dollar bills. And never think they love you for you. They don't. It's only your money, only your money and always will be. Just under the surface they'll despise you, always will. That's fair enough if you think about it—we're not Chinese and never will be."

"There's never an exception?"

"I don't think so. Not for a *quai loh,* my son. I don't think so. Never has been with me and I've known a few. Oh she'll give you her body, her children, even her life, but she'll always despise you. She has to, she's Chinese and we're *quai loh!*"

Ayeeyah, Gornt thought. That advice's proved itself time and time again. And saved me so much anguish. It'll be good to see the Old Man, he told himself. This year I'll give him a fine Christmas present: Struan's.

He was driving carefully down the left side of the winding road hugging the mountainside, the night good, the surface fine and the traffic light. Normally he would have been chauffeur-driven but tonight he wanted no witnesses to his meeting with Plumm.

No, he thought. Nor any witnesses when I meet Four Finger Wu. What the hell does that pirate want? Nothing good. Bound to be dangerous. Yes. But during the Korean War Wu did you a very large favor and perhaps now is the time he wants the favor repaid. There's always a reckoning sooner or later, and that's fair and that's Chinese law. You get a present, you give one back a little more valuable. You have a favor done . . .

In 1950 when the Chinese Communist armies in Korea were battering and bleeding their way south from the Yalu with monstrous losses, they were desperately short of all strategic supplies and very willing to pay mightily those who could slip through the blockade with the supplies they needed. At that time, Rothwell-Gornt was also in desperate straits because of their huge losses at Shanghai the previous year thanks to the conquest by Mao. So in December of 1950, he and his father had borrowed heavily and secretly bought a huge shipment of penicillin, morphine, sulfanilamides and other medical supplies in the Philippines, avoiding the obligatory export license. These they smuggled onto a hired ocean-going junk with one of their trusted crews and sent it to Wampoa, a bleak island in the Pearl River near Canton. Payment was to be in gold on delivery, but en route, in the secret backwaters of the Pearl River Estuary, their junk had been intercepted by river pirates favoring Chiang Kai-shek's Nationalists and a ransom demanded. They had no money to ransom the cargo, and if the Nationalists found out that Rothwell-Gornt was dealing with their hated Communist enemy, their own future in Asia was lost forever.

Through his compradore Gornt had arranged a meeting in Aberdeen Harbor with Four Finger Wu, supposedly one of the biggest smugglers in the Pearl River Estuary.

"Where ship now?" Four Finger Wu had asked in execrable pidgin English.

Gornt had told him as best he could, conversing in pidgin, not being able to speak Haklo, Wu's dialect.

"Perhaps, perhaps not!" Four Finger Wu smiled. "I phone three day. *Nee choh wah* password. Three day, *heya?*"

On the third day he phoned. "Bad, good, don' know. Meet two day Aberdeen. Begin Hour of Monkey." That hour was ten o'clock at night. Chinese split the day into twelve, two-hour segments, each with a name, always in the same sequence, beginning at 4:00 A.M. with the Cock, then at 6:00 A.M. with the Dog, and so on; Boar, Rat, Ox, Tiger, Rabbit, Dragon, Snake, Monkey, Horse and Sheep.

At the Hour of the Monkey on Wu's junk at Aberdeen two days later, he had been given the full payment for his shipment in gold *plus an extra 40 percent.* A staggering 500 percent profit.

Four Finger Wu had grinned. "Make better trade than *quai loh,* never mind. 28,000 taels of gold." A tael was a little more than an ounce. "Next time me ship. Yes?"

"Yes."

"You buy, me ship, me sell, 40 percent mine, sale price."

"Yes." Gornt had thankfully tried to press a much larger percentage on him this time but Wu had refused.

"40 percent only, sale price." But Gornt had understood that now he was in the smuggler's debt.

The gold was in five-tael smuggler bars. It was valued at the official rate of $35 U.S. an ounce. But on the black market, smuggled into Indonesia, India or back into China, it was worth two or three times as much . . . sometimes more. On this one shipment again with Wu's help, Rothwell-Gornt had made a million and a half U.S. and were on the road to recovery.

After that there had been three more shipments, immensely profitable to both sides. Then the war had ceased and so had their relationship.

Never a word since then, Gornt thought. Until the phone call this afternoon.

"Ah, old friend, can see? Tonight?" Four Finger Wu had said. "Can do? Anytime—I wait. Same place as old days. Yes?"

So now the favor's to be returned. Good.

Gornt switched on the radio. Chopin. He was driving the winding road automatically, his mind on the meetings ahead, the engine almost silent.

He slowed for an advancing truck, then swung out and accelerated on the short straight to overtake a slow-moving taxi. Going quite fast now he braked sharply in good time nearing the blind corner, then something seemed to snap in the innards of the engine, his foot sank to the floorboards, his stomach turned over and he went into the hairpin too fast.

In panic he jammed his foot on the brake again and again but nothing happened, his hands whirling the wheel around. He took the first corner badly, swerving drunkenly as he came out of it onto the wrong side of the road. Fortunately there was nothing coming at him but he overcorrected and lurched for the mountainside, his stomach twisting with nausea, overcorrected again, going very fast now and the next corner leapt at him. Here the grade was steeper, the road more winding and narrow. Again he cornered badly but once through he had a split second to grab the hand brake and this slowed him only a little, the new corner was on him, and he came out of it way out of his lane, oncoming headlights blinding him.

The taxi skittered in panic to the shoulder and almost went over the side, its horn blaring but he was passed by a fraction of an inch, lurching petrified for the correct side, and then went on down the hill out of control. A moment of straight road and he managed to jerk the gear lever into low as he hurtled into another blind corner, the engine howling now. The sudden slowing would have pitched him through the windshield but for his seat belt, his hands almost frozen to the wheel.

He got around this corner but again he was out too far and he missed the oncoming car by a millimeter, skidded back to his side once more, swerved, overcorrecting, slowing a little now but there was no letup in the grade or twisting road ahead. He was still going too fast into the new hairpin and coming out of the first part he was too far over. The heavily laden truck grinding up the hill was helpless.

Panic-stricken he tore the wheel left and just managed to get around the truck with a glancing blow. He tried to jerk the gear lever into reverse but it wouldn't go, the cogs shrieking in protest. Then, aghast, he saw slow traffic ahead in his lane, oncoming traffic in the other and the road vanish around the next bend. He was lost so he turned left into the mountainside, trying to ricochet and stop that way.

There was a howl of protesting metal, the back side window shattered and he bounced away. The oncoming car lurched for the far shoulder, its horn blaring. He closed his eyes and braced for the head-on collision but somehow it didn't happen and he was past and just had enough strength to jerk the wheel hard over again and went into the mountainside. He hit with a glancing blow. The front left fender ripped away. The car ploughed into the shrub and earth, then slammed into a rock outcrop, reared up throwing Gornt aside, but as the car fell back the near-side wheel went into the storm drain and held, and, just before smashing into the paralyzed little Mini ahead, it stopped.

Gornt weakly pulled himself up. The car was still half upright. Sweat was pouring off him and his heart was pounding. He found it hard to breathe or to think. Traffic both ways was stopped, snarled. He heard some horns hooting impatiently below and above, then hurried footsteps.

"You all right, old chap?" the stranger asked.

"Yes, yes I think so. My, my brakes went." Gornt wiped the sweat off his forehead, trying to get his brain to work. He felt his chest, then moved his feet and there was no pain. "I . . . the brakes went . . . I was turning a corner and . . . and then everything . . ."

"Brakes, eh? Not like a Rolls. I thought you were pretending to be Stirling Moss. You were very lucky. I thought you'd had it twenty times. If I were you I'd switch off the engine."

"What?" Then Gornt realized the engine was still gently purring and the radio playing so he turned the ignition off and, after a moment, pulled the keys out.

"Nice car," the stranger said, "but it's a right proper mess now. Always liked this model. '62, isn't it?"

"Yes. Yes it is."

"You want me to call the police?"

Gornt made the effort and thought a moment, his pulse still pounding in his ears. Weakly he unsnapped the seat belt. "No. There's a police station just back up the hill. If you'd give me a lift to there?"

"Delighted, old chap." The stranger was short and rotund. He looked around at the other cars and taxis and trucks that were stopped in both directions, their Chinese drivers and Chinese passengers gawking at them from their windows. "Bloody people," he muttered sourly. "You could be dying in the street and you'd be lucky if they stepped over you." He opened the door and helped Gornt out.

"Thanks." Gornt felt his knees shaking. For a moment he could not dominate his knees and he leaned against the car.

"You sure you're all right?"

"Oh yes. It's . . . that frightened me to death!" He looked at the damage, the nose buried into earth and shrub, a huge score down the right side, the car jammed well into the inside curve. "What a bloody mess!"

"Yes, but it hasn't telescoped a sausage! You were bloody lucky you were in a good car, old chap." The stranger let the door swing and it closed with a muted click. "Great workmanship. Well, you can leave it here. No one's likely to steal it." The stranger laughed, leading the way to his own car which was parked, its blinker lights on, just behind. "Hop in, won't take a jiffy."

It was then Gornt remembered the mocking half-smile on Dunross's face that he had taken for bravado as he left. His mind cleared. Would there have been time for Dunross to tamper . . . with his knowledge of engines . . . surely he wouldn't . . . ?

"Son of a bitch," he muttered, aghast.

"Not to worry, old chap," the stranger said, as he eased past the wreck, making the turn. "The police'll make all the arrangements for you."

Gornt's face closed. "Yes. Yes they will."

13

"Grand dinner, Ian, better than last year's," Sir Dunstan Barre said expansively from across the table.

"Thank you." Dunross raised his glass politely and took a sip of the fine cognac from the brandy snifter.

Barre gulped his port then refilled his glass, more florid than usual. "Ate too much, as usual, by God! Eh Phillip? Phillip!"

"Yes . . . oh yes . . . much better . . ." Phillip Chen muttered.

"Are you all right, old chap?"

"Oh yes . . . it's just . . . oh yes."

Dunross frowned, then let his eyes rove the other tables, hardly listening to them.

There were just the three of them now at this round table that had seated twelve comfortably. At the other tables spread across the terraces and lawns, men were lounging over their cognac, port and cigars, or standing in clusters, all the ladies now inside the house. He saw Bartlett standing over near the buffet tables that an hour ago had been groaning under the weight of roast legs of lamb, salads, sides of rare beef, vast hot steak-and-kidney pies, roast potatoes and vegetables of various kinds, and the pastries and cakes and ice cream sculptures. A small army of servants was cleaning away the debris. Bartlett was in deep conversation with Chief Superintendent Roger Crosse and the American Ed Langan. In a little while I'll deal with him, he told himself grimly—but first Brian Kwok. He looked around. Brian Kwok was not at his table, the one that Adryon had hosted, or at any of the others, so he sat back patiently, sipped his cognac and let himself drift.

Secret files, MI-6, Special Intelligence, Bartlett, Casey, Gornt, no Tsuyan and now Alan Medford Grant very dead. His phone call before dinner to Kiernan, Alan Medford Grant's assistant in London, had been a shocker. "It was sometime this morning, Mr. Dunross," Kiernan had said. "It was raining, very slippery and he was a motorcycle enthusiast as you

know. He was coming up to town as usual. As far as we know now there
were no witnesses. The fellow who found him on the country road near
Esher and the A3 highway, just said he was driving along in the rain and
then there in front of him was the bike on its side and a man sprawled in
a heap on the edge of the road. He said as far as he could tell, AMG was
dead when he reached him. He called the police and they've begun
inquiries but . . . well, what can I say? He's a great loss to all of us."

"Yes. Did he have any family?"

"Not that I know of, sir. Of course I informed MI-6 at once."

"Oh?"

"Yes sir."

"Why?"

There was heavy static on the line. "He'd left instructions with me, sir.
If anything happened to him I was to call two numbers at once and cable
you, which I did. Neither number meant anything to me. The first turned
out to be the private number of a high-up official in MI-6—he arrived
within half an hour with some of his people and they went through
AMG's desk and private papers. They took most of them when they left.
When he saw the copy of the last report, the one we'd just sent you, he
just about hit the roof, and when he asked for copies of all the others and
I told him, following AMG's instructions, I always destroyed the office
copy once we'd heard you had received yours, he just about had a hemorrhage. It seems AMG didn't really have Her Majesty's Government's permission to work for you."

"But I have Grant's assurance in writing he'd got clearance from HMG
in advance."

"Yes sir. You've done nothing illegal but this MI-6 fellow just about
went bonkers."

"Who was he? What was his name?"

"I was told, *told*, sir, not to mention any names. He was very pompous
and mumbled something about the Official Secrets Act."

"You said two numbers?"

"Yes sir. The other was in Switzerland. A woman answered and after
I'd told her, she just said, oh, so sorry, and hung up. She was foreign, sir.
One interesting thing, in AMG's final instructions he had said not to tell
either number about the other but, as this gentleman from MI-6 was, to
put it lightly, incensed, I told him. He called at once but got a busy line
and it was busy for a very long time and then the exchange said it had
been temporarily disconnected. He was bloody furious, sir."

"Can you carry on AMG's reports?"

"No sir. I was just a feeder—I collated information that he got. I just
wrote the reports for him, answered the phone when he was away, paid
office bills. He spent a good part of the time on the Continent but he
never said where he'd been, or volunteered anything. He was . . . well,
he played his cards close to his nose. I don't know who gave him anything

—I don't even know his office number in Whitehall. As I said, he was very secretive. . . ."

Dunross sighed and sipped his brandy. Bloody shame, he thought. Was it an accident—or was he murdered? And when do MI-6 fall on my neck? The numbered account in Switzerland? That's not illegal either, and no one's business but mine and his.

What to do? There must be a substitute somewhere.

Was it an accident? Or was he killed?

"Sorry?" he asked, not catching what Barre had said.

"I was just saying it was bloody funny when Casey didn't want to go and you threw her out." The big man laughed. "You've got balls, old boy."

At the end of the dinner just before the port and cognac and cigars had arrived, Penelope had got up from her table where Linc Bartlett was deep in conversation with Havergill and the ladies had left with her, and then Adryon at her table, and then, all over the terraces, ladies had begun trickling away after her. Lady Joanna, who was sitting on Dunross's right, had said, "Come on girls, time to powder."

Obediently the other women got up with her and the men politely pretended not to be relieved with their exodus.

"Come along, dear," Joanna had said to Casey, who had remained seated.

"Oh I'm fine, thanks."

"I'm sure you are but, er, come along anyway."

Then Casey had seen everyone staring. "What's the matter?"

"Nothing, dear," Lady Joanna had said. "It's custom that the ladies leave the men alone for a while with the port and cigars. So come along."

Casey had stared at her blankly. "You mean we're sent off while the men discuss affairs of state and the price of tea in China?"

"It's just good manners, dear. When in Rome . . ." Lady Joanna had watched her, a slight, contemptuous smile on her lips, enjoying the embarrassed silence and the shocked looks of most of the men. All eyes went back to the American girl.

"You can't be serious. That custom went out before the Civil War," Casey said.

"In America I'm sure it did." Joanna smiled her twisted smile. "Here it's different, this is part of England. It's a matter of manners. Do come along, dear."

"I will—dear," Casey said as sweetly. "Later."

Joanna had sighed and shrugged and raised an eyebrow at Dunross and smiled crookedly and gone off with the other ladies. There was a stunned silence at the table.

"Tai-pan, you don't mind if I stay, do you?" Casey had said with a laugh.

"Yes, I'm sorry but I do," he had told her gently. "It's just a custom, nothing important. It's really so the ladies can get first crack at the loo and the pails of water."

Her smile faded and her chin began to jut. "And if I prefer not to go?"

"It's just our custom, Ciranoush. In America it's custom to call someone you've just met by his first name, it's not here. Even so . . ." Dunross stared back calmly, but just as inflexibly. "There's no loss of face in it."

"I think there is."

"Sorry about that—I can assure you there isn't."

The others had waited, watching him and watching her, enjoying the confrontation, at the same time appalled by her. Except Ed Langan who was totally embarrassed for her. "Hell, Casey," he said, trying to make a joke of it, "you can't fight City Hall."

"I've been trying all my life," she had said sharply—clearly furious. Then, abruptly, she had smiled gloriously. Her fingers drummed momentarily on the tablecloth and she got up. "If you gentlemen will excuse me . . ." she had said sweetly and sailed away, an astonished silence in her wake.

"I hardly threw her out," Dunross said.

"It was bloody funny, even so," Barre said. "I wonder what changed her mind? Eh Phillip?"

"What?" Phillip Chen asked absently.

"For a moment I thought she was going to belt poor old Ian, didn't you? But something she thought of changed her mind. What?"

Dunross smiled. "I'll bet it's no good. That one's as touchy as a pocketful of scorpions."

"Great knockers, though," Barre said.

They laughed. Phillip Chen didn't. Dunross's concern for him increased. He had tried to cheer him up all evening but nothing had drawn the curtain away. All through dinner Phillip had been dulled and monosyllabic. Barre got up with a belch. "Think I'll take a leak while there's space." He lurched off into the garden.

"Don't pee on the camellias," Ian called after him absently, then forced himself to concentrate. "Phillip, not to worry," he said, now that they were alone. "They'll find John soon."

"Yes, I'm sure they will," Phillip Chen said dully, his mind not so much swamped by the kidnapping as appalled by what he had discovered in his son's safety deposit box this afternoon. He had opened it with the key that he had taken from the shoebox.

"Go on, Phillip, take it, don't be a fool," his wife Dianne had hissed. "Take it—if we don't the tai-pan will!"

"Yes, yes I know." Thank all gods I did, he thought, still in shock, remembering what he had found when he'd rifled through the contents. Manila envelopes of various sizes, mostly itemized, a diary and phone book. In the envelope marked "debts" betting slips for 97,000 HK for current debts to illegal, off-course gamblers in Hong Kong. A note in favor of

Miser Sing, a notorious moneylender, for 30,000 HK at 3 percent per month interest; a long overdue sight demand note from the Ho-Pak Bank for $20,000 U.S. and a letter from Richard Kwang dated last week saying unless John Chen made some arrangements soon he would have to talk to his father. Then there were letters which documented a growing friendship between his son and an American gambler, Vincenzo Banastasio, who assured John Chen that his debts were not pressing: ". . . take your time, John, your credit's the best, anytime this year's fine . . ." and, attached, was the photocopy of a perfectly legal, notorized promissory note binding his son, his heirs or assignees, to pay Banastasio, on demand, $485,000 U.S., plus interest.

Stupid, stupid, he had raged, knowing his son had not more than a fifth of those assets, so he himself would have to pay the debt eventually.

Then a thick envelope marked "Par-Con" had caught his attention.

This contained a Par-Con employment contract signed by K. C. Tcholok, three months ago, hiring John Chen as a private consultant to Par-Con for ". . . $100,000 down ($50,000 of which is hereby acknowledged as already paid) and, once a satisfactory deal is signed between Par-Con and Struan's, Rothwell-Gornt or any other Hong Kong company of Par-Con's choosing, a further one million dollars spread over a five-year period in equal installments; and within thirty days of the signing of the above said contract, a debt to Mr. Vincenzo Banastasio of 85 Orchard Road, Las Vegas, Nevada, of $485,000 paid off, the first year's installment of $200,000, along with the balance of $50,000 . . ."

"In return for what," Phillip Chen had gasped helplessly in the bank vault.

But the long contract spelled out nothing further except that John Chen was to be a "private consultant in Asia." There were no notes or papers attached to it.

Hastily he had rechecked the envelope in case he had missed anything but it was empty. A quick leafing through the other envelopes produced nothing. Then he happened to notice a thin airmail envelope half stuck to another. It was marked "Par-Con II." It contained photocopies of handwritten notes from his son to Linc Bartlett.

The first was dated six months ago and confirmed that he, John Chen, would and could supply Par-Con with the most intimate knowledge of the innermost workings of the whole Struan complex of companies, ". . . of course this has to be kept totally secret, but for example, Mr. Bartlett, you can see from the enclosed Struan balance sheets for 1954 through 1961 (when Struan's went public) what I advise is perfectly feasible. If you look at the chart of Struan's corporate structure, and the list of some of the important stockholders of Struan's and their secret holdings, including my father's, you should have no trouble in any takeover bid Par-Con cares to mount. Add to these photocopies the other thing I told you about—I swear to God that you can believe me—I guarantee success. I'm putting my life on the line, that should be collateral enough, but if you'll advance me fifty of the first hundred now, I'll agree to let you have possession on arrival—on your undertaking to return it to me once your deal's set—or for use against Struan's. I guarantee to use it against Struan's. In the end Dunross has to do anything you want. Please reply to the usual post box and destroy this as we have agreed."

"Possession of what?" Phillip Chen had muttered, beside himself with anxiety. His hands were shaking now as he read the second letter. It was dated three weeks ago. "Dear Mr. Bartlett. This will confirm your arrival dates. Everything's prepared. I look forward to seeing you again and meeting Mr. K. C. Tcholok. Thanks for the fifty cash which arrived safely—all future monies are to go to a numbered account in Zurich—I'll give you the bank details when you arrive. Thank you also for agreeing to our unwritten understanding that if I can assist you in the way I've claimed I can, then I'm in for 3 percent of the action of the new Par-Con (Asia) Trading Company.

"I enclose a few more things of interest: note the date that Struan's demand notes (countersigned by my father) become due to pay Toda Shipping for their new super container ships—September 1, 11 and 15. There's not enough money in Struan's till to meet them.

"Next: to answer Mr. Tcholok's question about my father's position in any takeover or proxy fight. He can be neutralized. Enclosed photocopies are a sample of many that I have. These show a very close relationship with White Powder Lee and his cousin, Wu Sang Fang who's also known as Four Finger Wu, from the early fifties, and secret ownership with them —even today—of a property company, two shipping companies and Bangkok trading interests. Though outwardly, now, both pose as respectable businessmen, property developers and shipping millionaires, it's common knowledge they have been successful pirates and smugglers for years—and there's a very strong rumor in Chinese circles that they are the High Dragons of the opium trade. If my father's connection with them was made public it would take his face away forever, would sever the very close links he has with Struan's, and all the other *hongs* that exist today, and most important, would destroy forever his chance for a knighthood, the one thing he wants above all. Just the threat of doing this would be enough to neutralize him—even make him an ally. Of course I realize these papers and the others I have need further documentation to stick in a court of law but I have this already in abundance in a safe place. . . ."

Phillip Chen remembered how, panic-stricken, he had searched frantically for the further documentation, his mind shrieking that it was impossible for his son to have so much secret knowledge, impossible for him to have Struan's balance sheets of the prepublic days, impossible to know about Four Finger Wu and those secret things.

Oh gods that's almost everything I know—even Dianne doesn't know half of that! What else does John know—what else has he told the American?

Beside himself with anxiety he had searched every envelope but there was nothing more.

"He must have another box somewhere—or safe," he had muttered aloud, hardly able to think.

Furiously he had scooped everything into his briefcase, hoping that a more careful examination would answer his questions—and slammed the box shut and locked it. At a sudden thought, he had reopened it. He had pulled the slim tray out and turned it upside down. Taped to the underside were two keys. One was a safety deposit box key with the number carefully filed off. He stared at the other, paralyzed. He recognized it at once. It was the key to his own safe in his house on the crest. He would have bet his life that the only key in existence was the one that he always wore around his neck, that had never been out of his possession—ever since his father had given it to him on his deathbed sixteen years ago.

"*Oh ko,*" he said aloud, once more consumed with rage.

Dunross said, "You all right? How about a brandy?"

"No, no thank you," Phillip Chen said shakily, back in the present now. With an effort he pulled his mind together and stared at the tai-pan, knowing he should tell him everything. But he dare not. He dare not until he knew the extent of the secrets stolen. Even then he dare not. Apart from many transactions the authorities could easily misconstrue, and others that could be highly embarrassing and lead to all sorts of court cases, civil if not criminal—stupid English law, he thought furiously, stupid to have one law for everyone, stupid not to have one law for the rich and another for the poor, why else work and slave and gamble and scheme to be rich—apart from all this he would still have had to admit to Dunross that he had been documenting Struan secrets for years, that his father had done so before him—balance sheets, stockholdings and other secret, very very private personal family things, smugglings and payoffs—and he knew it would be no good saying I did it just for protection, to protect the House, because the tai-pan would rightly say, yes but it was to protect the House of Chen and not the Noble House, and he would rightly turn on him, turn his full wrath on him and his brood, and in the holocaust of a fight against Struan's he was bound to lose—Dirk Struan's will had provided for that—and everything that almost a century and a half had built up would vanish.

Thank all gods that everything was not in the safe, he thought fervently. Thank all gods the other things are buried deep.

Then, suddenly, some words from his son's first letter ripped to the forefront of his mind, ". . . Add to these photocopies *the other thing* I told you about . . ."

He paled and staggered to his feet. "If you'll excuse me, tai-pan . . . I, er, I'll say good night. I'll just fetch Dianne and I . . . I'll . . . thank you, good night." He hurried off toward the house.

Dunross stared after him, shocked.

"Oh, Casey," Penelope was saying, "may I introduce Kathren Gavallan —Kathren's Ian's sister."

"Hi!" Casey smiled at her, liking her at once. They were in one of the antechambers on the ground floor among other ladies who were talking or fixing their makeup or standing in line, waiting their turn to visit the adjoining powder room. The room was large, comfortable and mirrored. "You both have the same eyes—I'd recognize the resemblance anywhere," she said. "He's quite a man, isn't he?"

"We think so," Kathren replied with a ready smile. She was thirty-eight, attractive, her Scots accent pleasing, her flowered silk dress long and cool. "This water shortage's a bore, isn't it?"

"Yes. Must be very difficult with children."

"No, chérie, the children, they just love it," Susanne deVille called out. She was in her late forties, chic, her French accent slight. "How can you insist they bathe every night?"

"My two are the same." Kathren smiled. "It bothers us parents, but it doesn't seem to bother them. It's a bore though, trying to run a house."

Penelope said, "God, I hate it! This summer's been ghastly. You're lucky tonight, usually we'd be dripping!" She was checking her makeup in the mirror. "I can't wait till next month. Kathren, did I tell you we're going home for a couple of weeks leave—at least I am. Ian's promised to come too but you never know with him."

"He needs a holiday," Kathren said and Casey noticed shadows in her eyes and care rings under her makeup. "Are you going to Ayr?"

"Yes, and London for a week."

"Lucky you. How long are you staying in Hong Kong, Casey?"

"I don't know. It all depends on what Par-Con does."

"Yes. Andrew said you had a meeting all day with them."

"I don't think they went much for having to talk business with a woman."

"That is the understatement," Susanne deVille said with a laugh, lifting her skirts to pull down her blouse. "Of course my Jacques is half French so he understands that women are in the business. But the English . . ." Her eyebrows soared.

"The tai-pan didn't seem to mind," Casey said, "but then I haven't had any real dealings with him yet."

"But you have with Quillan Gornt," Kathren said, and Casey, very much on guard even in the privacy of the ladies' room, heard the undercurrent in her voice.

"No," she replied. "I haven't—not before tonight—but my boss has."

Just before dinner she had had time to tell Bartlett the story of Gornt's father and Colin Dunross.

"Jesus! No wonder Adryon went cross-eyed!" Bartlett had said. "And in the billiard room too." He had thought a moment then he had shrugged. "But all that means is that this puts more pressure on Dunross."

"Maybe. But their enmity goes deeper than anything I've experienced, Linc. It could easily backfire."

"I don't see how—yet. Gornt was just opening up a flank like a good general should. If we hadn't had John Chen's advance information, what Gornt said could've been vital to us. Gornt's got no way of knowing we're ahead of him. So he's stepping up the tempo. We haven't even got our big guns out yet and they're both wooing us already."

"Have you decided yet which one to go with?"

"No. What's your hunch?"

"I haven't got one. Yet. They're both formidable. Linc, do you think John Chen was kidnapped because he was feeding us information?"

"I don't know. Why?"

"Before Gornt arrived I was intercepted by Superintendent Armstrong. He questioned me about what John Chen had said last night, what we'd talked about, exactly what was said. I told him everything I could remember—except I never mentioned I was to take delivery of 'it.' Since I still don't know what 'it' is."

"It's nothing illegal, Casey."

"I don't like not knowing. Not now. It's getting . . . I'm getting out of my depth, the guns, this brutal kidnapping and the police so insistent."

"It's nothing illegal. Leave it at that. Did Armstrong say there was a connection?"

"He volunteered nothing. He's a strong, silent English gentleman police officer and as smart and well trained as anything I've seen in the movies. I'm sure he was sure I was hiding something." She hesitated. "Linc, what's John Chen got that's so important to us?"

She remembered how he had studied her, his eyes deep and blue and quizzical and laughing.

"A coin," he had said calmly.

"What?" she had asked, astounded.

"Yes. Actually half a coin."

"But Linc, what's a coi—"

"That's all I'm telling you now, Casey, but you tell me does Armstrong figure there's some connection between Chen's kidnapping and the guns?"

"I don't know." She had shrugged. "I don't think so, Linc. I couldn't even give you odds. He's too cagey that one." Again she had hesitated. "Linc, have you made a deal, any deal with Gornt?"

"No. Nothing firm. Gornt just wants Struan out and wants to join with us to smash them. I said we'd discuss it Tuesday. Over dinner."

"What're you going to tell the tai-pan after dinner?"

"Depends on his questions. He'll know it's good strategy to probe enemy defenses."

Casey had begun to wonder who's the enemy, feeling very alien even here among all the other ladies. She had felt only hostility except from these two, Penelope and Kathren Gavallan—and a woman she had met earlier in the line for the toilet.

"Hello," the woman had said softly. "I hear you're a stranger here too."

"Yes, yes I am," Casey had said, awed by her beauty.

"I'm Fleur Marlowe. Peter Marlowe's my husband. He's a writer. I think you look super!"

"Thanks. So do you. Have you just arrived too?"

"No. We've been here for three months and two days but this is the first really English party we've been to," Fleur said, her English not as clipped as the others. "Most of the time we're with Chinese or by ourselves. We've a flat in the Old V and A annex. God," she added, looking at the toilet door ahead. "I wish she'd hurry up—my back teeth are floating."

"We're staying at the V and A too."

"Yes, I know. You two are rather famous." Fleur Marlowe laughed.

"Infamous! I didn't know they had apartments there."

"They're not, really. Just two tiny bedrooms and a sitting room. The kitchen's a cupboard. Still, it's home. We've got a bath, running water, and the loos flush." Fleur Marlowe had big gray eyes that tilted pleasingly and long fair hair and Casey thought she was about her age.

"Your husband's a journalist?"

"Author. Just one book. He mostly writes and directs films in Hollywood. That's what pays the rent."

"Why're you with Chinese?"

"Oh, Peter's interested in them." Fleur Marlowe had smiled and whispered conspiratorially, looking around at the rest of the women, "They're rather overpowering aren't they—more English than the English. The old school tie and all that balls."

Casey frowned. "But you're English too."

"Yes and no. I'm English but I come from Vancouver, B.C. We live in the States, Peter and I and the kids, in good old Hollywood, California. I really don't know what I am, half of one, half of the other."

"We live in L.A. too, Linc and I."

"I think he's smashing. You're lucky."

"How old are your kids?"

"Four and eight—thank God we're not water rationed yet."

"How do you like Hong Kong?"

"It's fascinating, Casey. Peter's researching a book here so it's marvelous for him. My God, if half the legends are true . . . the Struans and Dunrosses and all the others, and your Quillan Gornt."

"He's not mine. I just met him this evening."

"You created a minor earthquake by walking across the room with him." Fleur laughed. "If you're going to stay here, talk to Peter, he'll fill you in on all sorts of scandals." She nodded at Dianne Chen who was powdering her nose at one of the mirrors. "That's John Chen's stepmother, Phillip Chen's wife. She's wife number two—his first wife died. She's Eurasian and hated by almost everyone, but she's one of the kindest persons I've ever known."

"Why's she hated?"

"They're jealous, most of them. After all, she's wife of the compradore of the Noble House. We met her early on and she was terrific to me. It's . . . it's difficult living in Hong Kong for a woman, particularly an outsider. Don't really know why but she treated me like family. She's been grand."

"She's Eurasian? She looks Chinese."

"Sometimes it's hard to tell. Her maiden name's T'Chung, so Peter says, her mother's Sung. The T'Chungs come from one of Dirk Struan's mistresses and the Sung line's equally illegitimate from the famous painter, Aristotle Quance. Have you heard of him?"

"Oh yes."

"Lots of, er, our best Hong Kong families are, well, old Aristotle spawned four branches . . ."

At that moment the toilet door opened and a woman came out and Fleur said, "Thank God!"

While Casey was waiting her turn she had listened to the conversations of the others with half an ear. It was always the same: clothes, the heat, the water shortages, complaints about *amahs* and other servants, how expensive everything was or the children or schools. Then it was her turn and afterward, when she came out, Fleur Marlowe had vanished and Penelope had come up to her. "Oh I just heard about your not wanting to leave. Don't pay any attention to Joanna," Penelope had said quietly. "She's a pill and always has been."

"It was my fault—I'm not used to your customs yet."

"It's all very silly but in the long run it's much easier to let the men have their way. Personally I'm glad to leave. I must say I find most of their conversation boring."

"Yes, it is, sometimes. But it's the principle. We should be treated as equals."

"We'll never be equal, dear. Not here. This is the Crown Colony of Hong Kong."

"That's what everyone tells me. How long are we expected to stay away?"

"Oh, half an hour or so. There's no set time. Have you known Quillan Gornt long?"

"Tonight was the first time I'd met him," Casey said.

"He's—he's not welcome in this house," Penelope said.

"Yes, I know. I was told about the Christmas party."

"What were you told?"

She related what she knew.

There was a sharp silence. Then Penelope said, "It's not good for strangers to be involved in family squabbles, is it?"

"No." Casey added, "But then all families squabble. We're here, Linc and I, to start a business—we're hoping to start a business with one of your big companies. We're outsiders here, we know that—that's why we're looking for a partner."

"Well, dear, I'm sure you'll make up your mind. Be patient and be cautious. Don't you agree, Kathren?" she asked her sister-in-law.

"Yes, Penelope. Yes I do." Kathren looked at Casey with the same level gaze that Dunross had. "I hope you choose correctly, Casey. Everyone here's pretty vengeful."

"Why?"

"One reason's because we're such a closely knit society, very interrelated, and everyone knows everyone else—and almost all their secrets. Another's because hatreds here go back generations and have been nurtured for generations. When you hate you hate with all your heart. Another's because this is a piratical society with very few curbs so you can get away with all sorts of vengeances. Oh yes. Another's because here the stakes are high—if you make a pile of gold you can keep it legally even if it's made outside the law. Hong Kong's a place of transit—no one ever comes here to stay, even Chinese, just to make money and leave. It's the most different place on earth."

"But the Struans and Dunrosses and Gornts have been here for generations," Casey said.

"Yes, but individually they came here for one reason only: money. Money's our god here. And as soon as you have it, you vanish, European, American—and certainly the Chinese."

"You exaggerate, Kathy dear," Penelope said.

"Yes. It's still the truth. Another reason's that we live on the edge of catastrophe all the time: fire, flood, plague, landslide, riots. Half our population is Communist, half Nationalist, and they hate each other in a way no European can ever understand. And China—China can swallow us any moment. So you live for today and to hell with everything, grab what you can because tomorrow, who knows? Don't get in the way! People are rougher here because everything really is precarious, and nothing lasts in Hong Kong."

"Except the Peak," Penelope said. "And the Chinese."

"Even the Chinese want to get rich quickly to get out quickly—them more than most. You wait, Casey, you'll see. Hong Kong will work its magic on you—or evil, depending how you see it. For business it's the most exciting place on earth and soon you'll feel you're at the center of the earth. It's wild and exciting for a man, my God, it's marvelous for a man but for us it's awful and every woman, every wife, hates Hong Kong with a passion however much they pretend otherwise."

"Come on, Kathren," Penelope began, "again you exaggerate."

"No. No I don't. We're all threatened here, Penn, you know it! We women fight a losing battle . . ." Kathren stopped and forced a weary smile. "Sorry, I was getting quite worked up. Penn, I think I'll find Andrew and if he wants to stay I'll slip off if you don't mind."

"Are you feeling all right, Kathy?"

"Oh yes, just tired. The young one's a bit of a trial but next year he'll be off to boarding school."

"How was your checkup?"

"Fine." Kathy smiled wearily at Casey. "When you've the inclination give me a call. I'm in the book. Don't choose Gornt. That'd be fatal. 'Bye, darling," she added to Penelope and left.

"She's such a dear," Penelope said. "But she does work herself into a tizzy."

"Do you feel threatened?"

"I'm very content with my children and my husband."

"She asked whether you feel threatened, Penelope." Susanne deVille deftly powdered her nose and studied her reflection. "Do you?"

"No. I'm overwhelmed at times. But . . . but I'm not threatened any more than you are."

"Ah, chérie, but I am Parisienne, how can I be threatened? You've been to Paris, m'selle?"

"Yes," Casey said. "It's beautiful."

"It is the world," Susanne said with Gallic modesty. "Ugh, I look at least thirty-six."

"Nonsense, Susanne." Penelope glanced at her watch. "I think we can start going back now. Excuse me a second. . . ."

Susanne watched her go then turned her attention back to Casey. "Jacques and I came out to Hong Kong in 1946."

"You're family too?"

"Jacques's father married a Dunross in the First World War—an aunt of the tai-pan's." She leaned forward to the mirror and touched a fleck of powder away. "In Struan's it is important to be family."

Casey saw the shrewd Gallic eyes watching her in the mirror. "Of course, I agree with you that it is nonsense for the ladies to leave after dinner, for clearly, when we have gone, the heat she has left too, no?"

Casey smiled. "I think so. Why did Kathren say 'threatened'? Threatened by what?"

"By youth, of course by youth! Here there are tens of thousands of chic, sensible, lovely young Chinoise with long black hair and pretty, saucy derrières and golden skins who really understand men and treat sex for what it is: food, and often, barter. It is the gauche English puritan who has twisted the minds of their ladies, poor creatures. Thank God I was born French! Poor Kathy!"

"Oh," Casey said, understanding at once. "She's found out that Andrew's having an affair?"

Susanne smiled and did not answer, just stared at her reflection. Then she said, "My Jacques . . . of course he has affairs, of course all the men have affairs, and so do we if we're sensible. But we French, we understand that such transgressions should not interfere with a good marriage. We put correctly the amount of importance on to it, *non?*" Her dark brown eyes changed a little. *"Oui!"*

"That's tough, isn't it? Tough for a woman to live with?"

"Everything is tough for a woman, *chérie,* because men are such *cretins.*" Susanne deVille smoothed a crease away then touched perfume behind her ears and between her breasts. "You will fail here if you try to play the game according to masculine rules and not according to *feminine* rules. You have a rare chance here, mademoiselle, if you are woman enough. And if you remember that the Gornts are all poisonous. Watch your Linc Bartlett, Ciranoush, already there are ladies here who would like to possess him, and humble you."

14

Upstairs on the second floor the man came cautiously out of the shadows of the long balcony and slipped through the open French windows into the deeper darkness of Dunross's study. He hesitated, listening, his black clothes making him almost invisible. The distant sounds of the party drifted into the room making the silence and the waiting more heavy. He switched on a small flashlight.

The circle of light fell on the picture over the mantelpiece. He went closer. Dirk Struan seemed to be watching him, the slight smile taunting. Now the light moved to the edges of the frame. His hand reached out delicately and he tried it, first one side and then the other. Silently the picture moved away from the wall.

The man sighed.

He peered at the lock closely then took out a small bunch of skeleton keys. He selected one and tried it but it would not turn. Another. Another failure. Another and another, then there was a slight click and the key almost turned, almost but not quite. The rest of the keys failed too.

Irritably he tried the almost-key again but it would not work the lock.

Expertly his fingers traced the edges of the safe but he could find no secret catch or switch. Again he tried the almost-key, this way and that, gently or firmly, but it would not turn.

Again he hesitated. After a moment he pushed the painting carefully back into place, the eyes mocking him now, and went to the desk. There were two phones on it. He picked up the phone that he knew had no other extensions within the house and dialed.

The ringing tone went on monotonously, then stopped. "Yes?" a man's voice said in English.

"Mr. Lop-sing please," he said softly, beginning the code.

"There's no Lop-ting here. Sorry, you have a wrong number."

This code response was what he wanted to hear. He continued, "I want to leave a message."

"Sorry, you have a wrong number. Look in your phone book."

Again the correct response, the final one. "This is Lim," he whispered, using his cover name. "Arthur please. Urgent."

"Just a moment."

He heard the phone being passed and the dry cough he recognized at once. "Yes, Lim? Did you find the safe?"

"Yes," he said. "It's behind the painting over the fireplace but none of the keys fit. I'll need special equip—" He stopped suddenly. Voices were approaching. He hung up gently. A quick, nervous check that everything was in place and he switched off the flashlight and hurried for the balcony that ran the length of the north face. The moonlight illuminated him for an instant. It was Wine Waiter Feng. Then he vanished, his black waiter's clothes melding perfectly with the darkness.

The door opened. Dunross came in followed by Brian Kwok. He switched on the lights. At once the room became warm and friendly. "We won't be disturbed here," he said. "Make yourself at home."

"Thanks." This was the first time Brian Kwok had been invited upstairs.

Both men were carrying brandy snifters and they went over to the cool of the windows, the slight breeze moving the gossamer curtains, and sat in the high-backed easy chairs facing one another. Brian Kwok was looking at the painting, its own light perfectly placed. "Smashing portrait."

"Yes." Dunross glanced over and froze. The painting was imperceptibly out of place. No one else would have noticed it.

"Something's the matter, Ian?"

"No. No nothing," Dunross said, recovering his senses that had instinctively reached out, probing the room for an alien presence. Now he turned his full attention back to the Chinese superintendent, but he wondered deeply who had touched the painting and why. "What's on your mind?"

"Two things. First, your freighter, *Eastern Cloud*."

Dunross was startled. "Oh?" This was one of Struan's many coastal tramps that plied the trade routes of Asia. *Eastern Cloud* was a ten thousand tonner on the highly lucrative Hong Kong, Bangkok, Singapore, Calcutta, Madras, Bombay route, with a sometimes stop at Rangoon in Burma —all manner of Hong Kong manufactured goods outward bound, and all manner of Indian, Malayan, Thai and Burmese raw materials, silks, gems, teak, jute, foodstuffs, inbound. Six months ago she had been impounded by Indian authorities in Calcutta after a sudden customs search had discovered 36,000 taels of smugglers' gold in one of the bunkers. A little over one ton.

"The gold's one thing, your Excellency, that's nothing to do with us," Dunross had said to the consul general of India in Hong Kong, "but to impound our ship's something else!"

"Ah, very so sorry, Mr. Dunross sah. The law is the law and the smuggling of gold into India very serious indeed sah and the law says any ship with smuggled goods aboard may be impounded and sold."

"Yes, *may* be. Perhaps, Excellency, in this instance you could prevail on the authorities . . ." But all of his entreaties had been shuttled aside and attempted high-level intercessions over the months, here, in India, even in London, had not helped. Indian and Hong Kong police inquiries had produced no evidence against any member of his crew but, even so, *Eastern Cloud* was still tied up in Calcutta harbor.

"What about *Eastern Cloud?*" he asked.

"We think we can persuade the Indian authorities to let her go."

"In return for what?" Dunross asked suspiciously.

Brian Kwok laughed. "Nothing. We don't know who the smugglers are, but we know who did the informing."

"Who?"

"Seven odd months ago you changed your crewing policy. Up to that time Struan's had used exclusively Cantonese crew on their ships, then, for some reason you decided to employ Shanghainese. Right?"

"Yes." Dunross remembered that Tsu-yan, also Shanghainese, had suggested it, saying that it would do Struan's a lot of good to extend help to some of their northern refugees. "After all, tai-pan, they're just as good mariners," Tsu-yan had said, "and their wages are very competitive."

"So Struan's signed on a Shanghainese crew into *Eastern Cloud*—this was the first I believe—and the Cantonese crew that wasn't hired lost all face so they complained to their triad Red Rod leader wh—"

"Come off it for God's sake, our crews aren't triads!"

"I've said many times the Chinese are great joiners, Ian. All right, let's call the triad with Red Rod rank their union representative—though I know you don't have unions either—but this bugger said in no uncertain terms, *oh ko* we really have lost face because of those northern louts, I'll fix the bastards, and he tipped an Indian informer here who, for a large part of the reward, agreed of course in advance, and passed on the info to the Indian consulate."

"What?"

Brian Kwok beamed. "Yes. The reward was split twenty-eighty between the Indian and the Cantonese crew of the *Eastern Cloud* that should have been—Cantonese face was regained and the despised Shanghainese northern trash put into a stinking Indian pokey and their face lost instead."

"Oh Christ!"

"Yes."

"You have proof?"

"Oh yes! But let's just say that our Indian friend is helping us with future inquiries, in return for, er, services rendered, so we'd prefer not to name him. Your 'union shop steward'? Ah, one of his names was Big Mouth Tuk and he was a stoker on *Eastern Cloud* for three odd years. *Was* because, alas, we won't see him again. We caught him in full 14K regalia last week—in very senior Red Rod regalia—courtesy of a friendly Shanghainese informer, the brother of one of your crew that languished in said stinky Indian pokey."

"He's been deported?"

"Oh yes, quick as a wink. We really don't approve of triads. They are criminal gangs nowadays and into all sorts of vile occupations. He was off to Taiwan where I believe he won't be welcome at all—seeing as how the northern Shanghainese Green Pang triad society and the southern Cantonese 14K triad society are still fighting for control of Hong Kong. Big Mouth Tuk was a 426 all right—"

"What's a 426?"

"Oh, thought you might know. All officials of triads are known by numbers as well as symbolic titles—the numbers always divisible by the mystical number three. A leader's a 489, which also adds up to twenty-one, which adds up to three, and twenty-one's also a multiple of three, representing creation, times seven, death, signifying rebirth. A second rank's a White Fan, 438, a Red Rod's a 426. The lowest's a 49."

"That's not divisible by three, for God's sake!"

"Yes. But four times nine is thirty-six, the number of the secret blood oaths." Brian Kwok shrugged. "You know how potty we Chinese are over numbers and numerology. He was a Red Rod, a 426, Ian. We caught him. So triads exist, or existed, on one of your ships at least. Didn't they?"

"So it seems." Dunross was cursing himself for not prethinking that of course Shanghainese and Cantonese face would be involved so of course there'd be trouble. And now he knew he was in another trap. Now he had seven ships with Shanghainese crews against fifty-odd Cantonese.

"Christ, I can't fire the Shanghainese crews I've already hired and if I don't there'll be more of the same and loss of face on both sides. What's the solution to that one?" he asked.

"Assign certain routes exclusively to the Shanghainese, but only after consulting with their 426 Red Rod . . . sorry, with their shop stewards, and of course their Cantonese counterparts—*only* after consulting with a well-known soothsayer who suggested to you it would be fantastic joss to both sides to do this. How about Old Blind Tung?"

"Old Blind Tung?" Dunross laughed. "Perfect! Brian you're a genius! One good turn deserves another. For your ears only?"

"All right."

"Guaranteed?"

"Yes."

"Buy Struan's first thing tomorrow morning."

"How many shares?"

"As many as you can afford."

"How long do I hold them?"

"How are your *cojones*?"

Brian whistled tonelessly. "Thanks." He thought a moment, then forced his mind once more onto the matters in hand. "Back to *Eastern Cloud.* Now we come to one of the interesting bits, Ian. 36,000 taels of gold is legally worth $1,514,520 U.S. But melted down into the smugglers' five-tael bars and secretly delivered on shore in Calcutta, that shipment'd be worth two, perhaps three times that amount to private buyers—say 4.5 million U.S., right?"

"I don't know. Exactly."

"Oh, but I do. The lost profit's over 3 million—the lost investment about one and a half."

"So?"

"So we all know Shanghainese are as secretive and cliquey as Cantonese, or Chu Chow or Fukenese or any other tiny groupings of Chinese. So of course the Shanghainese crew were the smugglers—have to be, Ian, though we can't prove it, yet. So you can bet your bottom dollar that Shanghainese also smuggled the gold out of Macao to Hong Kong and onto *Eastern Cloud,* that Shanghainese money bought the gold originally in Macao, and that therefore certainly part of that money was Green Pang funds."

"That doesn't follow."

"Have you heard from Tsu-yan yet?"

Dunross watched him. "No. Have you?"

"Not yet but we're making inquiries." Brian watched him back. "My first point is that the Green Pang has been mauled and criminals loathe losing their hard-earned money, so Struan's can expect lots of trouble unless you nip the trouble in the bud as I've suggested."

"Not all Green Pang are criminals."

"That's a matter of opinion, Ian. Second point, for your ear only: We're sure Tsu-yan's in the gold-smuggling racket. My third and last point is that if a certain company doesn't want its ships impounded for smuggling gold, it could easily lessen the risk by reducing its gold imports into Macao."

"Come again?" Dunross said, pleasantly surprised to hear that he had managed to keep his voice sounding calm, wondering how much Special Intelligence knew and how much they were guessing.

Brian Kwok sighed and continued to lay out the information that Roger Crosse had given him. "Nelson Trading."

With a great effort, Dunross kept his face impassive. "Nelson Trading?"

"Yes. Nelson Trading Company Limited of London. As you know, Nelson Trading has the Hong Kong Government's exclusive license for the purchase of gold bullion on the international market for Hong Kong's jewelers, and, vastly more important, the equally exclusive monopoly for transshipment of gold bullion *in bond,* through Hong Kong to Macao—along with a minor second company, Saul Feinheimer Bullion Company, also of London. Nelson Trading and Feinheimer's have several things in common. Several directors for example, the same solicitors for example."

"Oh?"

"Yes. I believe you're also on the board."

"I'm on the board of almost seventy companies," Dunross said.

"True and not all of those are wholly or even partially owned by Struan's. Of course, some could be wholly owned through nominees, secretly, couldn't they?"

"Yes, of course."

"It's fortunate in Hong Kong we don't have to list directors—or holdings, isn't it?"

"What's your point, Brian?"

"Another coincidence: Nelson Trading's registered head offices in the city of London are in the same building as your British subsidiary, Struan London Limited."

"That's a big building, Brian, one of the best locations in the city. There must be a hundred companies there."

"Many thousands if you include all the companies registered with solicitors there—all the holding companies that hold other companies with nominee directors that hide all sorts of skeletons."

"So?" Dunross was thinking quite clearly now, pondering where Brian had got all this information, wondering too where in the hell all this was leading. Nelson Trading had been a secret, wholly owned subsidiary through nominees ever since it was formed in 1953 specifically for the Macao gold trade—Macao being the only country in Asia where gold importation was legal.

"By the way, Ian, have you met that Portuguese genius from Macao, Signore Lando Mata?"

"Yes. Yes I have. Charming man."

"Yes he is—and so well connected. The rumor is that some fifteen years ago he persuaded the Macao authorities to create a monopoly for the importation of gold, then to sell the monopoly to him, and a couple of friends, for a modest yearly tax: about one U.S. dollar an ounce. He's the same fellow, Ian, who first got the Macao authorities to legalize gambling . . . and curiously, to grant him and a couple of friends the same monopoly. All very cosy, what?"

Dunross did not answer, just stared back at the smile and at the eyes that did not smile.

"So everything went smoothly for a few years," Brian continued, "then in '54 he was approached by some Hong Kong gold enthusiasts—our Hong Kong gold law was changed in '54—who offered a now legal improvement on the scheme: their company buys the gold bullion legally in the world bullion markets on behalf of this Macao syndicate at the legal $35 an ounce and brings it to Hong Kong openly by plane or by ship. On arrival, our own Hong Kong customs fellows legally guard and supervise the transshipment from Kai Tak or the dock to the Macao ferry or the Catalina flying boat. When the ferry or flying boat arrives in Macao it's met by

Portuguese Customs officials and the bullion, all in regulation four-hundred-ounce bars, is transshipped under guard to cars, taxis actually, and taken to the bank. It's a grotty, ugly little building that does no ordinary banking, has no known customers—except the syndicate—never opens its door—except for the gold—and doesn't like visitors at all. Guess who owns it? Mr. Mata and his syndicate. Once inside their bank the gold vanishes!" Brian Kwok beamed like a magician doing his greatest trick. "Fifty-three tons this year so far. Forty-eight tons last year! Same the year before and the year before that and so on."

"That's a lot of gold," Dunross said helpfully.

"Yes it is. Very strangely the Macao authorities or the Hong Kong ones don't seem to care that what goes in never seems to come out. You with me still?"

"Yes."

"Of course, what really happens is that once inside the bank the gold's melted down from the regulation four-hundred-ounce bars into little pieces, into two, or the more usual five-tael bars which are much more easily carried, and smuggled. Now we come to the only illegal part of the whole marvelous chain: getting the gold out of Macao and smuggling it into Hong Kong. Of course, it's not illegal to remove it from Macao, only to smuggle it into Hong Kong. But you know and I know that it's relatively easy to smuggle anything into Hong Kong. And the incredible beauty of it all is that once in Hong Kong, *however the gold gets there*—it's perfectly legal for *anyone* to own it and no questions asked. Unlike say in the States or Britain where no citizen is ever allowed to own any gold bullion privately. Once legally owned, it can be legally exported."

"Where's all this leading to, Brian?" Dunross sipped his brandy.

Brian Kwok swilled the ancient, aromatic spirit in the huge glass and let the silence gather. At length he said, "We'd like some help."

"We? You mean Special Intelligence?" Dunross was startled.

"Yes."

"Who in SI? You?"

Brian Kwok hesitated. "Mr. Crosse himself."

"What help?"

"He'd like to read all your Alan Medford Grant reports."

"Come again?" Dunross said to give himself time to think, not expecting this at all.

Brian Kwok took out a photocopy of the first and last page of the intercepted report and offered it. "A copy of this has just come into our possession." Dunross glanced at the pages. Clearly they were genuine. "We'd like a quick look at all the others."

"I don't follow you."

"I didn't bring the whole report, just for convenience, but if you want it you can have it tomorrow," Brian said and his eyes didn't waver. "We'd appreciate it—Mr. Crosse said he'd appreciate the help."

The enormity of the implications of the request paralyzed Dunross for a moment.

"This report—and the others if they still exist—are private," he heard himself say carefully. "At least all the information in them is private to me personally, and to the Government. Surely you can get everything you want through your own intelligence channels."

"Yes. Meanwhile, Superintendent Crosse'd really appreciate it, Ian, if you'd let us have a quick look."

Dunross took a sip of his brandy, his mind in shock. He knew he could easily deny that the others existed and burn them or hide them or just leave them where they were, but he did not wish to avoid helping Special Intelligence. It was his duty to assist them. Special Intelligence was a vital part of Special Branch and the Colony's security and he was convinced that, without them, the Colony and their whole position in Asia would be untenable. And without a marvelous counterintelligence, if a twentieth of AMG's reports were true, all their days were numbered.

Christ Jesus, in the wrong hands . . .

His chest felt tight as he tried to reason out his dilemma. Part of that last report had leapt into his mind: about the traitor in the police. Then he remembered that Kiernan had told him that his back copies were the only ones in existence. How much was private to him and how much was known to British Intelligence? Why the secrecy? Why didn't Grant get permission? Christ, say I was wrong about some things being farfetched! In the wrong hands, in enemy hands, much of the information would be lethal.

With an effort he calmed his mind and concentrated. "I'll consider what you said and talk to you tomorrow. First thing."

"Sorry, Ian. I was told to in—to impress upon you the urgency."

"Were you going to say *insist?*"

"Yes. Sorry. We wish to ask for your assistance. This is a formal request for your cooperation."

"And *Eastern Cloud* and Nelson Trading are barter?"

"*Eastern Cloud*'s a gift. The information was also a gift. Nelson Trading is no concern of ours, except for passing interest. Everything said was confidential. To my knowledge, we have no records."

Dunross studied his friend, the high cheekbones and wide, heavy-lidded eyes, straight and unblinking, the face good-looking and well proportioned with thick black eyebrows.

"Did you read this report, Brian?"

"Yes."

"Then you'll understand my dilemma," he said, testing him.

"Ah, you mean the bit about a police traitor?"

"What was that?"

"You're right to be cautious. Yes, very correct. You're referring to the bit about a hostile being possibly at superintendent level?"

"Yes. Do you know who he is?"

"No. Not yet."

"Do you suspect anyone?"

"Yes. He's under surveillance now. There's no need to worry about that, Ian, the back copies'll just be seen by me and Mr. Crosse. They'll have top classification never mind."

"Just a moment, Brian—I haven't said they exist," Dunross told him, pretending irritation, and at once he noticed a flash in the eyes that could have been anger or could have been disappointment. The face had remained impassive. "Put yourself in my position, a layman," he said, his senses fine-honed, continuing the same line, "I'd be pretty bloody foolish to keep such info around, wouldn't I? Much wiser to destroy it—once the pertinent bits have been acted on. Wouldn't I?"

"Yes."

"Let's leave it at that for tonight. Until say ten in the morning."

Brian Kwok hesitated. Then his face hardened. "We're not playing parlor games, Ian. It's not for a few tons of gold, or some stock market shenanigans or a few gray area deals with the PRC however many millions're involved. This game's deadly and the millions involved are people and unborn generations and the Communist plague. Sevrin's bad news. The KGB's very bad news—and even our friends in the CIA and KMT can be equally vicious if need be. You'd better put a heavy guard on your files here tonight."

Dunross stared at his friend impassively. "Then your official position is that this report's accurate?"

"Crosse thinks it could be. Might be wise for us to have a man here just in case, don't you think?"

"Please yourself, Brian."

"Should we put a man out at Shek-O?"

"Please yourself, Brian."

"You're not being very cooperative, are you?"

"You're wrong, old chum. I'm taking your points very seriously," Dunross said sharply. "When did you get the copy and how?"

Brian Kwok hesitated. "I don't know, and if I knew I don't know if I should tell you."

Dunross got up. "Come on then, let's go and find Crosse."

"But why do the Gornts and the Rothwells hate the Struans and Dunrosses so much, Peter?" Casey asked. She and Bartlett were strolling the beautiful gardens in the cool of the evening with Peter Marlowe and his wife, Fleur.

"I don't know all the reasons yet," the Englishman said. He was a tall man of thirty-nine with fair hair, a patrician accent and a strange intensity behind his blue-gray eyes. "The rumor is that it goes back to the Brocks—

that there's some connection, some family connection between the Gornt family and the Brock family. Perhaps to old Tyler Brock himself. You've heard of him?"

"Sure," Bartlett said. "How did it start, the feud?"

"When Dirk Struan was a boy he'd been an apprentice seaman on one of Tyler Brock's armed merchantmen. Life at sea was pretty brutal then, life anywhere really, but my God in those days at sea . . . Anyway, Tyler Brock flogged young Struan unmercifully for an imagined slight, then left him for dead somewhere on the China coast. Dirk Struan was fourteen then, and he swore before God and the devil that when he was a man he'd smash the House of Brock and Sons and come after Tyler with a cat-o'-nine-tails. As far as I know he never did though there's a story he beat Tyler's eldest son to death with a Chinese fighting iron."

"What's that?" Casey asked uneasily.

"It's like a mace, Casey, three or four short links of iron with a spiked ball on one end and a handle on the other."

"He killed him for revenge on his father?" she said, shocked.

"That's another bit I don't know yet, but I'll bet he had a good reason." Peter Marlowe smiled strangely. "Dirk Struan, old Tyler and all the other men who made the British Empire, conquered India, opened up China. Christ, they were giants! Did I mention Tyler was one-eyed? One of his eyes was torn out by a whipping halyard in a storm in the 1830's when he was racing his three-masted clipper, the *White Witch*, after Struan with a full cargo of opium aboard. Struan was a day ahead in his clipper, *China Cloud*, in the race from the British opium fields of India to the markets of China. They say Tyler just poured brandy into the socket and cursed his sailors aloft to put on more canvas." Peter Marlowe hesitated, then he continued, "Dirk was killed in a typhoon in Happy Valley in 1841 and Tyler died penniless, bankrupt, in '63."

"Why penniless, Peter?" Casey asked.

"The legend is that Tess, his eldest daughter—Hag Struan to be—had plotted her father's downfall for years—you know she married Culum, Dirk's only son? Well, Hag Struan secretly plotted with the Victoria Bank, which Tyler had started in the 1840's and with Cooper-Tillman, Tyler's partners in the States. They trapped him and brought down the great House of Brock and Sons in one gigantic crash. He lost everything—his shipping line, opium hulks, property, warehouses, stocks, everything. He was wiped out."

"What happened to him?"

"I don't know, no one does for certain, but the story is that that same night, October thirty-first, 1863, old Tyler went to Aberdeen—that's a harbor on the other side of Hong Kong—with his grandson, Tom, who was then twenty-five, and six sailors, and they pirated an oceangoing lorcha—that's a ship with a Chinese hull but European rigged—and put out to sea. He was mad with rage, so they say, and he hauled up the Brock pennant to the masthead and he had pistols in his belt and a bloody cutlass in his hand—they'd killed four men to pirate the ship. At the neck of the harbor a cutter came after him and he blew it out of the water—in those days almost all boats were armed with cannon because of pirates—these seas have always been infected with pirates since time immemorial. So old Tyler put to sea, a good wind blowing from the east and a storm coming. At the mouth of Aberdeen he started bellowing out curses. He cursed Hag Struan and cursed the island, and cursed the Victoria Bank that had betrayed him, and the Coopers of Cooper-Tillman, but most of all he cursed the tai-pan who'd been dead more than twenty years. And old Tyler Brock swore revenge. They say he screamed out that he was going north to plunder and he was going to start again. He was going to build his House again and then, '. . . and then I be back by God . . . I be back and I be venged and then I be Noble House by God. . . . I be back. . . .'"

Bartlett and Casey felt a chill go down their backs as Peter Marlowe coarsened his voice. Then he continued, "Tyler went north and was never heard of again, no trace of him or the lorcha or his crew, ever. Even so, his presence is still here—like Dirk Struan's. You'd better remember, in any dealing with the Noble House you've got to deal with those two as well, or their ghosts. The night Ian Dunross took over as tai-pan, Struan's lost their freighter flagship, *Lasting Cloud*, in a typhoon. It was a gigantic financial disaster. She foundered off Formosa—Taiwan—and was lost with all hands except one seaman, a young English deckhand. He'd been on the bridge and he swore that they'd been lured onto the rocks by false lights and that he heard a maniac laughing as they went down."

Casey shivered involuntarily.

Bartlett noticed it and slipped his arm casually through hers and she smiled at him.

He said, "Peter, people here talk about people who've been dead a hundred years as though they're in the next room."

"Old Chinese habit," Peter Marlowe replied at once. "Chinese believe the past controls the future and explains the present. Of course Hong Kong's only a hundred and twenty years old so a man of eighty today'd . . . Take Phillip Chen, the present compradore, for example. He's sixty-five now—his grandfather was the famous Sir Gordon Chen, Dirk Struan's illegitimate son who died in 1907 at the age of eighty-six. So Phillip Chen would have been nine then. A sharp boy of nine'd remember all sorts of stories his revered grandfather would have told him about *his* father, the tai-pan, and May-may, his famous mistress. The story is that old Sir Gordon Chen was one hell of a character, truly an ancestor. He had two official wives, eight concubines of various ages, and left the sprawling Chen family rich, powerful and into everything. Ask Dunross to show you his portraits—I've only seen copies but, my, he was a handsome man. There're dozens of people alive here today who knew him—one of the original great founders. And my God, Hag Struan died only forty-six years

ago. Look over there. . . ." He nodded at a wizened little man, thin as a
bamboo and just as strong, talking volubly to a young woman. "That's
Vincent McGore, tai-pan of the fifth great *hong*, International Asian
Trading. He worked for Sir Gordon for years and then the Noble House."
He grinned suddenly. "Legend says he was Hag Struan's lover when he
was eighteen and just off the cattle boat from some Middle Eastern port—
he's not really Scots at all."

"Come off it, Peter," Fleur said. "You just made that up!"

"Do you mind," he said, but his grin never left him. "She was only
seventy-five at the time."

They all laughed.

"That's the truth?" Casey asked. "For real?"

"Who knows what's truth and what's fiction, Casey? That's what I was
told."

"I don't believe it," Fleur said confidently. "Peter makes up stories."

"Where'd you find out all this, Peter?" Bartlett asked.

"I read some of it. There are copies of newspapers that go back to 1870
in the Law Court library. Then there's the *History of the Law Courts of
Hong Kong*. It's as seamy a great book as you'll ever want if you're interested in Hong Kong. Christ, the things they used to get up to, so-called
judges and colonial secretaries, governors and policemen, and the tai-pans,
the highborn and the lowborn. Graft, murder, corruption, adultery, piracy,
bribery . . . it's all there!

"And I asked questions. There are dozens of old China hands who love
to reminisce about the old days and who know a huge amount about Asia
and Shanghai. Then there are lots of people who hate, or are jealous and
can't wait to pour a little poison on a good reputation or a bad one. Of
course, you sift, you try to sift the true from the false and that's very hard,
if not impossible."

For a moment Casey was lost in thought. Then she said, "Peter, what
was Changi like? Really like?"

His face did not change but his eyes did. "Changi was genesis, the
place of beginning again." His tone made them all chilled and she saw
Fleur slip her hand into his and in a moment he came back. "I'm fine,
darling," he said. Silently, somewhat embarrassed, they walked out of the
path onto the lower terrace, Casey knowing she had intruded. "We
should have a drink. Eh, Casey?" Peter Marlowe said kindly and made it
all right again.

"Yes. Thank you, Peter."

"Linc," Peter Marlowe said, "there's a marvelous strain of violence that
passes from generation to generation in these buccaneers—because that's
what they are. This is a very special place—it breeds very special people."
After a pause, he added thoughtfully, "I understand you may be going
into business here. If I were you I'd be very, very careful."

15

Dunross, with Brian Kwok in tow, was heading for Roger Crosse, chief of Special Intelligence, who was on the terrace chatting amiably with Armstrong and the three Americans, Ed Langan, Commander John Mishauer the uniformed naval officer, and Stanley Rosemont, a tall man in his fifties. Dunross did not know that Langan was FBI, or that Mishauer was U.S. Naval Intelligence, only that they were at the consulate. But he did know that Rosemont was CIA though not his seniority. Ladies were still drifting back to their tables, or chattering away on the terraces and in the garden. Men were lounging over drinks, and the party was mellow like the night. Some couples were dancing in the ballroom to sweet and slow music. Adryon was among them, and he saw Penelope stoically coping with Havergill. He noticed Casey and Bartlett in deep conversation with Peter and Fleur Marlowe, and he would have dearly loved to be overhearing what was being said. That fellow Marlowe could easily become a bloody nuisance, he thought in passing. He knows too many secrets already and if he was to read our book . . . No way, he thought. Not till hell freezes! That's one book he'll never read. How Alastair could be so stupid!

Some years ago Alastair Struan had commissioned a well-known writer to write the history of Struan's to celebrate their 125 years of trading and had passed over old ledgers and trunks of old papers to him unread and unsifted. Within the year the writer had produced an inflammatory tapestry that documented many happenings and transactions that were thought to have been buried forever. In shock they had thanked the writer and paid him off with a handsome bonus and the book, the only two copies, put in the tai-pan's safe.

Dunross had considered destroying them. But then, he thought, life is life, joss is joss and providing only we read them, there's no harm.

"Hello, Roger," he said, grimly amused. "Can we join you?"

"Of course, tai-pan." Crosse greeted him warmly, as did the others. "Make yourself at home."

The Americans smiled politely at the joke. They chatted for a moment about inconsequential things and Saturday's races and then Langan, Rosemont and Commander Mishauer, sensing that the others wanted to converse privately, politely excused themselves. When they were alone, Brian Kwok summarized exactly what Dunross had told him.

"We will certainly appreciate your help, Ian," Crosse said, his pale eyes penetrating. "Brian's right about it possibly being quite dicey—if of course AMG's other reports exist. Even if they don't, some nasties might want to investigate."

"Just exactly how and when did you get the copy of my latest one?"

"Why?"

"Did you get it yourselves—or from a third party?"

"Why?"

Dunross's voice hardened. "Because it's important."

"Why?"

The tai-pan stared at him and the three men felt the power of his personality. But Crosse was equally willful.

"I can partially answer your question, Ian," he said coolly. "If I do, will you answer mine?"

"Yes."

"We acquired a copy of your report this morning. An intelligence agent —I presume in England—tipped a friendly amateur here that a courier was en route to you with something that'd interest us. This Hong Kong contact asked us if we'd be interested in having a look at it—for a fee of course." Crosse was so convincing that the other two policemen who remembered the real story were doubly impressed. "This morning, the photocopy was delivered to my home by a Chinese I'd never met before. He was paid—of course you understand in these things you don't ask for a name. Now, why?"

"When this morning?"

"At 6:04 if you want an exact time. But why is this important to you?"

"Because Alan Medford Gr—"

"Oh, Father, sorry to interrupt," Adryon said, rushing up breathlessly, a tall, good-looking young man in tow, his crumpled sacklike dinner jacket and twisted tie and scruffy brown-black shoes out of place in all this elegance. "Sorry to interrupt but can I do something about the music?"

Dunross was looking at the young man. He knew Martin Haply and his reputation. The English-trained Canadian journalist was twenty-five, and had been in the Colony for two years and was now the scourge of the business community. His biting sarcasm and penetrating exposés of personalities and of business practices that were legitimate in Hong Kong but nowhere else in the Western world were a constant irritation.

"The music, Father," Adryon repeated, running on, "it's ghastly. Mother said I had to ask you. Can I tell them to play something different, please?"

"All right, but don't turn my party into a happening."

She laughed and he turned his attention back to Martin Haply. "Evening."

"Evening, tai-pan," the young man said with a confident, challenging grin. "Adryon invited me. I hope it was all right to come after dinner?"

"Of course. Have fun," Dunross said, and he added dryly, "There are a lot of your friends here."

Haply laughed. "I missed dinner because I was on the scent of a dilly."

"Oh?"

"Yes. Seems that certain interests in conjunction with a certain great bank have been spreading nasty rumors about a certain Chinese bank's solvency."

"You mean the Ho-Pak?"

"It's all nonsense though. The rumors. Just more Hong Kong shenanigans."

"Oh?" All day Dunross had heard rumors about Richard Kwang's Ho-Pak Bank being overextended. "Are you sure?"

"Have a column on it in tomorrow's *Guardian*. Talking about the Ho-Pak though," Martin Haply added breezily, "did you hear that upwards of a hundred people took all their money out of the Aberdeen branch this afternoon? Could be the beginning of a run and—"

"Sorry, Father . . . come on Martin, can't you see Father's busy." She leaned up and kissed Dunross lightly and his hand automatically went around her and hugged her.

"Have fun, darling." He watched her rush off, Haply following. Cocky son of a bitch, Dunross thought absently, wanting tomorrow's column now, knowing Haply to be painstaking, unbribable and very good at his job. Could Richard be overextended?

"You were saying, Ian? Alan Medford Grant?" broke into his thoughts.

"Oh, sorry, yes." Dunross sat back at the table, compartmentalizing those problems. "AMG's dead," he said quietly.

The three policemen gaped at him. "What?"

"I got a cable at one minute to eight this evening, and talked to his assistant in London at 9:11." Dunross watched them. "I wanted to know your 'when' because it's obvious there'd be plenty of time for your KGB spy—if he exists—to have called London and had poor old AMG murdered. Wouldn't there?"

"Yes." Crosse's face was solemn. "What time did he die?"

Dunross told them the whole of his conversation with Kiernan but he withheld the part about the call to Switzerland. Some intuition warned him not to tell. "Now, the question is: was it accident, coincidence or murder?"

"I don't know," Crosse said. "But I don't believe in coincidences."

"Nor do I."

"Christ," Armstrong said through his teeth, "if AMG hadn't had clearance . . . Christ only knows what's in those reports, Christ and you, Ian. If you've got the only existing copies this makes them potentially more explosive than ever."

"If they exist," Dunross said.

"Do they?"

"I'll tell you tomorrow. At 10 o'clock." Dunross got up. "Will you excuse me, please," he said politely with his easy charm. "I must see to my other guests now. Oh, one last thing. What about *Eastern Cloud?*"

Roger Crosse said, "She'll be released tomorrow."

"One way or the other?"

Crosse appeared shocked. "Good Lord, tai-pan, we weren't bartering! Brian, didn't you say we were just trying to help out?"

"Yes sir."

"Friends should always help out friends, shouldn't they, tai-pan?"

"Yes. Absolutely. Thank you."

They watched him walk away until he was lost.

"Do they or don't they?" Brian Kwok muttered.

"Exist? I'd say yes," Armstrong said.

"Of course they exist," Crosse said irritably. "But where?" He thought a moment, then added more irritably and both men's hearts skipped a beat, "Brian, while you were with Ian, Wine Waiter Feng told me none of his keys would fit."

"Oh, that's bad, sir," Brian Kwok said cautiously.

"Yes. The safe here won't be easy."

Armstrong said, "Perhaps we should look at Shek-O, sir, just in case."

"Would you keep such documents there—if they exist?"

"I don't know, sir. Dunross's unpredictable. I'd say they were in his penthouse at Struan's, that'd be the safest place."

"Have you been there?"

"No sir."

"Brian?"

"No sir."

"Neither have I." Crosse shook his head. "Bloody nuisance!"

Brian Kwok said thoughtfully, "We'd only be able to send in a team at night, sir. There's a private lift to that floor but you need a special key. Also there's supposed to be another lift from the garage basement, nonstop."

"There's been one hell of a slipup in London," Crosse said. "I can't understand why those bloody fools weren't on the job. Nor why AMG didn't ask for clearance."

"Perhaps he didn't want insiders to know he was dealing with an outsider."

"If there was one outsider, there could have been others." Crosse sighed, and, lost in thought, lit a cigarette. Armstrong felt the smoke hunger pangs. He took a swallow of his brandy but that did not ease the ache.

"Did Langan pass on his copy, sir?"

"Yes, to Rosemont here and in the diplomatic bag to his FBI HQ in Washington."

"Christ," Brian Kwok said sourly, "then it'll be all over Hong Kong by morning."

"Rosemont assured me it would not." Crosse's smile was humorless. "However, we'd better be prepared."

"Perhaps Ian'd be more cooperative if he knew, sir."

"No, much better to keep that to ourselves. He's up to something though."

Armstrong said, "What about getting Superintendent Foxwell to talk to him, sir, they're old friends."

"If Brian couldn't persuade him, no one can."

"The governor, sir?"

Crosse shook his head. "No reason to involve him. Brian, you take care of Shek-O."

"Find and open his safe, sir?"

"No. Just take a team out there and make sure no one else moves in. Robert, go to HQ, get on to London. Call Pensely at MI-5 and Sinders at MI-6. Find out exact times on AMG, everything you can, check the tai-pan's story. Check everything—perhaps other copies exist. Next, send back a team of three agents here to watch this place tonight, particularly to guard Dunross, without his knowledge of course. I'll meet the senior man at the junction of Peak Road and Culum's Way in an hour, that'll give you enough time. Send another team to watch Struan's building. Put one man in the garage—just in case. Leave me your car, Robert. I'll see you in my office in an hour and a half. Off you both go."

The two men sought out their host and made their apologies and gave their thanks and went to Brian Kwok's car. Going down Peak Road in the old Porsche, Armstrong said what they both had been thinking ever since Dunross had told them. "If Crosse's the spy he'd have had plenty of time to phone London, or to pass the word to Sevrin, the KGB or who the hell ever."

"Yes."

"We left his office at 6:10—that'd be 11:00 A.M. London time—so it couldn't've been us, not enough time." Armstrong shifted to ease the ache in his back. "Shit, I'd like a cigarette."

"There's a packet in the glove compartment, old chum."

"Tomorrow—I'll smoke tomorrow. Just like AA, like a bloody addict!" Armstrong laughed but there was no humor in it. He glanced across at his friend. "Find out quietly who else's read the AMG file today—apart from Crosse—quick as you can."

"My thought too."

"If he's the only one who read it . . . well, it's another piece of evidence. It's not proof but we'd be getting there." He stifled a nervous yawn, feeling very tired. "If it's him we really are up shit's creek."

Brian was driving very fast and very well. "Did he say when he gave the copy to Langan?"

"Yes. At noon. They had lunch."

"The leak could be from them, from the consulate—that place's like a sieve."

"It's possible but my nose says no. Rosemont's all right, Brian—and Langan. They're professionals."

"I don't trust them."

"You don't trust anyone. They've both asked their HQs to check the Bartlett and Casey Moscow frankings."

"Good. I think I'll send a telex to a friend in Ottawa. They might have something on file on them also. That Casey's a bird amongst birds, isn't she though? Was she wearing anything underneath that sheath?"

"Ten dollars to a penny you never find out."

"Done."

As they turned a corner, Armstrong looked at the city below and the harbor, the American cruiser lit all over tied up at the dockyard, Hong Kong side. "In the old days we'd have had half a dozen warships here of our own," he said sadly. "Good old Royal Navy!" He had been in destroyers during the war, lieutenant R.N. Sunk twice, once at Dunkirk, the second time on D Day plus three, off Cherbourg.

"Yes. Pity about the Navy, but, well, time marches on."

"Not for the better, Brian. Pity the whole bloody Empire's up the spout! It was better when it wasn't. The whole bloody world was better off! Bloody war! Bloody Germans, bloody Japs . . ."

"Yes. Talking about Navy, how was Mishauer?"

"The U.S. Naval Intelligence fellow? He was okay," Armstrong said wearily. "He talked a lot of shop. He whispered to the Old Man that the U.S.'re going to double their Seventh Fleet. It's so supersecret he didn't even want to trust the phone. There's going to be a big land expansion in Vietnam."

"Bloody fools—they'll get chewed up like the French. Don't they read the papers, let alone intelligence reports?"

"Mishauer whispered also their nuclear carrier's coming in the day after tomorrow for an eight-day R and R visit. Another top secret. He asked us to double up on security—and wet-nurse all Yankees ashore."

"More bloody trouble."

"Yes." Armstrong added thinly, "Particularly as the Old Man mentioned a Soviet freighter 'limped in' for repairs on the evening tide."

"Oh Christ!" Brian corrected an involuntary swerve.

"That's what I thought. Mishauer almost had a coronary and Rosemont swore for two minutes flat. The Old Man assured them of course none of the Russian seamen'll be allowed ashore without special permission, as usual, and we'll tail them all, as usual, but a couple'll manage to need a doctor or whatever, suddenly, and mayhaps escape the net."

"Yes." After a pause Brian Kwok said, "I hope we get those AMG files, Robert. Sevrin is a knife in the guts of China."

"Yes."

They drove in silence awhile.

"We're losing our war, aren't we?" Armstrong said.

"Yes."

16

The Soviet freighter, *Sovetsky Ivanov*, was tied up alongside in the vast Wampoa Dockyard that was built on reclaimed land on the eastern side of Kowloon. Floodlights washed her. She was a twenty-thousand tonner that plied the Asian trade routes out of Vladivostok, far to the north. Atop her bridge were many aerials and modern radar equipment. Russian seamen lounged at the foot of the fore and the aft gangways. Nearby, a uniformed policeman, a youthful Chinese, in neat regulation khaki drills, short pants, high socks, black belt and shoes, was at each gangway. A shore-going seaman had his pass checked by his shipmates and then by the constable, and then, as he walked toward the dockyard gates, two Chinese in civilian clothes came out of the shadows and began to dog his footsteps—openly.

Another seaman went down the aft gangway. He was checked through and then, soon, more silent Chinese plainclothes police began to follow him.

Unnoticed, a rowing boat eased silently from the blind side of the ship's stern and ducked into the shadows of the wharf. It slid quietly along the high wall toward a flight of dank sea steps half a hundred yards away. There were two men in the boat and the rowlocks were muffled. At the foot of the sea steps the boat stopped. Both men began listening intently.

At the forward gangway a third seaman going ashore reeled raucously down the slippery steps. At the foot he was intercepted and his pass checked and an argument began. He was refused permission by the shore guard and he was clearly drunk, so, cursing loudly, he let fly at one of them, but this man sidestepped and gave him a haymaker which was returned in kind. Both policemen's attention zeroed on the one-sided brawl. The tousled, thickset man who sat in the aft of the rowing boat ran up the sea steps, across the floodlit wharf and railway tracks, and vanished into the alleyways of the dockyard without being seen. Leisurely the rowing boat began to return the way it had come, and in a moment, the brawl ceased. The helpless drunk was carried back aboard, not unkindly.

Deep in the dockyard's byways, the tousled man sauntered now. From time to time, casually and expertly, he glanced behind to ensure he was not being followed. He wore dark tropicals and neat rubber-soled shoes. His ship's papers documented him as Igor Voranski, seaman first class, Soviet Merchant Marine.

He avoided the dock gates and the policeman who watched them and followed the wall for a hundred yards or so to a side door. The door opened onto an alley in the Tai-wan Shan resettlement area—a maze of corrugated iron, plywood and cardboard hovels. His pace quickened. Soon he was out of the area and into brightly lighted streets of shops and stalls and crowds that eventually led him to Chatham Road. There he hailed a taxi.

"Mong Kok, quick as you can," he said in English. "Yaumati Ferry."

The driver stared at him insolently. "Eh?"

"*Ayeeyah!*" Voranski replied at once and added in harsh, perfect Cantonese, "Mong Kok! Are you deaf! Have you been sniffing the White Powder? Do you take me for a foreign devil tourist from the Golden Mountain—me who is clearly a Hong Kong person who has lived here twenty years? *Ayeeyah!* Yaumati Ferry on the other side of Kowloon. Do you need directions? Are you from Outer Mongolia? Are you a stranger, eh?"

The driver sullenly pulled the flag down and sped off, heading south and then west. The man in the back of the car watched the street behind. He could see no trailing car but he still did not relax.

They're too clever here, he thought. Be cautious!

At Yaumati Ferry station he paid off the taxi and gave the man barely the correct tip then went into the crowds and slid out of them and hailed another taxi. "Golden Ferry."

The driver nodded sleepily, yawned and headed south.

At the ferry terminal he paid off the driver almost before he had stopped and joined the crowds that were hurrying for the turnstiles of the Hong Kong ferries. But once through the turnstiles he did not go to the ferry gate but instead went to the men's room and then, out once more, he opened the door of a phone booth and went in. Very sure now that he had not been followed he was more relaxed.

He put in a coin and dialed.

"Yes?" a man's voice answered in English.

"Mr. Lop-sing please."

"I don't know that name. There's no Mr. Lop-*ting* here. You have a wrong number."

"I want to leave a message."

"Sorry you have a wrong number. Look in your phone book!"

Voranski relaxed, his heart slowing a little. "I want to speak to Arthur," he said, his English perfect.

"Sorry, he's not here yet."

"He was told to be there, to wait my call," he said curtly. "Why is there a change?"

"Who is this please?"

"Brown," he snapped, using his cover name.

He was somewhat mollified as he heard the other voice instantly take on just deference. "Ah, Mr. Brown, welcome back to Hong Kong. Arthur's phoned to tell me to expect your call. He asked me to welcome you and to say everything's prepared for the meeting tomorrow."

"When do you expect him?"

"Any moment, sir."

Voranski cursed silently for he was obliged to report back to the ship by phone within the hour. He did not like divergences in any plan.

"Very well," he said. "Tell him to call me at 32." This was the code name for their safe apartment in Sinclair Towers. "Has the American arrived yet?"

"Yes."

"Good. He was accompanied?"

"Yes."

"Good. And?"

"Arthur told me nothing more."

"Have you met her yet?"

"No."

"Has Arthur?"

"I don't know."

"Has contact been made yet with either of them?"

"Sorry, I don't know. Arthur didn't tell me."

"And the tai-pan? What about him?"

"Everything's arranged."

"Good. How long would it take you to get to 32, if necessary?"

"Ten to fifteen minutes. Did you want us to meet you there?"

"I'll decide that later."

"Oh Mr. Brown, Arthur thought you might like a little company after such a voyage. Her name's Koh, Maureen Koh."

"That was thoughtful of him—very thoughtful."

"Her phone number's beside the phone at 32. Just ring and she'll arrive within half an hour. Arthur wanted to know if your superior was with you tonight—if he'd need companionship also."

"No. He'll join us as planned tomorrow. But tomorrow evening he will expect hospitality. Good night." Voranski hung up arrogantly, conscious of his KGB seniority. At that instant the booth door swung open and the Chinese barged in and another blocked the outside. "What the—"

The words died as he did. The stiletto was long and thin. It came out easily. The Chinese let the body fall. He stared down at the inert heap for a moment then cleaned the knife on the corpse and slid it back into its sheath in his sleeve. He grinned at the heavyset Chinese who still blocked

the glass windows in the upper part of the booth as though he was the
next customer, then put a coin in and dialed.

On the third ring a polite voice said, "Tsim Sha Tsui Police Station,
good evening."

The man smiled sardonically and said rudely in Shanghainese, "You
speak Shanghainese?"

A hesitation, a click, and now another voice in Shanghainese said,
"This is Divisional Sergeant Tang-po. What is it, caller?"

"A Soviet pig slipped through your mother-fornicating net tonight as
easily as a bullock shits, but now he's joined his ancestors. Do we of the
14K have to do all your manure-infected work for you?"

"What Sovie—"

"Hold your mouth and listen! His turtle-dung corpse's in a phone booth
at Golden Ferry, Kowloonside. Just tell your mother-fornicating superiors
to keep their eyes on enemies of China and not up their fornicating stink
holes!"

At once he hung up and eased out of the box. He turned back momentarily and spat on the body, then shut the door and he and his companion
joined the streams of passengers heading for the Hong Kong ferry.

They did not notice the man trailing them. He was a short, tubby
American dressed like all the other tourists with the inevitable camera
around his neck. Now he was leaning against the starboard gunnel melding into the crowd perfectly, pointing his camera this way and that as the
ferry skuttled toward Hong Kong Island. But unlike other tourists his film
was very special, so was his lens, and his camera.

"Hello, friend," another tourist said with a beam, wandering up to him.
"You having yourself a time?"

"Sure," the man said. "Hong Kong's a great place, huh?"

"You can say that again." He turned and looked at the view. "Beats the
hell outta Minneapolis."

The first man turned also but kept his peripheral vision locked onto the
two Chinese, then dropped his voice. "We got problems."

The other tourist blanched. "Did we lose him? He didn't double back,
Tom, I'm certain. I covered both exits. I thought you had him pegged in
the booth."

"You bet your ass he was pegged. Look back there, center row—the Chinese joker with the white shirt and the one next to him. Those two sons
of bitches knocked him off."

"Jesus!" Marty Povitz, one of the team of CIA agents assigned to cover
the *Sovetsky Ivanov*, carefully looked at the two Chinese. "Kuomintang?
Nationalists? Or Commies?"

"Shit, I don't know. But the stiff's still in a phone booth back there.
Where's Rosemont?"

"He's g—" Povitz stopped then raised his voice and became affable and
tourist again as passengers began to crowd nearer the exit. "Lookit there,"

he said, pointing to the crest of the Peak. The apartment buildings were tall and well lit and so were the houses that dotted the slopes, one particularly, one very high, the highest private mansion in Hong Kong. It was floodlit and sparkled like a jewel. "Say, whoever lives there's just about on top of the world, huh?"

Tom Connochie, the senior of the two, sighed. "Gotta be a tai-pan's house." Thoughtfully he lit a cigarette and let the match spiral into the black waters. Then, openly chatting tourist-style, he took a shot of the house and casually finished the roll of film, taking several more of the two Chinese. He reloaded his camera and, unobserved, passed the roll of exposed film to his partner. Hardly using his lips, he said, "Call Rosemont up there, soon as we dock—tell him we got problems—then go get these processed tonight. I'll phone you when these two've bedded down."

"You crazy?" Povitz said. "You're not tailing them alone."

"Have to, Marty, the film might be important. We're not risking that."

"No."

"Goddamnit, Marty, I'm tai-pan of this operation."

"Orders says two g—"

"Screw orders!" Connochie hissed. "Just call Rosemont and don't foul up the film." Then he raised his voice and said breezily, "Great night for a sail, huh?"

"Sure."

He nodded at the sparkle of light on the crest of the Peak, then focused on it through his super-powered telescopic lens viewfinder. "You live up there, you got it made, huh?"

Dunross and Bartlett were facing each other in the Long Gallery at the head of the staircase. Alone.

"Have you made a deal with Gornt?" Dunross asked.

"No," Bartlett said. "Not yet." He was as crisp and tough as Dunross and his dinner jacket fitted as elegantly.

"Neither you nor Casey?" Dunross asked.

"No."

"But you have examined possibilities?"

"We're in business to make money, Ian—as are you!"

"Yes. But there're ethics involved."

"Hong Kong ethics?"

"May I ask how long you have been dealing with Gornt?"

"About six months. Are you agreeing to our proposal today?"

Dunross tried to put away his tiredness. He had not wanted to seek out Bartlett tonight but it had been necessary. He felt the eyes from all the portraits on the walls watching him. "You said Tuesday. I'll tell you Tuesday."

"Then until then, if I want to deal with Gornt or anyone else, that's my right. If you accept our offer now, it's a deal. I'm told you're the best, the Noble House, so I'd rather deal with you than him—providing I get top dollar with all the necessary safeguards. I'm cash heavy, you're not. You're Asian heavy, I'm not. So we should deal."

Yes, Bartlett told himself, covering his foreboding, though delighted that his diversion this morning with Gornt had produced the confrontation so quickly and brought his opponent to bay—at the moment, Ian, you're just that, an opponent, until we finalize, if we finalize.

Is now the time to blitzkrieg?

He had been studying Dunross all evening, fascinated by him and the undercurrents and everything about Hong Kong—so totally alien to anything he had ever experienced before. New jungle, new rules, new dangers. Sure, he thought grimly, with both Dunross and Gornt as dangerous as a swamp full of rattlers and no yardstick to judge them by. I've got to be cautious like never before.

He felt his tension strongly, conscious of the eyes that watched from the walls. How far dare I push you, Ian? How far do I gamble? The profit potential's huge, the prize huge, but one mistake and you'll eat us up, Casey and me. You're a man after my own heart but even so still an opponent and governed by ghosts. Oh yes, I think Peter Marlowe was right in that though not in everything.

Jesus! Ghosts and the extent of the hatreds! Dunross, Gornt, Penelope, young Struan, Adryon . . . Adryon so brave after her initial fright.

He looked back at the cold blue eyes watching him. What would I do now, Ian, if I were you, you with your wild-ass heritage standing there so outwardly confident?

I don't know. But I know me and I know what Sun Tzu said about battlefields: only bring your opponent to battle at a time and a place of your own choosing. Well it's chosen and it's here and now.

"Tell me, Ian, before we decide, how are you going to pay off your three September notes to Toda Shipping?"

Dunross was shocked. "I beg your pardon?"

"You haven't got a charterer yet and your bank won't pay without one, so it's up to you, isn't it?"

"The bank . . . there's no problem."

"But I understand you've already overextended your line of credit 20 percent. Doesn't that mean you'll have to find a new line of credit?"

"I'll have one if I need it," Dunross said, his voice edgy, and Bartlett knew he had gotten under his guard.

"12 million to Toda's a lot of cash when you add it to your other indebtedness."

"What other indebtedness?"

"The installment of $6,800,000 U.S. due September 8 on your Orlin International Banking loan of 30 million unsecured; you've 4.2 million in consolidated corporate losses so far this year against a written-up paper profit of seven and a half last year; and 12 million from the loss of *Eastern Cloud* and all those contraband engines."

The color was out of Dunross's face. "You seem to be particularly well informed."

"I am. Sun Tzu said that you've got to be well informed about your allies."

The small vein in Dunross's forehead was pulsating. "You mean enemies."

"Allies sometimes become enemies, Ian."

"Yes. Sun Tzu also hammered about spies. Your spy can only be one of seven men."

Bartlett replied as harshly, "Why should I have a spy? That information's available from banks—all you've got to do is dig a little. Toda's bank's the Yokohama National of Japan—and they're tied in with Orlin in a lot of deals—so're we, Stateside."

"Whoever your spy is, he's wrong. Orlin will extend. They always have."

"Don't bet on it this time. I know those bastards and if they smell a killing, they'll have your ass so fast you'll never know what happened."

"A killing of Struan's?" Dunross laughed sardonically. "There's no way Orlin or any god-cursed bank could—or would want us wrecked."

"Maybe Gornt's got a deal cooking with them."

"Christ Jesus. . . ." Dunross held on to his temper with an effort. "Has he or hasn't he?"

"Ask him."

"I will. Meanwhile if you know anything, tell me now!"

"You've got enemies every which way."

"So have you."

"Yes. Does that make us good or bad partners?" Bartlett stared back at Dunross. Then his eyes fell on a portrait at the far end of the gallery. Ian Dunross was staring down at him from the wall, the likeness marvelous, part of a three-masted clipper in the background.

"Is that . . . Jesus, that's gotta be Dirk, Dirk Struan!"

Dunross turned and looked at the painting. "Yes."

Bartlett walked over and studied it. Now that he looked closer he could see that the sea captain was not Dunross, but even so, there was a curious similarity. "Jacques was right," he said.

"No."

"He's right." He turned and studied Dunross as though the man was a picture, comparing them back and forth. At length he said, "It's the eyes and the line of the jaw. And the taunting look in the eyes which says, 'You'd better believe I can kick the shit out of you anytime I want to.'"

The mouth smiled at him. "Does it now?"

"Yes."

"There's no problem on a line of credit, new or old."

"I think there is."

"The Victoria's our bank—we're big stockholders."

"How big?"

"We've alternate sources of credit if need be. But we'll get everything we want from the Vic. They're cash heavy too."

"Your Richard Kwang doesn't think so."

Dunross looked back from the portrait sharply. "Why?"

"He didn't say, Ian. He didn't say anything, but Casey knows bankers and she read the bottom line and that's what she thinks he thinks. I don't think she's much taken by Havergill either."

After a pause, Dunross said, "What else does she think?"

"That maybe we should go with Gornt."

"Be my guest."

"I may. What about Taipei?" Bartlett asked, wanting to keep Dunross off balance.

"What about it?"

"I'm still invited?"

"Yes, yes of course. That reminds me, you're released into my custody by kind permission of the assistant commissioner of police. Armstrong will be so informed tomorrow. You'll have to sign a piece of paper that you guarantee you'll return when I do."

"Thanks for arranging it. Casey is still not invited?"

"I thought we settled that this morning."

"Just asking. What about my airplane?"

Dunross frowned, off balance. "I suppose it's still impounded. Did you want to use it for the Taipei trip?"

"It'd be convenient, wouldn't it, then we could leave to suit ourselves."

"I'll see what I can do." Dunross watched him. "And your offer's firm until Tuesday?"

"Firm, just as Casey said. Until close of business Tuesday."

"Midnight Tuesday," Dunross countered.

"Do you always barter whatever the hell someone says?"

"Don't you?"

"Okay, midnight Tuesday. Then one minute into Wednesday all debts and friendships are canceled." Bartlett needed to keep the pressure on Dunross, needed the counteroffer now and not Tuesday so he could use it with or against Gornt. "The guy from Blacs, the chairman, what was his name?"

"Compton Southerby."

"Yes, Southerby. I was talking to him after dinner. He said they were all the way in back of Gornt. He implied Gornt also has a lot of Eurodollars on call if he ever needed them." Again Bartlett saw the piece of information slam home. "So I still don't know how you're going to pay Toda Shipping," he said.

Dunross didn't answer at once. He was still trying to find a way out of the maze. Each time he came back to the beginning: the spy must be Gavallan, deVille, Linbar Struan, Phillip Chen, Alastair Struan, David MacStruan, or his father, Colin Dunross. Some of Bartlett's information the banks would know—but not their corporate losses this year. That figure had been too accurate. That was the shocker. And the ". . . written-up paper profit."

He was looking at the American, wondering how much more inside knowledge the man had, feeling the trap closing on him with no way to maneuver, yet knowing he could not concede too much or he would lose everything.

What to do?

He glanced at Dirk Struan on the wall and saw the twisted half-smile and the look that said to him, Gamble laddie, where are thy balls?

Very well.

"Don't worry about Struan's. If you decide to join us, I want a two-year deal—20 million next year too," he said, going for broke. "I'd like 7 on signing the contract."

Bartlett kept the joy off his face. "Okay on the two-year deal. As to the cash flow, Casey offered 2 million down and then one and a half per month on the first of each month. Gavallan said that would be acceptable."

"It's not. I'd like 7 down, the rest spread monthly."

"If I agree to that I want title to your new Toda ships as a guarantee this year."

"What the hell do you want guarantees for?" Dunross snapped. "The whole point of the deal is that we'd be partners, partners in an immense expansion into Asia."

"Yes. But our 7 million cash covers your September payments to Toda Shipping, takes you off the Orlin hook and we get nothing in return."

"Why should I give you any concession? I can discount your contract immediately and get an advance of 18 of the 20 million you provide with no trouble at all."

Yes, you can, Bartlett thought—once the contract's signed. But before that you've got nothing. "I'll agree to change the down payment, Ian. But in return for what?" Casually he glanced at a painting opposite him, but he did not see it for all of his senses were concentrating on Dunross, knowing they were getting down to the short strokes. Title to the huge Toda bulk-cargo ships would cover all of Par-Con's risk whatever Dunross did.

"Don't forget," he added, "your 21 percent of the Victoria Bank stock is already in hock, signed over as collateral against your indebtedness to them. If you fail on the Toda payment or the Orlin, your old pal Havergill'll jerk the floor out. I would."

Dunross knew he was beaten. If Bartlett knew the exact amount of their secret bank holdings, Chen's secret holdings, together with their

open holdings, there was no telling what other power the American had
over him. "All right," he said. "I'll give you title to my ships for three
months, providing first, you guarantee to keep it secret between the two of
us; second, that our contracts are signed within seven days from today;
third, that you agree to the cash flow I've suggested. Last, you guarantee
not to leak one word of this until I make the announcement."

"When do you want to do that?"

"Sometime between Friday and Monday."

"I'd want to know in advance," Bartlett said.

"Of course. Twenty-four hours."

"I want title to the ships for six months, contracts within ten days."

"No."

"Then no deal," Bartlett said.

"Very well," Dunross said immediately. "Then let's return to the party."
He turned at once and calmly headed for the stairs.

Bartlett was startled with the abrupt ending of the negotiations. "Wait,"
he said, his heart skipping a beat.

Dunross stopped at the balustrade and faced him, one hand casually on
the bannister.

Grimly Bartlett tried to gauge Dunross, his stomach twisting uneasily.
He read finality in the eyes. "All right, title till January first, that's four
months-odd, secret to you, me and Casey, contracts next Tuesday—that
gives me time to get my tax people here—the cash flow as you laid it out
subject to . . . when's our meeting tomorrow?"

"It was at ten. Can we make it eleven?"

"Sure. Then it's a deal, subject to confirmation tomorrow at eleven."

"No. You've no need for more time. I might have but you haven't."
Again the thin smile. "Yes or no?"

Bartlett hesitated, all his instincts saying close now, stick out your hand
and close, you've everything you wanted. Yes—but what about Casey?
"This's Casey's deal. She can commit up to 20 million. You mind shaking
with her?"

"A tai-pan deals with a tai-pan on a closing, it's an old Chinese custom.
Is she tai-pan of Par-Con?"

"No," Bartlett said evenly. "I am."

"Good." Dunross came back and put out his hand, calling him, playing
with him, reading his mind. "Then it's a deal?"

Bartlett looked at the hand then into the cold blue eyes, his heart
pounding heavily. "It's a deal—but I want her to close it with you."

Dunross let his hand fall. "I repeat, who's tai-pan of Par-Con?"

Bartlett looked back levelly. "A promise is a promise, Ian. It's important
to her, and I promised she had the ball up to 20 million."

He saw Dunross begin to turn away, so he said firmly, "Ian, if I have to
choose between the deal and Casey, my promise to Casey, then that's no
contest. None. I'd consider it a fav—" He stopped. Both their heads jerked

around as there was a slight, involuntary noise from an eavesdropper in the shadows at the far end of the gallery where there was a group of high-backed settees and tall winged chairs. Instantly, Dunross spun on his heel and, catlike, hurtled silently to the attack. Bartlett's reactions were almost as fast. He, too, went quickly in support.

Dunross stopped at the green velvet settee. He sighed. It was no eavesdropper but his thirteen-year-old daughter, Glenna, fast asleep, curled up, all legs and arms like a young filly, angelic in her crumpled party dress, his wife's thin rope of pearls around her neck.

Bartlett's heart slowed and he whispered, "Jesus, for a moment . . . Hey, she's as cute as a button!"

"Do you have any children?"

"Boy and two girls. Brett's sixteen, Jenny's fourteen and Mary is thirteen. Unfortunately I don't see them very often." Bartlett, gaining his breath again, continued quietly, "They're on the East Coast now. Afraid I'm not very popular. Their mother . . . we, we were divorced seven years ago. She's remarried now but . . ." Bartlett shrugged, then looked down at the child. "She's a doll! You're lucky."

Dunross leaned over and gently picked up his child. She hardly stirred, just nestled closer to him, contentedly. He looked at the American thoughtfully. Then he said, "Bring Casey back here in ten minutes. I'll do what you ask—as much as I disapprove of it—because you wish to honor your promise." He walked away, surefooted, and disappeared into the east wing where Glenna's bedroom was.

After a pause, Bartlett glanced up at the portrait of Dirk Struan. The smile mocked him. "Go screw yourself," he muttered, feeling that Dunross had outsmarted him somehow. Then he grinned. "Eh, what the hell! Your boy's doing all right, Dirk old buddy!"

He went for the stairs. Then he noticed an unlit portrait in a half-hidden alcove. He stopped. The oil painting was of an old gray-bearded sea captain with one eye, hook-nosed and arrogant, his face scarred, a cutlass on the table beside him.

Bartlett gasped as he saw that the canvas was slashed and counterslashed, with a short knife buried in the man's heart, impaling the painting to the wall.

Casey was staring at the knife. She tried to hide her shock. She was alone in the gallery, waiting uneasily. Dance music wafted up from below —rhythm and blues music. A short wind tugged the curtains and moved a strand of her hair. A mosquito droned.

"That's Tyler Brock."

Casey spun around, startled. Dunross was watching her. "Oh, I didn't hear you come back," she said.

"Sorry," he said. "I didn't mean to make you jump."

"Oh, that's all right."

She looked back at the painting. "Peter Marlowe was telling us about him."

"He knows a lot about Hong Kong, but not everything, and not all his information's accurate. Some of it's quite wrong."

After a moment she said, "It's . . . it's a bit melodramatic, isn't it, leaving the knife like that?"

"Hag Struan did it. She ordered it left that way."

"Why?"

"It pleased her. She was tai-pan."

"Seriously, why?"

"I was serious." Dunross shrugged. "She hated her father and wanted us all to be reminded about our heritage."

Casey frowned, then motioned at a portrait on the opposite wall. "That's her?"

"Yes. It was done just after she was married." The girl in the painting was slim, about seventeen, pale blue eyes, fair hair. She wore a low-cut ball gown—tiny waist, budding bosom—an ornate green necklace encircling her throat.

They stood there looking at the picture for a moment. There was no name on the little brass plaque on the bottom of the ornate gilt frame, just the years, 1825–1917. Casey said, "It's an ordinary face, pretty but ordinary, except for the lips. They're thin and tight and disapproving—and tough. The artist captured a lot of strength there. It's a Quance?"

"No. We don't know who painted it. It was supposed to be her favorite portrait. There's a Quance of her in the Struan penthouse, painted about the same time. It's quite different, yet very much the same."

"Did she ever have a portrait done in later life?"

"Three. She destroyed them all, the moment they were finished."

"Are there any photos of her?"

"Not to my knowledge. She hated cameras—wouldn't have one in the house." Dunross laughed and she saw the tiredness in him. "Once a reporter for the *China Guardian* took her picture, just before the Great War. Within an hour she sent an armed crew from one of our merchantmen into their offices with orders to burn the place if she didn't get the negative and all copies back, and if the editor didn't promise to 'cease and desist from harassing her.' He promised."

"Surely you can't do that and get away with it?"

"No, you can't—unless you're tai-pan of the Noble House. Besides, everyone knew that Hag Struan didn't want her picture taken and this cocky young bastard had broken the rule. She was like the Chinese. She believed every time your picture's taken you lose part of your soul."

Casey peered at the necklace. "Is that jade?" she asked.

"Emeralds."

She gasped. "That must have been worth a fortune."

"Dirk Struan willed the necklace to her—it was never to leave Asia—it was to belong to the wife of each tai-pan of the Noble House, an heirloom to be passed on from lady to lady." He smiled oddly. "Hag Struan kept the necklace all her life, and, when she died, she ordered it burned with her."

"Jesus! Was it?"

"Yes."

"What a waste!"

Dunross looked back at the portrait. "No," he said, his voice different. "She kept Struan's the Noble House of Asia for almost seventy-five years. She was *the* tai-pan, the real tai-pan, though others had the title. Hag Struan fought off enemies and catastrophes and kept faith with Dirk's legacy and smashed the Brocks and did whatever was necessary. So what's a pretty bauble that probably cost nothing in the first place? It was probably pirated from the treasury of some Mandarin who stole it from someone else, whose peasants paid for it with sweat."

Casey watched him staring at the face, almost past it into another dimension. "I only hope I can do as well," he muttered absently, and it seemed to Casey he was saying it to *her*, to the girl in the picture.

Her eyes strayed beyond Dunross to the portrait of Dirk Struan and she saw again the marvelous likeness. There was a strong family resemblance in all the ten large portraits—nine men and the girl—that hung on the walls amid landscapes of all sizes of Hong Kong and Shanghai and Tien-sin and many seascapes of the elegant Struan clipper ships and some of their merchantmen. Below the portrait of each tai-pan was a small brass plaque with his name and the years of his life: "Dirk Dunross, 4th Tai-pan, 1852–1894, lost at sea in the India Ocean with all hands in *Sunset Cloud*" . . . "Sir Lochlin Struan, 3rd Tai-pan, 1841–1915" . . . "Alastair Struan, 9th Tai-pan, 1900–" . . . "Dirk Struan, 1798–1841" . . . "Ross Lechie Struan, 7th Tai-pan, 1887–1915, Captain Royal Scots Regiment, killed in action at Ypres" . . .

"So much history," she said, judging it time to break his thought pattern.

"Yes. Yes it is," he said, looking at her now.

"You're the 10th tai-pan?"

"Yes."

"Have you had your portrait done yet?"

"No."

"You'll have to, won't you?"

"Yes, yes in due course. There's no hurry."

"How do you become tai-pan, Ian?"

"You have to be chosen by the previous one. It's his decision."

"Have you chosen who'll follow you?"

"No," he said, but Casey thought that he had. Why should he tell me, she asked herself. And why are you asking him so many questions?

She looked away from him. A small portrait caught her attention. "Who's that?" she asked, disquieted. The man was misshapen, a hunchbacked dwarf, his eyes curious and his smile sardonic. "Was he a tai-pan too?"

"No. That's Stride Orlov, he was Dirk's chief captain. After *the tai-pan* was killed in the great typhoon and Culum took over, Stride Orlov became master of our clipper fleet. Legend has it he was a great seaman."

After a pause she said, "Sorry but there's something about him that gives me the creeps." There were pistols in Orlov's belt and a clipper ship in the background. "It's a frightening face," she said.

"He had that effect on everyone—except *the tai-pan* and Hag Struan—even Culum was supposed to have hated him." Dunross turned and studied her and she felt his probing. It made her feel warm and at the same time unsettled.

"Why did *she* like him?" she asked.

"The story is that right after the great typhoon when everyone in Hong Kong was picking up the pieces, Culum included, Devil Tyler started to take over the Noble House. He gave orders, assumed control, treated Culum and Tess like children . . . he sent Tess aboard his ship, the *White Witch*, and told Culum to be aboard by sunset or else. As far as Tyler was concerned the Noble House was now Brock-Struan and he was *the* tai-pan! Somehow or other—no one knows why or how Culum got the courage—my God, Culum was only twenty then and Tess barely sixteen—but Culum ordered Orlov to go aboard the *White Witch* and *fetch* his wife ashore. Orlov went alone, at once—Tyler was still ashore at the time. Orlov brought her back and in his wake left one man dead and another half a dozen with broken heads or limbs." Dunross was looking at her and she recognized the same half-mocking, half-violent, half-devilish smile that was on *the tai-pan*'s face. "Ever afterwards, Tess—Hag Struan to be—loved him, so they say. Orlov served our fleet well until he vanished. He was a fine man, and a great seaman, for all his ugliness."

"He vanished? He was lost at sea?"

"No. Hag Struan said he went ashore one day in Singapore and never returned. He was always threatening to leave and go home to Norway. So perhaps he went home. Perhaps he was knifed. Who knows, Asia's a violent place, though Hag Struan swore no man could kill Stride Orlov and that it must have been a woman. Perhaps Tyler ambushed him. Who knows?"

Inexorably her eyes went back to Tyler Brock. She was fascinated by the face and the implications of the knife. "Why did she do that to her father's image?"

"One day I'll tell you but not tonight, except to say that she hammered the knife into the wall with my grandfather's cricket bat and cursed before God and the devil anyone who took *her* knife out of *her* wall." He smiled at Casey and again she noticed an extraordinary tiredness in him and was glad because her own tiredness was creeping up on her and she did not want to make any mistakes now. He put out his hand. "We have to shake on a deal."

"No," Casey said calmly, glad to begin. "Sorry, I have to cancel out."

His smile evaporated. "What?"

"Yes. Linc told me the changes you want. It's a two-year deal—that ups our ante so I can't approve it."

"Oh?"

"No." She continued in the same flat but pleasant tone, "Sorry, 20 million's my limit so you'll have to close with Linc. He's waiting in the bar."

Understanding flashed over his face for an instant—and relief, she thought—and then he was calm again. "Is he now?" he said softly, watching her.

"Yes." She felt a wave of heat go through her, her cheeks began to burn and she wondered if the color showed.

"So we can't shake, you and I. It has to be Linc Bartlett?"

With an effort she kept her eyes unwavering. "A tai-pan should deal with a tai-pan."

"That's a basic rule, even in America?" His voice was soft and gentle.

"Yes."

"Is this your idea or his?"

"Does it matter?"

"Very much."

"If I say it's Linc's, he loses face, and if I say it's mine, he still loses face, though in a different way."

Dunross shook his head slightly and smiled. The warmth of it increased her inner warmth. Although she was very much in charge of herself, she felt herself responding to his unadulterated masculinity.

"We're all bound by face, aren't we, in some way or another," he said.

She did not answer, just glanced away to give herself time. Her eyes saw the portrait of the girl. How could such a pretty girl become known as the *Hag*, she wondered. It must be hateful to become old in face and body when you're young at heart and still strong and tough—so unfair for a woman. Will I be known one day as Hag Tcholok? Or "that old dyke Tcholok" if I'm still alone, unmarried, in the business world, the man's world, still working for the same things they work for—identity, power and money—and hated for being as good or better than they are at it? I don't care so long as we win, Linc and I. So play the part you've chosen tonight, she told herself, and thank the French lady for her advice. "Remember, child," her father had drummed into her, "remember that advice, good advice, comes from unexpected places at unexpected times." Yes, Casey thought happily, but for Susanne's reminder about how a lady should operate in this man's world, Ian, perhaps I wouldn't have given you that face-saving formula. But don't be mistaken, Ian Struan Dunross. This is my deal, and in this I'm tai-pan of Par-Con.

Casey felt an untoward glow as another current went through her. Never before had she articulated her actual position in Par-Con to herself. Yes, she thought, very satisfied, that's what I am.

She looked at the girl in the portrait critically and she saw, now, how wrong she had been before and how very special the girl was. Wasn't she *the tai-pan,* in embryo, even then?

"You're very generous," Dunross said, breaking into her thoughts.

"No," she replied at once, prepared, and glanced back at him, and she was thinking, If you want the truth, tai-pan, I'm not generous at all. I'm merely being demure and sweet and gentle because it makes you feel more at home. But she said none of this to him, only dropped her eyes and murmured with the right amount of softness, "It's you who're generous."

He took her hand and bowed over it and kissed it with old-fashioned gallantry.

She was startled and tried to cover it. No one had ever done that to her before. In spite of her resolve she was moved.

"Ah Ciranoush," he said with mock gravity, "any time you need a champion, send for me." Then he grinned suddenly. "I'll probably make a bog of it but never mind."

She laughed, all tension gone now, liking him very much. "You've got yourself a deal."

Casually he put his arm around her waist and gently propelled her toward the stairs. The contact with him felt good—too good, she thought. This one's no child. Be cautious.

17

11:58 P.M.:

Phillip Chen's Rolls screeched to a halt in the driveway of his house. He got out of the backseat, flushed with rage, Dianne nervously in tow. The night was dark, the lights of the city and ships and high rises blazing far below. "Bolt the gates, then you come inside too," he snapped to his equally nervous chauffeur, then hurried for the front door.

"Hurry up, Dianne," he said, irritably shoving his key into the lock.

"Phillip, what on earth's the matter with you? Why can't you tell me? Wh—"

"Shut up!" he shouted, his temper snapping, and she jerked to a halt, shocked. "Just shut up and do what you're told!" He ripped the front door open. "Get the servants here!"

"But Phi—"

"*Ah Sun! Ah Tak!*"

The two tousled, sleepy *amahs* appeared hastily out of the kitchen and gaped at him, shocked at his untoward rage. "Yes Father? Yes Mother?" they chorused in Cantonese. "What in the name of all gods ha—"

"Hold your tongues!" Phillip Chen roared, his neck red and now his face more red. "Go into that room and stay there until I tell you all to come out!" He pulled the door open. It was their dining room and the windows faced the road north. "All of you stay there until I tell you to come out and if any of you moves or looks out of the windows before I come back I'll . . . I'll have some friends put weights on you and get you all thrown into the harbor!"

The two *amahs* began wailing but everyone hurriedly obeyed him and he slammed the door shut.

"Stop it both of you!" Dianne Chen screeched at the *amahs*, then reached over and pinched one sharply on the cheek. This stopped the old woman's wailing and she gasped, her eyes rolling, "What's got into every-one? What's got into Father? Oh oh oh, his rage's gone to Java . . . oh oh oh. . . ."

"Shut up, Ah Tak!" Dianne fanned herself, seething, beside herself with fury. What in the name of all gods *has* got into him? Doesn't he trust me—me, his only true wife and the love of his life? In all my life . . . And to rush off like that from the tai-pan's party when everything was going so fine—us the talk of Hong Kong and everyone admiring my darling Kevin, fawning on him, now surely the new heir of the House of Chen, for everyone agrees John Chen would certainly have died of shock when his ear was cut off. Anyone would! I certainly would.

She shivered, feeling her own ear being cut again and being kidnapped as in her dream this afternoon when she had awoken in a cold sweat from her nap.

"*Ayeeyah*," she muttered to no one in particular. "Has he gone mad?"

"Yes, Mother," her chauffeur said confidently, "I think he has. It's the result of the kidnapping. I've never seen Father like this in all my yea—"

"Who asked you?" Dianne shrieked. "It's all your fault anyway! If you'd brought my poor John home instead of leaving him to his mealy-mouthed whores this would never have happened!"

Again the two *amahs* began whimpering at her fury and she turned her spleen on them for a moment, adding, "And as to you two, while I think of it, the quality of service in this house's enough to give anyone loose bowels. Have you asked me if I need a physic or aspirins? Or tea? Or a cold towel?"

"Mother," one of them said placatingly, hopefully pointing at the lacquered sideboard, "I can't make tea but would you like some brandy?"

"*Wat?* Ah, very good. Yes, yes, Ah Tak."

At once the old woman bustled over to the sideboard and opened it, brought out some cognac that she knew her mistress liked, poured it into a glass. "Poor Mother, to have Father in such a rage! Terrible! What's possessed him and why doesn't he want us to look out of the window?"

Because he doesn't want you turtle-dung thieves to see him dig up his secret safe in the garden, Dianne was thinking. Or even me. She smiled grimly to herself, sipping the fine smooth liquor, calmer in the knowledge that she knew where the iron box was buried. It was only right that she should have protected him by secretly watching him bury it, in case, God forbid, the gods took him from this earth before he could tell her where the secret hiding place was. It had been her duty to break her promise not to watch him that night during the Japanese Occupation when he had wisely scooped up all their valuables and hidden them.

She did not know what was in the box now. She did not care. It had been opened and closed many times, all in secret, as far as he was concerned. She did not care so long as she knew where her husband was, where all his deposit boxes of various kinds were, their keys, just in case.

After all, she told herself confidently, if he dies, without me the House of Chen will crumble. "Stop sniveling, Ah Sun!" She got up and closed the long drapes. Outside the night was dark and she could see nothing of the garden, only the driveway, the tall iron gates and the road beyond.

"More drink, Mother?" the old *amah* asked.

"Thank you, little oily mouth," she replied affectionately, the warmth of the spirit soothing her anger away. "And then you can massage my neck. I've got a headache. You two sit down, hold your tongues and don't make a sound till Father gets back!"

Phillip Chen was hurrying down the garden path, a flashlight in one hand, a shovel in the other. The path curled downward through well-tended gardens that meandered into a grove of trees and shrubs. He stopped a moment, getting his bearings, then found the place he sought. He hesitated and glanced back, even though he knew he was well hidden from the house now. Reassured that he could not be watched he switched on the flashlight. The circle of light wandered over the undergrowth and stopped at the foot of a tree. The spot appeared to be untouched. Carefully he pushed aside the natural mulch. When he saw the earth below had been disturbed he cursed obscenely. "Oh the swine . . . my own son!" Collecting himself with difficulty he began to dig. The earth was soft.

Ever since he had left the party he had been trying to remember exactly when he had last dug up the box. Now he was sure it had been in the spring when he needed the deeds to a row of slum dwellings in Wanchai that he had sold for fifty times cost to Donald McBride for one of his great new developments.

"Where was John then?" he muttered. "Was he in the house?"

As he dug he tried to recall but he could not. He knew that he would never have dug up the box when it was dangerous or when there were strangers in the house and that he would always have been circumspect. But John? Never would I have thought . . . John must have followed me somehow.

The shovel struck the metal. Carefully he cleaned off the earth and pulled the protective cloth away from the box and heavy lock and opened it. The hinges of the lid were well greased. His fingers shaking, he held the flashlight over the open box. All his papers and deeds and private balance sheets seemed to be in order and undisturbed, but he knew they must all have been taken out and read—and copied or memorized. Some of the information in his son's safety deposit box could only have come from here.

All the jewel boxes, big and small, were there. Nervously he reached out for the one he sought and opened it. The half-coin had vanished and the document explaining about the coin had vanished.

Tears of rage seeped down his cheeks. He felt his heart pounding and

smelled the damp earth and knew if his son was there he would happily
have strangled him with his own hands.

"Oh my son my son . . . all gods curse you to hell!"

His knees were weak. Shakily he sat on a rock and tried to collect his
wits. He could hear his father on his deathbed cautioning him: "Never
lose the coin my son—it's our key to ultimate survival and power over the
Noble House."

That was in 1937 and the first time he had learned the innermost secrets of the House of Chen: that he who became compradore became the
ranking leader in Hong Kong of the Hung Mun—the great secret triad society of China that, under Sun Yat-sen had become the 14K, originally
formed to spearhead China's revolt against their hated Manchu overlords;
that the compradore was the main, legitimate link between the Chinese
hierarchy on the Island and the inheritors of the 14K on the Mainland;
that because of Chen-tse Jin Arn, known as Jin-qua, the legendary chief
merchant of the co-*hong* that had possessed the Emperor's monopoly on all
foreign trade, the House of Chen was perpetually interlinked with the
Noble House by ownership and by blood.

"Listen carefully, my son," the dying man had whispered. "The tai-pan,
Great-Grandfather Dirk Struan, was Jin-qua's creation, as was the Noble
House. Jin-qua nurtured it, formed it *and* Dirk Struan. The tai-pan had
two concubines. The first was Kai-sung, one of Jin-qua's daughters by a
fifth wife. Their son was Gordon Chen, my father, your grandfather. The
tai-pan's second concubine was T'Chung Jin May-may, his mistress for six
years whom he married in secret just before the great typhoon that killed
them both. She was twenty-three then, a brilliant, favored granddaughter
of Jin-qua, sold to the tai-pan when she was seventeen to teach him
civilized ways without his knowing he was being taught. From them came
Duncan and Kate who took the surname *T'Chung* and were brought up
in my father's house. Father married off Kate to a Shanghai China Trader
called Peter Gavallan—Andrew Gavallan is also a cousin though he
doesn't know it. . . . So many stories to tell and now so little time to tell
them. Never mind, all the family trees are in the safe. There are so many.
We're all related, the Wu, Kwang, Sung, Kau, Kwok, Ng—all the old
families. Use the knowledge carefully. Here's the key to the safe.

"Another secret, Phillip, my son. Our line comes from my father's second wife. Father married her when he was fifty-three and she sixteen. She
was the daughter of John Yuan, the illegitimate son of the great American
Trader Jeff Cooper, and a Eurasian lady, Isobel Yau. Isobel Yau was the
oh-so-secret Eurasian daughter of Robb Struan, the tai-pan's half-brother
and cofounder of the Noble House, so we have blood from both sides of
the Struans. Alastair Struan is a cousin and Colon Dunross is a cousin—
the MacStruans are not, their history's in Grandfather's diaries. My son,
the English and Scots barbarians came to China and they never married
those whom they adored and most times abandoned when they returned to

the gray island of mist and rain and overcast. My God how I hate the English weather and loathe the past!

"Yes, Phillip, we're Eurasian, not of one side or the other. I've never been able to come to terms with it. It is our curse and our cross but it is up to all of us to make it a blessing. I pass our House on to you rich and strong like Jin-qua wished—do so to your son and make sure he does it to his. Jin-qua birthed us, in a way, gave us wealth, secret knowledge, continuity and power—and he gave us one of the coins. Here, Phillip, read about the coin."

The calligraphy of the ancient scroll was exquisite: "On this eighth day of the sixth month of the year 1841 by barbarian count, I, Chen-tse Jin Arn of Canton, Chief Merchant of the co-*hong,* have this day loaned to Green-Eyed Devil the tai-pan of the Noble House, chief pirate of all foreign devils who have made war on the Heavenly Kingdom and have stolen our island Hong Kong, forty lacs of silver . . . one million sterling in their specie . . . and have, with this bullion, saved him from being swallowed by One-Eye, his archenemy and rival. In return, the tai-pan grants us special trade advantages for the next twenty years, promises that one of the House of Chen will forever be compradore to the Noble House, and swears that he or his descendents will honor all debts and the debt of the coins. There are four of them. The coins are broken into halves. I have given the tai-pan four halves. Whenever one of the other halves is presented to him, or to a following tai-pan, he has sworn whatever favor is asked will be granted . . . *whether within their law, or ours, or outside it.*

"One coin I keep; one I give to the warlord Wu Fang Choi, my cousin; one will be given to my grandson Gordon Chen; and the last recipient I keep secret. Remember, he who reads this in the future, do not use the coin lightly, for the tai-pan of the Noble House must grant anything—*but only once.* And remember that though the Green-Eyed Devil himself will honor his promise and so will his descendents, he is still a mad-dog barbarian, cunning as a filthy Manchu because of *our* training, and as dangerous always as a nest of vipers."

Phillip Chen shuddered involuntarily, remembering the violence that was always ready to explode in Ian Dunross. He's a descendent of Green-Eyed Devil all right, he thought. Yes, him and his father.

Goddamn John! What possessed him? What devilment has he planned with Linc Bartlett? Has Bartlett got the coin now? Or does John still have it with him and now perhaps the kidnappers have it.

While his tired brain swept over the possibilities, his fingers checked the jewel boxes, one by one. Nothing was missing. The big one he left till last. There was a tightness in his throat as he opened it but the necklace was still there. A great sigh of relief went through him. The beauty of the emeralds in the flashlight gave him enormous pleasure and took away some of his anxiety. How stupid of Hag Struan to order them to be burned with her body. What an arrogant, awful, unholy waste that would have been! How wise of Father to intercept the coffin before the fire and remove them.

Reluctantly he put the necklace away and began to close up the safe. What to do about the coin? I almost used it the time the tai-pan took away our bank stock—and most of our power. Yes. But I decided to give him time to prove himself and this is the third year and nothing is yet proved, and though the American deal seems grand it is not yet signed. And now the coin is gone.

He groaned aloud, distraught, his back aching like his head. Below was all the city, ships tied up at Glessing's Point and others in the roads. Kowloon was equally brilliant and he could see a jetliner taking off from Kai Tak, another turning to make a landing, another whining high overhead, its lights blinking.

What to do? he asked himself exhaustedly. Does Bartlett have the coin? Or John? Or the Werewolves?

In the wrong hands it could destroy us all.

TUESDAY

18

Gornt said, "Of course Dunross could have buggered my brakes, Jason!"

"Oh come on, for God's sake! Climbing under your car during a party with two hundred guests around? Ian's not that stupid."

They were in Jason Plumm's penthouse above Happy Valley, the midnight air good though the humidity had increased again. Plumm got up and threw his cigar butt away, took a fresh one and lit it. The tai-pan of Asian Properties, the third largest *hong*, was taller than Gornt, in his late fifties, thin-faced and elegant, his smoking jacket red velvet. "Even Ian bloody Dunross's not that much of a bloody berk."

"You're wrong. For all his Scots cunning, he's an animal of sudden action, unpremeditated action, that's his failing. I think he did it."

Plumm steepled his fingers thoughtfully. "What did the police say?"

"All I told them was that my brakes had failed. There was no need to involve those nosy buggers, at least not yet. But Rolls brakes just *don't* go wrong by themselves for God's sake. Well, never mind. Tomorrow I'll make sure Tom Nikklin gets me an answer, an absolute answer, if there is one. Time enough for the police then."

"I agree." Plumm smiled thinly. "We don't need police to wash our various linens however droll—do we?"

"No." Both men laughed.

"You were very lucky. The Peak's no road to lose your brakes on. Must have been very unpleasant."

"For a moment it was, Jason, but then it was no problem, once I was over the initial shock." Gornt stretched the truth and sipped his whiskey and soda. They had eaten an elegant dinner on the terrace overlooking Happy Valley, the racecourse and city and sea beyond, just the two of them—Plumm's wife was in England on vacation and their children grown up and no longer in Hong Kong. Now they were sitting over cigars in great easy chairs in Plumm's book-lined study, the room luxurious though subdued, in perfect taste like the rest of the ten-room penthouse.

"Tom Nikklin'll find out if my car was tampered with if anyone can," he said with finality.

"Yes." Plumm sipped a glass of iced Perrier water. "Are you going to wind up young Nikklin again about Macao?"

"Me? You must be joking!"

"No. I'm not, actually," Plumm said with his mocking well-bred chuckle. "Didn't Dunross's engine blow up during the race three years ago and he bloody nearly killed himself?"

"Racing cars are always going wrong."

"Yes, yes they do frequently, though they're not always helped by the opposition." Plumm smiled.

Gornt kept his smile but inside he was not smiling. "Meaning?"

"Nothing, dear boy. Just rumors." The older man leaned over and poured more whiskey for Gornt, then used the soda syphon. "Rumor has it that a certain Chinese mechanic, for a small fee, put . . . put, as we say, a small spanner in the works."

"I doubt if that'd be true."

"I doubt if it could be proved. One way or another. It's disgusting, but some people will do anything for quite a small amount of money."

"Yes. Fortunately we're in the big-money market."

"My whole point, dear boy. Now." Plumm tapped the ash off his cigar. "What's the scheme?"

"It's very simple: providing Bartlett does not actually sign a deal with Struan's in the next ten days we can pluck the Noble House like a dead duck."

"Lots of people have thought that before and Struan's is still the Noble House."

"Yes. But at the moment, they're vulnerable."

"How?"

"The Toda Shipping notes, and the Orlin installment."

"Not true. Struan's credit is excellent—oh, they're stretched, but no more than anyone else. They'll just increase their line of credit—or Ian will go to Richard Kwang—or Blacs."

"Say Blacs won't help—they won't—and say Richard Kwang's neutralized. That leaves only the Victoria."

"Then Dunross'll ask the bank for more credit and we'll have to give it to him. Paul Havergill will put it to a vote of the board. We all know we can't outvote the Struan's block so we'll go along with it and save face, pretending we're very happy to oblige, as usual."

"Yes. But this time I'm happy to say Richard Kwang will vote against Struan's. That will tie up the board, the credit request will be delayed—he won't be able to make his payments, so Dunross goes under."

"For God's sake, Richard Kwang's not even on the board! Have you gone bonkers?"

Gornt puffed his cigar. "No, you've forgotten my game plan. The one called Competition. It was started a couple of days ago."

"Against Richard?"

"Yes."

"Poor old Richard!"

"Yes. He'll be our deciding vote. And Dunross'll never expect an attack from there."

Plumm stared at him. "Richard and Dunross are great friends."

"But Richard's in trouble. The run's started on the Ho-Pak. He'll do anything to save himself."

"I see. How much Ho-Pak stock did you sell short?"

"Lots."

"Are you sure Richard hasn't got the resources to stave off the run—that he can't pull in extra funds?"

"If he does, we can always abort, you and I."

"Yes, yes we can." Jason Plumm watched his cigar smoke spiral. "But just because Dunross won't meet those payments doesn't mean he's finished."

"I agree. But after the Ho-Pak 'disaster,' the news that Struan's have defaulted will send his stock plummeting. The market'll be very nervous, there'll be all the signs of a crash looming which we fuel by selling short. There's no board meeting scheduled for a couple of weeks unless Paul Havergill calls a special meeting. And he won't. Why should he? He wants their chunk of stock back more than anything else in the world. So everything will be fixed beforehand. He'll set the ground rules for rescuing Richard Kwang, and voting as Paul decides will be one of them. So the board lets Ian stew for a few days, then offers to extend credit and restore confidence—in return for Struan's piece of the bank stock—it's pledged against the credit anyway."

"Dunross'll never agree—neither he nor Phillip Chen, nor Tsu-yan."

"It's that or Struan's goes under—providing you hold tight and you've voting control. Once the bank gets his block of stock away from him . . . if you control the board, and therefore the Victoria Bank, then he's finished."

"Yes. But say he gets a new line of credit?"

"Then he's only badly mauled, maybe permanently weakened, Jason, but we make a killing either way. It's all a matter of timing, you know that."

"And Bartlett?"

"Bartlett and Par-Con are mine. He'll never go with Struan's sinking ship. I'll see to that."

After a pause Plumm said, "It's possible. Yes, it's possible."

"Are you in then?"

"After Struan's, how are you going to gobble up Par-Con?"

"I'm not. But *we* could—possibly." Gornt stubbed out his cigar. "Par-

Con's a long-term effort and a whole different set of problems. First Struan's. Well?"

"If I get Struan's Hong Kong property division—35 percent of their landholdings in Thailand and Singapore and we're fifty-fifty on their Kai Tak operation?"

"Yes, everything except Kai Tak—I need that to round off All Asia Airways, I'm sure you'll understand, old boy. But you've a seat on the board of the new company, ten percent of the stock at par, seats on Struan's of course, and all their subsidiaries."

"15 percent. And chairmanship of Struan's, alternate years with you?"

"Agreed, but I'm first." Gornt lit a cigarette. Why not? he thought expansively. By this time next year Struan's will be dismembered so your chairmanship is really academic, Jason old boy. "So everything's agreed? We'll put it in a joint memo if you like, one copy for each of us."

Plumm shook his head and smiled. "Don't need a memo, perish the thought! Here." He held out his hand. "I agree!"

The two men shook hands firmly. "Down with the Noble House!" They both laughed, very content with the deal they had made. Acquisition of Struan's landholdings would make Asian Properties the largest land company in Hong Kong. Gornt would acquire almost a total monopoly of all Hong Kong's air cargo, sea freighting and factoring—and preeminence in Asia.

Good, Gornt thought. Now for Four Finger Wu. "If you'll call me a taxi I'll be off."

"Take my car, my chauffeur will—"

"Thanks but no, I'd rather take a taxi. Really, Jason, thanks anyway."

So Plumm phoned down to the concierge of the twenty-story apartment building which was owned and operated by his Asian Properties. While they waited, they toasted each other and the destruction of Struan's and the profits they were going to make. A phone rang in the adjoining room.

"Excuse me a moment, old chap." Plumm went through the door and half-closed it behind him. This was his private bedroom which he used sometimes when he was working late. It was a small, very neat room, soundproofed, fitted up like a ship's cabin with a built-in bunk, hi-fi speakers that piped in the music, a small self-contained hot plate and refrigerator. And, on one side, was a huge bank of elaborate, shortwave, ham radio transceiver equipment which had been Jason Plumm's abiding hobby since his childhood.

He picked up the phone. "Yes?"

"Mr. Lop-sing please?" the woman's voice said.

"There's no Mr. Lop-*ting* here," he said easily. "Sorry, you have a wrong number."

"I want to leave a message."

"You have a wrong number. Look in your phone book."

"An urgent message for Arthur: Center radioed that the meeting's post-

poned until the day after tomorrow. Stand by for urgent instructions at
o6oo." The line went dead. Again a dial tone.

Plumm frowned as he put the phone back on its cradle.

Four Finger Wu stood at the gunnel of his junk with Goodweather
Poon watching Gornt get into the sampan that he had sent for him.

"He hasn't changed much in all this time, has he?" Wu said absently,
his narrowed eyes glittering.

"Foreign devils all look alike to me, never mind. How many years is it?
Ten?" Poon asked, scratching his piles.

"No, it's nearer twelve now. Good times then, *heya*," Wu said. "Lots of
profit. Very good, slipping upstream toward Canton, evading the foreign
devils and their lackeys, Chairman Mao's people welcoming us. Yes. Our
own people in charge and not a foreign devil anywhere—nor a fat official
wanting his hand touched with fragrant grease. You could visit all your
family and friends then and no trouble, *heya*? Not like now, *heya*?"

"The Reds're getting tough, very clever and very tough—worse than
the Mandarins."

Wu turned as his seventh son came on deck. Now the young man wore
a neat white shirt and gray trousers and good shoes. "Be careful," he
called out brusquely. "You're sure you know what to do?"

"Yes, Father."

"Good," Four Fingers said, hiding his pride. "I don't want any mistakes."

He watched him head awkwardly for the haphazard gangway of planks
that joined this junk to the next and thence across other junks to a make-
shift landing eight boats away.

"Does Seventh Son know anything yet?" Poon asked softly.

"No, no not yet," Wu said sourly. "Those dogmeat fools to be caught
with my guns! Without the guns, all our work will be for nothing."

"Evening, Mr. Gornt. I'm Paul Choy—my uncle Wu sent me to show
you the way," the young man said in perfect English, repeating the lie
that was now almost the real truth to him.

Gornt stopped, startled, then continued up the rickety stairs, his sea legs
better than the young man's. "Evening," he said. "You're American? Or
did you just go to school there, Mr. Choy?"

"Both." Paul Choy smiled. "You know how it is. Watch your head on
the ropes—and it's slippery as hell." He turned and began to lead the way
back. His real name was Wu Fang Choi and he was his father's seventh
son by his third wife, but, when he was born, his father Four Finger Wu
had sought a Hong Kong birth certificate for him, an unusual act for a

boat dweller, put his mother's maiden name on the birth certificate, added Paul and got one of his cousins to pose as the real father.

"Listen, my son," Four Finger Wu had said, as soon as Paul could understand, "when speaking Haklo aboard my ship, you can call me Father —but never in front of a foreign devil, even in Haklo. All other times I'm 'Uncle,' just one of many uncles. Understand?"

"Yes. But why, Father? Have I done something wrong? I'm sorry if I've offended you."

"You haven't. You're a good boy and you work hard. It's just better for the family for you to have another name."

"But why, Father?"

"When it's time you will be told." Then, when he was twelve and trained and had proved his value, his father had sent him to the States. "Now you're to learn the ways of the foreign devil. You must begin to speak like one, sleep like one, become one outwardly but never forget who you are, who your people are, or that all foreign devils are inferior, hardly human beings, and certainly not fornicating civilized."

Paul Choy laughed to himself. If Americans only knew—from tai-pan to meathead—and British, Iranians, Germans, Russians, every race and color, if they all really knew what even the lousiest coolie thought of them, they'd hemorrhage, he told himself for the millionth time. It's not that all the races of China despise foreigners, it's just that foreigners're just beneath any consideration. Of course we're wrong, he told himself. Foreigners are human and some are civilized—in their way—and far ahead of us technically. But we *are* better. . . .

"Why the smile?" Gornt asked, ducking under ropes, avoiding rubbish that scattered all the decks.

"Oh, I was just thinking how crazy life is. This time last month I was surfing at Malibu Colony, California. Boy, Aberdeen's something else, isn't it?"

"You mean the smell?"

"Sure."

"Yes it is."

"It's not much better at high tide. No one but me seems to smell the stench!"

"When were you last here?"

"Couple of years back—for ten days—after I graduated, B.A. in business, but I never seem to get used to it." Choy laughed. "New England it ain't!"

"Where did you go to school?"

"Seattle first. Then undergraduate school, University of Washington at Seattle. Then I got a master's at Harvard, Harvard Business School."

Gornt stopped. "Harvard?"

"Sure. I got an assist, a scholarship."

"That's very good. When did you graduate?"

"June last year. It was like getting out of prison! Boy, they really put your ass on the block if you don't keep up your grades. Two years of hell! After I got out I headed for California with a buddy, doing odd jobs here and there to make enough to keep surfing, having ourselves a time after sweating out so much school. Then . . ." Choy grinned. ". . . then a couple of months back Uncle Wu caught up with me and said it's time you went to work so here I am! After all, he paid for my education. My parents died years ago."

"Were you top of your class at Harvard?"

"Third."

"That's very good."

"Thank you. It's not far now, ours is the end junk."

They negotiated a precarious gangway, Gornt watched suspiciously by silent boat dwellers as they crossed from floating home to floating home, the families dozing or cooking or eating or playing mah-jong, some still repairing fishing nets, some children night fishing.

"This bit's slippery, Mr. Gornt." He jumped on to the tacky deck. "We made it! Home sweet home!" He tousled the hair of the sleepy little boy who was the lookout and said in Haklo, which he knew Gornt did not understand, "Keep awake, Little Brother, or the devils will get us."

"Yes, yes I will," the boy piped, his suspicious eyes on Gornt.

Paul Choy led the way below. The old junk smelled of tar and teak, rotting fish and sea salt and a thousand storms. Below decks the midship gangway opened on to the normal single large cabin for'ard that went the breadth of the ship and the length to the bow. An open charcoal fire burned in a careless brick fireplace with a sooty kettle singing over it. Smoke curled upward and found its way to the outside through a rough flue cut in the deck. A few old rattan chairs, tables and tiers of rough bunks lined one side.

Four Finger Wu was alone and he waved at one of the chairs and beamed. "*Heya*, good see," he said in halting, hardly understandable English. "Whiskey?"

"Thanks," Gornt said. "Good to see you too."

Paul Choy poured the good Scotch into two semiclean glasses.

"You want water, Mr. Gornt?" he asked.

"No, straight's fine. Not too much please."

"Sure."

Wu accepted his glass and toasted Gornt. "Good see you, *heya?*"

"Yes. Health!"

They watched Gornt sip his whiskey.

"Good," Gornt said. "Very good whiskey."

Wu beamed again and motioned at Paul. "Him sister son."

"Yes."

"Good school—Golden Country."

"Yes. Yes, he told me. You should be very proud."

"Wat?"

Paul Choy translated for the old man. "Ah thank, thank you. He talk good, *heya?*"

"Yes." Gornt smiled. "Very good."

"Ah, good never mind. Smoke?"

"Thank you." They watched Gornt take a cigarette. Then Wu took one and Paul Choy lit both of them. Another silence.

"Good with old frien'?"

"Yes. And you?"

"Good." Another silence. "Him sister son," the old seaman said again and saw Gornt nod and say nothing, waiting. It pleased him that Gornt just sat there, waiting patiently for him to come to the point as a civilized person should.

Some of these pink devils are learning at long last. Yes, but some have learned too fornicating well—*the* tai-pan for instance, him with those cold, ugly blue fish-eyes that most foreign devils have, that stare at you like a dead shark—the one who can even speak a little Haklo dialect. Yes, the tai-pan's too cunning and too civilized, but then he's had generations before him and his ancestors had the Evil Eye before him. Yes, but old Devil Green Eyes, the first of his line, who made a pact with my ancestor the great sea warlord, Wu Fang Choi and his son, Wu Kwok, and kept it, and saw that his sons kept it—and their sons. So this present tai-pan must be considered an old friend even though he's the most deadly of the line.

The old man suppressed a shudder and hawked and spat to scare away the evil spit god that lurked in all men's throats. He studied Gornt. Eeeee, he told himself, it must be vile to have to look at that pink face in every mirror—all that face hair like a monkey and a pallid white toad's belly skin elsewhere! Ugh!

He put a smile on his face to cover his embarrassment and tried to read Gornt's face, what was beneath it, but he could not. Never mind, he told himself gleefully, that's why all the time and money's been spent to prepare Number Seven Son—he'll know.

"Maybe ask favor?" he said tentatively.

The beams of the ship creaked pleasantly as she wallowed at her moorings.

"Yes. What favor, old friend?"

"Sister son—time go work—give job?" He saw astonishment on Gornt's face and this annoyed him but he hid it. "'Splain," he said in English then added to Paul Choy in guttural Haklo, "Explain to this Eater of Turtle Shit what I want. Just as I told you."

"My uncle apologizes that he can't speak directly to you so he's asked me to explain, Mr. Gornt," Paul Choy said politely. "He wants to ask if you'd give me a job—as a sort of trainee—in your airplane and shipping division."

Gornt sipped his whiskey. "Why those, Mr. Choy?"

"My uncle has substantial shipping interests, as you know, and he wants me to modernize his operation. I can give you chapter and verse on my background, if you'd consider me, sir—my second year at Harvard was directed to those areas—my major interest was transportation of all types. I'd been accepted in the International Division of the Bank of Ohio before my uncle jer—pulled me back." Paul Choy hesitated. "Anyway that's what he asks."

"What dialects do you speak, other than Haklo?"

"Mandarin."

"How many characters can you write?"

"About four thousand."

"Can you take shorthand?"

"Speedwriting only, sir. I can type about eighty words a minute but not clean."

"Wat?" Wu asked.

Gornt watched Paul Choy as the young man translated what had been said for his uncle, weighing him—and Four Finger Wu. Then he said, "What sort of trainee do you want to be?"

"He wants me to learn all there is to know about running shipping and airlines, the broking and freighting business also, the practical operation, and of course to be a profitable cog for you in your machine. Maybe my Yankee expertise, theoretical expertise, could help you somehow. I'm twenty-six. I've a master's. I'm into all the new computer theory. Of course I can program one. At Harvard I backgrounded in conglomerates, cash flows."

"And if you don't perform, or there's, how would you put it, a personality conflict?"

The young man said firmly, "There won't be, Mr. Gornt—leastways I'll work my can off to prevent that."

"Wat? What did he say? Exactly?" Four Fingers asked sharply in Haklo, noticing a change in inflection, his eyes and ears highly tuned.

His son explained, exactly.

"Good," Wu said, his voice a rasp. "Tell him exactly, if you don't do all your tasks to his satisfaction you'll be cast out of the family and my wrath will waste your days."

Paul Choy hesitated, hiding his shock, all his American training screaming to tell his father to go screw, that he was a Harvard graduate, that he was an American and had an American passport that *he'd* earned, whatever goddamn sampan or goddamn family he came from. But he kept his eyes averted and his anger off his face.

Don't be ungrateful, he ordered himself. You're not American, truly American. You're Chinese, and the head of your family has the right to rule. But for him you could be running a floating cathouse here in Aberdeen.

Paul Choy sighed. He knew that he was more fortunate than his eleven brothers. Four were junk captains here in Aberdeen, one lived in Bangkok and plied the Mekong River, one had a ferryboat in Singapore, another ran an import/export shipwright business in Indonesia, two had been lost at sea, one brother was in England—doing what he didn't know—and the last, the eldest, ruled the dozen feeder sampans in Aberdeen Harbor that were floating kitchens—and also three pleasure boats and eight ladies of the night.

After a pause Gornt asked, "What did he say? Exactly?"

Paul Choy hesitated, then decided to tell him, exactly.

"Thank you for being honest with me, Mr. Choy. That was wise. You're a very impressive young man," Gornt said. "I understand perfectly." Now for the first time since Wu had asked the original question he turned his eyes to the old seaman and smiled. "Of course. Glad to give nephew job."

Wu beamed and Paul Choy tried to keep the relief off his face.

"I won't let you down, Mr. Gornt."

"Yes, I know you won't."

Wu motioned at the bottle. "Whiskey?"

"No thank you. This is fine," Gornt said.

"When start job?"

Gornt looked at Paul Choy. "When would you like to start?"

"Tomorrow? Whenever's good for you, sir."

"Tomorrow. Wednesday."

"Gee, thanks. Eight o'clock?"

"Nine, eight thereafter. A six-day week of course. You'll have long hours and I'll push you. It'll be up to you how much you can learn and how fast I can increase your responsibilities."

"Thanks, Mr. Gornt." Happily Paul Choy translated for his father. Wu sipped his whiskey without hurrying. "What money?" he asked.

Gornt hesitated. He knew it had to be just the right sum, not too much, not too little, to give Paul Choy face and his uncle face. "1,000 HK a month for the first three months, then I'll review."

The young man kept his gloom off his face. That was hardly 200 U.S. but he translated it into Haklo.

"Maybe 2,000?" Wu said, hiding his pleasure. A thousand was the perfect figure but he was bargaining merely to give the foreign devil face and his son face.

"If he's to be trained, many valuable managers will have to take time away from their other duties," Gornt said politely. "It's expensive to train anyone."

"Much money Golden Mountain," Wu said firmly. "Two?"

"1,000 first month, 1,250 next two months?"

Wu frowned and added, "Month three, 1,500?"

"Very well. Months three and four at 1,500. And I'll review his salary after four months. And Paul Choy guarantees to work for Rothwell-Gornt for at least two years."

"Wat?"

Paul Choy translated again. Shit, he was thinking, how'm I going to vacation in the States on 50 bucks a week, even 60. Shit! And where the hell'm I gonna live? On a goddamn sampan? Then he heard Gornt say something and his brain twisted.

"Sir?"

"I said because you've been so honest with me, we'll give you free accommodation in one of our company houses—The Gables. That's where we put all our managerial trainees who come out from England. If you're going to be part of a foreign devil *hong* then you'd better mix with its future leaders."

"Yes sir!" Paul Choy could not stop the beam. "Yes sir, thank you sir."

Four Finger Wu asked something in Haklo.

"He wants to know where's the house, sir?"

"It's on the Peak. It's really very nice, Mr. Choy. I'm sure you'll be more than satisfied."

"You can bet your . . . yes sir."

"Tomorrow night be prepared to move in."

"Yes sir."

After Wu had understood what Gornt had said, he nodded his agreement. "All agree. Two year then see. Maybe more, *heya?*"

"Yes."

"Good. Thank old frien'." Then in Haklo, "Now ask him what you wanted to know . . . about the bank."

Gornt was getting up to go but Paul Choy said, "There's something else my uncle wanted to ask you, sir, if you can spare the time."

"Of course." Gornt settled back in his chair and Paul Choy noticed that the man seemed sharper now, more on guard.

"My uncle'd like to ask your opinion about the run on the Aberdeen branch of the Ho-Pak Bank today."

Gornt stared back at him, his eyes steady. "What about it?"

"There're all sorts of rumors," Paul Choy said. "My uncle's got a lot of money there, so've most of his friends. A run on that bank'd be real bad news."

"I think it would be a good idea to get his money out," Gornt said, delighted with the unexpected opportunity to feed the flames.

"Jesus," Paul Choy muttered, aghast. He had been gauging Gornt very carefully and he had noticed sudden tension and now equally sudden pleasure which surprised him. He pondered a moment, then decided to change tactics and probe. "He wanted to know if you were selling short."

Gornt said wryly, "He or you, Mr. Choy?"

"Both of us, sir. He's got quite a portfolio of stocks which he wants me to manage eventually," the young man said, which was a complete exaggeration. "I was explaining the mechanics of modern banking and the stock market to him—how it ticks and how Hong Kong's different from

Stateside. He gets the message very fast, sir." Another exaggeration. Paul Choy had found it impossible to break through his father's prejudices. "He asks if he should sell short?"

"Yes. I think he should. There have been lots of rumors that Ho-Pak's overextended—borrowing short and cheap, lending long and expensive, mostly on property, the classic way any bank would get into serious difficulties. For safety he should get all his money out and sell short."

"Next question, sir: Will Blacs, or the Victoria Bank do a bail-out?"

With an effort Gornt kept his face impassive. The old junk dipped slightly as waves from another chugging past lapped her sides. "Why should other banks do that?"

I'm trapped, Gornt was thinking, aghast. I can't tell the truth to them— there is no telling who else will get the information. At the same time, I daren't *not* tell the old bastard and his god-cursed whelp. He's asking for the return of *the* favor and I have to pay, that's a matter of face.

Paul Choy leaned forward in his chair, his excitement showing. "My theory's that if there's a real run on the Ho-Pak the others won't let it crash—not like the East India and Canton Bank disaster last year because it'd create shock waves that the market, the big operators in the market, wouldn't like. Everyone's waiting for a boom, and I bet the biggies here won't let a catastrophe wreck that chance. Since Blacs and the Victoria're the top bananas it figures they'd be the ones to do a bail-out."

"What's your point, Mr. Choy?"

"If someone knew in advance when Ho-Pak stock'd bottom out and either bank, or both, were launching a bail-out operation, that person could make a fortune."

Gornt was trying to decide what to do but he was tired now and not as sharp as he should be. That accident must have taken more out of me than I thought, he told himself. Was it Dunross? Was that bastard trying to even the score, repay me for *the* Christmas night or the Pacific Orient victory or fifty other victories—perhaps even the old Macao sore.

Gornt felt a sudden glow as he remembered the white hot thrill he had felt watching the road race, knowing that any moment the tai-pan's engine would seize up—watching the cars howl past lap after lap, and then Dunross, the leader, not coming in his turn—then waiting and hoping and then the news that he had spun out at Melco Hairpin in a metal screaming crash when his engine went. Waiting again, his stomach churning. Then the news that the whole racing car had exploded in a ball of fire but Dunross had scrambled out unscathed. He was both very sorry and very glad.

He didn't want Dunross dead. He wanted him alive and destroyed, alive to realize it.

He chuckled to himself. Oh it wasn't me who pressed the button that put that ploy into operation. Of course I did nudge young Donald Nikklin a little and suggest all sorts of ways and means that a little *h'eung yau* in the right hands . . .

His eyes saw Paul Choy and the old seaman waiting, watching him, and all of his good humor vanished. He pushed away his vagrant thoughts and concentrated.

"Yes, you're right of course, Mr. Choy. But your premise is wrong. Of course this is all theoretical, the Ho-Pak hasn't failed yet. Perhaps it won't. But there's no reason why any bank should do what you suggest, it never has in the past. Each bank stands or falls on its own merits, that's the joy of our free enterprise system. Such a scheme as you propose would set a dangerous precedent. It would certainly be impossible to prop up every bank that was mismanaged. Neither bank needs the Ho-Pak, Mr. Choy. Both have more than enough customers of their own. Neither has ever acquired other banking interests here and I doubt whether either would ever need to."

Horseshit, Paul Choy was thinking. A bank's committed to growth like any other business and Blacs and the Victoria are the most rapacious of all —except Struan's and Rothwell-Gornt. Shit, and Asian Properties and all the other *hongs*.

"I'm sure you're right, sir. But my uncle Wu'd appreciate it if you heard anything, one way or another."

He turned to his father and said in Haklo, "I'm finished now, Honored Uncle. This barbarian agrees the bank may be in trouble."

Wu's face lost color. "Eh? How bad?"

"I'll be the first in line tomorrow. You should take all your money out quickly."

"*Ayeeyah!* By all the gods!" Wu said, his voice raw, "I'll personally slit Banker Kwang's throat if I lose a single fornicating cash piece, even though he's my nephew!"

Paul Choy stared at him. "He is?"

"Banks are just fornicating inventions of foreign devils to steal honest people's wealth," Wu raged. "I'll get back every copper cash or his blood will flow! Tell me what he said about the bank!"

"Please be patient, Honored Uncle. It is polite, according to barbarian custom, not to keep this barbarian waiting."

Wu bottled his rage and said to Gornt in his execrable pidgin, "Bank bad, *heya*? Thank tell true. Bank bad custom, *heya*?"

"Sometimes," Gornt said cautiously.

Four Finger Wu unknotted his bony fists and forced calmness. "Thank for favor . . . yes . . . also want like sister son say *heya*?"

"Sorry, I don't understand. What does your uncle mean, Mr. Choy?"

After chatting with his father a moment for appearances, the young man said, "My uncle would consider it a real favor if he could hear privately, in advance, of any raid, takeover attempt or bail-out—of course it'd be kept completely confidential."

Wu nodded, only his mouth smiling now. "Yes. Favor." He put out his hand and shook with Gornt in friendly style, knowing that barbarians liked the custom though he found it uncivilized and distasteful, and contrary to correct manners from time immemorial. But he wanted his son trained quickly and it had to be with Second Great Company and he needed Gornt's information. He understood the importance of advance knowledge. Eeeee, he thought, without my friends in the Marine Police forces of Asia my fleets would be powerless.

"Go ashore with him, Nephew. See him into a taxi then wait for me. Fetch Two Hatchet Tok and wait for me, there, by the taxi stand."

He thanked Gornt again, then followed them to the deck and watched them go. His ferry sampan was waiting and he saw them get into it and head for the shore.

It was a good night and he tasted the wind. There was moisture on it. Rain? At once he studied the stars and the night sky, all his years of experience concentrating. Rain would come only with storm. Storm could mean typhoon. It was late in the season for summer rains but rains could come late and be sudden and very heavy and typhoon as late as November, as early as May, and if the gods willed, any season of the year.

We could use rain, he thought. But not typhoon.

He shuddered. Now we're almost into Ninth Month.

Ninth Month had bad memories for him. Over the years of his life, typhoon had savaged him nineteen times in that month, seven times since his father had died in 1937 and he had become Head of the House of the Seaborne Wu and Captain of the Fleets.

Of these seven times the first was that year. Winds of 115 knots tore out of the north/northwest and sank one whole fleet of a hundred junks in the Pearl River Estuary. Over a thousand drowned that time—his eldest son with all his family. In '49 when he had ordered all his Pearl River-based armada to flee the Communist Mainland and settle permanently into Hong Kong waters, he had been caught at sea and sunk along with ninety junks and three hundred sampans. He and his family were saved but he had lost 817 of his people. Those winds came out of the east. Twelve years ago from the east/northeast again and seventy junks lost. Ten years ago Typhoon Susan with her eighty-knot gales from the northeast, veering to east/southeast, had decimated his Taiwan-based fleet and cost another five hundred lives there, and another two hundred as far south as Singapore and another son with all his family. Typhoon Gloria in '57, one-hundred-knot gales, another multitude drowned. Last year Typhoon Wanda came and wrecked Aberdeen and most of the Haklo sea villages in the New Territories. Those winds came from the north/northwest and backed to northwest then veered south.

Wu knew the winds well and the number of the days well. September second, eighth, second again, eighteenth, twenty-second, tenth, and Typhoon Wanda first day. Yes, he thought, and those numbers add up to sixty-three, which is divisible by the magic number three, which then makes twenty-one which is three again. Will typhoon come on the third day of the Ninth Month this year? It never has before, never in all memory, but will it this year? Sixty-three is also nine. Will it come on the ninth day?

He tasted the wind again. There was more moisture in it. Rain was coming. The wind had freshened slightly. It came from north/northeast now.

The old seaman hawked and spat. Joss! If it's the third or ninth or second it's joss never mind. The only certain thing is that typhoon will come from some quarter or other and it will come in the Ninth Month—or this month which is equally bad.

He was watching the sampan now and he could see his son sitting amidships, alongside the barbarian, and he wondered how far he could trust him. The lad's smart and knows the foreign devil ways very well, he thought, filled with pride. Yes, but how far has he been converted to their evils? I'll soon find out never mind. Once the lad's part of the chain he'll be obedient. Or dead. In the past the House of Wu always traded in opium with or for the Noble House, and sometimes for ourselves. Once opium was honorable.

It still is for some. Me, Smuggler Mo, White Powder Lee, ah, what about them? Should we join into a Brotherhood, or not?

But the White Powders? Are they so different? Aren't they just stronger opium—like spirit is to beer?

What's the trading difference between the White Powders and salt? None. Except that now stupid foreign devil law says one's contraband and the other isn't! *Ayeeyah,* up to twenty-odd years ago when the barbarians lost their fornicating war to the fiends from the Eastern Sea, the government monopolized the trade here.

Wasn't Hong Kong trade with China built on opium, greased only by opium grown in barbarian India?

But now that they've destroyed their own producing fields, they're trying to pretend the trade never happened, that it's immoral and a terrible crime worth twenty years in prison!

Ayeeyah, how can a civilized person understand a barbarian?

Disgustedly he went below.

Eeeee, he thought wearily. This has been a difficult day. First John Chen vanishes. Then those two Cantonese dogmeat fornicators are caught at the airport and my shipment of guns is stolen by the fornicating police. Then this afternoon the tai-pan's letter arrived by hand: "Greetings Honored Old Friend. On reflection I suggest you put Number Seven Son with the enemy—better for him, better for us. Ask Black Beard to see you tonight. Telephone me afterwards." It was signed with the tai-pan's chop and "Old Friend."

"Old Friend" to a Chinese was a particular person or company who had done you an extreme favor in the past, or someone in business who had proved trustworthy and profitable over the years. Sometimes the years went over generations.

Yes, Wu thought, this tai-pan's an old friend. It was he who had suggested the birth certificate and the new name for his Seventh Son, who suggested sending him to the Golden Country and had smoothed the waters there and the waters into the great university, and had watched over him there without his knowledge—the subterfuge solving his dilemma of how to have one of his sons trained in America without the taint of the opium connection.

What fools barbarians are! Yes, but even so, this tai-pan is not. He's truly an old friend—and so is the Noble House.

Wu remembered all the profits he and his family had made secretly over the generations, with or without the help of the Noble House, in peace and war, trading where barbarian ships could not: contraband, gold, gasoline, opium, rubber, machinery, medical drugs, anything and everything in short supply. Even people, helping them escape from the Mainland or to the Mainland, their passage money considerable. With and without but mostly with the assistance of the Noble House, with this tai-pan and before him Old Hawk Nose, his old cousin, and before him, Mad Dog, his father, and before him the cousin's father, the Wu clan had prospered.

Now Four Finger Wu had 6 percent of the Noble House, purchased over the years and hidden with their help in a maze of nominees but still in his sole control, the largest share of their gold transmittal business, along with heavy investments here, in Macao, Singapore and Indonesia and in property, shipping, banking.

Banking, he thought grimly. I'll cut my nephew's throat after I've fed him his Secret Sack if I lose one copper cash!

He was below now and he went into the seamy, littered main cabin where he and his wife slept. She was in the big straw-filled bunk and she turned over in half-sleep. "Are you finished now? Are you coming to bed?"

"No. Go to sleep," he said kindly. "I've work to do."

Obediently she did as she was told. She was his *tai-tai*, his chief wife, and they had been married for forty-seven years.

He took off his clothes and changed. He put on a clean white shirt and clean socks and shoes, and the creases of his gray trousers were sharp. He closed the cabin door quietly behind him and came nimbly on deck feeling very uncomfortable and tied in by the clothes. "I'll be back before dawn, Fourth Grandson," he said.

"Yes, Grandfather."

"You stay awake now!"

"Yes, Grandfather."

He cuffed the boy gently then went across the gangways and stopped at the third junk.

"Goodweather Poon?" he called out.

"Yes . . . yes?" the sleepy voice said. The old man was curled up on old sacking, dozing.

"Assemble all the captains. I'll be back within two hours."

Poon was immediately alert. "We sail?" he asked.

"No. I'll be back in two hours. Assemble the captains!"

Wu continued on his way and was bowed into his personal ferry sampan. He peered at the shore. His son was standing beside his big black Rolls with the good luck number plate—the single number 8—that he had purchased for 150,000 HK in the government auction, his uniformed chauffeur and his bodyguard, Two Hatchet Tok, waiting deferentially beside him. As always he felt pleasure seeing his great machine and this overrode his growing concern. Of course, he was not the only dweller in the sea villages who owned a Rolls. But, by custom, his was always the largest and the newest. 8, *baat*, was the luckiest number because it rhymed with *faat* which meant "expanding prosperity."

He felt the wind shift a point and his anxiety increased. Eeeee, this has been a bad day but tomorrow will be worse.

Has that lump of dogmeat John Chen escaped to the Golden Country or is he truly kidnapped? Without that piece of dung I'm still the tai-pan's running dog. I'm tired of being a running dog. The 100,000 reward for John Chen is money well invested. I'd pay twelve times that for John Chen and his fornicating coin. Thank all gods I put spies in Noble House Chen's household.

He stabbed his hand shoreward. "Be quick, old man," he ordered the boatman, his face grim. "I've a lot to do before dawn!"

19

2:23 P.M.:

The day was hot and very humid, the sky sultry, clouds beginning a buildup. Since the opening this morning there had been no letup in the milling, noisy, sweating crowds inside and outside the small Aberdeen branch of the Ho-Pak Bank.

"I've no more money to pay out, Honorable Sung," the frightened teller whispered, sweat marking her neat *chong-sam*.

"How much do you need?"

"$7,457 for customer Tok-sing but there must be fifty more people waiting."

"Go back to your window," the equally nervous manager replied. "Delay. Pretend to check the account further—Head Office swore another consignment left their office an hour ago . . . perhaps the traffic . . . Go back to your window, Miss Pang." Hastily he shut the door of his office after her and, sweating, once more got on the phone. "The Honorable Richard Kwang please. Hurry. . . ."

Since the bank had opened promptly at ten o'clock, four or five hundred people had squirmed their way up to one of the three windows and demanded their money in full and their savings in full and then, blessing their joss, had shoved and pushed their way out into the world again.

Those with safety deposit boxes had demanded access. One by one, accompanied by an official, they had gone below to the vault, ecstatic or faint with relief. There the official had used his key and the client his key and then the official had left. Alone in the musty air the sweating client had blessed the gods that his joss had allowed him to be one of the lucky ones. Then his shaking hands had scooped the securities or cash or bullion or jewels and all the other secret things into a briefcase or suitcase or paper bag—or stuffed them into bulging pockets, already full with bank notes. Then, suddenly frightened to have so much wealth, so open and vulnerable, all the wealth of their individual world, their happiness had evaporated and they had slunk away to let another take their place, equally nervous, and, initially, equally ecstatic.

The line had started to form long before dawn. Four Finger Wu's people took the first thirty places. This news had rushed around the harbor, so others had joined instantly, then others, then everyone with any account whatsoever as the news spread, swelling the throng. By ten, the nervous, anxious gathering was of riot proportions. Now a few uniformed police were strolling among them, silent and watchful, their presence calming. More came as the day grew, their numbers quietly and carefully orchestrated by East Aberdeen police station. By noon a couple of Black Maria police vans were in one of the nearby alleys with a specially trained riot platoon in support. And European officers.

Most of the crowd were simple fisherfolk and locals, Haklos and Cantonese. Perhaps one in ten was born in Hong Kong. The rest were recent migrants from the People's Republic of China, the Middle Kingdom, as they called their land. They had poured into the Hong Kong sanctuary fleeing the Communists or fleeing the Nationalists, or famine, or just simple poverty as their forebears had done for more than a century. Ninety-eight of every hundred of Hong Kong's population were Chinese and this proportion had been the same ever since the Colony began.

Each person who came out of the bank told anyone who asked that they had been paid in full. Even so, the others who waited were sick with apprehension. All were remembering the crash of last year, and a lifetime in their home villages of other crashes and failures, frauds, rapacious money lenders, embezzlements and corruptions and how easy it was for a life's savings to evaporate through no fault of your own, whatever the government, Communist, Nationalist or warlord. For four thousand years it had always been the same.

And all loathed their dependence on banks—but they had to put their cash somewhere safe, life being what it was and robbers as plentiful as fleas. *Dew neh loh moh* on all banks, most were thinking, they're inventions of the devil—of the foreign devils! Yes. Before foreign devils came to the Middle Kingdom there was no paper money, just real money, silver or gold or copper—mostly silver and copper—that they could feel and hide, that would never evaporate. Not like filthy paper. Rats can eat paper, and men. Paper money's another invention of the foreign devil. Before they came to the Middle Kingdom life was good. Now? *Dew neh loh moh* on all foreign devils!

At eight o'clock this morning, the anxious bank manager had called Richard Kwang. "But Honored Lord, there must be five hundred people already and the queue goes from here all along the waterfront."

"Never mind, Honorable Sung! Pay those who want their cash. Don't worry! Just talk to them, they're mostly just superstitious fisherfolk. Talk them out of withdrawing. But those who insist—pay! The Ho-Pak's as strong as Blacs or the Victoria! It's a malicious lie that we're overstretched!

Pay! Check their savings books carefully and don't hurry with each client. Be methodical."

So the bank manager and the tellers had tried to persuade their clients that there was really no need for any anxiety, that false rumors were being spread by malicious people.

"Of course you can have your money, but don't you think . . ."

"*Ayeeyah*, give her the money," the next in line said irritably, "she wants her money, I want mine, and there's my wife's brother behind me who wants his and my auntie's somewhere outside. *Ayeeyah*, I haven't got all day! I've got to put to sea. With this wind there'll be a storm in a few days and I have to make a catch. . . ."

And the bank had begun to pay out. In full.

Like all banks, the Ho-Pak used its deposits to service loans to others—all sorts of loans. In Hong Kong there were few regulations and few laws. Some banks lent as much as 80 percent of their cash assets because they were sure their clients would never require back all their money at the same time.

Except today at Aberdeen. But, fortunately, this was only one of eighteen branches throughout the Colony. The Ho-Pak was not yet threatened.

Three times during the day the manager had had to call for extra cash from Head Office in Central. And twice for advice.

At one minute past ten this morning Four Finger Wu was grimly sitting beside the manager's desk with Paul Choy, and Two Hatchet Tok standing behind him.

"You want to close all your Ho-Pak accounts?" Mr. Sung gasped shakily.

"Yes. Now," Wu said and Paul Choy nodded.

The manager said weakly, "But we haven't en—"

Wu hissed, "I want all my money now. Cash or bullion. Now! Don't you understand?"

Mr. Sung winced. He dialed Richard Kwang and explained quickly. "Yes, yes, Lord." He offered the phone. "Honorable Kwang wants to speak to you, Honorable Wu."

But no amount of persuasion would sway the old seaman. "No. *Now.* My money, and the money of my people *now*. And also from those other accounts, the, er, those special ones wherever they are."

"But there isn't that amount of cash in that branch, Honored Uncle," Richard Kwang said soothingly. "I'd be glad to give you a cashier's check."

Wu exploded. "I don't want checks; I want money! Don't you understand? Money!" He did not understand what a cashier's check was so the frightened Mr. Sung began to explain. Paul Choy brightened. "That'll be all right, Honored Uncle," he said. "A cashier's check's . . ."

The old man roared, "How can a piece of paper be like cash money? I want money, my money now!"

"Please let me talk to the Honorable Kwang, Great Uncle," Paul Choy said placatingly, understanding the dilemma. "Perhaps I can help."

Wu nodded sourly. "All right, talk, but get my cash money."

Paul Choy introduced himself on the telephone and said, "Perhaps it'd be easier in English, sir." He talked a few moments then nodded, satisfied. "Just a moment, sir." Then in Haklo, "Great Uncle," he said, explaining, "the Honorable Kwang will give you payment in full in government securities, gold or silver at his Head Office, and a piece of paper which you can take to Blacs, or the Victoria for the remainder. But, if I may suggest, because you've no safe to put all that bullion in, perhaps you'll accept Honorable Kwang's cashier's check—with which I can open accounts at either bank for you. Immediately."

"*Banks!* Banks are foreign devil lobster-pot traps for civilized lobsters!"

It had taken Paul Choy half an hour to convince him. Then they had gone to the Ho-Pak's Head Office but Wu had left Two Hatchet Tok with the quaking Mr. Sung. "You stay here, Tok. If I don't get my money you will take it out of this branch!"

"Yes, Lord."

So they had gone to Central and by noon Four Finger Wu had new accounts, half at Blacs, half at the Victoria. Paul Choy had been staggered by the number of separate accounts that had had to be closed and opened afresh. And the amount of cash.

Twenty-odd million HK.

In spite of all his pleading and explaining the old seaman had refused to invest some of his money in selling Ho-Pak short, saying that that was a game for *quai loh* thieves. So Paul had slipped away and gone to every stockbroker he could find, trying to sell short on his own account. "But, my dear fellow, you've no credit. Of course, if you'll give me your uncle's chop, or assurance in writing, of course. . . ."

He discovered that stockbrokering firms were European, almost exclusively, the vast majority British. Not one was Chinese. All the seats on the stock exchange were European held, again the vast majority British. "That just doesn't seem right, Mr. Smith," Paul Choy said.

"Oh, I'm afraid our locals, Mr., Mr. . . . Mr. Chee was it?"

"Choy, Paul Choy."

"Ah yes. I'm afraid all our locals aren't really interested in complicated, modern practices like broking and stock markets—of course you know our locals are all immigrants? When we came here Hong Kong was just a barren rock."

"Yes. But I'm interested, Mr. Smith. In the States a stockbr—"

"Ah yes, America! I'm sure they do things differently in America, Mr. Chee. Now if you'll excuse me . . . good afternoon."

Seething, Paul Choy had gone from broker to broker but it was always the same. No one would back him without his father's chop.

Now he sat on a bench in Memorial Square near the Law Courts and the Struan's highrise and Rothwell-Gornt's, and looked out at the harbor, and thought. Then he went to the Law Court library and talked his way past the pedantic librarian. "I'm from Sims, Dawson and Dick," he said airily. "I'm their new attorney from the States. They want some quick information on stock markets and stockbroking."

"Government regulations, sir?" the elderly Eurasian asked helpfully.

"Yes."

"There aren't any, sir."

"Eh?"

"Well, practically none." The librarian went to the shelves. The requisite section was just a few paragraphs in a giant tome.

Paul Choy gaped at him. "This's all of it?"

"Yes sir."

Paul Choy's head reeled. "But then it's wide open, the market's wide open!"

The librarian was gently amused. "Yes, compared to London, or New York. As to stockbroking, well, anyone can set up as a broker, sir, providing someone wants them to sell shares and there's someone who wants them to buy and both are prepared to pay commission. The problem is that the, er, the existing firms control the market completely."

"How do you bust this monopoly?"

"Oh I wouldn't want to, sir. We're really for the status quo in Hong Kong."

"How do you break in then? Get a piece of the action?"

"I doubt if you could, sir. The, the British control everything very carefully," he said delicately.

"That doesn't seem right."

The elderly man shook his head and smiled gently. He steepled his fingers, liking the young Chinese he saw in front of him, envying him his purity—and his American education. "I presume you want to play the market on your own account?" he asked softly.

"Yeah . . ." Paul Choy tried to cover his mistake and stuttered, "At least . . . Dawson said for me—"

"Come now, Mr. Choy, you're not from Sims, Dawson and Dick," he said, chiding him politely. "If they'd hired an American—an unheard-of innovation—oh I would have heard of it along with a hundred others, long before you even arrived here. You must be Mr. Paul Choy, the great Wu Sang Fang's nephew, who has just come back from Harvard in America."

Paul Choy gaped at him. "How'd you know?"

"This is Hong Kong, Mr. Choy. It's a very tiny place. We have to know what's going on. That's how we survive. You do want to play the market?"

"Yes. Mr. . . . ?"

"Manuel Perriera. I'm Portuguese from Macao." The librarian took out a fountain pen and wrote in beautiful copybook writing an introduction on the back of one of his visiting cards. "Here. Ishwar Soorjani's an old friend. His place of business is just off the Nathan Road in Kowloon. He's a Parsee from India and deals in money and foreign exchange and buys and sells stocks from time to time. He might help you—but remember if he loans money, or credit, it will be expensive so you should not make any mistakes."

"Gee thanks, Mr. Perriera." Paul Choy stuck out his hand. Surprised, Perriera took it. Paul Choy shook warmly then began to rush off but stopped. "Say, Mr. Perriera . . . the stock market. Is there a long shot? Anything? Any way to get a piece of the action?"

Manuel Perriera had silver-gray hair and long, beautiful hands, and pronounced Chinese features. He considered the youth in front of him. Then he said softly, "There's nothing to prevent you from forming a company to set up your own stock market, a Chinese stock market. That's quite within Hong Kong law—or lack of it." The old eyes glittered. "All you need is money, contacts, knowledge and telephones. . . ."

"My money please," the old *amah* whispered hoarsely. "Here's my savings book." Her face was flushed from the heat within the Ho-Pak branch at Aberdeen. It was ten minutes to three now and she had been waiting since dawn. Sweat streaked her old white blouse and black pants. A long graying ratty queue hung down her back. "*Ayeeyah,* don't shove," she called out to those behind her. "You'll get your turn soon!"

Wearily the young teller took the book and glanced again at the clock. *Ayeeyah!* Thank all gods we close at three, she thought, and wondered anxiously through her grinding headache how they were going to close the doors with so many irritable people crammed in front of the grilles, pressed forward by those outside.

The amount in the savings book was 323.42 HK. Following Mr. Sung's instructions to take time and be accurate she went to the files trying to shut her ears to the stream of impatient, muttered obscenities that had gone on for hours. She made sure the amount was correct, then checked the clock again as she came back to her high stool and unlocked her cash drawer and opened it. There was not enough money in her till so she locked the drawer again and went to the manager's office. An undercurrent of rage went through the waiting people. She was a short clumsy woman. Eyes followed her, then went anxiously to the clock and back to her again.

She knocked on his door and closed it after her. "I can't pay Old Ah Tam," she said helplessly. "I've only 100 HK, I've delayed as much . . ."

Manager Sung wiped the sweat off his upper lip. "It's almost three so make her your last customer, Miss Cho." He took her through a side door to the vault. The safe door was ponderous. She gasped as she saw the empty shelves. At this time of the day usually the shelves were filled with neat stacks of notes and paper tubes of silver, the notes clipped together in their hundreds and thousands and tens of thousands. Sorting the money after closing was the job she liked best, that and touching the sensuous bundles of new, crisp, fresh bills.

"Oh this is terrible, Honorable Sung," she said near to tears. Her thick glasses were misted and her hair askew.

"It's just temporary, just temporary, Miss Cho. Remember what the Honorable Haply wrote in today's *Guardian!*" He cleared the last shelf, committing his final reserves, cursing the consignment that had not yet arrived. "Here." He gave her 15,000 for show, made her sign for it, and took 15 for each of the other two tellers. Now the vault was empty.

When he came into the main room there was a sudden electric, exciting hush at the apparently large amount of money, cash money.

He gave the money to the other two tellers, then vanished into his office again.

Miss Cho was stacking the money neatly in her drawer, all eyes watching her and the other tellers. One packet of 1,000 she left on the desk. She broke the seal and methodically counted out 320, and three ones and the change, recounted it and slid it across the counter. The old woman stuffed it into a paper bag, and the next in line irritably shoved forward and thrust his savings book into Miss Cho's face. "Here, by all the gods. I want seven thous—"

At that moment, the three o'clock bell went and Mr. Sung appeared instantly and said in a loud voice, "Sorry, we have to close now. All tellers close your—" The rest of his words were drowned by the angry roar.

"By all gods I've waited since dawn . . ."

"*Dew neh loh moh* but I've been here eight hours. . . ."

"*Ayeeyah*, just pay me, you've enough . . ."

"Oh please please please please . . ."

Normally the bank would just have shut its doors and served those within, but this time, obediently, the three frightened tellers locked their tills in the uproar, put up their CLOSED signs and backed away from the outstretched hands.

Suddenly the crowd within the bank became a mob.

Those in front were shoved against the counter as others fought to get into the bank. A girl shrieked as she was slammed against the counter. Hands reached out for the grilles that were more for decoration than protection. Everyone was enraged now. One old seaman who had been next in line reached over to try to jerk the till drawer open. The old *amah* was jammed in the seething mass of a hundred or more people and she fought to get to one side, her money clasped tightly in her scrawny hands. A young woman lost her footing and was trampled on. She tried to get up but the milling legs defied her so, in desperation, she bit into one leg and got enough respite to scramble up, stockings ripped, *chong-sam* torn and now in panic. Her panic whipped the mob further then someone shouted, "Kill the motherless whore's son . . ." and the shout was taken up, "Killlllllll!"

There was a split second of hesitation, then, as one, they surged forward.

"*Stop!*"

The word blasted through the atmosphere in English and then in Haklo and then in Cantonese and then in English again.

The silence was sudden and vast.

The uniformed chief inspector stood before them, unarmed and calm, an electric megaphone in his hand. He had come through the back door into an inner office and now he was looking at them.

"It's three o'clock," he said softly in Haklo. "The law says banks close at three o'clock. This bank is now closed. Please turn around and go home! Quietly!"

Another silence, angrier this time, then the beginning of a violent swell and one man muttered sullenly, "What about my fornicating money . . ." and others almost took up the shout but the police officer moved fast, very fast, directly at the man, fearlessly lifted the countertop and went straight at him into the mob. The mob backed off.

"Tomorrow," the police officer said gently, towering over him. "You'll get all your money tomorrow." The man dropped his eyes, hating the cold blue fish-eyes and the nearness of a foreign devil. Sullenly he moved back a pace.

The policeman looked at the rest of them, into their eyes. "You at the back," he ordered, instantly selecting the man with unerring care, his voice commanding yet with the same quiet confidence, "Turn around and make way for the others."

Obediently the man did as he was ordered. The mob became a crowd again. A moment's hesitation then another turned and began to push for the door. "*Dew neh loh moh* I haven't got all day, hurry up," he said sourly.

They all began to leave, muttering, furious—but individually, not as a mob. Sung and the tellers wiped the sweat off their brows, then sat trembling behind the safety of the counter.

The chief inspector helped the old *amah* up. A fleck of blood was at the corner of her mouth. "Are you all right, Old Lady?" he asked in Haklo.

She stared at him without understanding. He repeated it in Cantonese.

"Ah, yes . . . yes," she said hoarsely, still clasping her paper bag tight against her chest. "Thank you, Honored Lord." She scuttled away into the crowd and vanished. The room emptied. The Englishman went out to the sidewalk after the last person and stood in the doorway, whistling tonelessly as he watched them stream away.

"Sergeant!"

"Yes sir."

"You can dismiss the men now. Have a detail here at nine tomorrow. Put up barriers and let the buggers into the bank just three at a time. Yourself and four men'll be more than enough."

"Yes sir." The sergeant saluted. The chief inspector turned back into the bank. He locked the front door and smiled at Manager Sung. "Rather humid this afternoon, isn't it?" he said in English to give Sung face—all educated Chinese in Hong Kong prided themselves in speaking the international language.

"Yes sir," Sung replied nervously. Normally he liked him and admired this chief inspector greatly. Yes, he thought. But this was the first time he had actually seen a *quai loh* with the Evil Eye, daring a mob, standing alone like a malevolent god in front of the mob, daring it to move, to give him the opportunity to spit fire and brimstone.

Sung shuddered again. "Thank you, Chief Inspector."

"Let's go into your office and I can take a statement."

"Yes, please." Sung puffed himself up in front of his staff, taking command again. "The rest of you make up your books and tidy up."

He led the way into his office and sat down and beamed. "Tea, Chief Inspector?"

"No thank you." Chief Inspector Donald C. C. Smyth was about five foot ten and well built, fair hair and blue eyes and a taut sunburned face. He pulled out a sheaf of papers and put them on the desk. "These are the accounts of my men. At nine tomorrow, you will close their accounts and pay them. They'll come to the back door."

"Yes of course. I would be honored. But I will lose face if so many valuable accounts leave me. The bank is as sound as it was yesterday, Chief Inspector."

"Of course. Meanwhile tomorrow at nine. In cash please." He handed him some more papers. And four savings books. "I'll take a cashier's check for all of these. Now."

"But Chief Inspector, today was extraordinary. There's no problem with the Ho-Pak. Surely you could . . ."

"Now." Smyth smiled sweetly. "Withdrawal slips are all signed and ready."

Sung glanced at them. All were Chinese names that he knew were nominees of nominees of this man whose nickname was the Snake. The accounts totaled nearly 850,000 HK. And that's just in this branch alone, he thought, very impressed with the Snake's acumen. What about the Victoria and Blacs and all the other branches in Aberdeen?

"Very well," he said wearily. "But I'll be very sorry to see so many accounts leave the bank."

Smyth smiled again. "The whole of the Ho-Pak's not broke yet, is it?"

"Oh no, Chief Inspector," Sung said, shocked. "We have published assets worth a billion HK and cash reserves of many tens of millions. It's just these simple people, a temporary problem of confidence. Did you see Mr. Haply's column in the *Guardian?*"

"Yes."

"Ah." Sung's face darkened. "Malicious rumors spread by jealous taipans and other banks! If Haply claims that, of course it's true."

"Of course! Meanwhile I am a little busy this afternoon."

"Yes. Of course. I'll do it at once. I, er, I see in the paper you've caught one of those evil Werewolves."

"We've a triad suspect, Mr. Sung, just a suspect."

Sung shuddered. "Devils! But you'll catch them all . . . devils, sending an ear! They must be foreigners. I'll wager they're foreigners never mind. Here, sir, I've made the checks . . ."

There was a knock on the door. A corporal came in and saluted. "Excuse me, sir, a bank truck's outside. They say they're from Ho-Pak's Head Office."

"*Ayeeyah*," Sung said, greatly relieved, "and about time. They promised the delivery at two. It's more money."

"How much?" Smyth asked.

"Half a million," the corporal volunteered at once, handing over the manifest. He was a short, bright man with dancing eyes.

"Good," Smyth said. "Well, Mr. Sung, that'll take the pressure off you, won't it."

"Yes. Yes it will." Sung saw the two men looking at him and he said at once, expansively, "If it wasn't for you, and your men . . . With your permission I'd like to call Mr. Richard Kwang now. I feel sure he would be honored, as I would be, to make a modest contribution to your police benevolent fund as a token of our thanks."

"That's very thoughtful, but it's not necessary, Mr. Sung."

"But I will lose terrible face if you won't accept, Chief Inspector."

"You're very kind," Smyth said, knowing truly that without his presence in the bank and that of his men outside, Sung and the tellers and many others would be dead. "Thank you but that's not necessary." He accepted the cashier's checks and left.

Mr. Sung pleaded with the corporal who, at length, sent for his superior. Divisional Sergeant Mok declined also. "Twenty thousand times," he said.

But Mr. Sung insisted. Wisely. And Richard Kwang was equally delighted and equally honored to approve the unsolicited gift. 20,000 HK. In immediate cash. "With the bank's great appreciation, Divisional Sergeant Mok."

"Thank you, Honorable Manager Sung," Mok said politely, pocketing it, pleased to be in the Snake's division and totally impressed that 20,000 was the exact fair market figure the Snake had considered their afternoon's work was worth. "I hope your great bank stays solvent and you weather this storm with your usual cleverness. Tomorrow will be orderly, of course. We will be here at nine A.M. promptly for our cash. . . ."

The old *amah* still sat on the bench on the harbor wall, catching her breath. Her ribs hurt but then they always hurt, she thought wearily. Joss.

Her name was Ah Tam and she began to get up but a youth sauntered up to her and said, "Sit down, Old Woman, I want to talk to you." He was short and squat and twenty-one, his face pitted with small pox scars. "What's in that bag?"

"What? What bag?"

"The paper bag you clutch to your stinking old rags."

"This? Nothing, Honored Lord. It's just my poor shopping that—"

He sat on the bench beside her and leaned closer and hissed, "Shut up, Old Hag! I saw you come out of the fornicating bank. How much have you got there?"

The old woman held on to the bag desperately, her eyes closed in terror and she gasped, "It's all my savings, Hon—"

He pulled the bag out of her grasp and opened it. "*Ayeeyah!*" The notes were old and he counted them. "$323!" he said scornfully. "Who are you *amah* to—a beggar? You haven't been very clever in this life."

"Oh yes, you're right, Lord!" she said, her little black eyes watching him now.

"My *h'eung yau's* 20 percent," he said and began to count the notes.

"But Honored Sir," she said, her voice whining now, "20 is too high, but I'd be honored if you'd accept 5 with a poor old woman's thanks."

"15."

"6!"

"10 and that's my final offer. I haven't got all day!"

"But sir, you are young and strong, clearly a 489. The strong must protect the old and weak."

"True, true." He thought a moment, wanting to be fair. "Very well, 7 percent."

"Oh how generous you are, sir. Thank you, thank you." Happily she watched him count 22 dollars, then reach into his jeans pocket and count out 61 cents. "Here." He gave her the change and the remainder of her money back.

She thanked him profusely, delighted with the bargain she had made. By all the gods, she thought ecstatically, 7 percent instead of, well, at least 15 would be fair. "Have you also money in the Ho-Pak, Honored Lord?" she asked politely.

"Of course," the youth said importantly as though it were true. "My Brotherhood's account has been there for years. We have . . ." He doubled the amount he first thought of. ". . . we have over 25,000 in this branch alone."

"Eeeee," the old woman crooned. "To be so rich! The moment I saw you I knew you were 14K . . . and surely an Honorable 489."

"I'm better than that," the youth said proudly at once, filled with bravado. "I'm . . ." But he stopped, remembering their leader's admonition to be cautious, and so did not say, I'm Kin Sop-ming, Smallpox Kin, and I'm one of the famous Werewolves and there are four of us. "Run along, old woman," he said, tiring of her. "I've more important things to do than talk with you."

She got up and bowed and then her old eyes spotted the man who had been in the line in front of her. The man was Cantonese, like her. He was a rotund shopkeeper she knew who had a poultry street stall in one of Aberdeen's teeming marketplaces. "Yes," she said hoarsely, "but if you want another customer I see an easy one. He was in the queue before me. Over $8,000 he withdrew."

"Oh, where? Where is he?" the youth asked at once.

"For a 15 percent share?"

"7—and that's final. 7!"

"All right. 7. Look, over there!" she whispered. "The fat man, plump as a Mandarin, in the white shirt—the one who's sweating like he's just enjoyed the Clouds and the Rain!"

"I see him." The youth got up and walked quickly away to intercept the man. He caught up with him at the corner. The man froze and bartered for a while, paid 16 percent and hurried off, blessing his own acumen. The youth sauntered back to her.

"Here, Old Woman," he said. "The fornicator had $8,162. 16 percent is . . ."

"$1305.92 and my 7 percent of that is $91.41," she said at once.

He paid her exactly and she agreed to come tomorrow to spot for him.

"What's your name?" he asked.

"Ah Su, Lord," she said, giving a false name. "And yours?"

"Mo Wu-fang," he said, using a friend's name.

"Until tomorrow," she said happily. Thanking him again she waddled off, delighted with her day's profit.

His profit had been good too. Now he had over 3,000 in his pockets where this morning he had had only enough for the bus. And it was all windfall for he had come to Aberdeen from Glessing's Point to post another ransom note to Noble House Chen.

"It's for safety," his father, their leader, had said. "To put out a false scent for the fornicating police."

"But it will bring no money," he had said to him and to the others disgustedly. "How can we produce the fornicating son if he's dead and buried? Would you pay off without some proof that he was alive? Of course not! It was a mistake to hit him with the shovel."

"But the fellow was trying to escape!" his brother said.

"True, Younger Brother. But the first blow didn't kill him, only bent his head a little. You should have left it at that!"

"I would have but the evil spirits got into me so I hit him again. I only hit him four times! Eeeee, but these highborn fellows have soft skulls!"

"Yes, you're right," his father had said. He was short and balding with many gold teeth, his name Kin Min-ta, Baldhead Kin. *Dew neh loh moh* but it's done so there's no point in remembering it. Joss. It was his own fault for trying to escape! Have you seen the early edition of *The Times?*"

"No—not yet, Father," he had replied.

"Here, let me read it to you: 'The Chief of all the Police said today that they have arrested a triad who they suspect is one of the Werewolves, the dangerous gang of criminals who kidnapped John Chen. The authorities expect to have the case solved any moment.'"

They all laughed, he, his younger brother, his father and the last member, his very good friend, Dog-eared Chen—Pun Po Chen—for they knew it was all lies. Not one of them was a triad or had triad connections, and none had ever been caught for any crime before, though they had formed their own Brotherhood and his father had, from time to time, run a small gambling syndicate in North Point. It was his father who had proposed the first kidnapping. Eeee, that was very clever, he thought, remembering. And when John Chen had, unfortunately, had himself killed because he stupidly tried to escape, his father had also suggested cutting off the ear and sending it. "We will turn his bad joss into our good. 'Kill one to terrify ten thousand!' Sending the ear will terrify all Hong Kong, make us famous and make us rich!"

Yes, he thought, sitting in the sun at Aberdeen. But we haven't made our riches yet. Didn't I tell father this morning: "I don't mind going all the way to post the letter, Father, that's sensible and what Humphrey Bogart would order. But I still don't think it will bring us any ransom."

"Never mind and listen! I've a new plan worthy of Al Capone himself. We wait a few days. Then we phone Noble House Chen. If we don't get immediate cash, then we snatch the compradore himself! Great Miser Chen himself!"

They had all stared at him in awe.

"Yes, and if you don't think he'll pay up quickly after seeing his son's ear—of course we'll tell him it was his son's ear . . . perhaps we'll even dig up the body and show him, *heya?*"

Smallpox Kin beamed, recalling how they had all chortled. Oh how they had chortled, holding their bellies, almost rolling on the floor of their tenement apartment.

"Now to business. Dog-eared Chen, we need your advice again."

Dog-eared Chen was a distant cousin of John Chen and worked for him as a manager of one of the multitudinous Chen companies. "Your information about the son was perfect. Perhaps you can supply us with the father's movements too?"

"Of course, Honored Leader, that's easy," Dog-eared Chen had said. "He's a man of habit—and easily frightened. So is his *tai-tai—ayeeyah,* that mealy-mouthed whore knows which side of the bed she sleeps in! She'll pay up very quickly to get him back. Yes, I'm sure he'll be very cooperative now. But we'll have to ask double what we would settle for because he's an accomplished negotiator. I've worked for the fornicating House of Chen all my working life so I know what a miser he is."

"Excellent. Now, by all the gods, how and when should we kidnap Noble House Chen himself?"

20

Sir Dunstan Barre was ushered into Richard Kwang's office with the deference he considered his due. The Ho-Pak Building was small and unpretentious, off Ice House Street in Central, and the office was like most Chinese offices, small, cluttered and drab, a place for working and not for show. Most times two or three people would share a single office, running two or three separate businesses there, using the same telephone and same secretary for all. And why not, a wise man would say? A third of the overhead means more profit for the same amount of labor.

But Richard Kwang did not share his office. He knew it did not please his *quai loh* customers—and the few that he had were important to his bank and to him for face and for the highly sought after peripheral benefits they could bring. Like the possible, oh so important election as a voting member to the super-exclusive Turf Club, or membership in the Hong Kong Golf Club or Cricket Club—or even *the* Club itself—or any of the other minor though equally exclusive clubs that were tightly controlled by the British tai-pans of great *hongs* where all the really big business was conducted.

"Hello, Dunstan," he said affably. "How are things going?"

"Fine. And you?"

"Very good. My horse had a great workout this morning."

"Yes. I was at the track myself."

"Oh, I didn't see you!"

"Just popped in for a minute or two. My gelding's got a temperature—we may have to scratch him on Saturday. But Butterscotch Lass was really flying this morning."

"She almost pipped the track record. She'll definitely be trying on Saturday."

Barre chuckled. "I'll check with you just before race time and you can tell me the inside story then! You can never trust trainers and jockeys, can you—yours or mine or anyone's!"

They chatted inconsequentially, then Barre came to the point.

Richard Kwang tried to cover his shock. "Close all your corporate accounts?"

"Yes, old boy. Today. Sorry and all that but my board thinks it wise for the moment, until you weath—"

"But surely you don't think we're in trouble?" Richard Kwang laughed. "Didn't you see Haply's article in the *Guardian?* '. . . malicious lies spread by certain tai-pans and a certain big bank. . . .'"

"Oh yes, I saw that. More of his poppycock, I'd say. Ridiculous! Spread rumors? Why should anyone do that? Huh, I talked to both Paul Havergill and Southerby this morning and they said Haply better watch out this time if he implies it's them or he'll get a libel suit. That young man deserves a horsewhipping! However . . . I'd like a cashier's check now—sorry, but you know how boards are."

"Yes, yes I do." Richard Kwang kept his smile on the surface of his face but he hated the big florid man even more than usual. He knew that the board was a rubber stamp for Barre's decisions. "We've no problems. We're a billion-dollar bank. As to the Aberdeen branch, they're just a lot of superstitious locals."

"Yes, I know." Barre watched him. "I heard you had a few problems at your Mong Kok branch this afternoon too, also at Tsim Sha Tsui . . . at Sha Tin in the New Territories, even, God help us, on Lan Tao." Lan Tao Island was half a dozen miles east of Hong Kong, the biggest island in the whole archipelago of almost three hundred islands that made up the Colony—but almost unpopulated because it was waterless.

"A few customers withdrew their savings," Richard Kwang said with a scoff. "There's no trouble."

But there was trouble. He knew it and he was afraid everyone knew it. At first it was just at Aberdeen. Then, during the day, his other managers had begun to call with ever increasing anxiety. He had eighteen branches throughout the Colony. At four of them, withdrawals were untoward and heavy. At Mong Kok, a bustling hive within the teaming city of Kowloon, a line had formed in early afternoon. Everyone had wanted all their money. It was nothing like the frightening proportions at Aberdeen, but enough to show a clear indication of failing confidence. Richard Kwang could understand that the sea villages would hear about Four Finger Wu's withdrawals quickly, and would rush to follow his lead—but what about Mong Kok? Why there? And why Lan Tao? Why at Tsim Sha Tsui, his most profitable branch, which was almost beside the busy Golden Ferry Terminal where 150,000 persons passed by daily, to and from Hong Kong?

It must be a plot!

Is my enemy and arch-rival Smiler Ching behind it? Is it those fornicators, those jealous fornicators at Blacs or the Victoria?

Is Thin Tube of Dung Havergill masterminding the attack? Or is it

Compton Southerby of Blacs—he's always hated me. These filthy *quai loh!* But why should they attack me? Of course I'm a much better banker than them and they're jealous but my business is with civilized people and hardly touches them. Why? Or has it leaked somehow that against my better judgment, over my objections, my partners who control the bank have been insisting that I borrow short and cheap and lend long and high on property deals, and now, through their stupidity, we are temporarily overextended and cannot sustain a run?

Richard Kwang wanted to shout and scream and tear his hair out. His secret partners were Lando Mata and Tightfist Tung, major shareholders of Macao's gambling and gold syndicate, along with Smuggler Mo, who had helped him form and finance the Ho-Pak ten years ago. "Did you see Old Blind Tung's predictions this morning?" he asked, the smile still on his face.

"No. What'd he say?"

Richard Kwang found the paper and passed it over. "All the portents show we're ready for boom. The lucky eight is everywhere in the heavens and we're in the eighth month, my birthday is the eighth of the eighth month. . . ."

Barre read the column. In spite of his disbelief in soothsayers, he had been too long in Asia to dismiss them totally. His heart quickened. Old Blind Tung had a vast reputation in Hong Kong. "If you believe him we're in for the biggest boom in the history of the world," he said.

"He's usually much more cautious. *Ayeeyah,* that would be good, *heya?*"

"Better than good. Meanwhile Richard old boy, let's finish our business, shall we?"

"Certainly. It's all a typhoon in an oyster shell, Dunstan. We're stronger than ever—our stock's hardly a point off." When the market had opened, there had been a mass of small offerings to sell, which, if not reacted to at once would have sent their stock plummeting. Richard Kwang had instantly ordered his brokers to buy and to keep buying. This had stabilized the stock. During the day, to maintain the position, he had had to buy almost five million shares, an unheard of number to be traded in one day. None of his experts could pinpoint who was selling big. There was no reason for a lack of confidence, other than Four Finger Wu's withdrawals. All gods curse that old devil and his fornicating, too smart Harvard-trained nephew! "Why not le—"

The phone rang. "'Scuse me," then curtly into the phone, "I said no interruptions!"

"It's Mr. Haply from the *Guardian,* he says it's important," his secretary, his niece, Mary Yok said. "And the tai-pan's secretary called. The Nelson Trading board meeting's brought forward to this afternoon at five o'clock. Mr. Mata called to say he would be there too."

Richard Kwang's heart skipped three beats. Why? he asked himself, aghast. *Dew neh loh moh* it was supposed to be postponed to next week. *Oh ko* why? Then quickly he put aside that question to consider Haply. He decided that to answer now in front of Barre was too dangerous. "I'll call him back in a few minutes." He smiled at the red-faced man in front of him. "Leave everything for a day or two, Dunstan, we've no problems."

"Can't, old boy. Sorry. There was a special meeting, have to settle it today. The board insisted."

"We've been generous in the past—you've forty million of our money unsecured now—we're joint venturing another seventy million with you on your new building program."

"Yes, indeed you are, Richard, and your profit will be substantial. But they're another matter and those loans were negotiated in good faith months ago and will be settled in good faith when they're due. We've never defaulted on a payment to the Ho-Pak or anyone else." Barre passed the newspaper back and with it, signed documents imprinted with his corporate seal. "The accounts are consolidated so one check will suffice."

The amount was a little over nine and a half million.

Richard Kwang signed the cashier's check and smiled Sir Dunstan Barre out, then, when it was safe, cursed everyone in sight and went back into his office, slamming the door behind him. He kicked his desk then picked up the phone and shouted at his niece to get Haply and almost broke the phone as he slammed it back onto its cradle.

"*Dew neh loh moh* on all filthy *quai loh*," he shrieked to the ceiling and felt much better. That lump of dogmeat! I wonder . . . oh, I wonder if I could prevail on the Snake to forbid any lines at all tomorrow? Perhaps he and his men could break a few arms.

Gloomily Richard Kwang let his mind drift. It had been a rotten day. It had begun badly at the track. He was sure his trainer—or jockey—was feeding Butterscotch Lass pep pills to make her run faster to shorten her odds—she'd be favorite now—then Saturday they'd stop the pills and back an outsider and clean up without him being in on the profit-making. Dirty dog bones, all of them! Liars! Do they think I own a racehorse to lose money?

The banker hawked and spat into the spittoon.

Maggot-mouthed Barre and dog bone Uncle Wu! Those withdrawals will take most of my cash. Never mind, with Lando Mata, Smuggler Mo, Tightfist Tung and the tai-pan I'm quite safe. Oh I'll have to shout and scream and curse and weep but nothing can really touch me or the Ho-Pak. I'm too important to them.

Yes, it had been a rotten day. The only bright spot had been his meeting this morning with Casey. He had enjoyed looking at her, enjoyed her clean-smelling, smart, crisp Americanness of the great outdoors. They had fenced pleasantly about financing and he felt sure he could get all or certainly part of their business. Clearly the pickings would be huge. She's so naive, he thought. Her knowledge of banking and finance's impressive but of the Asian world, nil! She's so naive to be so open with their plans. Thank all gods for Americans.

"I love America, Miss Casey. Yes. Twice a year I go there, to eat good steaks and go to Vegas—and to do business of course."

Eeeee, he thought happily, the whores of the Golden Country are the best and most available *quai loh* in the world, and *quai lohs*'re so cheap compared to Hong Kong girls! Oh oh oh! I get such a good feeling pillowing them, with their great deodorized armpits, their great tits and thighs and rears. But in Vegas it's the best. Remember the golden-haired beauty that towered over me but lying down she . . .

His private phone rang. He picked it up, irritated as always that he had had to install it. But he had had no option. When his previous secretary of many years had left to get married, his wife had planted her favorite niece firmly in her place, of course to spy on me, he thought sourly. Eeeee, what can a man do?

"Yes?" he asked, wondering what his wife wanted now.

"You didn't call me all day. . . . I've been waiting for hours!"

His heart leapt at the unexpected sound of the girl's voice. He dismissed the petulance, her Cantonese sweet like her Jade Gate. "Listen, Little Treasure," he said, his voice placating. "Your poor Father's been very busy today. I've—"

"You just don't want your poor Daughter anymore. I'll have to throw myself in the harbor or find another person to cherish me oh oh oh. . . ."

His blood pressure soared at the sound of her tears. "Listen, Little Oily Mouth, I'll see you this evening at ten. We'll have an eight-course feast at Wanchai at my fav—"

"Ten's too late and I don't want a feast I want a steak and I want to go to the penthouse at the V and A and drink champagne!"

His spirit groaned at the danger of being seen and reported secretly to his *tai-tai*. Oh oh oh! But, in front of his friends and his enemies and all Hong Kong he would gain enormous face to escort his new mistress there, the young exotic rising star in TV's firmament, Venus Poon.

"At ten I'll call f—"

"Ten's too late. Nine."

Rapidly he tried to sort out all his meetings tonight to see how he could accommodate her. "Listen, Little Treasure, I'll se—"

"Ten's too late. Nine. I think I will die now that you don't care anymore."

"Listen. Your Father has three meetings and I th—"

"Oh my head hurts to think you don't want me anymore oh oh oh. This abject person will have to slit her wrists, or. . . ." He heard the change in her voice and his stomach twisted at the threat, "Or answer the phone calls of others, lesser than her revered Father of course, but just as rich nonetheless and m—"

"All right, Little Treasure. At nine!"

"Oh you do *love* me don't you!" Though she was speaking Cantonese Venus Poon used the English word and his heart flipped. English was the language of love for modern Chinese, there were no romantic words in their own language. "Tell me!" she said imperiously. "Tell me you *love* me!"

He told her, abjectly, then hung up. The mealy-mouthed little whore, he thought irritably. But then, at nineteen she's a right to be demanding and petulant and difficult if you're almost sixty and she makes you feel twenty and the Imperial Yang blissful. Eeeee, but Venus Poon's the best I've ever had. Expensive but, eeee, she's got muscles in her Golden Gully that only the legendary Emperor Kung wrote about!

He felt his yang stir and scratched pleasantly. I'll give that little baggage what for tonight. I'll buy an extra specially large device, ah yes, a ring with bells on it. Oh oh oh! That'll make her wriggle!

Yes, but meanwhile think about tomorrow. How to prepare for tomorrow?

Call your High Dragon friend, Divisional Sergeant Tang-po at Tsim Sha Tsui and enlist his help to see that his branch and all branches in Kowloon are well policed. Phone Blacs and Cousin Tung of the huge Tung Po Bank and Cousin Smiler Ching and Havergill to arrange extra cash against the Ho-Pak's securities and holdings. Ah yes, phone your very good friend Joe Jacobson, VP of the Chicago Federal and International Merchant Bank—his bank's got assets of four billion and he owes you lots of favors. Lots. There're lots of *quai loh* who're deeply in your debt, and civilized people. Call them all!

Abruptly Richard Kwang came out of his reverie as he remembered the tai-pan's summons. His soul twisted. Nelson Trading's deposits in bullion and cash were huge. *Oh ko* if Nels—

The phone jangled irritably. "Uncle, Mr. Haply's on the line."

"Hello, Mr. Haply, how nice to talk to you. Sorry I was engaged before."

"That's all right, Mr. Kwang. I just wanted to check a couple of facts if I may. First, the riot at Aberdeen. The police w—"

"Hardly a riot, Mr. Haply. A few noisy, impatient people, that's all," he said, despising Haply's Canadian-American accent, and the need to be polite.

"I'm looking at some photos right now, Mr. Kwang, the ones that're in this afternoon's *Times*—it looks like a riot all right."

The banker squirmed in his chair and fought to keep his voice calm. "Oh—oh well I wasn't there so . . . I'll have to talk to Mr. Sung."

"I did, Mr. Kwang. At 3:30. Spent half an hour with him. He said if it hadn't been for the police they'd've torn the place apart." There was a hesitation. "You're right to play it down, but, say, I'm trying to help, and I can't without the facts, so if you'll level with me . . . How many folks wanted their money out at Lan Tao?"

Richard Kwang said, "18," halving the real figure.

"Our guy said 36. 82 at Sha Tin. How about Mong Kok?"

"A cupful."

"My guy said 48, and there was a good 100 left at closing. How about Tsim Sha Tsui?"

"I haven't got the figures yet, Mr. Haply," Richard Kwang said smoothly, consumed with anxiety, hating the staccato questioning.

"All the evening editions're heavy with the Ho-Pak run. Some're even using the word."

"Oh ko. . . ."

"Yeah. I'd say you'd better get ready for a real hot day tomorrow, Mr. Kwang. I'd say your opposition's very well organized. Everything's too pat to be a coincidence."

"I certainly appreciate your interest." Then Richard Kwang added delicately, "If there's anything I can do . . ."

Again the irritating laugh. "Have any of your big depositors pulled out today?"

Richard Kwang hesitated a fraction of a moment and he heard Haply jump into the breach. "Of course I know about Four Finger Wu. I meant the big British *hongs*."

"No, Mr. Haply, not yet."

"There's a strong rumor that Hong Kong and Lan Tao Farms's going to change banks."

Richard Kwang felt that barb in his Secret Sack. "Let's hope it's not true, Mr. Haply. Who're the tai-pans and what big bank or banks? Is it the Victoria or Blacs?"

"Perhaps it's Chinese. Sorry, I can't divulge a news source. But you'd better get organized—it sure as hell looks as though the big guys are after you."

21

4:25 P.M.:

"They don't sleep together, tai-pan," Claudia Chen said.

"Eh?" Dunross looked up absently from the stack of papers he was going through.

"No. At least they didn't last night."

"Who?"

"Bartlett and your Cirrannousshee."

Dunross stopped working. "Oh?"

"Yes. Separate rooms, separate beds, breakfast together in the main room—both neat and tidy and dressed in modest robes which is interesting because neither wears anything in bed."

"They don't?"

"No, at least they didn't last night."

Dunross grinned and she was glad that her news pleased him. It was his first real smile of the day. Since she had arrived at 8:00 A.M. he had been working like a man possessed, rushing out for meetings, hurrying back again: the police, Phillip Chen, the governor, twice to the bank, once to the penthouse to meet whom she did not know. No time for lunch and, so the doorman had told her, the tai-pan had arrived with the dawn.

She had seen the weight on his spirit today, the weight that sooner or later bowed all tai-pans—and sometimes broke them. She had seen Ian's father withered away by the enormous shipping losses of the war years, the catastrophic loss of Hong Kong, of his sons and nephews—bad joss piling on bad joss. It was the loss of Mainland China that had finally crushed him. She had seen how Suez had broken Alastair Struan, how that tai-pan had never recovered from that debacle and how bad joss had piled on bad joss for him until the Gornt-mounted run on their stock had shattered him.

It must be a terrible strain, she thought. All our people to worry about and our House, all our enemies, all the unexpected catastrophes of nature and of man that seem to be ever present—and all the sins and piracies and devil's work of the past that are waiting to burst forth from our own Pandora's box as they do from time to time. It's a pity the tai-pans aren't Chinese, she thought. Then the sins of the past would be so much gossamer.

"What makes you sure, Claudia?"

"No sleep things for either—pajamas or filmy things." She beamed.

"How do you know?"

"Please, tai-pan, I can't divulge my sources!"

"What else do you know?"

"Ah!" she said, then blandly changed the conversation. "The Nelson Trading board meeting's in half an hour. You wanted to be reminded. Can I have a few minutes beforehand?"

"Yes. In a quarter of an hour. Now," he said with a finality she knew too well. "What else do you know?"

She sighed, then importantly consulted her notepad. "She's never been married. Oh, lots of suitors but none have lasted, tai-pan. In fact, according to rumors, none have . . ."

Dunross's eyebrows shot up. "You mean she's a virgin?"

"Of that we're not sure—only that she has no reputation for staying out late, or overnight, with a gentleman. No. The only gentleman she goes out socially with is Mr. Bartlett and that's infrequently. Except on business trips. He, by the way, tai-pan, he's quite a gadabout—*swinger* was the term used. No one lady bu—"

"Used by whom?"

"Ah! Mr. Handsome Bartlett doesn't have one special girl friend, tai-pan. Nothing steady as they say. He was divorced in 1956, the same year that your Cirrrannnousshee joined his firm."

"She's not my Ciranoush," he said.

Claudia beamed more broadly. "She's twenty-six. She's Sagittarius."

"You got someone to snitch her passport—or got someone to take a peek?"

"Very good gracious no, tai-pan." Claudia pretended to be shocked. "I don't spy on people. I just ask questions. But 100 says she and Mr. Bartlett have been lovers at some time or another."

"That's no bet, I'd be astounded if they weren't. He's certainly in love with her—and she with him. You saw how they danced together. That's no bet at all."

The lines around her eyes crinkled. "Then what odds will you give me they've never been lovers?"

"Eh? What d'you know?" he asked suspiciously.

"Odds, tai-pan?"

He watched her. Then he said, "A thousand to . . . I'll give you ten to one."

"Done! A hundred. Thank you tai-pan. Now, about the Nels—"

"Where'd you get all this information? Eh?"

She extracted a telex from the papers she was carrying. The rest she put into his *in* tray. "You telexed our people in New York the night before last for information on her and to recheck Bartlett's dossier. This's just arrived."

He took it and scanned it. His reading was very fast and his memory almost photographic. The telex gave the information Claudia had related in bald terms without her embroidered interpretation and added that K. C. Tcholok had no known police record, $46,000 in a savings account at the San Fernando Savings and Loan, and $8,700 in her checking account at the Los Angeles and California Bank.

"It's shocking how easy it is in the States to find out how much you've got in the bank, isn't it, Claudia?"

"Shocking. I'd never use one, tai-pan."

He grinned. "Except to borrow from! Claudia, just give me the telex next time."

"Yes, tai-pan. But isn't my way of telling certain things more exciting?"

"Yes. But where's it say about the nakedness? You made that up!"

"Oh no, that's from my own source here. Third Toiletma—" Claudia stopped just too late to avoid falling into his trap.

His smile was seraphic. "So! A spy in the V and A! Third Toiletmaid! Who? Which one, Claudia?"

To give him face she pretended to be annoyed. "*Ayeeyah!* A spymaster may reveal nothing, *heya?*" Her smile was kindly. "Here's a list of your calls. I've put off as many as I can till tomorrow—I'll buzz you in good time for the meeting."

He nodded but she saw that his smile had vanished and now he was lost in thought again. She went out and he did not hear the door close. He was thinking about spymasters and AMG and his meeting with Brian Kwok and Roger Crosse this morning at ten, and the one coming at six o'clock.

The meeting this morning had been short, sharp and angry. "First, is there anything new on AMG?" he had asked.

Roger Crosse had replied at once, "It was, apparently, an accident. No suspicious marks on the body. No one was seen nearby, no car marks, impact marks or skid marks—other than the motorcycle. Now, the files, Ian—oh by the way we know now you've got the only copies existent."

"Sorry but I can't do what you asked."

"Why?" There had been a sour edge to the policeman's voice.

"I'm still not admitting one way or the other that they exist but y—"

"Oh for chrissake, Ian, don't be ridiculous! Of course the copies exist. Do you take us for bloody fools? If they didn't, you'd've come out with it last night and that would have been that. I strongly advise you to let us copy them."

"And I strongly advise you to have a tighter hold on your temper."

"If you think I've lost my temper, Ian, then you know very little about

me. I formally ask you to produce those documents. If you refuse I'll in-
voke my powers under the Official Secrets Act at six o'clock this evening
and tai-pan or not, of the Noble House or not, friend or not, by one minute past six, you'll be under arrest. You'll be held incommunicado and
we'll go through all your papers, safes, deposit boxes until we've found
them! Now kindly produce the files!"

Dunross remembered the taut face and the iced eyes staring at him, his
real friend Brian Kwok in shock. "No."

Crosse had sighed. The threat in the sound had sent a tremor through
him. "For the last time, why?"

"Because, in the wrong hands, I think they'd be damaging to Her
Maj—"

"Good sweet Christ, I'm head of Special Intelligence!"

"I know."

"Then kindly do as I ask."

"Sorry. I spent most of the night trying to work out a safe way to giv—"

Roger Crosse had got up. "I'll be back at six o'clock for the files. Don't
burn them, Ian. I'll know if you try and I'm afraid you'll be stopped. Six
o'clock."

Last night while the house slept, Dunross had gone to his study and
reread the files. Rereading them now with the new knowledge of AMG's
death and possible murder, the involvement of MI-5 and -6, probably the
KGB, and Crosse's astounding anxiety; and then the added thought that
perhaps some of the material might not yet be available to the Secret Service, together with the possibility that many of the pieces he had dismissed
as too farfetched were not—now all the reports took on new importance.
Some of them blew his mind.

To hand them over was too risky. To keep them now, impossible.

In the quiet of the night Dunross had considered destroying them. Finally he concluded it was his duty not to. For a moment he had considered leaving them openly on his desk, the French windows wide to the
terrace darkness, and going back to sleep. If Crosse was so concerned
about the papers then he and his men would be watching now. To lock
them in the safe was unsafe. The safe had been touched once. It would be
touched again. No safe was proof against an absolute, concerted professional attack.

There in the darkness, his feet perched comfortably, he had felt the excitement welling, the beautiful, intoxicating lovely warmth of danger surrounding him, physical danger. Of enemies nearby. Of being perched on
the knife edge between life and void. The only thing that detracted from
his pleasure was the knowledge that Struan's was betrayed from within,
the same question always grinding: Is the Sevrin spy the same as he who
gave their secrets to Bartlett? One of seven? Alastair, Phillip, Andrew,
Jacques, Linbar, David MacStruan in Toronto, or his father. All unthinkable.

His mind had examined each one. Clinically, without passion. All had the opportunity, all the same motive: jealousy, and hatred, in varying degrees. But not one would sell the Noble House to an outsider. Not one. Even so, one of them did.

Who?

The hours passed.

Who? Sevrin, what to do about the files, was AMG murdered, how much of the files're true?

Who?

The night was cool now and the terrace had beckoned him. He stood under the stars. The breeze and the night welcomed him. He had always loved the night. Flying alone above the clouds at night, so much better than the day, the stars so near, eyes always watching for the enemy bomber or enemy night fighter, thumb ready on the trigger . . . ah, life was so simple then, kill or be killed.

He stood there for a while, then, refreshed, he went back and locked the files away and sat in his great chair facing the French windows, on guard, working out his options, choosing one. Then, satisfied, he had dozed an hour or so and awoke, as usual, just before dawn.

His dressing room was off his study which was next door to their master bedroom. He had dressed casually and left silently. The road was clear. Sixteen seconds were clipped from his record. In his penthouse he bathed and shaved and changed into a tropical suit, then went to his office on the floor below. It was very humid today with a curious look to the sky. A tropical storm's coming, he had thought. Perhaps we'll be lucky and it won't pass us by like all the others and it'll bring rain. He turned away from his windows and concentrated on running the Noble House.

There was a pile of overnight telexes to deal with on all manner of negotiations and enterprises, problems and business opportunities throughout the Colony and the great outside. From all points of the compass. As far north as the Yukon where Struan's had an oil-prospecting joint venture with the Canadian timber and mining giant, McLean-Woodley. Singapore and Malaya and as far south as Tasmania for fruit and minerals to carry to Japan. West to Britain, east to New York, the tentacles of the new international Noble House that Dunross dreamed about were beginning to reach out, still weak, still tentative, and without the sustenance he knew was vital to their growth.

Never mind. Soon they'll be strong. The Par-Con deal will make our web like steel, with Hong Kong the center of the earth and us the nucleus of the center. Thank God for the telex and telephones.

"Mr. Bartlett please."

"Hello?"

"Ian Dunross, good morning, sorry to disturb you so early, could we postpone our meeting till 6:30?"

"Yes. Is there a problem?"

"No. Just business. I've a lot to catch up with."

"Anything on John Chen?"

"Not yet, no. Sorry. I'll keep you posted though. Give my regards to Casey."

"I will. Say, that was some party last night. Your daughter's a charmer!"

"Thanks. I'll come to the hotel at 6:30. Of course Casey's invited. See you then. 'Bye!"

Ah Casey! he thought.

Casey and Bartlett. Casey and Gornt. Gornt and Four Finger Wu.

Early this morning he had heard from Four Finger Wu about his meeting with Gornt. A pleasant current had swept through him on hearing that his enemy had almost died. The Peak Road's no place to lose your brakes, he thought.

Pity the bastard didn't die. That would have saved me lots of anguish. Then he dismissed Gornt and rethought Four Finger Wu.

Between the old seaman's pidgin and his Haklo they could converse quite well. Wu had told him everything he could. Gornt's comment on the Ho-Pak, advising Wu to withdraw his money, was surprising. And cause for concern. That and Haply's article.

Does that bugger Gornt know something I don't?

He had gone to the bank. "Paul, what's going on?"

"About what?"

"The Ho-Pak."

"Oh. The run? Very bad for our banking image, I must say. Poor Richard! We're fairly certain he's got all the reserves he needs to weather his storm but we don't know the extent of his commitments. Of course I called him the moment I read Haply's ridiculous article. I must tell you, Ian, I also called Christian Toxe and told him in no uncertain terms he should control his reporters and that he'd better cease and desist or else."

"I was told there was a queue at Tsim Sha Tsui."

"Oh? I hadn't heard that. I'll check. Even so, surely the Ching Prosperity and the Lo Fat banks will support him. My God, he's built up the Ho-Pak into a major banking institution. If he went broke God knows what'll happen. We even had some withdrawals at Aberdeen ourselves. No, Ian, let's hope it'll all blow over. Talking about that, do you think we'll get some rain? It feels dicey today, don't you think? The news said there might be a storm coming through. Do you think it'll rain?"

"I don't know. Let's hope so. But not on Saturday!"

"My God yes! If the races were rained out that would be terrible. We can't have that. Oh, by the way, Ian, it was a lovely party last night. I enjoyed meeting Bartlett and his girl friend. How're your negotiations with Bartlett proceeding?"

"First class! Listen, Paul . . ."

Dunross smiled to himself, remembering how he had dropped his voice even though in Havergill's office . . . Havergill's office which overlooked

the whole of Central District was book-lined and very carefully soundproofed. "I've closed my deal. It's two years initially. We sign the papers
within seven days. They're putting up 20 million cash in each of the
years, succeeding ones to be negotiated."

"Congratulations, my dear fellow. Heartiest congratulations! And the
down payment?"

"Seven."

"That's marvelous! That covers everything nicely. It'll be marvelous to
have the Toda specter away from the balance sheet—and with another million for Orlin, well, perhaps they'll give you more time, then at long last
you can forget all the bad years and look forward to a very profitable future."

"Yes."

"Have you got your ships chartered yet?"

"No. But I'll have charterers in time to service our loan."

"I noticed your stock's jumped two points."

"It's on the way now. It's going to double, within thirty days."

"Oh? What makes you think so?"

"The boom."

"Eh?"

"All the signs point that way, Paul. Confidence's up. Our Par-Con deal
will lead the boom. It's long overdue."

"That would be marvelous! When do you make the initial announcement about Par-Con?"

"Friday, after the market closes."

"Excellent. My thought entirely. By Monday everyone will be on the
bandwagon!"

"But let's keep everything in the family until then."

"Of course. Oh, did you hear Quillan almost killed himself last night.
It was just after your party. His brakes failed on the Peak Road."

"Yes I heard. He should have killed himself—that would have sent Second Great Company's stock skyrocketing with happiness!"

"Come now, Ian! A boom eh? You really think so?"

"Enough to want to buy heavily. How about a million credit—to buy
Struan's?"

"Personal—or for the House?"

"Personal."

"We would hold the stock?"

"Of course."

"And if the stock goes down?"

"It won't."

"Say it does, Ian?"

"What do you suggest?"

"Well, it's all in the family so why don't we say if it goes two points below market at today's closing, we can sell and debit your account with the loss?"

"Three. Struan's is going to double."

"Yes. Meanwhile, let's say two until you sign the Par-Con deal. The House is rather a lot over on its revolving credit already. Let's say two, eh?"

"All right."

I'm safe at two, Dunross thought again, reassuring himself. I think.

Before he had left the bank he had gone by Johnjohn's office. Bruce Johnjohn, second deputy chief manager and heir apparent to Havergill, was a stocky, gentle man with a hummingbird's vitality. Dunross had given him the same news. Johnjohn had been equally pleased. But he had advised caution on projecting a boom and, contrary to Havergill, was greatly concerned with the Ho-Pak run.

"I don't like it at all, Ian. It's very smelly."

"Yes. What about Haply's article?"

"Oh, it's all nonsense. We don't go in for those sort of shenanigans. Blacs? Equally foolish. Why should we want to eliminate a major Chinese bank, even if we could. The Ching Bank might be the culprit. Perhaps. Perhaps old Smiler Ching would—he and Richard have been rivals for years. It could be a combination of half a dozen banks, Ching included. It might even be that Richard's depositors are really scared. I've heard all sorts of rumors for three months or so. They're in deep with dozens of dubious property schemes. Anyway, if he goes under it'll affect us all. Be bloody careful, Ian!"

"I'll be gald when you're upstairs, Bruce."

"Don't sell Paul short—he's very clever and he's been awfully good for Hong Kong and the bank. But we're in for some hairy times in Asia, Ian. I must say I think you're very wise to try to diversify into South America— it's a huge market and untapped by us. Have you considered South Africa?"

"What about it?"

"Let's have lunch next week. Wednesday? Good. I've an idea for you."

"Oh? What?"

"It'll wait, old chum. You heard about Gornt?"

"Yes."

"Very unusual for a Rolls, what?"

"Yes."

"He's very sure he can take Par-Con away from you."

"He won't."

"Have you seen Phillip today?"

"Phillip Chen? No, why?"

"Nothing."

"Why?"

"Bumped into him at the track. He seemed . . . well, he looked awful and very distraught. He's taking John's . . . he's taking the kidnapping very badly."

"Wouldn't you?"

"Yes. Yes I would. But I didn't think he and his Number One Son were that close."

Dunross thought about Adryon and Glenna and his son Duncan who was fifteen and on holiday on a friend's sheep station in Australia. What would I do if one of them were kidnapped? What would I do if a mutilated ear came through the mails at me like that?

I'd go mad.

I'd go mad with rage. I'd forget everything else and I'd hunt down the kidnappers and then, and then my vengeance would last a thousand years. I'd . . .

There was a knock on the door. "Yes? Oh hello, Kathy," he said, happy as always to see his younger sister.

"Sorry to interrupt, Ian dear," Kathy Gavallan said in a rush from the door to his office, "but Claudia said you had a few minutes before your next appointment. Is it all right?"

"'Course it's all right," he said with a laugh, and put aside the memo he was working on.

"Oh good, thanks." She closed the door and sat in the high chair that was near the window.

He stretched to ease the ache in his back and grinned at her. "Hey, I like your hat." It was pale straw with a yellow band that matched her cool-looking silk dress. "What's up?"

"I've got multiple sclerosis."

He stared at her blankly. "What?"

"That's what the tests say. The doctor told me yesterday but yesterday I couldn't tell you or . . . Today he checked the tests with another specialist and there's no mistake." Her voice was calm and her face calm and she sat upright in the chair, looking prettier than he had ever seen her. "I had to tell someone. Sorry to say it so suddenly. I thought you could help me make a plan, not today, but when you've time, perhaps over the weekend. . . ." She saw his expression and she laughed nervously. "It's not as bad as that. I think."

Dunross sat back in his big leather chair and fought to get his shocked mind working. "Multiple . . . that's dicey, isn't it?"

"Yes. Yes it is. Apparently it's something that attacks your nervous system that they can't cure yet. They don't know what it is or where or how you . . . how you get it."

"We'll get other specialists. No, even better, you go to England with Penn. There'd be specialists there or in Europe. There's got to be some form of cure, Kathy, got to be!"

"There isn't, dear. But England is a good idea. I'm . . . Dr. Tooley said he'd like me to see a Harley Street specialist for treatment. I'd love to go with Penn. I'm not too advanced and there's nothing to be too concerned about, if I'm careful."

"Meaning?"

"Meaning that if I take care of myself, take their medication, nap in the afternoon to stop getting tired, I'll still be able to take care of Andrew and the house and the children and play a little tennis and golf occasionally, but only one round in the mornings. You see, they can arrest the disease but they can't repair the damage already done so far. He said if I don't take care of myself and rest—it's rest mostly he said—if I don't rest, it will start up again and then each time you go down a plateau. Yes. And then you can never get back up again. Do you see, dear?"

He stared at her, keeping his agony for her bottled. His heart was grinding in his chest and he had eight plans for her and he thought Oh Christ poor Kathy! "Yes. Well, thank God you can rest all you want," he said, keeping his voice calm like hers. "Do you mind if I talk to Tooley?"

"I think that would be all right. There's no need to be alarmed, Ian. He said I'd be all right if I took care of myself, and I told him I'd be ever so good so he needn't have any worries on that score." Kathy was surprised that her voice was calm and her hands and fingers rested in her lap so easily, betraying none of the horror she felt within. She could almost feel the disease bugs or microbes or viruses seeping through her system, feeding on her nerves, eating them away oh so slowly, second by second hour by hour until there would be more tingling and more numbness in her fingers and her toes, then her wrists and ankles and legs and and and and and oh Jesus Christ God almighty . . .

She took a little tissue out of her purse and gently dabbed beside her nose and forehead. "It's awfully humid today, isn't it?"

"Yes. Kathy, why is it so sudden?"

"Well it isn't dear, not really. They just couldn't diagnose it. That's what all the tests were for." It had begun as a slight dizziness and headaches about six months ago. She'd noticed it most when she was playing golf. She would be standing over her ball, steadying herself, but her eyes would go dizzy and she could not focus and the ball would split and become two and three and two again and they would never stay still. Andrew had laughed and told her to see an optician. But it wasn't glasses, and aspirins did not help, nor stronger pills. Then dear old Tooley, their family doctor forever, had sent her to Matilda Hospital on the Peak for tests and more tests and brain scans in case there was a tumor but they had shown nothing, nor had all the other tests. Only the awful spinal tap gave a clue. Other tests confirmed it. Yesterday. Oh sweet Jesus was it only yesterday they condemned me to the wheelchair, at length to become a helpless slobbering thing?

"You've told Andrew?"

"No dear," she said, pulled once more back from the brink. "I haven't told him yet. I couldn't, not yet. Poor dear Andrew does get into a tizzy so easily. I'll tell him tonight. I couldn't tell him before I told you. I had to tell you first. We always used to tell you everything first, didn't we? Lechie, Scotty and I? You always used to know first. . . ." She was remembering when they were all young, all the lovely happy times here in Hong Kong and in Ayr at Castle Avisyard, at their lovely old rambling house on the crest of the hill amid the heather, overlooking the sea—Christmas and Easter and the long summer holidays, she and Ian—and Lechie, the oldest, and Scott, her twin brother—such happy days when Father wasn't there, all of them terrified of their father except Ian who was always their spokesman, always their protector, who always took the punishments—no supper tonight, and write five hundred times I will not argue anymore, a child's place is to be seen and not heard—who took all the beatings and never complained. Oh poor Lechie and Scotty . . .

"Oh Ian," she said, her tears welling suddenly, "I'm so sorry." Then she felt his arms wrap around her and she felt safe at last and the nightmare softened. But she knew it would never go away. Not now. Never. Nor would her brothers come back, except in her dreams, nor would her darling Johnny. "It's all right, Ian," she said through her tears. "It's not for me, not me really. I was just thinking about Lechie and Scotty and home at Ayr when we were small, and my Johnny, and I was oh ever so sad for all of them. . . ."

Lechie was the first to die. Second Lieutenant, Highland Light Infantry. He was lost in 1940 in France. Nothing was ever found of him. One moment he had been there beside the road, and then he was gone, the air filled with acrid smoke from the barrage that the Nazi panzers had laid down on the little stone bridge over the stream on the way to Dunkirk. For all the war years they had all lived in the hope that Lechie was now a POW in some good prison camp—not one of those terrible ones. And after the war, the months of searching but never a sign, never a witness, not even the littlest sign and then they, the family, and at length Father had laid Lechie's ghost to rest.

Scott had been sixteen in '39 and he'd gone to Canada for safety, there to finish schooling, and then, already a pilot, the day he was eighteen, in spite of Father's howling protests, he had joined the Canadian Air Force, wanting blood vengeance for Lechie. And he had got his wings at once and joined a bomber squadron and had come over well in time for D Day. Gleefully he had blown many a town to pieces and many a city to pieces until February 14, 1945, now Squadron Leader, DFC and Bar, coming home from the supreme holocaust of Dresden, his Lancaster had been jumped by a Messerschmitt and though his copilot had brought the crippled plane to rest in England, Scotty was dead in the left seat.

Kathy had been at his funeral and Ian had been there—in uniform, come home on leave from Chungking where he had been attached to Chiang Kai-shek's air force after he was shot down and grounded. She had wept on Ian's shoulder, wept for Lechie and wept for Scotty and wept for her Johnny. She was a widow then. Flight Lieutenant John Selkirk, DFC, another happy god of war, inviolate, invincible, had been blown out of the sky, torched out of the sky, the debris burning on the way to earth.

Johnny had had no funeral. There was nothing to bury. Like Lechie. Just a telegram came. One for each of them.

Oh Johnny my darling my darling my darling . . .

"What an awful waste, Ian dear, all of them. And for what?"

"I don't know, little Kathy," he said, still holding her. "I don't know. And I don't know why I made it and why they didn't."

"Oh I'm ever so glad you did!" She gave him a little hug and gathered herself. Somehow she put away her sadness for all of them. Then she dried her tears, took out a small mirror and looked at herself. "God, I look a mess! Sorry." His private bathroom was concealed behind a bookcase and she went there and repaired her makeup.

When she came back he was still staring out of the window. "Andrew's out of the office at the moment but the moment he comes back I'll tell him," he said.

"Oh no dear, that's my job. I must do that. I must. That's only fair." She smiled up at him and touched him. "I love you, Ian."

"I love you, Kathy."

22

The cardboard box that the Werewolves had sent to Phillip Chen was on Roger Crosse's desk. Beside the box was the ransom note, key ring, driver's license, pen, even the crumpled pieces of torn newspaper that had been used for packing. The little plastic bag was there, and the mottled rag. Only its contents were missing.

Everything had been tagged.

Roger Crosse was alone in the room and he stared at the objects, fascinated. He picked up a piece of the newspaper. Each had been carefully smoothed out, most were tagged with a date and the name of the Chinese newspaper it had come from. He turned it over, seeking hidden information, a hidden clue, something that might have been missed. Finding nothing, he put it back neatly and leaned on his hands, lost in thought.

Alan Medford Grant's report was also on his desk, near the intercom. It was very quiet in the room. Small windows overlooked Wanchai and part of the harbor toward Glessing's Point.

His phone jangled. "Yes?"

"Mr. Rosemont, CIA, and Mr. Langan, FBI, sir."

"Good." Roger Crosse replaced his phone. He unlocked his top desk drawer and carefully put the AMG file on top of the decoded telex and relocked it. The middle drawer contained a high-quality tape recorder. He checked it and touched a hidden switch. Silently the reels began to turn. The intercom on his desk contained a powerful microphone. Satisfied, he relocked this drawer. Another hidden desk switch slid a bolt open on the door soundlessly. He got up and opened the door.

"Hello, you two, please come in," he said affably. He closed the door behind the two Americans and shook hands with them. Unnoticed, he slid the bolt home again. "Take a seat. Tea?"

"No thanks," the CIA man said.

"What can I do for you?"

Both men were carrying manila envelopes. Rosemont opened his and took out a sheaf of good-quality eight-by-ten photos, clipped into two sections. "Here," he said, passing over the top section.

They were various shots of Voranski running across the wharf, on the streets of Kowloon, getting into and out of taxis, phoning, and many more of his Chinese assassins. One photograph showed the two Chinese leaving the phone booth with a clear glimpse of the crumpled body in the background.

Only Crosse's superb discipline kept him from showing astonishment, then blinding rage. "Good, very good," he said gently, putting them on the desk, very conscious of the ones Rosemont had retained in his hand. "So?"

Rosemont and Ed Langan frowned. "You were tailing him too?"

"Of course," Crosse said, lying with his marvelous sincerity. "My dear fellow, this is Hong Kong. But I do wish you'd let us do our job and not interfere."

"Rog, we, er, we don't want to interfere, just want to backstop you."

"Perhaps we don't need backstopping." There was a sharpness to his voice now.

"Sure." Rosemont took out a cigarette and lit it. He was tall and thin with gray crew-cut hair and good features. His hands were strong, like all of him. "We know where the two killers're holed up. We think we know," he said. "One of our guys thinks he's pegged them."

"How many men have you got watching the ship?"

"Ten. Our guys didn't notice any of yours tailing this one. The diversion almost spooked us too."

"Very dicey," Crosse said agreeably, wondering what diversion.

"Our guys never got to go through his pockets—we know he made two calls from the booth. . . ." Rosemont noted Crosse's eyes narrow slightly. That's curious, he thought. Crosse didn't know that. If he doesn't know that, maybe his operators weren't tailing the target either. Maybe he's lying and the Commie was loose in Hong Kong until he was knifed. "We radioed a mug shot back home—we'll get a call back fast. Who was he?"

"His papers said, Igor Voranski, seaman first class, Soviet merchant marine."

"You have a file on him, Rog?"

"It's rather unusual for you two to call together, isn't it? I mean, in the movies, we're always led to believe the FBI and CIA are always at odds."

Ed Langan smiled. "Sure we are—like you and MI-5—like the KGB, GRU and fifty other Soviet operations. But sometimes our cases cross—we're internal U.S., Stan's external, but we're both out for the same thing: security. We thought . . . we're asking if we could all cooperate. This could be a big one, and we're . . . Stan and I're out of our depth."

"That's right," Rosemont said, not believing it.

"All right," Crosse said, needing their information. "But you first."

Rosemont sighed. "Okay, Rog. We've had a buzz for some time there's something hotting up in Hong Kong—we don't know what—but it sure as hell's got tie-ins to the States. I figure the AMG file's the link. Lookit: take Banastasio—he's Mafia. Big-time. Narcotics, the lot. Now take Bartlett and the guns. Guns—"

"Is Bartlett tied into Banastasio?"

"We're not sure. We're checking. We are sure the guns were put aboard in L.A.—Los Angeles—where the airplane's based. Guns! Guns, narcotics and our growing interest in Vietnam. Where do narcotics come from? The Golden Triangle. Vietnam, Laos and the Yunnan Province of China. Now we're into Vietnam and—"

"Yes, and you're ill-advised to be there, old chum—I've pointed that out fifty times."

"We don't make policy, Rog, any more than you do. Next: Our nuclear carrier's here and the goddamn *Sovetsky Ivanov* arrives last night. That's too convenient, maybe the leak came from here. Then Ed tips you off and we get AMG's wild-assed letters from London and now there's Sevrin! Turns out the KGB've plants all over Asia and you've a high-placed hostile somewheres."

"That's not yet proved."

"Right. But I know about AMG. He's nobody's fool. If he says Sevrin's in place and you've a mole, you've a mole. Sure we've got hostiles in the CIA too, so've the KGB. I'm sure Ed has in the FBI—"

"That's doubtful," Ed Langan interrupted sharply. "Our guys are hand-picked and trained. You get your firemen from all over."

"Sure," Rosemont said, then added to Crosse, "Back to narcotics. Red China's our big enemy and—"

"Again, you're wrong, Stanley. The PRC's not the big enemy anywhere. Russia is."

"China's Commie. Commies're the enemy. Now, it'd be real smart to flood the States with cheap narcotics and Red China . . . okay the People's Republic of China can open the dam gates."

"But they haven't. Our Narcotics Branch's the best in Asia—they've never come up with anything to support your misguided official theory that they're behind the trade. Nothing. The PRC are as anti-drug traffic as the rest of us."

"Have it your way," Rosemont said. "Rog, you got a file on this agent? He's KGB, isn't he?"

Crosse lit a cigarette. "Voranski was here last year. That time he went under the cover name of Sergei Kudryov, again seaman first class, again off the same ship—they're not very inventive, are they?" Neither of the two men smiled. "His real name's Major Yuri Bakyan, First Directorate, KGB, Department 6."

Rosemont sighed heavily.

The FBI man glanced at him. "Then you're right. It all ties in."

"Maybe." The tall man thought a moment. "Rog, what about his contacts from last year?"

"He acted like a tourist, staying at the Nine Dragons in Kowloon. . . ."

"That's in AMG's report, that hotel's mentioned," Langan said.

"Yes. We've been covering it for a year or so. We've found nothing. Bakyan—Voranski—did ordinary tourist activities. We had him on twenty-four-hour surveillance. He stayed a couple of weeks, then, just before the ship sailed, sneaked back aboard."

"Girl friend?"

"No. Not a regular one. He used to hang out at the Good Luck Dance Hall in Wanchai. Quite a cocksman, apparently, but he asked no questions and met no one out of the ordinary."

"He ever visit Sinclair Towers?"

"No."

"Pity," Langan said, "that'd've been dandy. Tsu-yan's got a place there. Tsu-yan knows Banastasio, John Chen knows Banastasio, and we're back to guns, narcotics, AMG and Sevrin."

"Yeah," Rosemont said, then added, "Have you caught up with Tsu-yan yet?"

"No. He got to Taipei safely, then vanished."

"You think he's holed up there?"

"I would imagine so," Crosse said. But inside he believed him dead, already eliminated by Nationalist, Communist, Mafia or triad. I wonder if he could have been a double agent—or the supreme devil of all intelligence services, a triple agent?

"You'll find him—or we will—or the Taiwan boys will."

"Roger, did Voranski lead you anywhere?" Langan asked.

"No. Nowhere, even though we've had tabs on him for years. He's been attached to the Soviet Trade Commission in Bangkok, he spent time in Hanoi, and Seoul, but no covert activities we know of. Once the cheeky bugger even applied for a British passport and almost got one. Luckily our fellows vet all applications and spotted flaws in his cover. I'm sorry he's dead—you know how hard it is to identify nasties. Waste of a lot of time and effort." Crosse paused and lit a cigarette. "His major's rank is quite senior which suggests something very smelly. Perhaps he was just another of their specials who was ordered to cruise Asia and get into deep cover for twenty or thirty years."

"Those bastards have had their game plan set for so long it stinks!" Rosemont sighed. "What're you going to do with the corpse?"

Crosse smiled. "I got one of my Russian-speaking fellows to call the captain of the ship—Gregor Suslev. He's a Party member, of course, but fairly harmless. Has a sporadic girl friend with a flat in Mong Kok—a bar girl who gets a modest allowance from him and entertains him when he's here. He goes to the races, theater, Macao gambling a couple of times, speaks good English. Suslev's under surveillance. I don't want any of your hotshots ponging on one of our known hostiles."

"So Suslev's regular here then?"

"Yes, he's been plying these waters for years, based out of Vladivostok—he's an ex-submarine commander by the way. He wanders around the fringe here, mostly under the weather."

"What do you mean?"

"Drunk, but not badly so. Cavorts with a few of our British pinkos like Sam and Molly Finn."

"The ones who're always writing letters to the papers?"

"Yes. They're more of a nuisance than a security risk. Anyway, under instructions, my Russian-speaking fellow told Captain Suslev we were frightfully sorry but it seemed that one of his seamen had had a heart attack in a phone booth at Golden Ferry Terminal. Suslev was suitably shocked and quite reasonable. In Voranski's pocket there 'happened' to be an accurate, verbatim report of the assassin's phone conversation. We put it in Russian as a further sign of our displeasure. They're all professionals aboard that ship, and sophisticated enough to know we don't remove their agents without very great cause and provocation. They know we just watch the ones we know about and, if we're really very irritated, we deport them." Crosse looked across at Rosemont, his eyes hard though his voice stayed matter-of-fact. "We find our methods more effective than the knife, garrotte, poison or bullet."

The CIA man nodded. "But who would want to kill him?"

Crosse glanced at the photos again. He did not recognize the two Chinese, but their faces were clear and the body in the background unbelievable evidence. "We'll find them. Whoever they are. The one who phoned our police station claimed they were 14K. But he only spoke Shanghainese with a Ningpo dialect, so that's unlikely. Probably he was a triad of some sort. He could be Green Pang. He was certainly a trained professional—the knife was used perfectly, with great precision—one moment alive, the next dead and no sound. Could be one of your CIA's trainees in Chiang Kai-shek's intelligence agency. Or perhaps the Korean CIA, more of your trainees—they're anti-Soviet too, aren't they? Possibly PRC agents, but that's improbable. Their agents don't usually go in for *quai loh* murder, and certainly not in Hong Kong."

Rosemont nodded and let the censure pass. He gave Crosse the remaining photos, wanting the Englishman's cooperation and needing it. "These're shots of the house they went into. And the street sign. Our guy couldn't read characters but it translates, 'Street of the First Season, Number 14.' It's a rotten little alley in back of the bus depot in North Point."

Crosse began to examine them with equal care. Rosemont glanced at his watch, then got up and went to the single window that faced part of the harbor. "Look!" he said proudly.

The other two went over to him. The great nuclear carrier was just rounding North Point heading for the navy yard, Hong Kong side. She was dressed overall, all her obligatory flags stiff in the breeze, crowds of white-clothed sailors on her vast deck, with neat lines of her vicious fighter jet airplanes. Almost 84,000 tons. No smokestack, just a vast, ominous bridge complex, with an eleven-hundred-foot angled runway that could retrieve and launch jets simultaneously. The first of a generation.

"That's some ship," Crosse said enviously. This was the first time the colossus had entered Hong Kong since her commissioning in 1960. "Pretty," he said, hating the fact she was American and not British. "What's her top speed?"

"I don't know—that's classified along with most everything else." Rosemont turned to watch him. "Can't you send that goddamn Soviet spy ship to hell out of port?"

"Yes, and we could blow it up, but that would be equally foolish. Stanley, relax, you have to be a little civilized about these things. Repairing their ships—and some of them really do need it—is a good source of revenue, and intelligence, and they pay their bills promptly. Our ways have been tried and tested over the years."

Yes, Rosemont was thinking without rancor, but your ways don't work anymore. The British Empire's no more, the British raj no more and we've a different enemy now, smarter rougher dedicated totalitarian fanatic, with no Queensberry rules and a worldwide plan that's lavishly funded by whatever it takes. You British've no dough now, no clout, no navy, no army, no air force, and your goddamn government's filled with socialist and enemy pus, and *we* think they sold you out. You've been screwed from within, your security's the pits from Klaus Fuchs and Philby on down. Jesus, we won both goddamn wars for you, paid for most of it and both times you've screwed up the peace. And if it wasn't for *our* Strategic Air Command, our missiles, our nuclear strike force, our navy, our army, our air force our taxpayers our dough, you'd all be dead or in goddamn Siberia. Meanwhile, like it or not I got to deal with you. We need Hong Kong as a window and right now your cops to guard the carrier.

"Rog, thanks for the extra men," he said. "We sure appreciate it."

"We wouldn't want any trouble while she's here either. Pretty ship. I envy you having her."

"Her captain'll have the ship and crew under tight wraps—the shore parties'll all be briefed, and warned, and we'll cooperate a hundred percent."

"I'll see you get a copy of the list of bars I've suggested your sailors stay out of—some're known Communist hangouts, and some are frequented by our lads off H.M.S. *Dart*." Crosse smiled. "There'll still be the odd brawl."

"Sure. Rog, this Voranski killing's too much of a coincidence. Can I send a Shanghai speaker to assist the interrogation?"

"I'll let you know if we need help."

"Can we have our copies of the tai-pan's other AMG reports now? Then we can get out of your hair."

Crosse stared back at him twisting uneasily, even though he was prepared for the question. "I'll have to get approval from Whitehall."

Rosemont was surprised. "Our top man in England's been on to your Great White Father and it's approved. You should have had it an hour ago."

"Oh?"

"Sure. Hell, we'd no idea AMG was on the tai-pan's payroll let alone passing classified stuff for chrissake! The wires've been red hot since Ed got the top copy of AMG's last will and testament. We got an all-points from Washington on getting copies of the other reports and we're trying to trace the call to Switzerland but—"

"Say again?"

"Kiernan's call. The second call he made."

"I don't follow you."

Rosemont explained.

Crosse frowned. "My people didn't tell me about that. Nor did Dunross. Now why should Dunross lie—or avoid telling me that?" He related to them exactly what Dunross had told him. "There was no reason for him to hide that, was there?"

"No. All right, Rog: Is the tai-pan kosher?"

Crosse laughed. "If you mean is he a one hundred percent British Royalist freebooter whose allegiance is to his House, himself and the Queen—not necessarily in that order—the answer's an emphatic yes."

"Then if we can have our copies now, Rog, we'll be on our way."

"When I've got Whitehall's approval."

"If you'll check your decoding room—it's a Priority 1-4a. It says to let us have copies on receipt."

1-4a's were very rare. They called for immediate clearance and immediate action.

Crosse hesitated, wanting to avoid the trap he was in. He dared not tell them he did not yet have possession of the AMG reports. He picked up the phone and dialed. "This is Mr. Crosse. Is there anything for me from Source? A 1-4a?"

"No sir. Other than the one we sent up an hour ago—that you signed for," the SI woman said.

"Thank you." Crosse put the phone down. "Nothing yet," he said.

"Shit," Rosemont muttered, then added, "They swore they'd already beamed it out and you'd have it before we got here. It's got to be here any second. If you don't mind we'll wait."

"I've an appointment in Central shortly. Perhaps later this evening?"

Both men shook their heads. Langan said, "We'll wait. We've been ordered to send 'em back instantly by hand with a twenty-four-hour guard.

An army transport's due now at Kai Tak to carry the courier—we can't even copy them here."

"Aren't you overreacting?"

"You could answer that. What's in them?"

Crosse toyed with his lighter. It had Cambridge University emblazoned on it. He had owned it since his undergraduate days. "Is it true what AMG said about the CIA and the Mafia?"

Rosemont stared back at him. "I don't know. You guys used all sort of crooks during World War Two. We learned from you to take advantage of what we've got—that was your first rule. Besides," Rosemont added with utter conviction, "this war's our war and whatever it takes we're going to win."

"Yes, yes we must," Langan echoed, equally sure. "Because if we lose this one, the whole world's gone and we'll never get another chance."

On the closed-in bridge of the *Sovetsky Ivanov* three men had binoculars trained on the nuclear carrier. One of the men was a civilian and he wore a throat mike that fed into a tape recorder. He was giving an expert, technical running commentary of what he saw. From time to time the other two would add a comment. Both wore light naval uniform. One was Captain Gregor Suslev, the other his first officer.

The carrier was coming up the roads nicely, tugs in attendance, but no tug ropes. Ferries and freighters tooted a jaunty welcome. A marine band played on her aft deck. White-clad sailors waved at passing ships. The day was very humid and the afternoon sun cast long shadows.

"The captain's expert," the first officer said.

"Yes. But with all that radar even a child could handle her," Captain Suslev replied. He was a heavy-shouldered, bearded man, his Slavic brown eyes deepset in a friendly face. "Those sweepers aloft look like the new GE's for very long-range radar. Are they, Vassili?"

The technical expert broke off his transmission momentarily. "Yes, Comrade Captain. But look aft! They've four F5 interceptors parked on the right flight deck."

Suslev whistled tonelessly. "They're not supposed to be in service till next year."

"No," the civilian said.

"Report that separately as soon as she docks. That news alone pays for our voyage."

"Yes."

Suslev fine-tuned his focus now as the ship turned slightly. He could see the airplanes' bomb racks. "How many more F5's does she carry in her guts, and how many atomic warheads for them?"

They all watched the carrier for a moment.

"Perhaps we'll get lucky this time, Comrade Captain," the first officer said.

"Let's hope so. Then Voranski's death won't be so expensive."

"The Americans are fools to bring her here—don't they know every agent in Asia'll be tempted by her?"

"It's lucky for us they are. It makes our job so much easier." Once more Suslev concentrated on the F5's that looked like soldier hornets among other hornets.

Around him the bridge was massed with advanced surveillance equipment. One radar was sweeping the harbor. A gray-haired impassive sailor watched the screen, the carrier a large clear blip among the myriad of blips.

Suslev's binoculars moved to the carrier's ominous bridge complex, then wandered the length of the ship. In spite of himself he shivered at her size and power. "They say she's never refueled—not since she was launched in 1960."

Behind him the door to the radio room that adjoined the bridge opened and a radio operator came up to him and saluted, offering the cable. "Urgent from Center, Comrade Captain."

Suslev took the cable and signed for it. It was a meaningless jumble of words. A last look at the carrier and he let the binoculars rest on his chest and strode off the bridge. His sea cabin was just aft on the same deck. The door was guarded, like both entrances to the bridge.

He relocked his cabin door behind him and opened the small, concealed safe. His cipher book was secreted in a false wall. He sat at his desk. Quickly he decoded the message. He read it carefully, then stared into space for a moment.

He read it a second time, then replaced the cipher book, closed the safe and burned the original of the cable in an ashtray. He picked up his phone. "Bridge? Send Comrade Metkin to my cabin!" While he waited he stood by the porthole lost in thought. His cabin was untidy. Photographs of a heavyset woman, smiling self-consciously, were on his desk in a frame. Another of a good-looking youth in naval uniform, and a girl in her teens. Books, a tennis racket and a newspaper on the half-made bunk.

A knock. He unlocked the door. The sailor who had been staring at the radar screen stood there.

"Come in, Dimitri." Suslev motioned at the decoded cable and relocked the door after him.

The sailor was short and squat, with graying hair and a good face. He was, officially, political commissar and therefore senior officer on the ship. He picked up the decoded message. It read: "Priority One. Gregor Suslev. You will assume Voranski's duties and responsibilities at once. London reports optimum CIA and MI-6 interest in information contained in blue-covered files leaked to Ian Dunross of Struan's by the British Intelligence coordinator, AMG. Order Arthur to obtain copies immediately. If Dunross has destroyed the copies, cable feasibility plan to detain him for chemical debriefing in depth." The sailor's face closed. He looked across at Captain Suslev. "AMG? Alan Medford Grant?"

"Yes."

"May that one burn in hell for a thousand years."

"He will, if there's any justice in this world or the next." Suslev smiled grimly. He went to a sideboard and took out a half-full vodka bottle and two glasses. "Listen, Dimitri, if I fail or don't return, you take command." He held up the key. "Unlock the safe. There're instructions about decoding and everything else."

"Let me go tonight in your place. You're more impor—"

"No. Thank you, old friend." Suslev clapped him warmly on the shoulders. "In case of an accident you assume command and carry out our mission. That's what we've been trained for." He touched glasses with him. "Don't worry. Everything will be fine," he said, glad he could do as he wished and very content with his job and his position in life. He was, secretly, deputy controller in Asia for the KGB's First Directorate, Department 6, that was responsible for all covert activities in China, North Korea and Vietnam; a senior lecturer in Vladivostok University's Department of Foreign Affairs, 2A–Counterintelligence; a colonel in the KGB; and, most important of all, a senior Party member in the Far East. "Center's given the order. You must guard our tails here. Eh?"

"Of course. You needn't worry about that, Gregor. I can do everything. But I worry about you," Metkin said. They had sailed together for several years and he respected Suslev very much though he did not know from where his overriding authority came. Sometimes he was tempted to try to find out. You're getting on, he told himself. You retire next year and you may need powerful friends and the only way to have the help of powerful friends is to know their skeletons. But Suslev or no Suslev your well-earned retirement will be honorable, quiet and at home in the Crimea. Metkin's heart beat faster at the thought of all that lovely countryside and grand climate on the Black Sea, dreaming the rest of his life away with his wife and sometimes seeing his son, an up-and-coming KGB officer presently in Washington, no longer at risk and in danger from within or without.

Oh God protect my son from betrayal or making a mistake, he prayed fervently, then at once felt a wave of nausea, as always, in case his superiors knew that he was a secret believer and that his parents, peasants, had brought him up in the Church. If they knew there would be no retirement in the Crimea, only some icy backwater and no real home ever again.

"Voranski," he said, as always cautiously hiding his hatred of the man. "He was a top operator, eh? Where did he slip?"

"He was betrayed, that was his problem," Suslev said darkly. "We will find his murderers and they will pay. If my name is on the next knife . . ." The big man shrugged, then poured more vodka with a sudden laugh. "So what, eh? It's in the name of the cause, the Party and Mother Russia!"

They touched glasses and drained them.

"When're you going ashore?"

Suslev bit on the raw liquor. Then, thankfully, he felt the great good warmth begin inside and his anxieties and terrors seemed less real. He motioned out of the porthole. "As soon as she's moored and safe," he said with his rolling laugh. "Ah, but she's a pretty ship, eh?"

"We've got nothing to touch that bastard, Captain, have we? Or those fighters. Nothing."

Suslev smiled as he poured again. "No, comrade. But if the enemy has no real will to resist they can have a hundred of those carriers and it doesn't matter."

"Yes, but Americans're erratic, one general can go off at half-cock, and they can smash us off the face of the earth."

"I agree, now they can, but they won't. They've no balls." Suslev drank again. "And soon? Just a little more time and we'll stick their noses up their asses!" He sighed. "It will be good when we begin."

"It'll be terrible."

"No, a short, almost bloodless war against America and then the rest'll collapse like the pus-infected corpse it is."

"Bloodless? What about their atom bombs? Hydrogen bombs?"

"They'll never use atomics or missiles against us, they're too scared, even now, of *ours!* Because they're *sure* we'll use them."

"Will we?"

"I don't know. Some commanders would. I don't know. We'll certainly use them back. But first? I don't know. The threat will always be enough. I'm sure we'll never need a fighting war." He lit a corner of the decoded message and put it in the ashtray. "Another twenty years of détente—ah what Russian genius invented that—we'll have a navy bigger and better than theirs, an air force bigger and better than theirs. We've got more tanks now and more soldiers, but without ships and airplanes we must wait. Twenty years is not long to wait for Mother Russia to rule the earth."

"And China? What about China?"

Suslev gulped the vodka and refilled both glasses again. The bottle was empty now and he tossed it onto his bunk. His eyes saw the burning paper in the ashtray twist and crackle, dying. "Perhaps China's the one place to use our atomics," he said matter-of-factly. "There's nothing there we need. Nothing. That'd solve our China problem once and for all. How many men of military age did they have at last estimate?"

"116 million between the ages of eighteen and twenty-five."

"Think of that! 116 million yellow devils sharing 5,000 miles of our frontiers . . . and then foreigners call us paranoiac about China!" He sipped the vodka, this time making it last. "Atomics'd solve our China problem once and for all. Quick, simple and permanent."

The other man nodded. "And this Dunross? The papers of AMG?"

"We'll get them from him. After all, Dimitri, one of our people is family, another one of his partners, another's in Special Intelligence, there's Arthur and Sevrin everywhere he turns, and then we've a dozen decadents to call on in his parliament, some in his government." They both began laughing.

"And if he's destroyed the papers?"

Suslev shrugged. "They say he's got a photographic memory."

"You'd do the interrogation here?"

"It'd be dangerous to do an in-depth chemic quickly. I've never done one. Have you?"

"No."

The captain frowned. "When you report tonight, get Center to ready an expert in case we need one—Koronski from Vladivostok if he's available."

Dimitri nodded, lost in thought. This morning's *Guardian*, lying half-crumpled on the captain's bunk, caught his eye. He went over and picked it up, his eyes alight. "Gregor—if we have to detain Dunross, why not blame them, then you've all the time you'll need?" The screaming headline read, SUSPECTS IN WEREWOLVES KIDNAP CASE. "If Dunross doesn't return . . . perhaps our man'd become tai-pan! Eh?"

Suslev began to chuckle. "Dimitri, you're a genius."

Rosemont glanced at his watch. He had waited long enough. "Rog, can I use your phone?"

"Certainly," Crosse said.

The CIA man stubbed out his cigarette and dialed the central CIA exchange in the consulate.

"This is Rosemont—give me 2022." That was the CIA communications center.

"2022. Chapman—who's this?"

"Rosemont. Hi, Phil, anything new?"

"No, excepting Marty Povitz reports a lot of activity on the bridge of the *Ivanov*, high-powered binoculars. Three guys, Stan. One's a civilian, others're the captain and the first officer. One of their short-range radar sweep's working overtime. You want us to notify the *Corregidor*'s captain?"

"Hell no, no need to make his tail wriggle more than needs be. Say, Phil, we get a confirm on our 40-41?"

"Sure Stan. It came in at . . . stand by one . . . it came in at 1603 local."

"Thanks, Phil, see you."

Rosemont lit another cigarette. Sourly Langan, a nonsmoker, watched him but said nothing as Crosse was smoking too.

"Rog, what are you pulling?" Rosemont asked harshly, to Langan's shock. "You got your Priority 1-4a at 1603, same time as we did. Why the stall?"

"I find it presently convenient," Crosse replied, his voice pleasant.

Rosemont flushed, so did Langan. "Well I don't and we've instructions, official instructions, to pick up our copies right now."

"So sorry, Stanley."

Rosemont's neck was now very red but he kept his temper. "You're not going to obey the 1-4a?"

"Not at the moment."

Rosemont got up and headed for the door. "Okay, Rog, but they'll throw the book at you." He ripped the bolt back, jerked the door open and left. Langan was on his feet, his face also set.

"What's the reason, Roger?" he asked.

Crosse stared back at him calmly. "Reason for what?"

Ed Langan began to get angry but stopped, suddenly appalled. "Jesus, Roger, you haven't got them yet? Is that it?"

"Come now, Ed," Crosse said easily, "you of all people should know we're efficient."

"That's no answer, Roger. Have you or haven't you?" The FBI man's level eyes stayed on Crosse, and did not phase Crosse at all. Then he walked out, closing the door after him. At once Crosse touched the hidden switch. The bolt slid home. Another hidden switch turned off his tape recorder. He picked up his phone and dialed. "Brian? Have you heard from Dunross?"

"No sir."

"Meet me downstairs at once. With Armstrong."

"Yes sir."

Crosse hung up. He took out the formal arrest document that was headed DETAINMENT ORDER UNDER THE OFFICIAL SECRETS ACT. Quickly he filled in "Ian Struan Dunross" and signed both copies. The top copy he kept, the other he locked in his drawer. His eyes roamed his office, checking it. Satisfied, he delicately positioned a sliver of paper in the crack of his drawer so that he alone would know if anyone had opened it or tampered with it. He walked out. Heavy security locks slid home after him.

23

Dunross was in the Struan boardroom with the other directors of Nelson Trading, looking at Richard Kwang. "No, Richard. Sorry, I can't wait till after closing tomorrow."

"It'll make no difference to you, tai-pan. It will to me." Richard Kwang was sweating. The others watched him—Phillip Chen, Lando Mata and Zeppelin Tung.

"I disagree, Richard," Lando Mata said sharply. "Madonna, you don't seem to realize the seriousness of the run!"

"Yes," Zeppelin Tung said, his face shaking with suppressed rage.

Dunross sighed. If it wasn't for his presence he knew they would all be raving and screaming at each other, the obscenities flying back and forth as they do at any formal negotiation between Chinese, let alone one as serious as this. But it was a Noble House law that all board meetings were to be conducted in English, and English inhibited Chinese swearing and also unsettled Chinese which was of course the whole idea. "The matter has to be dealt with now, Richard."

"I agree." Lando Mata was a handsome, sharp-featured Portuguese in his fifties, his mother's Chinese blood clear in his dark eyes and dark hair and golden complexion. His long fine fingers drummed continuously on the conference table and he knew Richard Kwang would never dare disclose that he, Tightfist Tung and Smuggler Mo controlled the bank. Our bank's one enterprise, he thought angrily, but our bullion's something else. "We can't have our bullion, or our cash, in jeopardy!"

"Never," Zeppelin Tung said nervously. "My father wanted me to make that clear too. He wants his gold!"

"*Madre de Dios,* we've almost fifty tons of gold in your vaults."

"Actually it's over fifty tons," Zeppelin Tung said, the sweat beading his forehead. "My old man gave me the figures—it's 1,792,668 ounces in 298,778 five-tael bars." The air in the large room was warm and humid, the windows open. Zeppelin Tung was a well-dressed, heavyset man of forty with small narrow eyes, the eldest son of Tightfist Tung, and his accent was upper-class British. His nickname came from a movie that Tightfist had seen the day of his birth. "Richard, isn't that right?"

Richard Kwang shifted the agenda paper in front of him which listed the quantity of gold and Nelson Trading's current balance. If he had to give up the bullion and cash tonight it would severely hurt the bank's liquidity and, when the news leaked, as of course it would, that would rock their whole edifice.

"What're you going to do, you dumbhead dog bone!" his wife had screamed at him just before he had left his office.

"Delay, delay and hope th—"

"No! Pretend to be sick! If you're sick you can't give them our money. You can't go to the meeting! Rush home and we'll pretend—"

"I can't, the tai-pan called personally. And so did that dog bone Mata! I daren't not go! Oh oh oh!"

"Then find out who's hounding us and pay him off! Where's your head? Who have you offended? You must have offended one of those dirty *quai lohs*. Find the man and pay him off or we'll lose the bank, lose our membership in the Turf Club, lose the horses, lose the Rolls and lose face forever! *Ayeeyah!* If the bank goes you'll never be Sir Richard Kwang, not that being Lady Kwang matters to me oh no! Do something! Find the . . ."

Richard Kwang felt the sweat running down his back but he kept his composure and tried to find a way out of the maze. "The gold's as safe as it could be and so's your cash. We've been Nelson Trading's bankers since the beginning, we've never had a sniff of trouble. We gambled heavily with you in the beginning—"

"Come now, Richard," Mata said, keeping his loathing hidden. "You don't gamble on gold. Certainly not on *our* gold." The gold belonged to the Great Good Luck Company of Macao which had also owned the gambling monopoly for almost thirty years. The present worth of the company was in excess of two billion U.S. Tightfist Tung owned 30 percent, personally, Lando Mata 40 percent personally—and the descendents of Smuggler Mo, who had died last year, the other 30 percent.

And between us, Mata was thinking, we own 50 percent of the Ho-Pak which you, you stupid lump of dog turd, have somehow put into jeopardy. "So sorry, Richard, but I vote Nelson Trading changes its bank—at least temporarily. Tightfist Tung is really very upset . . . and I have the Chin family's proxy."

"But Lando," Richard Kwang began, "there's nothing to worry about." His finger stabbed at the half-opened newspaper, the *China Guardian*, that lay on the table. "Haply's new article says again that we're sound—that it's all a storm in an oyster shell, all started by malicious ban—"

"That's possible. But Chinese believe rumors, and the run's a fact," Mata said sharply.

"My old man believes rumors," Zeppelin Tung said fervently. "He also believes Four Finger Wu. Four Fingers phoned him this afternoon telling him he'd taken out all his money and suggested he do the same, and within the hour we, Lando and I, we were in our Catalina and heading here and you know how I hate flying. Richard, you know jolly well if the old man wants something done *now*, it's done *now*."

Yes, Richard Kwang thought disgustedly, that filthy old miser would climb out of his grave for fifty cents cash. "I suggest we wait a day or so . . ."

Dunross was letting them talk for face. He had already decided what to do. Nelson Trading was a wholly owned subsidiary of Struan's so the other directors really had little say. But even though Nelson Trading had the Hong Kong Government's exclusive gold-importing license, without the Great Good Luck Company's gold business—which meant without Tightfist Tung and Lando Mata's favor—Nelson Trading's profits would be almost zero.

Nelson Trading got a commission of one dollar an ounce on every ounce imported for the company, delivered to the jetty at Macao, a further one dollar an ounce on exports from Hong Kong. As a further consideration for suggesting the overall Hong Kong scheme to the company, Nelson Trading had been granted 10 percent of the real profit. This year the Japanese Government had arbitrarily fixed their official rate of gold at 55 dollars an ounce—a profit of 15 dollars an ounce. On the black market it would be more. In India it would be almost 98 dollars.

Dunross glanced at his watch. In a few minutes Crosse would arrive.

"We've assets over a billion, Lando," Richard Kwang repeated.

"Good," Dunross said crisply jumping in, finalizing the meeting. "Then, Richard, it really makes no difference one way or another. There's no point in waiting. I've made certain arrangements. Our transfer truck will be at your side door at eight o'clock precisely."

"But—"

"Why so late, tai-pan?" Mata asked. "It's not six o'clock yet."

"It'll be dark then, Lando. I wouldn't want to shift 50 tons of gold in daylight. There might be a few villains around. You never know. Eh?"

"My God, you think . . . triads?" Zeppelin Tung was shocked. "I'll phone my father. He'll have some extra guards."

"Yes," Mata said, "call at once."

"No need for that," Dunross told him. "The police suggested that we don't make too much of a show. They said they'll be there in depth."

Mata hesitated. "Well if you say so, tai-pan. You're responsible."

"Of course," Dunross said politely.

"How do we know the Victoria's safe?"

"If the Victoria fails we might as well not be in China." Dunross picked up the phone and dialed Johnjohn's private number at the bank. "Bruce? Ian. We'll need the vault—8:30 on the dot."

"Very well. Our security people will be there to assist. Use the side door —the one on Dirk's Street."

"Yes."

"Have the police been informed?"

"Yes."

"Good. By the way, Ian, about . . . is Richard still with you?"

"Yes."

"Give me a call when you can—I'm at home this evening. I've been checking and things don't look very good at all for him. My Chinese banking friends are all very nervous—even the Mok-tung had a mini-run out at Aberdeen, so did we. Of course we'll advance Richard all the money he needs against his securities, bankable securities, but if I were you I'd get any cash you control out. Get Blacs to deal with your check first at clearing tonight." All bank clearing of checks and bank loans was done in the basement of the Bank of London, Canton and Shanghai at midnight, five days a week.

"Thanks, Bruce. See you later." Then to the others, "That's all taken care of. Of course the transfer should be kept quiet. Richard, I'll need a cashier's check for Nelson Trading balance."

"And I'll have one for my father's balance!" Zeppelin echoed.

Richard Kwang said, "I'll send the checks over first thing in the morning."

"Tonight," Mata said, "then they can clear tonight." His eyes lidded even more. "And, of course, another for my personal balance."

"There isn't enough cash to cover those three checks—no bank could have that amount," Richard Kwang exploded. "Not even the Bank of England."

"Of course. Please call whomever you wish to pledge some of your securities. Or Havergill, or Southerby." Mata's fingers stopped drumming. "They're expecting your call."

"What?"

"Yes. I talked to both of them this afternoon."

Richard Kwang said nothing. He had to find a way to avoid giving the money over tonight. If not tonight, he would gain a day's interest and by tomorrow perhaps it would not be necessary to pay. *Dew neh loh moh* on all filthy *quai loh* and half *quai loh*, who're worse! His smile was as sweet as Mata's. "Well, as you wish. If you'll both meet me at the bank in an hour . . ."

"Even better," Dunross said. "Phillip will go with you now. You can give him all the checks. Is that all right with you, Phillip?"

"Oh, oh yes, yes, tai-pan."

"Good, thank you. Then if you'll take them right over to Blacs, they'll clear at midnight. Richard, that gives you plenty of time. Doesn't it?"

"Oh yes, tai-pan," Richard Kwang said, brightening. He had just thought of a brilliant answer. A pretended heart attack! I'll do it in the car going back to the bank and then . . .

Then he saw the coldness in Dunross's eyes and his stomach twisted and he changed his mind. Why should they have so much of my money? he thought as he got up. "You don't need me for anything more at the moment? Good, come along, Phillip." They walked out. There was a vast silence.

"Poor Phillip, he looks ghastly," Mata said.

"Yes. It's no wonder."

"Dirty triads," Zeppelin Tung said with a shudder. "The Werewolves must be foreigners to send his ear like that!" Another shudder. "I hope they don't come to Macao. There's a strong rumor Phillip's dealing with them already, negotiating with the Werewolves in Macao."

"There's no truth to that," Dunross said.

"He wouldn't tell you if he was, tai-pan. I'd keep that secret from everyone too." Zeppelin Tung stared gloomily at the phone. "*Dew neh loh moh* on all filthy kidnappers."

"Is the Ho-Pak finished?" Mata asked.

"Unless Richard Kwang can stay liquid, yes. This afternoon Dunstan closed all his accounts."

"Ah, so once again a rumor's correct!"

"Afraid so!" Dunross was sorry for Richard Kwang and the Ho-Pak but tomorrow he would sell short. "His stock's going to plummet."

"How will that affect the boom you've forecast?"

"Have I?"

"You're buying Struan's heavily, so I hear." Mata smiled thinly. "So has Phillip, and his *tai-tai,* and her family."

"Anyone's wise to buy our stock, Lando, at any time. It's very underpriced."

Zeppelin Tung was listening very carefully. His heart quickened. He too had heard rumors about the Noble House Chens buying today. "Did you see Old Blind Tung's column today? About the coming boom? He was very serious."

"Yes," Dunross said gravely. When he had read it this morning he had chortled, and his opinion of Dianne Chen's influence had soared. In spite of himself Dunross had reread it and had wondered briefly if the soothsayer had really been forecasting his own opinion.

"Is Old Blind Tung a relation, Zep?" he asked.

"No, tai-pan, no, not that I know of. *Dew neh loh moh* but it's hot today. I'll be glad to get back to Macao—the weather's much better in Macao. Are you in the motor race this year, tai-pan?"

"Yes, I hope so."

"Good! Damn the Ho-Pak! Richard will give us our checks, won't he? My old man will bust a blood vessel if one penny cash is missing."

"Yes," Dunross said, then noticed a strangeness in Mata's eyes. "What's up?"

"Nothing." Mata glanced at Zeppelin. "Zep, it's really important we have your father's approval quickly. Why don't you and Claudia track him down."

"Good idea." Obediently the Chinese got to his feet and walked out, closing the door. Dunross turned his attention to Mata. "And?"

Mata hesitated. Then he said quietly, "Ian, I'm considering taking all my funds out of Macao and Hong Kong and putting them in New York."

Dunross stared at him, perturbed. "If you did that you'd rattle our whole system. If you withdraw, Tightfist will too, and the Chins, Four Fingers . . . and all the others."

"Which is more important, tai-pan, the system or your own money?"

"I wouldn't want the system shaken like that."

"You've closed with Par-Con?"

Dunross watched him. "Verbally yes. Contracts in seven days. Withdrawing will hurt us all, Lando. Badly. What's bad for us will be very bad for you and very very bad for Macao."

"I'll consider what you say. So Par-Con's coming into Hong Kong. Very good—and if American Superfoods' takeover of the H. K. General Stores goes through, that'll add another boost to the market. Perhaps Old Blind Tung wasn't exaggerating again. Perhaps we'll be lucky. Has he ever been wrong before?"

"I don't know. Personally I don't think he has a private connection with the Almighty, though a lot of people do."

"A boom would be very good, very good indeed. Perfect timing. Yes," Mata added strangely, "we could add a little fuel to the greatest boom in our history. Eh?"

"Would you assist?"

"Ten million U.S., between myself and the Chins—Tightfist won't be interested, I know. You suggest where and when."

"Half a million into Struan's last thing Thursday, the rest spread over Rothwell-Gornt, Asian Properties, Hong Kong Wharf, Hong Kong Power, Golden Ferries, Kowloon Investments and H. K. General Stores."

"Why Thursday? Why not tomorrow?"

"The Ho-Pak will bring the market down. If we buy in quantity Thursday just before closing, we'll make a fortune."

"When do you announce the Par-Con deal?"

Dunross hesitated. Then he said, "Friday, after the market closes."

"Good. I'm with you, Ian. Fifteen million. Fifteen instead of ten. You'll sell the Ho-Pak short tomorrow?"

"Of course. Lando, do you know who's behind the run on the Ho-Pak?"

"No. But Richard is overextended, and he hasn't been too wise. People talk, Chinese always distrust any bank, and they react to rumors. I think the bank will crash."

"Christ!"

"Joss." Mata's fingers stopped drumming. "I want to triple our gold imports."

Dunross stared at him. "Why? You're up to capacity now. If you push them too fast they'll make mistakes and your seizure rate will go up. At the moment you've balanced everything perfectly."

"Yes, but Four Fingers and others assure us they can make some substantial bulk shipments safely."

"No need to push them—or your market. No need at all."

"Ian, listen to me a moment. There's trouble in Indonesia, trouble in China, India, Tibet, Malaya, Singapore, ferment in the Philippines and now the Americans are going into Southeast Asia which will be marvelous for us and dreadful for them. Inflation will soar and then, as usual, every sensible businessman in Asia, particularly Chinese businessmen, will want to get out of paper money and into gold. We should be ready to service that demand."

"What've you heard, Lando?"

"Lots of curious things, tai-pan. For example, that certain top U.S. generals want a full-scale confrontation with the Communists. Vietnam's chosen."

"But the Americans'll never win there. China can't let them, any more than they could in Korea. Any history book will tell them China *always* crosses her borders to protect her buffer zones when any invader approaches."

"Even so, the confrontation will take place."

Dunross studied Lando Mata whose enormous wealth and longtime involvement in the honorable profession of trading, as he described it, gave him vast entrée into the most secretive of places. "What else have you heard, Lando?"

"The CIA has had its budget doubled."

"That has to be classified. No one could know that."

"Yes. But I know. Their security's appalling. Ian, the CIA's into everything in Southeast Asia. I believe some of their misguided zealots are even trying to wheedle into the opium trade in the Golden Triangle for the benefit of their friendly Mekong hill tribes—to encourage them to fight the Viet Cong."

"Christ!"

"Yes. Our brethren in Taiwan are furious. And there's a growing abundance of U.S. Government money pouring into airfields, harbors, roads. In Okinawa, Taiwan and particularly in South Vietnam. Certain highly connected political families are helping to supply the cement and steel on very favorable terms."

"Who?"

"Who makes cement? Perhaps in . . . say in New England?"

"Good sweet Christ, are you sure?"

Mata smiled humorlessly. "I even heard that part of a very large government loan to South Vietnam was expended on a nonexistent airfield that's still impenetrable jungle. Oh yes, Ian, the pickings are already huge. So please order triple shipments from tomorrow. We institute our new hydrofoil services next month—that'll cut the time to Macao from three hours to seventy-five minutes."

"Wouldn't the Catalina still be safer?"

"No. I don't think so. The hydrofoils can carry much more gold and can outrun anything in these waters—we'll have constant radar communications, the best, so we can outrun any pirates."

After a pause, Dunross said, "So much gold could attract all sorts of villains. Perhaps even international crooks."

Mata smiled his thin smile. "Let them come. They'll never leave. We've long arms in Asia." His fingers began drumming again. "Ian, we're old friends, I would like some advice."

"Glad to—anything."

"Do you believe in change?"

"Business change?"

"Yes."

"It depends, Lando," Dunross answered at once. "The Noble House's changed little in almost a century and a half, in other ways it's changed vastly." He watched the older man, and he waited.

At length Mata said, "In a few weeks the Macao Government is obliged to put the gambling concession up for bids again. . . ." Instantly Dunross's attention zeroed. All big business in Macao was conducted on monopoly lines, the monopoly going to the person or company that offered the most taxes per year for the privilege. ". . . This's the fifth year. Every five years our department asks for closed bids. The auction's open to anyone but, in practice, we scrutinize very particularly those who are invited to bid." The silence hung a moment, then Mata continued, "My old associate, Smuggler Mo's already dead. His offspring're mostly profligate or more interested in the Western world, gambling in southern France or playing golf, than in the health and future of the syndicate. For the Mo it's the age-old destiny: one-in-ten-thousand coolie strikes gold, harbors money, invests in land, saves money, becomes rich, buys young concubines who use him up quickly. Second generation discontented, spend money, mortgage land to buy face and ladies' favors. Third generation sell land, go bankrupt for same favors. Fourth generation coolie." His voice was calm, even gentle. "My old friend's dead and I've no feeling for his sons, or their sons. They're rich, hugely rich because of me, and they'll find their own level, good, bad or very bad. As to Tightfist . . ." Again his fingers stopped. "Tightfist's dying."

Dunross was startled. "But I saw him only a week or so ago and he looked healthy, frail as always, but full of his usual piss and vinegar."

"He's dying, Ian. I know because I was his interpreter with the Portuguese specialists. He didn't want to trust any of his sons—that's what he told me. It took me months to get him to go to see them but both doctors were quite sure: cancer of the colon. His system's riddled with it. They gave him a month, two months . . . this was a week ago." Mata smiled. "Old Tightfist just swore at them, told them they were wrong and fools and that he'd never pay for a wrong diagnosis." The lithe Portuguese laughed without humor. "He's worth over 600 million U.S. but he'll never pay that doctor bill, or do anything but continue to drink foul-smelling, foul-tasting Chinese herbal brews and smoke his occasional opium pipe. He just won't accept a Western, a *quai loh* diagnosis—you know him. You know him very well, eh?"

"Yes." When Dunross was on his school holidays his father would send him to work for certain old friends. Tightfist Tung had been one of them and Dunross remembered the hideous summer he had spent sweating in the filthy basement of the syndicate bank in Macao, trying to please his mentor and not to weep with rage at the thought of what he had to endure while all his friends were out playing. But now he was glad for that summer. Tightfist had taught him much about money—the value of it, how to make it, hold on to it, about usury, greed and the normal Chinese lending rate, in good times, of 2 percent a month.

"Take twice as much collateral as you need but if he has none then look at the eyes of the borrower!" Tightfist would scream at him. "No collateral, then of course charge a bigger interest. Now think, can you trust him? Can he repay the money? Is he a worker or a drone? Look at him, fool, *he's* your collateral! How much of my hard-earned money does he want? Is he a hard worker? If he is, what's 2 percent a month to him—or 4? Nothing. But it's my money that'll make the fornicator rich if it's his joss to be rich. The man himself's all the collateral you ever need! Lend a rich man's son anything if he's borrowing against his heritage and you have the father's chop—it'll all be thrown away on singsong girls but never mind, it's his money not yours! How do you become rich? You save! You save money, buy land with one third, lend one third and keep one third in cash. Lend only to civilized persons and never trust a *quai loh* . . ." he would cackle.

Dunross remembered well the old man with his stony eyes, hardly any teeth—an illiterate who could read but three characters and could write but three characters, those of his name—who had a mind like a computer, who knew to the nearest copper cash who owed him what and when it was due. No one had ever defaulted on one of his loans. It wasn't worth the incessant hounding.

That summer he had been thirteen and Lando Mata had befriended him. Then, as now, Mata was almost a wraith, a mysterious presence who moved in and out of Macao's government spheres as he wished, always in the background, hardly seen, barely known, a strange Asian who came and went at whim, gathered what he liked, harvesting unbelievable riches as and when it pleased him. Even today there were but a handful of people who knew his name, let alone the man himself. Even Dunross had never been to his villa on the Street of the Broken Fountain, the low sprawling building hidden behind the iron gates and the huge stone encircling walls, or knew anything about him really—where he came from, who his parents were or how he had managed to acquire those two monopolies of limitless wealth.

"I'm sorry to hear about old Tightfist," Dunross said. "He was always a rough old bastard, but no rougher to me than to any of his own sons."

"Yes. He's dying. Joss. And I've no feeling for any of his heirs. Like the Chins, they'll be rich, all of them. Even Zeppelin," Lando Mata said with a sneer. "Even Zeppelin'll get 50 to 75 million U.S."

"Christ, when you think of all the money gambling makes . . ."

Mata's eyes lidded. "Should I make a change?"

"If you want to leave a monument, yes. At the moment the syndicate only allows Chinese gambling games: fan-tan, dominoes and dice. If the new group was modern, far-seeing, and they modernized . . . if they built a grand new casino, with tables for roulette, vingt-et-un, chemin de fer, even American craps you'd have all Asia flocking to Macao."

"What're the chances of Hong Kong legalizing gambling?"

"None—you know better than I do that without gambling and gold Macao'd drift into the sea and it's a cornerstone of British and Hong Kong business policy never to let that happen. We have our horse racing—you've the tables. But with modern ownership, new hotels, new games, new hydrofoils you'd have so much revenue you'd have to open your own bank."

Lando Mata took out a slip of paper, glanced at it, then handed it over. "Here are four groups of three names of people who might be allowed to bid. I'd like your opinion."

Dunross did not look at the list. "You'd like me to choose the group of three you've already decided on?"

Mata laughed. "Ah, Ian, you know too much about me! Yes, I've chosen the group that should be successful, if their bid is substantial enough."

"Do any of the groups know now that you might take them as partners?"

"No."

"What about Tightfist—and the Chins? They won't lose their monopoly lightly."

"If Tightfist dies before the auction, a new syndicate will come to pass. If not, the change will be made but differently."

Dunross glanced at the list. And gasped. All the names were well-known Hong Kong and Macao Chinese, all substantial people, some with curious pasts. "Well, they're certainly all famous, Lando."

"Yes. To earn such great wealth, to run a gambling empire needs men of vision."

Dunross smiled with him. "I agree. Then why is it I'm not on the list?"

"Resign from the Noble House within the month and you can form your own syndicate. I guarantee your bid will be successful. I take 40 percent."

"Sorry, that's not possible, Lando."

"You could have a personal fortune of 500 million to a billion dollars within ten years."

Dunross shrugged. "What's money?"

"*Moh ching moh meng!*" No money no life.

"Yes, but there's not enough money in the world to make me resign. Still, I'll make a deal with you. Struan's'll run the gambling for you, through nominees."

"Sorry, no. It has to be all or nothing."

"We could do it better and cheaper than anyone, with more flair."

"If you resign. All or none, tai-pan."

Dunross's head hurt at the thought of so much money, but he heard Lando Mata's finality. "Fair enough. Sorry, I'm not available," he said.

"I'm sure you'd, you personally, would be welcomed as a . . . as a consultant."

"If I choose the correct group?"

"Perhaps." The Portuguese smiled. "Well?"

Dunross was wondering whether or not he could risk such an association. To be part of the Macao gambling syndicate was not like being a steward of the Turf Club. "I'll think about that and let you know."

"Good, Ian. Give me your opinion within the next two days, eh?"

"All right. Will you tell me what the successful bid is—if you decide to change?"

"An associate or consultant should have that knowledge. Now a last item and I must go. I don't think you'll ever see your friend Tsu-yan again."

Dunross stared at him. "What?"

"He called me from Taipei, yesterday morning, in quite a state. He asked if I'd send the Catalina for him, to pick him up privately. It was urgent he said, he'd explain when he saw me. He'd come straight to my home, the moment he arrived." Mata shrugged and examined his perfectly manicured nails. "Tsu-yan's an old friend, I've accommodated old friends before, so I authorized the flight. He never appeared, Ian. Oh he came with the flying boat—my chauffeur was on the jetty to meet him." Mata looked up. "It's all rather unbelievable. Tsu-yan was dressed in filthy coolie rags with a straw hat. He mumbled something about seeing me later that night and jumped into the first taxi and took off as though all the devils from hell were at his heels. My driver was stunned."

"There's no mistake? You're sure it was he?"

"Oh yes, Tsu-yan's well known—fortunately my driver's Portuguese and can take some initiative. He charged in pursuit. He says Tsu-yan's taxi headed north. Near the Barrier Gate the taxi stopped and then Tsu-yan fled on foot, as fast as he could run, through the Barrier Gate into China. My man watched him run all the way up to the soldiers on the PRC's side and then he vanished into the guardhouse."

Dunross stared at Mata in disbelief. Tsu-yan was one of the best-known capitalists and anti-Communists in Hong Kong and Taiwan. Before the fall of the Mainland he had been almost a minor warlord in the Shanghai area. "Tsu-yan'd never be welcome in the PRC," he said. "Never! He must be top of their shit list."

Mata hesitated. "Unless he was working for them."

"It's just not possible."

"Anything's possible in China."

Twenty stories below, Roger Crosse and Brian Kwok were getting out of the police car, followed by Robert Armstrong. A plainclothes SI man met them. "Dunross's still in his office, sir."

"Good." Robert Armstrong stayed at the entrance and the other two went for the elevator. On the twentieth floor they got out.

"Ah good evening, sir," Claudia said and smiled at Brian Kwok. Zeppelin Tung was waiting by the phone. He stared at the policemen in sudden shock, obviously recognizing them.

Roger Crosse said, "Mr. Dunross's expecting me."

"Yes sir." She pressed the boardroom button and, in a moment, spoke into her phone. "Mr. Crosse's here, tai-pan."

Dunross said, "Give me a minute, then show him in, Claudia." He replaced his phone and turned to Mata. "Crosse's here. If I miss you at the bank tonight, I'll catch up with you tomorrow morning."

"Yes. I'm . . . please call me, Ian. Yes. I want a few minutes with you privately. Tonight or tomorrow."

"At nine tonight," Dunross said at once. "Or anytime tomorrow."

"Call me at nine. Or tomorrow. Thank you." Mata walked across the room and opened a hardly noticeable door that was camouflaged as part of the bookshelves. This opened onto a private corridor which led to the floor below. He closed the door behind him.

Dunross stared after him thoughtfully. I wonder what's on his mind? He put the agenda papers in a drawer and locked it, then leaned back at the head of the table trying to collect his wits, his eyes on the door, his heart beating a little quicker. The phone rang and he jumped.

"Yes?"

"Father," Adryon said in her usual rush, "sorry to interrupt but Mother wanted to know what time you'd be in for dinner."

"I'll be late. Ask her to go ahead. I'll get something on the run. What time did you get in last night?" he asked, remembering that he had heard her car return just before dawn.

"Early," she said, and he was going to give her both barrels but he heard unhappiness under her voice.

"What's up, pet?" he asked.

"Nothing."

"What's up?"

"Nothing really. I had a grand day, had lunch with your Linc Bartlett—we went shopping but that twit Martin stood me up."

"What?"

"Yes. I waited a bloody hour for him. We had a date to go to the V and A for tea but he never showed up. Rotten twit!"

Dunross beamed. "You just can't rely on some people, can you, Adryon? Fancy! Standing you up! What cheek!" he told her, suitably grave, delighted that Haply was going to get what for.

"He's a creep! A twenty-four-carat creep!"

The door opened. Crosse and Brian Kwok came in. He nodded to them, beckoned them. Claudia shut the door after them.

"Got to go, darling. Hey pet, love you! 'Bye!" He put the phone down. "Evening," he said, no longer perturbed.

"The files please, Ian."

"Certainly, but first we've got to see the governor."

"First I want those files." Crosse pulled out the warrant as Dunross picked up the phone and dialed. He waited only a moment. "Evening, sir. Superintendent Crosse's here . . . yes sir." He held out the phone. "For you."

Crosse hesitated, hard-faced, then took it. "Superintendent Crosse," he said into the phone. He listened a moment. "Yes sir. Very well, sir." He replaced the phone. "Now, what the hell shenanigans are you up to?"

"None. Just being careful."

Crosse held up the warrant. "If I don't get the files, I've clearance from London to serve this on you at six P.M. today, governor or no."

Dunross stared back at him, just as hard. "Please go ahead."

"You're served, Ian Struan Dunross! Sorry, but you're under arrest!"

Dunross's jaw jutted a little. "All right. But first by God we *will* see the governor!"

24

6:20 P.M.:

The tai-pan and Roger Crosse were walking across the white pebbles toward the front door of the Governor's Palace. Brian Kwok waited beside the police car. The front door opened and the young equerry in Royal Navy uniform greeted them politely, then ushered them into an exquisite antechamber.

His Excellency, Sir Geoffrey Allison, D.S.O., O.B.E., was a sandyhaired man in his late fifties, neat, soft-spoken and very tough. He sat at an antique desk and watched them. "Evening," he said easily and waved them to seats. His equerry closed the door, leaving them. "It seems we have a problem, Roger. Ian has some rather private property that he legally owns and is reluctant to give you—that you want."

"Legally want, sir. I've London's authority under the Official Secrets Act."

"Yes, I know that, Roger. I talked to the minister an hour ago. He said, and I agree, we can hardly arrest Ian and go through the Noble House like a dose of salts. That really wouldn't be very proper, or very sensible, however serious we are in obtaining the AMG files. And, equally, it wouldn't be very proper or sensible to acquire them with cloaks and daggers—that sort of thing. Would it?"

Crosse said, "With Ian's cooperation none of that would be necessary. I've pointed out to him that Her Majesty's Government was completely involved. He just doesn't seem to get the message, sir. He should cooperate."

"I quite agree. The minister said the same. Of course when Ian came here this morning he did explain his reasons for being so, so cautious . . . quite proper reasons if I may say so! The minister agrees too." The gray eyes became piercing. "Just exactly who is the deep-cover Communist agent in my police? Who are the Sevrin plants?"

There was a vast silence. "I don't know, sir."

"Then would you be kind enough to find out very quickly. Ian was kind enough to let me read the AMG report you rightly intercepted." The

governor's face mottled, quoting from it, "'. . . this information should
be leaked privately to the police commissioner or governor *should they be
considered loyal* . . .' Bless my soul! What's going on in the world?"

"I don't know, sir."

"Well you're supposed to, Roger. Yes." The governor watched them.
"Now. What about the mole? What sort of man would he be?"

"You, me, Dunross, Havergill, Armstrong—anyone," Crosse said at once.
"But with one characteristic: I think this one's so deep that he's probably
almost forgotten who he really is, or where his real political interest and
loyalty lie. He'd be very special—like all of Sevrin." The thin-faced man
stared at Dunross. "They must be special—SI's checks and balances are really very good, and the CIA's, but we've never had a whiff of Sevrin before, not a jot or a tittle."

Dunross said, "How're you going to catch him?"

"How're you going to catch your plant in Struan's?"

"I've no idea." Would the Sevrin spy be the same as the one who betrayed our secrets to Bartlett? Dunross was asking himself uneasily. "If
he's top echelon, he's one of seven—all unthinkable."

"There you have it," Crosse said. "All unthinkable, but one's a spy. If
we get one, we can probably break the others out of him if he knows
them." Both the other men felt icy at the calm viciousness in his voice.
"But to get the one, someone has to make a slip, or we have to get a little
luck."

The governor thought a moment. Then he said, "Ian assures me there's
nothing in the previous reports that names anyone—or gives any clues. So
the other reports wouldn't help us immediately."

"They could, sir, in other areas, sir."

"I know." The words were quietly spoken but they said Shut up, sit
down and wait till I've finished. Sir Geoffrey let the silence hang for a
while. "So our problem seems to be simply a matter of asking Ian for his
cooperation. I repeat, I agree that his caution is justified." His face tightened. "Philby, Burgess and Maclean taught us all a fine lesson. I must
confess every time I make a call to London I wonder if I'm talking to another bloody traitor." He blew his nose in a handkerchief. "Well, enough
of that. Ian, kindly tell Roger the circumstances under which you'll hand
over the AMG copies."

"I'll hand them, personally, to the head or deputy head of MI-6 or
MI-5, providing I have his Excellency's guarantee in writing that the man
I give them to is who he purports to be."

"The minister agrees to this, sir?"

"If you agree, Roger." Again it was said politely but the undercurrent
said You'd better agree, Roger.

"Very well, sir. Has Mr. Sinders agreed to the plan?"

"He will be here on Friday, BOAC willing."

"Yes sir." Roger Crosse glanced at Dunross. "I'd better keep the files then until then. You can give me a sealed pa—"

Dunross shook his head. "They're safe until I deliver them."

Crosse shook his head. "No. If we know, others'd know. The others're not so clean-handed as we are. We must know where they are—we'd better have a guard, around the clock."

Sir Geoffrey nodded. "That's fair enough, Ian?"

Dunross thought a moment. "Very well. I've put them in a vault at the Victoria Bank." Crosse's neck became pink as Dunross produced a key and laid it on the desk. The numbers were carefully defaced. "There're about a thousand safety deposit boxes. I alone know the number. This's the only key. If you'll keep it, Sir Geoffrey. Then . . . well, that's about the best I can do to avoid risks."

"Roger?"

"Yes sir. If you agree."

"They're certainly safe there. Certainly not possible to break open all of them. Good, then that's all settled. Ian, the warrant's canceled. You do promise, Ian, to deliver them to Sinders the moment he arrives?" Again the eyes became piercing. "I have really gone to a lot of trouble over this."

"Yes sir."

"Good. Then that's settled. Nothing yet on poor John Chen, Roger?"

"No sir, we're trying everything."

"Terrible business. Ian, what's all this about the Ho-Pak? Are they really in trouble?"

"Yes sir."

"Will they go under?"

"I don't know. The word seems to be they will."

"Damnable! I don't like that at all. Very bad for our image. And the Par-Con deal?"

"It looks good. I hope to have a favorable report for you next week, sir."

"Excellent. We could use some big American firms here." He smiled. "I understand the girl's a stunner! By the way, the Parliamentary Trade Delegation's due from Peking tomorrow. I'll entertain them Thursday—you'll come of course."

"Yes sir. Will the dinner be stag?"

"Yes, good idea."

"I'll invite them to the races Saturday—the overflow can go into the bank's box, sir."

"Good. Thank you, Ian. Roger, if you'll spare me a moment."

Dunross got up and shook hands and left. Though he had come with Crosse in the police car, his own Rolls was waiting for him. Brian Kwok intercepted him. "What's the poop, Ian?"

"I was asked to let your boss tell you," he said.

"Fair enough. Is he going to be long?"

"I don't know. Everything's all right, Brian. No need to worry. I think I dealt with the dilemma correctly."

"Hope so. Sorry—bloody business."

"Yes." Dunross got into the back of the Silver Cloud. "Golden Ferry," he said crisply.

Sir Geoffrey was pouring the fine sherry into two exquisite, eggshell porcelain cups. "This AMG business is quite frightening, Roger," he said. "I'm afraid I'm still not inured to treachery, betrayal and the rotten lengths the enemy will go to—even after all this time." Sir Geoffrey had been in the Diplomatic Corps all of his working life, except for the war years when he was a staff officer in the British Army. He spoke Russian, Mandarin, French and Italian. "Dreadful."

"Yes sir." Crosse watched him. "You're sure you can trust Ian?"

"On Friday you won't need London's clearance to proceed. You have an Order in Council. On Friday we take possession."

"Yes sir." Crosse accepted the porcelain cup, its fragility bothering him. "Thank you, sir."

"I suggest you have two men in the bank vaults at all times, one SI, one CID for safety, and a plainclothes guard on the tai-pan—quietly, of course."

"I'll arrange about the bank before I leave. I've already put him under blanket surveillance."

"You've already done it?"

"On him? Yes sir. I presumed he'd manipulate the situation to suit his purposes. Ian's a very tricky fellow. After all, the tai-pan of the Noble House is never a fool."

"No. Health!" They touched glasses delicately. The ring of the pottery was beautiful. "This tai-pan's the best I've dealt with."

"Did Ian mention if he'd reread all the files recently, sir? Last night, for instance?"

Sir Geoffrey frowned, rethinking their conversation this morning. "I don't think so. Wait a minute, he did say . . . exactly he said, 'When I first read the reports I thought some of AMG's ideas were too farfetched. But now—and now that he's dead, I've changed my mind . . .' That could imply he's reread them recently. Why?"

Crosse was examining the paper-thin porcelain cup against the light. "I've often heard he's got a remarkable memory. If the files in the vaults are untouchable . . . well, I wouldn't want the KGB tempted to snatch him."

"Good God, you don't think they'd be that stupid, do you? The tai-pan?"

"It depends what importance they put on the reports, sir," Crosse said dispassionately. "Perhaps our surveillance should be relatively open—that should scare them off if they happen to have that in mind. Would you mention it to him, sir?"

"Certainly." Sir Geoffrey made a note on his pad. "Good idea. Damnable business. Could the Werewolves . . . could there be a link between the smuggled guns and the John Chen kidnapping?"

"I don't know, sir. Yet. I've put Armstrong and Brian Kwok on to the case. If there's a connection they'll find it." He watched the dying sunlight on the pale, powder blue translucence of the porcelain that seemed to enhance the golden sheen of the dry La Ina sherry. "Interesting, the play of colors."

"Yes. They're T'ang Ying—named after the director of the Emperor's factory in 1736. Emperor Ch'en Leung actually." Sir Geoffrey looked up at Crosse. "A deep-cover spy in my police, in my Colonial Office, my Treasury Department, the naval base, the Victoria, telephone company, and even the Noble House. They could paralyze us and create untold mischief between us and the PRC."

"Yes sir." Crosse peered at the cup. "Seems impossible that it should be so thin. I've never seen such a cup before."

"You're a collector?"

"No sir. Afraid I don't know anything about them."

"These're my favorites, Roger, quite rare. They're called *t'o t'ai*—without body. They're so thin that the glazes, inside and out, seem to touch."

"I'm almost afraid to hold it."

"Oh, they're quite strong. Delicate of course but strong. Who could be Arthur?"

Crosse sighed. "There's no clue in this report. None. I've read it fifty times. There must be something in the others, whatever Dunross thinks."

"Possibly."

The delicate cup seemed to fascinate Crosse. "Porcelain's a clay, isn't it?"

"Yes. But this type is actually made from a mixture of two clays, Roger, kaolin—after the hilly district of Kingtehchen where it's found—and *pan tun tse,* the so-called little white blocks. Chinese call these the flesh and the bones of porcelain." Sir Geoffrey walked over to the ornate leather-topped table that served as a bar and brought back the decanter. It was about eight inches high and quite translucent, almost transparent. "The blue's remarkable too. When the body's quite dry, cobalt in powder form's blown onto the porcelain with a bamboo pipe. Actually the color's thousands of individual tiny specks of blue. Then it's glazed and fired—at about 1300 degrees." He put it back on the bar, the touch of the workmanship and the sight of it pleasing him.

"Remarkable."

"There was always an Imperial Edict against their export. We *quai loh* were only entitled to articles made out of *hua shih,* slippery stone, or *tun ni*—brick mud." He looked at his cup again, as a connoisseur. "The genius who made this probably earned 100 dollars a year."

"Perhaps he was overpaid," Crosse said and the two men smiled with one another.

"Perhaps."

"I'll find Arthur, sir, and the others. You can depend on it."

"I'm afraid I have to, Roger. Both the minister and I agree. He will have to inform the Prime Minister—and the Chiefs of Staff."

"Then the information has to go through all sorts of hands and tongues and the enemy'll be bound to find out that we may be on to them."

"Yes. So we'll have to work fast. I bought you four days' grace, Roger. The minister won't pass anything on for that time."

"Bought, sir?"

"Figuratively speaking. In life one acquires and gives IOUs—even in the Diplomatic Corps."

"Yes sir. Thank you."

"Nothing on Bartlett and Miss Casey?"

"No sir. Rosemont and Langan have asked for up-to-date dossiers. There seems to be some connection between Bartlett and Banastasio—we're not sure yet what it is. Both he and Miss Tcholok were in Moscow last month."

"Ah!" Sir Geoffrey replenished the cups. "What did you do about that poor fellow Voranski?"

"I sent the body back to his ship, sir." Crosse told him the gist of his meeting with Rosemont and Langan and about the photographs.

"That's a stroke of luck! Our cousins are getting quite smart," the governor said. "You'd better find those assassins before the KGB do—or the CIA, eh?"

"I have teams around the house now. As soon as they appear we'll grab them. We'll hold them incommunicado of course. I've tightened security all around the Ivanov. No one else'll slip through the net, I promise you. No one."

"Good. The police commissioner said he'd ordered CID to be more alert too." Sir Geoffrey thought a moment. "I'll send a minute to the secretary about your not complying with the 1-4a. American liaison in London's sure to be very upset, but under the circumstances, how could you obey?"

"If I might suggest, it might be better to ask him not to mention we haven't got the files yet, sir. That information might also get into the wrong hands. Leave well alone, as long as we can."

"Yes, I agree." The governor sipped his sherry. "There's lots of wisdom in laissez-faire, isn't there?"

"Yes sir."

Sir Geoffrey glanced at his watch. "I'll phone him in a few minutes, catch him before lunch. Good. But there's one problem I can't leave alone: the Ivanov. This morning I heard from our unofficial intermediary that Peking views that ship's presence here with the greatest concern." The quite unofficial spokesman for the PRC in Hong Kong and the ranking Communist appointment was believed to be, presently, one of the dep-

JAMES CLAVELL

uty chairmen of the Bank of China, China's central bank through which passed all foreign exchange and all the billion U.S. dollars earned by supplying consumer goods and almost all Hong Kong's food and water. Britain had always maintained, bluntly, that Hong Kong was British soil, a Crown Colony. In all of Hong Kong's history, since 1841, Britain had never allowed any *official* Chinese representative to reside in the Colony. None.

"He went out of his way to jiggle me about the *Ivanov*," Sir Geoffrey continued, "and he wanted to register Peking's extreme displeasure that a Soviet spy ship was here. He even suggested I might think it wise to expel it. . . . After all, he said, we hear one of the Soviet KGB spies posing as a seaman had actually got himself killed on our soil. I thanked him for his interest and told him I'd advise my superiors—in due course." Sir Geoffrey sipped some sherry. "Curiously, he didn't appear irritated that the nuclear carrier was here."

"That's strange!" Crosse was equally surprised.

"Does that indicate another policy shift—a distinct significant foreign-policy change, a desire for peace with the U.S.? I can't believe that. Everything indicates pathological hatred of the U.S.A."

The governor sighed and refilled the cups. "If it leaked that Sevrin's in existence, that we're undermined here . . . God almighty, they'd go into convulsions, and rightly so!"

"We'll find the traitors, sir, don't worry. We'll find them!"

"Will we? I wonder." Sir Geoffrey sat down at the window seat and stared out at the manicured lawns and English garden, shrubs, flower beds surrounded by the high white wall, the sunset good. His wife was cutting flowers, wandering among the beds at the far end of the gardens, followed by a sour-faced, disapproving Chinese gardener. Sir Geoffrey watched her a moment. They had been married thirty years and had three children, all married now, and they were content and at peace with each other. "Always traitors," he said sadly. "The Soviets are past masters in their use. So easy for the Sevrin traitors to agitate, to spread a little poison here and there, so easy to get China upset, poor China who's xenophobic anyway! Oh how easy it is to rock our boat here! Worst of all, who's *your* spy? The police spy? He must be at least a chief inspector to have access to that information."

"I've no idea. If I had, he'd've been neutralized long since."

"What are you going to do about General Jen and his Nationalist undercover agents?"

"I'm going to leave them alone—they've been pegged for months. Much better to leave known enemy agents in situ than to have to ferret out their replacements."

"I agree—they'd certainly all be replaced. Theirs, and ours. Sad, so sad! We do it and they do it. So sad and so stupid—this world's such a paradise, could be such a paradise."

A bee hummed in the bay windows then flew back to the garden again as Sir Geoffrey eased the curtain aside. "The minister asked me to make sure our visiting MPs—our trade delegation to China that returns tomorrow—to make sure their security was optimum, judicious, though totally discreet."

"Yes sir. I understand."

"It appears that one or two of them might be future cabinet ministers if the Labour Party get in. It'd be good for the Colony to create a fine impression on them."

"Do you think they've a chance next time? The Labour Party?"

"I don't comment on those sort of questions, Roger." The governor's voice was flat, and reproving. "I'm not concerned with party politics—I represent Her Majesty the Queen—but personally I really do wish some of their extremists would go away and leave us to our own devices for clearly much of their left wing socialist philosophy is alien to our English way of life." Sir Geoffrey hardened. "It's quite obvious some of them do assist the enemy, willingly—or as dupes. Since we're on the subject, are any of our guests security risks?"

"It depends what you mean, sir. Two are left-wing trades unionists backbenchers, fire-eaters—Robin Grey and Lochin Donald McLean. McLean openly flaunts his B.C.P.—British Communist Party—affiliations. He's fairly high on our S-list. All the other Socialists are moderates. The Conservative members are moderate, middle-class, all ex-service. One's rather imperialist, the Liberal Party representative, Hugh Guthrie."

"And the fire-eaters? They're ex-service?"

"McLean was a miner, at least his father was. Most of his Communist life's been as a shop steward and unionist in the Scottish coalfields. Robin Grey was army, a captain, infantry."

Sir Geoffrey looked up. "You don't usually associate ex-captains with being fire-eating trades unionists, do you?"

"No sir." Crosse sipped his sherry, appreciating it, savoring his knowledge more. "Nor with being related to a tai-pan."

"Eh?"

"Robin Grey's sister is Penelope Dunross."

"Good God!" Sir Geoffrey stared at him, astounded. "Are you sure?"

"Yes sir."

"But why hasn't, why hasn't Ian mentioned it before?"

"I don't know, sir. Perhaps he's ashamed of him. Mr. Grey is certainly the complete opposite of Mrs. Dunross."

"But . . . Bless my soul, you're sure?"

"Yes sir. Actually, it was Brian Kwok who spotted the connection. Just by chance. The MPs had to furnish the usual personal information to the PRC to get their visas, date of birth, profession, next of kin, etcetera. Brian was doing a routine check to make sure all the visas were in order to avoid any problem at the border. Brian happened to notice Mr. Grey had put 'sister, Penelope Grey' as his next of kin, with an address, Castle Avisyard in Ayr. Brian remembered that that was the Dunross family home address." Crosse pulled out his silver cigarette case. "Do you mind if I smoke, sir?"

"No, please go ahead."

"Thank you. That was a month or so ago. I thought it important enough for him to follow up the information. It took us relatively little time to establish that Mrs. Dunross really was his sister and next of kin. As far as we know now, Mrs. Dunross quarreled with her brother just after the war. Captain Grey was a POW in Changi, caught in Singapore in 1942. He got home in the later part of 1945—by the way their parents were killed in the London blitz in '43. At that time she was already married to Dunross—they'd married in 1943, sir, just after he was shot down—she was a WAAF. We know brother and sister met when Grey was released. As far as we can tell now, they've never met again. Of course it's none of our affair anyway, but the quarrel must have been—"

Crosse stopped as there was a discreet knock and Sir Geoffrey called out testily, "Yes?"

The door opened. "Excuse me, sir," his aide said politely, "Lady Allison asked me to tell you that the water's just gone on."

"Oh, marvelous! Thank you." The door closed. At once Crosse got up but the governor waved him back to his seat. "No, please finish, Roger. A few minutes won't matter, though I must confess I can hardly wait. Would you like to shower before you go?"

"Thank you, sir, but we've our own water tanks at police HQ."

"Oh yes. I forgot. Go on. You were saying—the quarrel?"

"The quarrel must have been pretty serious because it seems to have been final. A close friend of Grey told one of our people a few days ago that as far as he knew, Robin Grey had no living relatives. They really must hate each other."

Sir Geoffrey stared at his cup, not seeing it. Suddenly he was remembering his own rotten childhood and how he had hated his father, hated him so much that for thirty years he had never called him, or written to him, and, when he was dying last year, had not bothered to go to him, to make peace with the man who had given him life. "People are terrible to each other," he muttered sadly. "I know. Yes. Family quarrels are too easy. And then, when it's too late, you regret it, yes, you really regret it. People are terrible to each other . . ."

Crosse watched and waited, letting him ramble, letting him reveal himself, cautious not to make the slightest movement to distract him, wanting to know the man's secrets, and skeletons. Like Alan Medford Grant, Crosse collected secrets. Goddamn that bastard and his god-cursed files! God curse Dunross and his devilry! How in the name of Christ can I get those files before Sinders?

Sir Geoffrey was staring into space. Then the water gurgled delightfully in the pipes somewhere in the walls and he came back into himself. He saw Crosse watching him. "Hmmm, thinking aloud! Bad habit for a governor, eh?"

Crosse smiled and did not fall into the trap. "Sir?"

"Well. As you said, it's really none of our business." The governor finished his drink with finality and Crosse knew that he was dismissed. He got up. "Thank you, sir."

When he was alone the governor sighed. He thought a moment then picked up the special phone and gave the operator the minister's private number in London.

"This is Geoffrey Allison. Is he in please?"

"Hello, Geoffrey!"

"Hello, sir. I've just seen Roger. He assures me that the hiding place and Dunross will be completely guarded. Is Mr. Sinders en route?"

"He'll be there on Friday. I presume there have been no repercussions from that seaman's unfortunate accident?"

"No sir. Everything seems to be under control."

"The P.M. was most concerned."

"Yes sir." The governor added, "About the 1-4a . . . perhaps we shouldn't mention anything to our friends, yet."

"I've already heard from them. They were distressingly irritated. So were our fellows. All right, Geoffrey. Fortunately it's a long weekend this week so I'll inform them Monday and draft his reprimand then."

"Thank you, sir."

"Geoffrey, that American senator you have with you at the moment. I think he should be guided."

The governor frowned. *Guided* was a code word between them, meaning "watched very carefully." Senator Wilf Tillman, a presidential hopeful, was visiting Hong Kong en route to Saigon for a well-publicized fact-finding mission.

"I'll take care of it as soon as I'm off the phone. Was there anything else, sir?" he asked, impatient now to bathe.

"No, just give me a private minute on what the senator's program has been." *Program* was another code which meant to furnish the Colonial Office with detailed information. "When you've time."

"I'll have it on your desk Friday."

"Thank you, Geoffrey. We'll chat at the usual time tomorrow." The line went dead.

The governor replaced the phone thoughtfully. Their conversation would have been electronically scrambled and, at either end, unscrambled. Even so, they were guarded. They knew the enemy had the most advanced and sophisticated eavesdropping equipment in the world. For any really classified conversation or meeting he would go to the permanently guarded, concrete, cell-like room in the basement that was meticulously rechecked by security experts for possible electronic bugs every week.

Bloody nuisance, Sir Geoffrey thought. Bloody nuisance all this cloak-and-dagger stuff! Roger? Unthinkable, even so, once there was Philby.

25

6:20 P.M.:

Captain Gregor Suslev waved jauntily to the police at the dockyard gates in Kowloon, his two plainclothes detectives fifty yards in tow. He was dressed in well-cut civilians and he stood by the curb a moment watching the traffic, then hailed a passing taxi. The taxi took off and a small gray Jaguar with Sergeant Lee, CID, and another plainclothes CID man driving, followed smartly.

The taxi went along Chatham Road in the usual heavy traffic, southward, skirting the railway line, then turned west along Salisbury Road on the southmost tip of Kowloon, passing the railway terminus, near the Golden Ferry Terminal. There it stopped. Suslev paid it off and ran up the steps of the Victoria and Albert Hotel. Sergeant Lee followed him as the other detective parked the police Jag.

Suslev walked with an easy stride and he stood for a moment in the immense, crowded foyer with its high ceilings, lovely and ornate, and old-fashioned electric fans overhead, and looked for an empty table among the multitude of tables. The whole room was alive with the clink of ice in cocktail glasses and conversation. Mostly Europeans. A few Chinese couples. Suslev wandered through the people, found a table, loudly ordered a double vodka, sat and began to read his paper. Then the girl was standing near him.

"Hello," she said.

"Ginny, *doragaya!*" he said with a great beam and hugged her, lifting her off her little feet to the shocked disapproval of every woman in the place and the covert envy of every man. "It's been a long time, *golubchik.*"

"*Ayeeyah,*" she said with a toss of her head, her short hair dancing, and sat down, conscious of the stares, enjoying them, hating them. "You late. Wat for you keep me wait? A lady no like wait in Victoria by her self, *heya?*"

"You're right, *golubchik!*" Suslev pulled out a slim package and gave it to her with another beam. "Here, all the way from Vladivostok!"

"Oh! How thank you?" Ginny Fu was twenty-eight and most nights she worked at the Happy Drinkers Bar in an alley off Mong Kok, half a mile or so to the north. Some nights she went to the Good Luck Ballroom. Most days she would pinch-hit for her friends behind the counter of tiny shops within shops when they were with a client. White teeth and jet eyes and jet hair and golden skin, her gaudy *chong-sam* slit high on her long, stockinged thighs. She looked at the present excitedly. "Oh thank, Gregor, thank very much!" She put it in her large purse and grinned at him. Then her eyes went to the waiter who was strolling up with Suslev's vodka, along with the smug, open contempt reserved by all Chinese for all young Chinese women who sat with *quai loh*. They must of course be third-class whores—who else would sit with a *quai loh* in a public place, particularly in the foyer of the Vic? He set down the drink with practiced insolence and stared back at her.

"*Dew neh loh moh* on all your pig-swill ancestors," she hissed in gutter Cantonese. "My husband here is a 489 in the police and if I say the word he'll have those insignificant peanuts you call your balls crushed off your loathsome body an hour after you leave work tonight!"

The waiter blanched. "Eh?"

"Hot tea! Bring me fornicating hot tea and if you spit in it I'll get my husband to put a knot in that straw you call your stalk!"

The waiter fled.

"What did you say to him?" Suslev asked, understanding only a few words of Cantonese, though his English was very good.

Ginny Fu smiled sweetly. "I just ask him bring tea." She knew the waiter would automatically spit in her tea now, or more probably, for safety, get a friend to do it for him, so she would not drink it and thus cause him to lose even more face. Dirty dog bone! "Next time no like, meet here, lotsa nasty peoples," she said imperiously, looking around, then crinkled her nose at a group of middle-aged Englishwomen who were staring at her. "Too much body stinky," she added loudly, tossing her hair again, and chortled to herself seeing them flush and look away. "This gift, Gregy. Thank so very!"

"Nothing," Suslev said. He knew she would not open the gift now—or in front of him—which was very good, sensible Chinese manners. Then, if she did not like the gift or was disappointed or cursed aloud that what was given was the wrong size, or wrong color, or at the miserliness of the giver or bad taste or whatever, then he could not lose face and she could not lose face. "Very sensible!"

"Wat?"

"Nothing."

"You looks good."

"You too." It was three months since his last visit and though his mistress in Vladivostok was a Eurasian with a White Russian mother and Chinese father, he enjoyed Ginny Fu.

"Gregy," she said, then dropped her voice, her smile saucy. "Finish drink. We begin holiday! I got vodka . . . I got other things!"

He smiled back at her. "That you have, *golubchik!*"

"How many day you got?"

"At least three but . . ."

"Oh!" She tried to hide her disappointment.

". . . I'm back and forth to my ship. We've tonight, most of it, and to-morrow and all tomorrow night. And the stars will shine!"

"Three month long time, Gregy."

"I'll be back soon."

"Yes." Ginny Fu put away her disappointment and became pragmatic again. "Finish drink and we begin!" She saw the waiter hurrying with her tea. Her eyes ground into the man as he put it down. "Huh! Clearly it's cold and not fresh!" she said disgustedly. "Who am I! A dirty lump of for-eign devil dogmeat? No, I'm a civilized person from the Four Provinces who, because her rich father gambled away all his money, was sold by him into concubinage to become Number Two Wife for this chief of police of the foreign devils! So go piss in your hat!" She got up.

The waiter backed off a foot.

"What's up?" Suslev asked.

"Don't pay for teas, Gregy. Not hot!" she said imperiously. "No give tip!"

Nonetheless Suslev paid and she took his arm and they walked out to-gether, eyes following them. Her head was high, but inside she hated the looks from all the Chinese, even the young, starched bellboy who opened the door—the image of her youngest brother whose life and schooling she paid for.

Dunross was coming up the steps. He waited for them to pass by, an amused glint in his eyes, then he was bowed in politely by the beaming bellboy. He headed through the throng for the house phone. Many no-ticed him at once and eyes followed him. He walked around a group of tourists, camera bedecked, and noticed Jacques deVille and his wife Su-sanne at a corner table. Both were set-faced, staring at their drinks. He shook his head, wearily amused. Poor old Jacques has been caught again and she's twisting his infidelity in its well-worn wound. Joss! He could al-most hear old Chen-chen laugh. "Man's life is to suffer, young Ian! Yes, it's the eternal yin warring on our oh so vulnerable yang. . . ."

Normally Dunross would have pretended not to notice them, leaving them to their privacy, but some instinct told him otherwise.

"Hello, Jacques—Susanne. How're things?"

"Oh hello, hello, tai-pan." Jacques deVille got up politely. "Would you care to join us?"

"No thanks, can't." Then he saw the depth of his friend's agony and he remembered the car accident in France. Jacques's daughter Avril and her husband! "What's happened? Exactly!" Dunross said it as a leader would say it, requiring an instant answer.

Jacques hesitated. Then he said, "Exactly, tai-pan: I heard from Avril. She phoned from Cannes just as I was leaving the office. She, she said, 'Daddy . . . Daddy, Borge's dead. . . . Can you hear me? I've been trying to reach you for two days . . . it was head-on, and the, the other man was . . . My Borge's dead . . . can you hear me. . . .'" Jacques's voice was flat. "Then the line went dead. We know she's in the hospital at Cannes. I thought it best for Susanne to go at once. Her, her flight's delayed so . . . so we're just waiting here. They're trying to get a call through to Cannes but I don't hope for much."

"Christ, I'm so sorry," Dunross said, trying to dismiss the twinge that had rushed through him as his mind had substituted Adryon for Avril. Avril was just twenty and Borge Escary a fine young man. They had been married just a year and a half and this was their first holiday after the birth of a son. "What time's the flight?"

"Eight o'clock now."

"Susanne, would you like us to look after the baby? Jacques, why not get on the flight—I'll take care of everything here."

"No," Jacques said. "Thanks but no. It's best that Susanne go. She'll bring Avril home."

"Yes," Susanne said, and Dunross noticed that she seemed to have sagged. "We have the *amahs* . . . it's best just me, tai-pan. *Merci*, but no, this way is best." A spill of tears went down her cheeks. "It's not fair is it? Borge was so nice a boy!"

"Yes. Susanne, I'll get Penn to go over daily so don't worry, we'll make sure the babe's fine and Jacques too." Dunross weighed them both. He was confident that Jacques was well in control. Good, he thought. Then he said as an order, "Jacques, when Susanne's safely on the flight go back to the office. Telex our man in Marseilles. Get him to arrange a suite at the Capitol, to meet her with a car and ten thousand dollars worth of francs. Tell him from me he's to be at her beck and call as long as she's there. He's to call me tomorrow with a complete report on Avril, the accident, who was driving and who the other driver was."

"Yes, tai-pan."

"You sure you're all right?"

Jacques forced a smile. "*Oui. Merci, mon ami.*"

"*Rien.* I'm so sorry, Susanne—call collect if we can do anything." He walked away. Our man in Marseilles is good, he thought. He'll take care of everything. And Jacques's a man of iron. Have I covered everything? Yes, I think so. It's dealt with for the moment.

God protect Adryon and Glenna and Duncan and Penn, he thought. And Kathy, and all the others. And me—until the Noble House is inviolate. He glanced at his watch. It was exactly 6:30. He picked up a

house phone. "Mr. Bartlett, please." A moment, then he heard Casey's
voice.

"Hello?"

"Ah, hello, Ciranoush," Dunross said. "Would you tell him I'm in the
lobby."

"Oh hello, sure! Would you like to come up? We're—"

"Why don't you come down? I thought, if you're not too busy I'd take
you on my next appointment—it might be interesting for you. We could
eat afterwards, if you're free."

"I'd love that. Let me check."

He heard her repeat what he had said and he wondered, very much,
about his bet with Claudia. Impossible that those two aren't lovers, he.
thought, or haven't been lovers, living so close together. Wouldn't be
natural!

"We'll be right down, tai-pan!" He heard the smile in her voice as he
hung up.

The Most High Headwaiter was hovering beside him now, waiting for
the rare honor of seating the tai-pan. He had been summoned by the Second Headwaiter the moment the news had arrived that Dunross had been
seen approaching the front door. His name was Afternoon Pok and he was
gray-haired, majestic, and ruled this shift with a bamboo whip.

"Ah Honored Lord, this is a pleasure," the old man said in Cantonese
with a deferential bow. "Have you eaten rice today?" This was the polite
way of saying good-day or good evening or how are you in Chinese.

"Yes, thank you, Elder Brother," Dunross replied. He had known Afternoon Pok most of his life. As long as he could remember, Afternoon Pok
had been the headwaiter in the foyer from noon till six, and many times
when Dunross was young, sent on an errand here, sore from a whipping
or cuffing, the old man would seat him in a corner table, slip him a pastry,
tap him kindly on the head and never give him a bill. "You're looking
prosperous!"

"Thank you, tai-pan. Oh, you are looking very healthy too! But you've
still only one son! Don't you think it's time your revered Chief Wife
found you a second wife?"

They smiled together. "Please follow me," the old man said importantly
and led the way to the choice table that had miraculously appeared in a
spacious, favored place acquired by four energetic waiters who had
squeezed other guests and the tables out of the way. Now they stood, almost at attention, all beaming.

"Your usual, sir?" the wine waiter asked. "I've a bottle of the '52."

"Perfect," Dunross said, knowing this would be the La Doucette that he
enjoyed so much. He would have preferred tea but it was a matter of face
to accept the wine. The bottle was already there, in an ice bucket. "I'm
expecting Mr. Bartlett and Miss Tcholok." Another waiter went at once to
wait for them at the elevator.

"If there's anything you need, please call me." Afternoon Pok bowed and walked off, every waiter in the foyer nervously conscious of him. Dunross sat down and noticed Peter and Fleur Marlowe trying to control two pretty, boisterous girls of four and eight and he sighed and thanked God his daughters were past that age. As he sipped the wine approvingly, he saw old Willie Tusk look over at him and wave. He waved back.

When he was a boy he used to come over from Hong Kong three or four times a week with business orders for Tusk from old Sir Ross Struan, Alastair's father—or, more likely, they were orders from his own father who, for years, had run the foreign division of the Noble House. Occasionally Tusk would service the Noble House in areas of his expertise—anything to do with getting anything out of Thailand, Burma or Malaya and shipping it anywhere, with just a little *h'eung yau* and his standard trading fee of 7½ percent.

"What's the half percent for, Uncle Tusk?" he remembered asking one day, peering up at the man he now towered over.

"That's what I call my dollymoney, young Ian."

"What's dollymoney?"

"That's a little extra for your pocket to give away to dollies, to ladies of your choice."

"But why do you give money to ladies?"

"Well that's a long story, laddie."

Dunross smiled to himself. Yes, a very long story. That part of his education had had various teachers, some good, some very good and some bad. Old Uncle Chen-chen had arranged for his first mistress when he was fourteen.

"Oh do you really mean it, Uncle Chen-chen?"

"Yes, but you're not to tell anyone or your father will have my guts for garters! Huh," the lovely old man had continued, "your father should have arranged it, or asked me to arrange it but never mind. Now wh—"

"But when do I, when do I . . . oh are you sure? I mean how, how much do I pay and when, Uncle Chen-chen? When? I mean before or, or after or when? That's what I don't know."

"You don't know lots! You still don't know when to talk and when not to talk! How can I instruct you if you talk? Have I all day?"

"No sir."

"*Eeeee,*" old Chen-chen had said with that huge smile of his, "eeeee, but how lucky you are! Your first time in a Gorgeous Gorge! It will be the first time, won't it? Tell the truth!"

"Er . . . well er er well . . . er, yes."

"Good!"

It wasn't till years after that Dunross had discovered that some of the most famous houses in Hong Kong and Macao had secretly bid for the privilege of servicing the first pillow time of a future tai-pan and the great-great-grandson of Green-Eyed Devil himself. Apart from the face the house would gain for generations to be the one chosen by the compradore of the Noble House, it would also be enormous joss for the lady herself. First Time Essence of even the meanest personage was an elixir of marvelous value—just as, in Chinese lore, for the elderly man, the yin juices of the virgin were equally prized and sought after to rejuvenate the yang.

"Good sweet Christ, Uncle Chen-chen!" he had exploded. "It's true? You actually sold me? You mean to tell me you sold me to a bloody house! Me?"

"Of course." The old man had peered up at him, and chuckled and chuckled, bedridden now in the great house of the Chens on the ridge of Struan's Lookout, almost blind now and near death but sweetly unresisting and content. "Who told you, who, eh? Eh, young Ian?"

It was Tusk, a widower, a great frequenter of Kowloon's dance halls and bars and houses who had been told it as a legend by one of the mamasans who had heard that it was a custom in the Noble House that the compradore had to arrange the first pillow time for the progeny of Green-Eyed Devil Struan. "Yes, old boy," Tusk had told him. "Dirk Struan said to Sir Gordon Chen, old Chen-chen's father, he'd put his Evil Eye on the House of Chen if they didn't choose correctly."

"Balls," Dunross had said to Tusk, who had continued, pained, that he was just passing on a legend which was now part of Hong Kong's folklore and, balls or not Ian old chum, your first bang-ditty-bang-bang was worth thousands Hong Kong to that old rake!

"I think that's pretty bloody awful, Uncle Chen-chen!"

"But why? It was a most profitable auction. It cost you nothing but gave you enormous pleasure. It cost me nothing but gave me 20,000 HK. The girl's house gained vast face and so did the girl. It cost her nothing but gave her years of a huge clientele who would want to share the specialness of your Number One choice!"

Elegant Jade had been the only name he knew her by. She had been twenty-two and very practiced, a professional since she had been sold to the house by her parents when she was twelve. Her house was called the House of a Thousand Pleasures. Elegant Jade was sweet and gentle— when it pleased her and a total dragon when it pleased her. He had been madly in love with her and their affair had lasted over two summer holidays from boarding school in England, which was the contract time that Chen-chen had arranged. The moment he had returned on the first day of the third summer he had hurried to the house, but she had vanished.

Even today Dunross could remember how distraught he had been, how he had tried to find her. But the girl had left no trace in her wake.

"What happened to her, Uncle Chen-chen? Really happened?"

The old man sighed, lying back in his huge bed, tired now. "It was time for her to go. It is always too easy for a young man to give too much to a girl, too much time, too much thought. It was time for her to go . . . after her you could choose for yourself and you needed to put your mind on the House and not on her. . . . Oh don't try to hide your desire, I understand, oh, how I understand! Don't worry, she was well paid, my son, you had no child by her . . ."

"Where is she now?"

"She went to Taiwan. I made sure she had enough money to begin her own house, she said that's what she wanted to do and . . . and part of my arrangement was that I bought her out of her contract. That cost me, was it 5 . . . or 10,000. . . . I can't remember. . . . Please excuse me, I'm tired now. I must sleep a little. Please come back tomorrow, my son. . . ."

Dunross sipped his wine, remembering. That was the only time that old Chen-chen ever called me my son, he thought. What a grand old man! If only I could be so wise, so kind and so wise, and worthy of him.

Chen-chen had died a week later. His funeral was the greatest Hong Kong had ever seen, with a thousand professional wailers and drums following the coffin to its burial place. The white-clad women had been paid to follow the coffin, wailing loudly to the Heavens, petitioning the gods to grease the way of this great man's spirit to the Void or rebirth or to whatever happens to the spirit of the dead. Chen-chen was a nominal Christian so he had had two services for safety, one Christian, the other Buddhist. . . .

"Hello, tai-pan!"

Casey was there with Linc Bartlett beside her. Both were smiling though both were looking a little tired.

He greeted them and Casey ordered a Scotch and soda and Linc a beer.

"How's your day been?" Casey asked.

"Up and down," he said after a pause. "How was yours?"

"Busy, but we're getting there," she said. "Your attorney, Dawson, canceled our date this morning—that's on again for tomorrow at noon. The rest of my day was on the phone and the telex to the States, getting things organized. Service is good here, this is a great hotel. We're all set to complete our side of the agreement."

"Good. I think I'll attend the meeting with Dawson," Dunross said. "That'll expedite matters. I'll get him to come over to our offices. I'll send a car for you at 11:10."

"No need for that, tai-pan. I know my way on the ferry," she said. "I went back and forth this afternoon. Best five cents American I've ever spent. How'd you keep the fares so low?"

"We carried forty-seven million passengers last year." Dunross glanced at Bartlett. "Will you be at the meeting tomorrow?"

"Not unless you want me for something special," he said easily. "Casey handles the legals initially. She knows what we want, and we've got Seymour Steigler III coming in on Pan Am's flight Thursday—he's our head counsel and tax attorney. He'll keep everything smooth with your attorneys so we can close in seven days, easy."

"Excellent." A smiling obsequious waiter brought their drinks and topped up Dunross's glass. When they were alone again Casey said quietly, "Tai-pan, your ships. You want them as a separate agreement? If the attorneys draw it up it won't be private. How do we keep it private?"

"I'll draw up the document and put our chop on it. That'll make it legal and binding. Then the agreement stays secret between the three of us, eh?"

"What's a chop, Ian?" Bartlett asked.

"It's the equivalent of a seal." Dunross took out a slim, oblong bamboo container, perhaps two inches long and half an inch square, and slid back the tight-fitting top. He took out the chop, which fitted the scarlet silk-lined box, and showed it to them. It was made of ivory. Some Chinese characters were carved in relief on the bottom. "This is my personal chop —it's hand-carved so almost impossible to forge. You stick this end in the ink . . ." The ink was red and almost solid, neatly in its compartment in one end of the box. ". . . and imprint the paper. Quite often in Hong Kong you don't sign papers, you just chop them. Most aren't legal without a chop. The company seal's the same as this, only a little bigger."

"What do the characters mean?" Casey asked.

"They're a pun on my name, and ancestor. Literally they mean 'illustrious, razor sharp, throughout the noble green seas.' The pun's on Green-Eyed Devil, as Dirk was called, the Noble House, and a dirk or knife." Dunross smiled and put it away. "It has other meanings—the surface one's 'tai-pan of the Noble House.' In Chinese . . ." He glanced around at the sound of a bicycle bell. The young bellhop was walking through the crowds carrying a small paging board aloft on a pole that bore the scrawled name of the person wanted. The page was not for them so he continued, "With Chinese writing, there are always various levels of meanings. That's what makes it complex, and interesting."

Casey was fanning herself with a menu. It was warm in the foyer though the ceiling fans were creating a gentle breeze. She took out a tissue and pressed it beside her nose. "Is it always this humid?" she asked.

Dunross smiled. "It's relatively dry today. Sometimes it's ninety degrees and ninety-five humidity for weeks on end. Autumn and spring are the best times to be here. July, August, September are hot and wet. Actually, though, they're forecasting rain. We might even get a typhoon. I heard on the wireless there's a tropical depression gathering southeast of us. Yes. If we're lucky it'll rain. There's no water rationing in the V and A yet, is there?"

"No," Bartlett said, "but after seeing the pails in your house last night, I don't think I'll ever take water for granted again."

"Nor me," Casey said. "It must be terribly hard."

"Oh, you get used to it. By the way my suggestion about the document is satisfactory?" Dunross asked Bartlett, wanting it settled and irritated with himself that he was trapped into having to ask. He was grimly amused to notice that Bartlett hesitated a fraction of a second and glanced imperceptibly at Casey before saying, "Sure."

"Ian," Bartlett continued, "I've got Forrester—the head of our foam division—coming in on the same flight. I thought we might as well get the show on the road. There's no reason to wait until we have papers, is there?"

"No." Dunross thought a moment and decided to test his theory. "How expert is he?"

"Expert."

Casey added, "Charlie Forrester knows everything there is to know about polyurethane foam—manufacturing, distribution and sales."

"Good." Dunross turned to Bartlett and said innocently, "Would you like to bring him to Taipei?" He saw a flash behind the American's eyes and knew that he had been correct. Squirm, you bastard, he thought, you haven't told her yet! I haven't forgotten the rough time you gave me last night, with all your secret information. Squirm out of this one with face! "While we're golfing or whatever, I'll put Forrester with my experts—he can check out possible sites and set that in motion."

"Good idea," Bartlett said, not squirming at all, and Dunross's opinion of him went up.

"Taipei? Taipei in Taiwan?" Casey asked excitedly. "We're going to Taipei? When?"

"Sunday afternoon," Bartlett said, his voice calm. "We're going for a couple of days, Ian an—"

"Perfect, Linc," she said with a smile. "While you're golfing, I can check things out with Charlie. Let me play next time around. What's your handicap, tai-pan?"

"Ten," Dunross answered, "and since Linc Bartlett knows I'm sure you do too."

She laughed. "I'd forgotten that vital statistic. Mine's fourteen on a very good day."

"Give or take a stroke or two?"

"Sure. Women cheat in golf as much as men."

"Oh?"

"Yes. But unlike men they cheat to lower their handicap. A handicap's a status symbol, right? The lower the score, the more the status! Women don't usually bet more than a few dollars so a low handicap's not that vital except for face. But men? I've seen them hit one deliberately into the rough to pick up two extra strokes if they were on a dynamite round that would drop their handicap a notch. Of course that was only if they weren't playing that particular round for money. What's the stake between your pairs?"

"500 HK."

She whistled. "A hole?"

"Hell, no," Bartlett said. "The game."

"Even so, I think I'd better kibitz this one."

Dunross said, "What's that mean?"

"To watch. If I'm not careful, Linc will put my end of Par-Con on the line." Her smile warmed both of them, and then, because Dunross had deliberately dropped Bartlett into the trap, he decided to extract him.

"That's a fine idea, Casey," he said, watching her carefully. "But on second thought, perhaps it would be better for you and Forrester to check out Hong Kong before Taipei—this will be our biggest market. And if your lawyer arrives Thursday you might wish to spend time with him here." He looked at Bartlett directly, the picture of innocence. "If you want to cancel our trip, that's all right too, you've plenty of time to go to Taipei. But I must go."

"No," Bartlett said. "Casey, you cover this end. Seymour will need all the help you can give him. I'll make a preliminary tour this time and we can do it together later."

She sipped her drink and kept her face clear. So I'm not invited, huh? she thought with a flash of irritation. "You're off Sunday?"

"Yes," Dunross said, sure that the finesse had worked, detecting no change in her. "Sunday afternoon I may be doing a hill climb in the morning, so that's the earliest I can make it."

"Hill climb? Mountain climbing, tai-pan?"

"Oh no. Just with a motorcar—in the New Territories. You're both welcome if you're interested." He added to Bartlett, "We could go directly to the airport. If I can clear your aircraft, I will. I'll ask about that tomorrow."

"Linc," Casey said, "what about Armstrong and the police? You're grounded here."

"I arranged that today," Dunross said, "he's parolled into my custody."

She laughed. "Fantastic! Just don't jump bail!"

"I won't."

"You're off Sunday, tai-pan? Back when?"

"Tuesday, in time for dinner."

"Tuesday's when we sign?"

"Yes."

"Linc, isn't that cutting it tight?"

"No. I'll be in constant touch. The deal's set. All we need is to put it on paper."

"Whatever you say, Linc. Everything will be ready for signature when you two get back. Tai-pan, I'm to deal with Andrew if there's any problem?"

"Yes. Or Jacques." Dunross glanced at the far corner. Now their table was occupied by others. Never mind, he told himself. Everything was done that could be done. "The phone service is good to Taipei so there's no need to worry. Now, are you free for dinner?"

"We certainly are," Bartlett said.

"What sort of food would you like?"

"How about Chinese?"

"Sorry, but you've got to be more specific," Dunross said. "That's like saying you want European cooking—which could run the gamut from Italian to boiled English."

"Linc, shouldn't we leave it to the tai-pan?" Casey said, and added, "Tai-pan, I have to confess, I like sweet and sour, egg rolls, chop suey and fried rice. I'm not much on anything far out."

"Nor am I," Bartlett agreed. "No snake, dog or anything exotic."

"Snake's very good in season," Dunross said. "Especially the bile—mixed with tea. It's very invigorating, a great pick-me-up! And little young chow dog stewed in oyster sauce is just perfect."

"You've tried it? You've tried dog?" She was shocked.

"I was told it was chicken. It tasted a lot like chicken. But never eat dog and drink whiskey at the same time, Casey. They say it turns the meat into lumps of iron that'll give you a very hard time indeed. . . ."

He was listening to himself make jokes and inconsequential small talk while he was watching Jacques and Susanne getting into a taxi. His heart went out to them and to Kathy and to all the others and he wanted to get on the plane himself, to rush there and bring Avril back safely—such a nice girl, part of his family. . . .

How in the name of Christ do you live as a man, rule the Noble House and stay sane? How do you help the family and make deals and live with all the rest of it?

"That's the joy and the hurt of being tai-pan," Dirk Struan had said to him in his dreams, many times.

Yes, but there's very little joy.

You're wrong and Dirk's right and you're being far too serious, he told himself. The only serious problems are Par-Con, the boom, Kathy, AMG's papers, Crosse, John Chen, Toda Shipping, and the fact that you turned down Lando Mata's offer, not necessarily in that order. So much money.

What is it I want out of life? Money? Power? Or all China?

He saw Casey and Bartlett watching him. Since these two've arrived, he thought, I've had nothing but trouble. He looked back at them. She was certainly worth looking at with her tight pants and clinging blouse. "Leave it to me," he said, deciding that tonight he would like some Cantonese food.

They heard the page bell and saw the paging board and the name was "Miss K. C. Shuluk." Dunross beckoned the youth. "He'll show you to the phone, Casey."

"Thanks." She got up. Eyes followed the long, elegant legs and her sensuous walk—the women jealous, hating her.

"You're a son of a bitch," Bartlett said calmly.

"Oh?"

"Yes." He grinned and that took the curse off everything. "20 to 1 says

Taipei was a probe—but I'm not calling you on it, Ian. No. I was rough last night—had to be, so maybe I deserved a roasting. But don't do that a second time with Casey or I'll hand you your head."

"Will you now?"

"Yes. She's off limits." Bartlett's eyes went back to Casey. He saw her pass the Marlowe table, stop a second and greet them and their children, then go on again. "She knows she wasn't invited."

Dunross was perturbed. "Are you sure? I thought . . . I didn't cover properly? The moment I realized you hadn't told her yet . . . Sorry, thought I'd covered."

"Hell, you were perfect! But five'll still get you ten she knows she wasn't invited." Bartlett smiled again, and, once more, Dunross wondered what was under the smile. I'll have to watch this bugger more closely, he thought. So Casey's off limits, is she? I wonder what he really meant by that?

Dunross had chosen the foyer deliberately, wanting to be seen with the now famous—or infamous Bartlett and his lady. He knew it would fuel rumors of their impending deal and that would further agitate the stock market and put the punters off balance. If the Ho-Pak crashed, provided it did not bring other banks down with it, the boom could still happen. If Bartlett and Casey would bend a little, he thought, and if I could really trust them, I could make a killing of killings. So many ifs. Too many. I'm out of control of this battle at the moment. Bartlett and Casey have all the momentum. How far will they cooperate?

Then something Superintendent Armstrong and Brian Kwok had said triggered a vagrant thought and his anxiety increased.

"What do you think of that fellow Banastasio?" he asked, keeping his voice matter-of-fact.

"Vincenzo?" Bartlett said at once. "Interesting guy. Why?"

"Just wondering," Dunross said, outwardly calm but inwardly shocked that he had been right. "Have you known him long?"

"Three or four years. Casey an' I have gone to the track with him a few times—to Del Mar. He's a big-time gambler there and in Vegas. He'll bet 50,000 on a race—so he told us. He and John Chen are quite friendly. Is he a friend of yours?"

"No. I've never met him but I heard John mention him once or twice," he said, "and Tsu-yan."

"How is Tsu-yan? He's another gambler. When I saw him in L.A., he couldn't wait to get to Vegas. He was at the track the last time we were there with John Chen. Nothing yet on John or the kidnappers?"

"No."

"Rotten luck."

Dunross was hardly listening. The dossier he had had prepared on Bartlett had given no indication of any Mafia connections—but Banastasio linked everything. The guns, John Chen, Tsu-yan and Bartlett.

Mafia meant dirty money and narcotics, with a constant search for legitimate fronts for the laundering of money. Tsu-yan used to deal heavily in medical supplies during Korea—and now, so the story went, he was heavily into gold smuggling in Taipei, Indonesia and Malaya with Four Finger Wu. Could Banastasio be shipping guns to . . . to whom? Had poor John Chen stumbled onto something and was he kidnapped for that reason?

Does that mean part of Par-Con's money is Mafia money—is Par-Con Mafia-dominated or controlled by Mafia?

"I seem to remember John saying Banastasio was one of your major stockholders," he said, stabbing into the dark again.

"Vincenzo's got a big chunk of stock. But he's not an officer or director. Why?"

Dunross saw that now Bartlett's blue eyes were concentrated and he could almost feel the mind waves reaching out, wondering about this line of questioning. So he ended it. "It's curious how small the world really is, isn't it?"

Casey picked up the phone, inwardly seething. "Operator, this is Miss Tcholok. You've a call for me?"

"Ah one moment plees."

So I'm not invited to Taipei, she was thinking furiously. Why didn't the tai-pan just come out and say it and not twist things around and why didn't Linc tell me about it too? Jesus, is he under the tai-pan's spell like I was last night? Why the secret? What else are they cooking?

Taipei, eh? Well I've heard it's a man's place so if all they're after's a dirty weekend it's fine with me. But not if it's business. Why didn't Linc say? What's there to hide?

Casey's fury began to grow, then she remembered what the French-woman had said about beautiful *Chinoise* so readily available and her fury turned to an untoward anxiety for Linc.

Goddamn men!

Goddamn men and the world they've made exclusively to fit themselves. And it's worse here than anywhere I've ever been.

Goddamn the English! They're all so smooth and smart and their manners great and they say please and thank you and get up when you come in and hold your chair for you but, just under the surface, they're just as rotten as any others. They're worse. They're hypocrites, that's what they are! Well I'll get even. One day we'll play golf, Mr. Tai-pan Dunross and you'd better be good because I can play down to ten on a good day—I learned about golf in a man's world early—so I'll rub your nose in it. Yes. Or maybe a game of pool—or billiards. Sure, and I know what reverse English is too.

Casey thought of her father with a sudden shaft of joy, and how he had taught her the rudiments of both games. But it was Linc who taught her how to stab low on the left side with the cue to give the ball a twist to the right to swerve around the eight ball—showed her when, foolishly, she had challenged him to a game. He had slaughtered her before he gave her any lessons.

"Casey, you'd better make sure you know all a man's weak points before you battle with him. I wiped the board with you to prove a point. I don't play games for pleasure—just to win. I'm not playing games with you. I want you, nothing else matters. Let's forget the deal we made and get married and . . ."

That was just a few months after she had started working for Linc Bartlett. She was just twenty and already in love with him. But she still wanted revenge on the other man more, and independent wealth more and to find herself more, so she had said, "No, Linc, we agreed seven years. We agreed up front, as equals. I'll help you get rich and I'll get mine on the way to your millions, and neither of us owes the other anything. You can fire me anytime for any reason, and I can leave for any reason. We're equals. I won't deny that I love you with all my heart but I still won't change our deal. But if you're still willing to ask me to marry you when I reach my twenty-seventh birthday, then I will. I'll marry you, live with you, leave you—whatever you want. But not now. Yes I love you but if we become lovers now I'll . . . I'll never be able to . . . I just can't, Linc, not now. There's too much I have to find out about myself."

Casey sighed. What a twisted crazy deal it is. Has all the power and dealing and wheeling—and all the years and tears and loneliness been worth it?

I just don't know. I just don't know. And Par-Con? Can I ever reach my goal: Par-Con *and* Linc, or will I have to choose between them?

"Ciranoush?" came through the earpiece.

"Oh! Hello, Mr. Gornt!" She felt a surge of warmth. "This is a pleasant surprise," she added, collecting her wits.

"I hope I'm not disturbing you?"

"Not at all. What can I do for you?"

"I wondered if you are able to confirm this Sunday yet, if you and Mr. Bartlett are available? I want to plan my boat party and I'd like the two of you as my honored guests."

"I'm sorry, Mr. Gornt, but Linc can't make it. He's all tied up."

She heard the hesitation and then the covered pleasure in his voice. "Would you care to come without him? I was thinking of having a few business friends. I'm sure you'd find it interesting."

It might be very good for Par-Con if I went, she thought. Besides, if Linc and the tai-pan are going to Taipei without me, why can't I go boating without them? "I'd love to," she said, warmth in her voice, "if you're sure I won't be in the way."

"Of course not: We'll pick you up at the wharf, just opposite the hotel, near the Golden Ferry. Ten o'clock—casual. Do you swim?"

"Sure."

"Good—the water's refreshing. Water-ski?"

"Love it!"

"Very good!"

"Can I bring anything? Food or wine or anything?"

"No. I think we'll have everything aboard. We'll go to one of the outer islands and picnic, water-ski—be back just after sunset."

"Mr. Gornt, I'd like to keep this excursion to ourselves. I'm told Confucius said, 'A closed mouth catches no flies.'"

"Confucius said many things. He once likened a lady to a moonbeam."

She hesitated, the danger signals up. But then she heard herself say lightly, "Should I bring a chaperone?"

"Perhaps you should," he said and she heard his smile.

"How about Dunross?"

"He'd hardly be a chaperone—merely the destruction of what could perhaps be a perfect day."

"I look forward to Sunday, Mr. Gornt."

"Thank you." The phone clicked off instantly.

You arrogant bastard! she almost said aloud. How much are you taking for granted? Just thank you and click and no good-bye.

I'm Linc's and not up for grabs.

Then why did you play the coquette on the phone and at the party? she asked herself. And why did you want that bastard to keep your Sunday date quiet?

Women like secrets too, she told herself grimly. Women like a lot of things men like.

26

The coolie was in the dingy gold vaults of the Ho-Pak Bank. He was a small, old man who wore a tattered grimy undershirt and ragged shorts. As the two porters lifted the canvas sack onto his bent back, he adjusted the forehead halter and leaned against it, taking the strain with his neck muscles, his hands grasping the two worn straps. Now that he had the full weight, he felt his overtaxed heart pumping against the load, his joints shrieking for relief.

The sack weighed just over ninety pounds—almost more than his own weight. The tally clerks had just sealed it. It contained exactly 250 of the little gold smuggler bars, each of five taels—a little over six ounces—just one of which would have kept him and his family secure for months. But the old man had no thought of trying to steal even one of them. All of his being was concentrated on how to dominate the agony, how to keep his feet moving, how to do his share of the work, to get his pay at the end of his shift, and then to rest.

"Hurry up," the foreman said sourly, "we've still more than twenty fornicating tons to load. Next!"

The old man did not reply. To do so would take more of his precious energy. He had to guard his strength zealously tonight if he was to finish. With an effort he set his feet into motion, his calves knotted and varicosed and scarred from so many years of labor.

Another coolie took his place as he shuffled slowly out of the dank concrete room, the shelves ladened with a seemingly never-ending supply of meticulous stacks of little gold bars that waited under the watchful eyes of the two neat bank clerks—waited to be loaded into the next canvas sack, to be counted and recounted, then sealed with a flourish.

On the narrow stairway the old man faltered. He regained his balance with difficulty, then lifted a foot to climb another step—only twenty-eight more now—and then another and he had just made the landing when his calves gave out. He tottered against the wall, leaning against it to ease the weight, his heart grinding, both hands grasping the straps, knowing he could never resettle the load if he stepped out of the harness, terrified lest the foreman or a subforeman would pass by. Through the spectrum of pain he heard footsteps coming toward him and he fought the sack higher onto his back and into motion once more. He almost toppled over.

"Hey, Nine Carat Chu, are you all right?" the other coolie asked in Shantung dialect, steadying the sack for him.

"Yes . . . yes . . ." He gasped with relief, thankful it was his friend from his village far to the north and the leader of his gang of ten. "Fornicate all gods, I . . . I just slipped. . . ."

The other man peered at him in the coarse light from the single bare light overhead. He saw the tortured, rheumy old eyes and the stretched muscles. "I'll take this one, you rest a moment," he said. Skillfully he eased off the weight and swung the sack to the floorboards. "I'll tell that motherless foreigner who thinks he's got brains enough to be a foreman that you've gone to relieve yourself." He reached into his ragged, torn pants pocket and handed the old man one of his small, screwed-up pieces of cigarette foil. "Take it. I'll deduct it from your pay tonight."

The old man mumbled his thanks. He was all pain now, barely thinking. The other man swung the sack onto his back, grunting with the effort, leaned against the head band, then, his calves knotted, slowly went back up the stairs, pleased with the deal he had made.

The old man slunk off the landing into a dusty alcove and squatted down. His fingers trembled as he smoothed out the cigarette foil with its pinch of white powder. He lit a match and held it carefully under the foil to heat it. The powder began to blacken and smoke. Carefully he held the smoking powder under his nostrils and inhaled deeply, again and again, until every grain had vanished into the smoke that he pulled oh so gratefully into his lungs.

He leaned back against the wall. Soon the pain vanished and left euphoria. It was all-pervading. He felt young again and strong again and now he knew that he would finish his shift perfectly and this Saturday, when he went to the races, he would win the double quinella. Yes, this would be his lucky week and he would put most of his winnings down on a piece of property, yes, a small piece of property at first but with the boom my property will go up and up and up and then I'll sell that piece and make a fortune and buy more and more and then I'll be an ancestor, my grandchildren flocking around my knees . . .

He got up and stood tall then went back down the stairs again and stood in line, waiting his turn impatiently. "Dew neh loh moh hurry up," he said in his lilting Shantung dialect, "I haven't all night! I've another job at midnight."

The other job was on a construction site in Central, not far from the Ho-Pak and he knew he was blessed to have two bonus jobs in one night on top of his regular day job as a construction laborer. He knew, too, that it was the expensive white powder that had transformed him and taken his fatigue and pain away. Of course, he knew the white powder was dangerous. But he was sensible and cautious and only took it when he was at the limit of strength. That he took it most days now, twice a day most days now, did not worry him. Joss, he told himself with a shrug, taking the new canvas sack on his back.

Once he had been a farmer and the eldest son of landowning farmers in the northern province of Shantung, in the fertile, shifting delta of the Yellow River where, for centuries, they had grown fruit and grain and soybeans, peanuts, tobacco and all the vegetables they could eat.

Ah, our lovely fields, he thought happily, climbing the stairs now, oblivious of his pounding heart, our lovely fields rich with growing crops. So beautiful! Yes. But then the Bad Times began thirty years ago. The Devils from the Eastern Sea came with their guns and their tanks and raped our earth, and then, after warlord Mao Tse-tung and warlord Chiang Kai-shek beat them off, they fought among themselves and again the land was laid waste. So we fled the famine, me and my young wife and my two sons and came to this place, Fragrant Harbor, to live among strangers, southern barbarians and foreign devils. We walked all the way. We survived. I carried my sons most of the way and now my sons are sixteen and fourteen and we have two daughters and they all eat rice once a day and this year will be my lucky year. Yes. I'll win the quinella or the daily double and one day we'll go home to my village and I'll take our lands back and plant them again and Chairman Mao will welcome us home and let us take our lands back and we'll live so happily, so rich and so happy. . . .

He was out of the building now, in the night, standing beside the truck. Other hands lifted the sack and stacked it with all the other sacks of gold, more clerks checking and rechecking the numbers. There were two trucks in the side street. One was already filled and waiting under its guards. A single unarmed policeman was watching idly as the traffic passed. The night was warm.

The old man turned to go. Then he noticed the three Europeans, two men and a woman, approaching. They stopped near the far truck, watching him. His mouth dropped open.

"*Dew neh loh moh!* Look at that whore—the monster with the straw hair," he said to no one in particular.

"Unbelievable!" another replied.

"Yes," he said.

"It's revolting the way their whores dress in public, isn't it?" a wizened old loader said disgustedly. "Flaunting their loins with those tight trousers. You can see every fornicating wrinkle in her lower lips."

"I'll bet you could put your whole fist and whole arm in it and never reach bottom!" another said with a laugh.

"Who'd want to?" Nine Carat Chu asked and hawked loudly and spat and let his mind drift pleasantly to Saturday as he went below again.

"I wish they wouldn't spit like that. It's disgusting!" Casey said queasily.

"It's an old Chinese custom," Dunross said. "They believe there's an evil god-spirit in your throat which you've got to get rid of constantly or it will choke you. Of course spitting's against the law but that's meaningless to them."

"What'd that old man say?" Casey asked, watching him plod back into the side door of the bank, now over her anger and very glad to be going to dinner with them both.

"I don't know—I didn't understand his dialect."

"I'll bet it wasn't a compliment."

Dunross laughed. "You'd win that one, Casey. They don't think much of us at all."

"That old man must be eighty if he's a day and he's carried his load as though it was a feather. How'd they stay so fit?"

Dunross shrugged and said nothing. He knew.

Another coolie heaved his burden into the truck, stared at her, hawked, spat and plodded away again. "Up yours too," Casey muttered and then parodied an awful hawk and a twenty-foot spit and they laughed with her. The Chinese just stared.

"Ian, what's this all about? What're we here for?" Bartlett asked.

"I thought you might like to see fifty tons of gold."

Casey gasped. "Those sacks're filled with gold?"

"Yes. Come along." Dunross led the way down the dingy stairs into the gold vault. The bank officials greeted him politely and the unarmed guards and loaders stared. Both Americans felt disquieted under the stares. But their disquiet was swamped by the gold. Neat stacks of gold bars on the steel shelves that surrounded them—ten to a layer, each stack ten layers high.

"Can I pick one up?" Casey asked.

"Help yourself," Dunross told them, watching them, trying to test the extent of their greed. I'm gambling for high stakes, he thought again. I have to know the measure of these two.

Casey had never touched so much gold in her life. Nor had Bartlett. Their fingers trembled. She caressed one of the little bars, her eyes wide, before she lifted it. "It's so heavy for its size," she muttered.

"These're called smuggler bars because they're easy to hide and to transport," Dunross said, choosing his words deliberately. "Smugglers wear a sort of canvas waistcoat with little pockets in it that hold the bars snugly. They say a good courier can carry as much as eighty pounds a trip—that's almost 1,300 ounces. Of course they have to be fit and well trained."

Bartlett was hefting two in each hand, fascinated by them. "How many make up eighty pounds?"

"About two hundred, give or take a little."

Casey looked at him, her hazel eyes bigger than usual. "Are these yours, tai-pan?"

"Good God, no! They belong to a Macao company. They're shifting it from here to the Victoria Bank. Americans or English aren't allowed by law to own even one of these. But I thought you might be interested because it's not often you see fifty tons all in one place."

"I never realized what *real* money was like before," Casey said. "Now I can understand why my dad's and uncle's eyes used to light up when they talked about gold."

Dunross was watching her. He could see no greed in her. Just wonder.

"Do banks make many shipments like this?" Bartlett asked, his voice throaty.

"Yes, all the time," Dunross said and he wondered if Bartlett had taken the bait and was considering a Mafioso-style hijack with his friend Banastasio. "We've a very large shipment coming in in about three weeks," he said, increasing the lure.

"What's fifty tons worth?" Bartlett asked.

Dunross smiled to himself remembering Zeppelin Tung with his exactitude of figures. As if it mattered! "63 million dollars legally, give or take a few thousand."

"And you're moving it just with a bunch of old men, two trucks that're not even armored and no guards?"

"Of course. That's no problem in Hong Kong, which's one of the reasons our police are so sensitive about guns here. If they've the only guns in the Colony, well, what can the crooks and nasties do except curse?"

"But where're the police? I didn't see but one and he wasn't armed."

"Oh, they're around, I suppose," Dunross said, deliberately underplaying it.

Casey peered at the gold bar, enjoying the touch of the metal. "It feels so cool and so permanent. Tai-pan, if it's 63 million legal, what's it worth on the black market?"

Dunross noticed tiny beads of perspiration now on her upper lip. "However much someone's prepared to pay. At the moment, I hear the best market's India. They'd pay about $80 to $90 an ounce, U.S., delivered into India."

Bartlett smiled crookedly and reluctantly put his four bars back onto their pile. "That's a lot of profit."

They watched in silence as another canvas bag was sealed, the bars checked and rechecked by both clerks. Again the two loaders lifted the sack onto a bent back and the man plodded out.

"What're those?" Casey asked, pointing to some much bigger bars that were in another part of the vault.

"They're the regulation four-hundred-ounce bars," Dunross said. "They weigh around twenty-five pounds apiece." The bar was stamped with a hammer and sickle and *99,999*. "This's Russian. It's 99.99 percent pure. South African gold is usually 99.98 percent pure so the Russian's sought after. Of course both're easy to buy in the London gold market." He let them look a while longer, then said, "Shall we go now?"

On the street there was still only one policeman and the sloppy, unarmed bank guards, the two truck drivers smoking in their cabins. Traffic eased past from time to time. A few pedestrians.

Dunross was glad to get out of the close confinement of the vault. He had hated cellars and dungeons ever since his father had locked him in a cupboard when he was very small, for a crime he could not now remember. But he remembered old Ah Tat, his *amah*, rescuing him and standing up for him—him staring up at his father, trying to hold back the terror tears that would not be held back.

"It's good to be out in the air again," Casey said. She used a tissue. Inexorably her eyes were dragged to the sacks in the nearly full truck. "That's real money," she muttered, almost to herself. A small shudder wracked her and Dunross knew at once that he had found her jugular.

"I could use a bottle of beer," Bartlett said. "So much money makes me thirsty."

"I could use a Scotch and soda!" she said, and the spell was broken.

"We'll stroll over to the Victoria and see the delivery begin, then we'll eat—" Dunross stopped. He saw the two men chatting near the trucks, partially in shadow. He stiffened slightly.

The two men saw him. Martin Haply of the *China Guardian* and Peter Marlowe.

"Oh, hello, tai-pan," young Martin Haply said, coming up to him with his confident grin. "I didn't expect to see you here. Evening, Miss Casey, Mr. Bartlett. Tai-pan, would you care to comment on the Ho-Pak matter?"

"What Ho-Pak matter?"

"The run on the bank, sir."

"I didn't know there was one."

"Did you happen to read my column about the various branches and the rumo—"

"My dear Haply," Dunross said with his easy charm, "you know I don't seek interviews or give them lightly . . . and never on street corners."

"Yes sir." Haply nodded at the sacks. "Transferring all this gold out's kinda rough for the Ho-Pak, isn't it? That'll put the kiss of death on the bank when all this leaks."

Dunross sighed. "Forget the Ho-Pak, Mr. Haply. Can I have a word in private?" He took the young man's elbow and guided him away with velvet firmness. When they were alone, half covered by one of the trucks, he let go of the arm. His voice dropped. Involuntarily, Haply flinched and moved back half a pace. "Since you are going out with my daughter, I just want you to know that I'm very fond of her and among gentlemen there are certain rules. I'm presuming you're a gentleman. If you're not,

God help you. You'll answer to me personally, immediately and without mercy." Dunross turned and went back to the others, full of sudden bonhomie. "Evening, Marlowe, how're things?"

"Fine, thank you, tai-pan." The tall man nodded at the trucks. "Astonishing, all this wealth!"

"Where did you hear about the transfer?"

"A journalist friend mentioned it about an hour ago. He said that some fifty tons of gold were being moved from here to the Victoria. I thought it'd be interesting to see how it was done. Hope it's not . . . hope I'm not treading on any corns."

"Not at all." Dunross turned to Casey and Bartlett. "There, you see, I told you Hong Kong was just like a village—you can never keep any secrets here for long. But all this"—he waved at the sacks—"this is all lead—fool's gold. The real shipment was completed an hour ago. It wasn't fifty tons, only a few thousand ounces. The majority of the Ho-Pak's bullion's still intact." He smiled at Haply who was not smiling but listening, his face set.

"This's all fake after all?" Casey gasped.

Peter Marlowe laughed. "I must confess I did think this whole operation was a bit haphazard!"

"Well, good night you two," Dunross said breezily to Marlowe and Martin Haply. He took Casey's arm momentarily. "Come on, it's time for dinner." They started down the street, Bartlett beside them.

"But tai-pan, the ones we saw," Casey said, "the one I picked up, that was fake? I'd've bet my life, wouldn't you have, Linc?"

"Yes," Bartlett agreed. "But the diversion was wise. That's what I'd've done."

They turned the corner, heading along toward the huge Victoria Bank building, the air warm and sticky.

Casey laughed nervously. "That golden metal was getting to me—and it was fake all the time!"

"Actually it was all real," Dunross said quietly and she stopped. "Sorry to confuse you, Casey. I only said that for Haply and Marlowe's benefit, to pour suspicion on their source. They could hardly prove it one way or another. I was asked to make the arrangements for the transfer little more than an hour ago—which I did, obviously, with great caution." His heart quickened. He wondered how many other people knew about the AMG papers and the vault and the box number in the vault.

Bartlett watched him. "I bought what you said, so I guess they did," he said, but he was thinking, Why did you bring us to see the gold? That's what I'd like to know.

"It's curious, tai-pan," Casey said with a little nervous laugh. "I knew, I just knew the gold was real to begin with. Then I believed you when you said it was fake, and now I believe you back again. Is it that easy to fake?"

"Yes and no. You only know for certain if you put acid on it—you've got to put it to the acid test. That's the only real test for gold. Isn't it?" he added to Bartlett and saw the half-smile and he wondered if the American understood.

"Guess that's right, Ian. For gold—or for people."

Dunross smiled back. Good, he thought grimly, we understand each other perfectly.

It was quite late now. Golden Ferries had stopped running and Casey and Linc Bartlett were in a small private hire-launch chugging across the harbor, the night grand, a good sea smell on the wind, the sea calm. They were sitting on one of the thwarts facing Hong Kong, arm in arm. Dinner had been the best they had ever eaten, the conversation filled with lots of laughter, Dunross charming. They'd ended with cognac atop the Hilton. Both were feeling marvelously at peace with the world and with themselves.

Casey felt the light pressure of his arm and she leaned against him slightly. "It's romantic, isn't it, Linc? Look at the Peak, and all the lights. Unbelievable. It's the most beautiful and exciting place I've ever been."

"Better than the south of France?"

"That was so different." They had had a holiday on the Côte d'Azur two years ago. It was the first time they had holidayed together. And the last. It had been too much of a strain on both of them to stay apart. "Ian's fantastic, isn't he?"

"Yes. And so are you."

"Thank you, kind sir, and so are you." They laughed, happy together.

At the wharf, Kowloon side, Linc paid the boat off and they strolled to the hotel, arm in arm. A few waiters were still on duty in the lobby.

"Evening, sir, evening, missee," the old elevator man said sibilantly, and, on their floor, Nighttime Chang scurried ahead of them to open the door of the suite. Automatically Linc gave him a dollar and they were bowed in. Nighttime Chang closed the door.

She bolted it.

"Drink?" he asked.

"No thanks. It'd spoil that brandy."

She saw him looking at her. They were standing in the center of the living room, the huge picture window displaying all of Hong Kong behind him, his bedroom to the right, hers to the left. She could feel the vein in her neck pulsing, her loins seemed liquid and he looked so handsome to her.

"Well, it's . . . thanks for a lovely evening, Linc. I'll . . . I'll see you tomorrow," she said. But she did not move.

"It's three months to your birthday, Casey."

"Thirteen weeks and six days."

"Why don't we finesse them and get married now. Tomorrow?"

"You've . . . you've been so wonderful to me, Linc, so good to be patient and put up with my . . . my craziness." She smiled at him. It was a tentative smile. "It's not long now. Let's do it as we agreed. Please?"

He stood there and watched her, wanting her. Then he said, "Sure." At his door he stopped. "Casey, you're right about this place. It is romantic and exciting. It's got to me too. Maybe, maybe you'd better get another room."

His door closed.

That night she cried herself to sleep.

WEDNESDAY

27

The two racehorses came out of the turn into the final stretch going very fast. It was false dawn, the sky still dark to the west, and the Happy Valley Racecourse was spotted with people at the morning workout.

Dunross was up on Buccaneer, the big bay gelding, and he was neck and neck with Noble Star, ridden by his chief jockey, Tom Leung. Noble Star was on the rails and both horses were going well with plenty in reserve. Then Dunross saw the winning post ahead and he had that sudden urge to jam in his heels and best the other horse. The other jockey sensed the challenge and looked across at him. But both riders knew they were there just to exercise and not to race, there to confuse the opposition, so Dunross bottled his almost blinding desire.

Both horses had their ears down now. Their flanks were wet with sweat. Both felt the bit in between their teeth. And now, well into the stretch, they pounded toward the winning post excitedly, the inner training sand track not as fast as the encircling grass, making them work harder. Both riders stood high in the stirrups, leaning forward, reins tight.

Noble Star was carrying less weight. She began to pull away. Dunross automatically used his heels and cursed Buccaneer. The pace quickened. The gap began to close. His exhilaration soared. This gallop was barely half a lap so he thought he would be safe. No opposing trainer could get an accurate timing on them so he kicked harder and the race was on. Both horses knew. Their strides lengthened. Noble Star had her nose ahead and then, feeling Buccaneer coming up fast, she took the bit, laid to and charged forward on her own account and drew away and beat Dunross by half a length.

Now the riders slackened speed and, standing easily, continued around the lovely course—a patch of green surrounded by massed buildings and tiers of high rises that dotted the mountainsides. When Dunross had cantered up the final stretch again, he broke off the exercising, reined in beside where the winner's circle would normally be and dismounted. He

slapped the filly affectionately on the neck, threw the reins to a stable
hand. The man swung into the saddle and continued her exercise.

Dunross eased his shoulders, his heart beating nicely, the taste of blood
in his mouth. He felt very good, his stretched muscles aching pleasantly.
He had ridden all of his life. Horse racing was still officially all amateur in
Hong Kong. When he was young he had raced two seasons and he would
have continued, but he had been warned off the course by his father, then
tai-pan and chief steward, and again by Alastair Struan when he took over
both jobs, and ordered to quit racing on pain of instant dismissal. So he
had stopped racing though he continued to exercise the Struan stable at
his whim. And he raced in the dawn when the mood was on him.

It was the getting up when most of the world slept, to gallop in half
light—the exercise and excitement, the speed, and the danger that cleared
his head.

Dunross spat the sweet sick taste of not winning out of his mouth.
That's better, he thought. I could have taken Noble Star today, but I'd've
done it in the turn, not in the stretch.

Other horses were exercising on the sand track, more joining the circuit
or leaving it. Knots of owners and trainers and jockeys were conferring,
ma-foos—stable hands—walking horses in their blankets. He saw Butterscotch Lass, Richard Kwang's great mare, canter past, a white star on her
forehead, neat fetlocks, her jockey riding her tightly, looking very good.
Over on the far side Pilot Fish, Gornt's prize stallion, broke into a controlled gallop, chasing another of the Struan string, Impatience, a new,
young, untried filly, recently acquired in the first balloting of this season.
Dunross watched her critically and thought she lacked stamina. Give her a
season or two and then we'll see, he thought. Then Pilot Fish ripped past
her and she skittered in momentary fright, then charged in pursuit until
her jockey pulled her in, teaching her to gallop at his whim and not at
hers.

"So, tai-pan!" his trainer said. He was a leather-faced, iron-hard Russian
émigré in his late sixties with graying hair and this was his third season
with Struan's.

"So, Alexi?"

"So the devil got into you and you gave him your heel and did you see
Noble Star surge ahead?"

"She's a trier. Noble Star's a trier, everyone knows that," Dunross replied calmly.

"Yes, but I'd've preferred only you and I to be reminded of it today
and not"—the small man jerked a calloused thumb at the onlookers and
grinned—". . . and not every *viblyadok* in Asia."

Dunross grinned back. "You notice too much."

"I'm paid to notice too much."

Alexi Travkin could outride, outdrink, outwork and outstay a man half
his age. He was a loner among the other trainers. Over the years he had

told various stories about his past—like most of those who had been caught in the great turmoils of Russia and her revolutions, China and her revolutions, and now drifted the byways of Asia seeking a peace they could never find.

Alexi Ivanovitch Travkin had come out of Russia to Harbin in Manchuria in 1919, then worked his way south to the International Settlement of Shanghai. There he began to ride winners. Because he was very good and knew more about horses than most men know about themselves, he soon became a trainer. When the exodus happened again in '49 he fled south, this time to Hong Kong where he stayed a few years then drifted south again to Australia and the circuits there. But Asia beckoned him so he returned. Dunross was trainerless at that time and offered him the stable of the Noble House.

"I'll take it, tai-pan," he had said at once.

"We haven't discussed money," Dunross had said.

"You're a gentleman, so am I. You'll pay me the best for face—and because I'm the best."

"Are you?"

"Why else do you offer me the post? You don't like to lose either."

Last season had been good for both of them. The first not so good. Both knew this coming season would be the real test.

Noble Star was walking past, settling down nicely.

"What about Saturday?" Dunross asked.

"She'll be trying."

"And Butterscotch Lass?"

"She'll be trying. So will Pilot Fish. So will all the others—in all eight races. This's a very special meeting. We'll have to watch our entries very carefully."

Dunross nodded. He caught sight of Gornt talking with Sir Dunstan Barre by the winner's circle. "I'll be very peed off if I lose to Pilot Fish."

Alexi laughed. Then added wryly, "In that case perhaps you'd better ride Noble Star yourself, tai-pan. Then you can shove Pilot Fish into the rails in the turn if he looks like a threat, or put the whip across his jockey's eyes. Eh?" The old man looked up at him. "Isn't that what you'd've done with Noble Star today if it'd been a race?"

Dunross smiled back. "As it wasn't a race you'll never know—will you?"

A ma-foo came up and saluted Travkin, handing him a note. "Message, sir. Mr. Choi'd like you to look at Chardistan's bindings when you've a moment."

"I'll be there shortly. Tell him to put extra bran in Buccaneer's feed today and tomorrow." Travkin glanced back at Dunross, who was watching Noble Star closely. He frowned. "You're not considering riding Saturday?"

"Not at the moment."

"I wouldn't advise it."

Dunross laughed. "I know. See you tomorrow, Alexi. Tomorrow I'll work Impatience." He clapped him in friendly style and left.

Alexi Travkin stared after him; his eyes strayed to the horses that were in his charge, and their opposition that he could see. He knew this Saturday would be vicious and that Noble Star would have to be guarded. He smiled to himself, pleased to be in a game where the stakes were very high.

He opened the note that was in his hand. It was short and in Russian: "Greetings from Kurgan, Highness. I have news of Nestorova . . ." Alexi gasped. The color drained from his face. By the blood of Christ, he wanted to shout. No one in Asia knows my home was in Kurgan, in the flatlands on the banks of the River Tobol, nor that my father was Prince of Kurgan and Tobol, nor that my darling Nestorova, my child-wife of a thousand lifetimes ago, swallowed up in the revolution while I was with my regiment . . . I swear to God I've never mentioned her name to anyone, not even to myself. . . .

In shock he reread the note. Is this more of their devilment, the Soviets —the enemy of all the Russians? Or is it a friend? Oh Christ Jesus let it be a friend.

After "Nestorova" the note had ended, "Please meet me at the Green Dragon Restaurant, in the alley just off 189 Nathan Road, the back room at three this afternoon." There was no signature.

Across the paddock, near the winning post, Richard Kwang was walking toward his trainer when he saw his sixth cousin, Smiler Ching, chairman of the huge Ching Prosperity Bank, in the stands, his binoculars trained on Pilot Fish.

"Hello, Sixth Cousin," he said affably in Cantonese, "have you eaten rice today?"

The sly old man was instantly on guard. "You won't get any money out of me," he said coarsely, his lips sliding back from protruding teeth that gave him a perpetual smiling grimace.

"Why not?" Richard Kwang said equally rudely. "I've got 17 fornicating millions on loan to you an—"

"Yes but that's on ninety-day call and well invested. We've always paid the 40 percent interest," the old man snarled.

"You miserable old dog bone, I helped you when you needed money! Now it's time to repay!"

"Repay what? What?" Smiler Ching spat. "I've repaid you a fortune over the years. I've taken the risks and you've reaped the profit. This whole disaster couldn't happen at a worse time! I've every copper cash out —every one! I'm not like some bankers. My money's always put to good use."

The good use was narcotics, so legend went. Of course Richard Kwang had never asked, and no one knew for certain, but everyone believed that Smiler Ching's bank was secretly one of the main clearinghouses for the trade, the vast majority of which emanated from Bangkok. "Listen, Cousin, think of the family," Richard Kwang began. "It's only a temporary problem. The fornicating foreign devils are attacking us. When that happens civilized people have to stick together!"

"I agree. But you're the cause of the run on the Ho-Pak. You are. It's on you—not on my bank. You've offended the fornicators somehow! They're after you—don't you read the papers. Yes, and you've got all your cash out on some very bad deals so I hear. You, Cousin, you've put your own head into the cangue. Get money out of that evil son of a Malayan whore half-caste partner of yours. He's got billions—or out of Tightfist. . . ." The old man suddenly cackled. "I'll give you 10 for every 1 that old fornicator loans you!"

"If I go down the toilet the Ching Prosperity Bank won't be far behind."

"Don't threaten me!" the old man said angrily. His lips had a flick of saliva permanently in the corners and then they worked over his teeth once and fell apart again in his grimace. "If you go down it won't be my fault—why wish your rotten joss on family? I've done nothing to hurt you—why try and pass your bad joss on to me? If today . . . *ayeeyah,* if today your bad joss spills over and those dog bone depositors start a run on me I won't last the day!"

Richard Kwang momentarily felt better that the Ching empire was equally threatened. Good, very good. I could use all his business—particularly the Bangkok connection. Then he saw the big clock over the totalizator and groaned. It was just past six now and at ten, banks would open and the stock market would open and though arrangements had been made with Blacs, the Victoria and the Bombay and Eastern Bank of Kowloon to pledge securities that should cover everything and to spare, he was still nervous. And enraged. He had had to make some very tough deals that he had no wish to honor. "Come on, Cousin, just 50 million for ten days—I'll extend the 17 million for two years and add another 20 in thirty days."

"50 million for three days at 10 percent interest a day, your present loan to be collateral and I'll also take deed to your property in Central as further collateral!"

"Go fornicate in your mother's ear! That property's worth four times that."

Smiler Ching shrugged and turned his binoculars back on Pilot Fish. "Is the big black going to beat Butterscotch Lass too?"

Richard Kwang looked at Gornt's horse sourly. "Not unless my weevilmouthed trainer and jockey join together to pull her or dope her!"

"Filthy thieves! You can't trust one of them! My horse's never come in the money once. Never. Not even third. Disgusting!"

"50 million for one week—2 percent a day?"

"5. Plus the Central pro—"

"Never!"

"I'll take a 50 percent share of the property."

"6 percent," Richard Kwang said.

Smiler Ching estimated his risk. And his potential profit. The profit was huge if. If the Ho-Pak didn't fail. But even if it did, the loan would be well covered by the property. Yes, the profit would be huge, provided there wasn't a real run on himself. Perhaps I could gamble and pledge some future shipments and raise the 50 million.

"15 percent and that's final," he said knowing that he would withdraw or change by noon once he saw how the market was, and the run was— and he would continue to sell Ho-Pak short to great profit. "And also you can throw in Butterscotch Lass."

Richard Kwang swore obscenely and they bargained back and forth then agreed that the 50 million was on call at two o'clock. In cash. He would also pledge Smiler Ching 39 percent of the Central property as added collateral, and a quarter share in his mare. Butterscotch Lass was the clincher.

"What about Saturday?"

"Eh?" Richard Kwang said, loathing the grimace and buck teeth.

"Our horse's in the fifth race, *heya*? Listen, Sixth Cousin, perhaps we'd better make an accommodation with Pilot Fish's jockey. We pull our horse —she'll be favorite—and back Pilot Fish and Noble Star for safety!"

"Good idea. We'll decide Saturday morning."

"Better to eliminate Golden Lady too, eh?"

"John Chen's trainer suggested that."

"Eeeee, that fool, to get himself kidnapped. I'll expect you to give me the real information on who's going to win. I want the winner too!" Smiler hawked and spat.

"All gods defecate, don't we all! Those filthy trainers and jockeys! Disgusting the way they puppet us owners. Who pays their salaries, *heya*?"

"The Turf Club, the owners, but most the punters who aren't in the know. I hear you were at the Old Vic last night for foreign devil food."

Richard Kwang beamed. His dinner with Venus Poon had been an enormous success. She had worn the new knee-length Christian Dior he had bought for her, black clinging silk and gossamer underneath. When he had seen her get out of his Rolls and come up the steps of the Old Vic his heart had turned over and his Secret Sack had jiggled.

She had been all smiles at the effect her entrance had on the entire foyer, her chunky gold bracelets glittering, and had insisted on walking up the grand staircase instead of using the elevator. His chest had been tight with suppressed glee and terror. They had walked through the formal, well-groomed diners, European and Chinese, many in evening dress—husbands and wives, tourists and locals, men at business dinners, lovers and would-be lovers of all ages and nationalities. He was wearing a new, Savile Row dark suit of the most expensive lightweight cashmere wool. As they moved toward the choice table that had cost him a red—100 dollars— he had waved to many friends, and groaned inwardly four times as he saw four of his Chinese intimates with their wives, bouffant and overjeweled. The wives had stared at him glassily.

Richard Kwang shuddered. Wives really are dragons and all the same, he thought. Oh oh oh! And your lies sound false to them even before you've spoken them. He had not gone home yet to face Mai-ling who would have already been told by at least three very good friends about Venus Poon. He would let her rant and scream and weep and tear her hair for a while to release her devil wind and would say that enemies had filled her head with bile—how can she listen to such evil women?—and then he would meekly tell her about the full-length mink that he had ordered three weeks ago, that he was to collect today in time for her to wear to the races Saturday. Then there would be peace in the house—until the next time.

He chortled at his acumen in ordering the mink. That he had ordered it for Venus Poon and had, this morning, just an hour ago in the warmth of her embrace, promised it to her tonight so she would wear it to the races on Saturday did not bother him at all. It's much too good for the strumpet anyway, he was thinking. That coat cost 40,000 HK. I'll get her another one. Ah, perhaps I could find a secondhand one. . . .

He saw Smiler Ching leering at him. "What?"

"Venus Poon, *heya?*"

"I'm thinking of going into film production and making her a star," he said grandly, proud of the cover story he had invented as part of his excuse to his wife.

Smiler Ching was impressed. "Eeee, but that's a risky business, *heya?*"

"Yes, but there are ways to . . . to insure your risk." He winked knowingly.

"*Ayeeyah,* you mean a nudie film? Oh! Let me know when you set the production, I might take a point or two. Venus Poon naked! *Ayeeyah,* all Asia'd pay to see that! What's she like at the pillow?"

"Perfect! Now that I've educated her. She was a virgin when I fir—"

"What joss!" Smiler Ching said, then added, "How many times did you scale the Ramparts?"

"Last night? Three times—each time stronger than before!" Richard Kwang leaned forward. "Her Flower Heart's the best I've ever seen. Yes. And her triangle! Lovely silken hair and her inner lips pink and delicate. Eeeee, and her Jade Gate . . . her Jade Gate's really heart-shaped and her 'one square inch' is a perfect oval, pink, fragrant, and the Pearl on the Step also pink. . . ." Richard Kwang felt himself beginning to sweat as he remembered how she had spread herself on the sofa and handed him a big magnifying glass. "Here," she had said proudly. "Examine the goddess your baldheaded monk's about to worship." And he had. Meticulously.

"The best pillow partner I've ever had," Richard Kwang continued expansively, stretching the truth. "I was thinking about buying her a large diamond ring. Poor Little Mealy Mouth wept this morning when I left the apartment I've given her. She was swearing suicide because she's so *in love* with me." He used the English word.

"Eeeee, you're a lucky man!" Smiler Ching spoke no English except the words of love. He felt eyes on his back and he glanced around. In the next section of the stands, fifty yards away, slightly above him, was the foreign devil policeman Big Mountain of Dung, the hated chief of the CID Kowloon. The cold fish-eyes were staring at him, binoculars hanging from the man's neck. *Ayeeyah*, Ching muttered to himself, his mind darting over the various checks and traps and balances that guarded his main source of revenue.

"Eh? What? What's the matter with you, Smiler Ching?"

"Nothing. I want to piss, that's all. Send the papers over at two o'clock if you want my money." Sourly he turned away to go to the toilet, wondering if the police were aware of the imminent arrival of the foreign devil from the Golden Mountain, a High Tiger of the White Powders with the outlandish name of Vincenzo Banastasio.

He hawked and spat loudly. Joss if they do, joss if they don't. They can't touch me, I'm only a banker.

Robert Armstrong had noted that Smiler Ching was talking to Banker Kwang and knew surely that the pair of them were up to no good. The police were well aware of the whispers about Ching and his Prosperity Bank and the narcotics trade but so far had no real evidence implicating him or his bank, not even enough circumstantial evidence to merit SB detention, interrogation and summary deportation.

Well, he'll slip sometime, Robert Armstrong thought calmly, and turned his binoculars back on to Pilot Fish, then to Noble Star, then to Butterscotch Lass, and then to Golden Lady, John Chen's mare. Which one's got the form?

He yawned and stretched wearily. It had been another long night and he had not yet been to bed. Just as he was leaving Kowloon Police HQ last night there had been a flurry of excitement as another anonymous caller phoned to say that John Chen had been seen out in the New Territories, in the tiny fishing village of Sha Tau Kwok which bisected the eastern tip of the border.

He had rushed out there with a team and searched the village, hovel by hovel. His search had had to be done very cautiously for the whole border area was extremely sensitive, particularly at the village where there was one of the three border checkpoints. The villagers were a hardy, tough, uncompromising bellicose lot that wanted to be left alone. Particularly by foreign devil police. The search had proved to be just another false alarm though they had uncovered two illegal stills, a small heroin factory that converted raw opium into morphine and thence into heroin, and had broken up six illegal gambling dens.

When Armstrong had got back to Kowloon HQ there was another call about John Chen, this time Hong Kong side in Wanchai, down near Glessing's Point in the dock area. Apparently John Chen had been seen being bundled into a tenement house, a dirty bandage over his right ear. This time the caller had given his name and driver's license number so that he could claim the reward of 50,000 HK, offered by Struan's and Noble House Chen. Again Armstrong had brought units to surround the area and had led the meticulous search. It was already five o'clock in the morning by the time he called off the operation and dismissed his men.

"Brian, it's me for bed," he said. "Waste of another *fang-pi* night."

Brian Kwok yawned too. "Yes. But while we're this side, how about breakfast at the Para and then, then let's go and look at the morning workouts?"

At once most of Robert Armstrong's tiredness fell away. "Great idea!"

The Para Restaurant in Wanchai Road near Happy Valley Racecourse was always open. The food was excellent, cheap and it was a well-known meeting place for triads and their girls. When the two policemen strode into the large, noisy, bustling, plate-clattering room a sudden silence fell. The proprietor, One Foot Ko, limped over to them and beamed them to the best table in the place.

"*Dew neh loh moh* on you too, Old Friend," Armstrong said grimly and added some choice obscenities in gutter Cantonese, staring back pointedly at the nearest group of gaping young thugs who nervously turned away.

One Foot Ko laughed and showed his bad teeth. "Ah, Lords, you honor my poor establishment. *Dim sum?*"

"Why not?" *Dim sum*—small chow or small foods—were bite-sized dough envelopes packed with minced shrimps or vegetables or various meats then steamed or deep-fried and eaten with a touch of soya, or saucers of chicken and other meats in various sauces or pastries of all kinds.

"Your Worships are going to the track?"

Brian Kwok nodded, sipping his jasmine tea, his eyes roving the diners, making many of them very nervous. "Who's going to win the fifth?" he asked.

The restaurateur hesitated, knowing he'd better tell the truth. He said carefully in Cantonese, "They say that neither Golden Lady, Noble Star, Pilot Fish or Butterscotch Lass has . . . has yet been touted as having an edge." He saw the cold black-brown eyes come to rest on him and he tried not to shudder. "By all the gods, that's what they say."

"Good. I'll come here Saturday morning. Or I'll send my sergeant. Then you can whisper in his ear if some foul play's contemplated. Yes.

And if it turns out one of those are doped or cut and I don't know about it on Saturday morning . . . perhaps your soups will addle for fifty years."

One Foot smiled nervously. "Yes, Lord. Let me see to your food no—"

"Before you go, what's the latest gossip on John Chen?"

"None. Oh very none, Honored Lord," the man said, a little perspiration on his upper lip. "Fragrant Harbor's as clean of information on him as a virgin's treasure. Nothing, Lord. Not a dog's fart of a real rumor though everyone's looking. I hear there's an extra great reward."

"What? How much?"

"100,000 extra dollars if within three days."

Both policemen whistled. "Offered by whom?" Armstrong asked.

One Foot shrugged, his eyes hard. "No one knows, Sire. They say by one of the Dragons—or all the Dragons. 100,000 and promotion if within three days—if he's recovered alive. Please, now let me see about your food."

They watched him go. "Why did you lean on One Foot?" Armstrong asked.

"I'm tired of his mealy-mouthed hypocrisy—and all these rotten little thugs. The cat-o'-nine-tails'd solve our triad problems."

Armstrong called for a beer. "When I leaned on Sergeant Tang-po I didn't think I'd get such action so fast. 100,000's a lot of money! This can't be just a simple kidnapping. Jesus Christ that's a lot of reward! There's got to be something special about John."

"Yes. If it's true."

But they had arrived at no conclusions and when they came to the track, Brian Kwok had gone to check in with HQ and now Armstrong had his binoculars trained on the mare. Butterscotch Lass was leaving the track to walk back up the hill to the stables. She looks in great fettle, he thought. They all do. Shit, which one?

"Robert?"

"Oh hello, Peter."

Peter Marlowe smiled at him. "Are you up early or going to bed late?"

"Late."

"Did you notice the way Noble Star charged without her jockey doing a thing?"

"You've sharp eyes."

Peter Marlowe smiled and shook his head. He pointed at a group of men around one of the horses. "Donald McBride told me."

"Ah!" McBride was an immensely popular racing steward, a Eurasian property developer who had come to Hong Kong from Shanghai in '49. "Has he given you the winner? He'll know if anyone does."

"No, but he invited me to his box on Saturday. Are you racing?"

"Do you mind! I'll see you in the members' box—I don't cavort with the nobs!"

They both watched the horses for a while. "Golden Lady looks good."

"They all do."

"Nothing on John Chen yet?"

"Nothing." Armstrong caught sight of Dunross in his binoculars, talking to some stewards. Not far away was the SI guard that Crosse had assigned to him. Roll on Friday, the policeman thought. The sooner we see those AMG files the better. He felt slightly sick and he could not decide if it was apprehension about the papers, or Sevrin, or if it was just fatigue. He began to reach for a cigarette—stopped. You don't need a smoke, he ordered himself. "You should give up smoking, Peter. It's very bad for you."

"Yes. Yes I should. How's it going with you?"

"No trouble. Which reminds me, Peter, the Old Man approved your trip around the border road. Day after tomorrow, Friday, 6:00 A.M. on the dot at Kowloon HQ. That all right?"

Peter Marlowe's heart leaped. At long last he could look into Mainland China, into the unknown. In all the borderland of the New Territories there was only one accessible lookout that tourists could use to see into China, but the hill was so far away you could not see much at all. Even with binoculars. "How terrific!" he said, elated. At Armstrong's suggestion he had written to the commissioner and applied for this permission. The border road meandered from shore to shore. It was forbidden to all traffic and all persons—except locals in certain areas. It ran in a wide stretch of no-man's-land between the Colony and China. Once a day it was patrolled under very controlled circumstances. The Hong Kong Government had no wish to rock any PRC boats.

"One condition, Peter: You don't mention it or talk about it for a year or so."

"My word on it."

Armstrong suppressed another yawn. "You'll be the only Yank who's ever gone along it, perhaps ever will."

"Terrific! Thanks."

"Why did you become a citizen?"

After a pause Peter Marlowe said, "I'm a writer. All my income comes from there, almost all of it. Now people are beginning to read what I write. Perhaps I'd like the right to criticize."

"Have you ever been to any Iron Curtain countries?"

"Oh yes. I went to Moscow in July for the film festival. One of the films I wrote was the American entry. Why?"

"Nothing," Armstrong said, remembering Bartlett's and Casey's Moscow franks. He smiled. "No reason."

"One good turn deserves another. I heard a buzz about Bartlett's guns."

"Oh?" Armstrong was instantly attentive. Peter Marlowe was very rare in Hong Kong inasmuch as he crossed social strata and was accepted as a friend by many normally hostile groups.

"It's just talk probably but some friends have a theory—"

"Chinese friends?"

"Yes. They think the guns were a sample shipment, bound for one of our piratical Chinese citizens—at least, one with a history of smuggling—for shipment to one of the guerrilla bands operating in South Vietnam, called Viet Cong."

Armstrong grunted. "That's farfetched, Peter, Hong Kong's not the place to transit guns."

"Yes. But this shipment was special, the first, and it was asked for in a hurry and was to be delivered in a hurry. You've heard of Delta Force?"

"No," Armstrong said, staggered that Peter Marlowe had already heard of what Rosemont, CIA, had assured them in great secrecy was a very classified operation.

"I understand it's a group of specially trained U.S. combat soldiers, Robert, a special force who're operating in Vietnam in small units under the control of the American Technical Group, which's a cover name for the CIA. It seems they're succeeding so well that the Viet Cong need modern weapons fast and in great quantity and are prepared to pay handsomely. So these were rushed here on Bartlett's plane."

"Is he involved?"

"My friends doubt it," he said after a pause. "Anyway, the guns're U.S. Army issue, Robert, right? Well, once this shipment was approved, delivery in quantity was going to be easy."

"Oh, how?"

"The U.S. is going to supply the arms."

"What?"

"Sure." Peter Marlowe's face settled. "It's really very simple: Say these Viet Cong guerrillas were provided *in advance* with all exact U.S. shipment dates, exact destinations, quantities and types of arms—small arms to rockets—when they arrived in Vietnam?"

"Christ!"

"Yes. You know Asia. A little *h'eung yau* here and there and constant hijacking'd be simple."

"It'd be like them having their own stockpile!" Armstrong said, appalled. "How're the guns going to be paid for? A bank here?"

Peter Marlowe looked at him. "Bulk opium. Delivered here. One of our banks here supplies the financing."

The police officer sighed. The beauty of it fell into place. "Flawless," he said.

"Yes. Some rotten bastard traitor in the States just passes over schedules. That gives the enemy all the guns and ammunition they need to kill off our own soldiers. The enemy pays for the guns with a poison that costs them nothing—I imagine it's about the only salable commodity they've got in bulk and can easily acquire. The opium's delivered here by the Chinese smuggler and converted to heroin because this's where the expertise is. The traitors in the States make a deal with the Mafia who sell the heroin at enormous profit to more kids and so subvert and destroy the most important bloody asset we have: youth."

"As I said, flawless. What some buggers'll do for money!" Armstrong sighed again and eased his shoulders. He thought a moment. The theory tied in everything very neatly. "Does the name Banastasio mean anything?"

"Sounds Italian." Peter Marlowe kept his face guileless. His informants were two Portuguese Eurasian journalists who detested the police. When he had asked them if he could pass on the theory, da Vega had said, "Of course, but the police'll never believe it. Don't quote us and don't mention any names, not Four Finger Wu, Smuggler Pa, the Ching Prosperity, or Banastasio or anyone."

After a pause, Armstrong said, "What else have you heard?"

"Lots, but that's enough for today—it's my turn to get the kids up, cook breakfast and get them toddling off to school." Peter Marlowe lit a cigarette and again Armstrong achingly felt the smoke need in his own lungs. "Except one thing, Robert. I was asked by a friendly member of the press to tell you he'd heard there's to be a big narcotics meeting soon in Macao."

The blue eyes narrowed. "When?"

"I don't know."

"What sort of meeting?"

"Principals. 'Suppliers, importers, exporters, distributors' was the way he put it."

"Where in Macao?"

"He didn't say."

"Names?"

"None. He did add that the meeting'll include a visiting VIP from the States."

"Bartlett?"

"Christ, Robert, I don't know and he didn't say that. Linc Bartlett seems a jolly nice fellow, and straight as an arrow. I think it's all gossip and jealousy, trying to implicate him."

Armstrong smiled his jaundiced smile. "I'm just a suspicious copper. Villains exist in very high places, as well as in the boghole. Peter, old fellow, give your friendly journalist a message: If he wants to give me information, phone me direct."

"He's frightened of you. So am I!"

"In my hat you are." Armstrong smiled back at him, liking him, very glad for the information and that Peter Marlowe was a safe go-between who could keep his mouth shut. "Peter, ask him where in Macao and when and who and—" At a sudden thought, Armstrong said, stabbing into the unknown, "Peter, if you were to choose the best place in the Colony to smuggle in and out, where'd you pick?"

"Aberdeen or Mirs Bay. Any fool knows that—they're just the places that've always been used first, ever since there was a Hong Kong."

384

JAMES CLAVELL

Armstrong sighed. "I agree." Aberdeen, he thought. What Aberdeen smuggler? Any one of two hundred. Four Finger Wu'd be first choice. Four Fingers with his big black Rolls and lucky 8 number plate, that bloody thug Two Hatchet Tok and that young nephew of his, the one with the Yankee passport, the one from Yale, was it Yale? Four Fingers would be first choice. Then Goodweather Poon, Smuggler Pa, Ta Sap-fok, Fisherman Pok . . . Christ, the list's endless, just of the ones we know about. In Mirs Bay, northeast beside the New Territories? The Pa Brothers, Big Mouth Fang and a thousand others . . .

"Well," he said, very very glad now for the information—something tweaking him about Four Finger Wu though there had never been any rumor that he was in the heroin trade. "One good turn deserves another: Tell your journalist friend our visiting members of Parliament, the trade delegation, come in today from Peking . . . What's up?"

"Nothing," Peter Marlowe said, trying to keep his face clear. "You were saying?"

Armstrong watched him keenly, then added, "The delegation arrives on the afternoon train from Canton. They'll be at the border, transferring trains at 4:32—we just heard of the change of plan last night so perhaps your friend could get an exclusive interview. Seems they've made very good progress."

"Thanks. On my friend's behalf. Yes thanks. I'll pass it on at once. Well, I must be off. . . ."

Brian Kwok came hurrying toward them. "Hello, Peter." He was breathing quite hard. "Robert, sorry but Crosse wants to see us right now."

"Bloody hell!" Armstrong said wearily. "I told you it'd be better to wait before checking in. That bugger never sleeps." He rubbed his face to clear his tiredness away, his eyes red-rimmed. "You get the car, Brian, and I'll meet you at the front entrance."

"Good." Brian Kwok hurried away. Perturbed, Armstrong watched him go.

Peter Marlowe said as a joke, "The Town Hall's on fire?"

"In our business the Town Hall's always on fire, lad, somewhere." The policeman studied Peter Marlowe. "Before I leave, Peter, I'd like to know what's so important about the trade delegation to you."

After a pause the man with the curious eyes said, "I used to know one of them during the war. Lieutenant Robin Grey. He was provost marshal of Changi for the last two years." His voice was flat now, more flat and more icy than Armstrong had imagined possible. "I hated him and he hated me. I hope I don't meet him, that's all."

Across the winner's circle Gornt had his binoculars trained on Armstrong as he walked after Brian Kwok. Then, thoughtfully, he turned them back on Peter Marlowe who was wandering toward a group of trainers and jockeys.

"Nosy bugger!" Gornt said.

"Eh? Who? Oh Marlowe?" Sir Dunstan Barre chuckled. "He's not nosy, just wants to know everything about Hong Kong. It's your murky past that fascinates him, old boy, yours and the tai-pan's."

"You've no skeletons, Dunstan?" Gornt asked softly. "You're saying you and your family're lily white?"

"God forbid!" Barre was hastily affable, wanting to turn Gornt's sudden venom into honey. "Good God no! Scratch an Englishman find a pirate. We're all suspect! That's life, what?"

Gornt said nothing. He despised Barre but needed him. "I'm having a bash on my yacht on Sunday, Dunstan. Would you care to come—you'll find it interesting."

"Oh? Who's the honored guest?"

"I thought of making it stag only—no wives, eh?"

"Ah! Count me in," Barre said at once, brightening. "I could bring a lady friend?"

"Bring two if you like, old chap, the more the merrier. It'll be a small, select, safe group. Plumm, he's a good sort and his girl friend's lots of fun." Gornt saw Marlowe change direction as he was called over to a group of stewards dominated by Donald McBride. Then, at a sudden thought, he added, "I think I'll invite Marlowe too."

"Why if you think he's nosy?"

"He might be interested in the real stories about the Struans, our founding pirates and the present-day ones." Gornt smiled with the front of his face and Barre wondered what devilment Gornt was planning.

The red-faced man mopped his brow. "Christ, I wish it would rain. Did you know Marlowe was in the Hurricanes—he got three of the bloody Boche in the Battle of Britain before he got sent out to Singapore and that bloody mess. I'll never forgive those bloody Japs for what they did to our lads there, here, or in China."

"Nor will I," Gornt agreed darkly. "Did you know my old man was in Nanking in '37, during the rape of Nanking?"

"No, Christ, how did he get out?"

"Some of our people hid him for a few days—we'd had associates there for generations. Then he pretended to the Japs that he was a friendly correspondent for the London *Times* and talked his way back to Shanghai. He still has nightmares about it."

"Talking about nightmares, old chap, were you trying to give Ian one last night by going to his party?"

"You think he got even by taking care of my car?"

"Eh?" Barre was appalled. "Good God! You mean your car was tampered with?"

"The master cylinder was ruptured by a blow of some kind. The mechanic said it could've been done by a rock thrown up against it."

Barre stared at him and shook his head. "Ian's not a fool. He's wild, yes, but he's no fool. That'd be attempted murder."

"It wouldn't be the first time."

"If I were you I'd not say that sort of thing publicly, old chap."

"You're not public, old chap. Are you?"

"No. Of cour—"

"Good." Gornt turned his dark eyes on him. "This is going to be a time when friends should stick together."

"Oh?" Barre was instantly on guard.

"Yes. The market's very nervous. This Ho-Pak mess could foul up a lot of all our plans."

"My Hong Kong and Lan Tao Farms's as solid as the Peak."

"You are, providing your Swiss bankers continue to grant you your new line of credit."

Barre's florid face whitened. "Eh?"

"Without their loan you can't take over Hong Kong Docks and Wharves, Royal Insurance of Hong Kong and Malaya, expand into Singapore or complete a lot of other tricky little deals you've on your agenda—you and your newfound friend, Mason Loft, the whiz kid of Threadneedle Street. Right?"

Barre watched him, cold sweat running down his back, shocked that Gornt was privy to his secrets. "Where'd you hear about those?"

Gornt laughed. "I've friends in high places, old chap. Don't worry, your Achilles' heel's safe with me."

"We're . . . we're in no danger."

"Of course not." Gornt turned his binoculars back on his horse. "Oh by the way, Dunstan, I might need your vote at the next meeting of the bank."

"On what?"

"I don't know yet." Gornt looked down at him. "I just need to know that I can count on you."

"Yes. Yes of course." Barre was wondering nervously what Gornt had in mind and where the leak was. "Always happy to oblige, old chap."

"Thank you. You're selling Ho-Pak short?"

"Of course. I got all my money out yesterday, thank God. Why?"

"I heard Dunross's Par-Con deal won't go through. I'm considering selling him short too."

"Oh? The deal's not on? Why?"

Gornt smiled sardonically. "Because, Dunstan—"

"Hello, Quillan, Dunstan, sorry to interrupt," Donald McBride said, bustling up to them, two men in tow. "May I introduce Mr. Charles Biltzmann, vice-president of American Superfoods. He'll be heading up the new General Stores–Superfoods merger and based in the Colony from now on. Mr. Gornt and Sir Dunstan Barre."

The tall, sandy-haired American wore a gray suit and tie and rimless glasses. He stuck out his hand affably. "Glad to meet you. This's a nice little track you've got here."

Gornt shook hands without enthusiasm. Next to Biltzmann was Richard Hamilton Pugmire, the present tai-pan of H.K. General Stores, a steward of the Turf Club, a short arrogant man in his late forties who carried his smallness as a constant challenge. "Hello, you two! Well, who's the winner of the fifth?"

Gornt towered over him. "I'll tell you after the race."

"Oh come on, Quillan, you know it'll be fixed before the horses even parade."

"If you can prove that I'm sure we'd all like to know. I certainly would, wouldn't you, Donald?"

"I'm sure Richard was just joking," Donald McBride replied. He was in his sixties, his Eurasian features pleasing, and the warmth of his smile pervaded him. He added to Biltzmann, "There're always these rumors about race fixing but we do what we can and when we catch anyone—off with his head! At least off the course he goes."

"Hell, races get fixed in the States too but I guess here where it's all amateur and wide open, it's got to be easier," Biltzmann said breezily. "That stallion you have, Quillan. He's Australian, partial pedigree, isn't he?"

"Yes," Gornt said abruptly, detesting his familiarity.

"Don here was explaining some of the rules of your racing. I'd sure like to be part of your racing fraternity—hope I can get to be a voting member too."

The Turf Club was very exclusive and very tightly controlled. There were two hundred voting members and four thousand nonvoting members. Only voting members could get into the members' box. Only voting members could own horses. Only voting members could propose two persons a year to be nonvoting members—the stewards' decision, approval or nonapproval being final, their voting secret. And only voting members could become a steward.

"Yes," Biltzmann repeated, "that'd be just great."

"I'm sure that could be arranged," McBride said with a smile. "The club's always looking for new blood—and new horses."

"Do you plan to stay in Hong Kong, Mr. Biltzmann?" Gornt asked.

"Call me Chuck. I'm here for the duration," the American replied. "I suppose I'm Superfoods of Asia's new tai-pan. Sounds great, doesn't it?"

"Marvelous!" Barre said, witheringly.

Biltzmann continued happily, not yet tuned to English sarcasm, "I'm the fall guy for our board in New York. As the man from Missouri said, the buck stops here." He smiled but no one smiled with him. "I'll be here at least a couple of years and I'm looking forward to every minute. We're getting ready to settle in right now. My bride arrives tomorrow an—"

"You're just married, Mr. Biltzmann?"

"Oh no, that's just a, an American expression. We've been married twenty years. Soon as our new place's fixed the way she wants it, we'd be happy for you to come to dinner. Maybe a barbecue? We got the steaks organized, all prime, T-bones and New Yorks, being flown over once a month. And Idaho potatoes," he added proudly.

"I'm glad about the potatoes," Gornt said and the others settled back, waiting, knowing that he despised American cooking—particularly charcoaled steaks and hamburgers and "gooped-up baked potatoes," as he called them. "When does the merger finalize?"

"End of the month. Our bid's accepted. Everything's agreed. I certainly hope our American know-how'll fit into this great little island."

"I presume you'll build a mansion?"

"No sir. Dickie here," Biltzmann continued, and everyone winced, "Dickie's got us the penthouse of the company's apartment building on Blore Street, so we're in fat city."

"That's convenient," Gornt said. The others bit back their laughter. The oldest and most famous of the Colony's Houses of Easy Virtue had always been on Blore Street at Number One. Number One, Blore Street, had been started by one of Mrs. Fotheringill's "young ladies," Nellie Blore, in the 1860's, with money reportedly given her by Culum Struan, and was still operating under its original rules—European or Australian ladies only and no foreign gentlemen or natives allowed.

"Very convenient," Gornt said again. "But I wonder if you'd qualify."

"Sir?"

"Nothing. I'm sure Blore Street is most apt."

"Great view, but the plumbing's no good," Biltzmann said. "My bride'll soon fix that."

"She's a plumber too?" Gornt asked.

The American laughed. "Hell no, but she's mighty handy around the house."

"If you'll excuse me I have to see my trainer." Gornt nodded to the others and turned away with, "Donald, have you a moment? It's about Saturday."

"Of course, see you in a moment, Mr. Biltzmann."

"Sure. But call me Chuck. Have a nice day."

McBride fell into step beside Gornt. When they were alone Gornt said, "You're surely not seriously suggesting he should be a voting member?"

"Well, yes." McBride looked uncomfortable. "It's the first time a big American company's made a bid to come into Hong Kong. He'd be quite important to us."

"That's no reason to let him in here, is it? Make him a nonvoting member. Then he can get into the stands. And if you want to invite him to your box, that's your affair. But a voting member? Good God, he'll probably have 'superfoods' as his racing colors!"

"He's just new and out of his depth, Quillan. I'm sure he'll learn. He's decent enough even though he does make a few gaffes. He's quite well off an—"

"Since when has money been an open sesame to the Turf Club? Good God, Donald, if that was the case, every upstart Chinese property gambler or stock market gambler who'd made a killing on our market'd swamp us. We wouldn't have room to fart."

"I don't agree. Perhaps the answer's to increase the voting membership."

"No. Absolutely not. Of course you stewards will do what you like. But I suggest you reconsider." Gornt was a voting member but not a steward. The two hundred voting members elected the twelve stewards annually by secret ballot. Each year Gornt's name was put on the open list of nominees for steward and each year he failed to get enough votes. Most stewards were reelected by the membership automatically until they retired, though from time to time there was lobbying.

"Very well," McBride said, "when his name's proposed I'll mention your opposition."

Gornt smiled thinly. "That'll be tantamount to getting him elected."

McBride chuckled. "I don't think so, Quillan, not this time. Pug asked me to introduce him around. I must admit he gets off on the wrong foot every time. I introduced him to Paul Havergill and Biltzmann immediately started comparing banking procedures here with those in the States, and not very pleasantly either. And with the tai-pan . . ." McBride's graying eyebrows soared. ". . . he said he was sure glad to meet him as he wanted to learn about Hag Struan and Dirk Struan and all the other pirates and opium smugglers in his past!" He sighed. "Ian and Paul'll certainly blackball him for you, so I don't think you've much to worry about. I really don't understand why Pug sold out to them anyway."

"Because he's not his father. Since old Sir Thomas died General Stores've been slipping. Still, Pug makes 6 million U.S. personally and has a five-year unbreakable contract—so he has all the pleasure and none of the headaches and the family's taken care of. He wants to retire to England, Ascot and all that."

"Ah! That's a very good deal for old Pug!" McBride became more serious. "Quillan, the fifth race—the interest's enormous. I'm worried there'll be interference. We're going to increase surveillance on all the horses. There're rumors th—"

"About doping?"

"Yes."

"There're always rumors and someone will always try. I think the stewards do a very good job."

"The stewards agreed last night that we'd institute a new rule: in future we'll have an obligatory chemical analysis before and after each race, as they do at the major tracks in England or America."

"In time for Saturday? How're you going to arrange that?"

"Dr. Meng, the police pathologist, has agreed to be responsible—until we have an expert arranged."

"Good idea," Gornt said.

McBride sighed. "Yes, but the Mighty Dragon's no match for the Local Serpent." He turned and left.

Gornt hesitated, then went to his trainer who stood beside Pilot Fish talking with the jockey, another Australian, Bluey White. Bluey White was ostensibly a manager of one of Gornt's shipping divisions—the title given to him to preserve his amateur status.

"G'day, Mr. Gornt," they said. The jockey touched his forelock.

"Morning." Gornt looked at them a moment and then he said quietly, "Bluey, if you win, you've a 5,000 bonus. If you finish behind Noble Star, you're fired."

The tough little man whitened. "Yes, guv!"

"You'd better get changed now," Gornt said, dismissing him.

"I'll win," Bluey White said as he left.

The trainer said uneasily, "Pilot Fish's in very good fettle, Mr. Gornt. He'll be try—"

"If Noble Star wins you're fired. If Noble Star finishes ahead of Pilot Fish you're fired."

"My oath, Mr. Gornt." The man wiped the sudden sweat off his mouth. "I don't fix who ge—"

"I'm not suggesting you do anything. I'm just telling you what's going to happen to you." Gornt nodded pleasantly and strode off. He went to the club restaurant, which overlooked the course, and ordered his favorite breakfast, eggs Benedict with his own special hollandaise that they kept for his exclusive use, and Javanese coffee that he also supplied.

On his third cup of coffee the waiter came over. "Excuse me, sir, you're wanted on the telephone."

He went to the phone. "Gornt."

"Hello, Mr. Gornt, this's Paul Choy . . . Mr. Wu's nephew. . . . I hope I'm not disturbing you."

Gornt covered his surprise. "You're calling rather early, Mr. Choy."

"Yes sir, but I wanted to be in early the first day," the young man said in a rush, "so I was the only one here a couple of minutes ago when the phone rang. It was Mr. Bartlett, Linc Bartlett, you know, the guy with the smuggled guns, the millionaire."

Gornt was startled. "Bartlett?"

"Yes sir. He said he wanted to get hold of you, implied it was kinda urgent, said he'd tried your home. I put two and two together and came up with you might be at the workout and I'd better get off my butt. I hope I'm not disturbing you?"

"No. What did he say?" Gornt asked.

"Just that he wanted to talk to you, and were you in town? I said I didn't know, but I'd check around and leave a message and give him a call back."

"Where was he calling from?"

"The Vic and Albert. Kowloon side 662233, extension 773—that's his office extension, not his suite."

Gornt was very impressed. "A closed mouth catches no flies, Mr. Choy."

"Jesus, Mr. Gornt, that's one thing you never need worry about," Paul Choy said fervently. "My old Uncle Wu wopped that into us all like there was no tomorrow."

"Good. Thanks, Mr. Choy. I'll see you shortly."

"Yes sir."

Gornt hung up, thought a moment, then dialed the hotel. "773 please."

"Linc Bartlett."

"Good morning Mr. Bartlett, this's Mr. Gornt. What can I do for you?"

"Hey, thanks for returning my call. I've had disturbing news which sort of ties in with what we were discussing."

"Oh?"

"Yes. Does Toda Shipping mean anything to you?"

Gornt's interest soared. "Toda Shipping's a huge Japanese conglomerate, shipyards, steel mills, heavy engineering. Struan's have a two-ship deal with them, bulk vessels I believe. Why?"

"It seems Toda have some notes due from Struan's, $6 million in three installments—on the first, eleventh, and fifteenth of next month—and another $6 million in 90 days. Then there's another 6.8 million due on the eighth to Orlin International Bank—you know them?"

With a great effort Gornt kept his voice matter-of-fact. "I've, I've heard of them," he said, astounded that the American would have such details of the debts. "So?" he asked.

"So I heard Struan's have only 1.3 million in cash, with no cash reserves and not enough cash flow to make payment. They're not expecting a significant block of income until they get 17 million as their share of one of Kowloon Investments' property deals, not due until November, and they're 20 percent overextended at the Victoria Bank."

"That's . . . that's very intimate knowledge," Gornt gasped, his heart thumping in his chest, his collar feeling tight. He knew about the 20 percent overdraft—Plumm had told him—all the directors of the bank would know. But not the details of their cash, or their cash flow.

"Why're you telling me this, Mr. Bartlett?"

"How liquid are you?"

"I've already told you, I'm twenty times stronger than Struan's," he said automatically, the lie coming easily, his mind churning the marvelous opportunities all this information unlocked. "Why?"

"If I go through with the Struan deal he'll be using my cash down payment to get off the Toda and Orlin hooks—if his bank doesn't extend his credit."

"Yes."

"Will the Vic support him?"

"They always have. Why?"

"If they don't, then he's in big trouble."

"Struan's are substantial stockholders. The bank is obliged to support them."

"But he's overdrawn there and Havergill hates him. Between Chen's stock, Struan's and their nominees, they've 21 percent. . . ."

Gornt almost dropped the phone. "Where the hell did you get that information? No outsider could possibly know that!"

"That's right," he heard the American say calmly, "but that's a fact. Could you muster the other 79 percent?"

"What?"

"If I had a partner who could put the bank against him just this once and he couldn't get credit elsewhere . . . bluntly: it's a matter of timing. Dunross's mortally overextended and that means he's vulnerable. If his bank won't give him credit, he's got to sell something—or get a new line of credit. In either case he's wide open for an attack and ripe for a takeover at a fire-sale price."

Gornt mopped his brow, his brain reeling. "Where the hell did you get all this information?"

"Later, not now."

"When?"

"When we're down to the short strokes."

"How . . . how sure are you your figures are correct?"

"Very. We've his balance sheets for the last seven years."

In spite of his resolve Gornt gasped. "That's impossible!"

"Want to bet?"

Gornt was really shaken now and he tried to get his mind working. Be cautious, he admonished himself. For chrissake control yourself. "If . . . if you've all that, if you know that and get one last thing . . . their interlocking corporate structure, if you knew that we could do anything we want with Struan's."

"We've got that too. You want in?"

Gornt heard himself say calmly, not feeling calm at all, "Of course. When could we meet? Lunch?"

"How about now? But not here, and not at your office. This has to be kept very quiet."

Gornt's heart hurt in his chest. There was a rotten taste in his mouth and he wondered very much how far he could trust Bartlett. "I'll . . . I'll send a car for you. We could chat in the car."

"Good idea, but why don't I meet you Hong Kong side. The Golden Ferry Terminal in an hour."

"Excellent. My car's a Jag—license's 8888. I'll be by the taxi rank."

He hung up and stared at the phone a moment, then went back to his table.

"Not bad news I hope, Mr. Gornt?"

"Er, no, no not at all. Thank you."

"Some more of your special coffee? It's freshly made."

"No, no thank you. I'd like a half bottle of the Taittinger Blanc de Blancs. The '55." He sat back feeling very strange. His enemy was almost in his grasp—if the American's facts were true and if the American was to be trusted and not in some devious plot with Dunross.

The wine came but he hardly tasted it. His whole being was concentrated, sifting, preparing.

Gornt saw the tall American come through the crowds and, for a moment, he envied him his lean, trim figure and the easy, careless dress—jeans, openneck shirt, sports coat—and his obvious confidence. He saw the elaborate camera, smiled sardonically, then looked for Casey. When it was obvious Bartlett was alone he was disappointed. But this disappointment did not touch the glorious anticipation that had possessed him ever since he had put the phone down.

Gornt leaned over and opened the side door. "Welcome Hong Kong side, Mr. Bartlett," he said with forced joviality, starting the engine. He drove off along Gloucester Road toward Glessing's Point and the Yacht Club. "Your inside information's astonishing."

"Without spies you can't operate, can you?"

"You can, but then that's amateur. How's Miss Casey? I thought she'd be with you."

"She's not in this. Not yet."

"Oh?"

"No. No, she's not in on the initial attack. She's more valuable if she knows nothing."

"She knows nothing of this? Not even your call to me?"

"No. Nothing at all."

After a pause he said, "I thought she was your executive VP . . . your right arm you called her."

"She is, but I'm boss of Par-Con, Mr. Gornt."

Gornt saw the level eyes and, for the first time, felt that that was true and that his original estimation was wrong. "I've never doubted it," he said, waiting, his senses honed, waiting him out.

Then Bartlett said, "Is there somewhere we can park—I've got something I want to show you."

"Certainly." Gornt was driving along the sea front on Gloucester Road in the usual heavy traffic. In a moment he found a parking place near

Causeway Bay typhoon shelter with its massed, floating islands of boats of all sizes.

"Here." Bartlett handed him a typed folder. It was a detailed copy of Struan's balance sheet for the year before the company went public. Gornt's eyes raced over the figures. "Christ," he muttered. "So *Lasting Cloud*'s cost them 12 million?"

"It almost broke them. Seems they had all sorts of wild-assed cargo aboard. Jet engines for China, uninsured."

"Of course they'd be uninsured—how the hell can you insure contraband?" Gornt was trying to take in all the complicated figures. His mind was dazed. "If I'd known half of this I'd've got them the last time. Can I keep it?"

"When we've made a deal I'll give you a copy." Bartlett took the folder back and gave him a paper. "Try this one on for size." It showed, graphically, Struan's stockholdings in Kowloon Investments and detailed how, through nominee companies, the tai-pan of Struan's exercised complete control over the huge insurance-property-wharfing company that was supposedly a completely separate company and quoted as such on the stock exchange.

"Marvelous," Gornt said with a sigh, awed by the beauty of it. "Struan's have only a tiny proportion of the stock publicly held but retain 100 percent control, and perpetual secrecy."

"In the States whoever figured this out'd be in jail."

"Thank God Hong Kong laws aren't the same, and that this's all perfectly legal, if a trifle devious." The two men laughed.

Bartlett pocketed the paper. "I've got similar details of the rest of their holdings."

"Bluntly, what have you in mind, Mr. Bartlett?"

"A joint attack on Struan's, starting today. A blitzkrieg. We go 50-50 on all spoils. You get the Great House on the Peak, the prestige, his yacht —and 100 percent of the box at the Turf Club including his stewardship."

Gornt glanced at him keenly. Bartlett smiled. "We know that's kind of special to you. But everything else right down the middle."

"Except their Kai Tak operations. I need that for my airline."

"All right. But then I want Kowloon Investments."

"No," Gornt said, immediately on guard. "We should split that 50-50, and everything 50-50."

"No. You need Kai Tak, I need Kowloon Investments. It'll be a great nucleus for Par-Con's jump into Asia."

"Why?"

"Because all great fortunes in Hong Kong are based on property. K. I. will give me a perfect base."

"For further raids?"

"Sure," Bartlett said easily. "Your friend Jason Plumm's next on the list. We could swallow his Asian Properties easy. 50-50. Right?"

Gornt said nothing for a long time. "And after him?"

"Hong Kong and Lan Tao Farms."

Again Gornt's heart leapt. He had always hated Dunstan Barre and that hatred was tripled last year when Barre had been given a knighthood in the Queen's Birthday Honors List—an honor maneuvered, Gornt was sure, with judicious contributions to the Conservative Party fund. "And how would you swallow him?"

"There's always a time when any army, any country, any company's vulnerable. Every general or company president has to take chances, sometime, to stay ahead. You've got to, to stay ahead. There's always some enemy snapping at your heels, wanting yours, wanting your place in the sun, wanting your territory. You've got to be careful when you're vulnerable."

"Are you vulnerable now?"

"No. I was two years ago but not now. Now I've the muscle I need—we need. If you're in."

A flock of seabirds were dipping and weaving and cawing overhead. "What do you want me to do?"

"You're the pathfinder, the spearhead. I defend the rear. Once you've punched a hole through his defense, I'll deliver the knockout. We sell Struan's short—I guess you've already taken a position on the Ho-Pak?"

"I've sold short, yes. Modestly." Gornt told the lie easily.

"Good. In the States you could get their own accountants to leak the cash flow facts to the right big mouth. That'd soon be all over town. Could the same ploy work here?"

"Probably. But you'd never get their accountants to do that."

"Not for the right fee?"

"No. But rumors could be started." Gornt smiled grimly. "It's very bad of Dunross to hide his inept position from his shareholders. Yes. That's possible. And then?"

"You sell Struan's short, as soon as the market opens. Big."

Gornt lit a cigarette. "I sell short, and what do you do?"

"Nothing openly. That's our ace in the hole."

"Perhaps it really is, and I'm being set up," Gornt said.

"What if I cover all losses? Would that be proof enough I'm with you?"

"What?"

"I pay all losses and take half the profit for today, tomorrow and Friday. If we haven't got him on the run by Friday afternoon you buy back in, just before closing, and we've failed. If it looks like we've got him, we sell heavily, to the limit, just before closing. That'll sweat him out over the weekend. Monday I jerk the rug and our blitzkrieg's on. It's infallible."

"Yes. If you're to be trusted."

"I'll put $2 million in any Swiss bank you name by ten o'clock today. That's 10 million HK which sure as hell's enough to cover any shorting losses you might have. $2 million with no strings, no paper, no promissory note, just your word it's to cover any losses, that if we win we split profits and the rest of the deal as it's been laid out—50–50 except Kowloon Investments for me, Struan's at Kai Tak Airport for you, and for Casey and me, voting membership at the Turf Club. We'll put it to paper Tuesday—after he's crashed."

'You'll put up 2 million U.S., and it's my decision as to when I buy to cover any losses?" Gornt was incredulous.

"Yes. 2 million's the extent of my gamble. So how can you get hurt? You can't. And because he knows how you feel about him, if you mount the attack he won't be suspicious, won't be prepared for a flanking blitz from me."

"This all depends on whether your figures are correct—the amounts and the dates."

"Check them out. There must be a way you can do that—enough to convince yourself."

"Why the sudden change, Mr. Bartlett? You said you'd wait till Tuesday—perhaps later."

"We've done some checking and I don't like the figures I've come up with. We owe Dunross nothing. We'd be crazy to go with him when he's so weak. As it is, what I'm offering you is a great gamble, great odds: the Noble House against 2 lousy million. If we win that'd be parlayed into hundreds of millions."

"And if we fail?"

Bartlett shrugged. "Maybe I'll go home. Maybe we'll work out a Rothwell-Gornt-Par-Con deal. You win sometimes and you lose a lot more times. But this raid's too good not to try it. Without you it'd never work. I've seen enough of Hong Kong to know it has its own special rules. I've no time to learn them. Why should I—when I've got you."

"Or Dunross?"

Bartlett laughed and Gornt read no guile in him. "You're not stretched, you're not vulnerable, he is—that's his bad luck. What d'you say? Is the raid on?"

"I'd say you're very persuasive. Who gave you the information—and the document?"

"Tuesday I'll tell you. When Struan's have crashed."

"Ah, there's a payoff to Mister X?"

"There's always a payoff. It'll come off the top, but no more than 5 percent—any more comes out of my share."

"Two o'clock Friday, Mr. Bartlett? That's when I decide to buy back in and perhaps lose your 2 million—or we confer and continue the surge?"

"Friday at two."

"If we continue over the weekend you'll cover any further risk with further funds?"

"No. You won't need any more. 2 million's tops. By Friday afternoon either his stock will be way down and we'll have him running scared, or not. This's no long-term, well-organized raid. It's a once, er, a onetime attempt to fool's mate an opponent." Bartlett grinned happily. "I risk 2 lousy million for a game that will go down in history books. In less than a week we knock off the Noble House of Asia!"

Gornt nodded, torn. How far can I trust you, Mr. Bloody Raider, you with the key to Devil Dunross? He glanced out of the window and watched a child skulling a boat among the junks, the sea as safe and familiar to her as dry land. "I'll think about what you said."

"How long?"

"Till eleven."

"Sorry, this's a raid, not a business deal. It's now—or not at all!"

"Why?"

"There's a lot to do, Mr. Gornt. I want this settled now or not at all."

Gornt glanced at his watch. There was plenty of time. A call to the right Chinese newspaper and whatever he told them would be on the stands in an hour. He smiled grimly to himself. His own ace in the hole was Havergill. Everything dovetailed perfectly.

A seabird cawed and flew inland, riding some thermals toward the Peak. He watched it. Then his eyes noticed the Great House on the crest, white against the green of the slopes.

"It's a deal," he said and stuck out his hand.

Bartlett shook. "Great. This is strictly between us?"

"Yes."

"Where d'you want the 2 million?"

"The Bank of Switzerland and Zurich, in Zurich, account number 181819." Gornt reached into his pocket, noticing his fingers were trembling. "I'll write it down for you."

"No need. The account's in your name?"

"Good God, no! Canberra Limited."

"Canberra Limited's 2 million richer! And in three days with any luck, you'll be tai-pan of the Noble House. How about that!" Bartlett opened the door and got out. "See you."

"Wait," Gornt said, startled, "I'll drop you wh—"

"No thanks. I've got to get to a phone. Then at 9:15 I've an interview with your friend Orlanda, Miss Ramos—thought there was no harm in it. After that maybe I'll take a few pictures." He waved cheerily and walked off.

Gornt wiped the sweat off his hands. Before leaving the club he had phoned Orlanda to phone Bartlett and make the date. That's very good, he thought, still in shock. She'll keep an eye on him once they're lovers, and they will be, Casey or not. Orlanda has too much to gain.

He watched Bartlett, envying him. In a few moments the American had vanished into the crowds of Wanchai.

Suddenly he was very tired. It's all too pat, too fine, too easy, he told himself. And yet . . . and yet! Shakily he lit a cigarette. Where did Bartlett get those papers?

Inexorably his eyes went back to the Great House on the Peak. He was possessed by it and by a hatred so vast that it swept his mind back to his ancestors, to Sir Morgan Brock whom the Struans broke, to Gorth Brock whom Dirk Struan murdered, to Tyler Brock whom his daughter betrayed. Without wishing it, he renewed the oath of vengeance that he had sworn to his father, that his father had sworn to his—back to Sir Morgan Brock who, penniless, destroyed by his sister, Hag Struan, paralyzed, a shell of a man, had begged for vengeance on behalf of all the Brock ghosts on the Noble House and all the descendents of the most evil man who had ever lived.

Oh gods give me strength, Quillan Gornt prayed. Let the American be telling the truth. I will have vengeance.

28

10:50 A.M.:

The sun bore down on Aberdeen through a slight overcast. The air was sultry, ninety-two degrees Fahrenheit with ninety percent humidity. It was low tide. The smell of rotting kelp and offal and exposed mudflats added to the oppressive weight of the day.

There were five hundred or more sullen impatient people jamming against one another, trying to surge through the bottleneck of barriers ahead that the police had erected outside this branch of Ho-Pak. The barriers allowed only one person through at a time. Men and women of all ages, some with infants, were constantly jostling each other, no one waiting a turn, everyone trying to inch forward to get to the head of the line.

"Look at the bloody fools," Chief Inspector Donald C.C. Smyth said. "If they'd stretch out and not crowd they'd all get through quicker, and we could leave one copper here to keep order and the rest of us could go to lunch instead of getting the riot squad ready. Do it!"

"Yes sir," Divisional Sergeant Mok said politely. *Ayeeyah,* he was thinking as he walked over to the squad car, the poor fool still doesn't understand that we Chinese are not stupid foreign devils—or devils from the Eastern Sea—who'll line up patiently for hours. Oh no, we civilized persons understand life and it's every man for himself. He clicked on the police transmitter. "Divisional Sergeant Mok! The chief inspector wants a riot squad here on the double. Park just behind the fish market but keep in contact!"

"Yes sir."

Mok sighed and lit a cigarette. More barriers had been erected across the street, outside Blacs and the Victoria Aberdeen branches, and more at the Ching Prosperity Bank around the corner. His khaki uniform was ironed sharp on the creases and there were big sweat rings under his arms. He was very concerned. This crowd was very dangerous and he did not want a repetition of yesterday. If the bank shut its doors before three he was sure the crowd would tear the place apart. He knew that if he still had any money in there, he would be the first to tear the door open to get *his* money. *Ayeeyah*, he thought, very thankful for the Snake's authority that had unlocked all their money this morning to the last penny.

"Piss on all banks!" Mok muttered to no one. "All gods, let the Ho-Pak pay all customers today! Let it fail tomorrow! Tomorrow's my day off so let it fail tomorrow." He stubbed out his cigarette.

"Sergeant Major?"

"Yes?"

"Look over there!" the eager young plainclothes detective said, hurrying up to him. He wore spectacles and was in his early twenties. "By the Victoria Bank. The old woman. The old *amah*."

"Where? Oh yes, I see her." Mok watched her for a while but detected nothing untoward. Then he saw her scuttle through the crowd and whisper to a young tough, wearing jeans, who was leaning against a railing. She pointed to an old man who had just come out of the bank. At once the young tough sauntered after him and the old *amah* squeezed and squirmed and cursed her way back to the head of the barrier where she could see those who entered and those who came out.

"That's the third time, sir," the young detective said. "The old *amah* points out someone who's just come out of the bank to the tough, then off he goes. In a few minutes he comes back again. That's the third time. I'm sure I saw him slip her something once. I think it was money."

"Good! Very good, Spectacles Wu. It's bound to be a triad shakedown. The old hag's probably his mother. You follow the young bastard and I'll intercept him the other way. Keep out of sight!"

Divisional Sergeant Mok slipped around the corner, down a busy alley lined with stalls and street hawkers and open shops, moving carefully through the crowds. He turned into another alley just in time to catch a glimpse of some money being passed over by the old man. He waited until Wu had blocked the other end of the alley, then he walked ponderously forward.

"What's going on here?"

"What? Eh? Nothing, nothing at all," the old man said nervously, sweat running down his face. "What's the matter? I've done nothing!"

"Why did you give this young man money, *heya*? I saw you give him money!" The young thug stared back at Mok insolently, unafraid, knowing he was Smallpox Kin, one of the Werewolves who had all Hong Kong petrified. "Is he accosting you? Trying to squeeze you? He looks like a triad!"

"Oh! I . . . I . . . I owed him 500 dollars. I've just got it out of the bank and I paid him." The old man was clearly terrified but he blustered on, "He's my cousin." A crowd began to collect. Someone hawked and spat.

"Why're you sweating so much?"

"All gods fornicate all pigs! It's hot! Everyone's sweating. Everyone!"

"That's fornicating right," someone called out.

Mok turned his attention on the youth who waited truculently. "What's your name?"

"Sixth Son Wong!"

"Liar! Turn out your pockets!"

"Me, I've done nothing! I know the law. You can't search people without a warran—"

Mok's iron fist snapped out and twisted the youth's arm and he squealed. The crowd laughed. They fell silent as Spectacles Wu came out of nowhere to search him. Mok held Smallpox Kin in a vise. Another uneasy undercurrent swept through the onlookers as they saw the rolls of money, and change. "Where'd you get all this?" Mok snarled.

"It's mine. I'm . . . I'm a moneylender and I'm collecting forn—"

"Where's your place of business?"

"It's . . . it's in Third Alley, off Aberdeen Road."

"Come on, we'll go and look."

Mok released the young man who, unafraid, still stared back angrily. "First give me my money!" He turned to the crowd and appealed to them. "You saw him take it! I'm an honest moneylender! These're servants of the foreign devils and you all know them! Foreign devil law forbids honest citizens being searched!"

"Give him back his fornicating money!" someone shouted.

"If he's a moneylender . . ."

The crowd began to argue back and forth and then Smallpox Kin saw a small opening in the crowd and he darted for it. The crowd let him pass and he fled up the alley, vanishing into the traffic, but when Spectacles Wu charged in pursuit they closed up and jostled him and became a little uglier. Mok called him back. In the momentary melee the old man had disappeared. Wearily Mok said, "Let the motherless turd go! He was just a triad—another triad turd who preys on law-abiding people."

"What're you going to do with his fornicating money?" someone called out from the back of the crowd.

"I'm going to give it to an old woman's rest home," Mok shouted back equally rudely. "Go defecate in your grandmother's ear!"

Someone laughed and the crowd began to break up and then they all went about their business. In a moment Mok and Spectacles Wu were standing like stones in a river, the passersby eddying around them. Once back on the main street, Mok wiped his brow. "Dew neh loh moh!"

"Yes. Why're they like that, Sergeant Major?" the young detective asked. "We're only trying to help them. Why didn't the old man just admit that triad bastard was squeezing him?"

"You don't learn about mobs of people in schoolbooks," Mok said kindly, knowing the anxiety of the youth to succeed. Spectacles Wu was new, one of the recent university graduates to join the force. He was not one of Mok's private unit. "Be patient. Neither of them wanted anything to do with us because we're police and they all still believe we'll never help them, only ourselves. It's been the same in China since the first policeman."

"But this is Hong Kong," the youth said proudly. "We're different. We're British police."

"Yes." Mok felt a sudden chill. He did not wish to disillusion the youth. I used to be loyal too, loyal to the Queen and to the *quai loh* flag. I learned differently. When I needed help and protection and security I got none. Never once. The British used to be rich and powerful but they lost the war to those Eastern Sea Devils. The war took all their face away and humbled them and put the great tai-pans into Stanley Prison like common thieves—even the tai-pans of the Noble House and Great Bank and even the great high governor himself—put them away like common criminals, into Stanley with all their women and all the children and treated them like turds!

And then after the war, even though they had humbled the Eastern Devils, they never regained their power, or their face.

Now in Hong Kong and in all Asia, now it's not the same and never will be as before. Now every year the British get poorer and poorer and less powerful and how can they protect me and my family from evildoers if they're not rich and powerful? They pay me nothing and treat me like dogmeat! Now my only protection is money, money in gold so that we can flee if need be—or money in land or houses if we do not need to flee. How can I educate my sons in England or America without money? Will the grateful Government pay? Not a fornicating brass cash, and yet I'm supposed to risk my life to keep the streets clean of fornicating triads and pickpockets and rioting lumps of leper turd!

Mok shivered. The only safety for my family is in my own hands as always. Oh how wise the teachings of our ancestors are! Was the police commissioner loyal to me when I needed money, even steerage money, for my son to go to school in America? No. But the Snake was. He loaned me 10,000 dollars at only 10 percent interest so my son went like a Mandarin by Pan American aircraft, with three years of school money, and now he's a qualified architect with a Green Card and next month he'll have an American passport and then he can come back and no one will be able to touch him. He can help protect my generation and will protect his own and his son's and his son's sons!

Yes, the Snake gave me the money, long since paid back with full interest out of money he helped me earn. I shall be loyal to the Snake—until he turns. One day he'll turn, all *quai loh* do, all snakes do, but now I'm a High Dragon and neither gods nor devils nor the Snake himself can hurt my family or my bank accounts in Switzerland and Canada.

"Come along, we'd better go back, young Spectacles Wu," he said kindly and when he got back to the barriers he told Chief Inspector Smyth what had happened.

"Put the money in our kitty, 'Major," Smyth said. "Order a grand banquet for our lads tonight."

"Yes sir."

"It was Detective Constable Wu? The one who wants to join SI?"

"Yes sir. Spectacles is very keen."

Smyth sent for Wu, commended him. "Now, where's that old *amah*?"

Wu pointed her out. They saw her looking at the corner the thug had gone around, waiting impatiently. After a minute she squirmed out of the swarm and hobbled away, muttering obscenities.

"Wu," Smyth ordered, "follow her. Don't let yourself be seen. She'll lead you to the rotten little bugger who fled. Be careful, and when she goes to ground, phone the 'major."

"Yes sir."

"Do *not* take any risks—perhaps we can catch the whole gang, there's bound to be a gang."

"Yes sir."

"Off you go." They watched him following her. "That lad's going to be good. But not for us, 'Major, eh?"

"No sir."

"I think I'll recommend him to SI. Perhaps—"

Suddenly there was an ominous silence, then shouts and an angry roar. The two policemen rushed back around the corner. In their absence the crowd had shoved aside parts of the barricade, overpowering the four policemen, and now were surging into the bank. Manager Sung and his assistant were vainly trying to close the doors against the shouting, cursing throng. The barricades began to buckle.

"Get the riot squad!"

Mok raced for the squad car. Fearlessly Smyth rushed to the head of the line with his bullhorn. The tumult drowned his order to stop fighting. More reinforcements came running from across the street. Quickly and efficiently they charged to Smyth's support, but the mob was gathering strength. Sung and his tellers slammed the door shut but it was forced open again. Then a brick came out of the crowd and smashed one of the plate-glass windows. There was a roar of approval. The people in front were trying to get out of the way and those at the back were trying to get to the door. More bricks were hurtled at the building, then pieces of wood grabbed from a building site nearby. Another stone went through the glass and it totally shattered. Roaring, the mob surged forward. A girl fell and was crushed.

"Come on," Smyth shouted, "give me a hand!" He grabbed one of the barriers and, with four other policemen, used it as a shield and shoved it against the front of the mob, forcing them back. Above the uproar he shouted for them to use their shoulders and they fought the frenzied crowd. Other policemen followed his lead. More bricks went into the bank and then the shout went up, "Kill the fornicating bank thieves, kill them, they've stolen our money . . ."

"Kill the fornicators . . ."

"I want my money . . ."

"Kill the foreign devils . . ."

Smyth saw the mood of those near him change and his heart stopped as they took up the shout and forgot the bank and their hands reached out for him. He had seen that look before and knew he was a dead man. That other time was during the riots of '56 when 200,000 Chinese suddenly went on a senseless rampage in Kowloon. He would have been killed then if he had not had a Sten gun. He had killed four men and blasted a path to safety. Now he had no gun and he was fighting for his life. His hat was ripped away, someone grabbed his Sam Browne belt and a fist went into his groin, another into his face and talons clawed at his eyes. Fearlessly, Mok and others charged into the milling mess to rescue him. Someone hacked at Mok with a brick, another with a piece of wood that tore a great gash in his cheek. Smyth was engulfed, his hands and arms desperately trying to protect his head. Then the riot squad's Black Maria, siren screaming, skidded around the corner. The ten-man team fell on the crowd roughly and pulled Smyth away. Blood seeped from his mouth, his left arm dangled uselessly.

"You all right, sir?"

"Yes, for chrissake get those sodding barriers up! Get those bastards away from the bank—fire hoses!"

But the fire hoses weren't necessary. At the first violent charge of the riot squad the front of the mob had wilted and now the rest had retreated to a safe distance and stood there watching sullenly, some of them still shouting obscenities. Smyth grabbed the bullhorn. In Cantonese he said, "If anyone comes within twenty yards, he'll be arrested and deported!" He tried to catch his breath. "If anyone wants to visit the Ho-Pak, line up a hundred yards away."

The scowling crowd hesitated, then as Mok and the riot squad came forward fast, they retreated hastily and began to move away, treading on each other.

"I think my bloody shoulder's dislocated," Smyth said and cursed obscenely.

"What do we do about those bastards, sir?" Mok asked, in great pain, breathing hard, his cheek raw and bleeding, his uniform ripped.

Smyth held his arm to take the growing pain away and looked across the street at the sullen, gawking crowd. "Keep the riot squad here. Get another from West Aberdeen, inform Central. Where's my bloody hat? If I catch the bas—"

"Sir!" one of his men called out. He was kneeling beside the girl who had been trampled on. She was a bar girl or a dance hall girl: she had that sad, sweet oh so hard, young-old look. Blood was dribbling from her mouth, her breathing coming in hacking gasps.

"Christ, get an ambulance!"

As Smyth watched helplessly, the girl choked in her own blood and died.

Christian Toxe, editor of the *Guardian*, was scribbling notes, the phone jammed against his ear. "What was her name, Dan?" he asked over the hubbub of the newsroom.

"I'm not sure. One savings book said Su Tzee-Ian," Dan Yap the reporter on the other end of the phone at Aberdeen told him. "There was $4,360 in it—the other was in the name . . . Hang on a second, the ambulance's just leaving now. Can you hear all right, Chris, the traffic's heavy here."

"Yes. Go on. The second savings book?"

"The second book was in the name of Tak H'eung fah. Exactly 3,000 in that one."

Tak H'eung fah seemed to touch a memory. "Do any of the names mean anything?" Toxe asked. He was a tall rumpled man in his untidy cubbyhole of an office.

"No. Except one means Wisteria Su and the other Fragrant Flower Tak. She was pretty, Chris. Might have been Eurasian. . . ."

Toxe felt a sudden ice shaft in his stomach as he remembered his own three daughters, six and seven and eight, and his lovely Chinese wife. He tried to push that perpetual cross back into the recess of his mind, the secret worry of was it right to mix East and West, and what does the future hold for them, my darlings, in this lousy rotten bigoted world?

With an effort he concentrated again. "That's quite a lot of money for a dance hall girl, isn't it?"

"Yes. I'd say she had a patron. One interesting bit: in her purse was a crumpled envelope dated a couple of weeks ago with a mushy love letter in it. It was addressed to . . . hang on . . . to Tak H'eung fah, apartment 14, Fifth Alley, Tsung-pan Street in Aberdeen. It was soppy, swearing eternal love. Educated writing though."

"English?" Toxe asked surprised, writing swiftly.

"No. Characters. There was something about the writing—could be a *quai loh*."

"Did you get a copy?"

"The police wouldn't le—"

"Get a photocopy. Beg borrow or steal a photocopy in time for the afternoon edition. A week's bonus if you do it."

"Cash this afternoon?"

"All right."

"You have it."

"Any signature?"

" 'Your only love.' The *love* was in English."

"Mr. Toxe! Mrs. Publisher's on line two!" The English secretary called out through the open door, her desk just outside the glass partition.

"Oh Christ, I'll . . . I'll call her back. Tell her I've got a big story breaking." Then into the phone again, "Dan, keep on this story—keep close to the police, go with them to the dead girl's flat—if it's her flat. Find out who owns it—who her people are, where they live. Call me back!" Toxe hung up and called out to his assistant editor, "Hey, Mac!"

The lean, dour, gray-haired man got up from his desk and wandered in. "Aye?"

"I think we should put out an extra. Headline . . ." He scrawled on a piece of paper, "Mob Kills Fragrant Flower!"

"How about 'Mob Murders Fragrant Flower'?"

"Or, 'First Death at Aberdeen'?"

" 'Mob Murders' is better."

"That's it then. Martin!" Toxe called out. Martin Haply looked up from his desk and came over. Toxe ran his fingers through his hair as he told them both what Dan Yap had related. "Martin, do a follow-up: 'The beautiful young girl was crushed by the feet of the mob—but who were the real killers? Is it an incompetent government who refuses to regulate our outdated banking system? Are the killers those who started the rumors? Is the run on the Ho-Pak as simple as it sounds . . .' etcetera."

"Got it." Haply grinned and went back to his desk in the main office. He gulped a cold cup of coffee out of a plastic cup and started to type, his desk piled high with reference books, Chinese newspapers and stock market reports. Teletypes chattered in the background. A few silent copy boys and trainees delivered or picked up copy.

"Hey, Martin! What's the latest from the stock market?"

Martin Haply dialed a number without looking at the phone, then called back to the editor. "Ho-Pak's down to 24.60, four points from yesterday. Struan's are down a point though there's been some heavy buying. Hong Kong Lan Tao up three points—the story's just been confirmed. Dunstan Barre took their money out yesterday."

"They did? Then you were right again! Shit!"

"Victoria's off half a point—all banks are edgy and no buyers. There's a rumor a line's forming outside Blacs and the Victoria's head office in Central." Both men gasped.

"Send someone to check the Vic!" Mac hurried out. Jesus Christ, Toxe thought, his stomach churning, Jesus Christ if a run starts on the Vic the whole sodding island'll collapse and my sodding savings with it.

He leaned back in his old chair and put his feet on the desk, loving his job, loving the pressure and immediacy.

"Do you want me to call her?" his secretary asked. She was round and unflappable.

"Who? Oh shit, Peg, I'd forgotten. Yes—call the Dragon."

The Dragon was the wife of the publisher, Mong Pa-tok, the present head of the sprawling Mong family who owned this paper and three Chinese newspapers and five magazines, whose antecedents went back to the earliest days. The Mongs were supposed to have descended from the first editor-owner-publisher of the paper, Morley Skinner. The story was that Dirk Struan had given Skinner control of the paper in return for helping him against Tyler Brock and his son Gorth by hushing up the killing of Gorth in Macao. It was said Dirk Struan had provoked the duel. Both men had used fighting irons. Once, some years ago, Toxe had heard old Sarah Chen in her cups relate that when the Brocks came to collect Gorth's body they did not recognize him. The old woman had added that her father, Sir Gordon Chen, had had to mobilize most of Chinatown to prevent the Brocks from setting afire the Struan warehouses. Tyler Brock had set Tai-ping Shan alight instead. Only the great typhoon that came that night stopped the whole city from going up in flames—the same holocaust that had destroyed Dirk Struan's Great House and him and his secret Chinese wife, May-may.

"She's on line two."

"Eh? Oh! All right, Peg." Toxe sighed.

"Ah Mr. Toxe, I was waiting your call, *heya?*"

"What can I do for you, or Mr. Mong?"

"Your pieces on the Ho-Pak Bank, yesterday and today, that the adverse rumors about the Ho-Pak are untrue and started by tai-pans and another big bank. I see more today."

"Yes. Haply's quite sure."

"My husband and I hear this not true. No tai-pans or banks are putting out rumors or have put out rumors. Perhaps wise to drop this attack."

"It's not an attack, Mrs. Mong, just an attitude. You know how susceptible Chinese are to rumors. The Ho-Pak's as strong as any bank in the Colony. We feel sure the rumors were started by a bi—"

"Not by tai-pans and not big bank. My husband and I not like this attitude never mind. Please to change," she said and he heard the granite in her voice.

"That's editorial policy and I have control over editorial policy," he said grimly.

"*We* are publisher. It is *our* newspaper. *We* tell you to stop so you will stop."

"You're ordering me to stop?"

"Of course it is order."

"Very well. As you order it, it's stopped."

"Good!" The phone went dead. Christian Toxe snapped his pencil and threw it against the wall and began to curse. His secretary sighed and discreetly closed the door and when he was done Toxe opened the door. "Peg, how about some coffee? Mac! Martin!"

Toxe sat back at his desk. The chair creaked. He mopped the sweat off his cheeks and lit a cigarette and inhaled deeply.

"Yes, Chris?" Haply asked.

"Martin, cancel the piece I asked for and do another on Hong Kong banking and the need to have some form of banking insurance. . . ."

Both men gaped at him.

"Our publisher doesn't like the rumors approach."

Martin Haply flushed. "Well screw him! You heard the guys yourself at the tai-pan's party!"

"That proves nothing. You've no proof. We're stopping that approach. It's not proven so I can't take a stand."

"But, lo—"

Toxe's neck went purple. "*It's bloody well stopped,*" he roared. "*Understand?*"

Haply began to say something but changed his mind. Choked with rage he turned on his heel and left. He walked across the big room and jerked the front door open and slammed it behind him.

Christian Toxe exhaled. "He's got a lousy bloody temper that lad!"

He stubbed his cigarette out and lit another. "Christ, I'm smoking too much!" Still seething, his brown eyes watched the older man. "Someone must have called her, Mac. Now what would you like as a return favor if you were Mrs. Dragon Mong?"

Suddenly Mac beamed. "Na a voting membership of the Turf Club!"

"Go to the head of the class!"

Singh, the Indian reporter, came in with a foot of teletype. "You might need this for the extra, Chris."

It was a series of Reuters reports from the Middle East. "Teheran 0832 hours: High-level diplomatic sources in Iran report sudden extensive Soviet military maneuvers have begun close to their north border near the oil-rich border area of Azerbaijan where more rioting took place. Washington is reported to have asked permission to send observers to the area."

The next paragraph was: "Tel Aviv 0600 hours: The Knesset confirmed late last night that another huge irrigation project had been funded to further divert the waters of the River Jordan into the southern Negev Desert. There was immediate adverse and hostile reaction from Jordan, Egypt and Syria."

"Negev? Isn't Israel's brand spanking new atomic plant in the Negev?" Toxe asked.

"Aye. Now there's another splendid addition to the peace conference tables. Would the water be for that?"

"I don't know Mac, but this's certainly going to parch a few Jordanian and Palestinian throats. Water water everywhere but not a drop to shower in. I wish to Christ it would rain. Singh, tidy up these reports and we'll put them on the back page. They won't sell a single bloody paper. Do a follow-up piece on the Werewolves for the front page: 'The police have a

vast dragnet out but the vicious kidnappers of Mr. John Chen continue to
elude them. According to sources close to the family of his father, compradore of Struan's, no ransom note has yet been received but one is expected
imminently. The *China Guardian* asks all its readers to assist in the capture of these fiends . . .' That sort of thing."

At Aberdeen Spectacles Wu saw the old woman come out of the tenement building, a shopping basket in her hand, and join the noisy crowds
in the narrow alley. He followed cautiously feeling very pleased with himself. While he had waited for her to reappear he had struck up a conversation with a street hawker whose permanent place of business was a
patch of broken pavement opposite. The hawker sold tea and small bowls
of hot congee—rice gruel. Wu had ordered a bowl, and during his meal,
the hawker had told him about the old woman, Ah Tam, who had been in
the neighborhood since last year. She'd come to the Colony from a village
near Canton with the huge waves of immigrants who had flooded over the
border last summer. She didn't have any family of her own and the people
she worked for had no sons around twenty, though he had seen her with a
young man early this morning. "She says her village was Ning-tok. . . ."
It was then that Wu had felt a glow at this stroke of luck. Ning-tok was
the same village his own parents had come from and he spoke that dialect.
Now he was twenty paces behind her and he watched her haggle
brilliantly for vegetables, selecting only the very best onions and greens,
all just a few hours fresh from the fields in the New Territories. She
bought very little so he knew that the family she worked for was poor.
Then she was standing in front of the poultry stall with its layers of
barely alive, scrawny chickens crammed helplessly into cages, their legs
tied. The rotund stall owner bartered with her, both sides enjoying the
foul language, insults, choosing this bird, then that, then another, prod-
ding them, discarding them, until the bargain was made. Because she was
a good, salty trader, the man allowed his profit to be shaved. Then he
strangled the bird deftly without thought, tossing the carcass to his five-
year-old daughter, who squatted in a pile of feathers and offal, for plucking and cleaning.
"Hey, Mr. Poultryman," Wu called out, "I'd like a bird at the same
price. That one!" He pointed at a good choice and paid no attention to the
man's grumbling. "Elder Sister," he said to her politely, "clearly you have
saved me a great deal of cash. Would you like to have a cup of tea while
we wait for our birds to be cleaned?"
"Ah thank you, yes, these old bones are tired. We'll go there!" Her
gnarled finger pointed to a stall opposite. "Then we can watch to make
sure we get what we paid for." The poultry man muttered an obscenity
and they laughed.
She shoved her way across the street, sat down on a bench, ordered tea

and a cake and was soon telling Wu how she hated Hong Kong and living among strangers. It was easy for him to butter her up by using the odd word of Ning-tok patois; then pretending to be equally surprised when she switched to that dialect and told him she came from the same village and oh how wonderful it was to find a neighbor after all these months among foreigners! She told him that she had worked for the same family in Ning-tok ever since she was seven. But, sadly, three years ago her mistress—the child that she had brought up, now an old lady like herself—had died. "I stayed in the house but it had fallen on hard times. Then last year the famine was bad. Many in the village decided to come to this place. Chairman Mao's people didn't mind, in fact they encouraged us—'Useless Mouths' as they called us. Somehow we got split up and I managed to get over the border and found my way to this place here, penniless, hungry, with no family, no friends, nowhere to turn. At length I got a job and now I work as a cook-*amah* for the family Ch'ung who're street cleaners. The dog bones pay me nothing but my keep and my food and chief wife Ch'ung's a maggot-mouthed hag but soon I'll be rid of all of them! You said your father came here with his family ten years ago?"

"Yes. We owned a field near the bamboo glade beside the river. His name was Wu Cho-tam an—"

"Ah, yes I think I remember the family. Yes, I think so. Yes, and I know the field. My family was Wu Ting-top and their family owned the pharmacy at the crossroads for more than a hundred years."

"Ah, Honorable Pharmacy Wu? Oh yes of course!" Spectacles Wu did remember the family well. Pharmacy Wu had always been a Maoist sympathizer. Once he had had to flee the Nationalists. In this village of a thousand souls he had been well liked and trusted and he had kept life in the village as calm and as protected from outsiders as he could.

"So, you're one of Wu Cho-tam's sons, Younger Brother!" Ah Tam was saying. "Eeeee, in the early days it was so wonderful in Ning-tok but for the last years . . . terrible."

"Yes. We were lucky. Our field was fertile and we tilled the soil like always but after a few years outsiders came and accused all the landowners—as if we were exploiters! We only tilled our own field. Even so, from time to time some landowners were taken away, some shot, so one night ten years ago my father fled with all of us. Now my father is dead but I live with my mother not far away."

"There were many fleeings and famines in the early days. I hear that now it is better. Did you hear too? Outsiders came, wasn't it? They would come and they would leave. The village is not so bad again, Younger Brother, oh no! Outsiders leave us alone. Yes, they left my mistress and us alone because Father was important and one of Chairman Mao's supporters from the beginning. My mistress's name was Fang-ling, she's dead now. There's no collective near us so life is like it's always been, though we all have to study Chairman Mao's Red Book. The village isn't so bad, all my friends are there. . . . Hong Kong is a foul place and my village is home. Life without family is nothing. But now . . ." Then the old woman dropped her voice and chortled, carried away with pleasure. "But now the gods have favored me. In a month or two I'm going home, home forever. I'll have enough money to retire on and I'll buy the small house at the end of my street and perhaps a little field and . . ."

"Retire?" Wu said, leading her on. "Who has that sort of money, Elder Sister? You said you were paid nothing th—"

"Ah," the old woman replied, puffed up. "I've an important friend."

"What sort of friend?"

"A very important business friend who needs my help! Because I've been so useful he's promised to give me a huge amount of money—"

"You're making this all up, Elder Sister," he scoffed. "Am I a foolish stranger wh—"

"I tell you my friend's so important he can hold the whole island in thrall!"

"There are no such persons!"

"Oh yes there are!" She dropped her voice and whispered hoarsely, "What about the Werewolves!"

Spectacles Wu gaped at her. "What?"

She chortled again, delighted with the impact of her confidence. "Yes."

The young man took hold of his blown mind and put the pieces quickly back together; if this were true he would get the reward and the promotion and maybe an invitation to join Special Intelligence. "You're making this up!"

"Would I lie to someone from my own village? My friend's one of them I tell you. He's also a 489 and his Brotherhood's going to be the richest in all Hong Kong."

"Eeeee, how lucky you are, Elder Sister! And when you see him again please ask if perhaps he can use someone like me. I'm a street fighter by trade though my triad's poor and the leader stupid and a stranger. Is he from Ning-tok?"

"No. He's . . . he's my nephew," she said, and the young man knew it was a lie. "I'm seeing him later. Yes, he's coming later. He owes me some money."

"Eeeee, that's good, but don't put it in a bank and certainly not in the Ho-Pak or y—"

"Ho-Pak?" she said suspiciously, her little eyes narrowing suddenly in the creases of her face. "Why do you mention the Ho-Pak? What has the Ho-Pak to do with me?"

"Nothing, Elder Sister," Wu said, cursing himself for the slip, knowing her guard was now up. "I saw the queues this morning, that's all."

She nodded, not convinced, then saw that her chicken was packaged and ready so she thanked him for the tea and cake and scuttled off, muttering to herself. Most carefully he followed her. From time to time she would look back but she did not see him. Reassured, she went home.

The CIA man got out of his car and walked quickly into police head-quarters. The uniformed sergeant at the information desk greeted him. "Afternoon, Mr. Rosemont."

"I've an appointment with Mr. Crosse."

"Yes sir. He's expecting you."

Sourly Rosemont went to the elevator. This whole goddamn-piss-poor is-land makes me want to shit, and the goddamn British along with it.

"Hello, Stanley," Armstrong said. "What're you doing here?"

"Oh hi, Robert. Gotta meeting with your chief."

"I've already had that displeasure once today. At 7:01 precisely." The elevator opened. Rosemont went in and Armstrong followed.

"I hope you've got some good news for Crosse," Armstrong said with a yawn. "He's really in a foul mood."

"Oh? You in this meeting too?"

"Afraid so."

Rosemont flushed. "Shit, I asked for a private meeting."

"I'm private."

"You sure are, Robert. And Brian, and everyone else. But some bastard isn't."

Armstrong's humor vanished. "Oh?"

"No." Rosemont said nothing more. He knew he had hurt the English-man but he didn't care. It's the truth, he thought bitterly. The sooner these goddamn limeys open their goddamn eyes the better.

The elevator stopped. They walked down the corridor and were ushered into Crosse's room by Brian Kwok. Rosemont felt the bolts slide home behind him and he thought how goddamn foolish and useless and unnec-essary; the man's a knucklehead.

"I asked for a private meeting, Rog."

"It's private. Robert's very private, Brian is. What can I do for you, Stanley?" Crosse was politely cool.

"Okay, Rog, today I got a long list for you: first, you're personally 100 percent in the creek with me, my whole department, up to the director in Washington himself. I'm told to tell you—among other things—your mole's surpassed himself this time."

"Oh?"

Rosemont's voice was grating now. "For starters, we just heard from one of our sources in Canton that Fong-fong and all your lads were hit last night. Their cover's gone—they're blown." Armstrong and Brian Kwok looked shocked. Crosse was staring back at him and he read nothing in his face. "Got to be your mole, Rog. Got to be fingered from the tai-pan's AMG papers."

Crosse looked across at Brian Kwok. "Use the emergency wireless code. Check it!"

As Brian Kwok hurried out, Rosemont said again, "They're blown, the poor bastards."

"We'll check it anyway. Next?"

Rosemont smiled mirthlessly. "Next: Almost everything that was in the tai-pan's AMG papers's spread around the intelligence community in London—on the wrong side."

"God curse all traitors," Armstrong muttered.

"Yeah, that's what I thought, Robert. Next, another little gem—AMG was no accident."

"What?"

"No one knows the who, but we all know the why. The bike was hit by an auto. No make, no serial number, no witnesses, no nothing yet, but he was hit—and of course, fingered from here."

"Then why haven't I been informed by Source? Why's the information coming from you?" Crosse asked.

Rosemont's voice sharpened. "I just got off the phone to London. It's just past 5:00 A.M. there so maybe your people plan to let you know when they get to the office after a nice leisurely bacon and eggs and a goddamn cup of tea!"

Armstrong shot a quick glance at Crosse and winced at the look on his face.

"Your . . . your point's well taken, Stanley," Crosse said. "Next?"

"The photos we gave you of the guys who knocked off Voranski . . . what happened?"

"We had their place covered. The two men never reappeared, so I raided the place in the early hours. We went through that whole tenement, room by room, but found no one who looked anything like the photographs. We searched for a couple of hours and there were no secret doors or anything like that. They weren't there. Perhaps your fellow made a mistake. . . ."

"Not this time. Marty Povitz was sure. We had the place staked out soon as we deciphered the address but there was a time when it wasn't all covered, front and back. I think they were tipped, again by your mole." Rosemont took out a copy of a telex and passed it over. Crosse read it, reddened and passed it over to Armstrong.

Decoded from Director, Washington, to Rosemont, Deputy Director Station Hong Kong: Sinders MI-6 brings orders from Source, London, that you are to go with him Friday to witness the handover of the papers and get an immediate photocopy.

"You'll get your copy in today's mail, Rog," the American said.

"I can keep this?" Crosse asked.

"Sure. By the way, we have a tail on Dunross too. W—"

Crosse said angrily, "Would you kindly not interfere in our jurisdiction!"

"I told you you were in Shitsville, Rog!" Tautly Rosemont placed another cable on the table.

> Rosemont, Hong Kong. You will hand this cable to Chief of SI personally. Until further orders Rosemont is authorized to proceed independently to assist in the uncovering of the hostile in any way he chooses. He is, however, required to stay within the law and keep you advised personally of what he is doing. Source 8–98/3.

Rosemont saw Crosse bite back an explosion. "What else've you authorized?" Crosse asked.

"Nothing. Yet. Next: We'll be at the bank on Fri—"

"You know where Dunross's put the files?"

"It's all over town—among the community. I told you your mole's been working overtime." Abruptly Rosemont flared, "Come on for chrissake, Rog, you know if you tell a hot item to someone in London, it's all over town! We've all got security problems but yours're worse!" With an effort the American simmered down. "You could've leveled with me about the Dunross screw-up—it would've saved us all a lot of heartache and a lotta face."

Crosse lit a cigarette. "Perhaps. Perhaps not. I was trying to maintain security."

"Remember me? I'm on our side!"

"Are you?"

"You bet your ass!" Rosemont said it very angrily. "And if it was up to me I'd have every safety deposit box open before sundown—and the hell with the consequences."

"Thank God you can't do that."

"For chrissake we're at war and God only knows what's in those other files. Maybe they'll finger your goddamn mole and then we can get the bastard and give him his!"

"Yes," Crosse said, his voice a whiplash, "or maybe there's nothing in the papers at all!"

"What do you mean?"

"Dunross agreed to hand the files over to Sinders on Friday. What if there's nothing in them? Or what if he burned the pages and gives us just the covers? What the hell do we do then?"

Rosemont gaped at him. "Jesus—is that a possibility?"

"Of course it's a possibility! Dunross's clever. Perhaps they're not there at all, or the vault ones are false or nonexistent. We don't know he put them there, he just says he put them there. Jesus Christ, there're fifty possibilities. You're so smart, you CIA fellows, you tell me which deposit box and I'll open it myself."

"Get the key from the governor. Give me and some of my boys private access for five hours an—"

"Out of the question!" Crosse snarled, suddenly red-faced, and Armstrong felt the violence strongly. Poor Stanley, you're the target today. He suppressed a shudder, remembering the times he had had to face Crosse. He had soon learned that it was easier to tell the man the truth, to tell everything at once. If Crosse ever really went after him in an interrogation, he knew beyond doubt he would be broken. Thank God he's never yet had reason to try, he thought thankfully, then turned his eyes on Rosemont who was flushed with rage. I wonder who Rosemont's informants are, and how he knows for certain that Fong-fong and his team have been obliterated.

"Out of the question," Crosse said again.

"Then what the hell do we do? Sit on our goddamn lard till Friday?"

"Yes. We wait. We've been ordered to wait. Even if Dunross has torn out pages, or sections, or disposed of whole files, we can't put him in prison—or force him to remember or tell us anything."

"If the director or Source decide he should be leaned on, there're ways. That's what the enemy'd do."

Crosse and Armstrong stared at Rosemont. At length Armstrong said coldly, "But that doesn't make it right."

"That doesn't make it wrong either. Next: For your ears only, Rog."

At once Armstrong got up but Crosse motioned him to stay. "Robert's my ears." Armstrong hid the laughter that permeated him at so ridiculous a statement.

"No. Sorry, Rog, orders—your brass and mine."

Armstrong saw Crosse hesitate perfectly. "Robert, wait outside. When I buzz come back in. Check on Brian."

"Yes sir." Armstrong went out and closed the door, sorry that he would not be present for the kill.

"Well?"

The American lit another cigarette. "Top secret. At 0400 today the whole Ninety-second Airborne dropped into Azerbaijan supported by large units of Delta Force and they've fanned out all along the Iran-Soviet border." Crosse's eyes widened. "This was at the direct request of the Shah, in response to massive Soviet military preparations just over the border and the usual Soviet-sponsored riots all over Iran. Jesus, Rog, can't you get some air conditioning in here?" Rosemont mopped his brow. "There's a security blanket all over Iran now. At 0600 support units landed at Teheran airport. Our Seventh Fleet's heading for the Gulf, the Sixth—that's the Mediterranean—is already at battle stations off Israel, the Second, Atlantic, is heading for the Baltic, NORAD's alerted, NATO's alerted, and all Poseidons are one step from Red."

"Jesus Christ, what the hell's going on?"

"Khrushchev is making another real play for Iran—always an optimum Soviet target right? He figures he has the advantage. It's right on his own border where his own lines of communication're short and ours huge. Yesterday the Shah's security people uncovered a 'democratic socialist' insurrection scheduled to explode in the next few days in Azerbaijan. So the Pentagon's reacting like mashed cats. If Iran goes so does the whole Persian Gulf, then Saudi Arabia and that wraps up Europe's oil and that wraps up Europe."

"The Shah's been in trouble before. Isn't this more of your overreacting?"

The American hardened. "Khrushchev backed down over Cuba—first goddamn time there's been a Soviet backoff—because JFK wasn't bluffing and the only thing Commies understand is force. *Big-massive-honest-to-goddamn force!* The Big K better back off this time too or we'll hand him his head."

"You'll risk blowing up the whole bloody world over some illiterate, rioting, fanatic nutheads who've probably got some right on their side anyway?"

"I'm not into politics, Rog, only into winning. Iran oil, Persian Gulf oil, Saudi oil're the West's jugular. We're not gonna let the enemy get it."

"If they want it they'll take it."

"Not this time, they won't. We're calling the operation Dry Run. The idea's to go in heavy, frighten 'em off and get out fast, quietly, so no one's the wiser except the enemy, and particularly no goddamn liberal fellow-traveler congressman or journalist. The Pentagon figures the Soviets don't believe we could possibly respond so fast, so massively from so far away, so they'll go into shock and run for cover and close everything down—until next time."

The silence thickened.

Crosse's fingers drummed. "What am I supposed to do? Why're you telling me this?"

"Because the brass ordered me to. They want all allied chief SIs to know because if the stuff hits the fan there'll be sympathy riots all over, as usual, well-coordinated rent-a-mob riots, and you'll have to be prepared. AMG's papers said that Sevrin had been activated here—maybe there's a tie-in. Besides, you here in Hong Kong are vital to us. You're the back door to China, the back door to Vladivostok and the whole of east Russia— and our best shortcut to their Pacific naval and atomic-sub bases." Rosemont took out another cigarette, his fingers shaking. "Listen, Rog," he said, controlling his grumbling anger, "let's forget all the interoffice shit, huh? Maybe we can help each other."

"What atomic subs?" Crosse said with a deliberate sneer, baiting him. "They haven't got atomic subs yet an—"

"Jesus Christ!" Rosemont flared. "You guys've got your heads up your

asses and you won't listen. You spout détente and try to muzzle us and
they're laughing their goddamn heads off. They got nuclear subs and missile sites and naval bases all over the Sea of Okhotsk!" Rosemont got up
and went to the huge map of China and Asia that dominated one wall
and stabbed the Kamchatka peninsula, north of Japan. ". . . Petropavlovsk, Vladivostok . . . they've giant operations all along this whole
Siberian coast, here at Komsomolsk at the mouth of the Amur and on
Sakhalin. But Petropavlovsk's the big one. In ten years, that'll be the
greatest war-port in Asia with support airfields, atomic-protected subpens
and atomic-safe fighter strips and missile silos. And from there they
threaten all Asia—Japan, Korea, China, the Philippines—not forgetting
Hawaii and our West Coast."

"U.S. forces are preponderant and always will be. You're overreacting
again."

Rosemont's face closed. "People call me a hawk. I'm not. Just a realist.
They're on a war footing. Our Midas III's have pinpointed all kinds of
crap, our . . ." He stopped and almost kicked himself for letting his
mouth run on. "Well, we know a lot of what they're doing right now, and
they're not making goddamn ploughshares."

"I think you're wrong. They don't want war any more than we do."

"You want proof? You'll get it tomorrow, soon as I've clearance!" the
American said, stung. "If it's proved, can we cooperate better?"

"I thought we were cooperating well now."

"Will you?"

"Whatever you want. Does Source want me to react in any specific
way?"

"No, just to be prepared. I guess this'll all filter down through channels
today."

"Yes." Crosse was suddenly gentle. "What's really bothering you,
Stanley?"

Rosemont's hostility left him. "We lost one of our best setups in East
Berlin, last night, a lot of good guys. A buddy of mine got hit crossing
back to us, and we're sure it's tied into AMG."

"Oh, sorry about that. It wasn't Tom Owen, was it?"

"No. He left Berlin last month. It was Frank O'Connell."

"Don't think I ever met him. Sad."

"Listen, Rog, this mole thing's the shits." He got up and went to the
map. He stared at it a long time. "You know about Iman?"

"Sorry?"

Rosemont's stubby finger stabbed a point on the map. The city was inland, 180 miles north of Vladivostok at a rail junction. "It's an industrial
center, railways, lots of factories."

"So?" Crosse asked.

"You know about the airfield there?"

"What airfield?"

"It's underground, whole goddamn thing, just out of town, built into a gigantic maze of natural caves. It's got to be one of the wonders of the world. It's atomic capable, Rog. The whole base was constructed by Japanese and Nazi slave labor in '45, '6 and '7. A hundred thousand men they say. It's all underground, Rog, with space for 2500 airplanes, air crews and support personnel. It's bombproof—even atomic proof—with eighty runways that lead out onto a gigantic airstrip that circles eighteen low hills. It took one of our guys nine hours to drive around it. That was back in '46—so what's it like now?"

"Improved—if it exists."

"It's operational now. A few guys, intelligence, ours and yours, even a few of the better newspaper guys, knew about it even in '46. So why the silence now? That base alone's a massive threat to all of us and no one screams a shit. Even China, and she sure as hell's got to know about Iman."

"I can't answer that."

"I can. I think that info's being buried, deliberately, along with a lot of other things." The American got up and stretched. "Jesus, the whole world's falling apart and I got a backache. You know a good chiropractor?"

"Have you tried Doc Thomas on Pedder Street? I use him all the time."

"I can't stand him. He makes you wait in line—won't give you an appointment. Thank God for chiropractors! Trying to get my son to be one instead of an M.D."

The phone rang and Crosse answered it.

"Yes Brian?" Rosemont watched Crosse as he listened. "Just a minute, Brian. Stanley, are we through now?"

"Sure. Just a couple of open, routine things."

"Right. Brian, come in with Robert as soon as you come up." Crosse put the phone down. "We couldn't establish contact with Fong-fong. You're probably correct. They'll be MPD'd or MPC'd in forty-eight hours."

"I don't understand."

"Missing Presumed Dead or Missing Presumed Captured."

"Rough. Sorry to bring bad news."

"Joss."

"With Dry Run and AMG, how about pulling Dunross into protective custody?"

"Out of the question."

"You have the Official Secrets Act."

"Out of the question."

"I'm going to recommend it. By the way, Ed Langan's FBI boys tied Banastasio in with Bartlett. He's a big shareholder in Par-Con. They say he supplied the dough for the last merger that put Par-Con into the big time."

"Anything on the Moscow visas for Bartlett and Tcholok?"

"Best we can find is that they went as tourists. Maybe they did, maybe it was a cover."

"Anything on the guns?" This morning Armstrong had told Crosse of Peter Marlowe's theory and he had ordered an immediate watch on Four Finger Wu and offered a great reward for information.

"The FBI're sure they were put aboard in L.A. It'd be easy—Par-Con's hangar's got no security. They also checked on the serial numbers you gave us. They were all out of a batch that had gotten 'mislaid' en route from the factory to Camp Pendleton—that's the Marine depot in southern California. Could be we've stumbled onto a big arms-smuggling racket. Over seven hundred M14's have gotten mislaid in the last six months. Talking about that . . ." He stopped at the discreet knock. He saw Crosse touch the switch. The door opened and Brian Kwok and Armstrong came back in. Crosse motioned them to sit. "Talking about that, you remember the CARE case?"

"The suspected corruption here in Hong Kong?"

"That's the one. We might have a lead for you."

"Good. Robert, you were handling that at one time, weren't you?"

"Yes sir." Robert Armstrong sighed. Three months ago one of the vice-consuls at the U.S. Consulate had asked the CID to investigate the handling of the charity to see whether some light-fingered administrators were involved in a little take-away for personal profit. The digging and interviewing was still proceeding. "What've you got, Stanley?"

Rosemont searched in his pockets then pulled out a typed note. It contained three names and an address: Thomas K. K. Lim (Foreigner Lim), Mr. Tak Chou-lan (Big Hands Tak), Mr. Lo Tup-lin (Bucktooth Lo), Room 720, Princes Building, Central. "Thomas K. K. Lim is American, well heeled and well connected in Washington, Vietnam and South America. He's in business with the other two jokers at that address. We got a tip that he's mixed up in a couple of shady deals with AID and that Big Hands Tak is heavy in CARE. It's not in our bailiwick so it's over to you." Rosemont shrugged and stretched again. "Maybe it's something. The whole world's on fire but we still gotta deal with crooks! Crazy! I'll keep in touch. Sorry about Fong-fong and your people."

He left.

Crosse told Armstrong and Brian Kwok briefly what he had been told about Operation Dry Run.

Brian Kwok said sourly, "One day one of those Yankee madmen're going to make a mistake. It's stupid putting atomics into hair-trigger situations."

Crosse looked at them and their guards came up. "I want that mole. I want him before the CIA uncover him. If they get him first . . ." The thin-faced man was clearly very angry. "Brian, go and see Dunross. Tell him AMG was no accident and not to go out without our people nearby.

Under any circumstances. Say I would prefer him to give us the papers early, confidentially. Then he has nothing to fear."

"Yes sir." Brian Kwok knew that Dunross would do exactly as he wanted but he kept his mouth shut.

"Our normal riot planning will cover any by-product of the Iran problem and from Dry Run. However, you'd better alert CID an—" He stopped. Robert Armstrong was frowning at the piece of paper Rosemont had given him. "What is it, Robert?"

"Didn't Tsu-yan have an office at Princes Building?"

"Brian?"

"We've followed him there several times, sir. He visited a business acquaintance. . . ." Brian Kwok searched his memory. ". . . Shipping. Name of Ng, Vee Cee Ng, nicknamed Photographer Ng. Room 721. We checked him out but everything was above board. Vee Cee Ng runs Asian and China Shipping and about fifty other small allied businesses. Why?"

"This address's 720. Tsu-yan could tie in with John Chen, the guns, Banastasio, Bartlett—even the Werewolves," Armstrong said.

Crosse took the paper. After a pause he said, "Robert, take a team and check 720 and 721 right now."

"It's not in my area, sir."

"How right you are!" Crosse said at once, heavy with sarcasm. "Yes. I know. You're CID Kowloon, Robert, not Central. However, I authorize the raid. Go and do it. Now."

"Yes sir." Armstrong left, red-faced.

The silence gathered.

Brian Kwok waited, staring stoically at the desk top. Crosse selected a cigarette with care, lit it, then leaned back in his chair. "Brian. I think Robert's the mole."

29

1:38 P.M.:

Robert Armstrong and a uniformed police sergeant got out of the squad car and headed through the crowds into the vast maw of the Princes Arcade with its jewelry and curio shops, camera shops and radio shops stuffed with the latest electronic miracles, that was on the ground floor of the old-fashioned, high-rise office building in Central. They eased their way toward a bank of elevators, joining the swarm of waiting people. Eventually he and the sergeant squeezed into an elevator. The air was heavy and fetid and nervous. The Chinese passengers watched them obliquely and uncomfortably.

On the seventh floor Armstrong and the sergeant got out. The corridor was dingy and narrow with nondescript office doors on either side. He stood for a moment looking at the board. Room 720 was billed as "Ping-sing Wah Developments," 721 as "Asian and China Shipping." He walked ponderously down the corridor, Sergeant Yat alongside.

As they turned the corner a middle-aged Chinese wearing a white shirt and dark trousers was coming out of room 720. He saw them, blanched, and ducked back in. When Armstrong got to the door he expected it to be locked but it wasn't and he jerked it open just in time to see the man in the white shirt disappearing out of the back door, another man almost jamming him in equal haste to flee. The back door slammed closed.

Armstrong sighed. There were two rumpled secretaries in the sleazy, untidy office suite of three cramped rooms, and they were gawking at him, one with her chopsticks poised in midair over a bowl of chicken and noodles. The noodles slid off her chopsticks and fell back into the soup.

"Afternoon," Armstrong said.

The two women gaped at him, then looked at the sergeant and back to him again.

"Where are Mr. Lim, Mr. Tak and Mr. Lo, please?"

One of the girls shrugged and the other, unconcerned, began to eat again. Noisily. The office suite was untidy and unkempt. There were two phones, papers strewn around, plastic cups, dirty plates and bowls and used chopsticks. A teapot and tea cups. Full garbage cans.

Armstrong took out the search warrant and showed it to them.

The girls stared at him.

Irritably Armstrong harshened his voice. "You speak English?"

Both girls jumped. "Yes sir," they chorused.

"Good. Give your names to the sergeant and answer his questions. Th—" At that moment the back door opened again and the two men were herded back into the room by two hard-faced uniformed policemen who had been waiting in ambush. "Ah, good. Well done. Thank you, Corporal. Now, where were you two going?"

At once the two men began protesting their innocence in voluble Cantonese.

"*Shut up!*" Armstrong snarled. They stopped. "Give me your names!" They stared at him. In Cantonese he said, "Give me your names and you'd better not lie or I will become very fornicating angry."

"He's Tak Chou-lan," the one with pronounced buck teeth said, pointing at the other.

"What's your name?"

"Er, Lo Tup-sop, Lord. But I haven't done anyt—"

"Lo Tup-sop? Not Lo Tup-lin?"

"Oh no, Lord Superintendent, that's my brother."

"Where is he?"

The buck-toothed man shrugged. "I don't know. Please what's go—"

"Where were you going in such a hurry, Bucktooth Lo?"

"I'd forgotten an appointment, Lord. Oh it was very important. It's urgent and I will lose a fortune, sir, if I don't go immediately. May I now please go, Honored Lo—"

"No! Here's my search warrant. We're going to search and take away any papers th—"

At once both men began to protest strenuously. Again Armstrong cut them short. "Do you want to be taken to the border right now?" Both men blanched and shook their heads. "Good. Now, where's Thomas K. K. Lim?" Neither answered so Armstrong stabbed his finger at the younger of the two men. "You, Mr. Bucktooth Lo! Where's Thomas K. K. Lim?"

"In South America, Lord," Lo said nervously.

"Where?"

"I don't know, sir, he just shares the office. That's his fornicating desk." Bucktooth Lo waved a nervous hand at the far corner. There was a messy desk and a filing cabinet and a phone there. "I've done nothing wrong, Lord. Foreigner Lim's a stranger from the Golden Mountain. Fourth Cousin Tak here just rents him space, Lord. Foreigner Lim just comes and goes as it pleases him and is nothing to do with me. Is he a foul criminal? If there's anything wrong I don't know anything about it!"

"Then what do you know about the thieving of funds from the CARE program?"

"Eh?" Both men gaped at him.

"Informers have given us proof you're all thieving charity money that belongs to starving women and children!"

At once both began protesting their innocence.

"Enough! The judge will decide! You will go to headquarters and give statements." Then he switched back into English once more. "Sergeant, take them back to headquarters. Corporal, let's st—"

"Honored sir," Bucktooth Lo began in halting, nervous English, "if I may to talk, in office, plees?" He pointed at the inner, equally untidy and cluttered office.

"All right."

Armstrong followed Lo, towering over him. The man closed the door nervously and began talking Cantonese quickly and very quietly. "I don't know anything about anything criminal, Lord. If something's amiss it's those other two fornicators, I'm just an honest businessman who wants to make money and send his children to university in America an—"

"Yes. Of course. What did you want to say to me privately before you go down to police headquarters?"

The man smiled nervously and went to the desk and began to unlock a drawer. "If anyone's guilty it's not me, Lord. I don't know anything about anything." He opened the drawer. It was filled with used, red, 100-dollar notes. They were clipped into thousands. "If you'll let me go, Lord . . ." He grinned up at him, fingering the notes.

Armstrong's foot lashed out and the drawer slammed and caught Lo's fingertips and he let out a howl of pain. He tore the drawer open with his good hand. "Oh oh oh my fornic—"

Armstrong shoved his face close to the petrified Chinese. "Listen, you dogmeat turd, it's against the law to try to bribe a policeman and if you claim your fingers're police brutality I'll personally grind your fornicating Secret Sack to mincemeat!"

He leaned back against the desk, his heart pounding, sickness in his throat, enraged at the temptation and sight of all that money. How easy it would be to take it and pay his debts and have more than enough over to gamble on the market and at the races, and then to leave Hong Kong before it was too late.

So easy. So much more easy to take than to resist—this time or all the other thousand times. There must be 30, 40,000 in that drawer alone. And if there's one drawer full there must be others and if I lean on this bastard he'll cough up ten times this amount.

Roughly he reached out and grabbed the man's hand. Again the man cried out. One fingertip was mashed and Armstrong thought Lo would lose a couple of fingernails and have plenty of pain but that was all. He was angry with himself that he had lost his temper but he was tired and knew it was not just tiredness. "What do you know about Tsu-yan?"

"Wat? Me? Nothing. Tsu-yan who?"

Armstrong grabbed him and shook him. "Tsu-yan! The gun-runner Tsu-yan!"

"Nothing, Lord!"

"Liar! The Tsu-yan who visits Mr. Ng next door!"

"Tsu-yan? Oh him? Gun-runner? I didn't know he's a gun-runner! I always thought he was a businessman. He's another Northerner like Photographer Ng—"

"Who?"

"Photographer Ng, Lord. Vee Cee Ng from next door. He and this Tsu-yan never come in here or talk to us. . . . Oh I need a doctor . . . oh my han—"

"Where's Tsu-yan now?"

"I don't know, Lord . . . oh my fornicating hand, oh oh oh. . . . I swear by all the gods I don't know him. . . . oh oh oh. . . ."

Irritably Armstrong shoved him in a chair and jerked open the door. The three policemen and two secretaries stared at him silently. "Sergeant, take this bugger to HQ and charge him with trying to bribe a policeman. Look at this. . . ." He beckoned him in and pointed at the drawer.

Sergeant Yat's eyes widened. "*Dew neh loh moh!*"

"Count it and get both men to sign the amount as correct and take it to HQ with them and turn it in."

"Yes sir."

"Corporal, you start going through the files. I'm going next door. I'll be back shortly."

"Yes sir."

Armstrong strode out. He knew that this money would be counted quickly, and any other money in the offices—if this drawer was full others would be—then the amount to be turned in would be quickly negotiated by the principals, Sergeant Yat and Lo and Tak, and the rest split among them. Lo and Tak would believe him to be in for a major share and his own men would consider him mad not to be. Never mind. He didn't care. The money was stolen, and Sergeant Yat and his men were all good policemen and their pay totally inadequate for their responsibilities. A little *h'eung yau* wouldn't do them any harm, it would be a godsend.

Won't it?

In China you have to be pragmatic, he told himself grimly as he knocked on the door of 721 and went in. A good-looking secretary looked up from her lunch—a bowl of pure white rice and slivers of roast pork and jet green broccoli steaming nicely.

"Afternoon." Armstrong flashed his ID card. "I'd like to see Mr. Vee Cee Ng, please."

"Sorry, sir," the girl said, her English good and her eyes blank. "He's out. Out for lunch."

"Where?"

"At his club, I think. He—he won't be back today until five."

"Which club?"

She told him. He had never heard of it but that meant nothing as there were hundreds of private Chinese lunching or dining or at mah-jong clubs.

"What's your name?"

"Virginia Tong. Sir," she added as an afterthought.

"Do you mind if I look around?" He saw her eyes flash nervously. "Here's my search warrant."

She took it and read it and he thought, full marks, young lady. "Do you think you could wait, wait till five o'clock?" she asked.

"I'll take a short look now."

She shrugged and got up and opened the inner office. It was small and empty but for untidy desks, phones, filing cabinets, shipping posters and sailing schedules. Two inner doors let off it and a back door. He opened one door on the 720 side but it was a dank, evil-smelling toilet and dirty washbasin. The back door was bolted. He slid the bolts back and went onto the dingy back-stairs landing that served as a makeshift fire escape and alternate means of exit. He rebolted it, watched all the time by Virginia Tong. The last door, on the far side, was locked.

"Would you open it please?"

"Mr. Vee Cee has the only key, sir."

Armstrong sighed. "I do have a search warrant, Miss Tong, and the right to kick the door in, if necessary."

She stared back at him so he shrugged and stood away from the door and readied to kick it in. Truly.

"Just . . . just a moment, sir," she stammered. "I . . . I'll see if there . . . if he left his key before he went out."

"Good. Thank you." Armstrong watched her open a desk drawer and pretend to search, then another drawer and another and then, sensing his impatience, she found a key under a money box. "Ah, here it is!" she said as though a miracle had happened. He noticed she was perspiring now. Good, he thought. She unlocked the door and stood back. This door opened directly onto another. Armstrong opened it and whistled involuntarily. The room beyond was large, luxurious, thick-carpeted with elegant suede leather sofas and rosewood furniture and fine paintings. He wandered in. Virginia Tong watched from the doorway. The fine antique rosewood, tooled leather desk was bare and clean and polished, a bowl of flowers on it, and some framed photographs, all of a beaming Chinese leading in a garlanded racehorse, and one of the same Chinese in dinner jacket shaking hands with the governor, Dunross nearby.

"That's Mr. Ng?"

"Yes sir."

Top-quality hi-fi and record player were to one side, and a tall cocktail cabinet. Another doorway let off this room. He pushed the half-opened door aside. An elegant, very feminine bedroom with a huge, unmade king-sized bed, mirror-lined ceiling and a decorator's bathroom off it, with perfumes, aftershave lotions, gleaming modern fittings and many buckets of water.

"Interesting," he said and looked at her.

She said nothing, just waited.

Armstrong saw that she had nylon-clad legs and was very trim with well-groomed nails and hair. I'll bet she's a dragon, and expensive. He turned away from her and looked around thoughtfully. Clearly this self-contained apartment had been made out of the adjoining suite. Well, he told himself with a touch of envy, if you're rich and you want a private, secret flat for an afternoon's nooky behind your office there's no law against that. None. And none against having an attractive secretary. Lucky bastard. I wouldn't mind having one of these places myself.

Absently he opened a desk drawer. It was empty. All the drawers were empty. Then he went through the bedroom drawers but found nothing of interest. One cupboard contained a fine camera and some portable lighting equipment and cleaning equipment but nothing suspicious.

He came back into the main room satisfied that he had missed nothing. She was still watching him, and though she tried to hide it, he could sense a nervousness.

That's understandable, he told himself. If I were her and my boss was out and some rotten *quai loh* came prying I'd be nervous too. No harm in having a private place like this. Lots of rich people have them in Hong Kong. His eye was caught by the rosewood cocktail cabinet. The key in the lock beckoned him. He opened it. Nothing out of the ordinary. Then his sharp, well-trained eyes noticed the untoward width of the doors. A moment's inspection and he opened the false doors. His mouth dropped open.

The side walls of the cabinet were covered with dozens of photographs of Jade Gates in all their glory. Each photograph was neatly framed and tagged with a typed name and a date. Involuntarily he let out a bellow of embarrassed laughter, then glanced around. Virginia Tong had vanished. Quickly he scanned the names. Hers was third from the last.

Another paroxysm of laughter was barely contained. The policeman shook his head helplessly. What some buggers'll do for fun—and I suppose some ladies for money! I thought I'd seen it all but this . . . Photographer Ng, eh? So that's where the nickname came from.

Now over his initial shock, he studied the photographs. Each of them had been taken with the same lens from the same distance.

Good God, he thought after a minute, astounded, there's really quite a lot of difference between . . . I mean if you can forget what you're looking at and just look, well, there's a fantastic amount of difference in the shape and size of the whole, the position and protuberance of the Pearl on the Step, the quality and quantity of pubicity and . . . *ayeeyah* there's one piece *bat jam gai*. He looked at the name. Mona Leung—now where have I heard that name before? That's curious—Chinese usually consider lack of pubicity unlucky. Now why . . . oh my God! He peered at the next name tag to make sure. There was no mistake. Venus Poon. *Ayeeyah*, he thought elatedly, so that's hers, that's what she really looks like, the darling of the telly who daily projects such sweet, virginal innocence so beautifully!

He concentrated on her, his senses bemused. I suppose if you compare hers with, say, say Virginia Tong's, well she does have a certain delicacy. Yes, but if you want my considered opinion I'd still rather have had the mystery and not seen these at all. None of them.

Idly his eyes went from name to name. "Bloody hell," he said, recognizing one: Elizabeth Mithy. She was once a secretary at Struan's, one of the band of wanderers from the small towns in Australia and New Zealand, girls who aimlessly found their way to Hong Kong for a few weeks, to stay for months, perhaps years, to fill minor jobs until they married or vanished forever. I'll be damned. Liz Mithy!

Armstrong was trying to be dispassionate but he could not help comparing Caucasian with Chinese and he found no difference. Thank God for that, he told himself, and chuckled. Even so he was glad the photographs were black and white and not in color.

"Well," he said out loud, still very embarrassed, "there's no law against taking photos that I know of, and sticking them in your own cabinet. The young ladies must've cooperated. . . ." He grunted, amused and at the same time disgusted. Damned if I'll ever understand the Chinese! "Liz Mithy, eh?" he muttered. He had known her slightly when she was in the Colony, knew that she was quite wild, but what could have possessed her to pose for Ng? If her old man knew, he'd hemorrhage. Thank God we don't have children, Mary and I.

Be honest, you bleed for sons and daughters but you can't have them, at least Mary can't, so the doctors say—so you can't.

With an effort Armstrong buried that everlasting curse again and relocked the cabinet and walked out, closing the doors after him.

In the outer office Virginia Tong was polishing her nails, clearly furious.

"Can you get Mr. Ng on the phone, please?"

"No, not until four," she said sullenly without looking at him.

"Then please call Mr. Tsu-yan instead," Armstrong told her, stabbing in the dark.

Without looking up the number, she dialed, waited impatiently, chatted gutturally for a moment in Cantonese and slammed the phone down. "He's away. He's out of town and his office doesn't know where he is."

"When did you last see him?"

"Three or four days ago." Irritably she opened her appointments calendar and checked it. "It was Friday."

"Can I look at that please?"

She hesitated, shrugged and passed it over, then went back to polishing her nails.

Quickly he scanned the weeks and the months. Lots of names he knew: Richard Kwang, Jason Plumm, Dunross—Dunross several times—Thomas K. K. Lim—the mysterious American Chinese from next door—Johnjohn from the Victoria Bank, Donald McBride, Mata several times. Now who's Mata? he asked himself, never having heard the name before. He was about to give the calendar back to her then he flipped forward. "Saturday 10:00 A.M.—V. Banastasio." His heart twisted. This coming Saturday.

He said nothing, just put the appointment calendar back on her desk, and leaned back against one of the files, lost in thought. She paid no attention to him. The door opened.

"Excuse me, sir, phone for you!" Sergeant Yat said. He was looking much happier so Armstrong knew the negotiation must have been fruitful. He would have liked to know how much, exactly, but then, face would be involved and he would have to take action, one way or another.

"All right, Sergeant, stay here till I get back," he said, wanting to make sure no secret phone calls were made. Virginia Tong did not look up as he left.

In the other office Bucktooth Lo was still moaning, nursing his hand, and the other man, Big Hands Tak, was pretending to be nonchalant, going through some papers, loudly berating his secretary for her inefficiency. As he came in both men started loudly protesting their continued innocence and Lo groaned with increasing vigor.

"Quiet! Why did you jam your fingers in the drawer?" Armstrong asked and added without waiting for a reply, "People who try to bribe honest policemen deserve to be deported at once." In the aghast silence he picked up the phone. "Armstrong."

"Hello, Robert, this is Don, Don Smyth at East Aberdeen . . ."

"Oh, hello!" Armstrong was startled, not expecting to hear from the Snake, but he kept his voice polite though he loathed him and loathed what he was suspected of doing within his jurisdiction. It was one thing for constables and the lower ranks of Chinese police to supplement their income from illicit gambling. It was another for a British officer to sell influence, and to squeeze like an old-fashioned Mandarin. But though almost everyone believed Smyth was on the make, there was no proof, he had never been caught, and had never been investigated. Rumor had it that he was protected by certain VIP individuals who were deeply involved with him as well as in their own graft. "What's up?" he asked.

"Had a bit of luck. I think. You're heading up the John Chen kidnapping, aren't you?"

"That's right." Armstrong's interest soared. Smyth's graft had nothing to do with the quality of his police work—East Aberdeen had the lowest crime rate in the Colony. "Yes. What've you got?"

Smyth told him about the old *amah* and what had happened with Sergeant Mok and Spectacles Wu, then added, "He's a bright young chap, that, Robert. I'd recommend him for SI if you want to pass it on. Wu followed the old bird back to her fairly filthy lair, then called us. He obeys orders too, which is rare these days. On a hunch I told him to wait around and if she came out, to follow her. What do you think?"

"A twenty-four-carat lead!"

"What's your pleasure? Wait, or pull her in for real questioning?"

"Wait. I'll bet the Werewolf never comes back but it's worth waiting until tomorrow. Keep the place under surveillance and keep me posted."

"Good. Oh very good!"

Armstrong heard Smyth chortle down the phone and he could not think why he was so happy. Then he remembered the huge reward that the High Dragons had offered. "How's your arm?"

"It's my shoulder. Bloody thing's dislocated and I lost my favorite sodding hat. Apart from that everything's fine. Sergeant Mok's going through all our mug shots now and I've got one of my lads doing an Identi-Kit on him—I think I even saw the sod myself. His face is quite pockmarked. If we've got him on file we'll have him nailed by sundown."

"Excellent. How's it going down there?"

"Everything under control but it's bad. The Ho-Pak's still paying out but too slowly—everyone knows they're stalling. I hear it's the same all over the Colony. They're finished, Robert. The queue'll go on till every last cent's out. There's another run on the Vic here and no letup in the crowds. . . ."

Armstrong gasped. "The Vic?"

"Yes, they're handing out cash by the bagful and taking nothing in. Triads are swarming . . . the pickings must be huge. We arrested eight pickpockets and busted up twenty-odd fights. I'd say it's very bad."

"Surely the Vic's okay?"

"Not in Aberdeen it isn't, old lad. Me, I'm liquid. I've closed all my accounts. I took every cent out. I'm all right. If I were you I'd do the same."

Armstrong felt queasy. His life's savings were in the Victoria. "The Vic's got to be all right. All the government funds're in it."

"Right you are. But nothing in their constitution says your money's protected too. Well, I've got to get back to work."

"Yes. Thanks for the info. Sorry about your shoulder."

"I thought I was going to have my bloody head bashed in. The sods'd just started the old 'kill the *quai loh*' bit. I thought I was a goner."

Armstrong shivered in spite of himself. Ever since the '56 riots it was a recurring nightmare of his that he was back in that insane, screaming mob again. It was in Kowloon. The mob had just overturned the car with the

Swiss consul and his wife in it and set it afire. He and other policemen
had charged through the mob to rescue them. When they got to the car
the man was already dead and the young wife afire. By the time they'd
dragged her out, all her clothes had burned off her and her skin came
away like a pelt. And all around, men, women and young people were raving, "*Kill the quai loh . . .*"

He shivered again, his nostrils still smelling burned flesh. "Christ, what
a bastard!"

"Yes, but all in the day's work. I'll keep you posted. If that bloody
Werewolf comes back to Aberdeen he'll be in a net tighter than a gnat's
arsehole."

30

2:20 P.M.:

Phillip Chen stopped flipping through his mail, his face suddenly ashen. The envelope was marked, "Mr. Phillip Chen to open personally."

"What is it?" his wife asked.

"It's from them." Shakily he showed it to her. "The Werewolves."

"Oh!" They were at their lunch table that was set haphazardly in a corner of the living room of the house far up on the crest of Struan's Lookout. Nervously she put down her coffee cup. "Open it, Phillip. But, but better use your handkerchief in . . . in case of fingerprints," she added uneasily.

"Yes, yes of course, Dianne, how stupid of me!" Phillip Chen was looking very old. His coat was over his chair and his shirt damp. There was a slight breeze from the open window behind him but it was hot and humid and a brooding afternoon haze had settled over the Island. Carefully he used an ivory paper knife and unfolded the paper. "Yes, it's . . . it's from the Werewolves. It's . . . it's about the ransom."

"Read it out."

"All right: 'To Phillip Chen, compradore of the Noble House, greetings. I beg to inform you now how the ransom money is to be paid. 500,000 to you is as meaningless as a pig's scream in a slaughterhouse but to us poor farmers would be a heritage for our star—'"

"Liars!" Dianne hissed, her lovely gold and jade necklace glittering in a shaft of muted sunlight. "As if farmers would kidnap John or mutilate him like that. Dirty stinky foreign triads! Go on, Phillip."

"'. . . would be a heritage for our starving grandchildren. That you have already consulted the police is to us like pissing in the ocean. But now you will not consult. No. Now you will keep secret or the safety of your son will be endangered and he will not return and everything bad will be your own fault. Beware, our eyes are everywhere. If you try to betray us, the worst will happen and everything will be your own fault. Tonight at six o'clock I will phone you. Tell no one, not even your wife. Meanw—'"

"Dirty triads! Dirty whores' sons to try to spread trouble between husband and wife," Dianne said angrily.

"'. . . meanwhile prepare the ransom money in used 100-dollar notes. . . .'" Irritably Phillip Chen glanced at his watch. "I don't have much time to get to the bank. I'll have—"

"Finish the letter!"

"All right, be patient, my dear," he said placatingly, his overtaxed heart skipping a beat as he recognized the edge to her voice. "Where was I? Ah yes, '. . . notes. If you obey my instructions faithfully, you may have your son back tonight. . . .' Oh God I hope so," he said, breaking off momentarily, then continued, "'Do not consult the police or try to trap us. Our eyes are watching you even now. Written by the Werewolf.'" He took off his glasses. His eyes were red-rimmed and tired. Sweat was on his brow. "'Watching you even now?' Could one of the servants . . . or the chauffeur be in their pay?"

"No, no of course not. They've all been with us for years."

He wiped the sweat off, feeling dreadful, wanting John back, wanting him safe, wanting to strangle him. "That means nothing. I'd . . . I'd better call the police."

"Forget them! Forget them until we know what you have to do. Go to the bank. Get 200,000 only—you should be able to settle for that. If you get more you might be tempted to give it all to them if tonight . . . if they really mean what they say."

"Yes . . . very wise. If we could settle for that . . ." He hesitated. "What about the tai-pan? Do you think I should tell the tai-pan, Dianne? He, he might be able to help."

"Huh!" she said scornfully. "What help can he give us? We're dealing with dog-bone triads not foreign devil crooks. If we need help we have to stay with our own." Her eyes began boring into him. "And now you'd better tell me what's really the matter, why you were so angry the night before last and why you've been like a spiteful cat with a thorn in its rump ever since and not attending to business!"

"I've been attending to business," he said defensively.

"How many shares have you bought? Eh? Struan shares? Have you taken advantage of what the tai-pan told us about the coming boom? Do you remember what Old Blind Tung forecast?"

"Of course, of course I remember!" he stuttered. "I've, I've secretly doubled our holdings and have equally secret orders out with various brokers for half as much again."

Dianne Chen's abacus mind glowed at the thought of that vast profit, and all the private profit she would be making on all the shares she had bought on her own behalf, pledging her entire portfolio. But she kept her face cold and her voice icy. "And how much did you pay?"

"They averaged out at 28.90."

"Huh! According to today's paper Noble House opened at 28.80," she said with a disapproving sniff, furious that he had paid five cents less a share than she had. "You should have been at the market this morning instead of moping around here, sleeping your life away."

"I wasn't feeling very well, dear."

"It all goes back to the night before last. What sent you into that unbelievable rage? *Heya?*"

"It was nothing." He got up, hoping to flee. "Noth—"

"Sit down! *Nothing* that you shouted at me, me your faithful wife in front of the servants? *Nothing* that I was ordered into my own dining room like a common whore? *Heya?*" Her voice began rising and she let herself go, knowing instinctively that this was the perfect time, now that they were alone in the house, knowing that he was defenseless and she could press her advantage. "You think it's nothing that you abuse me, me who has given you the best years of her life, working and slaving and guarding you for twenty-three years? Me, Dianne Mai-wei T'Chung who has the blood of the great Dirk Struan in her veins, who came to you virgin, with property in Wanchai, North Point and even on Lan Tao, with stocks and shares and the best schooling in England? Me who never complains about your snoring and whoring or about the brat you sired out of that dance-hall girl you've sent to school in America!"

"*Eh?*"

"Oh I know all about you and her and all the others and all the other nasty things you do, and that you never loved me but just wanted my property and a perfect decoration to your drab life. . . ."

Phillip Chen was trying to close his ears but he could not. His heart was pounding. He hated rows and hated the shriek to her voice that, somehow, was perfectly tuned to set his teeth on edge, his brain oscillating and his bowels in turmoil. He tried to interrupt her but she overrode him, battering him, accusing him of all sorts of dalliances and mistakes and private matters that he was shocked she knew about.

". . . and what about your club?"

"Eh, what club?"

"The private Chinese lunch club with forty-three members called the 74 in a block off Pedder Street that contains a gourmet chef from Shanghai, teen-age hostesses and bedrooms and saunas and devices that dirty old men need to raise their Steamless Stalks? Eh?"

"It's nothing like that at all," Phillip Chen spluttered, aghast that she knew. "It's a pl—"

"Don't lie to me! You put up 87,000 good U.S. greenbacks as the down payment with Shitee T'Chung and those two mealy-mouthed friends of yours and even now pay 4,000 HK-a-month fees. Fees for what? You'd better . . . Where do you think you're going?"

Meekly he sat down again. "I—I was—I want to go to the bathroom."

"Huh! Whenever we have a discussion you want the bathroom! You're just ashamed of the way you treat me and guilty. . . ." Then, seeing him about to explode back at her, she switched abruptly, her voice crooningly gentle. "Poor Phillip! Poor boy! Why were you so angry? Who's hurt you?"

So he told her, and once he began the telling he felt better and his anguish and fear and fury started to melt away. Women are clever and cunning in these things, he told himself confidently, rushing on. He told her about opening John's safety deposit in the bank, about the letters to Linc Bartlett and about finding a duplicate key to his own safe in their bedroom. "I brought all the letters back," he said, almost in tears, "they're upstairs, you can read them for yourself. My own son! He's betrayed us!"

"My God, Phillip," she gasped, "if the tai-pan found out you and Father Chen-chen were keeping . . . if he knew he'd ruin us!"

"Yes, yes I know! That's why I've been so upset! By the rules of Dirk's legacy he has the right and the means. We'd be ruined. But, but that's not all. John knew where our secret safe was in the garden an—"

"*Wat?*"

"Yes, and he dug it up." He told her about the coin.

"*Ayeeyah!*" She stared at him in absolute shock, half her mind filled with terror, the other half with ecstasy, for now, whether John came back or not, he had destroyed himself. John would never inherit now! My Kevin's Number One Son now and future compradore to the Noble House! Then her fears drowned her excitement and she muttered, aghast, "If there's still a House of Chen."

"What? What did you say?"

"Nothing, never mind. Wait a moment, Phillip, let me think. Oh the rotten boy! How could John do this to us, we who have cherished him all his life! You . . . you'd better go to the bank. Get 300,000 out—in case you need to barter more. We must get John back at all costs. Would he keep the coin with him, on him, or would it be in his other safety deposit box?"

"It'd be in the box—or hidden at his flat in Sinclair Towers."

Her face closed. "How can we search that place with *her* in residence? That wife of his? That strumpet Barbara! If she suspects we're after something . . ." Her mind caught a vagrant thread. "Phillip, does it mean, *whoever* presents the coin gets whatever they want?"

"Yes."

"Eeeeee! What power!"

"Yes."

Now her mind was working cleanly. "Phillip," she said, in control again, everything else forgotten, "we need all the help we can get. Phone your cousin Four Fingers . . ." He looked at her, startled, then began to smile. ". . . arrange with him to have some of his street fighters follow you secretly to protect you when you pay over the ransom, then to follow the Werewolf to his lair and to rescue John whatever the cost. Whatever you do don't tell him about the coin—just that you want help to rescue poor John. That's it. We must get poor John back at all costs."

"Yes," he replied, much happier now. "Four Fingers is the perfect choice. He owes us a favor or two. I know where I can reach him this afternoon."

"Good. Off you go to the bank, but give me the key to the safe. I'll cancel my hairdressing appointment and I'll read John's papers at once."

"Very good." He got up immediately. "The key's upstairs," he said, lying, and hurried out, not wanting her prying into the safe. There were a number of things there he did not want her to know about. I'd better hide them somewhere else, he thought uneasily, just in case. His euphoria evaporated and his overwhelming anxiety returned. Oh my poor son, he told himself near tears. Whatever possessed you? I was a good father to you and you'll always be my heir and I've loved you like I loved your mother. Poor Jennifer, poor little thing, dying birthing my first-born son. O all gods: let me get my poor son back again, safe again, whatever he's done, let us extract ourselves from all this madness, and I'll endow a new temple for all of you equally!

The safe was behind the brass bedstead. He pulled it away from the wall, opened the safe and took out all of John's papers, then his very private deeds, letters and promissory notes which he stuffed into his coat pocket and went downstairs again.

"Here are John's letters," he said. "I thought I'd save you the trouble of moving the bed."

She noticed the bulge in his coat pocket but said nothing.

"I'll be back by 5:30 P.M. sharp."

"Good. Drive carefully," she said absently, her whole being concentrated on a single problem—how to get the coin for Kevin and herself. Secretly.

The phone rang. Phillip Chen stopped at the front door as she picked it up. "*Weyyyy?*" Her eyes glazed. "Oh hello, tai-pan, how're you today?" Phillip Chen blanched.

"Just fine thank you," Dunross said. "Is Phillip there?"

"Yes, yes just a minute." She could hear many voices behind Dunross's voice and she thought she heard an undercurrent of covered urgency which increased her dread. "Phillip, it's for you," she said, trying to keep the nervousness out of her voice. "The tai-pan!" She held up the phone, motioning him silently to keep the earpiece a little away from his ear so she could hear too.

"Yes, tai-pan?"

"Hello, Phillip. What're your plans this afternoon?"

"Nothing particular. I was just leaving to go to the bank, why?"

"Before you do that, drop by the exchange. The market's gone mad. The run on the Ho-Pak's Colony-wide now and the stock's teetering even though Richard's supporting it for all he's worth. Any moment it'll crash. The run's spilling over to lots of other banks, I hear—the Ching Prosperity, even the Vic . . ." Phillip Chen and his wife glanced at each other, perturbed. "I heard the Vic's got problems at Aberdeen and at Central. Everything's down, all our blue chips: the V and A, Kowloon Investments, Hong Kong Power, Rothwell-Gornt, Asian Properties, H.K.L.F., Zong Securities, Solomon Textiles, us . . . everyone."

"How many points are we off?"

"From this morning? Three points."

Phillip Chen gasped and almost dropped the phone. "What?"

"Yes," Dunross agreed pleasantly. "Someone's started rumors about us. It's all over the market that we're in trouble, that we can't pay Toda Shipping next week—nor the Orlin installment. I think now we're being sold short."

31

Gornt was sitting beside his stockbroker, Joseph Stern, in the exchange watching the big board delightedly. It was warm and very humid in the large room that was packed and noisy, phones ringing, sweating brokers, Chinese clerks and runners. Normally the exchange was calm and leisurely. Today it was not. Everyone was tense and concentrating. And uneasy. Many had their coats off.

Gornt's own stock was off a point but that did not bother him a bit. Struan's was down 3.50 now and Ho-Pak tottering. Time's running out for Struan's, he thought, everything's primed, everything's begun. Bartlett's money had been put into his Swiss bank within the hour, no strings —just 2 million transferred from an unknown account into his. Seven phone calls began the rumors. Another call to Japan confirmed the accuracy of the Struan payment dates. Yes, he thought, the attack's begun.

His attention went to the Ho-Pak listing on the board as some more sell offerings were written up by a broker. There were no immediate buyers.

Since he had secretly started selling Ho-Pak short on Monday just before the market closed at three o'clock—long before the run had started in earnest—he was millions ahead. On Monday the stock had sold at 28.60, and now, even with all the support Richard Kwang was giving it, it was down to 24.30—off more points than the stock had moved ever since the bank was formed eleven years ago.

4.30 times 500,000 makes 2,150,000, Gornt was thinking happily, all in honest-to-God HK currency if I wanted to buy back in right now which isn't bad for forty-eight hours of labor. But I won't buy back in yet, oh dear no. Not yet. I'm sure now that the stock will crash, if not today, tomorrow, Thursday. If not then, Friday—Monday at the latest, for no bank in the world can sustain such a run. Then, when the crash comes I'll buy back in at a few cents on the dollar and make twenty times half a million.

"Sell 200,000," he said, beginning to sell short openly now—the other shares hidden carefully among his secret nominees.

"Good God, Mr. Gornt," his stockbroker gasped. "The Ho-Pak'll have to put up almost 5 million to cover. That'll rock the whole market."

"Yes," he said jovially.

"We'll have a hell of a time borrowing the stock."

"Then do it."

Reluctantly his stockbroker began to leave but one of the phones rang. "Yes? Oh hello, Daytime Chang," he said in passable Cantonese. "What can I do for you?"

"I hope you can save all my money, Honorable Middleman. What is Noble House selling for?"

"25.30."

There was a screech of dismay. "Woe woe woe, there's barely half a dog-bone hour of trading left, woe woe woe! Please sell! Please sell all Noble House companies at once, Noble House, Good Luck Properties and Golden Ferry, also . . . what's Second Great Company selling at?"

"23.30."

"*Ayeeyah*, one point off from this morning? All gods bear witness to foul joss! Sell. Please to sell everything at once!"

"But Daytime Chang, the market's really quite sound an—"

"At once! Haven't you heard the rumors? Noble House will crash! Eeeee, sell, waste not a minute! Hold a moment, my associate Fung-tat wants to talk to you too."

"Yes, Third Toiletmaid Fung?"

"Just like Daytime Chang, Honorable Middleman! Sell! Before I'm lost! Sell and call us back with prices oh oh oh! Please hurry!"

He put the phone down. This was the fifth panic call he had had from old customers and he did not like it at all. Stupid to panic, he thought, checking his stock book. Between the two of them, Daytime Chang and Third Toiletmaid Fung had invested over 40,000 HK in various stocks. If he sold now they would be ahead, well ahead, but for the Struan losses today which would shave off most of their profit.

Joseph Stern was head of the firm of Stern and Jones that had been in Hong Kong for fifty years. They had become stockbrokers only since the war. Before that they were moneylenders, dealers in foreign exchange and ship's chandlers. He was a small, dark-haired man, mostly bald, in his sixties, and many people thought he had Chinese blood in him a few generations back.

He walked to the front of the board and stopped beside the column that listed Golden Ferry. He wrote down the combined Chang and Fung holdings in the sell column. It was a minor offering.

"I'll buy at 30 cents off listing," a broker said.

"There's no run on Golden Ferry," he said sharply.

"No, but it's a Struan company. Yes or no?"

"You know very well Golden Ferry's profits are up this quarter."

"Tough titty! Christ, isn't it bloody hot? Don't you think we could afford air conditioning in the exchange? Is it yes or no, old chap?"

Joseph Stern thought a moment. He did not want to fuel the nervousness. Only yesterday Golden Ferry had soared a dollar because all the business world knew their annual meeting was next week, it had been a good year and it was rumored there was going to be a stock split. But he knew the first rule of all exchanges: yesterday has nothing to do with today. The client had said, Sell.

"20 cents off market?" he asked.

"30. Last offer. What the hell do you care, you still get paid. Is it 30 off?"

"All right." Stern worked his way down the board, selling most of their stocks without trouble though each time he had to concede on price. With difficulty he borrowed the Ho-Pak stock. Now he stopped at the column listing the bank. There were many sell orders. Most of them were small figures. He wrote 200,000 at the bottom of the list in the sell column. A shock wave went through the room. He paid no attention, just looked at Forsythe, who was Richard Kwang's broker. Today he was the only buyer of Ho-Pak.

"Is Quillan trying to wreck the Ho-Pak?" a broker asked.

"It's already under siege. Do you want to buy the shares?"

"Not on your bloody life! Are you selling Struan short too?"

"No. No I'm not."

"Christ, I don't like this at all."

"Keep calm, Harry," someone else said. "The market's come alive for once, that's all that counts."

"Great day, what?" another broker said to him. "Is the crash on? I'm totally liquid myself, sold out this morning. Is it going to be a crash?"

"I don't know."

"Shocking about Struan's, isn't it?"

"Do you believe all the rumors?"

"No, of course not, but one word to the wise is sufficient they say, what?"

"I don't believe it."

"Struan's off 3½ points in one day, old boy, a lot of people believe it," another broker said. "I sold out my Struan's this morning. Will Richard sustain the run?"

"That's in the hands of . . ." Joseph Stern was going to say God but he knew that Richard Kwang's future was in the hands of his depositors and that they had already decided. "Joss," he said sadly.

"Yes. Thank God we get our commissions either way, feast or famine, jolly good, what?"

"Jolly good," Stern echoed, privately loathing the smug, self-satisfied upper-class English accent of the exclusive British public schools, schools that, because he was Jewish, he had never been able to attend. He saw

Forsythe put the phone down and look at the board. Once more he tapped his offering. Forsythe beckoned him. He walked through the throng, eyes watching him.

"Are you buying?" he asked.

"In due course, Joseph, old boy!" Forsythe added softly, "Between you and me, can't you get Quillan off our backs? I've reason to believe he's in cahoots with that berk Southerby."

"Is that a public accusation?"

"Oh come on, it's a private opinion, for chrissake! Haven't you read Haply's column? Tai-pans and a big bank spreading rumors? You know Richard's sound. Richard's as sound as . . . as the Rothschilds! You know Richard's got over a billion in res—"

"I saw the crash of '29, old chap. There were trillions in reserve then but even so everyone went broke. It's a matter of cash, credit and liquidity. And confidence. You'll buy our offering, yes or no?"

"Probably."

"How long can you keep this up?"

Forsythe looked at him. "Forever. I'm just a stockbroker. I just follow orders. Buy or sell I make a quarter of one percent."

"If the client pays."

"He has to. We have his stock, eh? We have rules. But while I think of it, go to hell."

Stern laughed. "I'm British, I'm going to heaven, didn't you know." Uneasily, he walked back to his desk. "I think he'll buy before the market closes."

It was a quarter to three. "Good," Gornt said. "Now I wa—" He stopped. They both looked back as there was an undercurrent. Dunross was escorting Casey and Linc Bartlett to the desk of Alan Holdbrook—Struan's in-house broker—on the other side of the hall.

"I thought he'd left for the day," Gornt said with a sneer.

"The tai-pan never runs away from trouble. It's not in his nature." Stern watched them thoughtfully. "They look pretty friendly. Perhaps the rumors are all wrong and Ian'll make the Par-Con deal and make the payments."

"He can't. That deal's going to fall through," Gornt said. "Bartlett's no fool. Bartlett'd be mad to throw in with that tottering empire."

"I didn't even know until a few hours ago that Struan's were indebted to the Orlin Bank. Or that the Toda payments were due in a week or so. Or the even more nonsensical rumor that the Vic won't support the Noble House. Lot of nonsense. I called Havergill and that's what he said."

"What else would he say?"

After a pause, Stern said, "Curious that all that news surfaced today."

"Very. Sell 200,000 Struan's."

Stern's eyes widened and he plucked at his bushy eyebrows. "Mr. Gornt, don't you think th—"

"No. Please do as I ask."

"I think you're wrong this time. The tai-pan's too clever. He'll get all the support he needs. You'll get burned."

"Times change. People change. If Struan's have extended themselves and can't pay . . . Well, my dear fellow, this's Hong Kong and I hope the buggers go to the wall. Make it 300,000."

"Sell at what figure, Mr. Gornt?"

"At market."

"It'll take time to borrow the shares. I'll have to sell in much smaller lots. I'll hav—"

"Are you suggesting my credit's not good enough or you can't perform normal stockbroking functions?"

"No. No of course not," Stern replied, not wanting to offend his biggest customer.

"Good, then sell Struan's short. Now."

Gornt watched him walk away. His heart was beating nicely.

Stern went to Sir Luis Basilio of the old stockbroking firm of Basilio and Sons, who had a great block of Struan's personally, as well as many substantial clients with more. He borrowed the stock then walked to the board and wrote the huge offering in the sell column. The chalk scraped loudly. Gradually the room fell silent. Eyes switched to Dunross and Alan Holdbrook and the Americans, then to Gornt and back to Dunross again. Gornt saw Linc Bartlett and Casey watching him and he was glad she was there. Casey was wearing a yellow silk skirt and blouse, very Californian, a green scarf tying her golden hair back. Why is she so sexual, Gornt asked himself absently. A strange invitation seemed to surround her. Why? Is it because no man yet has ever satisfied her?

He smiled at her, nodding slightly. She half-smiled back and he thought he noticed a shadow there. His greeting to Bartlett was polite and returned equally politely. His eyes held Dunross and the two men stared at each other.

The silence mounted. Someone coughed nervously. Everyone was conscious of the immensity of the offering and the implications of it.

Stern tapped his offering again. Holdbrook leaned forward and consulted with Dunross who half shrugged and shook his head, then began talking quietly to Bartlett and Casey.

Joseph Stern waited. Then someone offered to buy a portion and they haggled back and forth. Soon 50,000 shares had changed hands and the new market price was 24.90. He changed the 300,000 to 250,000 and again waited. He sold a few more but the bulk remained. Then, as there were no takers, he came back to his seat. He was sweating.

"If that number stays there overnight it'll do Struan's no good at all."

"Yes." Gornt still watched Casey. She was listening intently to Dunross. He sat back and thought a moment. "Sell another 100,000 Ho-Pak—and 200,000 Struan's."

"Good God, Mr. Gornt, if Struan's gets brought down the whole market'll totter, even your own company'll lose."

"There'll be an adjustment, lots of adjustments, certainly."

"There'll be a bloodbath. If Struan's go, so will other companies, thousands of investors'll be wiped out an—"

"I really don't need a lecture on Hong Kong economics, Mr. Stern," Gornt said coldly. "If you don't want to follow instructions I'll take my business elsewhere."

Stern flushed. "I'll . . . I'll have to round up the shares first. That number . . . to get that sum . . ."

"Then I suggest you hurry up! I want that on the board today!" Gornt watched him go, enjoying the moment immensely. Cocky bastard, he was thinking. Stockbrokers are just parasites, every one of them. He felt quite safe. Bartlett's money was in his account. He could buy back Ho-Pak and Struan's even now and be millions ahead. Contentedly his eyes strayed back to Casey. She was watching him. He could read nothing in her expression.

Joseph Stern was weaving through the brokers. Again he stopped at the Basilio desk. Sir Luis Basilio looked away from the board and smiled up at him. "So, Joseph? You want to borrow more Noble House shares?"

"Yes, please."

"For Quillan?" Sir Luis asked. He was a fine old man, small, elegant, very thin, and in his seventies—this year's chairman of the committee that ran the exchange.

"Yes."

"Come, sit down, let's talk a moment, old friend. How many do you want now?"

"200,000."

Sir Luis frowned. "300,000 on the board—another 2? Is this an all-out attack?"

"He . . . he didn't say that but I think it is."

"It's a great pity those two can't make peace with one another."

"Yes."

The older man thought a moment, then said even more quietly, "I'm considering suspending dealing in Ho-Pak shares, and, since lunch, Noble House shares. I'm very worried. At this precise moment a Ho-Pak crash, coupled with a Noble House crash, could wreck the whole market. Madonna, it's unthinkable for the Noble House to crash, it would pull down hundreds of us, perhaps all Hong Kong, unthinkable!"

"Perhaps the Noble House needs overhauling. Can I borrow 200,000 shares?"

"First answer me this, yes or no, and if yes when: Should we suspend the Ho-Pak? Should we suspend Struan's? I've polled all the other members of the committee except you. They're divided almost equally."

"Neither have ever been suspended. It would be bad to suspend either.

This's a free society—in its best sense, I think. You should let it work itself
out, let them sort themselves out, the Struans, and the Gornts and all the
rest, let the best get to the top and the worst . . ." Stern shook his head
wearily. "Ah but it's easy for me to say that, Luis, I'm not a big investor in
either."

"Where's your money?"

"Diamonds. All Jews need small things, things you can carry and things
you can hide, things you can convert easily."

"There's no need for you to be afraid here, Joseph. How many years
has your family been here and prospered? Look at Solomon—surely he and
his family are the richest in all Asia."

"For Jews fear is a way of life. And being hated."

Again the old man sighed. "Ah this world, this lovely world, how lovely
it should be." A phone rang and he picked it up delicately, his hands tiny,
his Portuguese sounding sweet and liquid to Stern though he understood
none of it. He only caught "Señor Mata" said deferentially several times
but the name meant nothing to him. In a moment Sir Luis replaced the
receiver very thoughtfully. "The financial secretary called just after lunch,
greatly perturbed. There's a deputation from Parliament here and a bank
crash would look extremely bad for all of us," he said. He smiled a pixyish
smile. "I suggested he introduce legislation for the governor's signature to
govern banks like they had in England and the poor fellow almost had a
fit. I really mustn't pull his leg so much." Stern smiled with him. "As if
we need government interference here!" The eyes sharpened. "So Joseph,
do you vote to let well alone—or suspend either or both of the stocks, if so
when?"

Stern glanced at the clock. If he went to the board now he would have
plenty of time to write up both sell offerings and still be able to challenge
Forsythe. It was a good feeling to know that he held the fate of both
houses in his hands, if only temporarily. "Perhaps it would be very good,
perhaps bad. What's the voting so far?"

"I said, almost equal." There was another burst of excitement and both
men looked up. Some more Struan shares were changing hands. The new
market price dropped to 24.70. Now Phillip Chen was leaning over Holdbrook's desk.

"Poor Phillip, he doesn't look well at all," Sir Luis said compassionately.

"No. Pity about John. I liked him. What about the Werewolves? Do
you think the papers are overplaying it?"

"No. No, I don't." The old eyes twinkled. "No more than you, Joseph."

"What?"

"You've decided to pass. You want to let today's time run out, don't
you? That's what you want, isn't it?"

"What better solution could there be?"

"If I wasn't so old I'd agree with you. But being so old and not knowing about tomorrow, or if I shall live to see tomorrow, I prefer my drama

today. Very well. I'll discount your vote this time and now the committee's deadlocked so I will decide, as I'm allowed to do. You can borrow 200,000 Noble House shares until Friday, Friday at two. Then I may ask for them back—I have to think of my own House, eh?" The sharp but kindly eyes in the lined face urged Stern to his feet. "What are you going to do now, my friend?"

Joseph Stern smiled sadly. "I'm a stockbroker."

He went to the board and wrote in the Ho-Pak sell column with a firm hand. Then in the new silence he went to the Struan column and wrote the figure clearly, conscious that he was on center stage now. He could feel the hate and the envy. More than 500,000 Noble House shares were now on offer, more than at any one time in the history of the exchange. He waited, wanting the clock to run out. There was a flurry of interest as Soorjani, the Parsee, bought some blocks of shares but it was well known he was nominee for many of the Struan and Dunross family and supporters. And though he bought 150,000, it made little difference to the enormity of Gornt's offering. The quiet was hurting. One minute to go now.

"*We buy!*" The tai-pan's voice shattered the silence.

"All my shares?" Stern asked hoarsely, his heart racing.

"Yes. Yours and all the rest. At market!"

Gornt was on his feet. "With what?" he asked sardonically. "That's almost 9 million cash."

Dunross was on his feet too, a taunting half-smile on his face. "The Noble House is good for that—and millions more. Has anyone ever doubted it?"

"I doubt it—and I sell short tomorrow!"

At that moment the finish bell sounded shrilly, the tension broke and there was a roar of approval.

"Christ what a day. . . ."

"Good old tai-pan. . . ."

"Couldn't stand much more of that . . ."

"Is Gornt going to beat him this time . . . ?"

"Maybe those rumors are all nonsense . . ."

"Christ I made a bloody fortune in commissions . . ."

"I think Ian's running scared. . . ."

"Don't forget he's got five days to pay for the shares . . ."

"He can't buy like that tomorrow . . ."

"Christ, tomorrow! What's going to happen tomorrow . . ."

Casey shifted in her seat, her heart thumping. She pried her eyes off Gornt and Dunross and looked back at Bartlett, who sat staring at the board, whistling tonelessly. She was awed—awed and a little frightened.

Just before coming here to meet Dunross, Linc Bartlett had told her his plan, about his call to Gornt and all about the meeting with him. "Now you know it all, Casey," he had said softly, grinning at her. "Now they're both set up and we control the battlefield, all for 2 million. Both're at each other's throats, both going for the jugular, each ready to cannibalize the other. Now we wait. Monday's D Day. If Gornt wins, we win. If Dunross wins, we win. Either way we become the Noble House."

32

Alexi Travkin who trained the racehorses of the Noble House went up the busy alley off Nathan Road in Kowloon and into the Green Dragon Restaurant. He wore a small .38 under his left arm and his walk was light for a man of his age.

The restaurant was small, ordinary and drab, with no tablecloths on the dozen or so tables. At one of them, four Chinese were noisily eating soup and noodles, and, as he came in, a bored waiter by the cash register looked up from his racing form and began to get up with a menu. Travkin shook his head and walked through the archway that led to the back.

The little room contained four tables. It was empty but for one man.

"*Zdrastvuytye,*" Suslev said lazily, his light clothes well cut.

"*Zdrastvuytye,*" Travkin replied, his Slavic eyes narrowing even more. Then he continued in Russian, "Who're you?"

"A friend, Highness."

"Please don't call me that, I'm not a highness. Who're you?"

"Still a friend. Once you were a prince. Will you join me?" Suslev politely motioned to a chair. There was an opened bottle of vodka on his table and two glasses. "Your father Nicoli Petrovitch was a prince too, like his father and back for generations, Prince of Kurgan and even Tobol."

"You talk in ciphers, friend," Travkin said, outwardly calm, and sat opposite him. The feel of the .38 took away some of his apprehension. "From your accent you're Muscovite—and Georgian."

Suslev laughed. "Your ear is very good, Prince Kurgan. Yes I'm Muscovite but I was born in Georgia. My name's unimportant but I'm a friend wh—"

"Of me, Russia or the Soviets?"

"Of all three. Vodka?" Suslev asked, lifting the bottle.

"Why not?" Travkin watched the other man pour the two glasses, then without hesitation he picked up the wrong glass, the one farthest from him, and lifted it. "Health!"

Without hesitation Suslev picked up the other, touched glasses, drained it and poured again. "Health!"

"You're the man who wrote to me?"

"I have news of your wife."

"I have no wife. What do you want from me, *friend?*" The way Travkin used the word it was an insult. He saw the flash of anger as Suslev looked up from his glass and he readied.

"I excuse your rudeness this once, Alexi Ivanovitch," Suslev said with dignity. "You've no cause to be rude to me. None. Have I insulted you?"

"Who are you?"

"Your wife's name is Nestorova Mikail and her father was Prince Anotoli Zergeyev whose lands straddle Karaganda, which is not so far away from your own family lands east of the Urals. He was a Kazaki, wasn't he, a great prince of the Kazaki, whom some people call Cossacks?"

Travkin kept his gnarled hands still and his face impassive, but he could not keep the blood from draining from his face. He reached out and poured two more glasses, the bottle still half full. He sipped the spirit. "This's good vodka, not like the piss in Hong Kong. Where did you get it?"

"Vladivostok."

"Ah. Once I was there. It's a flat dirty town but the vodka's good. Now, what's your real name and what do you want?"

"You know Ian Dunross well?"

Travkin was startled. "I train his horses . . . I've . . . this is my third year, why?"

"Would you like to see the Princess Nestor—"

"Good sweet Christ Jesus whoever you are, I told you I have no wife. Now, for the last time, what do you want from me?"

Suslev filled his glass and his voice was even more kindly. "Alexi Ivanovitch Travkin, your wife the princess today is sixty-three. She lives in Yakutsk on th—"

"On the Lena? In Siberia?" Travkin felt his heart about to explode. "What *gulag* is that, you turd?"

Through the archway in the other room, which was empty now, the waiter looked up momentarily, then yawned and went on reading.

"It's not a *gulag*, why should it be a *gulag?*" Suslev said, his voice hardening. "The princess went there of her own accord. She's lived there since she left Kurgan. Her . . ." Suslev's hand went into his pocket and he brought out his wallet. "This is her *dacha* in Yakutsk," he said, putting down a photograph. "It belonged to her family, I believe." The cottage was snowbound, within a nice glade of trees, the fences well kept, and it was pretty with good smoke coming out of the chimney. A tiny bundled-up figure waved gaily at the camera—too far away for the face to be seen clearly.

"And that's my wife?" Travkin said, his voice raw.

"Yes."

"I don't believe you!"

Suslev put down a new snapshot. A portrait. The lady was white-haired and in her fifties or sixties and though the cares of a whole world marked her, her face was still elegant, still patrician. The warmth of her smile reached out and broke him.

"You . . . you KGB turd," he said hoarsely, sure that he recognized her. "You filthy rotten mother-eating . . ."

"To have found her?" Suslev said angrily. "To have seen that she was looked after and left in peace and not troubled and not sent to . . . to the correction places she and your whole class deserved?" Irritably he poured himself another drink. "I'm Russian and proud of it—you're émigré and you left. My father and his were *owned* by one of your class. My father died at the barricades in 1916, and my mother—and before they died they were starving. They . . ." With an effort he stopped. Then he said in a different voice, "I agree there's much to forgive and much to forget on both sides, and that's all past now but I tell you we Soviets, we're not all animals—not all of us. We're not all like Bloody Beria and the murdering archfiend Stalin. . . . Not everyone." He found his pack of cigarettes. "Do you smoke?"

"No. Are you KGB or GRU?" KGB stood for the Committee for State Security; GRU for the Chief Intelligence Directorate of the General Staff. This was not the first time Travkin had been approached by one of them. Before, he had always been able to slough them off with his drab, unimportant cover story. But now he was trapped. This one knew too much about him, too much truth. Who are you, bastard? And what do you really want? he thought as he watched Suslev light a cigarette.

"Your wife knows you're alive."

"Impossible. She's dead. She was murdered by mobs when our pal— when our house in Kurgan was sacked, put to the torch, torn apart—the prettiest, most unarmed mansion within a hundred miles."

"The masses had the right t—"

"Those weren't my people and they were led by imported Trotskyites who afterwards murdered my peasants by the thousands—until they themselves were all purged by more of their own vermin."

"Perhaps, perhaps not," Suslev said coldly. "Even so, Prince of Kurgan and Tobol, she escaped with one old servant and fled east thinking she could find you, could escape after you through Siberia to Manchuria. The servant came originally from Austria. Pavchen was her name."

The breath seemed to have vanished from Travkin's lungs. "More lies," he heard himself say, no longer believing it, his spirit ripped apart by her lovely smile. "My wife's dead. She'd never go so far north."

"Ah but she did. Her escape train was diverted northwards. It was autumn. Already the first snows had come so she decided to wait the winter out in Yakutsk. She had to. . . ." Suslev put down another snapshot.

". . . she was with child. This is your son and his family. It was taken last year." The man was good-looking, in his forties, wearing a Soviet major's air force uniform, self-consciously smiling at the camera, his arm around a fine woman in her thirties with three happy children, a babe, a beaming girl of six or seven missing front teeth, a boy of about ten trying to be serious. "Your wife called him Pietor Ivanovitch after your grandfather."

Travkin did not touch the photo. He just stared at it, his face chalky. Then he pried his eyes away and poured a drink for himself, and as an afterthought, one for Suslev. "It's . . . it's all a brilliant reconstruction," he said, trying to sound convincing. "Brilliant."

"The child's name is Victoria, the girl is Nichola after your grandmother. The boy is Alexi. Major Ivanovitch is a bomber pilot."

Travkin said nothing. His eyes went back to the portrait of the beautiful old lady and he was near tears but his voice was still controlled. "She knows I'm alive, eh?"

"Yes."

"For how long?"

"Three months. About three months ago. One of our people told her."

"Who're they?"

"Do you want to see her?"

"Why only three months—why not a year—three years?"

"It was only six months ago we discovered who you were."

"How did you do that?"

"Did you expect to remain anonymous forever?"

"If she knows I'm alive and one of your people told her then she'd've written. . . . Yes. They would have asked her to do that if . . ." Travkin's voice was strange. He felt out of himself, in a nightmare, as he tried to think clearly. "She would have written a letter."

"She has. I will give it to you within the next few days. Do you want to see her?"

Travkin forced his agony down. He motioned at the family portrait. "And . . . and he knows I'm alive too?"

"No. None of them do. That was not at our suggestion, Alexi Ivanovitch. It was your wife's idea. For safety—to protect him, she thought. As if we would wreak vengeance for the sins of the fathers on the sons! She waited out two winters in Yakutsk. By that time peace had come to Russia so she stayed. By that time she presumed you dead, though she hoped you were alive. The boy was brought up believing you dead, and knew nothing of you. He still doesn't. As you can see, he's a credit to you both. He was head of his local school, then went to university as all gifted children do nowadays. . . . Do you know, Alexi Ivanovitch, in my day I was the first of my whole province ever to get to a university, the very first, ever from a *peasant* family. We're fair in Russia today."

"How many corpses have you made to become what you are now?"

"A few," Suslev said darkly, "all of them criminals or enemies of Russia."

"Tell me about them."

"I will. One day."

"Did you fight the last war—or were you a commissar?"

"Sixteenth Tank Corps, Forty-fifth Army. I was at Sebastopol . . . and at Berlin. Tank commander. Do you want to see your wife?"

"More than my whole life is worth, if this really is my wife and if she's alive."

"She is. I can arrange it."

"Where?"

"Vladivostok."

"No, here in Hong Kong."

"Sorry, that's impossible."

"Of course." Travkin laughed without mirth. "Of course, friend. Drink?" He poured the last of the vodka, splitting it equally. "Health!"

Suslev stared at him. Then he looked down at the portrait and the snapshot of the air force major and his family and picked them up, lost in thought. The silence grew. He scratched his beard. Then he said decisively, "All right. Here in Hong Kong," and Travkin's heart leapt.

"In return for what?"

Suslev stubbed his cigarette out. "Information. And cooperation."

"What?"

"I want to know everything you know about the tai-pan of the Noble House, everything you did in China, who you know, who you met."

"And the cooperation?"

"I will tell you later."

"And in return you'll bring my wife to Hong Kong?"

"Yes."

"When?"

"By Christmas."

"How can I trust you?"

"You can't. But if you cooperate she will be here at Christmas." Travkin was watching the two photos Suslev toyed with in his fingers, then he saw the look in his eyes and his stomach twisted. "Either way, you must be honest with me. With or without your wife, Prince Kurgan, we always have your son and your grandchildren hostage."

Travkin sipped his drink, making it last. "Now I believe you are what you are. Where do you want to start?"

"The tai-pan. But first I want to piss." Suslev got up and asked the waiter where the toilet was and went out through the kitchen.

Now that Travkin was alone despair gripped him. He picked up the snapshot of the cottage that was still on the table and peered at it. Tears filled his eyes. He brushed them away and felt the gun that nestled beneath his shoulder but that did not help him now. With all his inner strength he resolved to be wise and not believe, but in his heart he knew he had seen her picture and that he would do anything, risk anything to see her.

For years he had tried to avoid these hunters, knowing that he was always pursued. He had been the leader of the Whites in his area across the Trans-Siberian Railroad and he had killed many Reds. At length he had wearied of the killing and in 1919 had left for Shanghai and a new home until the Japanese armies came, escaping them to join Chinese guerrillas, fighting his way south and west to Chungking, there to join other marauders, English, French, Australian, Chinese—anyone who would pay —until the Japanese unconditionally surrendered, and so back to Shanghai again, soon to flee once more. Always fleeing, he thought.

By the blood of Christ, my darling, I know you're dead. I know it. I was told by someone who saw the mob sack our palace, saw them swarm over you. . . .

But now?

Are you really alive?

Travkin looked at the kitchen door with hatred, knowing he would forever be haunted until he was certain about her. Who is that shit eater? he thought. How did they find me?

Grimly he waited and waited and then in sudden panic went to find him. The toilet was empty. He rushed into the street but it was filled with other people. The man had vanished.

There was a vile taste in Travkin's mouth now and he was sick with apprehension. In the name of God, what does he want with the tai-pan?

33

"Hello, Ian," Penelope said. "You're home early! How was your day?"

"Fine, fine," Dunross said absently. Apart from all the disasters, just before he left the office he had had a call from Brian Kwok saying, among other things, that AMG was probably murdered and warned him to take serious precautions.

"Oh, it was one of those, was it?" she said at once. "How about a drink? Yes. How about champagne?"

"Good idea." Then he noticed her smile and smiled back and felt much better. "Penn, you're a mind reader!" He tossed his briefcase onto a sideboard and followed her into one of the sitting rooms of the Great House. The champagne was already in an ice bucket, opened, with two glasses partially filled and another waiting for him in the ice.

"Kathy's upstairs. She's reading Glenna a bedtime story," Penelope said, pouring for him. "She . . . she's just told me about . . . about the, about the disease."

"Oh." He accepted the glass. "Thanks. How's Andrew taking it? He didn't mention anything today."

"She's going to tell him tonight. The champagne was to give her some courage." Penelope looked up at him, anguished. "She's going to be all right, isn't she, Ian?"

"I think so. I had a long talk with Doc Tooley. He was encouraging, gave me the names of the top three experts in England and another three in America. I've cabled for appointments with the three in England and Doc Ferguson's air-mailing them case histories—they'll be there when you arrive."

She sipped her wine. A light breeze made the sultry day much better. The French doors were open to the garden. It was near six o'clock. "Do you think we should go at once? Will a few days make any difference?"

"I don't think so."

"But we should go?"

"If it were you, Penn, we'd've been on the first plane the very first moment."

"Yes. If I'd told you."

"You would have told me."

"Yes. I suppose I would. I've made reservations for tomorrow. Kathy thought it a good idea too. The BOAC flight."

He was startled. "Claudia never mentioned it."

She smiled. "I made them myself. I'm really quite capable. I've reservations for Glenna, me and Kathy. We could take the case histories with us. I thought Kathy should go without any of her children. They'll be perfectly all right with the *amahs*."

"Yes, that's much the best. Doc Tooley was adamant about her taking it easy. That's the main thing he said, lots of rest." Dunross smiled at her. "Thanks, Penn."

She was staring at the beads of condensation on the outside of the bottle and the ice bucket. "Bloody awful, isn't it?"

"Worse, Penn. There's no cure. He thinks . . . he thinks the medication will arrest it." He finished his glass and poured for both of them. "Any messages?"

"Oh, sorry! Yes, they're on the sideboard. There was a long-distance call from Marseilles a moment ago."

"Susanne?"

"No. A Mr. Deland."

"He's our agent there."

"Rotten about young Borge."

"Yes." Dunross skimmed the messages. Johnjohn at the bank, Holdbrook, Phillip Chen, and the inevitable catchall "please call Claudia." He sighed. It was only half an hour since he left the office and he was going to call her anyway. No rest for the wicked, he thought, and smiled to himself.

He had enjoyed besting Gornt at the exchange. That he did not have the money at the moment to pay did not worry him. There's five days of grace, he thought. Everything's covered—with joss. Ah yes, joss!

Since his stockbroker had called him in panic at a few minutes past ten about the rumors sweeping the exchange and how their stock was shifting, he had been bolstering his defenses against the sudden, unexpected attack. With Phillip Chen, Holdbrook, Gavallan and deVille he had marshaled all the major stockholders they could reach and told them that the rumors Struan's couldn't meet their obligations were nonsense and suggested they refuse to lend Gornt any big blocks of Struan stock but to keep him dangling, letting him have a few shares here and there. He told the selected few in the strictest confidence that the Par-Con deal was signed, sealed and about to be chopped, and that this was a marvelous opportunity to smash Rothwell-Gornt once and for all.

"If Gornt sells short, let him. We pretend to be vulnerable but support the stock. Then Friday we announce, our stock'll soar and he'll lose his shirt, tie and trousers," he had told them all. "We get back our airline along with his, and with his ships and ours together, we'll dominate all air and surface inbound and outbound trade in Asia."

If we could really smash Gornt, he thought fervently, we'd be safe for generations. And we could, given joss, Par-Con and more joss. Christ, but it's going to be very dicey!

He had exuded confidence all day, not feeling confident at all. Many of his big stockholders had called nervously but he had quieted them. Both Tightfist Tung and Four Finger Wu owned major blocks of stock through devious nominees. He had phoned both this afternoon to get their agreement not to loan or sell their major holdings for the next week or so. Both had agreed but it had not been easy with either of them.

All in all, Dunross thought, I've fought off the initial onslaught. Tomorrow will tell the real story—or Friday: is Bartlett enemy, friend or Judas?

He felt his anger rising but he pushed it back. Be calm, he told himself, think calmly. I will but it's bloody curious that everything Bartlett said the night of the party—all those very secret things he had so readily and suddenly produced to shatter my defenses—miraculously went through the market today like a typhoon. Who's the spy? Who gave him the info? Is he the Sevrin spy too? Well, never mind for the moment, everything's covered. I think.

Dunross went to the phone and asked the operator to get Mr. Deland, person to person, and to call him back.

"Would Susanne be there yet?" Penelope asked.

"I think so. If her plane's on time. It's about eleven, Marseilles time, so it shouldn't be an emergency. Bloody shame about Borge! I liked him."

"What's Avril going to do?"

"She's going to be all right. Avril's going to come home to bring up the child and soon she'll meet a Prince Charming, a new one, and her son'll join Struan's and meanwhile she'll be protected and cherished."

"Do you believe that, Ian—about the Prince Charming?"

"Yes," he said firmly. "I believe everything will be all right. It's going to be all right, Penn, for her, for Kathy, for . . . for everyone."

"You can't carry everyone, Ian."

"I know. But no one, no one in the family will ever need for anything while I'm alive and that's going to be forever."

His wife looked at him and remembered the first time she had seen him, a godlike youth sitting in his shattered fighter that should have crashed but somehow miraculously hadn't. Ian, just sitting there, then getting out, holding the terror down, she seeing in his eyes for the first time what death was like but him dominating it and coming back and just accepting the cup of tea saying, "Oh, jolly good, thanks. You're new, aren't you?" in his lovely patrician accent that was so far from her own background.

Such a long time ago, a thousand years ago, another lifetime, she thought. Such wonderful ghastly terrible beautiful agonizing days: will he die today or come back today? Will I die today, in the morning bombing or in the evening one? Where's Dad and Mum and is the phone just bombed out of service as usual or has the rotten little terraced house in Streatham vanished along with all the other thousands like it?

One day it had and then she had no past. Just Ian and his arms and strength and confidence, and she terrified that he would go like all the others. That was the worst part, she told herself. The waiting and anticipating and knowing how mortal the Few were and we all are. My God how quickly we had to grow up!

"I hope it is forever, darling," she said in her cool, flat voice, wanting to hide the immensity of her love. "Yes. I want you to be immortal!"

He grinned at her, loving her. "I'm immortal, Penn, never mind. After I'm dead I'll still be watching over you and Glenna and Duncan and Adryon and all the rest."

She watched him. "Like Dirk Struan does?"

"No," he said serious now. "He's a presence I'll never match. He's perpetual—I'm temporary." His eyes were watching hers. "You're rather serious tonight, aren't you?"

"You're rather serious tonight, aren't you?"

They laughed.

She said, "I was just thinking how transient life is, how violent, unexpected, how cruel. First John Chen and now Borge, Kathy . . ." A little shiver went through her, ever petrified she would lose him. "Who's next?"

"Any one of us. Meanwhile be Chinese. Remember under heaven all crows are black. Life is good. Gods make mistakes and go to sleep so we do the best we can and never trust a *quai loh!*"

She laughed, at peace again. "There are times, Ian Struan Dunross, when I quite like you. Do you th—" The phone rang and she stopped and thought, God curse that bloody phone. If I was omnipotent I'd outlaw all phones after 6:00 P.M. but then poor Ian'd go mad, and the bloody Noble House'd crumble and that's poor Ian's life. I'm second, so are the children and that's as it should be. Isn't it?

"Oh hello, Lando," Dunross was saying, "what's new?"

"Hope I'm not disturbing you, tai-pan."

"Not at all," he replied, all his energy concentrated. "I've just got in. What can I do for you?"

"Sorry, but I'm withdrawing the 15 million support I promised for tomorrow. Temporarily. The market makes me nervous."

"Nothing to worry about," Dunross said, his stomach churning. "Gornt's up to his tricks. That's all."

"I'm really very worried. It's not just Gornt. It's the Ho-Pak and the way the whole market's reacting," Mata said. "With the bank run seeping over to the Ching Prosperity and even the Vic . . . all the signs are very bad so I want to wait and see."

"Tomorrow's the day, Lando. Tomorrow. I was counting on you."

"Have you tripled our next gold consignment as I asked?"

"Yes, I did that personally. I've Zurich's telexed confirms in the usual code."

"Excellent, excellent!"

"I'll need your letter of credit tomorrow."

"Of course. If you'll send a messenger to my home now I'll give you my check for the full amount."

"Personal check?" Dunross held on to his astonishment. "On which bank, Lando?"

"The Victoria."

"Christ, that's a lot of money to remove just now."

"I'm not removing it, I'm just paying for some gold. I'd rather have some of my funds in gold outside Hong Kong for the next week or so, and this's an ideal moment to do it. You can get them to telex it first thing tomorrow. First thing. Yes. I'm not withdrawing funds, Ian, just paying for gold. If I were you I'd try to get liquid too."

Again his stomach fell over. "What have you heard?" he asked, his voice controlled.

"You know me, I'm just more cautious than you, tai-pan. The cost of my money comes very high."

"No more than mine."

"Yes. We'll consult tomorrow, then we'll see. But don't count on our 15 million. Sorry."

"You've heard something. I know you too well. What is it? *Chi pao pu chu huo.*" Literally, Paper cannot wrap up a fire, meaning a secret cannot be kept forever.

There was a long pause, then Mata said in a lower voice, "Confidentially, Ian, old Tightfist's selling heavily. He's getting ready to unload *all* his holdings. That old devil may be dying but his nose is as sensitive to the loss of a brass cash as ever and I've never known him to be wrong."

"All his holdings?" Dunross asked sharply. "When did you talk to him?"

"We've been in contact all day. Why?"

"I reached him after lunch and he promised he wouldn't sell or loan any Struan's. Has he changed his mind?"

"No. I'm sure he hasn't. He can't. He hasn't any Struan stock."

"He has 400,000 shares!"

"He *did* have, tai-pan, though actually the number was nearer 600,000—Sir Luis had very few shares of his own, he's one of Tightfist's many nominees. He's unloaded all 600,000 shares. Today."

Dunross bit back an obscenity. "Oh?"

"Listen, my young friend, this is all in the strictest confidence but you should be prepared: Tightfist ordered Sir Luis to sell or loan all his Noble

House stock the moment the rumors started this morning. 100,000 was spread throughout the brokers and sold immediately, the remainder. . . . the half million shares you bought from Gornt were Tightfist's. The moment it was evident there was a major assault on the House and Gornt was selling short, Tightfist told Sir Luis to go ahead and loan it all, except for a token 1,000 shares, which he's kept. For face. Yours. When the exchange closed, Tightfist was very pleased. On the day he's almost 2 million ahead."

Dunross was standing rock still. He heard that his voice was matter-of-fact and level and controlled and that pleased him, but he was in shock. If Tightfist had sold, the Chins would sell and a dozen other friends would follow his lead and that meant chaos. "The old bugger!" he said, bearing him no grudge. It was his own fault, he had not reached Tightfist in time. "Lando, what about your 300,000 shares—plus?"

He heard the Portuguese hesitate and his stomach twisted again. "I've still got them. I bought at 16 when you first went public so I'm not worried yet. Perhaps Alastair Struan was right when he advised against going public—the Noble House's only vulnerable because of that."

"Our growth rate's five times Gornt's and without going public we could never have weathered the disasters I inherited. We're supported by the Victoria. We've still got our bank stock and a majority vote on the board so they have to support us. We're really very strong and once this temporary situation's over we'll be the biggest conglomerate in Asia."

"Perhaps. But perhaps you'd have been wiser to accept our proposal instead of leaving yourself constantly open to the risk of takeovers or market disasters."

"I couldn't then. I can't now. Nothing's changed." Dunross smiled grimly. Lando Mata, Tightfist Tung and Gambler Chin collectively had offered him 20 percent of their gold and gambling syndicate revenue for 50 percent of Struan's—if he kept it as a wholly private-owned company.

"Come, tai-pan, be sensible! Tightfist and I will give you 100 million cash today for 50 percent ownership. U.S. dollars. Your position as tai-pan will not be touched, you will head the new syndicate and manage our gold and gambling monopolies, secretly or openly—with 10 percent of all profit as a personal fee."

"Who appoints the next tai-pan?"

"You do—in consultation."

"There, you see! It's impossible. A 50 percent control gives you power over Struan's and that I'm not allowed to give. That would negate Dirk's legacy, make my oath invalid and give away absolute control. Sorry, it's not possible."

"Because of an oath to an unknown, unknowable god in which you don't believe—on behalf of a murdering pirate who's been dead over a hundred years?"

"For whatever reason the answer is, thank you, no."

"You could easily lose the whole company."

"No. Between the Struans and the Dunrosses we have 60 percent voting control and I alone vote all the stock. What I'd lose is everything material we own, and cease to be the Noble House, and that by the Lord
God, is not going to happen either."

There was a long silence. Then Mata said, his voice friendly as always,
"Our offer is good for two weeks. If joss is against you and you fail, the
offer to head the new syndicate stands. I shall sell or lend my stock at 21."

"Below 20—not at 21."

"It will go that low?"

"No. Just a habit I have. 20 is better than 21."

"Yes. Good. Then let us see what tomorrow brings. I wish you good
joss. Good night, tai-pan."

Dunross put down the phone and sipped the last of his champagne. He
was up the creek without a paddle. That old bugger Tightfist, he thought
again, admiring his cleverness—to agree so reluctantly not to sell or barter
any Struan shares, knowing that only 1,000 remained, knowing the revenue from almost 600,000 was already safe—that old bastard's a great negotiator. It's so very clever of both Lando and Tightfist to make the new
offer now. 100 million! Jesus Christ, that'd stop Gornt farting in church! I
could use that to smash him to pieces, and in short order take over Asian
Properties and put Dunstan into an early retirement. Then I could pass
the House over to Jacques or Andrew in great shape and . . .

And then what? What would I do then? Retire to the moors and shoot
grouse? Throw vast parties in London? Or go into Parliament and sleep in
the Back Bench while the bloody Socialists give the country to the Communists? Christ, I'd be bored to bloody death! I'd . . .

"What?" He was startled. "Oh sorry, Penn, what did you say?"

"I just said that all sounded like bad news!"

"Yes. Yes it was." Then Dunross grinned and all his anxiety dropped
away. "It's joss! I'm tai-pan," he said happily. "You've got to expect it." He
picked up the bottle. It was empty. "I think we deserve another . . . No,
pet, I'll get it." He went to the concealed refrigerator that was set into a
vast old Chinese scarlet, lacquered sideboard.

"How do you cope, Ian?" she asked. "I mean, it always seems to be
something bad, ever since you took over—and there's always some disaster,
every phone call, you work all the time, never take a holiday . . . ever
since we came back to Hong Kong. First your father and then Alastair
and then . . . Isn't it ever going to stop pouring cats and dogs?"

"Of course not—that's the job."

"Is it worth it?"

He concentrated on the cork, knowing there was no future in this conversation. "Of course."

To you it is, Ian, she thought. But not to me. After a moment she said,
"Then it's all right for me to go?"

"Yes, yes of course. I'll watch Adryon and don't worry about Duncan. You just have a great time and hurry back."

"Are you going to do the hill climb Sunday?"

"Yes. Then I'm going to Taipei, back Tuesday. I'm taking Bartlett."

She thought about Taipei and wondered if there was a girl there, a special girl, a Chinese girl, half her age, with lovely soft skin and warmth, not much warmer than herself or softer or trimmer but half her age, with a ready smile, without the years of survival bowing her—the rotten growing-up years, the good and terrible war years, and childbearing years and child-rearing years and the exhausting reality of marriage, even to a good man.

I wonder I wonder I wonder. If I was a man . . . there're so many beauties here, so anxious to please, so readily available. If you believe a tenth of what the others say.

She watched him pour the fine wine, the bubbles and froth good, his face strong and craggy and greatly pleasing, and she wondered, Does any woman possess any man for more than a few years?

"What?" he asked.

"Nothing," she said, loving him. She touched his glass. "Be careful on the hill climb."

"Of course."

"How do you cope with being tai-pan, Ian?"

"How do you cope with running a home, bringing up the kids, getting up at all hours, year after year, keeping the peace, and all the other things you've had to do? I couldn't do that. Never could. I'd've given up the ghost long ago. It's part training and part what you're born to do."

"A woman's place is in the home?"

"I don't know about others, Penn, but so long as you're in my home all's good in my world." He popped the cork neatly.

"Thank you, dear," she said and smiled. Then she frowned. "But I'm afraid I don't have much option and never had. Of course it's different now and the next generation's lucky, they're going to change things, turn things around and give men their comeuppance once and for all."

"Oh?" he said, most of his mind back on Lando Mata and tomorrow and how to get the 100 million without conceding control.

"Oh yes. The girls of the next generation aren't going to put up with the boring 'a woman's place is by the sink.' God how I hate housework, how every woman hates housework. Our daughters are going to change all that! Adryon for one. My God I'd hate to be her husband."

said, pouring. "This's great champagne. Remember how we did? Remember how we used to bitch, still do, about our parents' attitudes?"

"True. But our daughters have the pill and that's a whole new kettle of fish an—"

"Eh?" Dunross stared at her, shocked. "You mean Adryon's on the pill? Jesus Christ how long . . . do you mean sh—"

"Calm down, Ian, and listen. That little pill's unlocked womanhood from fear forever—men too, in a way. I think very few people realize what an enormous social revolution it's going to create. Now women can all make love without fear of having a child, they can use their bodies as men use their bodies, for gratification, for pleasure, and without shame." She looked at him keenly. "As to Adryon, she's had access to the pill since she was seventeen."

"What?"

"Of course. Would you prefer her to have a child?"

"Jesus Christ, Penn, of course not," Dunross spluttered, "but Jesus Christ who? You . . . you mean she's having an affair, had affairs or. . . ."

"I sent her to Dr. Tooley. I thought it best she should see him."

"You what?"

"Yes. When she was seventeen, she asked me what to do, said most of her friends were on the pill. As there are various types I wanted her to have expert advice. Dr. Too— What are you so red about, Ian? Adryon's nineteen now, twenty next month, it's all very ordinary."

"It isn't by God. It just isn't!"

"Och laddie but it is," she said, aping the broad Scots accent of Granny Dunross whom he had adored, "and my whole point is that the lassies of today know what they're aboot and dinna ye dare mention it to Adryon that I've told ye or I'll take my stick to your britches!"

He stared at her.

"Health!" Smugly she raised her glass. "Did you see the *Guardian* Extra this afternoon?"

"Don't change the subject, Penn. Don't you think I should talk to her?"

"Absolutely not. No. It's a . . . it's a very private matter. It's really her body and her life and whatever you say, Ian, she has the right to do with her life what she pleases and really nothing you say will make any difference. It'll all be very embarrassing for both of you. There's face involved," she added and was pleased with her cleverness. "Oh of course Adryon'll listen and take your views to heart but you really must be adult and modern for your own sake, as well as hers."

Suddenly an uncontrollable wave of heat went through his face.

"What is it?" she asked.

"I was thinking about . . . I was just thinking."

"About who was, is or could be her lover?"

"Yes."

Penelope Dunross sighed. "For your own sanity, Ian, don't! She's very sensible, over nineteen . . . well, quite sensible. Come to think of it I haven't seen her all day. The little rotter rushed out with my new scarf before I could catch her. You remember the blouse I lent her? I found it scrumpled up on her bathroom floor! I shall be very glad to see her off on her own and in her own apartment."

"She's too young for God's sake!"

"I don't agree, dear. As I was saying, there's really nothing you can do about progress, and the pill is a marvelous fantastic unbelievable leap forward. You really must be more sensible. Please?"

"It's . . . Christ, it's a bit sudden, that's all."

She laughed outright. "If we were talking about Glenna I could unders— Oh for God's sake, Ian, I'm only joking! It never really occurred to me that you wouldn't have presumed Adryon was a very healthy, well-adjusted though foul-tempered, infuriating, very frustrated young lady, most of whose frustrations spring from trying to please us with our old-fashioned ideas."

"You're right." He tried to sound convincing but he wasn't and he said sourly, "You're right even so . . . you're right."

"Laddie, dinna ye think ye'd better visit our Shrieking Tree?" she asked with a smile. It was an ancient clan custom in the old country that somewhere near the dwelling of the oldest woman of the laird's family would be the Shrieking Tree. When Ian was young, Granny Dunross was the oldest, and her cottage was in a glade in the hills behind Kilmarnock in Ayrshire where the Struan lands were. The tree was a great oak. It was the tree that you went out to when the deevil—as old Granny Dunross called it—when the deevil was with you, and alone, you shrieked whatever curses you liked. ". . . and then, lassie," the lovely old woman had told her the first night, ". . . and then, lassie, there would be peace in the home and never a body has need to really curse a husband or wife or lover or child. Aye, just a wee tree and the tree can bear all the curse words that the deevil himself invented. . . ."

Penelope was remembering how old Granny Dunross had taken her into her heart and into the clan from the first moment. That was just after she and Ian were married and visiting for the second time, Ian on sick leave, still on crutches, his legs badly burned but healing, the rest of him untouched in the flaming crash-landing but for his mad, all-consuming anger at being grounded forever, she so pleased secretly, thanking God for the reprieve.

"But whisht, lassie," Granny Dunross had added with a chuckle that night when the winter winds were whining off the moors, sleet outside, and they all warm and toasty in front of the great fire, safe from the bombing, well fed and never a care except that Ian should get well quickly, ". . . there was a time when this Dunross was six and, och aye, he had a terrible temper even then and his father Colin was off in those heathen foreign parts as always, so this Dunross would come to Ayr on holiday from boarding school. Aye, and sometimes he would come to see me and I'd tell him tales o' the clan and his grandfather and great-grandfather but this time nothing would take away the deevil that possessed him. It was a night like this and I sent him out, the poor wee bairn, aye I sent him out to the Shrieking Tree. . . ." The old woman had chuckled and chuckled and sipped whiskey and continued, "Aye and the young deevil went out, cock of the walk, the gale under his kilt, and he cursed the tree. Och aye, surely the wee beasties in the forest fled before his wrath and then he came back. 'Have you given it a good drubbing,' I asked him. 'Aye,' he said in his wee voice. 'Aye, Grandma, I gave it a good drubbing, the very best ever.'

" 'Good,' I said. 'And now you're at peace!'

" 'Well, not really, Grandmother, but I am tired.' And then, lassie, at that moment, there was an almighty crash and the whole house shook and I thought it was the end of the world but the wee little bairn ran out to see what had happened and a lightning bolt had blasted the Shrieking Tree to pieces. 'Och aye, Granny,' he said in his piping little voice when he came back, his eyes wide, 'that really was the very best I ever did. Can I do it again!' "

Ian had laughed. "That's all a story, I don't remember that at all. You're making it up, Granny!"

"Whisht on you! You were five or six and the next day we went into the glade and picked the new tree, the one you'll see tomorrow, lassie, and blessed it in the clan's name and I told young Ian to be a mite more careful next time!"

They had laughed together and then, later that night, she had woken up to find Ian gone and his crutches gone. She had watched and waited. When he came back he was soaked but tired and at peace. She pretended sleep until he was in bed again. Then she turned to him and gave him all the warmth she had.

"Remember, lassie," Granny Dunross had said to her privately the day they left, "if ye want to keep your marriage sweet, make sure this Dunross always has a Shrieking Tree nearby. Dinna be afeared. Pick one, always pick one wherever you go. This Dunross needs a Shrieking Tree close by though he'll never admit it and will never use it but rarely. He's like the Dirk. He's too strong. . . ."

So wherever they had gone they had had one. Penelope had insisted. Once, in Chungking, where Dunross had been sent to be an Allied liaison officer after he was well again, she had made a bamboo their Shrieking Tree. Here in Hong Kong it was a huge jacaranda that dominated the whole garden. "Don't you think you should pay her a wee visit?" The tree was always a her for him and a him for her. Everyone should have a Shrieking Tree, Penelope thought. Everyone.

"Thanks," he said. "I'm okay now."

"How did Granny Dunross have so much wisdom and stay so marvelous after so much tragedy in her life?"

"I don't know. Perhaps they built them stronger in those days."

"I miss her." Granny Dunross was eighty-five when she died. She was

Agnes Struan when she married her cousin Dirk Dunross—Dirk McCloud Dunross, whom his mother Winifred, Dirk Struan's only daughter, had named after her father in remembrance. Dirk Dunross had been fourth tai-pan and he had been lost at sea in *Sunset Cloud* driving her homeward. He was only forty-two when he was lost, she thirty-one. She never married again. They had had three sons and one daughter. Two of her sons were killed in World War I, the eldest at Gallipoli at twenty-one, the other gassed at Ypres in Flanders, nineteen. Her daughter Anne had married Gaston deVille, Jacques's father. Anne had died in the London bombing where all the deVilles had fled except Jacques who had stayed in France and fought the Nazis with the Maquis. Colin, the last of her sons, Ian's father, also had three sons and a daughter, Kathren. Two sons also were killed in World War II. Kathren's first husband, Ian's squadron leader, was killed in the Battle of Britain. "So many deaths, violent deaths," Penelope said sadly. "To see them all born and all die . . . terrible. Poor Granny! Yet when she died she seemed to go so peacefully with that lovely smile of hers."

"Perhaps it was joss. But the others, that was joss too. They only did what they had to, Penn. After all, our family history's ordinary in that. We're British. War's been a way of life for centuries. Look at your family —one of your uncles was lost at sea in the navy in the Great War, another in the last at El Alamein, your parents killed in the blitz . . . all very ordinary." His voice hardened. "It's not easy to explain to any outsider, is it?"

"No. We all had to grow up so quickly, didn't we, Ian?" He nodded and after a moment she said, "You'd better dress for dinner, dear, you'll be late."

"Come on, Penn, for God's sake, you take an hour longer than me. We'll put in a quick appearance and leave directly after chow. Wh—" The phone rang and he picked it up. "Yes? Oh hello, Mr. Deland."

"Good evening, tai-pan. I wish to report about Mme. deVille's daughter and son-in-law, M. Escary."

"Yes, please go ahead."

"I am sad to have the dishonor of bringing such bad tidings. The accident was a, how do you say, sideswipe on the upper Corniche just outside Eze. The driver of the other car was drunk. It was at two in the morning about, and when the police arrived, M. Escary was already dead and his wife, unconscious. The doctor says she will mend, very well, but he is afraid that her, her internal organs, her childbearing organs may have permanent hurt. She may require an operation. He—"

"Does she know this?"

"No, m'sieu, not yet, but Mme. deVille was told, the doctor told her. I met her as you ordered and have taken care of everything. I have asked for a specialist in these things from Paris to consult with the Nice Hospital and he arrives this afternoon."

"Is there any other damage?"

"Externally, *non*. A broken wrist, a few cuts, nothing. But . . . the poor lady is distraught. It was glad . . . I was glad that her mother came, that helped, has helped. She stays at the Métropole in a suite and I met her airplane. Of course I will be in the constant touch."

"Who was driving?"

"Mme. Escary."

"And the other driver?"

There was a hesitation. "His name is Charles Sessonne. He's a baker in Eze and he was coming home after cards and an evening with some friends. The police have . . . Mme. Escary swears his car was on the wrong side of the road. He cannot remember. Of course he is very sorry and the police have charged him with drunk driving an—"

"Is this the first time?"

"*Non. Non,* once before he was stopped and fined."

"What'll happen under French law?"

"There will be a court and then . . . I do not know, m'sieu. There were no other witnesses. Perhaps a fine, perhaps jail; I do not know. Perhaps he will remember he was on the right side, who knows? I'm sorry."

Dunross thought a moment. "Where does this man live?"

"Rue de Verte 14, Eze."

Dunross remembered the village well, not far from Monte Carlo, high above, and the whole of the Côte d'Azur below and you could see beyond Monte Carlo into Italy, and beyond Cap Ferrat to Nice. "Thank you, Mr. Deland. I've telexed you 10,000 U.S. for Mme. deVille's expenses and anything else. Whatever's necessary please do it. Call me at once if there's anything . . . yes and ask the specialist to call me immediately after he's examined Mme. Escary. Have you talked with Mr. Jacques deVille?"

"No, tai-pan. You did not instruct this. Should I phone?"

"No. I'll call him. Thank you again." Dunross hung up and told Penelope everything, except about the internal injuries.

"How awful! How . . . how senseless!"

Dunross was looking out at the sunset. It was at his suggestion the young couple had gone to Nice and Monte Carlo where he and Penelope had had so much fun, and marvelous food, marvelous wine and a little gambling. Joss, he thought, then added, Christ all bloody mighty!

He dialed Jacques deVille's house but he was not there. He left a message for him to return the call. "I'll see him at the dinner tonight," he said, the champagne now tasteless. "Well, we'd better get changed."

"I'm not going, dear."

"Oh but . . ."

"I've lots to do to get ready for tomorrow. You can make an excuse for me—of course you have to go. I'll be ever so busy. There's Glenna's school things—and Duncan gets back on Monday and his school things have to be sorted. You'll have to put him on the aircraft, make sure he has his passport . . . You can easily make an excuse for me tonight as I'm leaving."

He smiled faintly. "Of course, Penn, but what's the real reason?"

"It's going to be a big do. Robin's bound to be there."

"They're not back till tomorrow!"

"No, it was in the *Guardian*'s Extra. They arrived this afternoon. The whole delegation. They're sure to be invited." The banquet was being given by a multimillionaire property developer, Sir Shi-teh T'Chung, partially to celebrate the knighthood he had received in the last Honors List, but mostly to launch his latest charity drive for the new wing of the new Elizabeth Hospital. "I've really no wish to go, and so long as you're there, everything'll be all right. I really want an early night too. Please."

"All right. I'll deal with these calls, then I'll be off. I'll see you though before I go." Dunross walked upstairs and went into his study. Lim was waiting there, on guard. He wore a white tunic and black pants and soft shoes. "Evening, Lim," Dunross said in Cantonese.

"Good evening, tai-pan." Quietly the old man motioned him to the window. Dunross could see two men, Chinese, loitering across the street outside the high wall that surrounded the Great House, near the tall, open iron gates. "They've been there some time, tai-pan."

Dunross watched them a moment, disquieted. His own guard had just been dismissed and Brian Kwok, who was also a guest at Sir Shi-teh's tonight, would come by shortly and go with him, acting as a substitute. "If they don't go away by dusk call Superintendent Crosse's office." He wrote the number down, then added in Cantonese, his voice abruptly hard, "While I think of it, Lim, if I want any foreign devil car interfered with, I will order it." He saw the old eyes staring back at him impassively. Lim Chu had been with the family since he was seven, like his father before him, and *his* father, the first of his line who, in the very old days, before Hong Kong had existed, had been Number One Boy and looked after the Struan mansion in Macao.

"I don't understand, tai-pan."

"You cannot wrap fire in paper. The police are clever and old Black Beard's a great supporter of police. Experts can examine brakes and deduce all sorts of information."

"I know nothing of police." The old man shrugged then beamed. "Tai-pan, I do not climb trees to find a fish. Nor do you. May I mention that in the night I could not sleep and I came here. There was a shadow on the veranda balcony. The moment I opened the study door the shadow slid down the drainpipe and vanished into the shrubs." The old man took out a torn piece of cloth. "This was on the drainpipe." The cloth was nondescript.

Dunross studied it, perturbed. He glanced at Dirk Struan's oil painting over the fireplace. It was perfectly in position. He moved it away and saw

that the hair he had delicately balanced on a hinge of the safe was un-
touched. Satisfied, he replaced the picture, then checked the locks on the
French windows. The two men were still loitering. For the first time
Dunross was very glad that he had an SI guard.

34

It was hot and humid in Phillip Chen's study and he was sitting beside the phone staring at it nervously. The door swung open and he jumped. Dianne sailed in.

"There's no point in waiting anymore, Phillip," she said irritably. "You'd better go and change. That devil Werewolf won't call tonight. Something must have happened. Do come along!" She wore an evening *chong-sam* in the latest, most expensive fashion, her hair bouffant, and she was bejeweled like a Christmas tree. "Yes. Something must have happened. Perhaps the police . . . huh, it's too much to expect they caught him. More likely that *fang pi* devil's playing with us. You'd better change or we'll be late. If you hurr—"

"I really don't want to go," he snapped back at her. "Shitee T'Chung's a bore and now that he's Sir Shitee he's a double one." Years ago Shi-teh had adulterated down to become the nickname *Shitee* to his intimate friends. "Anyway, it's hardly eight o'clock and dinner's not till 9:30 and he's always late, his banquets are always at least an hour late. For God's sake, you go!"

"*Ayeeyah* you've got to come. It's a matter of face," she replied, equally ill-tempered. "My God, after today at the stock market . . . if we don't go we'll lose terrible face and it's sure to push the stock down further! All Hong Kong will laugh at us. They can't wait. They'll say we're so ashamed the House can't pay its bills that we won't show our face in public. Huh! And as for Shitee's new wife, Constance, that mealy-mouthed whore can't wait to see me humbled!" She was near screeching. Her losses on the day exceeded 100,000 of her own secret private dollars. When Phillip had called her from the stock market just after three to relate what had happened she had almost fainted. "*Oh ko* you have to come or we'll be ruined!"

Miserably her husband nodded. He knew what gossips and rumor-mongers would be at the banquet. All day he had been inundated with questions, moans and panic. "I suppose you're right." He was down almost a million dollars on the day and if the run continued and Gornt won he knew he would be wiped out. Oh oh oh why did I trust Dunross and buy so heavily? he was thinking, so angry that he wanted to kick someone. He looked up at his wife. His heart sank as he recognized the signs of her awesome displeasure at the world in general, and him in particular. He quaked inside. "All right," he said meekly. "I won't be a moment."

When he got to the door the phone rang. Once more his heart twisted and he felt sick. There had been four calls since around six. Each had been a business call decrying the fate of the stock, and were the rumors true and *oh ko*, Phillip, I'd better sell—each time worse than the last. "*Weyyyy?*" he asked angrily.

There was a short pause, then an equally rude voice said in crude Cantonese, "You're in a foul temper whoever you are! Where are your fornicating manners?"

"Who's this? Eh, who's calling?" he asked in Cantonese.

"This is the Werewolf. The Chief Werewolf, by all the gods! Who're you?"

"Oh!" The blood drained from Phillip Chen's face. In panic he beckoned his wife. She rushed forward and bent to listen too, everything else forgotten except the safety of the House. "This . . . this is Honorable Chen," he said cautiously. "Please, what's . . . what's your name?"

"Are your ears filled with wax? I said I was the Werewolf. Am I so stupid to give you my name?"

"I'm . . . I'm sorry but how do I know you're . . . you're telling me the truth?"

"How do I know who you are? Perhaps you're a dung-eating policeman. Who are you?"

"I'm Noble House Chen. I swear it!"

"Good. Then I wrote you a letter saying I'd call about 6:00 P.M. today. Didn't you get the letter?"

"Yes, yes I got the letter," Phillip Chen said, trying to control a relief that was mixed with rage and frustration and terror. "Let me talk to my Number One Son, please."

"Every generation thinks they're going to change the world," Dunross

"That's not possible, no, not possible! Can a frog think of eating a swan? Your son's in another part of the Island . . . actually he's in the New Territories, not near a telephone but quite safe, Noble House Chen, oh yes, quite safe. He lacks for nothing. Do you have the ransom money?"

"Yes . . . at least I could only raise 100,000. Th—"

"All gods bear witness to my fornicating patience!" the man said angrily. "You know very well we asked for 500,000! 5 or 10 it's still like one hair on ten oxen to you!"

"Lies!" Phillip Chen shrieked. "That's all lies and rumors spread by my enemies! I'm not that rich. . . . Didn't you hear about the stock market today?" Phillip Chen groped for a chair, his heart pounding, and sat down still holding the phone so she could listen too.

"*Ayeeyah*, stock market! We poor farmers don't deal on the stock market! Do you want his other ear?"

Phillip Chen blanched. "No. But we must negotiate. Five is too much. One and a half I can manage."

"If I settle for one and a half I will be the laughingstock of all China! Are you accusing me of displaying a lamb's head but selling dogmeat? One and a half for the Number One Son of Noble House Chen? Impossible! It's face! Surely you can see that."

Phillip Chen hesitated. "Well," he said reasonably, "you have a point. First I want to know when I get my son back."

"As soon as the ransom's paid! I promise on the bones of my ancestors! Within a few hours of getting the money he'll be put on the main Sha Tin Road."

"Ah, he's in Sha Tin now?"

"*Ayeeyah*, you can't trap me, Noble House Chen. I smell dung in this conversation. Are the fornicating police listening? Is the dog acting fierce because his master's listening? Have you called the police?"

"No, I swear it. I haven't called the police and I'm not trying to trap you, but please, I need assurances, reasonable assurances." Phillip Chen was beaded with sweat. "You're quite safe, you have my oath, I haven't called the police. Why should I? If I call them how can we negotiate?"

There was another long hesitation, then the man said, somewhat mollified, "I agree. But we have your son so any trouble that happens is your fault and not ours. All right, I'll be reasonable too. I will accept 400,000, but it must be tonight!"

"That's impossible! You ask me to fish in the sea to catch a tiger! I didn't get your letter till after the banks were closed but I've got 100,000 cash, in small bills. . . ." Dianne nudged him and held up two fingers. "Listen, Honorable Werewolf, perhaps I can borrow more tonight. Perhaps . . . listen, I will give you two tonight. I'm sure I can raise that within the hour. 200,000!"

"May all gods smite me dead if I sell out for such a fornicating pittance. 350,000!"

"200,000 within the hour!"

"His other ear within two days or 300,000 tonight!"

Phillip Chen wailed and pleaded and flattered and cursed and they negotiated back and forth. Both men were adept. Soon both were caught up in the battle of wits, each using all his powers, the kidnapper using threats, Phillip Chen using guile, flattery and promises. At length, Phillip Chen said, "You are too good for me, too good a negotiator. I will pay 200,000 tonight and a further 100,000 within four months."

"Within one month!"

"Three!" Phillip Chen was aghast at the flow of obscenities that followed and he wondered if he had misjudged his adversary.

"Two!"

Dianne nudged him again, nodding agreement. "Very well," he said, "I agree. Another 100,000 in two months."

"Good!" The man sounded satisfied, then he added, "I will consider what you say and call you back."

"But wait a moment, Honorable Werewolf. When wil—"

"Within the hour."

"Bu—" The line went dead. Phillip Chen cursed, then mopped his brow again. "I thought I had him. God curse the motherless dog turd!"

"Yes." Dianne was elated. "You did very well, Phillip! Only two now and another hundred in two months! Perfect! Anything can happen in two months. Perhaps the dirty police will catch them and then we won't have to pay the hundred!" Happily she took out a tissue and blotted the perspiration off her upper lip. Then her smile faded. "What about Shitee T'Chung? We've got to go but you'll have to wait."

"Ah, I have it! Take Kevin, I'll come later. There'll be plenty of space for me whenever I get there. I'll . . . I'll wait for him to call back."

"Excellent! How clever you are! We've got to get our coin back. Oh very good! Perhaps our joss has changed and the boom will happen like Old Blind Tung forecast. Kevin's so concerned for you, Phillip. The poor boy's so upset that you have all these troubles. He's very concerned for your health." She hurried out, thanking the gods, knowing she would be back long before John Chen returned safely. Perfect, she was thinking, Kevin can wear his new white sharkskin dinner jacket. It's time he began to live up to his new position. "Kevinnnnn!"

The door closed. Phillip Chen sighed. When he had gathered his strength, he went to the sideboard and poured himself a brandy. After Dianne and Kevin had left, he poured himself another. At a quarter to nine the phone rang again.

"Noble House Chen?"

"Yes . . . yes, Honorable Werewolf?"

"We accept. But it has to be tonight!"

Phillip Chen sighed. "Very well. Now wh—"

"You can get all the money?"

"Yes."

"The notes will be hundreds as I asked?"

"Yes. I have 100,000 and can get another hundred from a friend . . ."

"You have rich friends," the man said suspiciously. "Mandarins."

"He's a bookmaker," Phillip Chen said quickly, cursing himself for his slip. "When you hung up I . . . I made the arrangements. Fortunately this happened to be one of his big nights."

"All right. Listen, take a taxi—"

"Oh but I have a car an—"

"I know you have a fornicating car and I know the license number," the man said rudely, "and we know all about you and if you try to betray us to the police you will never see your son again and you will be next on our list! Understand?"

"Yes . . . yes, of course, Honorable Werewolf," Phillip Chen said placatingly. "I'm to take a taxi—where to?"

"The triangle garden at Kowloon Tong. There's a road called Essex Road. There's a wall fence there and a hole in the wall. An arrow drawn on the pavement of the road has its arrowhead pointing at the hole. You put your hand in this hole and you'll get a letter. You read it then our street fighters will approach you and say 'Tin koon chi fook' and you hand the bag over."

"Oh! Isn't it possible I can hand it to the wrong man?"

"You won't. You understand the password and everything?"

"Yes . . . yes."

"How long will it take you to get there?"

"I can come at once. I'll . . . I can get the other money on the way, I can come at once."

"Then come immediately. Come alone, you cannot come with anyone else. You will be watched the moment you leave the door."

Phillip Chen mopped his brow. "And my son? When do I ge—"

"Obey instructions! Beware and come alone."

Again the phone went dead. His fingers were shaking as he picked up the glass and drained the brandy. He felt the warm afterglow but it took away none of his apprehension. When he had collected himself, he dialed a very private number. "I want to speak to Four Finger Wu," he said in Wu's dialect.

"One moment please." There were some muffled Haklo voices, and then, "Is this Mr. Chen, Mr. Phillip Chen?" the voice asked in American English.

"Oh!" he said, startled, then added cautiously, "Who's this?"

"This's Paul Choy, Mr. Chen. Mr. Wu's nephew. My uncle had to go out but he left instructions for me to wait until you called. He's made some arrangements for you. This is Mr. Chen?"

"Yes, yes, it is."

"Ah, great. Have you heard from the kidnappers?"

"Yes, yes I have." Phillip Chen was uneasy talking to a stranger but now he had no option. He told Paul Choy the instructions he had been given.

"Just a moment, sir."

He heard a hand being put over the phone and again muffled, indistinct talking in Haklo dialect for a moment. "Everything's set, sir. We'll send a cab to your house—you're phoning from Struan's Lookout?"

"Yes—yes, I'm home."

"The driver'll be one of our guys. There'll be more of my uncle's, er, people scattered over Kowloon Tong so not to worry, you'll be covered every foot of the way. Just hand over the money and, er, and they'll take care of everything. My uncle's chief lieut—er, his aide, says not to worry, they'll have the whole area swarming . . . Mr. Chen?"

"Yes, I'm still here. Thank you."

"The cab'll be there in twenty minutes."

Paul Choy put down the phone. "Noble House Chen says thank you, Honorable Father," he told Four Finger Wu placatingly in their dialect, quaking under the stony eyes. Sweat was beading his face. He tried unsuccessfully to hide his fear of the others. It was hot and stuffy in the crowded main cabin of this ancient junk that was tied up in a permanent berth to an equally ancient dock in one of Aberdeen's multitude of estuaries. "Can I go with your fighters, too?"

"Do you send a rabbit against a dragon?" Four Finger Wu snarled. "Are you trained as a street fighter? Am I a fool like you? Treacherous like you?" He jerked a horny thumb at Goodweather Poon. "Lead the fighters!" The man hurried out. The others followed.

Now the two of them were alone in the cabin.

The old man was sitting on an upturned keg. He lit another cigarette, inhaled deeply, coughed and spat loudly on the deck floor. Paul Choy watched him, the sweat running down his back, more from fear than from the heat. Around them were some old desks, filing cabinets, rickety chairs and two phones, and this was Four Fingers's office and communications center. It was mostly from here that he sent messages to his fleets. Much of his business was regular freighting but wherever the Silver Lotus flag flew, his order to his captains was: Anything, shipped anywhere, at any time—at the right price.

The tough old man coughed again and glared at him under shaggy eyebrows. "They teach you curious ways in the Golden Mountain, *heya*?"

Paul Choy held his tongue and waited, his heart thumping, and wished he had never come back to Hong Kong, that he was still Stateside, or even better in Honolulu surfing in the Great Waves or lying on the beach with his girl friend. His spirit twisted at the thought of her.

"They teach you to bite the hand that feeds you, *heya*?"

"No, Honored Father, sorr—"

"They teach that my money is yours, my wealth yours and my chop yours to use as you wish, *heya*?"

"No, Honored Lord. I'm sorry to displease you," Paul Choy muttered, wilting under the weight of his fear.

This morning, early, when Gornt had jauntily come into the office from the meeting with Bartlett, it was still before the secretaries were due so Paul Choy had asked if he could help him. Gornt had told him to get several people on the phone. Others he had dialed himself on his private line.

Paul Choy had thought nothing of it at the time until he happened to overhear part of what was, obviously, inside information about Struan's being whispered confidentially over the phone. Remembering the Bartlett call earlier, deducing that Gornt and Bartlett had had a meeting—a successful one judging by Gornt's good humor—and realizing Gornt was relating the same confidences over and over, his curiosity peaked. Later, he happened to hear Gornt saying to his solicitor, ". . . selling short . . . No, don't worry, nothing's going to happen till I'm covered, not till about eleven. . . . Certainly. I'll send the order, chopped, as soon as . . ."

The next call he was asked to make was long distance to the manager of the Bank of Switzerland and Zurich that, discreetly, he listened to. ". . . I'm expecting a large draft of U.S. dollars this morning, before eleven. Phone me the instant, the very instant it's in my account . . ."

So, bemused, he had put the various pieces of the equation together and come up with a theory: If Bartlett has arranged a sudden secret partnership with Gornt, Struan's known enemy, to launch one of his raids, if Bartlett also takes part of the risk, or most of it—by secretly putting large sums in one of Gornt's numbered Swiss accounts to cover any sell-short losses—and lastly, if he's talked Gornt into being the front guy while he sits on the fence, the stuff is going to hit the fan in the exchange and Struan's stock has got to go down.

This precipitated an immediate business decision: Jump in quickly and sell Struan's short before the big guys and we'll make a bundle.

He remembered how he had almost groaned aloud because he had no money, no credit, no shares and no means to borrow any. Then he recalled what one of his instructors at Harvard Business School had kept drumming into them: A faint heart never laid a lovely lady. So he'd gone into a private office and phoned his newfound friend, Ishwar Soorjani, the moneylender and dealer in foreign exchange whom he had met through the old Eurasian at the library. "Say, Ishwar, your brother's head of Soorjani Stockbrokers, isn't he?"

"No, Young Master. Arjan is my very first cousin. Why?"

"If I wanted to sell a stock short would you back me?"

"Certainly, as I told you before, buying or selling I support you to the holster, if you have reasonable cash to cover any losses . . . or the equivalent. No cash or equivalent so sorry."

"Say I had some red-hot information?"

"The road to hell and debtor's prison is flooded to drowning with red-hot information, Young Master. I advise against red-hot informations."

"Boy," Paul Choy said unhappily, "I could make us a few 100,000 before three."

"Oh? Would you care to whisper the illustrious name of the stock?"

"Would you back me for . . . for 20,000 U.S.?"

"Ah, so sorry, Young Master, I'm a moneylender not a money giver. My ancestors forbid it!"

"20,000 HK?"

"Not even 10 dollars in your Rebel Dixie redbacks."

"Gee, Ishwar, you're not much help."

"Why not ask your illustrious uncle? His chop . . . and I would instantly go to half a million. HK."

Paul Choy knew that among his father's cash and assets transferred from the Ho-Pak to the Victoria had been many stock certificates and a list of securities held by various stockbrokers. One was for 150,000 Struan shares. Jesus, he thought, if I'm right the old man might get dumped. If Gornt presses the raid the old man could get caught.

"Good idea, Ishwar. I'll call you back!" At once he had phoned his father but he could not reach him. He left messages wherever he could and began to wait. His anxiety grew. Just before ten he heard Gornt's secretary answer the phone. "Yes? . . . Oh, one moment please. . . . Mr. Gornt? A person-to-person call from Zurich. . . . You're through."

Once more he had tried to reach his father, wanting to give him the urgent news. Then Gornt had sent for him. "Mr. Choy, would you please run this over to my solicitor at once." He handed over a sealed envelope. "Give it to him personally."

"Yes sir."

So he had left the office. At every phone he had stopped and tried to reach his father. Then he had delivered the note, personally, watching the solicitor's face carefully. He saw glee. "Is there a reply, sir?" he asked politely.

"Just say everything will be done as ordered." It was a few minutes past ten.

Outside the office door and going down in the elevator Paul Choy had weighed the pluses and the minuses. His stomach twisting uneasily, he stopped at the nearest phone. "Ishwar? Say, I've an urgent order from my uncle. He wants to sell his Struan stock. 150,000 shares."

"Ah, wise wise, there are terrible rumors speeding around."

"I suggested you and Soorjani's should do it for him. 150,000 shares. He asks can you do it instantly? Can you do that?"

"Like a bird on the wing. For the Esteemed Four Fingers we will go forth like Rothschilds! Where are the shares?"

"In the vault."

"I will need his chop at once."

"I'm going to get it now but he said to sell at once. He said to sell in small blocks so as not to shock the market. He wants the very best price. You'll sell at once?"

"Yes, never fear, at once. And we will get the best price!"

"Good. And most important, he said to keep this secret."

"Verily, Young Master, you may trust us implicitly. And the stock that you yourself wished to sell short?"

"Oh that . . . well that'll have to wait . . . until I've credit *heya?*"

"Wise very wise."

Paul Choy shivered. His heart was pounding now in the silence and he watched his father's cigarette, not the angry face, knowing those cold black eyes were boring into him, deciding his fate. He remembered how he had almost shouted with excitement when the stock had begun to fall almost immediately, monitoring it moment by moment, then ordering Soorjani to buy back in just before close and feeling light-headed and in euphoria. At once he had phoned his girl, spending nearly 30 of his valuable U.S. dollars telling her how fantastic his day had been and how much he missed her. She said how much she missed him too and when was he coming back to Honolulu? Her name was Mika Kasunari and she was *sansei*, third-generation American of Japanese descent. Her parents hated him because he was Chinese, as he knew his father would hate her because she was Japanese except they were both American, both of them, and they had met and fallen in love at school.

"Very soon, honey," he had promised her ecstatically, "guaranteed by Christmas! After today my uncle'll surely give me a bonus. . . ."

The work that Gornt gave him for the rest of the day he breezed through. Late in the afternoon Goodweather Poon had phoned to say his father would see him in Aberdeen at 7:30 P.M. Before he went there he had collected Soorjani's check made out to his father. 615,000 HK less brokerage.

Elated, he had come to Aberdeen and given him the check, and when he told him what he had done he was aghast at the extent of his father's rage. The tirade had been interrupted by Phillip Chen's phone call.

"I'm deeply sorry I've offended you, Hon—"

"So my chop is yours, my wealth is yours *heya?*" Four Finger Wu shouted suddenly.

"No, Honored Father," he gasped, "but the information was so good and I wanted to protect your stock as well as make money for you."

"But not for you *heya?*"

"No, Honored Father. It was for you. To make you money, and help repay all the money you invested in me . . . they were your shares and it's your money. I tried to ca—"

"That's no fornicating excuse! You come with me!"

Shakily Paul Choy got up and followed the old man onto the deck. Four Finger Wu cursed his bodyguard away and pointed a stubby finger at the befouled muddy waters in the harbor. "If you weren't my son," he hissed, "if you weren't my son you'd be feeding the fish there, your feet in a chain, this very moment."

"Yes, Father."

"If you ever again use my name, my chop, my anything without my approval you're a dead man."

"Yes, Father," Paul Choy muttered, petrified, realizing that his father had the means, the will and the authority to put that threat into effect without fear of retaliation. "Sorry, Father. I swear I'll never do that again."

"Good. If you'd lost one bronze cash you'd be there now. It's only because you fornicating won that you're alive now."

"Yes, Father."

Four Finger Wu glared at his son and continued to hide his delight at the huge windfall. 615,000 HK less a few dollars. Unbelievable! All with a few phone calls and inside knowledge, he was thinking. That's as miraculous as having ten tons of opium leap ashore over the heads of the Customs boat! The boy's paid for his education twenty times over and he's here hardly three weeks. How clever . . . but also how dangerous!

He shivered at the thought of other minions making decisions themselves. *Dew neh loh moh* then I would be in their power and surely in jail for their mistakes and not my own. And yet, he told himself helplessly, this is the way barbarians act in business. Number Seven Son is trained as a barbarian. All gods bear witness, I did not wish to create a viper!

He looked at his son, not understanding him, hating his direct way of speaking, the barbarian way and not in innuendo and obliquely like a civilized person.

And yet . . . and yet better than 600,000 HK in one day. If I had talked to him beforehand I would never have agreed and I would have lost all that profit! *Ayeeyah!* Yes, my stock would be down all that fortune in one day . . . oh oh oh!

He groped for a box and sat down, his heart thumping at that awful thought.

His eyes were watching his son. What to do about him? he asked himself. He could feel the weight of the check in his pocket. It seemed unbelievable that his son could make that amount of money for him in a few hours, without moving the stock from its hiding place.

"Explain to me why that black-faced foreign devil with the foul name owes me so much money!"

Paul Choy explained the mechanics patiently, desperate to please.

The old man thought about that. "Then tomorrow I should do the same and make the same?"

"No, Honored Father. You take your gains and keep them. Today was almost a certainty. It was a sudden attack, a raid. We do not know how the Noble House will react tomorrow, or if Gornt really intends to continue the raid. He can buy back in and be way ahead too. It would be dangerous to follow Gornt tomorrow, very dangerous."

Four Finger Wu threw his cigarette away. "Then what should I do tomorrow?"

"Wait. The foreign devil market's nervous and in the hands of foreign devils. I counsel you to wait and see what happens with the Ho-Pak and the Victoria. May I use your name to ask the foreign devil Gornt about the Ho-Pak?"

"What?"

Patiently Paul Choy refreshed his father's memory about the bank run and possible stock manipulation.

"Ah, yes, I understand," the old man said loftily. Paul Choy said nothing, knowing he did not. "Then we . . . then I just wait?"

"Yes, Honored Father."

Four Fingers pulled out the check distastefully. "And this fornicating piece of paper? What about this?"

"Convert it into gold, Honored Father. The price hardly varies at all. I could talk to Ishwar Soorjani, if you wish. He deals in foreign exchange."

"And where would I keep the gold?" It was one thing to smuggle other people's gold but quite another to have to worry about your own.

Paul Choy explained that physical possession of the gold was not necessary to own it.

"But I don't trust banks," the old man said angrily. "If it's my gold it's my gold and not a bank's!"

"Yes, Father. But this would be a Swiss bank, not in Hong Kong, and completely safe."

"You guarantee it with your life?"

"Yes, Father."

"Good." The old man took out a pen and signed his name on the back with instructions to Soorjani to convert it at once into gold. He gave it to his son. "On your head, my son. And we wait tomorrow? We don't make money tomorrow?"

"There might be an opportunity for further profit but I could not guarantee it. I might know around noon."

"Call me here at noon."

"Yes, Father. Of course if we had our own exchange we could manipulate a hundred stocks . . ." Paul Choy let the idea hang in the air.

"What?"

Carefully the young man began to explain how easy it would be for them to form their own exchange, a Chinese-dominated exchange, and the limitless opportunities for profit their own exchange would give. He talked for an hour, gaining confidence with the minutes, explaining as simply as he could.

"If it's so easy, my son, why hasn't Tightfist Tung done it—or Big Noise Sung—or Moneybags Ng—or that half-barbarian gold-smuggler from Macao—or Banker Kwang or dozens of others, *heya?*"

"Perhaps they've never had the idea, or courage. Perhaps they want to work within the foreign devil system—the Turf Club, Cricket Club, knighthoods, and all that English foolishness. Perhaps they are afraid to go against the tide or they haven't got the knowledge. We have the knowledge and expertise. Yes. And I've a friend in the Golden Mountain, a good friend, who was at school with me who co—"

"What friend?"

"He's Shanghainese and a dragon in stocks, a broker in New York now. Together, with the cash support, we could do it. I know we could."

"*Ayeeyah!* With a northern barbarian?" Four Finger Wu scoffed. "How could you trust him?"

"I think you could trust him, Honored Father—of course you'd set boundaries against weeds like a good market gardener does."

"But all business power in Hong Kong is in the hands of foreign devils. Civilized persons couldn't support an opposition exchange."

"You may be right, Honored Father," Paul Choy agreed cautiously, keeping his excitement off his face and out of his voice. "But all Chinese love to gamble. Yet at the moment there's not one civilized person stockbroker! Why do foreign devils keep us out? Because we'd outplay them. For us the stock market's the greatest profession in the world. Once our people in Hong Kong see our market is wide open to civilized persons and *their* companies, they'll flock to us. Foreign devils will be forced to open up their own exchange to us as well. We're better gamblers than they are. After all, Honorable Father"—he waved his hand at the shore, at the tall high rises and the boats and junks and floating restaurants—"this could be all yours! It's in stocks and shares and the stock market that the modern man *owns* the might of his world."

Four Fingers smoked leisurely. "How much would your stock market cost, Number Seven Son?"

"A year of time. An initial investment of . . . I don't know exactly." The young man's heart was grinding. He could sense his father's avarice. The implications of forming a Chinese stock exchange in this unregulated capitalistic society were so far-reaching to him that he felt faint. It would be so easy given time and . . . and how much? "I could give you an estimate within a week."

Four Fingers turned his shrewd old eyes on his son and he could read his son's excitement, and his greed. Is it for money, or for power? he asked himself.

It's for both, he decided. The young fool doesn't know that they're both the same. He thought about Phillip Chen's power and the power of the Noble House and the power of the half-coin that John Chen had stolen. Phillip Chen and his wife are fools too, he told himself. They should remember that there are always ears on the other side of walls and once a jealous mother knows a secret it is a secret no longer. Nor can secrets be kept in hotels, among foreign devils, who always presume servants cannot speak the barbarian tongue, nor have long ears and sharp eyes.

Ah sons, he mused. Sons are certainly the wealth of a father—but sometimes also cause the death of the father.

A man's a fool to trust a son. Completely. *Heya?*

"Very well, my son," he said easily. "Give me your plan, written down, and the amount. And I will decide."

* * *

Phillip Chen got out of the taxi at the grass triangle in Kowloon Tong, the attaché case clutched to his chest. The driver turned the meter off and looked at him. The meter read 17.80 HK. If it had been left up to Phillip he would not have taken the same taxi all the way from Struan's Lookout, which meant using the taxi ferry, the meter running all the time. No. He would have crossed the harbor by the Golden Ferry for 15 cents, and got another taxi in Kowloon and saved at least 8 dollars. Terrible waste of money, he thought.

Carefully he counted out 18 dollars. As an afterthought he added a thirty-cent tip, feeling generous. The man drove off and left him standing near the grassy triangle.

Kowloon Tong was just another suburb of Kowloon, a multitudinous nest of buildings, slums, alleys, people and traffic. He found Essex Road, that skirted the garden, and walked around the road. The attaché case seemed to be getting heavier and he felt sure everyone knew it contained 200,000 HK. His nervousness increased. In an area like this you could buy the death of a man for a few hundred if you knew whom to ask—and for this amount, you could hire an army. His eyes were on the broken pavement. When he had gone almost all the way around the triangle he saw the arrow on the pavement pointing at the wall. His heart was weighty in his chest, hurting him. It was quite dark here, with few streetlights. The hole was formed by some bricks that had fallen away. He could see what looked like a crumpled-up newspaper within the hole. He hastily took it out, made sure there was nothing else left, then went over to a seat under a lamp and sat down. When his heart had slowed and his breathing become more calm he opened the newspaper. In it was an envelope. The envelope was flat and some of his anxiety left him. He had been petrified that he was going to get the other ear.

The note said: "Walk to Waterloo Road. Go north toward the army camp, staying on the west side of the road. Beware, we are watching you now."

A shiver went through him and he looked around. No one seemed to be watching him. Neither friend nor foe. But he could feel eyes. His attaché case became even more leaden.

All gods protect me, he prayed fervently, trying to gather his courage to continue. Where the devil are Four Finger Wu's men?

Waterloo Road was nearby, a busy main thoroughfare. He paid the crowds no attention, just plodded north feeling naked, seeing no one in particular. The shops were all open, restaurants bustling, the alleyways more crowded. In the nearby embankment a goods train whistled mournfully, going north, mixing with the blaring horns that all traffic used indiscriminately. The night was bleak, the sky overcast and very humid.

Wearily he walked half a mile, crossing side streets and alleys. In a knot of people he stopped to let a truck pass, then went across the mouth of another narrow alleyway, moving this way and that as oncomers jostled him. Suddenly two young men were in front of him, barring his path, and one hissed, "Tin koon chi fook!"

"Eh?"

Both wore caps pulled down low, both wore dark glasses, their faces similar. "Tin koon chi fook!" Smallpox Kin repeated malevolently. "Dew neh loh moh give me the bag!"

"Oh!" Blankly Phillip Chen handed it to him. Smallpox Kin grabbed it. "Don't look around, and keep on walking north!"

"All right, but please keep your prom—" Phillip Chen stopped. The two youths were gone. It seemed that they had only been in front of him a split second. Still in shock he forced his feet into motion, trying to etch the little he had seen of their faces on his memory. Then an oncoming woman shoved him rudely and he swore, their faces fading. Then someone grabbed him roughly.

"Where's the fornicating bag?"

"What?" he gasped, staring down at the evil-looking thug who was Goodweather Poon.

"Your bag—where's it gone?"

"Two young men . . ." Helplessly he pointed backward. The man cursed and hurried past, weaving in and out of the crowd, put his fingers to his lips and whistled shrilly. Few people paid any attention to him. Other toughs began to converge, then Goodweather Poon caught sight of the two youths with the attaché case as they turned off the well-lit main road into an alley. He broke into a run, others following him.

Smallpox Kin and his younger brother went into the crowds without hurrying, the alley unlit except for the bare bulbs of the dingy stalls and stores. They grinned, one to another. Completely confident now, they took off their glasses and caps and stuffed them into their pockets. Both were very similar—almost twins—and now they melted even more into the raucous shoppers.

"Dew neh loh moh that old bastard looked frightened to death!" Smallpox Kin chortled. "In one step we have reached heaven!"

"Yes. And next week when we snatch him he'll pay up as easily as an old dog farts!"

They laughed and stopped a moment in the light of a stall and peeked into the bag. When they both saw the bundle of notes both sighed. "Ayeeyah, truly we've reached heaven with one step, Elder Brother. Pity the son is dead and buried."

Smallpox Kin shrugged as they went on, turning into a smaller alley, then another, surefooted in the darkening maze. "Honorable Father's right. We have turned ill luck into good. It wasn't your fault that bastard's head was soft! Not at all! When we dig him up and leave him on the Sha Tin Road with the note on his fornicating chest. . . ." He stopped a moment and they stepped aside in the bustling, jostling crowds to allow a laden, broken-down truck to squeeze past. As they waited he happened to glance back. At the far end of this alley he saw three men change direction, seeing him, then begin to hurry toward him.

"*Dew neh loh moh* we're betrayed," he gasped then shoved his way forward and took to his heels, his brother close behind.

The two youths were very fast. Terror lent cunning to their feet as they rushed through the cursing crowd, maneuvering around the inevitable potholes and small stalls, the darkness helping them. Smallpox Kin led the charge. He ducked between some stalls and fled down the narrow unlit passageway, the attaché case clutched tightly. "Go home a different way, Young Brother," he gasped.

At the next corner he rushed left and his brother went directly on. Their three pursuers split up as well, two following him. It was almost impossible to see now in the darkness and the alleys twisted and turned and never a dead end. His chest was heaving but he was well ahead of his pursuers. He fled into a shortcut and at once turned into a bedraggled store that, like all the rest, served as a dwelling. Careless of the family huddled around a screeching television he rushed through them and out the back door, then doubled back to the end of the alley. He peered around the corner with great caution. A few people watched him curiously but continued on their way without stopping, wanting no part of what clearly was trouble.

Then, hoping he was safe, he slid into the crowds and walked away quietly, his head down. His breath was still labored and his head was filled with obscenities and he swore vengeance on Phillip Chen for betraying them. All gods bear witness, he thought furiously, when we kidnap him next week, before we let him go I'll slice off his nose! How dare he betray us to the police! Hey, wait a moment, were those police?

He thought about that as he wandered along in the stream, cautiously doubling back from time to time, just in case. But now he was sure he was not followed. He let his mind consider the money and he beamed. Let's see, what will I do with my 50,000! I'll put 40 down on an apartment and rent it out at once. *Ayeeyah*, I'm a property owner! I'll buy a Rolex and a revolver and a new throwing knife. I'll give my wife a bracelet or two, and a couple to White Rose at the Thousand Pleasure Whorehouse. Tonight we'll have a feast. . . .

Happily he continued on his way. At a street stall he bought a small cheap suitcase and, in an alley, secretly transferred the money into it. Farther down the street in another side alley he sold Phillip Chen's good leather attaché case to a hawker for a handsome sum after haggling for five minutes. Now, very pleased with himself, he caught a bus for Kowloon City where his father had rented a small apartment in an assumed name as one of their havens, far away from their real home in Wanchai near Glessing's Point. He did not notice Goodweather Poon board the bus, nor the other two men, nor the taxi that followed the bus.

Kowloon City was a festering mess of slums and open drains and squalid dwellings. Smallpox Kin knew he was safe here. No police ever came, except in great strength. When China had leased the New Territories for ninety-nine years in 1898 it had maintained suzerainty over Kowloon City in perpetuity. In theory the ten square acres were Chinese territory. The British authorities left the area alone provided it remained quiet. It was a seething mass of opium dens, illegal gambling schools, triad headquarters, and a sanctuary for the criminal. From time to time the police would sweep through. The next day the Kowloon City would become as it had always been.

The stairs to the fifth-floor apartment in the tenement building were rickety and messy, the plaster cracked and mildewed. He was tired now. He knocked on the door, in their secret code. The door opened.

"Hello, Father, hello, Dog-eared Chen," he said happily. "Here's the cash!" Then he saw his younger brother. "Oh good, you escaped too?"

"Of course! Dung-eating police in civilian clothes! We ought to kill one or two for their impertinence." Kin Pak waved a .38. "We ought to have vengeance!"

"Perhaps you're right, now that we've got the first money," Father Kin said.

"I don't think we should kill any police, that would send them mad," Dog-eared Chen said shakily.

"*Dew neh loh moh* on all police!" young Kin Pak said and pocketed the gun.

Smallpox Kin shrugged. "We've got the cash th—"

At that moment the door burst open. Goodweather Poon and three of his men were in the room, knives out. Everyone froze. Abruptly Father Kin slid a knife out of his sleeve and ducked left but before he could throw it Goodweather Poon's knife was flailing through the air and it thwanged into his throat. He clawed at it as he fell backward. Neither Dog-eared Chen nor the brothers had moved. They watched him die. The body twitched, the muscles spasmed for a moment, then was still.

"Where's Number One Son Chen?" Goodweather Poon said, a second knife in his hand.

"We don't know any Num—"

Two of the men fell on Smallpox Kin, slammed his hands outstretched on the table and held them there. Goodweather Poon leaned forward and sliced off his index finger. Smallpox Kin went gray. The other two were paralyzed with fear.

"Where's Number One Son Chen?"

Smallpox Kin was staring blankly at his severed finger and the blood that was pulsing onto the table. He cried out as Goodweather Poon lunged again. "Don't don't," he begged, "he's dead . . . dead and we've buried him I swear it!"

"Where?"

"Near the Sha . . . the Sha Tin Road. Listen," he screeched desperately, "we'll split the money with you. We'll—" He froze as Goodweather Poon put the tip of his knife into his mouth.

"Just answer questions, you fornicating whore's turd, or I'll slit your tongue. Where's Number One Son's things? The things he had on him?"

"We, we sent everything to Noble House Chen, everything except the money he had. I swear it." He whimpered at the pain. Suddenly the two men put pressure on one of his elbows and he cried out, "All gods bear witness it's the truth!" He screamed as the joint went, and fainted. Across the room Dog-eared Chen groaned with fear. He started to cry out but one of the men smashed him in the face, his head crashed against the wall and he collapsed, unconscious.

Now all their eyes went to Kin Pak. "It's true," Kin Pak gasped in terror at the suddenness of everything. "Everything he told you. It's true!"

Goodweather Poon cursed him. Then he said, "Did you search Noble House Chen before you buried him?"

"Yes, Lord, at least I didn't, he . . ." Shakily he pointed at his father's body. "He did."

"You were there?"

The youth hesitated. Instantly Poon darted at him, moving with incredible speed for such an old man. His knife knicked Kin Pak's cheek a deliberate fraction below his eyes and stayed there. "Liar!"

"I was there," the youth choked out, "I was going to tell you, Lord, I was there. I won't lie to you I swear it!"

"The next time you lie it will be your left eye. You were there, *heya*?"

"Yes . . . yes, Lord!"

"Was he there?" he said pointing at Smallpox Kin.

"No, Lord."

"Him?"

"Yes. Dog-eared was there!"

"Did you search the body?"

"Yes, Lord, yes I helped our father."

"All his pockets, everything?"

"Yes yes everything."

"Any papers? Notebook, diary? Jewelry?"

The youth hesitated, frantic, trying to think, the knife never moving away from his face. "Nothing, Lord, that I remember. We sent all his things to Noble House Chen, except, except the money. We kept the money. And his watch—I'd forgotten his watch! It's, it's that one!" He pointed at the watch on his father's outstretched wrist.

Goodweather Poon swore again. Four Finger Wu had told him to recapture John Chen, to get any of his possessions the kidnappers still had, particularly any coins or parts of coins, and then, equally anonymously, to dispose of the kidnappers. I'd better phone him in a moment, he thought. I'd better get further instructions. I don't want to make a mistake.

"What did you do with the money?"

"We spent it, Lord. There were only a few hundred dollars and some change. It's gone."

One of the men said, "I think he's lying!"

"I'm not, Lord, I swear it!" Kin Pak almost burst into tears. "I'm not. Pl—"

"Shut up! Shall I cut this one's throat?" the man said genially, motioning at Smallpox Kin who was still unconscious, sprawled across the table, the pool of blood thickening.

"No, no, not yet. Hold him there." Goodweather Poon scratched his piles while he thought a moment. "We'll go and dig up Number One Son Chen. Yes that's what we'll do. Now, Little Turd, who killed him?"

At once Kin Pak pointed at his father's body. "He did. It was terrible. He's our father and he hit him with a shovel . . . he hit him with a shovel when he tried to escape the night . . . the night we got him." The youth shuddered, his face chalky, his fear of the knife under his eye consuming him. "It, it wasn't my fault, Lord."

"What's your name?"

"Soo Tak-gai, Lord," he said instantly, using their prearranged emergency names.

"Him?" The finger pointed at his brother.

"Soo Tak-tong."

"Him?"

"Wu-tip Sup."

"And him?"

The youth looked at his father's body. "He was Goldtooth Soo, Lord. He was very bad but we . . . we, we had to obey. We had to obey him, he was our, our father."

"Where did you take Number One Son Chen before you killed him?"

"To Sha Tin, Lord, but I didn't kill him. We snatched him Hong Kong side then put him in the back of a car we stole and went to Sha Tin. There's an old shack our father rented, just outside the village . . . he planned everything. We had to obey him."

Poon grunted and nodded at his men. "We'll search here first." At once they released Smallpox Kin, the unconscious youth who slumped to the floor, leaving a trail of blood. "You, bind up his finger!" Hastily Kin Pak grabbed an old dishcloth and, near vomiting, began to tie a rough tourniquet around the stump.

Poon sighed, not knowing what to do first. After a moment he opened the suitcase. All their eyes went to the mountain of notes. They all felt the greed. Poon shifted the knife into his other hand and closed the suitcase. He left it in the center of the table and started to search the dingy apartment. There was just a table, a few chairs and an old iron bedstead with a soiled mattress. Paper was peeling off the walls, the windows mostly boarded up and glassless. He turned the mattress over, then searched it but it concealed nothing. He went into the filthy, almost empty kitchen and switched on the light. Then into the foul-smelling toilet. Smallpox Kin whimpered, coming around.

In a drawer Goodweather Poon found some papers, ink and writing brushes. "What's this for?" he asked, holding up one of the papers. On it was written in bold characters: "This Number One Son Chen had the stupidity to try to escape us. No one can escape the Werewolves! Let all Hong Kong beware. Our eyes are everywhere!" "What's this for, *heya?*"

Kin Pak looked up from the floor, desperate to please. "We couldn't return him alive to Noble House Chen so our father ordered that . . . that tonight we were to dig Number One Son up and put that on his chest and put him beside the Sha Tin Road."

Goodweather Poon looked at him. "When you start to dig you'd better find him quickly, the first time," he said malevolently. "Yes. Or your eyes, Little Turd, won't be anywhere."

35

Orlanda Ramos came up the wide staircase of the vast *Floating Dragon* restaurant at Aberdeen and moved through the noisy, chattering guests at Sir Shi-teh T'Chung's banquet looking for Linc Bartlett—and Casey.

The two hours that she had spent with Linc this morning for the newspaper interview had been revealing, particularly about Casey. Her instincts had told her the sooner she brought the enemy to battle the better. It had been easy to have them both invited tonight—Shi-teh was an old associate of Gornt and an old friend. Gornt had been pleased with her idea.

They were on the top deck. There was a nice smell of the sea coming through the large windows, the night good though humid, overcast, and all around were the lights of the high rises and the township of Aberdeen. Out in the harbor, nearby, were the brooding islands of junks, partially lit, where 150,000 boat people lived their lives.

The room they were in, scarlet and gold and green, stretched half the length and the whole breadth of the boat, off the central staircase. Ornate wood and plaster gargoyles and unicorns and dragons were everywhere throughout the three soaring decks of the restaurant ablaze with lights and packed with diners. Below decks, the cramped kitchens held twenty-eight cooks, an army of helpers, a dozen huge cauldrons—steam, sweat and smoke. Eighty-two waiters serviced the *Floating Dragon*. There were seats for four hundred on each of the first two decks and two hundred on the third. Sir Shi-teh had taken over the whole top deck and now it was well filled with his guests, standing in impatient groups amid the round tables that seated twelve.

Orlanda felt fine tonight and very confident. She had again dressed meticulously for Bartlett. This morning when she had had the interview with him she had worn casual American clothes and little makeup, and the loose, silk blouse that she had selected so carefully did not flaunt her bralessness, merely suggested it. This daring new fashion pleased her greatly, making her even more aware of her femininity. Tonight she wore delicate white silk. She knew her figure was perfect, that she was envied for her open, unconscious sensuality.

That's what Quillan did for me, she thought, her lovely head high and the curious half-smile lighting her face—one of the many things. He made me understand sensuality.

Havergill and his wife were in front of her and she saw their eyes on her breasts. She laughed to herself, well aware that, even discreetly, she would be the only woman in the room who had dared to be so modern, to emulate the fashion that had begun the year before in Swinging London.

"Evening, Mr. Havergill, Mrs. Havergill," she said politely, moving around them in the crush. She knew him well. Many times he had been invited onto Gornt's yacht. Sometimes Gornt's yacht would steam out from the Yacht Club, Hong Kong side, with just her and Quillan and his men friends aboard and go over to Kowloon, to the sea-washed steps beside the Golden Ferry where the girls would be waiting, dressed in sun clothes or boating clothes.

In her early days with Quillan she too had had to wait Kowloon side, honoring the golden rule in the Colony that discretion was all important and when you live Hong Kong side you play Kowloon side, live Kowloon side, play Hong Kong side.

In the days when Quillan's wife was bedridden and Orlanda was openly, though still most discreetly, Quillan's mistress, Quillan would take her with him to Japan and Singapore and Taiwan but never Bangkok. In those days Paul Havergill was Paul or more likely, Horny—Horny Hav-a-girl, as he was known to most of his intimates. But even then, whenever she would meet him in public, like tonight, it would always be Mr. Havergill. He's not a bad man, she told herself, remembering that though most of his girls never liked him, they fawned on him for he was reasonably generous and could always arrange a sudden loan at low interest for a friend through one of his banking associates, but never at the Vic.

Wise, she thought, amused, and a matter of face. Ah, but I could write such a book about them all if I wanted to. I never will—I don't think I ever will. Why should I, there's no reason. Even after Macao I've always kept the secrets. That's another thing Quillan taught me—discretion.

Macao. What a waste! I can hardly remember what that young man looked like now, only that he was awful at the pillow and, because of him, my life was destroyed. The fool was only a sudden, passing fancy, the very first. It was only loneliness because Quillan was away a month and everyone away, and it was lust for youth—just the youth-filled body that had attracted me and proved to be so useless. Fool! What a fool I was!

Her heart began fluttering at the thought of all those nightmares: being caught, being sent to England, having to fight the youth off, desperate to please Quillan, then coming back and Quillan so cool and never pillowing with him again. And then the greater nightmare of adjusting to a life without him.

Terrifying days. That awful unquenchable desire. Being alone. Being
excluded. All the tears and the misery then trying to begin again but cautiously, always hoping he would relent if I was patient. Never anyone in
Hong Kong, always alone in Hong Kong, but when the urge was too
much, going away and trying but never satisfied. Oh Quillan, what a
lover you were!

Not long ago his wife had died and then, when the time was right,
Orlanda had gone to see him. To seduce him back to her. That night she
had thought that she had succeeded but he had only been toying with
her. "Put your clothes on, Orlanda. I was just curious about your body, I
wanted to see if it was still as exquisite as it was in *my* day. I'm delighted
to tell you it is—you're still perfection. But, so sorry, I don't desire you."
And all her frantic weepings and pleadings made no difference. He just
listened and smoked a cigarette then stubbed it out. "Orlanda, please don't
ever come here again uninvited," he had said so quietly. "You chose
Macao."

And he was right, I did, I took his face away. Why does he still support
me? she asked herself, her eyes wandering the guests, seeking Bartlett. Do
you have to lose something before you find its true value? Is that what life
is?

"Orlanda!"

She stopped, startled, as someone stepped in her way. Her eyes focused.
It was Richard Hamilton Pugmire. He was slightly shorter than she was.
"May I introduce Charles Biltzmann from America," he was saying with a
leer, his nearness making her skin crawl. "Charles's going to be, the, er,
the new tai-pan of General Stores. Chuck, this's Orlanda Ramos!"

"Pleased to meet you, ma'am!"

"How are you?" she said politely, instantly disliking him. "I'm sorry—"

"Call me Chuck. It's Orlanda? Say, that's a mighty pretty name, mighty
pretty dress!" Biltzmann produced his visiting card with a flourish. "Old
Chinese custom!"

She accepted it but did not reciprocate. "Thank you. Sorry, Mr. Biltzmann, would you excuse me? I have to join my friends an—" Before she
could prevent it, Pugmire took her arm, led her aside a pace and whispered throatily, "How about dinner? You look fantas—"

She jerked her arm away trying not to be obvious. "Go away, Pug."

"Listen, Orlan—"

"I've told you politely fifty times to leave me alone! Now *dew neh loh
moh* on you and all your line!" she said and Pugmire flushed. She had always detested him, even in the old days. He was always looking at her
behind Quillan's back, leching, and when she had been discarded, Pugmire had pestered her and tried every way to get her into bed—still did.
"If you ever call or talk to me again I'll tell all Hong Kong about you and
your peculiar habits." She nodded politely to Biltzmann, let his card drop

unnoticed and walked off. After a moment, Pugmire went back to the American.

"What a body!" Biltzmann said, his eyes still following her.

"She's—she's one of our well-known whores," Pugmire said with a sneer. "I wish to Christ they'd hurry up with the food. I'm starving."

"She's a tramp?" Biltzmann gaped at him.

"You can never tell here." Pugmire added, keeping his voice down, "I'm surprised Shitee T'Chung invited her. Still, I don't suppose he gives a shit now that his knighthood's dubbed and paid for. Years ago, Orlanda used to be a girlfriend of a friend but she was up to her old tricks of selling it on the side. He caught her at it and gave her the Big E."

"The Big E?"

"The Elbow—the shove."

Biltzmann could not take his eyes off her. "Jesus," he muttered, "I don't know about the Big E but I'd sure as hell like to give her the Big One."

"That's just a matter of money but I can assure you, old chap, she's not worth it. Orlanda's dreadful in the sack, I know, and nowadays you can never tell who's been there before, eh?" Pugmire laughed at the American's expression. "Never fancied her myself after the first time, but if you dip your wick there you'd better use precautions."

Dunross had just arrived and he was listening with half an ear to Richard Kwang who was talking grandly about the deals he had made to stave off the run, and how foul certain people were to spread such rumors.

"I quite agree, Richard," Dunross said, wanting to join the visiting MPs, who were at the far end of the room. "There really are a lot of bastards around. If you'll excuse me . . ."

"Of course, tai-pan." Richard Kwang dropped his voice but could not prevent some of his anxiety showing. "I might need a hand."

"Anything, of course, except money."

"You could talk to Johnjohn at the Vic for me. He'd—"

"He won't, you know that, Richard. Your only chance is one of your Chinese friends. What about Smiler Ching?"

"Huh, that old crook—wouldn't ask him for any of his dirty money!" Richard Kwang said with a sneer. Smiler Ching had reneged on their deal and had refused to lend him money—or credit. "That old crook deserves prison! There's a run on him too, but that's what he deserves! I think it's all started by the Communists, they're trying to ruin us all. The Bank of China! Did you hear about the queues at the Vic in Central? There're more at Blacs. Old Big Belly Tok's Bank of East Asia and Japan's gone under. They won't open their doors tomorrow."

"Christ, are you sure?"

"He called me tonight asking for 20 million. *Dew neh loh moh*, tai-pan, unless we all get help Hong Kong's going under. We've . . ." Then he saw Venus Poon in the doorway on the arm of Four Finger Wu and his heart skipped eight beats. This evening she had been furious when he did not arrive with the mink coat that he had promised her. She had wept and shouted and her *amah* had wailed and they would not accept his excuse that his furrier had let him down and they both had gone on and on until he promised without fail that before the races he would bring her the gift that he had promised.

"Are you taking me to Shi-teh's?"

"My wife changed her mind and now she's going, so I can't, but afterwards we'll go—"

"Afterwards I'll be tired! First no present and now I can't go to the party! Where's the aquamarine pendant you promised me last month? Where did my mink go? On your wife's back I'll bet! *Ayeeyah*, my hairdresser and her hairdresser are friends so I'll find out if it did. Oh woe woe woe you don't really love your Daughter anymore. I'll have to kill myself or accept Four Finger Wu's invitation."

"*Wat?*"

Richard Kwang remembered how he had almost had a hemorrhage then and there, and he had ranted and raved and screamed that her apartment cost him a fortune and her clothes cost thousands a week and she had ranted and raved and screamed back. "And what about the run on the bank? Are you solvent? What about my savings? Are they safe *heya?*"

"*Ayeeyah* you miserable whore, what savings? The savings I am going to put there for you? Huh! Of course they're safe, safe as the Bank of England!"

"Woe woe woe I'm penniless now. Your poor destitute Daughter! I'll have to sell myself or commit suicide. Yes, that's it! Poison . . . that's it! I think I'll take an overdose of . . . of aspirins. *Ah Poo! Bring me an overdose of aspirins!*"

So he had begged and pleaded and eventually she had relented and allowed him to take away the aspirins and he had promised to rush back to the apartment the very moment the banquet was over and now his eyes were almost staring out of his head because there, at the doorway, was Venus Poon on the arm of Four Finger Wu, both resplendent, he puffed with pride, and she demure and innocent, wearing the dress he'd just paid for.

"What's up, Richard?" Dunross asked, concerned.

Richard Kwang tried to speak, couldn't, just tottered away toward his wife who tore her baleful eyes off Venus Poon and put them back on him.

"Hello, dear," he said, his backbone jelly.

"Hello, dear," Mai-ling Kwang replied sweetly. "Who's that whore?"

"Which one?"

"That one."

"Isn't that the . . . what's her name . . . the TV starlet?"

"Isn't her name Itch-in-her-drawers Poon, the VD starlet?"

He pretended to laugh with her but he wanted to tear all his hair out. The fact that his latest mistress had come with someone else would not be lost on all Hong Kong. Everyone would interpret it as an infallible sign that he was in absolute financial trouble and that she had, wisely, left the sinking junk for a safer haven. And coming with his uncle, Four Finger Wu, was even worse. That would confirm that all Wu's wealth had been removed from the Ho-Pak, and therefore most probably Lando Mata and the gold syndicate had done the same. All the civilized population that counted were sure that Wu was the syndicate's prime smuggler now that Smuggler Mo was dead. Woe woe woe! Troubles never come singly.

"Eh?" he asked wearily. "What did you say?"

"I said, is the tai-pan going to approach the Victoria for us?"

He switched into Cantonese as Europeans were nearby. "Regretfully that son of a whore's in trouble himself. No, he won't help us. We're in great trouble which is not our fault. The day has been terrible, except for one thing: we made a fine profit today. I sold all our Noble House stock."

"Excellent. At what price?"

"We made 2.70 a share. It's all in gold now in Zurich. I'm putting it all in our joint account," he added carefully, twisting the truth, all the while trying to figure out a ploy to get his wife out of the room so he could go over to Four Finger Wu and Venus Poon to pretend to everyone that everything was fine.

"Good. Very good. That's better." Mai-ling was toying with her huge aquamarine pendant. Suddenly Richard Kwang's testicles chilled. This was the pendant he had promised Venus Poon. Oh woe woe woe . . .

"Are you feeling all right?" Mai-ling asked.

"I, er, I must have eaten some bad fish. I think I need to go to the bathroom."

"You'd better go now. I suppose we'll eat soon. Shitee's always so late!" She noticed him take a nervous sidelong look at Venus Poon and Uncle Wu and her eyes turned baleful again. "That whore's really quite fascinating. I'm going to watch her until you get back."

"Why don't we go together?" He took her arm and guided her down the stairs to the door that led to the bathrooms, greeting friends here and there, trying to exude confidence. The moment she was launched into the ladies' room he rushed back up, walked over to Zeppelin Tung who was near them. He chatted a moment, then pretended to see Four Fingers. "Oh hello, Honored Uncle," he said expansively. "Thank you for bringing her here. Hello, little oily mouth."

"What?" the old man said suspiciously. "I brought her for me not for you."

"Yes, and don't you oily mouth me," Venus Poon hissed and deliberately took the old man's arm and Richard Kwang almost spat blood. "I talked to my hairdresser tonight! My mink on her back! And isn't that my aquamarine pendant too, the one she's wearing right now! To think I almost committed suicide tonight because I thought I'd displeased my Honored Father . . . and all the time it was lies lies lies. Oh I almost want to commit suicide again."

"Eh, don't do that yet, Little Mealy Mouth," Four Finger Wu whispered anxiously, having already negotiated a deal in excess of Smiler Ching's offer. "Go away, Nephew, you're giving her indigestion. She won't be able to perform!"

Richard Kwang forced a glazed smile, muttered a few pleasantries and went off shakily. He headed for the staircase to wait for his wife, and someone said, "I see a certain filly's left the paddock for more manured grass!"

"What nonsense!" he replied at once. "Of course I asked the old fool to bring her since my wife is here. Why else would she be with him? Is that old fool hung like a bullock? Or even a bantam cock? No. *Ayeeyah*, not even Venus Poon with all the technique I taught her can get up what has no thread! It's good for his face to pretend otherwise, *heya*? Of course, and she wanted to see her Old Father and to be seen too!"

"Eeeee, that's clever, Banker Kwang!" the man said, and turned away and whispered it to another, who said caustically, "Huh, you'd swallow a bucket of shit if someone said it was stewed beef with black bean sauce! Don't you know old Four Finger's Stalk's nurtured by the most expensive salves and ointments and ginseng that money can buy? Why only last month his Number Six Concubine gave birth to a son! Eeeee, don't worry about him. Before he's through tonight, Venus Poon's in for a drubbing that'll make her Golden Gully cry out for mercy in eight dialects. . . ."

"Are you staying for dinner, tai-pan?" Brian Kwok asked, intercepting him. "When and if it arrives."

"Yes. Why?"

"Sorry I've got to go back to work. But there'll be someone else to chaperone you home."

"For God's sake, Brian, aren't you overreacting?" Dunross said as quietly.

Brian Kwok kept his voice down. "I don't think so. I've just phoned Crosse to see what happened about those two loiterers outside your house. The moment our fellows arrived they took to their heels."

"Perhaps they were just thugs who don't like police."

Brian Kwok shook his head. "Crosse asked again that you give us the AMG papers right now."

"Friday."

"He told me to tell you there's a Soviet spy ship in port. There's already been one killing—one of their agents, knifed."

Dunross was shocked. "What's that got to do with me?"

"You know that better than we do. You know what's in those reports.

Must be quite serious or you wouldn't be so difficult—or careful—yourself. Crosse said . . . Never mind him! Ian, look, we're old friends. I'm really very worried." Brian Kwok switched to Cantonese. "Even the wise can fall into thorns—poisoned thorns."

"In two days the police Mandarin arrives. Two days is not long."

"True. But in two days the spy may hurt us very much. Why tempt the gods? It is my ask."

"No. Sorry."

Brian Kwok hardened. In English he said, "Our American friends have asked us to take you into protective custody."

"What nonsense!"

"Not such nonsense, Ian. It's very well known you've a photographic memory. The sooner you turn the papers over the better. Even afterwards you should be careful. Why not tell me where they are and we'll take care of everything?"

Dunross was equally set-faced. "Everything's taken care of now, Brian. Everything stays as planned."

The tall Chinese sighed. Then he shrugged. "Very well. Sorry, but don't say you weren't warned. Are Gavallan and Jacques staying for dinner too?"

"No, I don't think so. I asked them just to put in an appearance. Why?"

"They could've gone home with you. Please don't go anywhere alone for a while, don't try to lose your guard. For the time being, if you have any, er, private dates call me."

"Me, a private date? Here in Hong Kong? Really, what a suggestion!"

"Does the name Jen mean anything?"

Dunross's eyes became stony. "You buggers can be too nosy."

"And you don't seem to realize you're in a very dirty game without Queensberry rules."

"I've got that message, by God."

" 'Night, tai-pan."

" 'Night, Brian." Dunross went over to the MPs who were in a group in one corner talking with Jacques deVille. There were only four of them now, the rest were resting after their long journey. Jacques deVille introduced him. Sir Charles Pennyworth, Conservative; Hugh Guthrie, Liberal; Julian Broadhurst and Robin Grey, both Labour. "Hello, Robin," he said.

"Hello, Ian. It's been a long time."

"Yes."

"If you'll excuse me, I'll be off," deVille said, his face careworn. "My wife's away and we've a young grandchild staying with us."

"Did you talk to Susanne in France?" Dunross asked.

"Yes, tai-pan. She's . . . she'll be all right. Thank you for calling Deland. See you tomorrow. Good night, gentlemen." He walked off.

Dunross glanced back at Robin Grey. "You haven't changed at all."

"Nor have you," Grey said, then turned to Pennyworth. "Ian and I met in London some years ago, Sir Charles. It was just after the war. I'd just become a shop steward." He was a lean man with thin lips, thin graying hair and sharp features.

"Yes, it was some years ago," Dunross said politely, continuing the pattern that Penelope and her brother had agreed to so many years ago—that neither side was blood kin to the other. "So, Robin, are you staying long?"

"Just a few days," Grey said. His smile was as thin as his lips. "I've never been in this workers' paradise before so I want to visit a few unions, see how the other ninety-nine percent live."

Sir Charles Pennyworth, leader of the delegation, laughed. He was a florid, well-covered man, an ex-colonel of the London Scottish Regiment, D.S.O. and Bar. "Don't think they go much on unions here, Robin. Do they, tai-pan?"

"Our labor force does very well without them," Dunross said.

"Sweated labor, tai-pan," Grey said at once. "According to some of your own statistics, government statistics."

"Not our statistics, Robin, merely your statisticians," Dunross said. "Our people are the highest paid in Asia after the Japanese and this is a free society."

"Free? Come off it!" Grey jeered. "You mean free to exploit the workers. Well, never mind, when Labour gets in at the next election we'll change all that."

"Come now, Robin," Sir Charles said. "Labour hasn't a prayer at the next election."

Grey smiled. "Don't bet on it, Sir Charles. The people of England want change. We didn't all go to war to keep up the rotten old ways. Labour's for social change—and getting the workers a fair share of the profits they create."

Dunross said, "I've always thought it rather unfair that Socialists talk about the 'workers' as though they do all the work and we do none. We're workers too. We work as hard if not harder with longer hours an—"

"Ah, but you're a tai-pan and you live in a great big house that was handed down, along with your power. All that capital came from some poor fellow's sweat, and I won't even mention the opium trade that started it all. It's fair that capital should be spread around, fair that everyone should have the same start. The rich should be taxed more. There should be a capital tax. The sooner the great fortunes are broken up the better for all Englishmen, eh, Julian?"

Julian Broadhurst was a tall, distinguished man in his mid-forties, a strong supporter of the Fabian Society, which was the intellectual brain trust of the socialist movement. "Well, Robin," he said with his lazy, almost diffident voice, "I certainly don't advocate as you do that we take to the barricades but I do think, Mr. Dunross, that here in Hong Kong you could do with a Trades Union Council, a minimum wage scale, elected legislature, proper unions and safeguards, socialized medicine, workman's compensation and all the modern British innovations."

"Totally wrong, Mr. Broadhurst. China would never agree to a change in our colonial status, they would never allow any form of city-state on her border. As to the rest, who pays for them?" Dunross asked. "Our unfettered system here's outperforming Britain twenty times and—"

"You pay for it out of all your profits, Ian," Robin Grey said with a laugh. "You pay a fair tax, not 15 percent. You pay the same as we do in Britain and—"

"God forbid!" Dunross said, hard put to keep his temper. "You're taxing yourself out of business and out of c—"

"Profit?" the last MP, the Liberal, Hugh Guthrie interrupted caustically. "The last bloody Labour Government wiped out our profits years ago with bloody stupid profligate spending, ridiculous nationalization, giving the Empire away piecemeal with fatuous stupid abandon, disrupting the Commonwealth and shoving poor old England's face in the bloody mud. Bloody ridiculous! Attlee and all that shower!"

Robin Grey said placatingly, "Come on, Hugh, the Labour Government did what the people wanted, what the masses wanted."

"Nonsense! The enemy wanted it. The Communists! In barely eighteen years you gave away the greatest empire the world's ever seen, made us a second-class power and allowed the sodding Soviet enemy to eat up most of Europe. Bloody ridiculous!"

"I agree wholeheartedly that communism's dreadful. But as to 'giving' away our empire, it was the wind of change, Hugh," Broadhurst said, calming him. "Colonialism had run its course. You really must take the long-term view."

"I do. I think we're up the creek without a paddle. Churchill's right, always was."

"The people didn't think so," Grey said grimly. "That's why he was voted out. The armed service vote did that, they'd had enough of him. As to the Empire, sorry Hugh old chap, but it was just an excuse to exploit natives who didn't know any better." Robin Grey saw their faces and read them. He was used to the hatred that surrounded him. He hated them more and always had. After the war he had wanted to stay in the Regular Army but he had been rejected—captains were two a penny then with decorations and great war service, while he spent the war a POW at Changi. So, filled with anger and resentment, he had joined Crawley's, a huge car manufacturer, as a mechanic. Quickly he had become a shop steward and union organizer, then into the lower ranks of the Trades Union General Council. Five years ago, he had become a Labour MP where he was now, a cutting, angry, hostile backbencher and protégé of the late left-wing Socialist Aneurin Bevan. "Yes, we got rid of Churchill and when we get in next year we'll sweep out a lot more of the old tired ways and upper-class infections back where they belong. We'll nationalize every industry an—"

"Really, Robin," Sir Charles said, "this is a banquet not a soapbox in Hyde Park. We all agreed to cut out politics while we were on the trip."

"You're right, Sir Charles. It was just that the tai-pan of the Noble House asked me." Grey turned to Dunross. "How is the Noble House?"

"Fine. Very fine."

"According to this afternoon's paper there's a run on your stock?"

"One of our competitors is playing silly buggers, that's all."

"And the bank runs? They're not serious either?"

"They're serious." Dunross was choosing his words carefully. He knew the anti–Hong Kong lobby in Parliament was strong and many members of all three parties were against its colonial status, against its nonvoting status and freewheeling nature—and most of all envious of its almost tax-free basis. Never mind, he thought. Since 1841 we've survived hostile Parliaments, fire, typhoon, pestilence, plague, embargo, depression, occupation and the periodic convulsions that China goes through, and somehow we always will.

"The run's on the Ho-Pak, one of our Chinese banks," Dunross said.

"It's the largest, isn't it?" Grey said.

"No. But it's large. We're all hoping it'll weather the problem."

"If it goes broke, what about all the depositors' money?"

"Unfortunately they lose it," Dunross said, backed into a corner.

"You need English banking laws."

"No, we've found our system operates very well. How did you find China?" Dunross asked.

Before Sir Charles could answer, Grey said, "Our majority view is that they're dangerous, hostile, should be locked up and the Hong Kong border sealed. They're openly committed to becoming a world irritant and their brand of communism is merely an excuse for dictatorship and exploitation of their masses."

Dunross and the other Hong Kong *yan* blanched as Sir Charles said sharply, "Come now, Robin, that's only your view and the Comm—the, er, and McLean's. I found just the opposite. I think China's very sincere in trying to deal with the problems of China, which are hideous, monumental and I think insoluble."

"Thank God there's going to be big trouble there," Grey said with a sneer. "Even the Russians knew it, why else would they get out?"

"Because they're enemies, they share a common five thousand miles of border," Dunross said trying to hold in his anger. "They've always distrusted each other. Because China's invader has always come out of the West, and Russia's always out of the East. Possession of China's always been Russia's obsession and preoccupation."

"Come now, Mr. Dunross," Broadhurst began. "You exaggerate, surely."

"It's to Russia's advantage to have China weak and divided, and Hong Kong disrupted. Russia *requires* China weak as a cornerstone of its foreign policy."

"At least Russia's civilized," Grey said. "Red China's fanatic, dangerous and heathen and should be cut off, particularly from here."

"Ridiculous!" Dunross said tightly. "China has the oldest civilization on earth. China desperately wants to be friends with the West. China's Chinese first and Communist second."

"Hong Kong and you 'traders' are keeping the Communists in power."

"Rubbish! Mao Tse-tung and Chou En-lai don't need us or the Soviets to stay in Peking!"

Hugh Guthrie said, "As far as I'm concerned Red China and Soviet Russia're equally dangerous."

"There's no comparison!" Grey said. "In Moscow they eat with knives and forks and understand food! In China we had nothing but rotten food, rotten hotels and lots of double-talk."

"I really don't understand you at all, old boy," Sir Charles said irritably. "You fought like hell to get on this committee, you're supposed to be interested in Asian affairs and you've done nothing but complain."

"Being critical's not complaining, Sir Charles. Bluntly, I'm for giving Red China no help at all. None. And when I get back I'm offering a motion to change Hong Kong's status entirely: to embargo everything from and to Communist China, to hold immediate and proper elections here, introduce proper taxes, proper unionism and proper British social justice!"

Dunross's chin jutted. "Then you'll destroy our position in Asia!"

"Of all the tai-pans, yes, the people no! Russia was right about China."

"I'm talking about the Free World! Christ almighty, it should be clear to everyone—Soviet Russia's committed to hegemony, to world domination and our destruction. China isn't," Dunross said.

"You're wrong, Ian. You can't see the wood for the trees," Grey said. "Listen! If Russia . . ."

Broadhurst interrupted smoothly. "Russia's just trying to solve her own problems, Mr. Dunross, one of them's the U.S. containment policy. They just want to be left alone and not surrounded by highly emotional Americans with their overfed hands on nuclear triggers."

"Balls! The Yanks're the only friends we've got," Hugh Guthrie said angrily. "As to the Soviets, what about the Cold War? Berlin? Hungary? Cuba, Egypt . . . they're swallowing us piecemeal."

Sir Charles Pennyworth sighed. "Life's strange and memories are so short. In '45, May second it was, in the evening, we joined up with the Russians at Wismar in northern Germany. I'd never been so proud or happy in my life, yes, proud. We sang and drank and cheered and toasted each other. Then my division and all of us in Europe, all the Allies had been held back for weeks to let the Russkies sweep into Germany all through the Balkans, Czechoslovakia and Poland and all the other places.

At the time I didn't think much about it, I was so thankful that the war was almost over at long last and so proud of our Russian allies, but you know, looking back, now I know we were betrayed, we soldiers were betrayed—Russian soldiers included. We got buggered. I don't really know how it happened, still don't, but I truly believe we were betrayed, Julian, by our own leaders, your bloody Socialists, along with Eisenhower, Roosevelt and his misguided advisors. I swear to God I still don't know how it happened but we lost the war, we won but we lost."

"Come now, Charles, you're quite wrong. We all won," Broadhurst said. "The people of the world won when Nazi Germany was sma—" He stopped, startled, as he saw the look on Grey's face. "What's the matter, Robin?"

Grey was staring at the other side of the room. "Ian! That man over there talking to the Chinese . . . do you know him? The tall bugger in the blazer."

Equally astonished, Dunross glanced at the other side of the room. "The sandy-haired fellow? You mean Marlowe, Pete—"

"Peter bloody Marlowe!" Grey muttered. "What's . . . what's he doing in Hong Kong?"

"He's just visiting. From the States. He's a writer. I believe he's writing or researching a book on Hong Kong."

"Writer, eh? Curious. Is he a friend of yours?"

"I met him a few days ago. Why?"

"That's his wife—the girl next to him?"

"Yes. That's Fleur Marlowe, why?"

Grey did not answer. There was a fleck of saliva at the corner of his lips.

"What's his connection with you, Robin?" Broadhurst asked, strangely perturbed.

With an effort Grey tore his eyes off Marlowe. "We were in Changi together, Julian, the Jap POW camp. I was provost marshal for the last couple of years, in charge of camp discipline." He wiped the sweat off his top lip. "Marlowe was one of the black marketeers there."

"Marlowe?" Dunross was astounded.

"Oh yes, Flight Lieutenant Marlowe, the great English gentleman," Grey said, his voice raw with bitterness. "Yes. He and his pal, an American called King, Corporal King, were the main ones. Then there was a fellow called Timsen, an Aussie. . . . But the American was the biggest, he was the King all right. A Texan. He had colonels on his payroll, English gentlemen all—colonels, majors, captains. Marlowe was his interpreter with the Jap and Korean guards . . . we mostly had Korean guards. They were the worst. . . ." Grey coughed. "Christ, it's such a short time ago. Marlowe and the King lived off the fat of the land—those two buggers ate at least one egg a day, while the rest of us starved. You can't imagine how . . ." Again Grey wiped the sweat off his lip without noticing it.

"How long were you a POW?" Sir Charles asked compassionately.

"Three and a half years."

"Terrible," Hugh Guthrie said. "My cousin bought it on the Burma railroad. Terrible!"

"It was all terrible," Grey said. "But it wasn't so terrible for those who sold out. On the Road or at Changi!" He looked at Sir Charles and his eyes were strange and bloodshot. "It's the Marlowes of the world who betrayed us, the ordinary people without privileges of birth." His voice became even more bitter. "No offense but now you're all getting your comeuppance and about time. Christ, I need a drink. Excuse me a moment." He stalked off, heading for the bar that was set up to one side.

"Extraordinary," Sir Charles said.

Guthrie said with a slight, nervous laugh, "For a moment I thought he was going for Marlowe."

They all watched him, then Broadhurst noticed Dunross frowning after Grey, his face set and cold. "Don't pay any attention to him, Mr. Dunross. I'm afraid Grey's very tiresome and a rather vulgar bore. He's . . . well he's not at all representative of the Labour echelon, thank God. You'd like our new leader, Harold Wilson, you'd approve of him. Next time you're in London I'd be glad to introduce you if you've time."

"Thank you. Actually I was thinking about Marlowe. It's hard to believe he 'sold out' or betrayed anyone."

"You never know about people, do you?"

Grey got a whiskey and soda and turned and went across the room. "Well, if it isn't Flight Lieutenant Marlowe!"

Peter Marlowe turned, startled. His smile vanished and the two men stared at one another. Fleur Marlowe froze.

"Hello, Grey," Marlowe said, his voice flat. "I heard you were in Hong Kong. In fact, I read your interview in the afternoon paper." He turned to his wife. "Darling, this is Robin Grey, MP." He introduced him to the Chinese, one of whom was Sir Shi-teh T'Chung.

"Ah, Mr. Grey, it's an honor to have you here," Shi-teh said with an Oxford English accent. He was tall, dark, good-looking, slightly Chinese and mostly European. "We hope your stay in Hong Kong will be good. If there's anything I can do, just say the word!"

"Ta," Grey said carelessly. They all noticed his rudeness. "So, Marlowe! You haven't changed much."

"Nor have you. You've done well for yourself." Marlowe added to the others, "We were in the war together. I haven't seen Grey since '45."

"We were POWs, Marlowe and I," Grey said, then added, "We're on opposite sides of the political blanket." He stopped and stepped out of the way to allow Orlanda Ramos to pass. She greeted Shi-teh with a smile and continued on. Grey watched her briefly, then turned back. "Marlowe old chap, are you still in trade?" It was a private English insult. "Trade" to someone like Marlowe who came from a long line of English officers meant everything common and lower class.

"I'm a writer," Marlowe said. His eyes went to his wife and his eyes smiled at her.

"I thought you'd still be in the RAF, regular officer like your illustrious forebears."

"I was invalided out, malaria and all that. Rather boring," Marlowe said, deliberately lengthening his patrician accent knowing that it would infuriate Grey. "And you're in Parliament? How very clever of you. You represent Streatham East? Wasn't that where you were born?"

Grey flushed. "Yes, yes it was . . ."

Shi-teh covered his embarrassment at the undercurrents between them. "I must, er, see about dinner." He hurried off. The other Chinese excused themselves and turned away.

Fleur Marlowe fanned herself. "Perhaps we should find our table, Peter," she said.

"A good idea, Mrs. Marlowe," Grey said. He was in as tight control as Peter Marlowe. "How's the King?"

"I don't know. I haven't seen him since Changi." Marlowe looked down on Grey.

"But you're in touch with him?"

"No. No, actually I'm not."

"You don't know where he is?"

"No."

"That's strange, seeing how close you two were." Grey ripped his eyes away and glanced at Fleur Marlowe and thought she was the prettiest woman he had ever seen. So pretty and fine and English and fair, just like his ex-wife Trina who went off with an American barely a month after he was reported missing in action. Barely a month. "Did you know we were enemies in Changi, Mrs. Marlowe?" he said with a gentleness that she found frightening.

"Peter's never discussed Changi with me, Mr. Grey. Or anyone that I know of."

"Curious. It was an awesome experience, Mrs. Marlowe. I've forgotten none of it. I . . . well, sorry to interrupt . . ." He glanced up at Marlowe. He began to say something but changed his mind and turned away.

"Oh, Peter, what an awful man!" Fleur said. "He gave me the creeps."

"Nothing to bother about, my darling."

"Why were you enemies?"

"Not now, my pet, later." Marlowe smiled at her, loving her. "Grey's nothing to us."

36

Linc Bartlett saw Orlanda before she saw him and she took his breath away. He couldn't help comparing her with Casey who was beside him talking to Andrew Gavallan. Orlanda was wearing white silk, floor-length, backless with a halter neck that, discreetly, somehow, seemed to offer her golden body. Casey wore her green that he had seen many times, her tawny hair cascading.

"Would you both like to come to Shi-teh's tonight?" Orlanda had asked him this morning. "It could be important for you and your Casey to be there."

"Why?"

"Because almost all business that counts in Hong Kong is done at this type of function, Mr. Bartlett. It could be very important for you to become involved with people like Shi-teh—and in the Turf Club, Cricket Club, even *the* Club itself, though that'd be impossible."

"Because I'm American?"

"Because someone has to die to create an opening—an English or Scotsman." She had laughed. "The waiting list's as long as Queen's Road! It's men only, very stuffy, old leather chairs, old men sleeping off their three-hour and ten-gin lunches, *The Times* and all that."

"Hell, that sounds exciting!"

She had laughed again. Her teeth were white and he could see no blemish in her. They had talked over breakfast and he had found her more than easy to talk to. And to be with. Her perfume was enticing. Casey rarely wore perfume—she said that she'd found it just another distraction to the businessmen she had to deal with. With Orlanda, breakfast had been coffee and toast and eggs and crisp bacon, American style, at a brand-new hotel she suggested, called the Mandarin. Casey didn't eat breakfast. Just coffee and toast sometimes, or croissants.

The interview had passed easily and the time too fast. He had never been in the company of a woman with such open and confident feminin-

ity. Casey was always so strong, efficient and cool and not feminine. By
choice, her choice and my agreement, he reminded himself.

"That's Orlanda?" Casey was looking at him, one eyebrow arched.

"Yes," he replied, trying unsuccessfully to read her. "What do you
think?"

"I think she's dynamite."

"Which way?"

Casey laughed. She turned to Gavallan who was trying to concentrate
and be polite but whose mind was taken up with Kathy. After Kathy had
told him this evening, he had not wanted to leave her but she had
insisted, saying that it was important for him to be there. "Do you know
her, Andrew?"

"Who?"

"The girl in white."

"Where? Oh! Oh yes, but only by reputation."

"Is it good or bad?"

"That, er, depends on your point of view, Casey. She's, she's Portuguese, Eurasian, of course. Orlanda was Gornt's friend for quite a few
years."

"You mean his mistress?"

"Yes, I suppose that's the word," he told her politely, disliking Casey's
directness intensely. "But it was all very discreet."

"Gornt's got taste. Did you know she was his steady, Linc?"

"She told me this morning. I met her at Gornt's a couple of days ago.
He said they were still friends."

"Gornt's not to be trusted," Gavallan said.

Casey said, "He's got heavy backers, in and outside Hong Kong, I was
told. Far as I know he's not stretched at the moment, as you are. You must
have heard he wants us to deal with him, not you."

"We're not stretched," Gavallan said. He looked at Bartlett. "We do
have a deal?"

"We sign Tuesday. If you're ready," Bartlett said.

"We're ready now."

"Ian wants us to keep it quiet till Saturday and that's fine with us,"
Casey said. "Isn't it, Linc?"

"Sure." Bartlett glanced back at Orlanda. Casey followed his eyes.

She had noticed her the first moment the girl had hesitated in the doorway. "Who's she talking to, Andrew?" The man was interesting-looking,
lithe, elegant and in his fifties.

"That's Lando Mata. He's also Portuguese, from Macao." Gavallan
wondered achingly if Dunross would manage to persuade Mata to come to
their rescue with all his millions. What would I do if I was tai-pan? he
asked himself wearily. Would I buy tomorrow, or make a deal with Mata
and Tightfist tonight? With their money, the Noble House would be safe
for generations, though out of our control. No point in worrying now.

Wait till you're tai-pan. Then he saw Mata smiling at Orlanda and then both of them looked over and began to thread their way toward them. His eyes watched her firm breasts, free under the silk. Taut nipples. Good God, he thought, awed, even Venus Poon wouldn't dare do that. When they came up he introduced them and stood back, odd man out, wanting to watch them.

"Hello," Orlanda said warmly to Casey. "Linc told me so much about you and how important you are to him."

"And I've heard about you too," Casey said as warmly. But not enough. You're much more lovely than Linc indicated, she thought. Very much more. So you're Orlanda Ramos. Beautiful and soft-spoken and feminine and a bitch piranha who has set her sights on my Linc. Jesus, what do I do now?

She heard herself making small talk but her mind was still thinking Orlanda Ramos through. On the one hand it would be good for Linc to have an affair, she thought. It would take the heat out of him. Last night was as lousy for him as it was for me. He was right about me moving out. But once this one's magic surrounds him could I extract him? Would she be just another girl like the others that were nothing to me and after a week or so, nothing to him either?

Not this one, Casey decided with finality. I've got two choices. I either stick to thirteen weeks and four days and do battle, or don't and do battle.

She smiled. "Orlanda, your dress is fantastic."

"Thanks. May I call you Casey?"

Both women knew the war had begun.

Bartlett was delighted that Casey obviously liked Orlanda. Gavallan watched, fascinated by the four of them. There was a strange warmth among them all. Particularly between Bartlett and Orlanda.

He turned his attention to Mata and Casey. Mata was suave, filled with old world charm, concentrating on Casey, playing her like a fish. I wonder how far he'll get with this one. Curious that Casey doesn't seem to mind Orlanda at all. Surely she's noticed that her boyfriend's smitten? Perhaps she hasn't. Or perhaps she couldn't care less and she and Bartlett are just business partners and nothing else. Perhaps she's a dyke after all. Or maybe she's just frigid like a lot of them. How sad!

"How do you like Hong Kong, Miss Casey?" Mata asked, wondering what she would be like in bed.

"Afraid I haven't seen much of it yet though I did go out to the New Territories on the hotel tour and peek into China."

"Would you like to go? I mean really go into China? Say to Canton? I could arrange for you to be invited."

She was shocked. "But we're forbidden to go into China . . . our passports aren't valid."

"Oh, you wouldn't have to use your passport. The PRC doesn't bother with passports. So few *quai loh* go into China there's no problem. They give you a written visa and they stamp that."

"But our State Department . . . I don't think I'd risk it right now."

Bartlett nodded. "We're not even supposed to go into the Communist store here. The department store."

"Yes, your government really is very strange," Mata said. "As if going into a store is subversive! Did you hear the rumor about the Hilton?"

"What about it?"

"The story is that they bought a marvelous collection of Chinese antiques for the new hotel, of course all locally." Mata smiled. "It seems that now the U.S. has decided they can't use any of it, even here in Hong Kong. It's all in storage. At least that's the story."

"It figures. If you can't make it in the States, you join the government," Bartlett said sourly.

"Casey, you should decide for yourself," Mata said. "Visit the store. It's called China Arts and Crafts on Queen's Road. The prices are very reasonable and the Communists really don't have horns and barbed tails."

"It's nothing like what I expected," Bartlett said. "Casey, you'd freak out at some of the things."

"You've been?" she asked, surprised.

"Sure."

"I took Mr. Bartlett this morning," Orlanda explained. "We happened to be passing. I'd be glad to go shopping with you if you wish."

"Thanks, I'd like that," Casey said as nicely, all her danger signals up. "But we were told in L.A. the CIA monitors Americans who go in and out because they're sure it's a Communist meeting place."

"It looked like an ordinary store to me, Casey," Bartlett said. "I didn't see anything except a few posters of Mao. You can't bargain though. All prices're written out. Some of the biggest bargains you ever did see. Pity we can't take them back home." There was a total embargo on all goods of Chinese origin into the States, even antiques that had been in Hong Kong a hundred years.

"That's no problem," Mata said at once, wondering how much he would make as a middleman. "If there's anything you want I'd be happy to purchase it."

"But we still can't get it into the States, Mr. Mata," Casey said.

"Oh that's easy too. I do it for American friends all the time. I just send their purchases to a company I have in Singapore or Manila. For a tiny fee they send it to you in the States with a certificate of origin, Malaya or the Philippines, whichever you'd prefer."

"But that'd be cheating. Smuggling."

Mata, Gavallan and Orlanda laughed outright and Gavallan said, "Trade's the grease of the world. Embargoed goods from the U.S. or Taiwan find their way to the PRC, PRC goods go to Taiwan and the U.S.—if they're sought after. Of course they do!"

"I know," Casey said, "but I don't think that's right."

"Soviet Russia's committed to your destruction but you still trade with her," Gavallan said to Bartlett.

"We don't ourselves," Casey said. "Not Par-Con, though we've been approached to sell computers. Much as we like profits they're a no-no. The government does, but only on very carefully controlled goods. Wheat, things like that."

"Wherever there's a willing buyer of anything, there'll always be a seller," Gavallan said, irritated by her. He glanced out of the windows and wished he was back in Shanghai. "Take Vietnam, your Algiers."

"Sir?" Casey said.

Gavallan glanced back at her. "I mean that Vietnam will bleed your economy to death as it did to France and as Algiers also did to France."

"We'll never go into Vietnam," Bartlett said confidently. "Why should we? Vietnam's nothing to do with us."

"I agree," Mata said, "but nevertheless the States is having a growing involvement there. In fact, Mr. Bartlett, I think you're being sucked into the abyss."

"In what way?" Casey asked.

"I think the Soviets have deliberately enticed you into Vietnam. You'll send in troops but they won't. You'll be fighting Viets and the jungle, and the Soviets will be the winners. Your CIA's already there in strength. They're running an airline. Even now airfields are being constructed with U.S. money, U.S. arms are pouring in. You've soldiers fighting there already."

"I don't believe it," Casey said.

"You can. They're called Special Forces, sometimes Delta Force. So sorry but Vietnam's going to be a big problem for your government unless it's very smart."

Bartlett said confidently, "Thank God it is. JFK handled Cuba. He'll handle Vietnam too. He made the Big K back off there and he can do it again. We won that time. The Soviets took their missiles out."

Gavallan was grimly amused. "You should talk to Ian about Cuba, old chap, that really gets him going. He says, and I agree, you lost. The Soviets sucked you into another trap. A fool's mate. He believes they built their sites almost openly—wanting you to detect them and you did and then there was a lot of saber-rattling, the whole world's frightened to death, and in exchange for the Soviet agreement to take the missiles out of Cuba your President tore up your Monroe Doctrine, the cornerstone of your whole security system."

"What?"

"Certainly. Didn't JFK give Khrushchev a written promise not to invade Cuba, not to permit an invasion from American territory—or from any other place in the Western Hemisphere? *Written,* by God! So now, a hostile European power, Soviet Russia, totally against your Monroe Doctrine, is openly established ninety miles off your coast, the borders of which are guaranteed in writing by your own President and ratified by your own Congress. The Big K pulled off a colossal coup never duplicated in your whole history. And all for nothing!" Gavallan's voice harshened. "Now Cuba's nicely safe, thank you very much, where it'll grow, expand and eventually infect all South America. Safe for Soviet subs, ships, aircraft. . . . Christ almighty that's certainly a marvelous victory!"

Casey looked at Bartlett, shocked. "But surely, Linc, surely that's not right."

Bartlett was as shocked. "I guess . . . if you think about it, Casey, I guess. . . . It sure as hell cost them nothing."

"Ian's convinced of it," Gavallan said. "Talk to him. As to Vietnam, no one here thinks President Kennedy can handle that either, much as we admire him personally. Asia's not like Europe, or the Americas. They think differently here, act differently and have different values."

There was a sudden silence. Bartlett broke it. "You think there'll be war then?"

Gavallan glanced at him. "Nothing for you to worry about. Par-Con should do very well. You've heavy industry, computers, polyurethane foam, government contracts into aerospace, petrochemicals, sonics, wireless equipment . . . With your goods and our expertise if there's a war, well, the sky's the limit."

"I don't think I'd like to profit that way," Casey said, irritated by him. "That's a lousy way to earn a buck."

Gavallan turned on her. "A lot of things on this earth are lousy, and wrong and unfair. . . ." He was going to give her both barrels, infuriated with the way she kept interrupting his conversation with Bartlett but he decided that now was not the time, nor the place, so he said pleasantly, "But of course you're right. No one wants to profit from death. If you'll excuse me I'll be going. . . . You know everyone has place cards? Dinner'll start any moment. Matter of face."

He walked off.

Casey said, "I don't think he likes me at all."

They laughed at the way she said it. "What you said was right, Casey," Orlanda told her. "You were right. War is terrible."

"You were here during it?" Casey asked innocently.

"Yes, but in Macao. I'm Portuguese. My mother told me it wasn't too bad there. The Japanese didn't trouble Macao because Portugal was neutral." Orlanda added sweetly, "Of course I'm only twenty-five now so I hardly remember any of it. I was not quite seven when the war ended. Macao's nice, Casey. So different from Hong Kong. You and Linc might like to go there. It's worth seeing. I'd love to be your guide."

I'll bet, Casey thought, feeling her twenty-six was old against Orlanda who had the skin of a seventeen-year-old. "That'd be great. But Lando, what's with Andrew? Why was he so teed off? Because I'm a woman VP and all that?"

"I doubt that. I'm sure you exaggerate," Mata said. "It's just that he's not very pro-American and it drives him mad that the British Empire's no more, that the U.S. is arbiter of the world's fate and making obvious mistakes, he thinks. Most British people agree with him, I'm afraid! It's part jealousy of course. But you must be patient with Andrew. After all, your government did give away Hong Kong in '45 to Chiang—only the British navy stopped that. America did side with Soviet Russia against them over Suez, did support the Jews against them in Palestine—there are dozens of examples. It's also true lots of us here think your present hostility to China's ill-advised."

"But they're as Communist as Russia. They went to war against us when we were only trying to protect freedom in South Korea. We weren't going to attack them."

"But historically, China's always crossed the Yalu when any foreign invader approached that border. *Always*. Your MacArthur was supposed to be a historian," Mata said patiently, wondering if she was as naive in bed, "he should have known. He—or your President—forced China into a path it did not want to take. I'm absolutely sure of that."

"But we weren't invaders. North Korea invaded the South. We just wanted to help a people be free. We'd nothing to gain from South Korea. We spend billions trying to help people stay free. Look what China did to Tibet—to India last year. Seems to me we're always the fall guy and all we want is to protect freedom." She stopped as a murmur of relief went through the room and people began heading for their tables. Waiters bearing silver-domed platters were trooping in. "Thank God! I'm starving!"

"Me too," Bartlett said.

"Shitee's early tonight," Mata said with a laugh. "Orlanda, you should have warned them it's an old custom always to have a snack before any of Shitee's banquets."

Orlanda just smiled her lovely smile and Casey said, "Orlanda warned Linc, who told me, but I figured I could last." She looked at her enemy who was almost half a head shorter, about five foot three. For the first time in her life she felt big and oafish. Be honest, she reminded herself, ever since you walked out of the hotel into the streets and saw all the Chinese girls and women with their tiny hands and feet and bodies and smallness, all dark-eyed and dark-haired, you've felt huge and alien. Yes. Now I can understand why they all gape at us so much. And as for the ordinary tourist, loud, overweight, waddling along . . .

Even so, Orlanda Ramos, as pretty as you are and as clever as you think you are, you're not the girl for Linc Bartlett. So you can blow it all out of your ass! "Next time, Orlanda," she said so nicely, "I'll remember to be very cautious about what you recommend."

"I recommend we eat, Casey. I'm hungry too."

Mata said, "I do believe we're all at the same table. I must confess I arranged it." Happily he led the way, more than ever excited by the challenge of getting Casey into bed. The moment he had seen her he had decided. Part of it was her beauty and tallness and beautiful breasts, such a welcome contrast to the smallness and sameness of the normal Asian girl. Part was because of the clues Orlanda had given him. But the biggest part had been his sudden thought that by breaking the Bartlett-Casey connection he might wreck Par-Con's probe into Asia. Far better to keep Americans and their hypocritical, impractical morality and meddling out of our area as long as we can, he had told himself. And if Dunross doesn't have the Par-Con deal, then he will have to sell me the control I want. Then, at long last, *I* become *the tai-pan* of the Noble House, all the Dunrosses and Struans notwithstanding.

Madonna, life is really very good. Curious that this woman could be the key to the best lock in Asia, he thought. Then he added contentedly, Clearly she can be bought. It's only a matter of how much.

37

Dinner was twelve courses. Braised abalone with green sprouts, chicken livers and sliced partridge sauce, shark's fin soup, barbecued chicken, Chinese greens and peapods and broccoli and fifty other vegetables with crabmeat, the skin of roast Peking duck with plum sauce and sliced spring onions and paper-thin pancakes, double-boiled mushrooms and fish maw, smoked pomfret fish with salad, rice Yangchow style, home sweet home noodles—then happiness dessert, sweetened lotus seeds and lily in rice gruel. And tea continuously.

Mata and Orlanda helped Casey and Bartlett. Fleur and Peter Marlowe were the only other Europeans at their table. The Chinese presented their visiting cards and received others in exchange. "Oh you can eat with chopsticks!" All the Chinese were openly astonished, then slid comfortably back into Cantonese, the bejeweled women clearly discussing Casey and Bartlett and the Marlowes. Their comments were slightly guarded only because of Lando Mata and Orlanda.

"What're they saying, Orlanda?" Bartlett asked quietly amid the noisy exuberance, particularly of the Chinese.

"They're just wondering about you and Miss Casey," she said as cautiously, not translating the lewd remarks about the size of Casey's chest, the wondering where her clothes came from, how much they cost, why she didn't wear any jewelry, and what it must be like to be so tall. They were saying little about Bartlett other than wondering out loud if he was really Mafia as one of the Chinese papers had suggested.

Orlanda was sure he wasn't. But she was sure also that she would have to be very circumspect in front of Casey, neither too forward nor too slow, and never to touch him. And to be sweet to her, to try to throw her off her stride.

Fresh plates for each course were laid with a clatter, the used ones whisked away. Waiters hurried to the dumbwaiters in the central section by the staircase to dispose of the old and grab steaming platters of the new.

The kitchens, three decks below, were an inferno with the huge four-feet-wide iron woks fired with gas that was piped aboard. Some woks for steaming, some for quick frying, some for deep frying, some for stewing, and many for the pure white rice. An open, wood-fired barbecue. An army of helpers for the twenty-eight cooks were preparing the meats and vegetables, plucking chickens, killing fresh fish and lobsters and crabs and cleaning them, doing the thousand tasks that Chinese food requires—as each dish is cooked freshly for each customer.

The restaurant opened at 10:00 A.M. and the kitchen closed at 10:45 P.M.—sometimes later when a special party was arranged. There could be dancing and a floor show if the host was rich enough. Tonight, though there was no late shift or floor show or dancing, they all knew that their share of the tip from Shitee T'Chung's banquet would be very good. Shitee T'Chung was an expansive host, though most of them believed that much of the charity money he collected went into his stomach or those of his guests or onto the backs of his lady friends. He also had the reputation of being ruthless to his detractors, a miser to his family, and vengeful to his enemies.

Never mind, the head chef thought. A man needs soft lips and hard teeth in this world and everyone knows which will last the longer. "Hurry up!" he shouted. "Can I wait all manure-infested night? Prawns! Bring the prawns!" A sweating helper in ragged pants and ancient, sweaty undershirt rushed up with a bamboo platter of the freshly caught and freshly peeled prawns. The chef cast them into the vast wok, added a handful of monosodium glutamate, whisked them twice and scooped them out, put a handful of steaming peapods on two platters and divided up the pink, glistening succulent prawns on top equally.

"All gods urinate on all prawns!" he said sourly, his stomach ulcer paining him, his feet and calves leaden from his ten-hour shift. "Send those upstairs before they spoil! *Dew neh loh moh* hurry . . . that's my last order. It's time to go home!"

Other cooks were shouting last orders and cursing as they cooked. They were all impatient to be gone. "Hurry it up!" Then one young helper carrying a pot of used fat stumbled and the fat sprayed onto one of the gas fires, caught with a whoosh and there was sudden pandemonium. A cook screamed as the fire surrounded him and he beat at it, his face and hair singed. Someone threw a bucket of water on the fire and spread it violently. Flames soared to the rafters, billowing smoke. Shouting, shoving cooks moving out of the fire were causing a bottleneck. The acrid, black, oil smoke began to fill the air.

The man nearest the single narrow staircase to the first deck grabbed one of the two fire extinguishers and slammed the plunger down and pointed the nozzle at the fire. Nothing happened. He did it again then someone else grabbed it from him with a curse, tried unsuccessfully to make it work, and cast it aside. The other extinguisher was also a dud. The staff had never bothered to test them.

"All gods defecate on these motherless foreign devil inventions!" a cook wailed and prepared to flee if the fire approached him. A frightened coolie choking on the smoke at the other end of the kitchen backed away from a shaft of flame into some jars and toppled them. Some contained thousand-year-old eggs and others sesame oil. The oil flooded the floor and caught fire. The coolie vanished in the sudden sheet of flame. Now the fire owned half the kitchen.

It was well past eleven o'clock and most diners had already left. The top deck of the *Floating Dragon* was still partially filled. Most of the Chinese, Four Finger Wu and Venus Poon among them, were walking out or had already left as the last course had already been served long since and it was polite Chinese custom to leave as soon as the last dish was finished, table by table. Only the Europeans were lingering over Cognac or port, and cigars.

Throughout the boat, tables of mah-jong were being set up by Chinese, and the clitter-clatter of the ivory tiles banging on the tables began to dominate.

"Do you play mah-jong, Mr. Bartlett?" Mata asked.

"No. Please call me Linc."

"You should learn—it's better than bridge. Do you play bridge, Casey?"

Linc Bartlett laughed. "She's a wiz, Lando. Don't play her for money."

"Perhaps we can have a game sometime. You play, don't you, Orlanda?" Mata said, remembering Gornt was an accomplished player.

"Yes, a little," Orlanda said softly and Casey thought grimly, I'll bet the bitch's a wiz too.

"I'd love a game," Casey said sweetly.

"Good," Mata said. "One day next week . . . oh, hello, tai-pan!"

Dunross greeted them all with his smile. "How did you enjoy the food?"

"It was fantastic!" Casey said, happy to see him and greatly aware of how handsome he looked in his tuxedo. "Would you like to join us?"

"Thanks bu—"

"Good night, tai-pan," Dianne Chen said, coming up to him, her son Kevin—a short, heavyset youth with dark curly hair and full lips—in tow.

Dunross introduced them. "Where's Phillip?"

"He was going to come but he phoned to say he was delayed. Well, good night . . ." Dianne smiled and so did Kevin and they headed for the door, Casey and Orlanda wide-eyed at Dianne's jewelry.

"Well, I must be off too," Dunross said.

"How was your table?"

"Rather trying," Dunross said with his infectious laugh. He had eaten with the MPs—with Gornt, Shi-teh and his wife at the Number One table

—and there had been sporadic angry outbursts above the clatter of plates. "Robin Grey's rather outspoken, and ill-informed, and some of us were having at him. For once Gornt and I were on the same side. I must confess our table got served first so poor old Shi-teh and his wife could flee. He took off like a dose of salts fifteen minutes ago."

They all laughed with him. Dunross was watching Marlowe. He wondered if Marlowe knew that Grey was his brother-in-law. "Grey seems to know you quite well, Mr. Marlowe."

"He has a good memory, tai-pan, though his manners are off."

"I don't know about that, but if he has his way in Parliament God help Hong Kong. Well, I just wanted to say hello to all of you." He smiled at Bartlett and Casey. "How about lunch tomorrow?"

"Fine," Casey said. "How about coming to the V and A?" She noticed Gornt get up to leave on the opposite side of the room and she wondered again who would win. "Just before dinner Andrew was say—"

Then, with all of them, she heard faint screams. There was a sudden hush, everyone listening.

"*Fire!*"

"Christ, look!" They all stared at the dumbwaiter. Smoke was pouring out. Then a small tongue of flame.

A split second of disbelief, then everyone jumped up. Those nearest the main staircase rushed for the doorway, crowding it, as others took up the shout. Bartlett leapt to his feet and dragged Casey with him. Mata and some of the guests began to run for the bottleneck.

"*Hold it!*" Dunross roared above the noise. Everyone stopped. "There's plenty of time. Don't hurry!" he ordered. "There's no need to run, take your time! There's no danger yet!" His admonition helped those who were overly frightened. They started easing out of the crammed doorway. But below, on the staircases, the shouts and hysteria had increased.

Not everyone had run at the first cry of danger. Gornt hadn't moved. He puffed his cigar, all his senses concentrated. Havergill and his wife had walked over to the windows to look out. Others joined them. They could see crowds milling around the main entrance two decks below. "I don't think we need to worry, my dear," Havergill said. "Once the main lot are out we can follow at leisure."

Lady Joanna, beside them, said, "Did you see Biltzmann rush off? What a berk!" She looked around and saw Bartlett and Casey across the room, waiting beside Dunross. "Oh, I'd've thought they'd've fled too."

Havergill said, "Oh come on, Joanna, not all Yankees are cowards!"

A sudden shaft of flame and thick black smoke poured out of the dumbwaiter. The shouting to hurry up began again.

On the far side of the room nearer the fire, Bartlett said hastily, "Ian, is there another exit?"

"I don't know," Dunross said. "Take a look outside. I'll hold the fort here." Bartlett took off quickly for the exit door to the half deck and

Dunross turned to the rest of them. "Nothing to worry about," he said, calming them and gauging them quickly. Fleur Marlowe was white but in control, Casey stared in shock at the people jamming the doorway, Orlanda petrified, near breaking. "Orlanda! It's all right," he said, "there's no danger . . ."

On the other side of the room Gornt got up and went nearer to the door. He could see the crush and knew that the stairs below would be jammed. Shrieks and some screams added to the fear here but Sir Charles Pennyworth was beside the doorway trying to get an orderly withdrawal down the stairs. More smoke billowed out and Gornt thought, Christ almighty, a bloody fire, half a hundred people and one exit. Then he noticed the unattended bar. He went to it and, outwardly calm, poured himself a whiskey and soda, but the sweat was running down his back.

Below on the crowded second-deck landing Lando Mata stumbled and brought a whole group down, Dianne Chen and Kevin with them, creating a blockage in this, the only escape route. Men and women shrieked impotently, crushed against the floor as others fell or stumbled over them in a headlong dash for safety. Above on the staircase, Pugmire held on to the banister and just managed to keep his feet, using his great strength to shove his back against the people and prevent more from falling. Julian Broadhurst was beside him, frightened too but equally controlled, using his height and weight with Pugmire. Together they held the breach momentarily, but gradually the weight of those behind overcame them. Pugmire felt his grip slipping. Ten steps below, Mata fought to his feet, trampled on a few people in his haste, then shoved on downstairs, his coat half torn from him. Dianne Chen clawed her way to her feet, dragging Kevin with her. In the shoving, milling mass of humanity she did not notice a woman grab her diamond pendant neatly and pocket it, then jostle away down the stairs. Smoke billowing up from the lower deck added to the horror. Pugmire's hold was broken. He was half-shoved into the wall by the human flood and Broadhurst missed his footing. Another small avalanche of people began. Now the stairs on both levels were clogged.

Four Finger Wu with Venus Poon had been on the first landing when the shout had gone up and he had darted down the last staircase and shoved his way out onto the drawbridge that led to the wharf, Venus Poon a few terrorized steps behind him. Safe on the wharf, he turned and looked back, his heart pounding, his breathing heavy. Men and women were stumbling out of the huge ornate doorway onto the jetty, some flames coming out of portholes near the waterline. A policeman who had been patrolling nearby ran up, watched aghast for a moment, then took to his heels for the nearest telephone. Wu was still trying to catch his breath when he saw Richard Kwang and his wife rush out pell-mell. He began to laugh and felt much better. Venus Poon thought the people looked very funny too. Onlookers were collecting in safety, no one doing anything to help, just gawking—which is only right, Wu thought in passing. One must never interfere with the decisions of the gods. The gods have their own rules and they decide a human's joss. It's my joss to escape and to enjoy this whore tonight. All gods help me to maintain my Imperial Iron until she screams for mercy.

"Come along, Little Mealy Mouth," Four Fingers said with a cackle, "we can safely leave them to their joss. Time's wasting."

"No, Father," she said quickly. "Any moment the TV cameras and press will arrive—we must think of our image, *heya?*"

"Image? It's the pillow and the Gorgeous G—"

"Later!" she said imperiously and he bit back the curse he was going to add. "Don't you want to be hailed as a hero?" she said sharply. "Perhaps even a knighthood like Shitee, *heya?*" Quickly she dirtied her hands and her face and carefully ripped one of the straps above her breast and went near to the gangway where she could see and be seen. Four Fingers watched her blankly. A *quai loh* honor like Shitee? he thought astounded. Eeeeee, why not! He followed her warily, taking great care not to get too close to any danger.

They saw a tongue of flame sweep out of the chimney on the top deck and frightened people looking down from the three decks of windows. People were collecting on the wharf. Others were stumbling out to safety in hysterics, many coughing from the smoke that was beginning to possess the whole restaurant. There was another shouting crush in the doorway, a few went down and some scuttled from under the milling feet, those behind shrieking at those in front to hurry, and again Four Fingers and other onlookers laughed.

On the top deck Bartlett leaned over the railings and looked down at the hull and the jetty below. He could see crowds on the wharf and milling, hysterical people fighting out of the entrance. There was no other staircase, ladder or escape possibility on either side. His heart was hammering but he was not afraid. There's no real danger, yet, he thought. We can jump into the water below. Easy. It's what, thirty, forty feet—no sweat if you don't belly flop. He ran back along the deck that used up half the length of the boat. Black smoke, sparks and a little flame surged out of the funnels.

He opened the top-deck door and closed it quickly in order not to create any added draft. The smoke was much worse and the flames coming out of the dumbwaiter were continuous now. The smoke smell on the air was acrid and carried the stench of burning meat. Almost everyone was crowded around the far doorway. Gornt was standing apart by himself watching them, sipping a drink. Bartlett thought, Jesus, there's one cold-blooded bastard! He skirted the dumbwaiter carefully, his eyes smarting from the smoke, and almost knocked over Christian Toxe who was hunched over the telephone shouting into it above the noise, ". . . I don't give a shit, get a photographer out here right now, and *then* phone the fire department!" Angrily Toxe slammed down the phone and muttering,

"Stupid bastards," went back to his wife, a matronly Chinese woman who stared at him blankly. Bartlett hurried toward Dunross. The tai-pan stood motionless beside Peter and Fleur Marlowe, Orlanda and Casey, whistling tonelessly.

"Nothing, Ian," he said quietly, noticing his voice sounded strange, "not a goddamn thing. No ladders, nothing. But we can jump, easy, if necessary."

"Yes. We're lucky being on this deck. The others may not be so lucky." Dunross watched the smoke and fire spurting from the dumbwaiter that was near the exit door. "We'll have to decide pretty soon which way to go," he said gently. "That fire could cut us off from the outside. If we go out we may never get back in and we'll have to jump. If we stay in, we can only use the stairs."

"Jesus," Casey muttered. She was trying to calm her racing heart and the feeling of claustrophobia that was welling up. Her skin felt clammy and her eyes were darting from the exit to the doorway and back again. Bartlett put an arm around her. "It's no sweat, we can jump anytime."

"Yes, sure, Linc." Casey was holding on grimly.

"You can swim, Casey?" Dunross asked.

"Yes. I . . . was caught in a fire once. Ever since then I've been frightened to death of them." It was a few years before when her little house in the Hollywood Hills of Los Angeles was in the path of one of the sudden summer conflagrations and she had been bottled in, the winding canyon road already burning below. She had turned on all the water sprinklers and begun to hose the roof. The clawing heat of the fire had reached out at her. Then the fire had crested, jumping from the top of one valley to the opposite side, to begin burning down both sides toward the valley floor, whipped by hundred-mile-an-hour gusts self-generated by the fire. The roaring flames obliterated trees and houses, came closer and there was no way out. In terror, she kept the hose on her roof. Cats and dogs from the homes above fled past her and one wild-eyed Alsatian cowered in the lee of her house. The heat and the smoke and the terror surrounded her and it went on and on but this part of the fire stopped fifty feet from her boundary. For no reason. Above, all the houses on her street had gone. Most of the canyon. A swath almost half a mile wide and two long burned for three days in the hills that bisected the city of Los Angeles.

"I'm all right, Linc," she said shakily. "I . . . I think I'd rather be outside than here. Let's get the hell out of here. A swim'd be great."

"I can't swim!" Orlanda was trembling. Then her control snapped and she got up to rush for the stairs.

Bartlett grabbed her. "Everything's going to be all right. Jesus, you'll never make it that way. Listen to the poor bastards down there, they're in real trouble. Stay put, huh? The stairs're no good." She hung on to him, petrified.

"You'll be all right," Casey said compassionately.

"Yes," Dunross said, his eyes on the fire and billowing smoke.

Marlowe said, "We, er, we're really in very good shape, tai-pan, aren't we? Yes. The fire's got to be from the kitchens. They'll get it under control. Fleur, pet, there'll be no need to go over the side."

"It's no sweat," Bartlett assured him. "There's plenty of sampans to pick us up!"

"Oh yes, but she can't swim either."

Fleur put her hand on her husband's arm. "You always said I should learn, Peter."

Dunross wasn't listening. He was consumed with fear and trying to dominate it. His nostrils were filled with the stench of burning meat that he knew oh so well and he was near vomiting. He was back in his burning Spitfire, shot out of the sky by a Messerschmitt 109 over the Channel, the cliffs of Dover too far away, and he knew the fire would consume him before he could tear the jammed and damaged cockpit canopy free and bail out, the horror-smell of scorching flesh, his own, surrounding him. In terror he smashed his fist impotently against the Perspex, his other beating at the flames around his feet and knees, choking from the acrid smoke in his lungs, half blinded. Then there was a sudden frantic roar as the cowl ripped away, an inferno of flames surged up and surrounded him and somehow he was out and falling away from the flames, not knowing if his face was gone, the skin of his hands and feet, his boots and flying overalls still smoking. Then the shuddering nauseating jerk as his chute opened, then the dark silhouette of the enemy plane hurtled toward him out of the sun and he saw the machine guns sparking and a tracer blew part of his calf away. He remembered none of the rest except the smell of burning flesh that was the same then as now.

"What do you think, tai-pan?"

"What?"

"Shall we stay or leave?" Marlowe repeated.

"We'll stay, for the moment," Dunross said and they all wondered how he could sound so calm and look so calm. "When the stairs clear we can walk out. No reason to get wet if we don't have to."

Casey smiled at him hesitantly. "These fires happen often?"

"Not here, but they do in Hong Kong, I'm afraid. Our Chinese friends don't care much about fire regulations . . ."

It was still only a few minutes since the first violent gust of fire had swirled up in the kitchen but now the fire had a full hold there and, through the access of the dumbwaiter, a strong hold on the central sections of the three decks above. The fire in the kitchen blocked half the room from the only staircase. Twenty terrified men were trapped on the wrong side. The rest of the staff had fled long since to join the heaving mass of people on the deck above. There were half a dozen portholes but these were small and rusted up. In panic one of the cooks rushed at the flaming barrier, screamed as the flames engulfed him, almost made it through but slipped and kept on screaming for a long while. A petrified moan burst from the others. There was no other escape possibility.

The head chef was trapped too. He was a portly man and he had been in many kitchen fires so he was not panicked. His mind ranged all the other fires, desperately seeking a clue. Then he remembered.

"Hurry," he shouted, "get bags of rice flour . . . rice . . . hurry!"

The others stared at him without moving, their terror numbing them, so he lashed out and smashed some of them into the storeroom, grabbed a fifty-pound sack himself and tore the top off. "Fornicate all fires hurry but wait till I tell you," he gasped, the smoke choking and almost blinding him. One of the portholes shattered and the sudden draft whooshed the flames at them. Terrified they grabbed a sack each, coughing as the smoke billowed.

"Now!" the head chef roared and hurled the sack at the flaming corridor between the stoves. The sack burst open and the clouds of flour doused some of the flames. Other sacks followed in the same area and more flames were swallowed. Another barrage of flour went over the flaming benches, snuffing them out. The passage was momentarily clear. At once the head chef led the charge through the remaining flames and they all followed him pell-mell, leaping over the two charred bodies, and gained the stairs at the far side before the flames gushed back and closed the path. The men fought their way up the narrow staircase and into the partial air of the landing, joining the milling mob that pushed and shoved and screamed and coughed their way through the black smoke into the open.

Tears streamed from most faces. The smoke was very heavy now in the lower levels. Then the wall behind the first landing where the shaft of the dumbwaiter was began to twist and blacken. Abruptly it burst open, scattering gargoyles, and flames gushed out. Those on the stairs below shoved forward in panic and those on the landing reeled back. Then, seeing they were so close to safety, the first ranks darted forward, skirting the inferno, jumping the stairs two at a time. Hugh Guthrie, one of the MPs, saw a woman fall. He held on to the banister and stopped to help her but those behind toppled him and he fell with others. He picked himself up, cursing, and fought a path clear for just enough time to drag the woman up before he was engulfed again and shoved down the last few stairs to gain the entrance safely.

Half the landing between the lower deck and the second deck was still free of flames though the fire had an unassailable hold and was fueling itself. The crowds were thinning now though more than a hundred still clogged the upper staircases and doorways. Those above were milling and cursing, not being able to see ahead.

"What's the holdup for chrissake. . . ."

"Are the stairs still clear . . . ?"

"For chrissake get on with it. . . ."

"It's getting bloody hot up here . . ."

"What a sodding carve-up. . . ."

Grey was one of those trapped on the second-deck staircase. He could see the flames gushing out of the wall ahead and knew the nearby wall would go any moment. He could not decide whether to retreat or to advance. Then he saw a child cowering against the steps under the banister. He managed to pull the little boy into his arms then pressed on, cursing those in front, darted around the fire, the way to safety below still jammed.

On the top deck Gornt and others were listening to the pandemonium below. There were only thirty or so people still here. He finished his drink, set the glass down and walked over to the group surrounding Dunross—Orlanda was still sitting, twisting her handkerchief in her hands, Fleur and Peter Marlowe still outwardly calm, and Dunross, as always, in control. Good, he thought, blessing his own heritage and training. It was part of British tradition that in danger, however petrified you are, you lose face by showing it. Then, too, he reminded himself, most of us have been bombed most of our lives, shot at, sunk, slammed into POW jails or been in the Services. Gornt's sister had been in the Women's Royal Naval Service—his mother an air raid warden, his father in the army, his uncle killed at Monte Cassino, and he himself had served with the Australians in New Guinea after escaping from Shanghai, and had fought his way into and through Burma to Singapore.

"Ian," he said, keeping his voice suitably nonchalant, "it sounds as though the fire's on the first landing now. I suggest a swim."

Dunross glanced back at the fire near the exit door. "Some of the ladies don't swim. Let's give it a couple of minutes."

"Very well. I think those who don't mind jumping should go on deck. That particular fire's really very boring."

Casey said, "I don't find it very boring at all."

They all laughed. "It's just an expression," Peter Marlowe explained.

An explosion below decks rocked the boat slightly. The momentary silence was eerie.

In the kitchen the fire had spread to the storage rooms and was surrounding the four remaining hundred-gallon drums of oil. The one that had blown up had torn a gaping hole in the floor and buckled the side of the boat. Burning embers and burning oil and some seawater poured into the scuppers. The force of the explosion had ruptured some of the great timbers of the flat-bottomed hull and water was seeping through the seams. Hordes of rats scrambled out of the way seeking an escape route.

Another of the thick metal drums blew up and ripped a vast hole in the side of the boat just below the waterline, scattering fire in all directions. The people on the wharf gasped and some reeled back though there was no danger. Others laughed nervously. Still another drum exploded and another shaft of flames sprayed everywhere. The ceiling supports and joists were seriously weakened and, oil soaked, began to burn. Above on the first deck, the feet of the frenzied escapees pounded dangerously.

Just above the first landing Grey still had the child in his arms. He held on to the banister with one hand, frightened, shoving people behind and in front of him. He waited his turn, then shielding the child as best he could, ducked around the flames on the landing and darted down the stairs, the way mostly clear. The carpet by the threshold was beginning to smoke and one heavyset man stumbled, the whole floor shaky.

"Come on," Grey shouted desperately to those behind. He made the threshold, others close behind and in front. Just as he reached the drawbridge the last two drums exploded, the whole floor behind him disappeared and he and the child and others were hurled forward like so much chaff.

Hugh Guthrie rushed out of the onlookers and pulled them to safety. "You all right, old chap?" he gasped.

Grey was half stunned, gasping for breath, his clothes smoldering, and Guthrie helped beat them out. "Yes . . . yes I think so . . ." he said half out of himself.

Guthrie gently lifted the unconscious child and peered at him. "Poor little bastard!"

"Is he dead?"

"I don't think so. Here . . ." Guthrie gave the little Chinese boy to an onlooker and both men charged back to the gateway to help the others who were still numbed by the explosion and helpless. "Christ all bloody mighty," he gasped as he saw that now the whole entrance was impassable. Above the uproar, they heard the wail of approaching sirens.

The fire on the top deck near the exit was building nastily. Frightened, coughing people were streaming back into the room, forced back up the stairs by the fire that now owned the lower deck. Pandemonium and the stench of fear were heavy on the air.

"Ian, we'd better get the hell out of here," Bartlett said.

"Yes. Quillan, would you please lead the way and take charge of the deck," Dunross said. "I'll hold this end."

Gornt turned and roared, "*Everyone this way!* You'll be safe on deck . . . one at a time. . . ." He opened the door and positioned himself by it and tried to bring order to the hasty retreat—a few Chinese, the remainder mostly British. Once in the open everyone was much less frightened and grateful to be away from the smoke.

Bartlett, waiting in the room, felt excitement but still no fear for he knew he could smash any one of the windows and get Casey and himself out and into the sea. People stumbled past. Flames from the dumbwaiter increased and there was a dull explosion below.

"How you doing, Casey?"

"Okay."

"Out you go!"

"When you go."

"Sure." Bartlett grinned at her. The room was thinning. He helped Lady Joanna through the doorway, then Havergill, who was limping, and his wife.

Casey saw that Orlanda was still frozen to her chair. Poor girl, she thought compassionately, remembering her own absolute terror in her own fire. She went over to her. "Come on," she said gently and helped her up. The girl's knees were trembling. Casey kept her arm around her.

"I . . . I've lost . . . my purse," Orlanda muttered.

"No, here it is." Casey picked it up from the chair and kept her arm around her as she half-pushed her past the flames into the open. The deck was crowded but once outside Casey felt enormously better.

"Everything's fine," Casey said encouragingly. She guided her to the railing. Orlanda held on tightly. Casey turned back to look for Bartlett and saw both him and Gornt watching her from inside the room. Bartlett waved at her and she waved back, wishing he were outside with her.

Peter Marlowe herded his wife onto the deck and came up to her. "You all right, Casey?"

"Sure. How you doing, Fleur?"

"Fine. Fine. It's . . . it's rather pleasant outside, isn't it?" Fleur Marlowe said, feeling faint and awful, petrified at the idea of jumping from this great height. "Do you think it's going to rain?"

"The sooner the better." Casey looked over the side. In the murky waters, thirty feet below, sampans were beginning to collect. All boatmen knew that those on the top would have to jump soon. From their vantage they could see that the fire possessed most of the first and second decks. A few people were trapped there, then one man hurled a chair through one of the windows, broke the glass away, scrambled through and fell into the sea. A sampan darted forward and threw him a line. Others who were trapped followed. One woman never came up.

The night was dark though the flames lit everything nearby, casting eerie shadows. The crowds on the wharf parted as the screaming fire engines pulled up. Immediately Chinese firemen and British officers dragged out the hoses. Another detachment joined up to the nearby fire hydrant and the first jet of water played onto the fire and there was a cheer. In seconds six hoses were in operation and two masked firemen with asbestos clothing and breathing equipment strapped to their backs rushed the entrance and began to drag those who were lying unconscious out of danger. Another huge explosion sprayed them with burning embers. One of the firemen doused everyone with water then directed the hose back on the entrance again.

The top deck was empty now except for Bartlett, Dunross and Gornt. They felt the deck sway under them and almost lost their footing. "Jesus Christ," Bartlett gasped, "we going to sink?"

"Those explosions could've blown her bottom out," Gornt said urgently. "Come on!" He went through the door quickly, Bartlett followed.

Now Dunross was alone. The smoke was very bad, the heat and stench revolting him. He made a conscious effort not to flee, dominating his terror. At a sudden thought he ran back across the room to the doorway of the main staircase to make sure there was no one there. Then he saw the inert figure of a man on the staircase. Flames were everywhere. He felt his own fear surging again but once more he held it down, darted forward and began to drag the man back up the stairs. The Chinese was heavy and he did not know if the man was alive or dead. The heat was scorching and again he smelt burning flesh and felt his bile rising. Then Bartlett was beside him and together they half-dragged, half-carried the man across the room out onto the deck.

"Thanks," Dunross gasped.

Quillan Gornt came over to them, bent down and turned the man over. The face was partially burned. "You could have saved yourself the heroics. He's dead."

"Who is he?" Bartlett asked.

Gornt shrugged. "I don't know. Do you know him, Ian?"

Dunross was staring at the body. "Yes. It's Zep . . . Zeppelin Tung."

"Tightfist's son?" Gornt was surprised. "My God, he's put on weight. I'd never have recognized him." He got to his feet. "We'd better get everyone ready to jump. This boat's a graveyard." He saw Casey standing by the railing. "Are you all right?" he asked, going over to her.

"Yes, thanks. You?"

"Oh yes."

Orlanda was still beside her, staring blankly at the water below. People were milling around the deck. "I'd better help get them organized," Gornt said. "I'll be back in a second." He walked off.

Another explosion jarred the boat again. The list began to increase. Several people climbed over the side and jumped. Sampans went in to rescue them.

Christian Toxe had his arm around his Chinese wife and he was staring sourly overboard.

"You're going to have to jump, Christian," Dunross said.

"Into Aberdeen Harbor? You must be bloody joking old chap! If you don't bounce off all the bloody effluvia you'll catch the bloody plague."

"It's that or a red-hot tail," someone called out with a laugh.

At the end of the deck Sir Charles Pennyworth was holding on to the railing as he worked his way down the boat encouraging everyone. "Come on, young lady," he said to Orlanda, "it's an easy jump."

She shook her head, petrified. "No . . . no not yet . . . I can't swim."

Fleur Marlowe put her arm around her. "Don't worry, I can't swim either. I'm staying too."

Bartlett said, "Peter, you can hold her hand, she'll be safe. All you have to do, Fleur, is hold your breath!"

"She's not going to jump," Marlowe said quietly. "At least, not till the last second."

"It's safe."

"Yes, but it's not safe for her. She's *enceinte.*"

"What?"

"Fleur's with child. About three months."

"Oh Jesus."

Flames roared skyward out of one of the flues. Inside the top deck restaurant tables were afire and the great carved temple screens at the far end were burning merrily. There was a great gust of sparks as the inner central staircase collapsed. "Jesus, this whole boat's a firetrap. What about the folk below?" Casey asked.

"They're all out long ago," Dunross said, not believing it. Now that he was in the open he felt fine. His successful domination of his fear made him light-headed. "The view here is quite splendid, don't you think?"

Pennyworth called out jovially, "We're in luck! The ship's listing this way so when she goes down we'll be safe enough. Unless she capsizes. Just like old times," he added. "I was sunk three times in the Med."

"So was I," Marlowe said, "but it was in the Bangka Strait off Sumatra."

"I didn't know that, Peter," Fleur said.

"It was nothing."

"How deep's the water here?" Bartlett asked.

"It must be twenty feet or more," Dunross said.

"That'll be en—" There was a *whoopwhoopwhoop* of sirens as the police launch came bustling through the narrow byways between the islands of boats, its searchlight darting here and there. When it was almost alongside the *Floating Dragon,* the megaphone sounded loudly, first in Chinese, "All sampans clear the area, clear the area . . ." Then in English, "Those on the top deck prepare to abandon ship! The hull's holed, prepare to abandon ship!"

Christian Toxe muttered sourly to no one, "Buggered if I'm going to ruin my only dinner jacket."

His wife tugged at his arm. "You never liked it anyway, Chris."

"I like it now, old girl." He tried to smile. "You can't bloody swim either."

She shrugged. "I'll bet you fifty dollar you and me we swim like a one hundred percent eel."

"Mrs. Toxe, you have a bet. But it's only fitting we're the last to go. After all, I want an eyewitness account." He reached into his pocket and found his cigarettes, gave her one, trying to feel brave, frightened for her safety. He searched for a match, couldn't find one. She reached into her purse and rummaged around. Eventually she found her lighter. It lit on the third go. Both were oblivious of the flames that were ten feet behind them.

Dunross said, "You smoke too much, Christian."

The deck twisted sickeningly. The boat began to settle. Water was pouring through the great hole in her side. Firemen used their hoses with great bravery but they had little effect on the conflagration. A murmur went through the crowd as the whole boat shuddered. Two of the mooring guys snapped.

Pennyworth was leaning against the gunnel, helping others to jump clear. Quite a few were jumping now. Lady Joanna fell awkwardly. Paul Havergill helped his wife over the side. When he saw she had surfaced he leaped too. The police launch was still blaring in Cantonese to clear the area. Sailors threw life jackets over the side as others launched a cutter. Then, led by a young marine inspector, half a dozen sailors dived over the side to help those in trouble, men, women and a few children. A sampan darted in to help Lady Joanna, Havergill and his wife. Gratefully they clambered aboard the rickety craft. Others from the top deck plunged into the water.

The *Floating Dragon* was listing badly. Someone slipped on the top deck and knocked Pennyworth off balance. He half-jumped, half-fell backward before he could catch himself and fell like a stone. His head smashed into the stern of the sampan, snapping his neck, and he slithered into the water and sank. In the pandemonium no one noticed him.

Casey was hanging on to the railings with Bartlett, Dunross, Gornt, Orlanda and the Marlowes. Nearby, Toxe was puffing away, trying to summon his courage. His wife stubbed her cigarette out carefully. Flames were surging from the air vents, skylights and exit door, then the ship grounded heavily and lurched as another of her anchoring cables snapped. Gornt's hold was torn away and he crashed headfirst into the railing, stunning himself. Toxe and his wife lost their balance and went over the side, badly. Peter Marlowe held on to his wife and just managed to prevent her being smashed into a bulkhead as Bartlett and Casey half-tumbled, half-stumbled past and fell in a heap at the railing, Bartlett protecting her as best he could, her high heels dangerous.

Below, in the water, sailors were helping people to the rescue boat. One saw Toxe and his wife rise to the surface for an instant fifteen yards away, both gasping and spluttering, before they choked, and, flailing, went down again. At once he dived for them and after a seeming eternity, grabbed her clothing and shoved her, half-drowned, to the surface. The young lieutenant swam over to where he had seen Toxe and dived but missed him in the darkness. He came up for air and dived once more into the blackness, groping helplessly. When his lungs were bursting, his outstretched fingers touched some clothing and he grabbed and kicked for the surface. Toxe clung on in panic, retching and choking from all the seawater he had swallowed. The young man broke his hold, turned Toxe over and hauled him to the cutter.

Above them, the boat was tilted dangerously and Dunross picked himself up. He saw Gornt inert in a heap and he stumbled over to him. He tried to lift him, couldn't.

"I'm . . . I'm all right," Gornt gasped, coming around, then he shook his head like a dog. "Christ, thanks . . ." He looked up and saw it was Dunross. "Thanks," he said, smiled grimly as he got up shakily. "I'm still selling tomorrow and by next week you'll have had it."

Dunross laughed. "Jolly good luck! The idea of burning to death or drowning with you fills me with equal dismay."

Ten yards away, Bartlett was lifting Casey up. The angle of the deck was bad now, the fire worse. "This whole goddamn tub could capsize any second."

"What about them?" she asked quietly, nodding at Fleur and Orlanda.

He thought a second, then said decisively, "You go first, wait below!"

"Got it!" At once she gave him her small purse. He stuffed it into a pocket and hurried away as she kicked off her shoes, unzipped her long dress and stepped out of it. At once she gathered up the light silk material into a rope, tied it around her waist, swung neatly over the railing and stood there poised on the edge a moment, gauged her impact point carefully, and leapt out into a perfect swan dive. Gornt and Dunross watched her go, their immediate danger forgotten.

Bartlett was beside Orlanda now. He saw Casey break the surface cleanly and before Orlanda could do anything he lifted her over the railing and said, "Hold your breath, honey," and dropped her carefully. They all watched her fall. She plummeted down feet first and went into the water a few yards from Casey who had already anticipated the spot and had swum down below the surface. She caught Orlanda easily, kicked for the surface, and Orlanda was breathing almost before she realized she was off the deck. Casey held her safely and swam strongly for the cutter, in perfect control.

Gornt and Dunross cheered lustily. The boat lurched again and they almost lost their footing as Bartlett stumbled over to the Marlowes.

"Peter, how's your swimming?" Bartlett asked.

"Average."

"Trust me with her? I was a lifeguard, beach bum, for years."

Before Marlowe could say no, Bartlett lifted Fleur into his arms and stepped over the railing onto the ledge and poised himself for a second. "Just hold your breath!" She put one arm around his neck and held her nose then he stepped into space, Fleur tightly and safely in his arms. He plunged into the sea cleanly, protecting her from the shock with his own legs and body, and kicked smoothly for the surface. Her head was hardly under a few seconds and she was not even spluttering though her heart was racing. In seconds she was at the cutter. She hung on to the side and they looked back.

When Peter Marlowe saw she was safe his heart began again. "Oh, jolly good," he muttered.

"Did you see Casey go?" Dunross asked. "Fantastic!"

"What? Oh, no, tai-pan."

"Just bra and pants with stockings attached and no ironworks and a dream dive. Christ, what a figure!"

"Oh those're pantyhose," Marlowe said absently, looking at the water below, gathering his courage. "They've just come out in the States, they're all the rage . . ."

Dunross was hardly listening. "Christ Agnes, what a figure." "Ah yes," Gornt echoed. "And what *cojones*."

The boat shrieked as the last of its mooring guys snapped. The deck toppled nauseatingly.

As one, the last three men went overboard. Dunross and Gornt dived, Peter Marlowe jumped. The dives were good but both men knew they were not as good as Casey's.

38

11:30 P.M.:

On the other side of the island the old taxi was grinding up the narrow street high above West Point in Mid Levels, Suslev sprawled drunkenly in the backseat. The night was dark and he was singing a sad Russian ballad to the sweating driver, his tie askew, coat off, his shirt streaked with sweat. The overcast had thickened and lowered, the humidity was worse, the air stifling.

"*Matyeryebyets!*" he muttered, cursing the heat, then smiled, the twisted obscenity pleasing him. He looked out the window. The city and harbor lights far below were misted by wisps of clouds, Kowloon mostly obscured. "It'll rain soon, comrade," he said to the driver, his English slurred, not caring if the man understood or not.

The ancient taxi was wheezing. The engine coughed suddenly and that reminded him of Arthur's cough and their coming meeting. His excitement quickened.

The taxi had picked him up at the Golden Ferry Terminal, then climbed to Mid Levels on the Peak, turned west, skirting Government House where the governor lived, and the Botanical Gardens. Passing the palace, Suslev had wondered absently when the Hammer and Sickle would fly atop the empty flagpole. Soon, he had thought contentedly. With Arthur's help and Sevrin's—very soon. Just a few more years.

He peered at his watch. He would be a little late but that did not worry him. Arthur was always late, never less than ten minutes, never more than twenty. Dangerous to be a man of habit in our profession, he thought. But dangerous or not, Arthur's an enormous asset and Sevrin, his creation, a brilliant, vital tool in our KGB armament, buried so deep, waiting so patiently, like all the other Sevrins throughout the world. Only ninety-odd thousands of us KGB officers and yet we almost rule the world. We've already changed it, changed it permanently, already we own half . . . and in such a short time, only since 1917.

So few of us, so many of *them*. But now our tentacles reach out into every corner. Our armies of assistants—informers, fools, parasites, traitors, the twisted self-deluders and misshapen, misbegotten believers we so deliberately recruit are in every land, feeding off one another like the vermin they all are, fueled by their own selfish wants and fears, all expendable sooner or later. And everywhere one of us, one of the elite, the KGB officers, in the center of each web, controlling guiding eliminating. Webs within webs up to the Presidium of all the Soviets and now so tightly woven into the fabric of Mother Russia as to be indestructible. We *are* modern Russia, he thought proudly. We're Lenin's spearhead. Without us and our techniques and our orchestrated use of terror there would be no Soviet Russia, no Soviet Empire, no driving force to keep the rulers of the Party all powerful—and nowhere on earth would there be a Communist state. Yes, we're the elite.

His smile deepened.

It was hot and sultry inside the taxi even though the windows were open as it curled upward through this residential area with its ribbons of great gardenless apartment blocks that sat on small pads chewed out of the mountainside. A bead of sweat trickled down his cheek and he wiped it off, his whole body feeling clammy.

I'd love a shower, he thought, letting his mind wander. A shower with cool sweet Georgian water, not this saline filth they put through Hong Kong's pipes. I'd love to be in the *dacha* near Tiflis, oh that would be grand! Yes, back in the *dacha* with Father and Mother and I'd swim in the stream running through our land and dry off in the sun, a great Georgian wine cooling in the stream and the mountains nearby. That's Eden if there ever was an Eden. Mountains and pastures, grapes and harvest and the air so clean.

He chuckled as he remembered the fabrication about his past he had told Travkin. That parasite! Just another fool, another tool to be used and, when blunt, discarded.

His father had been a Communist since the very early days—first in the Cheka, secretly, and then, since its inception in 1917, in the KGB. Now in his late seventies, still tall and upright and in honored retirement, he lived like an old-fashioned prince with servants and horses and bodyguards. Suslev was sure that he would inherit the same *dacha*, the same land, the same honor in due course. So would his son, a fledgling in the KGB, if his service continued to be excellent. His own work merited it, his record was impressive and he was only fifty-two.

Yes, he told himself confidently, in thirteen years I'm due for retirement. Thirteen great more years, helping the attack move forward, never easing up whatever the enemy does.

And who is the enemy, the real enemy?

All those who disobey us, all those who refuse our eminence—Russians most of all.

He laughed out loud.

The weary sour-faced young driver glanced up briefly at the rear mirror then went back to his driving, hoping his passenger was drunk enough to misread the meter and give him a great tip. He pulled up at the address he had been given.

Rose Court on Kotewall Road was a modern fourteen-story apartment block. Below were three floors of garage space and around it a small ribbon of concrete and below that, down a slight concrete embankment, was Sinclair Road and Sinclair Towers and more apartment blocks that nestled into the mountainside. This was a choice area to live. The view was grand, the apartments were below the clouds that frequently shrouded the upper reaches of the Peak where walls would sweat, linens would mildew and everything would seem to be perpetually damp.

The meter read 8.70 HK. Suslev peered at a bunch of notes, gave the driver 100 instead of a 10 and got out heavily. A Chinese woman was fanning herself impatiently. He lurched toward the apartment intercom. She told the driver to wait for her husband and looked after Suslev disgustedly.

His feet were unsteady. He found the button he sought and pressed it: Ernest Clinker, Esq., Manager.

"Yes?"

"Ernie, it's me, Gregor," he said thickly with a belch. "Are you in?"

The cockney voice laughed. "Not on your nelly! 'Course I'm in, mate! You're late! You sound as though you've been on a pub crawl! Beer's up, vodka's up, and me'n Mabel's here to greet you!"

Suslev headed for the elevator. He pressed the *down* button. On the lowest level he got out into the open garage and went to the far side. The apartment door was already open and a ruddy-faced, ugly little man in his sixties held out his hand. "Stone the bloody crows," Clinker said, a grin showing cheap false teeth, "you're a bit under the weather, ain'cher?" Suslev gave him a bear hug which was returned and they went inside.

The apartment was two tiny bedrooms, living room, kitchen, bathroom. The rooms were poorly furnished but pleasant, and the only real luxury a small tape deck that was playing opera loudly.

"Beer or vodka?"

Suslev beamed and belched. "First a piss, then vodka, then . . . then another and then . . . then bed." He belched hugely, lurching for the toilet.

"Right you are, Cap'n me old sport! Hey, Mabel, say hello to the Cap'n!" The sleepy old bulldog on her well-chewed mat opened one eye briefly, barked once and was almost instantly wheezily asleep again. Clinker beamed and went to the table and poured a stiff vodka and a glass of water. No ice. He drank some Guinness then called out, "How long you staying, Gregor?"

"Just tonight, *tovarich*. Perhaps tomorrow night. Tomorrow . . . tomorrow I've got to be back aboard. But tomorrow night . . . perhaps, eh?"

"What about Ginny? She throw you out again . . . ?"

In the nondescript van that was parked down the road, Roger Crosse, Brian Kwok and the police radio technician were listening to this conversation through a loudspeaker, the quality of the bug good with little static, the van packed with radio surveillance equipment. They heard Clinker chuckle and say again, "She threw you out, eh?"

"All evening we jig-jig and she . . . she says go stay with Ernie and leave me . . . leave me sleep!"

"You're a lucky bugger. She's a princess that one. Bring her over tomorrer."

"Yes . . . yes I . . . will. Yes she's the best."

They heard Suslev pour a bucket of water into the toilet and come back.

"Here, old chum!"

"Thank you." The sound of thirsty drinking. "I . . . I think . . . I think I want to lie down for . . . lie down. A few minutes . . ."

"A few hours more like! Don't you fret, I'll cook breakfast. Here, wanta 'nother drink. . . ."

The policemen in the van were listening carefully. Crosse had ordered the bug put into Clinker's apartment two years ago. Periodically it was monitored, always when Suslev was there. Suslev, always under loose surveillance, had met Clinker in a bar. Both men were submariners and they had struck up a friendship. Clinker had invited him to stay and from time to time Suslev did. At once Crosse had instituted a security check on Clinker but nothing untoward had been discovered. For twenty years Clinker had been a sailor with the Royal Navy. After the war he had drifted from job to job in the Merchant Marine, throughout Asia to Hong Kong, where he had settled when he retired. He was a quiet, easygoing man who lived alone and had been Rose Court's caretaker-janitor for five years now. Suslev and Clinker were a matched pair who drank a lot, caroused a lot and swapped stories. None of their hours of talk had produced anything considered valuable.

"He's had his usual tankful, Brian," Crosse said.

"Yes sir." Brian Kwok was bored and tried not to show it.

In the small living room Clinker gave Suslev his shoulder. "Come on, it's you for a kip." He stepped over the glass and helped Suslev into the small bedroom. Suslev lay down heavily and sighed.

Clinker closed the drapes then went over to another small tape deck and turned it on. In a moment heavy breathing and the beginnings of a snore came from the tape. Suslev got up soundlessly, his pretended drunkenness gone. Clinker was already on his hands and knees. He pulled away a mat and opened the trapdoor. Noiselessly, Suslev went down into it. Clinker grinned, slapped him on the back and closed the well-greased door after him. The trapdoor steps led to a rough tunnel that quickly joined the large, dry, subterranean culvert storm drain. Suslev picked his way carefully, using the flashlight that was in a bracket at the bottom of the steps. In a moment he heard a car grinding over Sinclair Road just above his head. A few more steps and he was below Sinclair Towers. Another trapdoor led to a janitor's closet. This let out onto some disused back stairs. He began to climb.

Roger Crosse was still listening to the heavy breathing, mixed with opera. The van was cramped and close, their shirts sweaty. Crosse was smoking. "Sounds like he's bedded down for the night," he said. They could hear Clinker humming and his movements as he cleared up the broken glass. A red warning light on the radio panel started winking. The operator clicked on the sender. "Patrol car 1423, yes?"

"Headquarters for Superintendent Crosse. Urgent."

"This's Crosse."

"Duty Office, sir. A report's just come in that the *Floating Dragon* restaurant's on fire . . ." Brian Kwok gasped. ". . . Fire engines're already there, and the constable said that as many as twenty may be dead or drowned. It seems the boat caught fire from the kitchen, sir. There were several explosions. They blew out most of the hull and . . . Just a moment sir, there's another report coming in from Marine."

They waited. Brian Kwok broke the silence. "Dunross?"

"The party was on the top deck?" Crosse asked.

"Yes sir."

"He's much too smart to get burned to death—or drowned," Crosse said softly. "Was the fire an accident, or deliberate?"

Brian Kwok did not answer.

The HQ voice came in again. "Marine reports that the boat's capsized. They say it's a proper carve-up and it looks like a few got sucked under."

"Was our agent with our VIP?"

"No sir, he was waiting on the wharf near his car. There was no time to get to him."

"What about the people caught on the top deck?"

"Hang on a moment, I'll ask. . . ."

Again a silence. Brian Kwok wiped the sweat off.

". . . They say, twenty or thirty up there jumped, sir. Unfortunately most of them abandoned ship a bit late, just before the boat capsized. Marine doesn't know how many were swamped."

"Stand by." Crosse thought a moment. Then he spoke into the mike again. "I'm sending Superintendent Kwok there at once in this transport. Send a team of frogmen to meet him. Ask the navy to assist, Priority One. I'll be at home if I'm needed." He clicked off the mike. Then to Brian Kwok, "I'll walk from here. Call me the moment you know about Dunross. If he's dead we'll visit the bank vaults at once and to hell with the consequences. Fast as you can now!"

He got out. The van took off up the hill. Aberdeen was over the spine of mountains and due south. He glanced at Rose Court a moment, then down across the street below to Sinclair Towers. One of his teams was still watching the entrance, waiting patiently for Tsu-yan's return. Where is that bastard? he asked himself irritably.

Very concerned, he walked off down the hill. Rain began to splatter him. His footsteps quickened.

Suslev took an ice-cold beer from the modern refrigerator and opened it. He drank gratefully. 32 Sinclair Towers was spacious, rich, clean and well furnished, with three bedrooms and a large living room. It was on the eleventh floor. There were three apartments to each floor around two cramped elevators and exit steps. Mr. and Mrs. John Chen owned 31. 33 belonged to a Mr. K. V. Lee. Arthur had told Suslev that K. V. Lee was a cover name for Ian Dunross who, following the pattern of his predecessors, had sole access to three or four private apartments spread around the Colony. Suslev had never met either John Chen or Dunross though he had seen them at the races and elsewhere many times.

If we have to interview the tai-pan what could be more convenient? he thought grimly. And with Travkin as an alternate bait. . . .

A sudden squall whipped the curtains that were drawn over open windows and he heard the rain. He shut the windows carefully and looked out. Great drops were streaking the windows. Streets and rooftops were already wet. Lightning went across the sky. The rumble of thunder followed. Already the temperature had dropped a few degrees. This'll be a good storm, he told himself gratefully, pleased to be out of Ginny Fu's tiny, sleazy fifth-floor walkup in Mong Kok, and equally happy not to be at Clinker's.

Arthur had arranged everything: Clinker, Ginny Fu, this safe house, the tunnel, certainly as well as he himself could have done in Vladivostok. Clinker was a submariner and cockney and everything he was supposed to be except that he had always detested the officer class. Arthur had said it had been easy to subvert Clinker to the cause, using the man's built-in suspicions, hatreds and secretiveness. "Ugly Ernie knows only a little about you, Gregor—of course that you're Russian and captain of the *Ivanov*. As to the tunnel, I told him you're having an affair with a married woman in Sinclair Towers, the wife of one of the Establishment tai-pans. I told him the tape-recorded snores and secrecy are because the rotten Peelers are after you and they've sneaked in and bugged his flat."

"Peelers?"

"That's the cockney nickname for police. It came from Sir Robert Peel, Prime Minister of England, who founded the first police force. Cockneys've always hated Peelers and Ugly Ernie would delight in outwitting them. Just be pro-*Royal* Navy and he's your dog until death. . . ."

Suslev smiled. Clinker's not a bad man, he thought, just a bore.

He sipped his beer as he wandered back into the living room. The afternoon paper was there. It was the *Guardian* Extra, the headlines screaming, MOB MURDERS FRAGRANT FLOWER, and a good photograph of the riot. He sat in an armchair and read quickly.

Then his sharp ears heard the elevator stop. He went to the table beside the door and slid the loaded automatic with its silencer from under it. He pocketed the gun and peered through the spy hole.

The doorbell was muted. He opened it and smiled. "Come in, old friend." He embraced Jacques deVille warmly. "It's been a long time."

"Yes, yes it has, comrade," deVille said as warmly. The last time he had seen Suslev was in Singapore, five years before, at a secret meeting arranged by Arthur just after deVille had been induced to join Sevrin. He and Suslev had met just as secretly the first time in the great port of Lyons in France in June '41, just days before Nazi Germany invaded Soviet Russia when the two countries were outwardly still allies. At that time deVille was in the Maquis and Suslev second-in-command and secret political commissar of a Soviet submarine that was ostensibly in for a refit from patrol in the Atlantic. It was then that deVille was asked if he would like to carry on the *real war*, the war against the capitalist enemy as a secret agent after the fascists had been destroyed.

He had agreed with all his heart.

It had been easy for Suslev to subvert him. Because of deVille's potential after the war, the KGB had secretly had him betrayed to the Gestapo, then rescued from a Gestapo prison death by Communist guerrillas. The guerrillas had given him false proof that he had been betrayed by one of his own men for money. DeVille was thirty-two then and, like many, infatuated with socialism and with some of the teachings of Marx and Lenin. He had never joined the French Communist Party but now, because of Sevrin, he was an honorary captain in the KGB Soviet Security Force.

"You seem tired, Frederick," Suslev said, using deVille's cover name. "Tell me what's wrong."

"Just a family problem."

"Tell me."

Suslev listened intently to deVille's sad story about his son-in-law and daughter. Since their meeting in 1941 Suslev had been deVille's controller. In 1947 he had ordered him out to Hong Kong to join Struan's. Before the war deVille and his father had owned a highly successful import-export business with close ties to Struan's—as well as family ties—so the change had been easy and welcome. DeVille's secret assignment was to become a member of the Inner Court and, at length, tai-pan.

"Where's your daughter now?" he asked compassionately.

DeVille told him.

"And the driver of the other car?" Suslev committed the name and address to memory. "I'll see that he's dealt with."

"No," deVille said at once. "It . . . it was an accident. We cannot punish a man for an accident."

"He was drunk. There is no excuse for drunk driving. In any event you are important to us. We take care of our own. I will deal with him."

DeVille knew there was no point in arguing. A gust of rain battered the windows. "*Merde,* but the rain's good. The temperature must be down five degrees. Will it last?"

"The storm front's reported to be big."

DeVille watched globules running down the pane, wondering why he had been summoned. "How are things with you?"

"Very good. Drink?" Suslev went to the mirrored bar. "There's good vodka."

"Vodka's fine, please. But a short one."

"If Dunross retired are you the next tai-pan?"

"I would think it's between four of us: Gavallan, David MacStruan, myself and Linbar Struan."

"In that order?"

"I don't know. Except Linbar's probably last. Thanks." DeVille accepted his drink. They toasted each other. "I'd bet on Gavallan."

"Who's this MacStruan?"

"A distant cousin. He's done his five years as a China Trader. At the moment he's heading up our expansion into Canada—we're trying to diversify and get into wood fibers, copper, all the Canadian minerals, mostly out of British Columbia."

"How good is he?"

"Very good. Very tough. A very dirty fighter. Forty-one, ex-lieutenant, Paratroopers. His left hand was almost ripped off over Burma by a tangle in the shrouds of his parachute. He just tied a tourniquet around it and carried on fighting. That earned him a Military Cross. If I was tai-pan I'd choose him." DeVille shrugged. "By our company law only the tai-pan can appoint his successor. He can do it anytime, even in his will if he wants. Whatever way it's done it's binding on the Noble House."

Suslev watched him. "Has Dunross made a will?"

"Ian's very efficient."

A silence gathered.

"Another vodka?"

"*Non, merci,* I'll stay with this one. Is Arthur joining us?"

"Yes. How could we tip the scales for you?"

DeVille hesitated, then shrugged.

Suslev poured himself another drink. "It would be easy to discredit this MacStruan and the others. Yes. Easy to eliminate them." Suslev turned and looked at him. "Even Dunross."

"No. That's not the solution."

"Is there another one?"

"Being patient." DeVille smiled but his eyes were very tired and shadows lurked there. "I would not like to be the cause of . . . of his removal or that of the others."

Suslev laughed. "It's not necessary to kill to eliminate! Are we barbarians? Or course not." He was watching his protégé closely. DeVille needs toughening, he was thinking. "Tell me about the American, Bartlett, and the Struan–Par-Con deal."

DeVille told him all he knew. "Bartlett's money will give us everything we need."

"Can this Gornt effect a takeover?"

"Yes and no. And possibly. He's tough and he truly hates us. It's a long-term rival—"

"Yes, I know." Suslev was surprised deVille kept repeating information he already had been given. It's a bad sign, he thought, and glanced at his watch. "Our friend's twenty-five minutes late. That's unusual." Both men were too seasoned to worry. Meetings such as this could never be completely firm because no one could ever control the unexpected happening.

"Did you hear about the fire in Aberdeen?" deVille asked at the sudden thought.

"What fire?"

"There was a bulletin over the wireless just before I came up." DeVille and his wife had apartment 20 on the sixth floor. "The *Floating Dragon* restaurant at Aberdeen burned down. Perhaps Arthur was there."

"Did you see him?" Suslev was suddenly concerned.

"No. But I could easily have missed him. I left well before dinner."

Suslev sipped his vodka thoughtfully. "Has he told you yet who the others are in Sevrin?"

"No. I asked him, judiciously, as you ordered, but he nev—"

"Order? I don't order you, *tovarich*, I just suggest."

"Of course. All he said was, 'We'll all meet in due course.'"

"We'll both know soon. He's perfectly correct to be cautious." Suslev had wanted to test deVille and test Arthur. It was one of the most basic rules in the KGB that you can never be too cautious about your spies however important they are. He remembered his instructor hammering into them another direct quote from Sun Tzu's *The Art of War*, which was obligatory reading for all Soviet military: "There are five classes of spies— local spies, inward spies, converted spies, doomed spies and surviving spies. When all five categories are working in concert, the state will be secure and the army inviolate. Local spies are those who are local inhabitants. Inward spies are officials of the enemy. Converted spies are the enemies' spies you have converted. Doomed spies are those fed false information and reported to the enemy who will torture this false information from them and so be deceived. Surviving spies are those who bring back news from the enemy camp. Remember, in the whole army, none should more liberally be rewarded. But if a secret piece of news is divulged by a spy before the time is ripe, he or she must be put to death, together with the person to whom the secret is told."

If the other AMG reports are like the one already discovered, Suslev thought dispassionately, then Dunross is doomed.

He was watching deVille, measuring him, liking him, glad that again he had passed that test—and Arthur. The last paragraph of *The Art of War*—so important a book to the Soviet elite that many knew the slim volume by heart—sprang into his mind: "It is only the enlightened ruler and wise general who will use the highest intelligence of the army for the purposes of spying. Spies are the most important element in war because upon them depends an army's ability to move."

That's what the KGB does, he thought contentedly. We try for the best talent in all the Soviets. We *are* the elite. We *need* spies of all five categories. We need these men, Jacques and Arthur and all the others.

Yes, we need them very much.

"Arthur's never given any clue who the others are. Nothing," deVille was saying, "only that there are seven of us."

"We must be patient," Suslev said, relieved that Arthur was correctly cautious too, for part of the plan was that the seven should never know each other, should never know that Suslev was Sevrin's controller and Arthur's superior. Suslev knew the identities of all the Sevrin moles. With Arthur he had approved all of them over the years, continually testing them all, honing their loyalties, eliminating some, substituting others. You always test, and the moment a spy wavers that's the time to neutralize or eliminate him—before he neutralizes or eliminates you. Even Ginny Fu, he thought, though she's not a spy and knows nothing. You can never be sure of anyone except yourself—that's what our Soviet system teaches. Yes. It's time I took her on the trip I've always promised. A short voyage next week. To Vladivostok. Once she's there she can be cleansed and rehabilitated and made useful, never to return here.

He sipped his vodka, rolling the fiery liquid around his tongue. "We'll give Arthur half an hour. Please," he said, motioning to a chair.

DeVille moved the newspaper out of the way and sat in the armchair. "Did you read about the bank runs?"

Suslev beamed. "Yes, *tovarich*. Marvelous."

"Is it a KGB operation?"

"Not to my knowledge," Suslev said jovially. "If it is there's promotion for someone." It was a key Leninistic policy to pay particular attention to Western banks that were at the core of Western strength, to infiltrate them to the highest level, to encourage and assist others to foment disaster against Western currencies but at the same time to borrow capital from them to the utter maximum, whatever the interest, the longer the loan the better, making sure that no Soviet ever defaulted on any repayment, *whatsoever the cost.* "The crash of the Ho-Pak will certainly bring down others. The papers say there might even be a run on the Victoria, eh?"

DeVille shivered in spite of himself and Suslev noticed it. His concern deepened. "*Merde,* but that would wreck Hong Kong," deVille said. "Oh, I know the sooner the better but . . . but being buried so deep, sometimes you forget who you really are."

"That's nothing to worry about. It happens to all of us. You're in turmoil because of your daughter. What father wouldn't be? It will pass."

"When can we do something? I'm tired, so tired of waiting."

"Soon. Listen," Suslev said to encourage him. "In January I was at a top echelon meeting in Moscow. Banking was high on our list. At our last count we're indebted to the capitalists nearly 30 billions in loans—most of that to America."

DeVille gasped. "Madonna, I had no idea you'd been so successful."

Suslev's smile broadened. "That's just Soviet Russia! Our satellites are in for another 6.3 billions. East Germany's just got another 1.3 billion to purchase capitalist rolling mills, computer technology and a lot of things we need." He laughed, drained his glass and poured another, the liquor oiling his tongue. "I really don't understand them, the capitalists. They delude themselves. We're openly committed to consume them but they give us the means to do it. They're astonishing. If we have time, twenty years—at the most twenty—by that time our debt will be 60, 70 billions and as far as they're concerned we'll still be a triple-A risk, never having defaulted on a payment ever . . . in war, peace or depression." He let out a sudden burst of laughter. "What was it the Swiss banker said? 'Lend a little and you have a debtor—lend a lot and you have a partner!' 70 billions, Jacques old friend, and we own them. 70 and we can twist their policies to suit ourselves and then at any moment of our own choosing the final ploy: 'So sorry, Mr. Capitalist Zionist Banker, we regret we're broke! Oh very sorry but we can no longer repay the loans, not even the interest on the loans. Very sorry but from this moment all our present currency's valueless. Our new currency's a red ruble, one red ruble's worth a hundred of your capitalist dollars. . . .'"

Suslev laughed, feeling very happy. ". . . and however rich the banks are collectively they'll never be able to write off 70 billions. Never. 70 plus by that time with all the Eastern Bloc billions! And if the sudden announcement's timed to one of their inevitable capitalistic recessions as it will be . . . they'll be up to their Hebrew bankers' noses in their own panic shit, begging us to save their rotten skins." He added contemptuously, "The stupid bastards deserve to lose! Why should we fight them when their own greed and stupidity's destroying them. Eh?"

DeVille nodded uneasily. Suslev frightened him. I must be getting old, he thought. In the early days it was so easy to believe in the cause of the masses. The cries of the downtrodden were so loud and clear then. But now? Now they're not so clear. I'm still committed, deeply committed. I regret nothing. France will be better Communist.

Will it?

I don't know anymore, not for certain, not as I used to. It's a pity for all people that there must be some "ism" or other, he told himself, trying to cover his anguish. Better if there were no "isms," just my beloved Côte d'Azur basking in the sun.

"I tell you, old friend, Stalin and Beria were geniuses," Suslev was saying. "They're the greatest Russians that have ever been."

DeVille just managed to keep the shock off his face. He was remembering the horror of the German occupation, the humbling of France, all the villages and hamlets and vineyards, remembering that Hitler would never have dared attack Poland and start it all without Stalin's nonaggression pact to protect his back. Without Stalin there would have been no war, no holocaust and we would all be better off. "Twenty million Russians? Countless millions of others," he said.

"A modest cost." Suslev poured again, his zeal and the vodka taking him. "Because of Stalin and Beria we have all Eastern Europe from the Baltic to the Balkans—Estonia, Lithuania, Latvia, Czechoslovakia, Hungary, Rumania, Bulgaria, all Poland, Prussia, half of Germany, Outer Mongolia." Suslev belched happily. "North Korea, and footholds everywhere else. Their Operation Lion smashed the British Empire. Because of their support the United Nations was birthed to give us our greatest weapon in our arsenal of many weapons. And then there's Israel." He began to laugh. "My father was one of the controllers of that program."

DeVille felt the hackles of his neck rise. "What?"

"Israel was a Stalin-Beria coup of monumental proportions! Who helped it, overt and covert, come into being? Who gave it immediate recognition? *We did*, and why?" Suslev belched again, "To cement into the guts of Arabia a perpetual cancer that will suppurate and destroy both sides and, along with them, bring down the industrial might of the West. Jew against Mohammedan against Christian. Those fanatics'll never live at peace with one another even though they could, easily. They will never bury their differences even if it costs them their stupid lives." He laughed and stared at his glass blearily, swirling the liquid around. DeVille watched him, hating him, wanting to give him the lie back, afraid to, knowing himself totally in Suslev's power. Once, some years ago, he had balked over sending some routine Struan figures to a box number in Berlin. Within a day, a stranger had phoned him at home. Such a call had never happened before. It was friendly. But he knew.

DeVille suppressed a shudder and kept his face clear as Suslev glanced up at him.

"Don't you agree, *tovarich?*" the KGB man said, beaming. "I swear I'll never understand the capitalists. They make enemies of four hundred million Arabs who have all the world's real oil reserves one day they will need so desperately. And soon we'll have Iran and the Gulf and the Strait of Hormuz. Then we'll have a hand on the West's tap, then they're ours and no need for war—just execution." Suslev drained his vodka and poured another.

DeVille watched him, loathing him now, wondering frantically about his own role. Is it for this that I have been almost a perfect mole, for sixteen years keeping myself prepared and ready, with no suspicion against me? Even Susanne suspects nothing and everyone believes I'm anti-Communist, pro-Struan's which is the arch-capitalistic creation in all Asia. Dirk Struan's thoughts permeate us. Profit. Profit for the tai-pan and the Noble House and then Hong Kong in that order and the hell with everyone except the Crown, England and China. And even if I don't become tai-pan, I can still make Sevrin the wrecker of China that Suslev and Arthur want it to be. But do I want to now? Now that, for the first time, I've really seen into this . . . this monster and all their hypocrisy?

"Stalin," he said, almost wincing under Suslev's gaze. "Did . . . you ever meet him?"

"I was near him once. Ten feet away. He was tiny but you could feel his power. That was in 1953 at a party Beria gave for some senior KGB officers. My father was invited and I was allowed to go with him." Suslev took another vodka, hardly seeing him, swept by the past and by his family's involvement in the movement. "Stalin was there, Beria, Malenkov . . . Did you know Stalin's real name was Iosif Vissarionovich Dzhugashvili? He was the son of a shoemaker, in Tiflis, my home, destined for the priesthood but expelled from the seminary there. Strange strange strange!"

They touched glasses.

"No need for you to be so solemn, comrade," he said, misreading deVille. "Whatever your personal loss. You're part of the future, part of the march to victory!" Suslev drained his glass. "Stalin must have died a happy man. We should be so lucky, eh?"

"And Beria?"

"Beria tried to take power too late. He failed. We in the KGB are like Japanese in that we too agree the only sin is failure. But Stalin . . . There's a story my father tells that when at Yalta, for no concession, Roosevelt agreed to give Stalin Manchuria *and the Kuriles* which guaranteed us dominance over China and Japan and all Asian waters, Stalin had a hemorrhage choking back his laughter and almost died!"

After a pause, deVille said, "And Solzhenitsyn and the *gulags?*"

"We're at war, my friend, there are traitors within. Without terror how can the few rule the many? Stalin knew that. He was a truly great man. Even his death served us. It was brilliant of Khrushchev to use him to 'humanize' the USSR."

"That was just another ploy?" deVille asked, shaken.

"That would be a state secret." Suslev swallowed a belch. "It doesn't matter, Stalin will be returned to his glory soon. Now, what about Ottawa?"

"Oh. I've been in contact with Jean-Charles an—" The phone rang abruptly. A single ring. Their eyes went to it, their breathing almost stopped. After twenty-odd seconds there was a second single ring. Both men relaxed slightly. Another twenty-odd seconds and the third ring became continuous. One ring meant "Danger leave immediately"; two, that the meeting was canceled; three that whoever was calling would be there shortly; three becoming continuous, that it was safe to talk. Suslev picked up the phone. He heard breathing, then Arthur asked in his curious accent, "Is Mr. Lop-sing there?"

"There's no Lop-*ting* here, you have a wrong number," Suslev said in a different voice, concentrating with an effort.

They went through the code carefully, Suslev further reassured by Arthur's slight, dry cough. Then Arthur said, "I cannot meet tonight. Would Friday at three be convenient?" Friday meant Thursday—tomorrow—Wednesday meant Tuesday, and so on. The three was a code for a meeting place: the Happy Valley Racecourse at the dawn workout.

Tomorrow at dawn!

"Yes."

The phone clicked off. Only the dial tone remained.

THURSDAY

39

About an hour before dawn in the pouring rain Goodweather Poon looked down at the half-naked body of John Chen and cursed. He had been through his clothes carefully and sifted through endless pounds of mud from the grave that the two youths, Kin Pak and Dog-eared Chen, had dug. But he had found nothing—no coins or parts of coins or jewelry, nothing. And Four Finger Wu had said earlier, "You find that half-coin, Goodweather Poon!" Then the old man had given him further instructions and Goodweather Poon was very pleased because that relieved him of any responsibility and he could then make no mistake.

He had ordered Dog-eared Chen and Kin Pak to carry the body down-stairs and had threatened Smallpox Kin, who nursed his mutilated hand, that if the youth moaned once more he would slice out his tongue. They had left Father Kin's body in an alley. Then Goodweather Poon had sought out the King of the Beggars of Kowloon City who was a distant cousin of Four Finger Wu. All beggars were members of the Beggars' Guild and there was one king in Hong Kong, one in Kowloon and one in Kowloon City. In olden days begging was a lucrative profession, but now, due to stiff prison sentences and fines and plenty of well-paying jobs, it was not.

"You see, Honored Beggar King, this acquaintance of ours has just died," Goodweather Poon explained patiently to the distinguished old man. "He has no relations, so he's been put out in Flowersellers' Alley. My High Dragon would certainly appreciate a little help. Perhaps you could arrange a quiet burial?" He negotiated politely then paid the agreed price and went off to their taxi and car that waited outside the city limits, happy that now the body would vanish forever without a trace. Kin Pak was already in the taxi's front seat. He got in beside him. "Guide us to John Chen," he ordered. "And be quick!"

"Take the Sha Tin Road," Kin Pak said importantly to the driver. Dog-eared Chen was cowering in the backseat with more of Goodweather Poon's fighters. Smallpox Kin and the others followed in the car.

The two vehicles went northwest into the New Territories on the Sha Tin–Tai Po road that curled through villages and resettlement areas and shantytowns of squatters, through the mountain pass, skirting the railway that headed north for the border, past rich market gardens heavy with the smell of dung. Just before the fishing village of Sha Tin with the sea on their right, they turned left off the main road onto a side road, the surface broken and puddled. In a glade of trees they stopped and got out.

It was warm in the rain, the land sweet-smelling. Kin Pak took the shovel and led the way into the undergrowth. Goodweather Poon held the flashlight as Kin Pak, Dog-eared Chen and Smallpox Kin searched. It was difficult in the darkness for them to find the exact place. Twice they had begun to dig, before Kin Pak remembered their father had marked the spot with a crescent rock. Cursing and soaked, at length they found the rock and began to dig. The earth was parched under the surface. Soon they had unearthed the corpse which was wrapped in a blanket. The smell was heavy. Though Goodweather Poon had made them strip the body and had searched diligently, nothing was to be found.

"You sent everything else to Noble House Chen?" he asked again, rain on his face, his clothes soaking.

"Yes," the young Kin Pak said truculently. "How many fornicating times do I have to tell you?" He was very weary, his clothes sodden, and he was sure he was going to die.

"All of you take your manure-infested clothes off. Shoes socks everything. I want to go through your pockets."

They obeyed. Kin Pak wore a string around his neck with a cheap circle of jade on it. Almost everyone in China wore a piece of jade for good luck, because everyone knew if an evil god caused you to stumble, the spirit of jade would get between you and the evil and take the brunt of the fall from you and shatter, saving you from shattering. And if it didn't, then the Jade God was regretfully sleeping and that was your joss never mind.

Goodweather Poon found nothing in Kin Pak's pockets. He threw the clothes back at him. By now he was soaked too and very irritable. "You can dress, and dress the corpse again. And hurry it up!"

Dog-eared Chen had almost 400 HK and a jade bracelet of good quality. One of the men took the jade and Poon pocketed the money and turned on Smallpox Kin. All their eyes popped as they saw the big roll of notes he found in the youth's pants pocket.

Goodweather Poon shielded it carefully from the rain. "Where in the name of Heavenly Whore did you get all this?"

He told them about shaking down the lucky ones outside the Ho-Pak and they laughed and complimented him on his sagacity. "Very good, very clever," Poon said. "You're a good businessman. Put your clothes on. What was the old woman's name?"

"She called herself Ah Tam." Smallpox Kin wiped the rain out of his eyes, his toes twisting into the mud, his mutilated hand on fire now and aching very much. "I'll take you to her if you want."

"Hey, I need the fornicating light here!" Kin Pak called out. He was on his hands and knees, fighting John Chen's clothes into place. "Can't someone give me a hand?"

"Help him!"

Dog-eared Chen and Smallpox Kin hurried to help as Goodweather Poon directed the circle of light back on the corpse. The body was swollen and puffy, the rain washing the dirt away. The back of John Chen's head was blood-matted and crushed but his face was still recognizable.

"*Ayeeyah*," one of his men said, "let's get on with it. I feel evil spirits lurking hereabouts."

"Just his trousers and shirt'll do," Goodweather Poon said sourly. He waited until the body was partially dressed. Then he turned his eyes on them. "Now which one of you motherless whores helped the old man kill this poor fornicator?"

Kin Pak said, "I already t—" He stopped as he saw the other two point at him and say in unison, "He did," and back away from him.

"I suspected it all along!" Goodweather Poon was pleased that he had at last got to the bottom of the mystery. He pointed his stubby forefinger at Kin Pak. "Get in the trench and lie down."

"We have an easy plan how to kidnap Noble House Chen himself that'll bring us all twice, three times what this fornicator brought. I'll tell you how, *heya?*" Kin Pak said.

Goodweather Poon hesitated a moment at this new thought. Then he remembered Four Fingers's instructions. "Put your face in the dirt in the trench!"

Kin Pak looked at the inflexible eyes and knew he was dead. He shrugged. Joss. "I piss on all your generations," he said and got into the grave and lay down.

He put his head on his arms in the dirt and began to shut out the light of his life. From nothing into nothing, always part of the Kin family, of all its generations, living forever in its perpetual stream, from generation to generation, down through history into the everlasting future.

Goodweather Poon took up one of the shovels and because of the youth's courage he dispatched him instantly by putting the sharp edge of the blade between his vertebrae and shoving downward. Kin Pak died without knowing it.

"Fill up the grave!"

Dog-eared Chen was petrified but he rushed to obey. Goodweather Poon laughed and tripped him and gave him a savage kick for his cowardice. The man half-fell into the trench. At once the shovel in Poon's hands whirled in an arc and crunched into the back of Dog-eared Chen's head and he collapsed with a sigh on top of Kin Pak. The others laughed and one said, "Eeeee, you used that like a foreign devil cricket bat! Good. Is he dead?"

Goodweather Poon did not answer, just looked at the last Werewolf, Smallpox Kin. All their eyes went to him. He stood rigid in the rain. It was then that Goodweather Poon noticed the string tight around his neck. He took up the flashlight and went over to him and saw that the other end was dangling down his back. Weighing it down was a broken half-coin, a hole bored carefully into it. It was a copper cash and seemed ancient.

"All gods fart in Tsao Tsao's face! Where did you get this?" he asked, beginning to beam.

"My father gave it to me."

"Where did he get it, little turd?"

"He didn't tell me."

"Could he have got it from Number One Son Chen?"

Another shrug. "I don't know. I wasn't here when they killed him. I'm innocent on my mother's head!"

With a sudden movement Goodweather Poon ripped the necklace off. "Take him to the car," he said to two of his fighters. "Watch him very carefully. We'll take him back with us. Yes, we'll take him back. The rest of you fill up the grave and camouflage it carefully." Then he ordered the last two of his men to pick up the blanket containing John Chen and to follow him. They did so awkwardly in the darkness.

He trudged off toward the Sha Tin Road, skirting the puddles. Nearby was a broken-down bus shelter. When the road was clear he motioned to his men and they quickly unwrapped the blanket and propped the body in a corner. Then he took out the sign that the Werewolves had made previously and stuck it carefully on the body.

"Why're you doing that, Goodweather Poon, heya? Why're you do—"

"Because Four Fingers told me to! How do I know? Keep your fornicating mouth sh—"

Headlights from an approaching car rounding the bend washed them suddenly. They froze and turned their faces away, pretending to be waiting passengers. Once the car was safely past they took to their heels. Dawn was streaking the sky, the rain lessening.

The phone jangled and Armstrong came out of sleep heavily. In the half-darkness he groped for the receiver and picked it up. His wife stirred uneasily and awoke.

"Divisional Sergeant Major Tang-po, sir, sorry to wake you, sir, but we've found John Chen. The Were—"

Armstrong was instantly awake. "Alive?"

"*Dew neh loh moh* no sir, his body was found near Sha Tin at a bus stop, a bus shelter, sir, and those fornicating Werewolves've left a note on his chest, sir: 'This Number One Son Chen had the stupidity to try to escape us. No one can escape the Werewolves! Let all Hong Kong beware. Our eyes are everywhere!' He w—"

Armstrong listened, appalled, while the excited man told how police at Sha Tin had been summoned by an early-morning bus passenger. At once they had cordoned off the area and phoned CID Kowloon. "What should we do, sir?"

"Send a car for me at once."

Armstrong hung up and rubbed the tiredness out of his eyes. He wore a sarong and it looked well on his muscular body.

"Trouble?" Mary stifled a yawn and stretched. She was just forty, two years younger than he, brown-haired, taut, her face friendly though lined.

He told her, watching her.

"Oh." The color had left her face. "How terrible. Oh, how terrible. Poor John!"

"I'll make the tea," Armstrong said.

"No, no I'll do that." She got out of bed, her body firm. "Will you have time?"

"Just a cuppa. Listen to the rain . . . about bloody time!" Thoughtfully Armstrong went off to the bathroom and shaved and dressed quickly as only a policeman or doctor can. Two gulps of the hot sweet tea and just before the toast the doorbell rang. "I'll call you later. How about curry tonight? We can go to Singh's."

"Yes," she said. "Yes, if you'd like."

The door closed behind him.

Mary Armstrong stared at the door. Tomorrow is our fifteenth anniversary, she thought. I wonder if he'll remember. Probably not. In fourteen times, he's been out on a case eight, once I was in hospital and the rest . . . the rest were all right, I suppose.

She went to the window and pulled the curtains back. Torrents of rain streaked the windows in the half-light, but now it was cool and pleasant. The apartment had two bedrooms and it was their furniture though the apartment belonged to the government and went with the job.

Christ, what a job!

Rotten for a policeman's wife. You spend your life waiting for him to come home, waiting for some rotten villain to knife him, or shoot him or hurt him—most nights you sleep alone or you're being woken up at all rotten hours with some more rotten disasters and off he goes again. Overworked and underpaid. Or you go to the Police Club and sit around with other wives while the men get smashed and you swap lies with the wives and drink too many pink gins. At least they have children.

Children! Oh God . . . I wish we had children.

But then, most of the wives complain about how tired they are, how exhausting children are, and about *amahs* and school and the expense . . . and everything. What the hell does this life mean? What a rotten waste! What a perfectly rotten—

The phone rang. "*Shut up!*" she shrieked at it, then laughed nervously. "Mary Mary quite contrary where did your temper go?" she chided herself and picked the phone up. "Hello?"

"Mary, Brian Kwok, sorry to wake you but is Rob—"

"Oh hello, dear. No, sorry, he's just left. Something about the Were-wolves."

"Yes, I just heard, that's what I was calling about. He's gone to Sha Tin?"

"Yes. Are you going too?"

"No. I'm with the Old Man."

"Poor you." She heard him laugh. They chatted for a moment then he rang off.

She sighed and poured herself another cup of tea, added milk and sugar and thought about John Chen. Once upon a time she had been madly in love with him. They had been lovers for more than two years and he had been her first. This was in the Japanese Internment Camp in Stanley Prison on the south part of the island.

In 1940 she had passed the Civil Service exam in England with honors and after a few months had been sent out to Hong Kong, around the Cape. She had arrived late in '41, just nineteen, and just in time to be interned with all European civilians, there to stay until 1945.

I was twenty-two when I got out and the last two years, we were lovers, John and I. Poor John, nagged constantly by his rotten father, and his sick mother, with no way to escape them and almost no privacy in the camp, cooped up with families, children, babes, husbands, wives, hatred hunger envy and little laughter all those years. Loving him made the camp bearable. . . .

I don't want to think about those rotten times.

Or the rotten time after the camp when he married his father's choice, a rotten little harpy but someone with money and influence and Hong Kong family connections. I had none. I should have gone home but I didn't want home—what was there to go home to? So I stayed and worked in the Colonial Office and had a good time, good enough. And then I met Robert.

Ah, Robert. You were a good man and good to me and we had fun and I was a good wife to you, still try to be. But I can't have children and you . . . we both want children and one day a few years ago, you found out about John Chen. You never asked me about him but I know you know and ever since then you've hated him. It all happened long before I met you and you knew about the camp but not about my lover. Remember how before we got married I said, Do you want to know about the past, my darling? And you said, No, old girl.

You used to call me old girl all the time. Now you don't call me anything. Just Mary sometimes.

Poor Robert! How I must have disappointed you!

Poor John! How you disappointed me, once upon a time so fine, now so very dead.

I wish I was dead too.

She began to cry.

40

"It's going to continue to rain, Alexi," Dunross said, the track already sodden, heavy overcast and the day gloomy.

"I agree, tai-pan. If it rains even part of tomorrow too, the going will be foul on Saturday."

"Jacques? What do you think?"

"I agree," deVille said. "Thank God for the rain but *merde* it would be a pity if the races were canceled."

Dunross nodded.

They were standing on the grass near the winner's circle at the Happy Valley Racecourse, the three men dressed in raincoats and hats. There was a bad weal across Dunross's face, and bruises, but his eyes were steady and clear and he stood with his easy confidence, watching the cloud cover, the rain still falling but not as strongly as in the night, other trainers and owners and bystanders scattered about the paddock and stands, equally pensive. A few horses were exercising, among them Noble Star, Buccaneer with a stable jockey up and Gornt's Pilot Fish. All of the horses were being exercised gingerly with very tight reins: the track and the approach to the track were very slippery. But Pilot Fish was prancing, enjoying the rain.

"This morning's weather report said the storm was huge." Travkin's sloe eyes were red-rimmed with tiredness and he watched Dunross. "If the rain stops tomorrow, the going'll still be soft on Saturday."

"Does that help or hurt Noble Star's chances, Alexi?" Jacques asked.

"As God wills, Jacques. She's never run in the wet." It was hard for Travkin to concentrate. Last evening the phone had rung and it was the KGB stranger again and the man had rudely cut through his questions of why he had vanished so suddenly. "It's not your privilege to question, Prince Kurgan. Just tell me everything you know about Dunross. Now. Everything. His habits, rumors about him, everything."

Travkin had obeyed. He knew that he was in a vise, knew that the stranger who must be KGB would be taping what he said to check the truth of what he related, the slightest variation of the truth perhaps a death knell for his wife or son or his son's wife or son's children—if they truly existed.

Do they? he asked himself again, agonized.

"What's the matter, Alexi?"

"Nothing, tai-pan," Travkin replied, feeling unclean. "I was thinking of what you went through last night." The news of the fire at Aberdeen had flooded the airwaves, particularly Venus Poon's harrowing eyewitness account which had been the focus of the reports. "Terrible about the others, wasn't it?"

"Yes." So far the known death count was fifteen burned and drowned, including two children. "It'll take days to find out really how many were lost."

"Terrible," Jacques said. "When I heard about it . . . if Susanne had been here we would have been caught in it. She . . . Curious how life is sometimes."

"Bloody firetrap! Never occurred to me before," Dunross said. "We've all eaten there dozens of times—I'm going to talk to the governor this morning about all those floating restaurants."

"But you're all right, you yourself?" Travkin asked.

"Oh yes. No problem." Dunross smiled grimly. "Not unless we all get the croup from swimming in that cesspit."

When the *Floating Dragon* had suddenly capsized, Dunross, Gornt and Peter Marlowe had been in the water right below. The megaphone on the police launch had shouted a frantic warning and they had all kicked out desperately. Dunross was a strong swimmer and he and Gornt had just got clear though the surge of water sucked them backward. As his head went under he saw the half-full cutter pulled into the maelstrom and capsized and Marlowe in trouble. He let himself go with the boiling torrent as the ship settled onto her side and lunged for Marlowe. His fingers found his shirt and held on and they swirled together for a moment, drawn a few fathoms down, smashing against the deck. The blow almost stunned him but he held on to Marlowe and when the drag lessened he kicked for the surface. Their heads came out of the water together. Marlowe gasped his thanks and struck out for Fleur who was hanging on to the side of the overturned cutter with others. Around them was chaos, people gasping and drowning and being rescued by sailors and by the strong. Dunross saw Casey diving for someone. Gornt was nowhere to be seen. Bartlett came up with Christian Toxe and kicked for a life belt. He made sure that Toxe had hold of the life ring securely before he shouted to Dunross, "I think Gornt got sucked down and there was a woman . . ." and at once dived again.

Dunross looked around. The *Floating Dragon* was almost on her side now. He felt a slight underwater explosion and water boiled around him for a moment. Casey came up for air, filled her lungs and slid under the surface again. Dunross dived too. It was almost impossible to see but he groped his way down along the top deck that was now almost vertical in the water. He swam around the wreck, searching, and stayed below as long as he could, then surfaced carefully for there were many swimmers still thrashing around. Toxe was choking out seawater, precariously hanging on to the life ring. Dunross swam over and paddled him toward a sailor, knowing Toxe could not swim.

"Hang on, Christian . . . you're okay now."

Desperately Toxe tried to talk through his retching. "My . . . my wife's . . . she's down th . . . down there . . . down . . ."

The sailor swam over. "I've got him, sir, you all right?"

"Yes . . . yes . . . he says his wife was sucked down."

"Christ! I didn't see anyone . . . I'll get some help!" The sailor turned and shouted at the police launch for assistance. At once several sailors dived overboard and began the search. Dunross looked for Gornt and could not see him. Casey came up panting and held on to the upturned cutter to catch her breath.

"You all right?"

"Yes . . . yes . . . thank God you're okay . . ." she gasped, her chest heaving. "There's a woman down there, Chinese I think, I saw her sucked down."

"Have you seen Gornt?"

"No. . . . Maybe he's . . ." She motioned at the launch. People were clambering up the gangway, others huddling on the deck. Bartlett surfaced for an instant and dived again. Casey took another great breath and slid into the depths. Dunross went after her slightly to her right.

They searched, the three of them, until everyone else was safe on the launch or in sampans. They never found the woman.

When Dunross had got home Penelope was deep asleep. She awoke momentarily. "Ian?"

"Yes. Go back to sleep, darling."

"Did you have a nice time?" she asked, not really awake.

"Yes, go back to sleep."

This morning, an hour ago, he had not awakened her when he left the Great House.

"You heard that Gornt made it, Alexi?" he said.

"Yes, yes I did, tai-pan. As God wills."

"Meaning?"

"After yesterday's stock market it would have been very convenient if he hadn't made it."

Dunross grinned and eased an ache in his back. "Ah, but then I would have been very put out, very put out indeed, for I'd not have had the pleasure of smashing Rothwell-Gornt myself, eh?"

After a pause deVille said, "It's astonishing more didn't die." They watched Pilot Fish as the stallion cantered past looking very good. De-Ville's eyes ranged the course.

"Is it true that Bartlett saved Peter Marlowe's wife?" Travkin asked.

"He jumped with her. Yes. Both Linc and Casey did a great job. Wonderful."

"Will you excuse me, tai-pan?" Jacques deVille nodded at the stands. "There's Jason Plumm—I'm supposed to be playing bridge with him tonight."

"See you at Prayers, Jacques." Dunross smiled at him and deVille walked off. He sighed, sad for his friend. "I'm off to the office, Alexi. Call me at six."

"Tai-pan . . ."

"What?"

Travkin hesitated. Then he said simply, "I just want you to know I . . . I admire you greatly."

Dunross was nonplussed at the suddenness and at the open, curious melancholy that emanated from the other man. "Thanks," he said warmly and clapped him on the shoulder. He had never touched him as a friend before. "You're not so bad yourself."

Travkin watched him walk off, his chest hurting him, tears of shame adding to the rain. He wiped his face with the back of his hand and went back to watching Noble Star, trying to concentrate.

In the periphery of his vision he saw someone and he turned, startled. The KGB man was in a corner of the stands, another man joining him now. The man was old and gnarled and well known as a punter in Hong Kong. Travkin searched his mind for the name. Clinker. That's it! Clinker!

He watched them blankly for a moment. Jason Plumm was in the stands just behind the KGB man and he saw Plumm get up to return Jacques deVille's wave and walk down the steps to meet him. Just then the KGB man glanced in his direction and he turned carefully, trying not to be sudden again. The KGB man had lifted binoculars to his eyes and Travkin did not know if he had been noticed or not. His skin crawled at the thought of those high-powered binoculars focused on him. Perhaps the man can lip-read, he thought, aghast. Christ Jesus and Mother of God, thank God I didn't blurt out the truth to the tai-pan.

His heart was grinding nastily and he felt sick. A flicker of lightning went across the eastern sky. Rain was puddling the concrete and the open, lower section of the stands. He tried to calm himself and looked around helplessly not knowing what to do, wanting very much to find out who the KGB man was. Absently he noticed Pilot Fish was finishing his workout in fine form. Beyond him Richard Kwang was talking intently to a group of other Chinese he did not know. Linbar Struan and Andrew Gavallan were leaning on the rails with the American Rosemont and others from the consulate he knew by sight. They were watching the horses, oblivious of the rain. Near the changing rooms, under cover, Donald McBride was talking to other stewards, Sir Shi-teh T'Chung, Pugmire and Roger Crosse among them. He saw McBride glance over to Dunross, wave and beckon him to join them. Brian Kwok was waiting for Roger Crosse on the outskirts of the stewards. Travkin knew both of them but not that they were in SI.

Involuntarily his feet began to move toward them. The foul taste of bile rose into his mouth. He dominated his urge to rush up to them and blurt out the truth. Instead he called over his chief *ma-foo.* "Send our string home. All of them. Make sure they're dry before they're fed."

"Yes sir."

Unhappily Travkin trudged for the changing rooms. From the corner of his eye he saw that the KGB man had his binoculars trained on him. Rain trickled down his neck and mixed with the fear-sweat.

"Ah, Ian, we were thinking that if it rains tomorrow, we'd better cancel the meet. Say at 6:00 P.M. tomorrow," McBride said. "Don't you agree?"

"No, actually I don't. I suggest we make a final decision at ten Saturday morning."

"Isn't that a little late, old boy?" Pugmire asked.

"Not if the stewards alert the wireless and television fellows. It'll add to the excitement. Particularly if you release that news today."

"Good idea," Crosse said.

"Then that's settled," Dunross said. "Was there anything else?"

"Don't you think . . . it's a matter of the turf," McBride said. "We don't want to ruin it."

"I quite agree, Donald. We'll make a final decision Saturday at ten. All in favor?" There were no dissenters. "Good! Nothing else? Sorry, but I've got a meeting in half an hour."

Shi-teh said uncomfortably, "Oh, tai-pan, I was terribly sorry about last night . . . terrible."

"Yes. Shitee, when we meet the governor in Council at noon we should suggest he implants new, very severe fire regulations on Aberdeen."

"Agreed," Crosse said. "It's a miracle more weren't lost."

"You mean close the restaurants down, old boy?" Pugmire was shocked. His company had an interest in two of them. "That'll hurt the tourist business badly. You can't put in more exits. . . . You'd have to start from scratch!"

Dunross glanced back at Shi-teh. "Why don't you suggest to the governor that he order all kitchens at once be put on barges that can be moored alongside their mother ship? He could order that fire trucks be kept nearby until the changes have been made. The cost'd be modest, it would be easy to operate and the fire hazard would be solved once and for all."

They all stared at him. Shi-teh beamed. "Ian, you're a genius!"

"No. I'm only sorry we didn't think of it before. Never occurred to me. Rotten about Zep . . . and Christian's wife, isn't it? Have they found her body yet?"

"I don't think so."

"God knows how many others went. Did the MPs get out, Pug?"

"Yes, old chap. Except Sir Charles Pennyworth. Poor sod got his head bashed in on a sampan when he fell."

Dunross was shocked. "I liked him! What bloody bad joss!"

"There were a couple of the others near me at one stage. That bloody radical bastard, what's his name? Grey, ah yes, Grey that's it. And the other one, the other bloody Socialist berk, Broadhurst. Both behaved rather well I thought."

"I hear your Superfoods got out too, Pug. Wasn't our 'Call me Chuck' first ashore?"

Pugmire shrugged uneasily. "I really don't know." Then he beamed. "I . . . er . . . I hear Casey and Bartlett did a very good job, what? Perhaps they should have a medal."

"Why don't you suggest it?" Dunross said, anxious to leave. "If there's nothing else . . ."

Crosse said, "Ian, if I were you I'd get a shot. There must be bugs in that bay that haven't been invented yet."

They all laughed with him.

"Actually I've done better than that. After we got out of the water I grabbed Linc Bartlett and Casey and we fled to Doc Tooley." Dunross smiled faintly. "When we told him we'd been swimming in Aberdeen Harbor he almost had a hemorrhage. He said, 'Drink this,' and like bloody berks we did and before we knew what was happening we were retching our hearts out. If I'd had any strength I'd've belted him but we were all on our hands and knees fighting for the loo not knowing which end was first. Then Casey started laughing between heaves and then we were rolling on the bloody floor!" He added with pretended sadness, "Then, before we knew what was happening, Old Sawbones was shoving pills down our throats by the barrel and Bartlett said, 'For chrissake, Doc, how about a suppository and then you've a hole in one!'" They laughed again.

"Is it true about Casey? That she stripped and dived like an Olympic star?" Pugmire asked.

"Better! Stark bollock naked, old boy," Dunross exaggerated airily. "Like Venus de Milo! Probably the best . . . everything . . . I've ever seen."

"Oh?" Their eyes popped.

"Yes."

"My God, but swimming in Aberdeen Harbor! That sewer!" McBride said, eyebrows soaring. "If you all live it'll be a miracle!"

"Doc Tooley said the very least'll be gastroenteritis, dysentery or the plague." Dunross rolled his eyes. "Well, here today gone tomorrow. Anything else?"

"Tai-pan," Shi-teh said, "I . . . hope you don't mind but I've . . . I'd like to start a fund for the victims' families."

"Good idea! The Turf Club should contribute too. Donald, would you canvass the other stewards today and get their approval? How about 100,000?"

"That's a bit generous, isn't it?" Pugmire said.

Dunross's chin jutted. "No. Then let's make it 150,000 instead. The Noble House will contribute the same." Pugmire flushed. No one said anything. "Meeting adjourned? Good. Morning." Dunross raised his hat politely and walked off.

"Excuse me a moment." Crosse motioned Brian Kwok to follow him. "Ian!"

"Yes, Roger?"

When Crosse came up to Dunross he said quietly, "Ian, we've a report that Sinders is confirmed on the BOAC flight tomorrow. We'll go straight to the bank from the airport if that's convenient."

"The governor will be there too?"

"I'll ask him. We should be there about six."

"If the plane's on time." Dunross smiled.

"Did you get *Eastern Cloud*'s formal release yet?"

"Yes, thanks. It was telexed yesterday from Delhi. I ordered her back here at once and she sailed on the tide. Brian, you remember the bet you wanted—the one about Casey. About her knockers—fifty dollars to a copper cash they're the best in Hong Kong?"

Brian Kwok reddened, conscious of Crosse's bleak stare. "Er, yes, why?"

"I don't know about the best, but like the judgment of Paris, you'd have one helluva problem if it—they—were put to the test!"

"Then it's true, she was starkers?"

"She was Lady Godiva to the rescue." Dunross nodded to both of them pleasantly and walked off with, "See you tomorrow."

They watched him go. At the exit an SI agent was waiting to follow him.

Crosse said, "He's got something cooking."

"I agree, sir."

Crosse tore his eyes off Dunross and looked at Brian Kwok. "Do you usually bet on a lady's mammary glands?"

"No sir, sorry sir."

"Good. Fortunately women aren't the only source of beauty, are they?"

"No sir."

"There're hounds, paintings, music, even a killing. Eh?"

"Yes sir."

"Wait here please." Crosse went back to the other stewards.

Brian Kwok sighed. He was bored and tired. The team of frogmen had met him at Aberdeen and though he had found out almost at once that Dunross was safe and had already gone home, he had had to wait most of the night helping to organize the search for bodies. It had been a ghoulish task. Then when he was about to go home Crosse had called him to be at Happy Valley at dawn so there had been no point in going to bed. Instead he had gone to the Para Restaurant and glowered at the triads and One Foot Ko.

Now he was watching Dunross. What's that bugger got in the reaches of his mind? he asked himself, a twinge of envy soaring through him. What couldn't I do with his power and his money!

He saw Dunross change direction for the nearby stand, then noticed Adryon sitting beside Martin Haply, both staring at the horses, oblivious of Dunross. *Dew neh loh moh,* he thought, surprised. Curious that they'd be together. Christ, what a beauty! Thank God I'm not father to that one. I'd go out of my mind.

Crosse and the others had also noticed Adryon and Martin Haply with astonishment. "What's that bastard doing with the tai-pan's daughter?" Pugmire asked, his voice sour.

"No good, that's certain," someone said.

"Blasted fellow creates nothing but trouble!" Pugmire muttered and the others nodded agreement. "Can't understand why Toxe keeps him on!"

"Bloody man's a Socialist that's why! He should be blackballed too."

"Oh come off it, Pug. Toxe's all right—so're some Socialists," Shi-teh said. "But he should fire Haply, and we'd all be better off!" They had all been subject to Haply's attacks. A few weeks ago he had written a series of scathing exposés of some of Shi-teh's trading deals within his huge conglomeration of companies and implied that all sorts of dubious contributions were being made to various VIPs in the Hong Kong Government for favors.

"I agree," Pugmire said, hating him too. Haply, with his accuracy, had reported the private details of Pugmire's forthcoming merger with Superfoods and had made it abundantly clear Pugmire benefited far more than his shareholders in General Stores who were barely consulted on the terms of the merger. "Rotten bastard! I'd certainly like to know where he gets his information."

"Curious Haply should be with her," Crosse said, watching their lips, waiting for them to speak. "The only major company he hasn't gone after yet is Struan's."

"You think it's Struan's turn and Haply's pumping Adryon?" one of the others asked. "Wouldn't that be smashing!"

Excitedly they watched Dunross go into the stands, the two young people still not having noticed him.

"Maybe he'll whip him like he did the other bastard," Pugmire said gleefully.

"Eh?" Shi-teh said. "Who? What was that?"

"Oh, I thought you knew. About two years ago one of the Vic's junior execs straight out from England started pursuing Adryon. She was sixteen, perhaps seventeen—he was twenty-two, as big as a house, bigger than Ian, his name was Byron. He thought he was Lord Byron on the rampage and he mounted a campaign. The poor girl was bowled over. Ian warned him a last time. The creep kept calling, so Ian invited him out to his gym at Shek-O, put on gloves—he knew the bugger fancied himself as a boxer— and proceeded to pulp him." The others laughed. "Within the week the bank had sent him packing."

"Did you see it?" Shi-teh asked.

"Of course not. They were alone for God's sake, but the bloody fool was really in a bad way. I wouldn't like to go against the tai-pan—not when his temper's up."

Shi-teh looked back at Dunross. "Perhaps he'll do the same to that little rotter," he said happily.

They watched. Hopefully. Crosse wandered off with Brian Kwok, going closer.

Dunross was running up the steps in the stands now with his easy strength and he stopped beside them. "Hello, darling, you're up early," he said.

"Oh hello, Dad," Adryon said, startled. "I didn't se— What happened to your face?"

"I ran into the back end of a bus. Morning, Haply."

"Morning, sir." Haply half got up and sat down again.

"A bus?" she said, then suddenly, "Did you prang the Jag? Oh, did you get a ticket?" she asked hopefully, having had three this year herself.

"No. You're up early aren't you?" he said, sitting beside her.

"Actually we're late. We've been up all night."

"Oh?" He held on to forty-eight immediate questions and said instead, "You must be tired."

"No. No, actually I'm not."

"What's this all about, a celebration?"

"No. Actually it's poor Martin." She put a gentle hand on the youth's shoulder. With an effort Dunross kept his smile as gentle as her hand. He turned his attention to the young Canadian. "What's the problem?"

Haply hesitated, then told him what had happened at the paper when the publisher had called and Christian Toxe, his editor, had canceled his rumor series. "That bastard's sold us out. He's allowed the publisher to censor us. I know I'm right. I know I'm right."

"How?" Dunross asked, thinking, What a callous little bastard you are!

"Sorry, I can't reveal my source."

"He really can't, Dad, that's an infringement of freedom of the press," Adryon said defensively.

Haply was bunching his fists, then absently he put his hand on

Adryon's knee. She covered it with one of her own. "The Ho-Pak's being shoved into the ground for nothing."

"Why?"

"I don't know. But Gor—but tai-pans are behind the raid and it doesn't make sense."

"Gornt's behind it?" Dunross frowned at this new thought.

"I didn't say Gornt, sir. No I didn't say that."

"He didn't, Father," Adryon said. "What should Martin do? Should he resign or just swallow his pride an—"

"I just can't, Adryon," Martin Haply said.

"Let Father talk, he'll know."

Dunross saw her turn her lovely eyes back on him and he felt a glow at her confident innocence that he had never felt before. "Two things: First you go back at once. Christian will need all the help he can get. Second, y—"

"Help?"

"Haven't you heard about his wife?"

"What about her?"

"Don't you know she's dead?"

They stared at him blankly.

Quickly he told them about Aberdeen. Both of them were shocked and Haply stuttered, "Jesus, we . . . we didn't listen to a radio or anything . . . we were just dancing and talking. . . ." He jumped up and started to leave then came back. "I . . . I'd better go at once. Jesus!"

Adryon was on her feet. "I'll drop you."

Dunross said, "Haply, would you ask Christian to emphasize in bold type that anyone who got dunked or went swimming should see their doctors right smartly—very important."

"Got it!"

Adryon said anxiously, "Father, did you see Doc Too—"

"Oh yes," Dunross said. "Cleansed inside and out. Off you go!"

"What was the second thing, tai-pan?" Haply asked.

"Second was that you should remember it's the publisher's money, therefore his newspaper and he can do what he likes. But publishers can be persuaded. I wonder, for instance, who got to him or her and why he and she agreed to call Christian. . . . if you're so sure your story's true."

Haply beamed suddenly. "Come on, honey," he said and shouted thanks. They ran off hand-in-hand.

Dunross stayed sitting in the stands for the moment. He sighed deeply, then got up and went away.

Roger Crosse was with Brian Kwok under cover near the jockeys' changing rooms and he had been lip-reading the tai-pan's conversation. He watched him leave, the SI guard following him. "No need to waste any more time here, Brian. Come along." He headed for the far exit. "I wonder if Robert found anything at Sha Tin."

"Those bloody Werewolves are going to have a field day. All Hong Kong'll be frightened to death. I'll bet we . . ." Brian Kwok stopped suddenly. "Sir! Look!" He nodded at the stands, noticing Suslev and Clinker among the scattered groups who watched out of the rain. "I wouldn't've thought he'd be up yet!"

Crosse's eyes narrowed. "Yes. That's curious. Yes." He hesitated, then changed direction, watching their lips carefully. "Since he's honored us we might as well have a little chat. Ah . . . they've seen us. Clinker really doesn't like us at all." Leisurely he led the way into the stands.

The big Russian put a smile on his face and slid out a thin flask and took a sip. He offered it to Clinker.

"No thanks, mate, I just drink beer." Clinker's cold eyes were on the approaching policemen. "Proper niffy around here, ain't it?" he said loudly.

"Morning, Clinker," Crosse said, equally coldly. Then he smiled at Suslev. "Morning, Captain. Filthy day, what?"

"We're alive, *tovarich*, alive, so how can a day be filthy, eh?" Suslev was filled with outward bonhomie, continuing his cover as a hail-fellow-well-met. "Will there be racing Saturday, Superintendent?"

"Probably. The final decision'll be made Saturday morning. How long will you be in port?"

"Not long, Superintendent. The repairs to the rudder go slowly."

"Not too slowly I hope. We all get very nervous if our VIP harbor guests don't get very rapid service." Crosse's voice was crisp. "I'll talk to the harbor master."

"Thank you, that's . . . that's very thoughtful of you. And it was thoughtful of your department . . ." Suslev hesitated, then turned to Clinker. "Old friend, do you mind?"

"Not on your nelly," Clinker said. "Narks make me nervous." Brian Kwok looked at him. Clinker looked back unafraid. "I'll be in me car." He wandered off.

Suslev's voice hardened. "It was thoughtful of your department to send back the body of our poor comrade Voranski. Have you found the murderers?"

"Unfortunately no. They could be hired assassins—from any point of the compass. Of course if he hadn't slipped ashore mysteriously he'd still be a useful operative of the . . . of whatever department he served."

"He was just a seaman and a good man. I thought Hong Kong was safe."

"Did you pass on the assassins' photographs and information about their phone call to your KGB superiors?"

"I'm not KGB, piss on KGB! Yes, the information was passed on . . . by my superior," Suslev said irritably. "You know how it is, Superintendent, for God's sake. But Voranski was a good man and his murderers must be caught."

"We'll find them soon enough," Crosse said easily. "Did you know Voranski was in reality Major Yuri Bakyan, First Directorate, Department 6, KGB?"

They saw shock on Suslev's face. "He was . . . he was just a friend to me and he came with us from time to time."

"Who arranges that, Captain?" Crosse said.

Suslev looked at Brian Kwok who stared back at him with unconcealed distaste. "Why're you so angry? What have I done to you?"

"Why's the Russian empire so greedy, particularly when it comes to Chinese soil?"

"Politics!" Suslev said sourly then added to Crosse, "I don't interfere in politics."

"You buggers interfere all the time! What's your KGB rank?"

"I don't have one."

Crosse said, "A little cooperation could go a long way. Who arranges your crews, Captain Suslev?"

Suslev glanced at him. Then he said, "A word in private, eh?"

"Certainly," Crosse said. "Wait here, Brian."

Suslev turned his back on Brian Kwok and led the way down the exit stairs onto the grass. Crosse followed. "What do you think of Noble Star's chances?" Suslev asked genially.

"Good. But she's never raced in the wet."

"Pilot Fish?"

"Look at him—you can see for yourself. He loves the wet. He'll be the favorite. You plan to be here Saturday?"

Suslev leaned on the railings. And smiled. "Why not?"

Crosse laughed softly. "Why not indeed?" He was sure they were quite alone now. "You're a good actor, Gregor, very good."

"So're you, comrade."

"You're taking a hell of a risk, aren't you?" Crosse said, his lips hardly moving now as he talked.

"Yes, but then all life's a risk. Center told me to take over until Voranski's replacement arrives—there are too many important contacts and decisions to be made on this trip. Not the least, Sevrin. And anyway, as you know, Arthur wanted it this way."

"Sometimes I wonder if he's wise."

"He's wise." The lines around Suslev's eyes crinkled with his smile. "Oh yes. Very wise. I'm pleased to see you. Center's very very pleased with your year's work. I've much to tell you."

"Who's the bastard who leaked Sevrin to AMG?"

"I don't know. It was a defector. As soon as we know, he's a dead man."

"Someone's betrayed a group of my people to the PRC. The leak had to come from the AMG file. You read my copy. Who else on your ship did? Someone's infiltrated your operation here!"

Suslev blanched. "I'll activate a security check immediately. It could have come from London, or Washington."

"I doubt it. Not in time. I think it came from here. And then there's Voranski. You're infiltrated."

"If the PRC . . . yes, it will be done. But who? I'd bet my life there's no spy aboard."

Crosse was equally grim. "There's always someone who can be subverted."

"You have an escape plan?"

"Several."

"I'm ordered to assist in any way. Do you want a berth on the *Ivanov?*"

Crosse hesitated. "I'll wait until I've read the AMG files. It would be a pity after such a long time . . ."

"I agree."

"It's easy for you to agree. If you're caught you just get deported and asked politely, please don't come back. Me? I wouldn't want to be caught alive."

"Of course." Suslev lit a cigarette. "You won't get caught, Roger. You're much too clever. You have something for me?"

"Look down there, along the rails. The tall man."

Casually Suslev put his binoculars to his eyes. He took his time about centering the man indicated, then looked away.

"That's Stanley Rosemont, CIA. You know they're tailing you?"

"Oh yes. I can lose them if I wish to."

"The man next to him's Ed Langan, FBI. The bearded fellow's Mishauer, American Naval Intelligence."

"Mishauer? That sounds familiar. Do you have files on them?"

"Not yet but there's a deviate in the consulate who's having a jolly affair with the son of one of our prominent Chinese solicitors. By the time you're back on your next trip he'll be happy to oblige your slightest wish."

Suslev smiled grimly. "Good." Again, casually, he glanced at Rosemont and the others, cementing their faces into his memory. "What's his job?"

"Deputy chief of station. CIA for fifteen years. OSS and all that. They've a dozen more cover businesses here and safe houses everywhere. I've sent a list in microdots to 32."

"Good. Center wants increased surveillance of all CIA movements."

"No problem. They're careless but their funding's big and growing."

"Vietnam?"

"Of course Vietnam."

Suslev chuckled. "Those poor fools don't know what they've been sucked into. They still think they can fight a jungle war with Korean or World War Two tactics."

"They're not all fools," Crosse said. "Rosemont's good, very good. By the way, they know about the Iman Air Base."

Suslev cursed softly and leaned on one hand, casually keeping it near his mouth to prevent any lip-reading.

". . . Iman and almost all about Petropavlovsk, the new sub base at Korsakov on Sakhalin. . . ."

Suslev cursed again. "How do they do it?"

"Traitors." Crosse smiled thinly.

"Why are you a double agent, Roger?"

"Why do you ask me that every time we meet?"

Suslev sighed. He had specific orders not to probe Crosse and to help him every way he could. And although he was KGB controller of all Far Eastern espionage activities, it was only last year that even he had been allowed into the secret of Crosse's identity. Crosse, in KGB files, had the highest secret classification, an importance on the level of a Philby. But even Philby didn't know that Crosse had been working for the KGB for the last seven years.

"I ask because I'm curious," he said.

"Aren't your orders not to be curious, comrade?"

Suslev laughed. "Neither of us obeys orders all the time, no? Center enjoyed your last report so much I've been told to tell you your Swiss account will be credited with an extra bonus of $50,000 on the fifteenth of next month."

"Good. Thank you. But it's not a bonus, it's payment for value received."

"What does SI know about the visiting delegation of Parliament?"

Crosse told him what he had told the governor. "Why the question?"

"Routine check. Three are potentially very influential—Guthrie, Broadhurst, and Grey." Suslev offered a cigarette. "We're maneuvering Grey and Broadhurst into our World Peace Council. Their anti-Chinese sentiments help us. Roger, would you please put a tail on Guthrie. Perhaps he has some bad habits. If he was compromised, perhaps photographed with a Wanchai girl, it might be useful later, eh?"

Crosse nodded. "I'll see what can be done."

"Can you find the scum who murdered poor Voranski?"

"Eventually." Crosse watched him. "He must have been marked for some time. And that's ominous for all of us."

"Were they Kuomintang? Or Mao's bandits?"

"I don't know." Crosse smiled sardonically. "Russia isn't very popular with any Chinese."

"Their leaders are traitors to communism. We should smash them before they get too strong."

"Is that policy?"

"Since Genghis Khan." Suslev laughed. "But now . . . now we have to be a little patient. You needn't be." He jerked a thumb backward at Brian Kwok. "Why not discredit that *matyeryebyets*? I don't like him at all."

"Young Brian's very good. I need good people. Inform Center that

Sinders, of MI-6, arrives tomorrow from London to take delivery of the AMG papers. Both MI-6 and the CIA suspect AMG was murdered. Was he?"

"I don't know. He should have been, years ago. How will you get a copy?"

"I don't know. I'm fairly certain Sinders'll let me read them before he goes back."

"And if he doesn't?"

Crosse shrugged. "We'll get to look at them one way or another."

"Dunross?"

"Only as a last resort. He's too valuable where he is and I'd rather have him where I can see him. What about Travkin?"

"Your information was invaluable. Everything checked." Suslev told him the substance of their meeting, adding, "Now he'll be our dog forever. He'll do anything we want. Anything. I think he'd kill Dunross if necessary."

"Good. How much of what you told him was true?"

Suslev smiled. "Not much."

"Is his wife alive?"

"Oh yes, *tovarich*, she's alive."

"But not in her own *dacha*?"

"Now she is."

"And before?"

Suslev shrugged. "I told him what I was told to tell him."

Crosse lit a cigarette. "What do you know about Iran?"

Again Suslev looked at him sharply. "Quite a lot. It's one of our eight remaining great targets and there's a big operation going on right now."

"The Ninety-second U.S. Airborne's on the Soviet-Iranian border right now!"

Suslev gaped at him. "What?"

Crosse related all that Rosemont had told him about Dry Run and when he came to the part about the U.S. forces having nuclear arms Suslev whitened palpably. "Mother of God! Those god-cursed Americans'll make a mistake one day and then we'll never be able to extricate ourselves! They're fools to deploy such weapons."

"Can you combat them?"

"Of course not, not yet," Suslev said irritably. "The core of our strategy's never to have a direct clash until America's totally isolated and there's no doubt about final victory. A direct clash would be suicide now. I'll get on to Center at once."

"Impress on them the Americans consider it just a dry run. Get Center to take your forces away and cool everything. Do it at once or there will be trouble. Don't give the U.S. forces any provocation. In a few days the Americans will go away. Don't leak the invasion to your inward spies in Washington. Let it come first from your people in the CIA."

"The Ninety-second's really there? That seems impossible."

"You'd better get your armies more airborne, more mobile with more firepower."

Suslev grunted. "The energies and resources of three hundred million Russians are channeled to solve that problem, *tovarich*. If we have twenty years . . . just twenty more years."

"Then?"

"In the eighties we rule the world."

"I'll be dead long since."

"Not you. You'll rule whatever province or country you want. England?"

"Sorry, the weather there's dreadful. Except for one or two days a year, most years, when it's the most beautiful place on earth."

"Ah, you should see my home in Georgia and the country around Tiflis." Suslev's eyes were sparkling. "That's Eden."

Crosse was watching everywhere as they talked. He knew they could not be overheard. Brian Kwok was sitting in the stand waiting, half-asleep. Rosemont and the others were studying him covertly. Down by the winner's circle Jacques deVille was strolling casually with Jason Plumm.

"Have you talked to Jason yet?"

"Of course, while we were in the stands."

"Good."

"What did he say about deVille?"

"That he doubted, too, if Jacques'd ever be chosen as tai-pan. After my meeting last night I agree—he's obviously too weak, or his resolve's softened." Suslev added, "It often happens with deep-cover assets who have nothing active to do but wait. That's the hardest of all jobs."

"Yes."

"He's a good man but I'm afraid he won't achieve his assignment."

"What do you plan for him?"

"I haven't decided."

"Convert him from an inward spy to a doomed spy?"

"Only if you or the others of Sevrin are threatened." For the benefit of any watchers Suslev tipped the flask to his lips and offered it to Crosse who shook his head. Both knew the flask contained only water. Suslev dropped his voice. "I have an idea. We're increasing our effort in Canada. Clearly the French Separatist Movement is a tremendous opportunity for us. If Quebec was to split from Canada it would send the whole North American continent reeling into a completely new power structure. I was thinking that it would be perfect if deVille took over Struan's in Canada. Eh?"

Crosse smiled. "Very good. Very very good. I like Jacques too. It would be a pity to waste him. Yes, that would be very clever."

"It's even better than that, Roger. He has some very important French-Canadian friends from his Paris days just after the war, all openly separatist, all left-wing inclined. A few of them are becoming a prominent national political force in Canada."

"You'd get him to drop his deep cover?"

"No. Jacques could give the separatist issue a push without jeopardizing himself. As head of an important branch of Struan's . . . and if one of his special friends became foreign minister or prime minister, eh?"

"Is that possible?"

"It's possible."

Crosse whistled. "If Canada swung away from the U.S. that would be a coup of coups."

"Yes."

After a pause, Crosse said, "Once upon a time a Chinese sage was asked by a friend to bless his newly born son. His benediction was, 'Let's pray he lives in interesting times.' Well, Gregor Petrovitch Suslev whose real name is Petr Oleg Mzytryk, we certainly live in interesting times. Don't we?"

Suslev was staring at him in shock. "Who told you my name?"

"Your superiors." Crosse watched him, his eyes suddenly pitiless. "You know me, I know you. That's fair, isn't it?"

"Of . . . of course. I . . ." The man's laugh was forced. "I haven't used that name for so long I'd . . . I'd almost forgotten it." He looked back at the eyes, fighting for control. "What's the matter? Why are you so edgy, eh?"

"AMG. I think we should close this meeting for now. Our cover's that I tried to subvert you but you refused. Let's meet tomorrow at seven." Seven was the code number for the apartment next to Ginny Fu's in Mong Kok. "Late. Eleven o'clock."

"Ten is better."

Crosse motioned carefully toward Rosemont and the others. "Before you go I need something for them."

"All right. Tomorrow I'll ha—"

"It must be now." Crosse hardened. "Something special—in case I can't get a look at Sinders's copy, I'll have to barter with them!"

"You divulge to no one the source. No one."

"All right."

"Never?"

"Never."

Suslev thought a moment, weighing possibilities. "Tonight one of our agents takes delivery of some top-secret material from the carrier. Eh?"

The Englishman's face lit up. "Perfect! Is that why you came?"

"One reason."

"When and where's the drop?"

Suslev told him, then added, "But I still want copies of everything."

"Of course. Good, that'll do just fine. Rosemont will be really in my debt. How long's your asset been aboard?"

"Two years, at least that's when he was first subverted."

"Does he give you good stuff?"

"Anything off that whore's valuable."

"What's his fee?"

"For this? $2,000. He's not expensive, none of our assets are, except you."

Crosse smiled equally mirthlessly. "Ah, but I'm the best you have in Asia and I've proved my quality fifty times. Up to now I've been doing it practically for love, old chap."

"Your costs, old chap, are the highest we have! We buy the entire NATO battle plan, codes, everything, yearly for less than $8,000."

"Those amateur bastards are ruining our business. It is a business, isn't it?"

"Not to us."

"Balls! You KGB folk are more than well rewarded. *Dachas*, places in Tiflis, special stores to shop in. Mistresses. But I have to tell you, squeezing money out of your company gets worse yearly. I'll expect a rather large increase for Dry Run and for the AMG matter when it's concluded."

"Talk to them direct. I've no jurisdiction over money."

"Liar."

Suslev laughed. "It's good—and safe—dealing with a professional. *Prosit!*" He raised his flask and drained it.

Crosse said abruptly, "Please leave angrily. I can feel binoculars!"

At once Suslev began cursing him in Russian, softly but vehemently, then shook a fist in the policeman's face and walked off.

Crosse stared after him.

On the Sha Tin Road Robert Armstrong was looking down at the corpse of John Chen as raincoated police rewrapped it in its blanket, then carried it through the gawking crowds to the waiting ambulance. Fingerprint experts and others were all around, searching for clues. The rain was falling more heavily now and there was a great deal of mud everywhere.

"Everything's messed up, sir," Sergeant Lee said sourly. "There're footprints but they could be anyone's."

Armstrong nodded and used a handkerchief to dry his face. Many onlookers were behind the crude barriers that had been erected around the area. Passing traffic on the narrow road was slowed and almost jammed, everyone honking irritably. "Keep the men sweeping within a hundred-yard area. Get someone out to the nearest village, someone might have seen something." He left Lee and went over to the police car. He got in, closing the door, and picked up the communicator. "This is Armstrong. Give me Chief Inspector Donald Smyth at East Aberdeen, please." He began to wait, feeling dreadful.

The driver was young and smart and still dry. "The rain's wonderful, isn't it, sir?"

Armstrong looked across sourly. The young man blanched. "Do you smoke?"

"Yes sir." The young man took out his pack and offered it. Armstrong took the pack. "Why don't you join the others? They need a nice smart fellow like yourself to help. Find some clues. Eh?"

"Yes sir." The young man fled into the rain.

Carefully Armstrong took out a cigarette. He contemplated it. Grimly he put it back and the pack into a side pocket. Hunching down into his seat, he muttered, "Sod all cigarettes, sod the rain, sod that smart arse and most of all sod the sodding Werewolves!"

In time the intercom came on crackling, "Chief Inspector Donald Smyth."

"Morning. I'm out at Sha Tin," Armstrong began, and told him what had happened and about finding the body. "We're covering the area but in this rain I don't expect to find anything. When the papers hear about the corpse and the message we'll be swamped. I think we'd better pick up the old *amah* right now. She's the only lead we have. Do your fellows still have her under surveillance?"

"Oh yes."

"Good. Wait for me, then we'll move in. I want to search her place. Have a team stand by."

"How long will you be?"

Armstrong said, "It'll take me a couple of hours to get there. Traffic's sodded up from here all the way back to the ferry."

"It is here too. All over Aberdeen. But it's not just the rain, old lad. There's about a thousand ghouls gawking at the wreck, then there're more bloody mobs already at the Ho-Pak, the Victoria . . . in fact every bloody bank in the vicinity, and I hear there's already about five hundred collecting outside the Vic in Central."

"Christ! My whole miserable bloody life savings're there."

"I told you yesterday to get liquid, old boy!" Armstrong heard the Snake's laugh. "And by the way, if you've any spare cash, sell Struan's short—I hear the Noble House is going to crash."